DAKWINSI STEPPE

The Young King

ed-Öma.

Kwan

The Naghaniin Host

kai
The Ragged Pillars

Mordaga's Castle

SIGHING DESERT

The Teeth of Shenkh

esh

Nishvalni-Oss

Anakhazhan

orn
Quarzhasaat

Valederia

.Elwher
ESHMIR

Bas'Uk

Ilmar

WEEPING WASTE

to PHUM
Yeshpotoom-Kahlai

ILMIORA Karlaak

ORG
Forest of Troos

.Gorjhan

to OKARA
CHANG SHAI

Nadsokor-Rignariom

Jadmar

IR
Old Hrolmar

.Uhaio

STRAITS OF VILMIR

Ma-ha-kil-agra,

Menii
Utkel

The Fortress of the Evening

ISLE OF THE
PURPLE TOWNS

.Oi Oi

Ufych-Sormeer

Chalal

THE
ROARING ROCKS

repesaz

.Raschil

agasaz

FILKHAR

losaz

ARGIMILIAR

.Alorasaz

PIKARAYD

The Dead Hills

.Ryfel

DOREL

For Jim Cawthorn-
The Master Cartographer
of Elric's World

John Collier 2021

THE
ELRIC
SAGA

VOLUME THREE

THE WHITE WOLF

THE ELRIC SAGA

VOLUME THREE

THE WHITE WOLF

BOOK 1: THE DREAMTHIEF'S DAUGHTER

BOOK 2: THE SKRAYLING TREE

BOOK 3: THE WHITE WOLF'S SON

BY MICHAEL MOORCOCK
WITH JOHN DAVEY, EDITOR AND BIBLIOGRAPHER

SAGA PRESS

LONDON SYDNEY **NEW YORK** TORONTO NEW DELHI

SAGA ꟲ PRESS

AN IMPRINT OF SIMON & SCHUSTER, INC.

1230 AVENUE OF THE AMERICAS, NEW YORK, NEW YORK 10020

Foreword: "The Return of the Thin White Duke" copyright © 2008 by Alan Moore
The Dreamthief's Daughter copyright © 2001, 2013 by Michael & Linda Moorcock
The Skrayling Tree copyright © 2003, 2013 by Michael & Linda Moorcock
The White Wolf's Son copyright © 2005, 2013 by Michael & Linda Moorcock

First Saga Press hardcover edition October 2022

SAGA PRESS and colophon are trademarks of Simon & Schuster, Inc.

For information about special discounts for bulk purchases, please contact Simon & Schuster Special Sales at 1-866-506-1949 or business@simonandschuster.com.

The Simon & Schuster Speakers Bureau can bring authors to your live event. For more information or to book an event, contact the Simon & Schuster Speakers Bureau at 1-866-248-3049 or visit our website at www.simonspeakers.com.

Interior design by Kathryn A. Kenney-Peterson

Manufactured in Spain

1   3   5   7   9   10   8   6   4   2

Library of Congress Cataloging-in-Publication Data is available.

ISBN 978-1-5344-4574-1
ISBN 978-1-5344-4576-5 (ebook)

CONTENTS

ART CREDITS

ENDPAPERS BY JOHN COLLIER

PAGE XIII BY JOHN PICACIO

PAGE 902 BY ROBERT GOULD

JACKET POSTER ILLUSTRATIONS BY ROBERT GOULD

THE RETURN OF
THE THIN WHITE DUKE

I remember Melniboné. Not the empire, obviously, but its aftermath, its débris: mangled scraps of silver filigree from brooch or breastplate, tatters of checked silk accumulating in the gutters of the Tottenham Court Road. Exquisite and depraved, Melnibonéan culture had been shattered by a grand catastrophe before recorded history began—probably sometime during the mid-1940s—but its shards and relics and survivors were still evident in London's tangled streets as late as 1968. You could still find reasonably priced bronze effigies of Arioch amongst the stalls on Portobello Road, and when I interviewed Dave Brock of Hawkwind for the English music paper SOUNDS in 1981 he showed me the black runesword fragment he'd been using as a plectrum since the band's first album. Though the cruel and glorious civilisation of Melniboné was by then vanished as though it had never been, its flavours and its atmospheres endured, a perfume lingering for decades in the basements and back alleys of the capital. Even the empire's laid-off gods and demons were effectively absorbed into the ordinary British social structure; its Law Lords rapidly became a cornerstone of the judicial system while its Chaos Lords went, for the most part, into industry or government. Former Melnibonéan Lord of Chaos Sir Giles Pyaray, for instance, currently occupies a seat at the Department of Trade and Industry, while his company Pyaray Holdings has been recently awarded major contracts as a part of the ongoing reconstruction of Iraq.

Despite Melniboné's pervasive influence, however, you will find few public figures ready to acknowledge their huge debt to this all-but forgotten world, perhaps because the wilful decadence and tortured romance that Melniboné exemplified has fallen out of favour with the resolutely medieval world view we embrace today throughout the globe's foremost Neoconservative theocracies. Just as with the visitor's centres serving the Grand Canyon that have been instructed to remove all reference to the canyon's geologic age lest they offend creationists, so too has any evidence for the existence of Melniboné apparently been stricken from the record. With its central governmental district renamed Marylebone and its distinctive azure ceremonial tartans sold off in job lots to boutiques in the King's Road, it's entirely possible that those of my own post-war generation might have never heard about Melniboné were it not for allusions found in the supposedly fictitious works of the great London writer, Michael Moorcock.

My own entry to the Moorcock oeuvre came, if I recall correctly, by way of a Pyramid Books "science fantasy" anthology entitled *The Fantastic Swordsmen*, edited by the ubiquitous L. Sprague de Camp and purchased from the first science fiction, fantasy and comics bookshop, Dark They Were and Golden Eyed, itself a strikingly neo-Melnibonéan establishment. The paperback, touchingly small and underfed to modern eyes, had pages edged a brilliant Naples yellow and came with the uninviting cover image of a blond barbarian engaged in butchering some sort of octopus, clearly an off-day from the usually inspired Jack Gaughan. The contents, likewise, while initially attractive to an undiscriminating fourteen-year-old boy, turned out upon inspection to be widely varied in their quality, a motley armful of fantastic tales swept up under the loose rubric of sword-and-sorcery, ranging from a pedestrian early outing by potboiler king John Jakes, through more accomplished works by the tormented would-be cowboy Robert Howard, or a dreamlike early Lovecraft piece, or one by Lovecraft's early model, Lord Dunsany, to a genuinely stylish and more noticeably modern offering from Fritz Leiber. Every story had a map appended to it, showing the geographies of the distinct imaginary worlds in which the various narratives were set, and all in all it was a decent and commendable collection for its genre, for its time,

And then, clearly standing aloof and apart from the surrounding mighty-thewed pulp and Dunsanian fairy tales, there was the Elric yarn by Michael Moorcock.

Now, at almost forty years' remove, I can't even recall which one it was—one of the precious handful from *The Stealer of Souls*, no doubt—but I still remember vividly its impact. Elric, decadent, hallucinatory and feverish, its alabaster hero battled with his howling, parasitic blade against a paranoiac backdrop that made other fantasy environments seem lazy and anaemic in their Chinese-takeaway cod orientalism or their snug Arcadian idylls. Unlike every other sword-wielding protagonist in the anthology, it was apparent that Moorcock's wan, drug-addicted champion would not be stigmatised by a dismaying jacket blurb declaring him to be in the tradition of J. R. R. Tolkien: The Melnibonéan landscape, seething, mutable, warped by the touch of fractal horrors, was an anti-matter antidote to Middle Earth, a toxic and fluorescing elf-repellent. Elric's world churned with a fierce and unselfconscious poetry, churned with the breakneck energies of its own furious pulp-deadline composition. Not content to stand there shuffling uneasily beneath its threadbare sword-and-sorcery banner, Moorcock's prose instead took the whole stagnant genre by its throat and pummelled it into a different shape, transmuted Howard's blustering over-compensation and the relatively tired and bloodless efforts of Howard's competitors into a new form, a delirious romance with different capabilities, delivered in a language that was adequate to all the tumult and upheaval of its times, a voice that we could recognise.

Moorcock was evidently writing from experience, with the extravagance and sheer exhilaration of his stories marking him as from a different stock than the majority of his contemporaries. The breadth and richness of his influences hinted that he was himself some kind of a Melnibonéan ex-pat, nurtured by the cultural traditions of his homeland, drawing from a more exotic pool of reference than that available to those who worked within the often stultifying literary conventions found in post-war England. When Moorcock commenced his long career while in his teens he showed no interest in the leading authors of the day, the former Angry Young Men who were in truth far more petulant than angry and had never been that young, cleaving instead to sombre, thoughtful voices such as that of Angus Wilson, or to marvellous, baroque outsiders such as Mervyn Peake. After solid apprentice work on his conventional blade-swinging hero Sojan in the weekly TARZAN comic book, or in the Sexton Blake adventures that he penned alongside notables such as the wonderful Jack Trevor Story (and, as rumour has it, even Irish genius Flann O'Brien), Moorcock emerged as a formidable rare beast with an extensive reach, as capable of championing the then-unpublished *Naked Lunch* by Burroughs (W. S.) as he was of appreciating the wild colour and invention that was to be found in Burroughs

(E. R.). Whether by virtue of his possibly Melnibonéan heritage or by some other means, Moorcock was consummately hip and brought the sensibilities of a progressive and much wider world of art and literature into a field that was, despite the unrestrained imagination promised by its sales pitch, for the most part both conservative and inward-looking.

Growing out of a mid-1950s correspondence between the young writer and his long-serving artist confederate James Cawthorn, the first Elric stories were an aromatic broth of Abraham Merritt and Jack Kerouac, of Bertolt Brecht, and Anthony Skene's Monsieur Zenith, the albino drug-dependent foe of Sexton Blake who'd turned out to have more charisma than his shrewd detective adversary. With the series finally seeing daylight in Carnell's SCIENCE FANTASY in 1961, it was immediately quite clear that a dangerous mutation had occurred within the narrow gene pool of heroic fantasy, a mutation just as elegant and threatening as Elvis Presley had turned out to be in the popular music of this decade, or that James Dean represented in its cinema. Most noticeably, Elric in no way conformed to the then-current definition of a hero, being instead a pink-eyed necromaniac invalid, a traitor to his kind and slayer of his wife, a sickly and yet terrifying spiritual vampire living without hope at the frayed limits of his own debatable humanity. Bad like Gene Vincent, sick like Lenny Bruce and haunted by addiction like Bill Burroughs, though Elric ostensibly existed in a dawn world of antiquity this was belied by his being so obviously a creature of his Cold War brothel-creeper times, albeit one whose languid decadence placed him slightly ahead of them and presciently made his pallid, well-outfitted figure just as emblematic of the psychedelic '60s yet to come.

By 1963, when first the character appeared in book form, Britain was beginning to show healthy signs of energetic uproar and a glorious peacock-feathered blossoming, against which setting Elric would seem even more appropriate. The Beatles had, significantly, changed the rules of English culture by erupting from a background of the popular and vulgar to make art more vital and transformative than anything produced by the polite society-approved and -vetted artistic establishment. The wrought-iron and forbidding gates had been thrown open so that artists, writers and musicians could storm in to explore subjects that seemed genuinely relevant to the eventful and uncertain world in which they found themselves; could define the acceptable according to their own rules. Within

five years, when I first belatedly discovered Elric sometime during 1968, provincial English life had been transmuted into a fantasmagoric territory, at least
psychologically, so that the exploits of this fated, chalk-white aesthete somehow
struck the perfect resonance, made Moorcock's anti-hero just as much a symbol
of the times as demonstrations at the US embassy in Grosvenor Square, or Jimi
Hendrix, or the OZ trial.

Naturally, by then Moorcock himself had moved on and was editing NEW
WORLDS, the last and the best of traditional science fiction magazines published
in England. Under Moorcock's guidance, the magazine became a vehicle for
modernist experiment, gleefully re-imagining the SF genre as a field elastic
enough to include the pathological and alienated "condensed novels" of J. G.
Ballard, the brilliantly skewed and subverted conventional science fiction tropes
of Barrington Bayley, and even the black urban comedies dished up by old Sexton Blake mucker Jack Trevor Story. Moorcock's own main contribution to the
magazine, aside from his task as commander of the entire risky, improbable
venture, came in the form of his Jerry Cornelius stories.

Cornelius, a multiphasic modern pierrot with his doings catalogued by most
of Moorcock's NEW WORLDS writing stable at one time or other, rapidly became
an edgy mascot for the magazine and also for the entire movement that the
magazine was spearheading, an icon of the fractured moral wasteland England
would become after the wild, fluorescent brushfire of the 1960s had burned
out. His début, starting in the pages of NEW WORLDS in 1965 and culminating
in Avon Books' publication of *The Final Programme* during 1968 was a spectacular affair—"Michael Moorcock's savagely satirical breakthrough in specu-
lative fiction, *The Final Programme*, a breathtakingly vivid, rapid-fire novel of
tomorrow that says things you may not want to hear about today!"—and a
mind-bending apparent change of tack for those readers who thought that they
knew Moorcock from his Elric or his Dorian Hawkmoon fantasies. Even its
dedication, "To Jimmy Ballard, Bill Burroughs, and the Beatles, who are pointing the way through," seemed dangerously avant-garde within the cosy rocket-
robot-raygun comfort zone of early '60s science fiction. As disorienting as *The
Final Programme* was, however, its relentless novelty was undercut by a peculiar
familiarity: Cornelius's exploits mirrored those of Elric of Melniboné almost
exactly, blow for blow. Even a minor character like the Melnibonéan servant,

Tanglebones, could turn up anagrammatised as the Cornelius family's retainer John Gnatbeelson. It became clear that far from abandoning his haunted and anaemic prince of ruins, Moorcock had in some way cleverly refracted that persona through a different glass, until it looked and spoke and acted differently, became a different creature fit for different times, while still retaining all the fascinating, cryptic charge of the original.

As Moorcock's work evolved into progressively more radical and startling forms over the coming decades, this process of refracting light and ideas through a prototypical Melnibonéan gemstone would continue. Even in the soaring majesty of *Mother London* or the dark symphony of Moorcock's Pyat quartet, it is still possible to hear the music of Tarkesh, the Boiling Sea, or Old Hrolmar. With these later works and with Moorcock's ascent to literary landmark, it has become fashionable to assert that only in such offerings as the exquisite *Vengeance of Rome* are we seeing the real Moorcock; that the staggering sweep of glittering fantasy trilogies that preceded these admitted masterpieces are in some way minor works, safely excluded from the author's serious canon. This is to misunderstand, I think, the intertextual and organic whole of Moorcock's writings. All the blood and passion that informs his work has the genetic markers of Melniboné, stamped clearly on each paragraph, each line. No matter where the various strands of Moorcock's sprawling opera ended up, or in what lofty climes, the bloodline started out with Elric. All the narratives have his mysterious, apocalyptic eyes.

These tales are among the first rush of that blood, the first pure spurts from what would prove to be a deep and never-ending fountain. Messy, uncontrolled and beautiful, the stories are the raw heart of Michael Moorcock, the spells that first drew me and all the numerous admirers of his work with whom I am acquainted into Moorcock's luminous and captivating web. Read them and remember the frenetic, fiery world and times that gave them birth. Read them and recall the days when all of us were living in Melniboné.

ALAN MOORE
NORTHAMPTON
31 JANUARY, 2007

THE DREAMTHIEF'S DAUGHTER

For my god-daughter, Oona von B
and for Berry and Co.

THE DREAMTHIEF'S DAUGHTER
CONTENTS

AUTHOR'S NOTE

On 10 May, 1941, a few months after Britain had unexpectedly won the crucial Battle of Britain and at last stopped the Nazi expansion, Rudolf Hess, Hitler's deputy and his oldest remaining friend within the Nazi hierarchy, flew to Scotland on his own initiative. He had crucial information for Churchill, he said. Arrested, he was interrogated by MI5, British military intelligence. What he told MI5 was immediately suppressed. Certain files have since disappeared. Some existing files have still not been made public. Hitler attacked the Soviet Union on 24 June, 1941. Many believe that Hess was appalled by Hitler's decision and was trying to make a final bargain with Churchill. Churchill never permitted a meeting with Hess, who died in mysterious circumstances in 1987.

BOOK ONE

Sleep, and I'll steal your silver;
Dream, and I'll steal your soul.

—Wheldrake,
The Knight of the Balance

I

Stolen Dreams

My name is Ulric, Graf von Bek, and I am the last of my earthly line. An unhealthy child, cursed with the family disease of albinism, I was born and raised in Bek, Saxony, in the early years of the century. I was trained to rule our province wisely and justly, to preserve the status quo, in the best traditions of the Lutheran Church.

My mother died giving birth to me. My father perished in a ghastly fire, when our old tower was partially destroyed. My brothers were all far older than I, and engaged mostly in military diplomacy abroad, so the estate, it was thought, would be my responsibility. It was not expected that I would wish to expose, any longer than necessary, my strange, ruby eyes to the light of common day. I accepted this sentence of virtual imprisonment as my due. It had been suffered by many ancestors before me. There were terrible tales of what had become of twin albino children born to my great-grandmother.

Any unease I had in this role was soon subdued as, in my questioning years, I made friends with the local Catholic priest and became an obsessive fencer. I would discuss theology with Fra. Cornelius in the morning and practise my swordplay every afternoon. All my bafflement and frustrations were translated into learning that subtle and dangerous art. Not the sort of silly swashbuckling boy-braggadocio nonsense affected by the nouveaux riches and ennobled bürgermeisters who perform half-invented rituals of ludicrous manliness at Heidelberg.

No real lover of the sword would subject the instrument to such vulgar, clattering nonsense. With precious few affectations, I hope, I became a true swordsman, an expert in the art of the duel to the death. For in the end, existentialist that I am, entropy alone is the only enemy worth challenging and to conquer entropy is to reach a compromise with death, always the ultimate victor in our conflicts.

There's something to be said for dedicating one's life to an impossible cause. Perhaps an easier decision for a solitary albino aristocrat full of the idealism of previous centuries, disliked by his contemporaries and a discomfort to his tenants. One given to reading and brooding. But not unaware, never unaware, that outside the old, thick walls of Bek, in my rich and complex Germany, the world was beginning to march to simplistic tunes, numbing the race mind so that it would deceive itself into making war again. Into destroying itself again.

Instinctively, while still a teenager, and after an inspiring school trip to the Nile Valley and other great sites of our civilisation, I plunged deeply into archaic studies.

Old Bek grew all around me. A towered manor house to which rooms and buildings had been added over the centuries, she emerged like a tree from the lush grounds and thickly wooded hills of Bek, surrounded by the cedars, poplars and cypresses my crusader forebears had brought from the Holy Land, by the Saxon oaks into which my earlier ancestors had bound their souls, so that they and the world were rooted in the same earth. Those ancestors had first fought against Charlemagne and then fought with him. They had sent two sons to Roncesvalles. They had been Irish pirates. They had served King Ethelred of England.

My tutor was old von Asch, black, shrunken and gnarled, whom my brothers called The Walnut, whose family had been smiths and swordsmen since the time their first ancestor struck the bronze weapon. He loved me. I was a vessel for his experience. I was willing to learn anything, try any trick to improve my skills. Whatever he demanded, I would eventually rise to meet that expectation. I was, he said, the living record of his family wisdom.

But von Asch's wisdom was nothing sensational. Indeed, his advice was subtle and appealed, as perhaps he knew, to my aestheticism, my love of the complex and the symbolic. Rather than impose his ideas on me, he planted them like seeds. They would grow if the conditions were right. This was the secret of his teaching. He somehow made you realise that you were doing it yourself, that the situation demanded certain responses and what he helped you to do was trust your intuition and use it.

Of course, there was his notion of the sword's song.

"You have to listen for the song," he said. "Every great individual sword has her own song. Once you find that song and hear it clearly, then you can fight with it, for the song is the very essence of the sword. The sword was not forged to decorate walls or be a lifted signal of victory and dominance, but to cut flesh, bone and sinew, and kill. She is not an extension of your manhood, nor an expression of your selfhood. She is an instrument of death. At her best, she kills injustice. If this notion is objectionable to you, my son—and I do not suggest for an instant that you apply it, simply that you acknowledge its truth—then you should put away the sword for ever. Fighting with swords is a refined art, but it is an art best enjoyed when also a matter of life and death."

To fight for the ultimate—against oblivion—seemed to me exactly the noble destiny the Raven Sword, our ancestral blade, deserved. Few down the centuries had shown much interest in this queerly wrought old longsword inscribed with mysterious runic verses. It was even considered something of an embarrassment. We had a few mad ancestors who had perhaps not been exemplary in their tormented curiosity and had put the sword to strange uses. There was a report in the Mirenburg press only in the last century. Some madman posing as a legendary creature called "Crimson Eyes" had run amok with a blade, killing at least thirty people before disappearing. For a while the von Beks had been suspected. The story of our albinism was well known there. But no person was ever brought to justice. He featured dramatically in the street literature of the day, like Jack the Ripper, Fantômas and Springheeled Jack.

Part of our vulgar and bloody past. We tended to want to forget the sword and its legends. But there were few in the empty, abandoned and lost rooms at Bek, which had no family to fill them any longer, who could remember. Only a few retainers too old for war or the city. And, of course, books.

When it was time for me to handle that sword whenever I wished, von Asch taught me her main songs—for this blade was a special blade.

There were extraordinary resonances to the steel, however you turned it. A vibrancy which seemed feral. Like a perfect musical instrument. She moved to those songs. She seemed to guide me. He showed me how to coax from her, by subtle strokes and movements of my fingers and wrists, her songs of hatred and contempt, sweet songs of yearning bloodlust, melancholy memories of battles fought, determined revenge. But no love songs. Swords, said von Asch, rarely had hearts. And it was unwise to rely on their loyalty.

This particular weapon, which we called Ravenbrand, was a big longsword of black iron with a slender, unusual leaf-shaped blade. Our family legend said that it was forged by Friar Corvo, the Venetian armourer, who wrote the famous treatise on the subject. But there is a tale that Corvo—the Raven Smith, as Browning called him—only found the sword, or at least the blade itself, and wrought nothing but the hilt.

Some said it was Satan's own blade. Others said it was the Devil Himself. The Browning poem describes how Corvo gave his soul to bring the sword to life again. One day I would go with our Ravenbrand to Venice and discover for myself what truth there might be to the story. Von Asch went off and never came back. He was searching for a certain kind of metal which he thought might be found on the Isle of Morn.

Then it was August 1914 and for the first months of that war I longed to be old enough to join it. As the realities were reported by the returning veterans— young men hardly older than myself—I began to wonder how such a war could ever be ended.

My brothers died of disease or were blown apart in some nameless pit. Soon I had no other living relative but my ancient grandfather, who lived in sheltered luxury on the outskirts of Mirenburg in Wäldenstein and would look at me from huge, pale, disappointed grey eyes which saw the end of everything he had worked for. After a while he would wave me away. Eventually he refused to have me at his bedside.

I was inducted in 1918. I joined my father's old infantry regiment and, with the rank of lieutenant, was sent immediately to the Western Front. The War lasted just long enough to demonstrate what cruel folly it was. We could rarely speak of what we'd witnessed.

Sometimes it seemed a million voices called out to us from no man's land, pleading only for a release from pain. *Help me, help me, help me.* English. French. German. Russian. And the voices of a dozen disparate empires. Which screamed at the sight of their own exposed organs and ruined limbs. Which implored God to take away their pain. To bless them with death. Voices which could soon be ours.

They did not leave me when I slept. They turned and twisted in millions, screaming and wailing for release throughout my constant dreams. At night I left one horror to inhabit another. There seemed little difference between them.

What was worse, my dreams did not confine themselves to the current conflict but embraced every war Man had instigated.

Vividly, and no doubt thanks to my intense reading, I began to witness huge battles. Some of them I recognised from history. Most, however, were merely the repetition, with different costumes, of the obscenity I witnessed twenty-four hours a day from the trenches.

Towards the end, one or two of the dreams had something else in common. A beautiful white hare who ran through the warring men, apparently unnoticed and unharmed. Once she turned and looked back at me and her ruby-coloured eyes were my own. I felt I should follow her. But gradually the nightmares faded. Real life proved hard enough, perhaps.

We, who were technically the instigators of the war and subject to the victor's view of history, were humiliated by the Treaty of Versailles in which the Europeans squabbled with ruthless greed over the spoils, disgusted President Woodrow Wilson and stripped Germany of everything, including machinery with which to rebuild. The result, of course, was that as usual the common people were forced to pay far too high a price for the follies of exiled nobles. We live, die, know sickness and health, comfort and discomfort, because of the egos of a few stupid men.

To be fair, some of those nobles, such as myself, elected to stay and work for the restoration of the German Federation, though I had no liking for the swaggering aggression of the defeated Prussians, who had thought themselves unbeatable. These proud nationalists were the ones who supplied the rhetoric which, by 1920, was fuelling what would be the Nazi and Bolshevik movements, admittedly towards rather different ends. Germany defeated, impoverished, shamed.

The Serbian Black Hand had fallen upon our world and blighted it almost beyond recognition. All that Bismarck had built up in us, a sense of unity and mission, had been diverted to serve the ambitions of a few greedy businessmen, industrialists, gun-makers and their royal allies, a sour echo which many of those, in Berlin for instance, chose to ignore, or turn into an art of bitter realism giving us the likes of Brecht and Weill. The sardonic, popular rhythms of *The Threepenny Opera* were the musical accompaniment to the story of our ruin.

Germany remained on the verge of civil war, between right and left. Between the communist fighters and the nationalist Freikorps. Civil war was the greatest danger we feared. We saw what it had done to Russia.

There is no faster way of plunging a country into chaos than to make panicky decisions aimed at averting that chaos. Germany was recovering. Many thinking people believed that if the other great powers had supported Germany then, we should have had no Adolf Hitler. Creatures like Hitler emerge frequently because of a vacuum. They are conjured whole from yearning nothingness by our own negativity, by our Faustian appetites and dark greed.

Our family and its fortunes had been greatly reduced by the war. My friend the priest had become a missionary in the former German colony of Rwanda. I became a rather sorry, solitary individual. I was frequently advised to sell Bek. Bustling black-marketeers and rising fascists would offer to buy my ancestral seat from me. They thought they could buy the authority of place in the same way they had bought their grand houses and large motorcars.

In some ways, by having to manage my estates rather more desperately than in the past, I learned a little of the uncertainty and horror facing the average German who saw his country on the brink of total ruin.

It was easy to blame the victors. True, their tax on us was punitive, unjust, inhuman and foolish; it was the poison which the Nazis in Munich and other parts of Bavaria began to use to their own advantage.

Even as their popular support began to slide, the Nazi Party was able to take control of almost all the power in Germany. A power they had originally claimed for the Jews. But recently, unlike the Jews, they actually did control the media. On the radio, in the newspapers and magazines and movies, they began to tell the people whom they should love and whom they should hate.

How do you kill a million or so of your neighbours?

Well, first you say they are Unlike. They are Not Us. Not human. Only like us on the surface. Pretending to be us. Evil underneath in spite of all common experience. Then you compare them to unclean animals and you accuse them of plotting against you. And very soon you have the necessary madness in place to produce a holocaust.

This is by no means a new phenomenon, of course. The American Puritans characterised everyone who disagreed with them as evil and godless and probably witches. Andrew Jackson helped start an imaginary war which he then pretended to win in order to steal the treaty lands of Indian nations. The British and Americans went into China to save the country from the opium they had originally sold it. The Turks had to characterise Armenians as godless monsters in order to begin their appalling slaughter of the Christians. But in my time, save for the embarrassments of Martin Luther's fulminations against Jewry, such talk was strange to me in Bek and I could not believe that ultimately a civilised nation would tolerate it.

Frightened nations, however, will accept too easily the threat of civil war and the promise of the man who says he will avert it. Hitler averted civil war because he had no need of it. His opposition was delivered into his hands by the ballot boxes of a country which, at that time, had one of the best democratic constitutions in the world, superior in many ways to the American.

Hitler's opponents were already in his power, thanks to the authority of the State he had seized. We could all see this, those of us who were horrified, but it was impossible to convince anyone. So many German people so badly needed stability they were willing to cleave to the Nazis. And it was easier to forget a Jewish neighbour's disappearance than it was the concerns of your own relatives.

And so ordinary people were led into complicity in that evil, through deed or word or that awful silence, to become part of it, to defend against their own consciences, to hate themselves as well as others, to choose a strutting self-esteem over self-respect, and so devalue themselves as citizens.

In this way a modern dictatorship makes us rule ourselves on its behalf. We learn to gloss our self-disgust with cheap rhetoric, sentimental talk, claims of good will, protestations of innocence, of victimhood. And those of us who refuse are ultimately killed.

For all my determination to pursue the cause of peace, I still maintained my swordsmanship. It had become much more than a mere *pasatiempo*. It remained something of a cause, I suppose, a method of controlling what little there was still in my own control. The skills needed to wield the Raven Blade were highly specialised, for while my sword was balanced so perfectly that I could easily spin it in one hand, it was of heavy, flexible steel and had a life of its own. It seemed to flow through my hands, even as I practised.

The blade was impossible to sharpen with ordinary stone. Von Asch had given me a special grindstone, which appeared to be imbedded with pieces of diamond. Not that the blade ever needed much sharpening.

Freudians, who were busily interpreting our chaos in those days, would have known what to think of my tendency to bond with my blade and my unwillingness to be separated from it. Yet I felt I drew power from the weapon. Not the kind of brute, predatory power the Nazis so loved, but a permanent sustenance.

I carried the sword with me whenever I travelled, which was rarely. A local maker had fashioned a long gun case, into which Ravenbrand fitted discreetly, so that to the casual eye, with the case over my shoulder, I looked like some bucolic landsman prepared for a day's shooting or even fishing.

I had it in my mind that whatever happened to Bek, the sword and I would survive. Whatever the symbolic meaning of the sword was, I cannot tell you, save that it had been handled by my family for at least a thousand years, that it was said to have been forged for Wotan, had turned the tide at Roncesvalles, leading the monstrous horses of Carolingian chivalry against the invading Berber, had defended the Danish royal line at Hastings and served the Saxon cause in exile in Byzantium and beyond.

I suppose I was also superstitious, if not completely crazy, because I sensed there was a bond between myself and the sword. Something more than tradition or romance.

Meanwhile the quality of civil life continued to decline in Germany.

Even the town of Bek with her dreaming gables, twisted old roofs and chimneys, green-glazed windows, weekly markets and ancient customs, was not immune to the twentieth-century jackboot.

In the years before 1933, a small division of self-titled Freikorps, made up mostly of unemployed ex-soldiers commanded by NCOs who had given themselves the rank of captain or higher, paraded occasionally through the streets. They were not based in Bek, where I refused to allow any such goings-on, but in a neighbouring city. They had too many rivals in the city to contend with, I suspect, and felt more important showing their strength to a town of old people and children, which had lost most of its men.

These private armies controlled parts of Germany and were constantly in conflict with rivals, with communist groups and politicians who sought to curb their power, warning that civil war was inevitable if the Freikorps were not brought under control. Of course, this is what the Nazis offered to do—to control the very forces they were using to sow the seeds of further uncertainty about the future of our poor, humiliated Germany.

I share the view that if the Allies had been more generous and not attempted to suck the last marrow from our bones, Hitler and the Freikorps would have had nothing to complain of. But our situation was manifestly unjust and in such a climate even the most moderate of burghers can somehow find himself condoning the actions of people he would have condemned out of hand before the war.

Thus, in 1933, fearing Russian-style civil conflict worse than tyranny, many of us voted for a "strong man," in the hope it would bring us stability.

Sadly, of course, like most "strong men," Hitler was merely a political construct, no more the man of iron his followers declared him to be than any other of his wretched, ranting psychopathic type.

There were a thousand Hitlers in the streets of Germany, a thousand dispossessed, twitching, feckless neurotics, eaten up with jealousy and frustrated hatred. But Hitler worked hard at his gift for cheap political oratory, drew power from the worst elements of the mob, and spoke in the grossest emotional terms of our betrayal not, as some perceived it, by the greed of our leaders and the rapacity of our conquerors, but by a mysterious, almost supernatural, force they called "International Jewry."

Normally such blatant nonsense would have gathered together only the marginal and less intelligent members of society, but, as financial crisis followed crisis, Hitler and his followers had persuaded more and more ordinary Germans and business leaders that fascism was the only way to salvation.

Look at Mussolini in Italy. He had saved his nation, regenerated it, made people fear it again. He had masculinised Italy, they said. Made it virile as Germany could be made virile again. It is how they think, these people. *Guns and boots, flags and prongs / Blacks and whites. Rights and wrongs . . .* As Wheldrake put it in one of those angry doggerel pieces he wrote just before his death in 1927.

Simple pursuits. Simple answers. Simple truths.

Intellect, learning and moral decency were mocked and attacked as though they were mortal enemies. Men asserted their own vulnerable masculinity by insisting, as they so often do, that women stay at home and have babies. For all their worship of these earth goddesses, women were actually treated with sentimental contempt. Women were kept from all real power.

We are slow to learn. Neither the English, French nor American experiments in social order by imposition came to any good, and the communist and fascist experiments, equally puritanical in their rhetoric, demonstrated the same fact— that ordinary human beings are far more complex than simple truth and simple truth is fine for argument and clarification, but it is not an instrument for government, which must represent complexity if it is to succeed. It was no surprise to many that juvenile delinquency reached epidemic proportions in Germany by 1940, although the Nazis, of course, could not admit the problem which was not supposed to exist in the world they had created.

By 1933, in spite of so many of us knowing what the Nazis were like, they had taken control of parliament. Our constitution was no more than a piece of paper, burning amongst great, inspired books, by Mann, Heine, Brecht, Zweig and Remarque, which the Nazis heaped in blazing pyres at crossroads and in town squares. An act they termed "cultural cleansing." It was the triumph of ignorance and bigotry.

Boots, blackjacks and whips became the instruments of political policy. We could not resist because we could not believe what had happened. We had relied upon our democratic institutions. We were in a state of national denial. The realities, however, were soon demonstrated to us.

It was intolerable for any who valued the old humane virtues of German life, but our protests were silenced in the most brutally efficient ways. Soon there were only a few of us who continued to resist.

As the Nazi grip tightened, fewer and fewer of us spoke out, or even grumbled. The storm troopers were everywhere. They would arrest people on an arbitrary basis "just to give them a taste of what they'll get if they step out of line."

Several journalists I knew, who had no political affiliations, were locked up for months, released, then locked up again. Not only would they not speak when they were released, they were terrified of speech.

Nazi policy was to cow the protesting classes. They succeeded fairly well, with the compliance of the church and the army, but they did not entirely extinguish opposition. I, for instance, determined to join the White Rose Society, swore to destroy Hitler and work against his interests in every way.

I advertised my sympathies as best I could and was eventually telephoned by a young woman. She gave her name as "Gertie" and told me that she would be in touch as soon as it was safe. I believed they were probably checking my credentials, making sure I was not a spy or a potential traitor.

Twice in the streets of Bek I was pointed out as an unclean creature, some kind of leper. I was lucky to get home without being harmed. After that, I went out as little as possible, usually after dark. Frequently accompanied by my sword. Stupid as it sounds, for the storm troopers were armed with guns, the sword gave me a sense of purpose, a kind of courage, a peculiar security.

Not long after the second incident, when I had been spat at by brownshirt boys, who had also attacked my old manservant Reiter as an aristocrat's lackey, those bizarre, terrifying dreams began again. With even greater intensity. Wagnerian, almost. Thick with armour and heavy warhorses, bloody banners, butchering steel and blaring trumpets. All the potent, misplaced romance of conflict. The kind of imagery which powered the very movement I was sworn to fight.

Slowly the dreams took shape and in them I was again plagued by voices in languages I could not understand, full of a litany of unlikely, tongue-twisting names. It seemed to me I was listening to a long list of those who had already died violent deaths since the beginning of time—and those who were yet to die.

The resumption of my nightmares caused me considerable distress and alarmed my old servants who spoke of fetching the doctor or getting me to Berlin to see a specialist.

Yet before I could decide what action to take, the white hare appeared again. She ran swiftly over corpses, between the legs of metal-covered men, under the guns and lances of a thousand conflicting nations and religions. I could not tell if she wished me to follow her. This time she did not look back. I longed for her to turn, to show me her eyes again, to determine if she was, in fact, a version of myself—a self freed at last from that eternal struggle. It was as if she signalled the ending of the horror. I needed to know what she symbolised. I tried to call out, but I was dumb. Then I was deaf. Then blind.

And suddenly the dreams were gone. I would wake in the morning with that strange feeling of rapidly fading memory, of a vanishing reality, as a powerful dream disappears, leaving only the sense of having experienced it. A sense, in my case, of confusion and deep, deep dread. All I could remember was the vision of a white hare racing across a field of butchered flesh. Not a particularly pleasant feeling, but offering a relief from that nightly conflict.

Not only my nightmares had been stolen, but also my ordinary, waking dreams, my dreams of a lifetime of quiet study and benign action. Such a monkish life was the best someone of my appearance could hope for in those days which were merely an uneasy pause in the conflict we began by calling the Great War to end wars. Now we think of it as an entire century of war, where one dreadful conflict followed another, half of them justified as holy wars, or moral wars, or wars to help distressed minorities, but almost all of which were actually inspired by the basest of emotions, the most short-term of goals, the cruellest greed and that appalling self-righteousness which no doubt the Christian Crusaders had when they brought blood and terror to Jerusalem in the name of God and human justice.

So many quiet dreams like mine were stolen in that century. So many noble men and women, honest souls, were rewarded only with agony and obscene death.

Soon, thanks to the compliance of the church, we were privileged to see in Bek's streets pictures of Adolf Hitler, Chancellor of Germany, dressed in silver, shining armour and mounted on a white horse, carrying the banner of Christ and the Holy Grail, recalling all the legendary saviours of our people.

These bigoted philistines despised Christianity and had made the swastika the symbol of modern Germany, but they were not above corrupting our noblest idealism and historical imagery to further their evil.

It is a mark, I think, of the political scoundrel, one who speaks most of the people's rights and hopes and uses the most sentimental language to blame all others but his own constituents for the problems of the world. Always a "foreign threat," fear of "the stranger." "Secret intruders, illegal aliens . . ."

I still hear those voices in modern Germany and France and America and all the countries we once thought of as far too civilised to allow such horror within their own borders.

After many years I still fear, I suppose, a recurrence of that terrible dream into which I finally plunged. A dream far more real than any reality I had known, a dream without end. A dream of eternity. An experience of the complexity of our multiverse in all its vast, limitless variety, with all its potential for evil and its capacity for good.

Perhaps the only dream that was not stolen from me.

2

Uninvited Relatives

I was still waiting for another call from "Gertie" when in the early months of 1934 I had an unexpected and rather alarming visitor to Bek.

My people are related through marriage and other kinships to the traditional rulers of Mirenburg, the capital of Wäldenstein, which the Nazis, and later the Soviets, would annex. Although predominantly of Slavic stock, the principality has for hundreds of years been culturally linked to Germany through language and common concerns. It was my family's practice to spend the Season in Mirenburg at least. Some members, such as my rather unwholesome Uncle Ricky, disgraced in Germany, chose to live there almost permanently.

The rulers of Mirenburg had not survived the tenor of the century. They, too, had known civil war, most of it instigated by foreign interests who had always sought to control Wäldenstein. The Badehoff-Krasny family had been restored to power, but more as clients of Austria than as independent rulers. They had married into the von Mincts, one of the great Mirenburg dynasties.

Hungary, of course, also possessed an interest in the tiny country. The current Prince of Wäldenstein was my cousin Gaynor, whose mother had been one of the most beautiful women in Buda-Pesht and was still reckoned a powerful political mind. I knew and admired my aunt. In middle years she was an impressive woman, maintaining her adopted country with all the skills of a Bismarck.

She was ailing now. The rise of fascism had shocked and exhausted her. Mussolini's successes were an abomination to her, and Hitler was inconceivably shallow and vicious in his political rhetoric, his ambitions and claims. But, as she said when last I saw her, Germany's soul had been stolen already. Hitler was merely addressing the corpse of German democracy. He had killed nothing. He had grown out of the grave, she said. Grown out of that corpse like an epidemic which had rapidly infected the entire country.

"And where is Germany's soul?" I asked. "Who stole it?"

"It's safe enough, I think." She had winked at me, crediting me with more wit than I possessed. And that was all she had said on the subject.

Prince Gaynor Paul St Odhran Badehoff-Krasny von Minct lacked his mother's calm intelligence but had all her wonderful Hungarian beauty and a charm which often disarmed his political opponents. At one time he had shared his mother's politics, but it seemed he had followed the road of many frustrated idealists in those days and saw fascism as the strong force that would revitalise an exhausted Europe and ease the pain of all those who still suffered the war's consequences.

Gaynor was no racialist. Wäldenstein was traditionally philo-Semitic (though not so tolerant of her gypsies) and his fascism, at least as he presented it to me, looked more to Mussolini than to Hitler. I still found the ideas either foolish or unpalatable, a mélange of kulak bigotry, certainly not in any serious philosophical or political tradition, for all their seduction of thinkers like Heidegger and their incorporation of a few misunderstood Nietzschean slogans.

It shocked me, however, to see him arrive in an official black Mercedes, festooned with swastikas, wearing the uniform of a captain in the "élite" SS, now superior to Röhm's SA, the original rough-and-ready Freikorps fighters who had become an embarrassment to Hitler. There was still a considerable amount of snow. It would not be until the summer that Ernst Röhm and all Hitler's other Nazi rivals and embarrassments were murdered in the so-called Night of the Long Knives. Röhm's great enemy, now rising rapidly in the Party, was the colourless little prude Heinrich Himmler, the boss of the SS, with his prissy pince-nez, an ex-chicken farmer, whose power would soon be second only to Hitler's.

My manservant Reiter disdainfully opened the door for them and took my cousin's card. He announced, in high sarcasm, the honour of the arrival of Captain Paul von Minct. Before they were taken below stairs by a determined Reiter, Gaynor was addressed as Captain von Minct both by his driver and by the skull-faced Prussian, Lieutenant Klosterheim, whose eyes glittered from within the deep caverns of their sockets.

Gaynor looked splendid and sinister in the black-and-silver uniform with its red-and-black swastika insignia. He was, as usual, completely engaging and amusing, making some self-deprecating murmur about his uniform even as he followed the servants up the stairs. I invited him, as soon as he was in his rooms and refreshed, to join me on the terrace before dinner. His driver and the secretary, Klosterheim, would take their supper in the servants' hall. Klosterheim had seemed to resent this a little, but then accepted it with the air of a man who had been insulted too many times for this to matter. I was glad he wasn't eating with us. His sickly, grey skin and almost fleshless head gave him the appearance of a dead man.

It was a relatively warm evening and the moon was already rising as the sun set, turning the surrounding landscape to glittering white and bloody shadow. This would probably be our last snow. I almost regretted its passing.

As I lit a cigarette, I saw a movement in the copse to my left and suddenly, from the bushes, darted a large white hare. She ran into a stain of scarlet sunlight then hesitated, looked to left and right and loped forward a few paces. She was an identical animal to the one I had seen in my dreams. I almost called to her. Instinctively I held my peace. Either the Nazis would think me mad, or they would be suspicious of me. Yet I wanted to reach out to the hare and reassure her that she was in no danger from me. I felt as a father might feel to a child.

Then the white hare had made her decision and was moving again. I watched her run, a faint powdering of snow rising like mist around her feet as she sped rapidly towards the darkness of the oaks on the far side. I heard a sound from the house and turned. When I looked back, the hare had vanished.

Gaynor came down in perfect evening dress and accepted a cigarette from my case. We agreed that the sun setting over the old oaks and cypresses, the soft, snowy roofs and leaning chimneys of Bek did the soul good. We said little while, as true romantics, we savoured a view Goethe would have turned into a cause. I mentioned to him that I had seen a snow hare, running across the far meadow. His response was odd.

He shrugged. "Oh, she'll be no bother to us," he said.

When it was twilight and growing a little chilly, we continued to sit outside under the moon exchanging superficial questions and answers about obscure relatives and common acquaintances. He mentioned a name. I said that to my astonishment he had joined the Nazi Party. Why would someone of that sort do such a thing? And I let the question hang.

He laughed.

"Oh, no, cousin. Never fear! I didn't volunteer. I'm only a nominal Nazi, an honorary captain in the SS. It makes them feel respectable. And it's a useful uniform for travelling in Germany these days. After a visit I made a few weeks ago to Berlin, they offered me the rank. I accepted it. They assured me that I would not be called up in time of war! I had a visit, a letter. You know how they cultivate people like ourselves. Why, Mussolini even made the king a fascist! It helps convince old fogies like you that the Nazis are no longer a bunch of uneducated, unemployed, unthinking butchers."

I told him that I remained a sceptic. All I saw were the same thugs with the spending power of a looted state willing to pay anything to cultivate those people whose association with their Party would give it authority in the wider world.

"Precisely," he said. "But we can use these thugs for our own ends, can't we? To improve the world? They know in their bones that they have no real moral position or political programmes. They know how to seize and hold power, but not much else. They need people like us, cousin. And the more people like us join them, the more they will become like us."

I told him that in my experience most people seemed to become like them. He said that it was because there were not yet enough of "us" running things. I suggested that this was dangerous logic. I had heard of no individuals corrupting power, but I had seen many individuals corrupted by it. He found this amusing. He said that it depended what you meant by power. And how you used that power when it was yours. To attack and slander tax-paying citizens because of their race and religion, I said. Power to do that? Of course not, he said. The Jewish Question was a nonsense. We all knew that. The poor old Jews were always the scapegoats. They'd survive this bit of political theatre. Nobody ever came to serious harm doing a few physical exercises in a well-ordered open-air environment. Hadn't I seen the film of those camps? They had every luxury. He had the grace to change the conversation as we went into dinner.

We spent the meal discussing the Nazi reorganisation of the legal system and what it meant for lawyers trained in a very different tradition. At that time we had not seen the ruin which fascism brought to all who professed it and still talked about the "good" and "bad" aspects of the system. It would be a year or two before ordinary people came to understand the fundamental evil which had settled on our nation. Gaynor's views were common. We had grown used to anti-Jewish rhetoric and understood it to have no meaning beyond gathering a few right-wing votes. Many of our Jewish friends refused to take it seriously, so why should we? We all failed to understand how the Nazis had made that rhetoric their reality.

Although the Nazis had developed concentration camps from the moment they came to power and used exactly the same methods at the beginning of their rule as they would at the end, we had no experience of such appalling cruelty and horror, and in our desire to avert the foulness of the trenches, we had created a worse foulness from our unthinking appetites and fears. Even when we received credible stories of Nazi brutality we thought them to be isolated cases. Even the Jews scarcely understood what was happening, and they were the chief objects of that brutality.

That is how we take for granted the fundamental social bargain of our democracy, whose deep, historic freedoms were won for us by our ancestors, step by noble step, through the centuries, the bones and sinews of our common compact. When those structures are forgotten or destroyed, we know no other way to think.

So familiar had their democratic freedoms and rights become to those citizens that they constantly asked "What have I done?" to brutes who had overturned the rule of law and replaced it with violence and raging hatred, with loathing and unwholesome sexuality. These were not policemen but torturers, thieves, rapists and murderers who had been given power by our own lack of moral courage and self-respect. And now they controlled us all! We have nothing to fear, the great FDR would tell us, but fear itself. Fear won in this case.

Although not of a superstitious disposition, I felt that real evil had fallen upon our world. Ironically, the century had started with the common belief that war and injustice were rapidly being eradicated. Had our complacency encouraged attack? It was as if some demonic force had been attracted by the stink of the Boer War's carnage, by Leopold's Congo, by the Armenian genocide, by the Great War, by the millions of corpses which filled the ditches, gutters and trenches of the world from Paris to Peking. Greedily feasting, the force grew strong enough to begin preying upon the living.

After dinner it was a bit chilly for the terrace, so we smoked our cigars by the fire in the study and enjoyed our brandy and soda and the familiarity of old-fashioned, civilised comforts. I realised that my cousin had not come for a vacation. Some sort of business brought him to Bek, and I wondered when he would raise the issue.

He had spent the past week in Berlin and was full of gossip about Hitler's new hierarchy. Göring was a great snob and liked to cultivate the aristocracy. So Prince Gaynor—whom the Germans preferred to call by the name of Paul von Minct—was the personal guest of the Reichsmarschall which, he said, was a great deal better than being Hitler's personal guest. Hitler, he assured me, was the most boring little man on the face of the planet. All he liked to do was drone on and on about his half-baked ideas while a flunky played the same Franz Lehár records over and over again. An evening with Hitler, he said, was like the longest evening you could imagine with your prissy maiden aunt. It was hard to believe his old friends, who said he used to keep them in fits of laughter with his impressions and jokes. Goebbels was too withdrawn to be good company and confined himself to sly remarks about the other Nazis, but Göring was great fun and had a genuine love of art to which his colleagues only pretended. He was making it his business to rescue threatened paintings from the Nazi censor. In fact his house in Berlin had become a haven, a repository for all kinds of art, including ancient German folk objects and weaponry.

Although that ironic, slightly mocking tone never left him, I was not convinced that Gaynor was merely playing along with the Nazis in order to keep Wäldenstein free from their direct influence. He said he accepted the realpolitik of the situation, but hoped that it would suit the new German masters to let his little country remain at least superficially independent. Yet I sensed more than this. I sensed his attraction to the whole perverse slew of corrupted romanticism. He was drawn by the enormous power he saw Hitler and Co. now wielding. I had the feeling that he did not want to share in that power; he wanted to take it all for himself. Perhaps he intended to set himself up as the new Prince of the Greater Germany? He joked that he had as much Jewish and Slavic blood as he had Aryan, but it seemed the Nazis turned a blind eye to some of one's ancestors if one was useful enough to them.

And it was clear that "Captain von Minct" was currently useful enough to the Nazis for them to equip him with a staff car, a driver and a secretary. And from his manner, it was obvious he was here on some connected business. I could only believe my eyes and use my intelligence. Had Gaynor been sent here to recruit me, too?

Or perhaps, I wondered, he had been sent to kill me. Then logic told me that he'd have many better means of doing that than inviting himself to dinner. The one thing the Nazis were unconcerned about was the murder of their opponents. They hardly needed to be clandestine about it.

I needed fresh air. I suggested we stroll onto the terrace. The moonlight was dramatic.

Abruptly, he proposed that his secretary, Lieutenant Klosterheim, join us. "He's a little touchy about being treated as an outsider and he's rather well-connected, I understand, to Goebbels's wife's people. An old mountain family. One of those which refused all honours and maintained their landsman status as a matter of pride. The family had some kind of fortress in the Harz Mountains for a thousand years. They call themselves yeomen-mountaineers, but my guess is they kept themselves through banditry during most of their history. He also has other relatives in the Church."

I no longer much cared. Gaynor's company had begun to irritate me and it was growing harder for me to remember that he was my guest. Klosterheim might relieve the atmosphere.

This fantasy was dispelled the moment the cadaverous, monkish figure in his tight SS uniform came out onto the terrace, his cap under his arm, his breath steaming with a whiteness which seemed colder than the surrounding air. I apologised for my rudeness and invited him to drink. He waved a pocket *Mein Kampf* at me and said he had plenty to engage him in his room. He carried the air of a fanatic and reminded me in many ways of his neurotic Führer. Gaynor seemed almost deferential to him.

Klosterheim agreed to take a small glass of Bénédictine. As I handed him his drink he spoke to Gaynor over my shoulder. "Have you made the proposition yet, Captain von Minct?"

Gaynor laughed. A little strained. I turned to ask him a question and he raised his hand. "A small matter, cousin, which can be discussed at any time. Lieutenant Klosterheim is very direct and efficient, but he sometimes lacks the subtler graces."

"We are not very gentlemanly at Klosterheim," said the lieutenant severely. "We have no time to cultivate fine manners, for life is hard and constantly threatened. We've defended your borders since time began. All we have are our ancient traditions. Our craggy fortresses. Our pride and our privacy."

I suggested that modern tourism might consequently be welcomed by his family and bring them some relief. Some ease, at last. A busload of Bavarians round the old place and one could put one's feet up for a week. I'd do the same, only all I had was a glorified farmhouse. I don't know what encouraged such levity in me. Perhaps it was a response to his unremitting sobriety. Something unpleasant glinted from his eye-sockets and then dulled again.

"Perhaps so," he said. "Yes. It would give us the easy life, eh?" He consumed his Bénédictine and made an awkward attempt at grace. "But Captain von Minct came here, I believe, to ease one of your burdens, Herr Count?"

"I have none that needs easing," I said.

"Of responsibility. Of stewardship." Gaynor was now cultivating a rather over-hearty manner. Klosterheim had no trouble sounding threatening but Gaynor wanted my approval as well as whatever it was he had come for.

"You know I place little value on our remaining heirlooms," I said, "except where they pertain to personal, family matters. Is there something you want?"

"You remember the old sword you used to play with before you went to the war? Black with age? Must have rusted through eventually. Rather like von Asch himself, your tutor. What did you do with that old sword in the end? Give it away? Sell it? Or did you place a more sentimental value on it?"

"Presumably, cousin, you speak of the sword Ravenbrand."

"Just so, cousin. Ravenbrand. I had forgotten you christened it with a nickname."

"It has never had a different name. It is as old as our family. It has all sorts of legendary nonsense attached to it, of course, but no evidence. Just the usual stories we invent to make generations of farmers seem more interesting. Ghosts and old treasure. No antiquarian or genuine historian would give credence to those legends. They are as familiar as they are unlikely." I became a little alarmed. Surely he had not come here to loot us of our oldest treasures, our responsibilities, our heritage? "But it has little commercial value, I understand. Uncle Ricky tried to sell it once. Took it all the way to Mirenburg to get it valued. He was very disappointed."

"It is more valuable as a pair. When matched to its twin," said Klosterheim, almost humorously. His mouth twisted in a peculiar rictus. Perhaps a smile. "Its counterweight."

I had begun to suspect that Klosterheim was not, as they say in Vienna, the full pfennig. His remarks seemed to bear only the barest connection to the conversation, as if his mind was operating on some other, colder plane altogether. It was easier to ignore him than ask him for explanations. How on earth could a sword be a "counterweight"? He was probably one of those mystical Nazis. It's an odd phenomenon I've noticed more than once, that fascination with the numinous and the supernatural and a preference for extremist right-wing politics. I have never been able to understand it, but many of the Nazis, including Hitler and Hess, were immersed in such stuff. As rational, no doubt, as their racialism. Dark abstractions which, when applied to real life, produce the most banal evils.

"Don't minimise your family's achievements, either." Gaynor recalled our ancient victories. "You've given Germany some famous soldiers."

"And rogues. And radicals."

"And some who were all three," said Gaynor, still hearty as a highwayman on the scaffold. All face.

"Your namesake, for instance," murmured Klosterheim. Even the act of speaking seemed to add a chill to the night air.

"Eh?"

Klosterheim's voice seemed to echo in his mouth. "He who sought and found—the Grail. Who gave your family its antique motto."

I shrugged at this and suggested we return inside. There was a fire going in the hearth and I had an unlikely frisson of nostalgia as I remembered the great family Christmases we had enjoyed, as only Saxons can enjoy their Yuletide festival, when my father and mother and brothers were all alive and friends came from Castle Auchy in Scotland and Mirenburg and France and America, together with more distant relatives, to enjoy that unchallenged fantasy of comfort and good will. War had destroyed all that. And now I stood by blackened oak and slate watching the smoke rise from out of a guttering, unhappy fire and did my best to remember my manners as I entertained the two gentlemen in black and silver who had come, I was now certain, to take away my sword.

"Do you the Devil's work." Klosterheim read the coat of arms which was imbedded above the hearth. I thought the thing was vulgar and would have removed it if it had not entailed ripping down the entire wall. A piece of Gothic nonsense, with its almost alchemical motifs and its dark admonishment which, according to my reading, had once meant something rather different than it seemed. "Do you still follow that motto, Herr Count?"

"There are more stories attached to the motto than to the sword. Unfortunately, as you know, our family curse of albinism was not always tolerated and some generations came to see it as a matter of shame, destroying much that had been recorded where it pertained to albinos like myself or, I suspect, anything which seemed a little strange to the kind of mentality which believes burning books to be burning unpalatable truths. Something we seem prone to, in Germany. So little record remains of any sense. But I understand the motto to be ironic in some way."

"Perhaps." Klosterheim looked capable of carrying only the heaviest of ironies. "But you lost the goblet, I understand. The Grail."

"My dear Herr Lieutenant, there isn't an old family in Germany that doesn't have at least one Grail legend attached to it and usually some cup or other which is supposed to represent the Grail. The same is true in England. Arthur had more Camelots than Mussolini has titles. They're all nineteenth-century inventions. Part of the Gothic revival. The Romantic movement. A nation reinventing herself. You must know of half a dozen such family legends. Wolfram von Eschenbach claimed it was granite. Few can be traced much past 1750. I can imagine, too, that with your recruitment of Wagner to the Nazi cause, your Leader has need of such symbols, but if we did have an old goblet it has long since gone from here."

"I agree these associations are ridiculous." Gaynor took himself closer to the fire. "But my father remembers your grandfather showing him a golden bowl that had the properties of glass and metals combined. Warm to the touch, he said, and vibrant."

"If there is such a family secret, cousin, then it has not been passed on to me. My grandfather died soon after the armistice. I was never in his confidence."

Klosterheim frowned, clearly unsure if he should believe me. Gaynor was openly incredulous. "You of all the von Beks would know of such things. Your father died because of his studies. You've read everything in the library. Von Asch passed what he knew on to you. Why, you yourself, cousin, are almost part of the museum. No doubt a better prospect than the circus."

"Very true," I said. I glanced at the hideous old "huntsman's clock" over the mantel and asked him if he would excuse me. It was time I turned in.

Gaynor began to try to charm his way out of what he now understood to be an insult, but his remark about me was no more offensive than most of his and Klosterheim's conversation. There was a certain coarseness about him I hadn't noticed in the past. No doubt he had the scent of his new pack on him. It was how he intended to survive.

"But we still have business," said Klosterheim.

Gaynor turned towards the fire.

"Business? You're here on business?" I pretended to be surprised.

Gaynor said quietly, not turning to look at me, "Berlin made a decision. About these special German relics."

"Berlin? Do you mean Hitler and Co.?"

"They are fascinated by such things, cousin."

"They are symbols of our old German power," said Klosterheim brusquely. "They represent what so many German aristocrats have lost—the vital blood of a brave and warlike people."

"And why would you want to take my sword from me?"

"For safe-keeping, cousin." Gaynor stepped forward before Klosterheim could reply. "So that it's not stolen by Bolsheviks, for instance. Or otherwise harmed. A state treasure, as I'm sure you will agree. Your name will be credited, of course, in any exhibition. And there would be some financial recompense, I'm sure."

"I know nothing of the so-called Grail. But what would happen if I refused to give up the sword?"

"It would make you, of course, an enemy of the State." Gaynor had the decency to glance down at his well-polished boots. "And therefore an enemy of the Nazi Party and all it stands for."

"An enemy of the Nazi Party?" I spoke thoughtfully. "Only a fool would antagonise Hitler and expect to survive, eh?"

"Very true, cousin."

"Well," I said, as I left the room, "the Beks have rarely been fools. I'd better sleep on the problem."

"I'm sure your dreams will be inspired," said Gaynor rather cryptically.

But Klosterheim was more direct. "We have put sentimentality behind us in modern Germany and are making our own traditions, Herr Count. That sword is no more yours than it is mine. The sword is Germany's, a symbol of our ancient power and valour. Of our blood. You cannot betray your blood."

I looked at the inbred mountaineer and the Slavic Aryan before me. I looked at my own bone-white hand, the pale nails and faintly darker veins. "Our blood? My blood. Who invented the myth of blood?"

"Myths are simply old truths disguised as stories," said Klosterheim. "That is the secret of Wagner's success."

"It can't be his music. Swords, bowls and tormented souls. Did you say the sword was one of a pair? Does the owner of the sister sword seek to own the set?"

Gaynor spoke from behind Klosterheim.

"The other sword, cousin, when last heard of, was in Jerusalem."

I suppose I could not help smiling as I made my way to bed, yet that sense of foreboding soon returned and by the time I put my head on my pillow I was already wondering how I could save my sword and myself from Hitler. Then, in a strange hypnagogic moment between waking and sleeping, I heard a voice say: "Naturally I accept paradox. Paradox is the stuff of the multiverse. The essence of humanity. We are sustained by paradox." It sounded like my own voice. Yet it carried an authority, a confidence and a power I had never known.

I thought at first someone was in the room, but then I had fallen back into slumber and found my nostrils suddenly filled with a remarkable stink. It was pungent, almost tangible, but not unpleasant. Acrid, dry. The smell of snakes, perhaps? Or lizards? Massive lizards. Creatures which flew as a squadron under the control of mortals and rained fiery venom down upon their enemies. An enemy that was not bound by any rules save to win at all costs, by whatever it chose to do and be.

Deep blue patterns like gigantic butterfly wings. It was a dream of flying, but unlike any I had heard of. I was seated in a great black saddle which appeared to have been carved from a single piece of ebony yet which fitted my body perfectly and from which radiated a kind of membrane blending with the living creature. I leaned forward to place my hand on a scaly skin that was hot to the touch, suggesting an alien metabolism, and something reared up in front of me, all rustle and clatter and jingling of harness, casting a vast shadow. The monstrous head of what I first took to be a dinosaur and then realised was a dragon, absolutely dwarfing me, its mouth carrying a bit of intricately decorated gold whose tasselled decorations were as long as my body and which threatened to sweep against me when the head turned and a vast, glowing yellow eye regarded me with an intelligence that was inconceivably ancient, drawing on experience of worlds which had never known mankind. And yet, was I foolish to read affection there?

Emerald green. The subtle language of colour and gesture.

Flamefang.

Was it my voice which spoke that name?

That vibrant stink filled my lungs. There was a hint of smoke wreathing the beast's huge nostrils and something like acid boiled between its long teeth. This beast's metabolism was extraordinary. Even as I dreamed I recalled stories of spontaneous combustion and would not have been surprised if my steed had suddenly burst into flames beneath the saddle. There was a sensual movement of huge bones and muscles and sinews, of scraping scales, a booming rush as the dragon's wings beat against gravity and all the laws of common sense and then, with another thrust which thrilled my whole body, we were airborne. The world fell away. It seemed so natural to fly. Another thrust and we had reached the clouds. It felt strangely familiar to be riding on the back of a monster, yet guiding her with all the gentle fluid ease of a Viennese riding master. A gentle touch above the ear with the staff, a fingertip movement of the reins.

While my left hand held the traditional dragon goad, the other gripped Ravenbrand, pulsing with a horrible darkness and perpetually running with blood, the runes in her blade glowing a brilliant scarlet. And I heard that voice again. My own voice.

Arioch! Arioch! Blood and souls for my Lord Arioch!

Such barbaric splendour, such splendid savagery, such ancient, sophisticated knowledge. But all offering a vocabulary of image, word and idea utterly alien to the Enlightenment humanist that was Ulric von Bek. Here were ideals of courage and battle prowess which whispered in my ear like enticing obscenities, thoroughly at odds with my training and traditions. Cruel, unthinkable ideas taken for granted. Here was a power greater than any modern human being could ever know. The power to transform reality. The power of sorcery in a war fought without machines, yet more terrifying, more all-encompassing than the Great War which had recently passed.

Arioch! Arioch!

I could not know who Arioch was, but something in my bones conjured a strong sense of subtle, alluring evil, an evil so sophisticated it could even believe itself to be virtuous. This was some of the scent I had smelled on Gaynor and Klosterheim, but nothing like the wholesome beast-stink of my dragon, her massive, sinuous multicoloured wings beating a leisurely course across the sky. Her scales clashed faintly and her spikey crests folded back against her spine. My modern eye marvelled at these natural aerodynamics which enabled such a creature to exist. Her heat was almost uncomfortable and every so often a droplet of venom would form on her lips and flash to earth, burning stone, trees, even setting water ablaze for a short while. What strange twist of fate had made us allies? Allies we were. Bonded in the same way that ordinary men are bonded to ordinary animals, almost telepathic, a deep empathetic heartbeat that made our blood one, our souls' fates united. When at the dawn of time had we come together to form this complementary union?

Now man and beast climbed higher and higher into the chilly upper air, steam wafting from the dragon's head and body, her tail and wings growing faintly sluggish as we reached our maximum altitude and looked down on a world laid out like a map. I felt an indescribable mixture of horror and ecstasy. This was how I imagined the dreams of opium- or hashish-eaters. Without end. Without meaning. A burning world. A martial world. A world which could have been my own, my twentieth-century world, but which I knew was not. Armies and flags. Armies and flags. And in their wake, the piled corpses of innocents. In the name of whom the flags are raised and the armies sent to war. To fight to the death to defend the virtues of the dead.

Now, as the clouds parted completely, I saw that the sky was filled with dragons. A great squadron of flying reptiles whose wings were at least thirty feet across and whose riders were dwarfed by their mounts. A squadron that waited lazily, adrift in the atmosphere, for me to lead it.

In sudden terror I woke up. And looked directly into the cold eyes of Lieutenant Klosterheim.

"My apologies, Count von Bek, but we have urgent business in Berlin and must leave within the hour. I thought you might have something to tell us."

Confused by my dream and furious at Klosterheim's graceless intrusion, I told him I would see him downstairs shortly.

In the breakfast room, where one of my old servants was blearily doing his best to attend to my guests, I found them munching ham and bread and calling for eggs and coffee.

Gaynor waved his cup at me as I came in. "My dear fellow. How kind of you to join us. We received word from Berlin that we must return immediately. I'm so sorry to be a bad guest."

I wondered how he had received such news. A private radio, perhaps, in the car?

"Well," I said, "we shall just have to be content with our dull tranquillity."

I knew what I was doing. I saw a contradiction in Klosterheim's eye. He was almost smiling as he glanced down at the table.

"What about the sword, cousin?" Gaynor impatiently directed the servant to unshell his eggs. "Have you decided to give it up to the care of the State?"

"I don't believe it has much value to the State," I said, "whereas it has great sentimental value to me."

Gaynor scowled and rose up in his chair. "Dear cousin, I am not speaking for myself, but if Berlin were to hear your words—you would not have a home, let alone a sword to keep in it!"

"Well," I said, "I'm one of those old-fashioned Germans. I believe that duty and honour come before personal comfort. Hitler, after all, is an Austrian and of that happy-go-lucky, tolerant nature, which thinks less of such things, I'm sure."

Gaynor was not slow to understand my irony. He seemed to relish it. But Klosterheim was angry again, I could tell.

"Could we perhaps see the sword, cousin?" Gaynor said. "Just to verify that it is the one Berlin seeks. It could be that it's the wrong blade altogether!"

I was in no mood to put myself or the sword in jeopardy. Fantastic as it seemed, I believed both my cousin and his lieutenant to be capable of hitting me over the head and stealing the sword if I showed it to them.

"I'll be delighted to show it to you," I said. "As soon as it comes back from Mirenburg, where I left it with a relative of von Asch's, to be cleaned and restored."

"Von Asch? In Mirenburg?" Klosterheim sounded alarmed.

"A relative," I said. "In Baudissingaten. Do you know the man?"

"Von Asch disappeared, did he not?" Gaynor interrupted.

"Yes. In the early days of the war. He wanted to visit a certain Irish island, where he expected to find metal of special properties for a sword he wished to make, but I suspect he was too old for the journey. We never heard from him again."

"And he told you nothing about the sword?"

"A few legends, cousin. But I scarcely remember them. They didn't seem remarkable."

"And he mentioned nothing of a sister sword?"

"Absolutely nothing. I doubt if ours is the blade you seek."

"I'm beginning to suspect that you're right. I'll do my best to put your point of view to Berlin, but it will be difficult to present it in a sympathetic light."

"They have called on the spirit of Old Germany," I said. "They'd be wise to respect that spirit and not coarsen its meaning to suit their own brutal agendas."

"And perhaps we would be wise to report such treacherous remarks before we are somehow contaminated by them ourselves." Klosterheim's strange, cold eyes flared like ice in sudden firelight.

Gaynor tried to make light of this threat. "I would remind you, cousin, that the Führer will look very positively on someone who bestows such a gift to the nation." He seemed a little too emphatic, revealing his desperation. He cleared his throat. "Any preconceptions that you, like so many of your class, are a traitor to the New Germany will be dispelled."

He was almost unconsciously speaking the language of deceit and obfuscation. The kind of double-talk which always signals a dearth of moral and intellectual content. He was already, whatever he had said to me, a Nazi.

I went with them to the outside door and stood on the steps as their driver brought the Mercedes around. It was still dark, with a sliver of moon on a pale horizon. I watched the black-and-chrome car move slowly away down the drive towards those ancient gates, each topped by a time-worn sculpture. Firedrakes. They reminded me of my dream.

They reminded me that my dream had been considerably less terrifying than my present reality.

I wondered when I would be receiving my next Nazi guests and whether they would be as easily refused as Gaynor and Klosterheim.

3

Visiting Strangers

That same evening I received a telephone call from the mysterious "Gertie." She suggested that around sunset I go down to the river which marked the northern edge of our land. There someone would contact me. There was a snap in the air. I was perfectly happy to stroll down through that lovely rolling parkland to the little bridge which connected, via a wicket gate, with a public path which had once been the main road to the town of Bek. The ruts were hardened into miniature mountain ranges. Few used the path. Now one rarely saw anything but an occasional pair of lovers or an old man walking his dog.

Just on that point of dusk between night and day, when a faint shivering mist had begun to rise from the river, I saw a tall figure appear on the bridge and wait patiently at the gate for me to unlock it. I moved forward quickly, apologetically. Somehow I had not seen the man approach. I opened the gate, welcoming him onto my land. He stepped swiftly through, closely followed by a slighter figure, who I thought at first must be a bodyguard, since it carried a longbow and a quiver of arrows.

"Are you Gertie's friends?" I asked the pre-arranged question.

"We know her very well," answered the archer. A woman's voice, low and commanding. Her face hooded against the evening chill, she stepped forward out of the tall man's shadow and took my hand. A strong, soft, dry handshake. The cloth of her cloak and the tunic beneath had a strange shimmering quality and the shades were unfamiliar. I wondered if this were some sort of stage costume. She might have been a German demigoddess in one of those interminable folk plays the Nazis encouraged everywhere. I invited them up to the house, but the man declined. His head lifted from within a darkness it seemed to carry as a kind of aura. He was gaunt, relatively young, and his blind eyes were glaring emeralds, as if he stared past me into a future so monstrous, so cruel and so agonising that he sought any distraction from its constant presence.

"I believe your house has already been microphoned," he said. "Even if it has not been, it's always wise to behave as if the Nazis could be listening. We'll stay out here for a while and then, when our business is done, perhaps go into the house for some refreshment?"

"You will be welcome."

His voice was surprisingly light and pleasant, with a faint Austrian accent. He introduced himself as Herr El and his handshake was also reassuring. I knew I was in the presence of a man of substance. His dark green cape and hat were familiar enough clothing in Germany to cause no comment, but they also had the effect of disguising him, for the great collar could be pulled around the face and the brim tugged down to put what remained in shadow. There was something familiar about him and I was sure we had met at least once before, probably in Mirenburg.

"You're here to help me join the White Rose Society, I presume?" I strolled with them through the ornamental shrubberies. "To fight against Hitler."

"We are certainly here to help you fight against Hitler," said the young woman, "since you, Count Ulric, are destined for specific duties in the struggle."

She, too, gave me the impression that we had met before. I was surprised at her outlandish costume, which I would have thought would attract unwanted attention in the streets of the average German town, but guessed she was taking part in some celebration, some charade. Were they on their way to a party?

"Perhaps you know that I had a visit from my cousin Gaynor yesterday. He has Germanised his name and calls himself Paul von Minct. He's become a Nazi, though he denies it."

"Like so many, Gaynor sees Hitler and company as furthering their own power. They cannot realise to what extent Hitler and his people are both fascinated by power and addicted to it. They desire it more than ordinary people. They think of nothing else. They are constantly scheming and counter-scheming, always ahead of the game, because most of us don't even know there's a game being played." He spoke with the urbanity of an old Franz Josef Viennese cosmopolitan. For me he represented a reassuring past, a less cynical time.

The young woman's face remained hidden, and she wore smoked glasses so that I could not see her eyes. I was surprised she could see at all as the dusk turned to darkness. She chose to sit on an old stone bench, she said, and listen to the last of the birdsong. Meanwhile Herr El and myself slowly walked amongst formal beds and borders which were just beginning to show the shoots of our first flowers. He asked me ordinary questions, mostly about my background, and I was happy to answer. I knew that the White Rose had to be more than careful. One informer and the best these people could hope for would be the guillotine.

He asked me what I hoped to achieve by joining. I said that the overthrow of Hitler was the chief reason. He asked me if I thought that would rid us of Nazis, and I was forced to admit that I did not.

"So how *are* we to defeat the Nazis?" asked Herr El, pausing beneath one of our old ornamental statues, so worn that the face was unrecognisable. "With machine guns? With rhetoric? With passive resistance?"

It was as if he was trying to dissuade me from joining, telling me that the society could not possibly have any effect.

I answered almost unthinkingly. "By example, sir, surely?"

He seemed pleased with this and nodded slightly. "It is pretty much all most of us have," he agreed. "And we can help people escape. How would you function in that respect, Count Ulric?"

"I could use my house. There are many secret parts. I could hide people. I could probably hide a radio, too. Obviously, we can get people into Poland and also to Hamburg. We're fairly well positioned as a staging post, I'd say. I can only make these offers, sir, because I am naïve. Whatever function you find for me, of course I will fulfil."

"I hope so," he said. "I will tell you at once that this house is not safe. They are too interested in it. Too interested in you. And something else here . . ."

"My old black sword, I think."

"Exactly. And a cup?"

"Believe me, Herr El, they spoke of a cup, but I have no idea what they meant. We have no legendary chalice at Bek. And if we had, we would not hide our honour!"

"Just so," murmured Herr El. "I do not believe you have the chalice either. But the sword is important. It must not become their property."

"Does it have more symbolic meaning than I know?"

"The meanings to be derived from that particular blade, Count Ulric, are, I would say, almost infinite."

"It's been suggested that the sword has a power of her own," I said.

"Indeed," he agreed. "Some even believe she has a soul."

I found this mystical tenor a little discomforting and attempted to change the subject. The air was growing cold again and I had begun to shiver a little. "My visitors of yesterday, who left this morning, looked as if they could use a soul or two. They've sold their own to the Nazis. Do you think Herr Hitler will last? My guess is that his rank and file will pull him down. They are already grumbling about betrayal."

"One should not underestimate a weakling who has spent most of his life dreaming of power, studying power, yearning for power. That he has no ability to handle power is unfortunate, but he believes that the more he has, the easier it will be for him to control. We are dealing with a mind, Count Ulric, that is at once deeply banal and profoundly mad. Because such minds are beyond our common experience, we do our best to make them seem more ordinary, more palatable to us. We give them motive and meaning which are closer to our own. Their motives are raw, dear count. Savage. Uncivilised. The naked basic greedy primeval stuff of existence, unrefined by any humanity, which is determined to survive at any cost or, if that is its only option, to be the last to die."

I found this a little melodramatic for my somewhat puritanical education. "Don't some of his followers call him Lucky Adolf?" I asked. "Isn't he just a nasty little street orator who has, by sheer chance, been elevated to the Chancellery? Are his banalities not simply those you will find in the head of any ordinary Austrian petite bourgeois? Which is why he's so popular."

"I agree that his ideas mirror those you'll find in any small-town shopkeeper, but they are elevated by a psychopathic vision. Even the words of Jesus, Count Ulric, can be reduced to sentimental banalities. Who can truly describe or even recognise genius? We can judge by action and by what those actions accomplish. Hitler's strength could be that he was dismissed too readily by people of our class and background. Not for the first time. The little Corsican colonel appeared to come from nowhere. Successful revolutionaries rarely announce themselves as anything but champions of the old virtues. The peasants supported Lenin because they believed he was going to return the Tsar to his throne."

"You don't believe in men of destiny then, Herr El?"

"On the contrary. I believe that every so often the world creates a monster which represents either its very best or its very worst desires. Every so often the monster goes out of control and it is left to certain of us, who call ourselves by various names, to fight that monster and to show that it can be wounded, if not destroyed. Not all of us use guns or swords. We'll use words and the ballot box. But sometimes the result is the same. For it is motive, in the end, which the public must examine in its leaders. And, given time, that is exactly what a mature democracy does. But when it is frightened and bullied into bigotry it no longer behaves like a mature democracy. And that is when the Hitlers move in. The public soon begins to see how little his actions and words suit their interest and his vote is dwindling by the time he makes his final lunge for power and, through luck and cunning, suddenly he finds himself in charge of a great, civilised nation which had failed once to understand the real brutality of war and desired never to know that reality again. I believe that Hitler represents the demonic aggression of a nation drowning in its own orthodoxies."

"And who represents the angelic qualities of that nation, Herr El? The communists?"

"The invisible people, mostly," he replied seriously. "The ordinary heroes and heroines of these appalling conflicts between corrupted Chaos and degenerate Law as the multiverse grows tired and her denizens lack the will or the means to help her renew herself."

"A gloomy prospect," I said quite cheerfully. I understood the philosophical position and looked forward to arguing it over a glass or two of punch. My spirits lightened considerably and I suggested that perhaps we could go discreetly into the house and draw the curtains before my people turned on the lamps.

He glanced towards the pale young "Diana," who had still to remove her dark spectacles, and she seemed to acquiesce. I led the way up the steps to the verandah and from there through French doors into my study, where I drew the heavy velvet curtains and lit the oil lamp which stood on my desk. My visitors looked curiously at my packed bookshelves, the clutter of documents, maps and old volumes over every surface, the lamplight giving everything golden warmth and contrast, their shadows falling upon my library as gracefully they moved from shelf to shelf. It was as if they had been deprived of books for too long. There was an almost greedy darting speed about the way they reached for titles that attracted them and I felt oddly virtuous, as if I had brought food to the starving. But even as they quested through my books, they continued to question me, continued to elaborate as if they sought the limits of my intellectual capacity. Eventually, they seemed satisfied. Then they asked if they could see Ravenbrand. I almost refused, so protective had I become of my trust. But I was certain of their credentials. They were not my enemies and they meant me no ill.

And so, overcoming my fear of betrayal, I led my visitors down into the system of cellars and tunnels which ran deep beneath our foundations and whose passages led, according to old stories, into mysterious realms. The most mysterious realm I had encountered was the cavern of natural rock, cold and strangely dry, in which I had buried our oldest heirloom, the Raven Sword. I stooped and drew back the stones which appeared to be part of the wall and, reaching into the cavity, brought out the hard case I had commissioned. I laid the case on an old deal table in the middle of the cave and took a key on my keychain to unlock it.

Even as I threw back the lid to show them the sword, some strange trick of the air caused the blade to begin murmuring and singing, like an old man in his dotage, and I was momentarily blinded not by a light, but by a blackness which seemed to blaze from the blade and was then gone. As I blinked against that strange phenomenon I thought I saw another figure standing near the wall. A figure of exactly the same height and general shape as myself, its white face staring hard into mine, its red eyes blazing with a mixture of anger and perhaps mocking intelligence. Then the apparition had gone and I was reaching into the case to take out the great two-handed sword, which could be used so readily in one. I offered the hilt to Herr El but he declined firmly, almost as if he was afraid to touch it. The woman, too, kept her distance from the sword and a moment or two later I closed the case, replacing it in the wall.

"She seems to behave a little differently in company," I said. I tried to make light of something which had disturbed me, yet I could not be absolutely sure what it was. I did not want to believe that the sword had supernatural qualities. The supernatural and I were best left to meet once a week, in the company of others, to hear a good sermon from the local pastor. I began to wonder if perhaps the couple were tricking me in some way, but I had no sense of levity or of deception. Neither had wanted to be near the blade. They shared my fear of its oddness.

"It is the Black Sword," Herr El told the huntress. "And soon we shall find out if it still has a soul."

I must have raised an eyebrow at this. I think he smiled. "I suppose I sound fanciful to you, Count Ulric. I apologise. I am so used to speaking in metaphor and symbol that I sometimes forget my ordinary language."

"I've heard many claims made for the sword," I said. "Not least by the one whose family almost certainly forged it. You know von Asch?"

"I know they are smiths. Does the family still live here in Bek?"

"The old man left just before the beginning of the war," I said. "He had some important journey of his own to make."

"You asked no questions?"

"It isn't my way."

He understood this. We were walking out of the chamber now, back up the narrow twisting stair that would take us to a corridor and from there to a door and another flight or two of steps where, if we were lucky, the air would become easier to breathe.

The scene felt far too close to something from a melodramatic version of Wagner for my taste and I was glad to be back in the study where my guests again began to move amongst my books even as we continued our strange conversation. They were not impolite, merely profoundly curious. It was no doubt their curiosity which had brought them to their present situation, that and a common feeling for humanity. Herr El was impressed by my first edition of Grimmelshausen. *Simplicissimus* was one of his favourite books, he said. Was I familiar with that period?

As much as any, I said. The Beks appeared to have shifted their loyalties as thoroughly as most families during the Thirty Years War, fighting originally for the Protestant cause but frequently finding themselves side by side with Catholics. Perhaps that was the nature of war?

He said he had heard a rumour that my namesake had written an account of those times. There were records in a certain monastery which referred to them. Did I have a version of it?

I had never heard of it, I said. The most famous memoirs were the fabrications of my scapegrace ancestor Manfred, who claimed to have gone to faraway lands by balloon and to have had supernatural adventures. He was an embarrassment to the rest of us. The account still existed, as I understood, in a bad English version, but even that had been heavily edited. The original was altogether too grotesque and fantastic to be even remotely credible. Even the English, with their taste for such stuff, gave it no great credence. For such a dull family, we occasionally threw up the most peculiar sorts. I spoke ironically, of course, of my own strange appearance.

"Indeed," said Herr El, accepting a glass of cognac. The young woman refused. "And here we are in a society which attempts to stamp out all difference, insists on conformism against all reality. Tidy minds make bad governors. Do you not feel we should celebrate and cultivate variety, Count Ulric, while we have the opportunity?"

While in no way antagonistic to them, I felt that perhaps these visitors, too, had come for something and been disappointed.

Then suddenly the young woman still cowled and wearing dark glasses murmured to the tall man who put down his unfinished drink and began to move rapidly, with her, towards the French doors and the verandah beyond.

"One of us will contact you again, soon. But remember, you are in great danger. While the sword is hidden, they will let you live. Fear not, Herr Count, you will serve the White Rose."

I saw them melt into the darkness beyond the verandah. I went outside to take a last breath or two of clear night air. As I looked down towards the bridge I thought I saw the white hare running again. For a flashing moment I thought she followed a white raven which flew just above her head. I saw nothing, however, of the man and the woman. Eventually, losing hope of seeing the hare or the bird again, I went inside, locked the doors and drew the heavy curtains.

That night I dreamed I flew again on the back of a dragon. This time the scene was peaceful. I soared over the slender towers and minarets of a fantastic city which blazed with vivid colours. I knew the name of the city. I knew that it was my home.

But home though it was, sight of it filled me with longing and anguish and at length I turned the dragon away, flying gracefully over the massing waters of a dark and endless ocean. Flying towards the great silver-gold disc of the moon which filled the horizon.

I was awakened early that morning by the sound of cars in the drive. When I was at last able to find my dressing gown and go to a front window I saw that there were three vehicles outside. All official. Two were Mercedes saloons and one was a black police van. I was familiar enough with the scene. No doubt someone had come to arrest me.

Or perhaps they only intended to frighten me.

I thought of leaving by a back door but then imagined the indignity of being caught by guards posted there. I heard voices in the hallway now. Nobody was shouting. I heard a servant say they would wake me.

I went back to my room and when the servant arrived I told him I would be down shortly. I washed, shaved and groomed myself, put on my army uniform and then began to descend the stairs to the hall where two Gestapo plain-clothes men, distinguished by identical leather coats, waited. The occupants of the other vehicles must, as I suspected, have been positioned around the house.

"Good morning, gentlemen." I paused on one of the bottom stairs. "How can we help you?" Banal remarks, but somehow appropriate here.

"Count Ulric von Bek?" The speaker had been less successful shaving. His face was covered in tiny nicks. His swarthy companion looked young and a little nervous.

"The same," I said. "And you, gentlemen, are—"

"I'm Lieutenant Bauer and this is Sergeant Stiftung. We understand you to be in possession of certain state property. My orders, count, are to receive that property or hold you liable for its safety. If, for instance, it has been lost, you alone can be held to account for failing in your stewardship. Believe me, sir, we have no wish to cause you any distress. This matter can be quickly brought to a satisfactory conclusion."

"I give you my family heirloom or you arrest me?"

"As you can see, Herr Count, we should in the end be successful. So would you like to reach that conclusion from behind the wire of a concentration camp or would you rather reach it in the continuing comfort of your own home?"

His threatening sarcasm made me impatient. "I would guess my company would be better in the camp," I told him.

And so, before I had had my breakfast, I was arrested, handcuffed and placed in the van whose hard seats were constantly threatening to throw me to the floor as we bumped over the old road from Bek. No shouts. No threats of violence. No swearing. Just a smooth transition. One moment I was free, captain of my own fate, the next I was a prisoner, no longer the possessor of my own body. The reality was beginning to impinge rapidly, well before the van stopped, and I was ordered far less politely to step into the coldness of some kind of courtyard. An old castle, perhaps? Something they had turned into a prison? The walls and cobbles were in bad repair. The place seemed to have been abandoned for some years. There was new barbed wire running along the top and a couple of roughly roofed machine-gun posts. Though my legs would hardly hold me at first, I was shoved through an archway and a series of dirty tunnels to emerge into a large compound full of the kind of temporary huts built for refugees during the war. I realised I had been brought to a fair-sized concentration camp, perhaps the nearest to Bek, but I had no idea of its name until I was bundled through another door, back into the main building and made to stand before some kind of reception officer, who seemed uncomfortable with the situation. I was, after all, in my army uniform, wearing my honours and not evidently a political agitator or foreign spy. I had been determined that they should be confronted by this evidence since, to me at least, it advertised the absurdity of their régime.

I was charged, it seemed, with political activities threatening the property and security of the State and was held under "protective custody." I had not been accused of a crime or allowed to defend myself. But there would have been no point. Everyone engaged in this filthy charade knew that this was merely a piece of play-acting, that the Nazis ruled above a law which they had openly despised, just as they despised the principles of the Christian religion and all its admonishments.

I was allowed to keep my uniform but had to give up my leather accoutrements. Then I was led deeper into the building to a small room, like a monk's cell. Here I was told I would stay until my turn came for interrogation.

I had a fair idea that the interrogation would be a little less subtle than that I'd enjoyed from Prince Gaynor or the Gestapo.

4

Camp Life

Better writers than I have experienced worse terrors and anguish than I knew in those camps and my case was, if anything, privileged compared to poor Mr Feldmann with whom I shared a cell during a "squeeze" when the Gestapo and their SA bully-boys were busier than usual.

Of course, I lost my uniform the first day. Ordered to shower and then finding nothing to wear but black-and-white-striped prison clothes, far too small for me, with a red "political" star sewn on them, I was given no choice. While I dressed, bellowing SA mocked me and made lewd comments reminding me of their leader Röhm's infamous proclivities. I had never anticipated this degree of fear and wretchedness, yet I never once regretted my decision. Their crudeness somehow sustained me. The worse I was treated, the more I was singled out for hardship, the more I came to understand how important my family heirlooms were to the Nazis. That such power should still seek more power revealed how fundamentally insecure these people were. Their creed had been the rationalisations of the displaced, the cowardly, the unvictorious. It was not a creed suited for command. Thus their brutality increased almost daily as their leader and his creatures came to fear even the most minor resistance to their will. And this meant, too, that they were ultimately vulnerable. Their children knew their vulnerability.

My initial interrogation had been harsh, threatening, but I had not suffered much physical violence so far. I think they were giving me a "taste" of camp life in order to soften me up. In other words, I still might find an open gate out of this hell if I learned my lesson. I was, indeed, learning lessons.

The Nazis were destroying the infrastructure of democracy and institution-alised law which they had exploited in order to gain their power. But without that infrastructure, their power could only be sustained by increased violence. Such violence, as we always see, ultimately destroys itself. Paradox is sometimes the most reassuring quality the multiverse possesses. It's a happy thought, for one of my background and experience, to know that God is indeed a paradox.

As a relatively honoured prisoner of the Sachsenburg camp, I was given a shared cell in the castle itself, which had been used as a prisoner-of-war camp during the Great War and was run on pretty much the same lines. We "inside" prisoners were given better treatment, slightly better food and some letter-writing privileges, while the "outside" prisoners, in the huts, were regimented in the most barbaric ways and killed almost casually for any violation of the many rules. For "insiders," there was always the threat of going "outside" if you failed to behave yourself.

Give a German of my kind daily terror and every misery, give him the threat of death and the sight of decent human beings murdered and tortured before his helpless eyes, and he will escape, if he can escape at all, into philosophy. There is a level of experience at which your emotions and mind, your soul perhaps, fail to function. They fail to absorb, if you like, the horror around them. You become a kind of zombie.

Yet even zombies have their levels of feeling and understanding, dim echoes of their original personalities—a whisper of generosity, a passing moment of sympathy. But anger, which must sustain you at these times, is the hardest to hold on to. Some zombies are able to give every appearance of still being human. They talk. They reminisce. They philosophise. They show no anger or despair. They are perfect prisoners.

I suppose I was lucky to share a cell first with a journalist whose work I had read in the Berlin papers, Hans Hellander, and then, by some bureaucratic accident when the "in" cells were filling too fast for the "out," we were joined by Erich Feldmann, who had written as "Henry Grimm" and had also been classified as a political, rather than with the yellow star of the Jew. Three philos-ophising zombies. With two bunks between us, sharing as best we could and sus-taining ourselves on swill and the occasional parcel from the foreign volunteers still allowed to work in Germany, we relived the comradeship we had all known in the trenches. Beyond the castle walls, in the "out" huts of the compounds, we frequently heard the most blood-curdling shrieks, the crack of shots, and other even more disturbing sounds, less readily identified.

Sleep brought me no benefit, no escape. The most peaceful dream I had was of a white hare running through snow, leaving a trail of blood. And still I dreamed of dragons and swords and mighty armies. Any Freudian would have found me a classic case. Perhaps I was, but to me those things were real—more vivid than life.

I thought that I began to see myself in these dreams. A figure almost always in shadow, with its face shaded, that regarded me from hard, steady eyes the colour and depth of rubies. Bleak eyes which held more knowledge than I would care for. Did I look at my future self?

Somehow I saw this doppelgänger as an ally, yet at the same time I was thoroughly afraid of him.

When it was my turn for a bunk, I slept well. Even on the floor of the prison, I usually achieved some kind of rest. The guards were a mixture of SA and members of the prison service, who did their best to follow old regulations and see that we were properly treated. This was impossible, by the old standards, but it still meant we occasionally saw a doctor and very rarely one of us was released back to his family.

We already knew we were privileged. That we were in one of the most comfortable camps in the country. Although still only hinting at the death factories of Auschwitz and Treblinka, Dachau and some of the other places were becoming recognised as murder camps and this, of course, long before the Nazis had ever considered making the Final Solution a reality.

I was not to know my own "lesson" was only just beginning. After about two months of this, I was summoned from my cell one day by SA Hauptsturmführer Hahn whom we'd come to fear, especially when he was accompanied, as now, by two uniformed thugs we knew as Fritzi and Franzi, since one was tall and thin while the other was short and fat. They reminded us of the famous cartoon characters. Hahn looked like most other SA officers, with a puffy face, a toothbrush moustache, a plug of a nose and two or three tiny receding chins. All he lacked to make him identical to his leader Röhm were the hideous scarred face and the rapacious proclivities which would make men hide their sons when he and his gang came to town.

I was marched between Fritzi and Franzi up and down stairs, through tunnels and corridors until I was brought at last to the commandant's office where Major Hausleiter, a corrupt old drunk who would have been drummed out of any decent army, awaited me. Since my reception, when he had seemed embarrassed, I had only seen him at a distance. Now he seemed nervous. Something was in the air and I had a feeling that Hausleiter would be the last to know what was really going on. He told me that I was being paroled on "humanitarian leave" under the charge of my cousin, now Major von Minct, for a "trial period." He advised me to keep my nose clean and co-operate with people who only had my good at heart. If I returned to Sachsenburg, it might not be with the same privileges.

Someone had found my clothes. Doubtless Gaynor or one of his people had brought them from Bek. The shirt and suit hung on my thinner-than-usual body, but I dressed carefully, tying the laces of my shoes, making a neat knot of my tie, determined to look as well as possible when I confronted my cousin.

Escorted into the castle courtyard by Fritzi and Franzi, I found Prince Gaynor waiting beside his car. Klosterheim was not with I him, but the glowering driver was the same.

Gaynor raised his hand in that ridiculous "salute" borrowed from American movie versions of Roman history and bid me good afternoon.

I got into the car without a word. I was smiling to myself.

When we were driving through the gates and leaving the prison behind, Gaynor asked me why I was smiling.

"I was simply amused by the lengths of play-acting you and your kind are willing to allow yourselves. And apparently without embarrassment."

He shrugged. "Some of us find it easier to ape the absurd. After all, the world has become completely absurd, has it not?"

"The humorous aspects are a little wasted on some of those camp inmates," I said. In prison I had met journalists, doctors, lawyers, scientists, musicians, most of whom had been brutalised in some way. "All we can see are degenerate brutes pulling down a culture because they cannot understand it. Bigotry elevated to the status of law and politics. A decline into a barbarism worse than we knew in the Middle Ages, with the ideas of that time turned into 'truth.' They are told obvious lies—that some six hundred and forty thousand Jewish citizens somehow control the majority of the population. Yet every German knows at least one 'good' Jew, which means that there are sixty million 'good' Jews in the country. Which means that the 'bad' Jews are heavily outnumbered by the 'good.' A problem Goebbels has yet to solve."

"Oh, I'm sure he will in time." Gaynor had removed his cap and was unbuttoning his uniform jacket. "The best lies are those which carry the familiarity of truth with them. And the familiar lie often sounds like the truth, even to the most refined of us. A resonant story, you know, will do the trick with the right delivery . . ."

I must admit the spring air was refreshing and I thoroughly enjoyed the long drive to Bek. I scarcely wanted it to end, since I had anxieties about what I might find at my home. After asking me how I had liked the camp, Gaynor said very little to me as we drove along. He was less full of himself than when I'd last seen him. I wondered if he had made promises to his masters which he'd been unable to keep.

It was dusk before we passed through Bek's gates and came to a stop in the drive outside the main door. The house was unusually dark. I asked what had happened to the servants. They had resigned, I was told, once they realised they had been working for a traitor. One had even died of shame.

I asked his name.

"Reiter, I believe."

I knew that feeling had returned. My spirits sank. My oldest, most faithful retainer. Had they killed him asking him questions about me?

"The coroner reported that Reiter died of shame, eh?"

"Officially, of course, it was the heart attack." Gaynor stepped out into the darkness and opened my door for me. "But I'm sure two resourceful fellows like us will be able to make ourselves at home."

"You're staying?"

"Naturally," he said. "You are in my custody, after all."

Together we ascended the steps. There was a crude padlock on the door. Gaynor called the driver to come forward and open it. Then we stepped into a house that smelled strongly of damp and neglect and worse. There was no gas or electricity, but the driver discovered some candles and oil lamps and with the help of these I surveyed the wreckage of my home.

It had been ransacked.

Most things of value were gone. Pictures had vanished from walls. Vases. Ornaments. The library had disappeared. Everything else was scattered and broken where Gaynor's thugs had clearly left it. Not a room in the house was undamaged. In some cases where there was nothing at all of value, men had urinated and defecated in the rooms. Only fire, I thought, could possibly cleanse the place now.

"The police seem to have been a little untidy in their searches," Gaynor said lightly. His face was thrown into sharp, demonic contrast by the oil lamp's light. His dark eyes glittered with unwholesome pleasure.

I knew too much self-discipline and was far too weak physically to throw myself on him, but the impulse was there. As anger came back, so, in a strange way, did life.

"Did you supervise this disgusting business?" I asked him.

"I'm afraid I was in Berlin during most of the search. By the time I arrived, Klosterheim and his people had created this. Naturally, I berated them."

He didn't expect to be believed. His tone of mockery remained.

"You were looking for a sword, no doubt."

"Exactly, cousin. Your famous sword."

"Famous, apparently, amongst Nazis," I retorted, "but not amongst civilised human beings. Presumably you found nothing."

"It's well hidden."

"Or perhaps it does not exist."

"Our orders are to tear the place down, stone by stone and beam by beam, until it is nothing but débris, if we have to. You could save all this, dear cousin. You could save yourself. You could be sure of spending your life in contentment, an honoured citizen of the Third Reich. Do you not yearn for these things, cousin?"

"Not at all, cousin. I'm more comfortable than I was in the trenches. I have better company. What I yearn for is altogether more general. And perhaps unattainable. I yearn for a just world in which educated men like yourself understand their responsibilities to the people, in which issues are decided by informed public debate, not by bigotry and filthy rhetoric."

"What? Sachsenburg hasn't shown you the folly of your childish idealism? Perhaps it's time for you to visit Dachau or some camp where you'll be far less comfortable than you were in those damned trenches. Ulric, don't you think those trenches meant something to me, too!" He had suddenly lost his mockery. "When I had to watch men of both sides dying for nothing, being lied to for nothing, being threatened for nothing. Everything for nothing. Nothing. Nothing. Nothing. And seeing all that nothing, are you surprised someone like myself might not grow cynical and realise that nothing is all we have in our future."

"Some come to the same realisation but decide we still have it in us to make a life on Earth. Through tolerance and good will, cousin."

He laughed openly at that. He waved a gauntleted hand around the ruins of my study.

"Well, well, cousin. Are you pleased with everything your good will has brought you?"

"It has left me with my dignity and self-respect." Sanctimonious as that sounded, I knew I might never have another chance to say it.

"Oh, dear Ulric. You have seen how we end, have you not? Writhing in filthy ditches trying to push our own guts back into our bodies? Shrieking like terrified rats? Climbing over the corpses of friends to get a crust of dirty bread? And worse. We all saw worse, did we not?"

"And better, perhaps. Some of us saw visions. Miracles. The Angel of Mons."

"Delusions. Criminal delusions. We cannot escape the truth. We must make what we can of our hideous world. In truth, cousin, it's safe to say that Satan rules in Germany today. Satan rules everywhere. Haven't you noticed? America, where they hang black men on a whim and where the Ku Klux Klan now puts state governors into office? England, which kills, imprisons and exiles thousands of Indians who naïvely seek the same rights as other citizens of the empire? France? Italy? All those civilised nations of the world, who brought us our great music, our literature, our philosophy and our sophisticated politics. What was the result of all this refinement? Gas warfare? Tanks? Battle aeroplanes? If I seem contemptuous of you, cousin, it is because you insist on seeking the delusion. I have respect only for people like myself, who see the truth for what it is and make sure their own lives are not made wretched by allegiance to some worthless principle, some noble ideal, which could well be the very ideal which sends us into the next war, and the next. The Nazis are right. Life is a matter of brute struggle. Nothing else is real. Nothing."

Again, I was amused. I found his ideas worthless and foolish, entirely self-pitying. The logic of a weak man who arrogantly assumed himself stronger than he was. I had seen others like him. Their own failures became the failures of whole classes, governments, races or nations. The most picturesque were inclined to blame the entire universe for their own inability to be the heroes they imagined themselves to be. Self-pity translated into aggression is an unpredictable and unworthy force.

"Your self-esteem seems to rise in direct proportion to the decline of your self-respect," I said.

As if from habit, he swung on me, raising his gloved fist. Then my eyes locked with his and he dropped his arm, turning away. "Oh, cousin, you understand so little of mankind's capacity for cruelty," he hissed. "I trust you'll have no further experience of it. Just tell me where the sword and cup are hidden."

"I know nothing of a cup and sword," I said. "Or its companion blade." That was the closest I came to lying. I wanted to go no further than that. My own sense of honour demanded I stop.

Gaynor sighed, tapping his foot on the old boards. "Where could you have hidden it? We found its case. No doubt where you left it for us. In that cellar. The first place we searched. I guessed you'd be naïve enough to bury your treasures as deep as you could. A few taps on the wall and we found the cavity. But we had underestimated you. What did you do with that sword, cousin?"

I almost laughed aloud. Had someone else stolen Ravenbrand? Someone who held it in no particular value? No wonder the house was in such a condition.

Gaynor was like a wolf. His eyes continued to search the walls and crannies. He paced nervously as he talked.

"We know the sword's in the house. You didn't take it away. You didn't give it to your visitors. So where did you put it, cousin?"

"The last I saw Ravenbrand it was in that case."

He was disgusted. "How can someone so idealistic be such a thoroughgoing liar. Who else could have taken the sword from the case, cousin? We interrogated all the servants. Even old Reiter didn't confess until his confession was clearly meaningless. Which left you, cousin. Not up the chimneys. Not under the floorboards. Not in a secret panel or a cupboard. We know how to search these old places. Not in the attics or the eaves or the beams or the walls, as far as we can discover. We know your father lost the cup. We got that out of Reiter. He heard one name, 'Miggea.' Do you know that name? No? Would you like to see Reiter, by the way? It might take you a while to spot something about him that you recognise."

Having nothing to gain from controlling my anger, I had the satisfaction of striking him one good blow on the ear, like a bad schoolboy.

"Be quiet, Gaynor. You sound as banal as a villain from a melodrama. Whatever you did to Reiter or do to me, I'm sure it's the foulest thing your fouler brain could invent."

"Flattering me at this late stage is a little pointless." He grumbled to himself as, rubbing his ear, he marched about the ruins of my study. He had become used to brutish power. He acted like a frustrated ape. He was trying to recover himself, but hardly knew how any more.

At last he regained some poise. "There are a couple of beds upstairs which are still all right. We'll sleep there. I'll let you consider your problem overnight. And then I'll cheerfully give you up to the mercies of Dachau."

And so, in the bedroom where my mother had given birth to me and where she had eventually died, I slept, handcuffed to the bedpost with my worst enemy in the other bed. My dreams were all of pale landscapes over which ran the white hare who led me to a tall man, standing alone in a glade. A man who was my double. Whose crimson eyes stared into my crimson eyes and who murmured urgent words I could not hear. And I knew a terror deeper than anything I had so far experienced. For a moment I thought I saw the sword. And I awoke screaming.

Much to Gaynor's satisfaction.

"So you've come to your senses," he said. He sat up in a bed covered with feminine linen. An incongruous sight. He jumped to the floor in his silk underwear and rang a bell. A few moments later, Gaynor's driver arrived with his uniform almost perfectly pressed. I was uncuffed and my own clothes were handed to me in a pillowcase. I did my best to look as smart as possible while Gaynor waited impatiently for his turn in the only surviving bathroom.

The driver served us bread and cheese on plates he had evidently cleaned himself. I saw rat droppings on the floor and recalled what I had to look forward to. Dachau. I ate the food. It might be my last.

"Is the sword somewhere in the grounds?" asked Gaynor. His manner had changed, had become eager.

I finished my cheese and smiled at him cheerfully. "I have no idea where the sword is," I said. I was light-hearted because I had no need to lie. "It appears to have vanished of its own volition. Perhaps it followed the cup."

My cousin was snarling as he stood up. His hand fell on the holstered pistol at his belt, at which I laughed more heartily. "What a charlatan you have become, Gaynor. Clearly you should be acting in films. Herr Pabst would snap you up if he could see you now. How can you know if I'm telling you the truth or not?"

"My orders are not to offer you any kind of public martyrdom." His voice was so low, so furious, that I could hardly hear it. "To make sure that you died quietly and well away from the public eye. It's the only thing, cousin, that makes me hold back from testing your grip on the truth myself. So you'll be returned to the pleasures of Sachsenburg and from there you'll be sent on to a *real* camp, where they know how to deal with vermin of your kind."

Then he kicked me deliberately in the groin and slapped my face.

I was still handcuffed.

Gaynor's driver led me from my house and back into the car.

This time Gaynor sat me in front with the driver while he lounged, smoking and scowling, in the back. As far as I know, he never looked at me directly again.

His masters were no doubt beginning to think they had overestimated him. As he had me. I guessed that the sword had been saved by Herr El, "Diana" and the White Rose Society and would be used by them against Hitler. My own death, my own silence, would not be wasted.

I made the best use I could of the journey and slept a little, ate all that was available, dozed again, so that we had driven back through the gates and were in the great black shadow of Sachsenburg Castle before I realised it.

Fritzi and Franzi were waiting for me. They came forward almost eagerly as I stepped from the car.

They were clearly pleased to see me home.

They had clubbed me to the ground, in fact, and were in the process of beating my skinny body black and blue before Gaynor's car had gone roaring back into the night. I heard a voice from a window above and then I was being dragged, almost insensible, back to my cell where Hellander and Feldmann attempted to deal with the worst of my bruises as I lay in agony on a bunk, convinced that more than one bone had been broken.

The next morning they didn't come for me. They came for Feldmann. They understood how to test me. I was by no means sure I would not fail.

When Feldmann returned he no longer had any teeth. His mouth was a weeping red wound and one of his eyes seemed permanently closed.

"For God's sake." He spoke indistinctly, every movement of his face painful. "Don't tell them where that sword is."

"Believe me," I told him, "I don't know where it is. But I wish with all my soul that I held it in my hands at this moment."

Small comfort to Feldmann. They took him again in the morning, while he screamed at them for the cowards they were, and they brought him back in the afternoon. Ribs were broken. Several fingers. A foot. He was breathing with difficulty, as if something pressed on his lungs.

He told me not to give up. That they were not defeating us. They were not dividing us.

Both Hellander and I were weeping as we did our best to ease his pain. But they took him again for a third day. And that night, with nothing left of him that had not been tortured, inside and out, he died in our arms. When I looked into Hellander's eyes I saw that he was terrified. We knew exactly what they were doing. He guessed that he would be next.

And then, even as Feldmann gave out his last, thin gasp of life, I looked beyond Hellander and saw, distinct yet vaguely insubstantial, my doppelgänger. That strange, cloaked albino whose eyes were mine.

And for the first time I thought I heard him speak.

"The sword," he said.

Hellander was looking away from me, looking to where the albino had stood. I asked him if he had seen anything. He shook his head. We laid Feldmann out on the flagstones and tried to say some useful service for him. But Hellander was wretched and I didn't know how to help him.

My dreams were of the white hare, of my doppelgänger in his hooded cape, of the lost black sword and of the young woman archer whom I had nicknamed Diana. No dragons or ornamented cities. No armies. No monsters. Just my own face staring at me, desperate to communicate something. And then the sword. I could almost feel it in my hands.

Half-roused, I heard Hellander moving uncomfortably. I asked him if he was all right. He said that he was fine.

In the morning I awoke to find his hanging body turning slowly in the air above Feldmann's. He had found his means of escape as I slept.

A full twenty-four hours passed before the guards removed the corpses from my cell.

5

Martial Music

Fritzi and Franzi came for me a couple of days later. Without bothering to move me, they took out their blackjacks and beat me up on the spot. Fritzi and Franzi enjoyed their work and had become very expert at it, commenting on my responses, the reaction of my strange, pale body to their blows. The peculiar colour of my bruises. They complained, however, that it was hard to get sounds out of me. A small problem they thought they would solve over time.

Shortly after they left, I received a visit from Klosterheim, now an SS captain, who offered me something from a hip flask which I refused. I had no intention of helping him drug me.

"A sequence of very unfortunate accidents, eh?" He looked around my cell. "You must find all this a bit depressing, Herr Count."

"Oh, it means I don't have to mix too much with Nazis," I said. "So I suppose I am at an advantage."

"Your notion of advantage is rather hard for me to grasp," he said. "It seems to get you in this sort of predicament. How long did it take our SA boys to finish off your friend Feldmann? Of course, you could be a little fitter, a little younger. How long was it? Three days?"

"Feldmann's triumph?" I said. "Three days in which every word he had written about you was proven. You confirmed his judgement in every detail. You gave extra authority to everything he published. No writer can feel better than that."

"These are martyr's victories, however. Intelligent men would call them meaningless."

"Only stupid men who believed themselves intelligent would call them that," I said. "And we all know how ludicrous such strutting fellows are." I was glad of his presence. My hatred of him took my mind off my injuries. "I'll tell you now, Herr Captain, that I have no sword to give you and no cup, either. Whatever you believe, you are wrong. I will be happy to die with you believing otherwise, but I would not like others to die on my behalf. In your assumption of power, sir, you have also assumed responsibility, whether you like it or not. You can't have one without the other. So I present you with your guilt."

I turned my back on him and he left immediately.

A few hours later Fritzi and Franzi arrived to carry on their experiments. When I passed out, I immediately had a vision of my doppelgänger. He was speaking urgently, but I still couldn't hear him. Then he vanished and was replaced by the black sword, whose iron, now constantly washed with blood, bore the same runes but they were alive—scarlet.

When I woke I was naked with no blanket on my bed. I understood at once that they meant to kill me. The standard method was to starve and expose a prisoner until they were too weak to withstand infection, usually pneumonia. They used it when you refused to die of a heart attack. Why this charade was perpetuated I was never sure. I guessed this "message" was a bluff. If they still thought I could lead them to the sword or the cup they set such store by, they wouldn't kill me.

In fact, Major Hausleiter came to my cell himself at one point. He had Klosterheim with him. I think he attempted to reason with me, but he was so inarticulate he made no sense. Klosterheim reminded me that his patience was over and made some other villainous, ridiculous threat. What do you threaten the damned with? I was too weak to offer any significant retort. But I managed something like a smile with my broken mouth.

I leaned forward, as if to whisper a secret, and watched with satisfaction as, drop by drop, my blood fell upon his perfect uniform. It took him a moment to realise what had happened. He pulled back in baffled disgust, pushing me away so that I fell to the floor.

The door slammed and there was silence. Nobody else was being tortured tonight. When I tried to rise I saw another figure sitting on my bunk. My doppelgänger made a gesture and then seemed to fold downwards onto the bare mattress.

I crawled to the bunk. My double had gone. But in his place was Raven-brand. My sword. The sword they all sought. I reached out to touch the familiar iron and as I did so it, too, vanished. Yet I knew I had imagined nothing. Somehow the sword would find me again.

Not before Fritzi and Franzi had returned once more. Even as they beat me they discussed my staying power. They thought I could take one more "general physical" and then they would let me rest up for a day or two or they would probably lose me. Major von Minct was arriving later. He might have some ideas.

As the door slammed and was locked, leaving me in darkness, I saw my doppelgänger clearly framed there. The figure almost glowed. Then it crossed to the bunk. I turned my head painfully, but the man was gone. I knew I was not hallucinating. I had a feeling that if I had the strength to get to my bed I would see the sword again.

Somehow the thought drove me to find energy from nothing. Bit by bit I crawled to the bunk and this time my hand touched cold metal. The hilt of the Raven Sword. Fraction by fraction I worked my fingers until they had closed around the hilt. Perhaps this was a dying man's delusion, but the metal felt solid enough. Even as my hand gripped it, the sword made a low crooning noise, one of welcome, like a cat purring. I was determined to hang on to it, not to let it vanish again, even though I had no strength to lift it.

Strangely the metal seemed to warm, passing energy into my hands and wrists, giving me the means to raise myself up onto the bunk and lie with my body shielding the sword from anyone looking into the cell. There was a fresh vibrancy about the metal. As if the sword were actually alive. While this thought was disturbing, it did not seem as bizarre as it might have done a few months earlier.

I do not really know if a day passed. My own head was full of images and stories. The sword had somehow infected me. It could have been later that night Franzi and Fritzi arrived. They had brought some prison clothes and were yelling at me to get up. They were taking me to see Major von Minct.

I had been gathering my strength and praying for this moment. I had the sword gripped in both hands and as I turned I lifted the blade and threw my body weight behind it. The point caught short fat Franzi in the stomach and slid into him with frightening ease. He began to gulp. Behind him Fritzi was transfixed, unsure what was happening.

Franzi screamed. It was a long, cold, anguished scream. When it stopped, I was standing on my feet, blocking Fritzi from reaching the door. He sobbed. Clearly something about me terrified him. Perhaps my sudden energy. I was full of an edgy, unnatural power. But I was glad of it. I had sucked Franzi's lifestuff from him and drawn it into my own body. Disgusting as this idea might be, I considered it without emotion even as, with familiar skill, I knocked Fritzi's bludgeon from his red, peasant hand and drove the point of my sword directly into his pumping heart. Blood gushed across the cell, covering my naked flesh.

And I laughed at this and suddenly on my lips there formed an alien word. One I had heard only in my dreams. There were other words, but I did not recognise them.

"*Arioch!*" I shrieked as I killed. "*Arioch!*"

Still naked, with broken ribs and ruined face, with one leg which would hardly support my weight, with arms that seemed too thin to hold that great iron battle-blade, I picked up Franzi's keys and padded down the darkness of the corridor, unlocking the cell doors as I went. There was no resistance until I reached the guardroom at the far end of the passage. Here a few fat SA lads sat around drowsing off their beer. They only knew they were being killed as they awoke to feel my iron entering their bodies and somehow adding to the power which now raged through my veins, making me forget all pain, all broken bones. I screamed out that single name and within moments turned the room into a charnel house, with bodies and limbs scattered everywhere.

Once the civilised man would have known revulsion, but that civilised man had been beaten out of me by the Nazis and all that was left was this raging, bloodthirsty, near-insensate revenging monster. I did not resist that monster. It wanted to kill. I let it kill. I think I was laughing. I think I called out for Gaynor to come and find me. I had the sword he wanted. Waiting for him.

Behind me in the corridors, prisoners were emerging, clearly not sure if this was a trick of some kind. I flung them every key in the guardroom and made my way out into the night. Even as I reached the courtyard, lights began to come on in the castle. They heard unfamiliar screams and disturbing noises from the prison quarters. I loped like an old, wounded wolf across the compound towards the ranks of huts where the less fortunate prisoners were kept. Anything that threatened me or tried to shoot at me, I killed. The sword was a scythe which swept away wooden gates, barbed wire and men, all at once. I hacked down the wooden legs of a machine-gun post and saw the thing collapse, bringing down the wire, making escape far easier. In no time at all I was at the huts, striking the padlocks and bolts off the doors.

I don't know how many Nazis I killed before every hut was opened and the prisoners, many of them still terrified, began to pour out. Up on the castle walls they had got a searchlight working and I heard the pop of their shots as they aimed into the prisoners, apparently at random. Then I saw a group of stripe-uniformed inmates swarm up the wall and reach the searchlight. Within seconds the compound was in darkness as other lights were smashed. I heard Major Hausleiter's voice, crazed with a dozen different kinds of fear, yelling over the general mêlée.

God knows what any of them made of me, holding a great leaf-bladed longsword in one ruined hand, with my bone-white skin covered in blood, my crimson eyes blazing with the ecstasy of unbridled vengeance as I called out an alien name.

Arioch! Arioch!

Whatever demon possessed me, it did not have my feelings about the sanctity of life. Had this monster always lain within me, waiting to be awakened? Or was it my doppelgänger, whom I confused with the sword itself, who drew such wild satisfaction from my unrelenting bloodletting?

Machine-gun fire now began to spatter around me. I ran with the other prisoners for the safety of the walls and huts. Some of the prisoners, who had clearly had experience of street fighting, quickly collected the weapons of the men I had killed. Soon shots were spitting back from the darkness and at least one machine gun was silenced.

The prisoners had no need of me. Their leaders were well-disciplined and able to make quick decisions.

With the camp now in total confusion, I went back into the castle and began to climb stairs, looking for Gaynor's quarters.

I had barely reached the second floor when ahead of me I met the same hooded huntress, whom I had seen earlier with Herr El, that mysterious "Diana" who had also appeared in my dreams. Her eyes, as usual, were hidden behind smoked glasses. Her pale hair was loose. She, like me, was an albino.

"You have no time for Gaynor," she said. "We must get away from here soon or it will be too late. They have a whole garrison of storm troopers in Sachsenburg village, and someone is bound to have got through on the telephone. Come, follow me. We have a car."

How had she got inside the prison? Had she brought me the sword? Or was it my doppelgänger? Did they work together? Was she my rescuer? Impressed by the White Rose's powers, I obeyed her. I had already put myself at the society's service and was prepared to follow their orders.

Some of the battle-lust was leaving me. But the strange, dark energy remained. I felt as if I had swallowed a powerful drug which could have destructive side effects. But I was careless of any consequences. I was at last taking revenge on the brutes who had already murdered so many innocents. I was not proud of the new emotions which raged through my body, but I did not reject them either.

I followed the hooded woman back into the mêlée of the compound towards the main gate. The guards were already dead. The huntress stopped to pull her arrows from their corpses as she unlocked the gates and led me through, just as the emergency lighting system began to flicker on. Now the freed prisoners flooded towards the gates and rushed past us into the night. At least some of them would not die nameless, painful and undignified deaths.

As we reached the open roadway, I heard a motor bellow into life. Headlights came on and I heard three short notes on a horn. My huntress led me towards the big car. A handsome man of about forty, wearing a dark uniform I couldn't identify, saluted from behind the steering wheel. He was already driving forward as we climbed in beside him. He spoke good German with a distinctly English accent. It seemed the British Secret Service was already in Germany. "Honoured to meet you, dear count. I'm Captain Oswald Bastable, GTA, at your service. Business has improved in this region lately. We've got some clothes for you in the back, but we'll have to stop later. The schedule's looking a bit tight at the moment." He turned to my companion. "He means to bring them to Morn."

A few shots spat up dirt around us and at least one bullet struck the car.

My battle-rage was passing now and I looked down at my ruined body, realising that I was a mass of blood and bruises. Stark naked. With a bloody longsword in the broken fingers of my right hand. I must have been a nightmarish sight. I tried to thank the Englishman, but was thrown back in my seat as with her famous roar the powerful Duesenberg bore us rapidly along a country road, straight towards a mass of approaching headlights. No doubt these were the storm troopers from Sachsenburg town.

Captain Bastable seemed unperturbed. He was slipping Nazi armbands on his sleeves. "You'd better act as if you're knocked out," he said to me. As the first truck approached, he slowed down and waved a commanding hand from the car. He gave the Hitler salute and spoke rapidly to the driver, telling him to be careful. Prisoners were escaping. They had taken many guards captive and forced them to wear prison stripes before turning them loose into the countryside. There was every chance that if they shot at a man without being sure who he was, they could be killing one of their own.

This preposterous story would create considerable confusion and probably save a few prisoners' lives. Saying he had urgent business in Berlin, Bastable convinced the storm troopers, who were rarely the brightest individuals, and they roared off into the night.

Bastable kept up his own high speed for several hours, until we were climbing a narrow road between masses of dark pines. I was reminded of the Harz Mountains where I had often hiked as a boy. At last I saw a sign for Magdeburg. Thirty kilometres. Sachsenburg lay, of course, to the east of Magdeburg, which was north of the Harz. Another sign at a crossroads. Halberstadt, Magdeburg and Berlin one way, Bad Harzburg, Hildesheim and Hanover the other. We took the Hanover road but, before Hildesheim, Bastable drove into a series of narrow, winding lanes, switching off his car's lights and slowing down. He was buying time, he hoped.

Eventually he stopped near a brook with wide shallow sides where I could easily climb down and wash myself thoroughly in the icy water. Cold as I was, I felt purified and dried myself with the towels Bastable had provided. I hesitated a little when I realised that the clothes he had brought for me were my own, but of the kind one wore for hunting, even down to the knee-high leather boots, tweed breeches and a three-eared cap—what they call a deerstalker in England—which I fastened under my chin. I must have looked like a whiteface clown posing as a country gentleman, but the cap covered my white hair and I could be less readily identified by anyone who had been given a description of us. I pulled on the stout jacket and was ready for anything. Psychologically, the clothes made me feel much better. I wasn't too sure they would look as good with a longsword as with a twelve-bore, but perhaps if I wrapped the sword in something it would be less incongruous.

Bastable had the manner and appearance of an experienced soldier. He was reading a map when I came back and shaking his head. "Every bloody town begins with an 'H' around here," he complained. "I get them mixed up. I think I should have taken a right at Holzminden. Or was it Höxter? Anyway, it looks as if I overshot my turning. We seem to be halfway to Hamm. It'll be daylight fairly soon and I want to get this car out of sight. We have friends in Detmold and in Lemgo. I think we can make it to Lemgo before dawn."

"Are you taking us out of the country?" I asked. "Is that our only choice?"

"Well, it will probably come to that." Bastable's handsome, somewhat aquiline face was thoughtful. "I'd hoped to get all the way tonight. It would have made a big difference. But if we hole up in Lemgo, which is pretty hard to reach, we'll still have a chance of getting clear of Gaynor. Of course, Klosterheim will probably guess where we're eventually heading if the car has been recognised. But I took roads that were little travelled. We'll sleep in Lemgo and be ready for the next part of our journey tomorrow evening."

I fell into an exhausted doze but woke up as the car began to bounce and flounder all over a steep, badly made road full of potholes, which Bastable was negotiating as best he could. Then suddenly, outlined against the first touch of dawn on the horizon, I saw the most extraordinary array of roofs, chimneys and gables, which made Bek look positively futuristic. This was an illustration from a children's fairy tale. We seemed to have driven in our huge modern motorcar to the world of Hansel and Gretel and entered a medieval fantasy.

We had arrived, of course, in Lemgo, that strangely self-conscious town which had embellished every aspect of its picture-book appearance in the most elaborate ways. Its quaintness disguised a dark and terrible history. I had been here once or twice on walking holidays but had stayed only briefly because of the tourists.

Our route from Sachsenburg had been circuitous and could well have thrown any pursuers off our scent. I asked no questions. I was too exhausted and I understood the White Rose Society needed to be discreet with its secrets. I was content at that moment to be free of what had been an extended nightmare.

I wondered if Lemgo had any significance for my liberators. It was the essence of German quaintness. A fortified town, a member of the Hanseatic League, it had known real power, but now it was almost determinedly a backwater, still under the patronage of the Dukes of Lippe, to whom we von Beks were distantly related. Its streets were a marvel, for the residents vied with one another to produce the most elaborate house-fronts, carved with every kind of beast and character from folklore, inscribed with biblical quotations and lines from Goethe, painted with coats of arms and tableaux showing the region's mythical history.

The bürgermeister's house had a relief depicting a lion attacking a mother and her child while two men vainly tried to frighten the creature away. The house known as Old Lemgo was festooned with plant patterns of every possible description, but the most elaborate house of all, I remembered, was called the Hexenbürgermeisterhaus, the sixteenth-century House of the Mayor of the Witches in Breitestrasse. I glimpsed it as the car moved quietly through the sleeping streets. Its massive front rose gracefully in scalloped gables to the niche at the top where Christ held the world in his hands, while further down Adam and Eve supported another gable. Every part of the woodwork was richly and fancifully carved. A quintessentially German building. Its sweetness, however, was marred a little when you knew that its name came from the famous witch-burner, Bürgermeister Rothmann. In 1667 he had burned twenty-five witches. It was his best year. The previous bürgermeister had burned men as well as women, including the pastor of St Nicholas's Church. Other pastors had fled or been driven from the town. The fine house of the hangman in Neuestrasse was inscribed with some pious motto. He had made a fat living killing witches. I could not help feeling that this place was somehow symbolic of the New Germany with its sentimentality, its folklore versions of history, its dark hatred of anything which questioned its cloying dreams of hearth and home. The town would never have seemed sinister to me before 1933. What should have been innocent nostalgia had become, in the present context, threatening, corrupted romanticism.

Bastable drove the car under an archway, through a double door and into a garage. Someone had been waiting and the doors were immediately closed. An oil lamp was turned up. Herr El stood there, smiling with relief. He moved to embrace me, but I begged him not to. The energy I seemed to have derived from the sword was still with me, but my bones remained broken and bruised.

We crossed a small quadrangle and entered another old door. The lintels of the doors were so low I had to bend to get through them. But the place was comfortable and there was a relaxing air to it, as if some protective spell had been cast around it. Herr El asked if he could examine me. I agreed and we went into a small room next to the kitchen. It seemed to be set up as a surgery. Perhaps Herr El was the doctor to the White Rose. I imagined him treating gunshot wounds here. As he examined me, he commented on the expert nature of the beatings. "Those fellows know what to do. They can keep a fit man going for a long time, I'd imagine. You yourself, Count von Bek, were in surprisingly good condition. All that exercise with your sword seems to have paid dividends. I'd guess you'll heal in no time. But the men who did this were scientists!"

"Well," I said grimly, "they're passing their knowledge on to their fellow scientists in Hell now."

Herr El let out a long sigh. He dressed my wounds and bandaged me himself. He clearly had medical training. "You'll have to do your best with this. Ideally, you should rest, but there'll be little time for that after today. Do you know what's happening?"

"I understand that I'm being taken to a place of safety via some secret underground route," I said.

His smile was thin. "With luck," he said. He asked me to tell him all that I could remember. When I remarked how I had become possessed, how some hellish self had taken me over, he put a sympathetic hand on my arm. But he could not or would not reveal the mystery of it.

He gave me something to help me sleep. As far as I knew that sleep was dreamless and uninterrupted until I felt the young woman shaking me gently and heard her calling me to get up and have something to eat. There was a certain urgency in her voice which made me immediately alert. A quick shower, some ham and hard-boiled eggs, a bit of decent bread and butter, which reminded me suddenly how good ordinary food could be, and I was hurrying back to the garage where Bastable waited in the driving seat, the young woman beside him. She now carried her arrows in a basket and her bow had become a kind of staff. She had aged herself by about seventy years. Bastable wore his SS-style uniform and I was back in my country clothes, with a hat hiding my white hair and smoked glasses hiding my red eyes.

The young woman turned to me as I climbed into the Duesenberg. "We can deceive almost anyone but von Minct and Klosterheim. They suspect who we really are and do not underestimate us. Gaynor, as you call him, has a remarkable instinct. How he found us so quickly is impossible to understand, but his own car has already passed through Kassel and it's touch and go who'll reach our ultimate destination first." I asked her where that was. She named another picturesque town which possessed an authentic legend. "The town of Hameln, only a few miles from here. It's reached by an atrocious road."

Some might almost call it the most famous town in Germany. It was known throughout the world, and especially in England and America, for its association with rats, children and a harlequin piper.

Again we drove frequently without lights, doing everything we could to make sure that the car was not recognised. A less sturdy machine would have given up long since, but the American car was one of the best ever produced, as good as the finest Rolls-Royce or Mercedes and capable of even greater speeds. The thump of its engine, as it cruised at almost fifty miles an hour, was like the steady, even beat of a gigantic heart. Admiring the brash, optimistic romanticism of its styling, I wondered if America was to be our eventual destination, or if I was to learn to fight Hitler closer to home.

Crags and forests fled by in the moonlight. Monasteries and hamlets, churches and farms. Everything that was most enduring and individual about Germany. Yet this history, this folklore and mythology, was exactly what the Nazis had co-opted for themselves, identifying it with all that was least noble about Germans and Germany. A nation's real health can be measured, I sometimes think, by the degree in which it sentimentalises experience.

At last we saw the Weser, a long dark scar of water in the distance, and on its banks the town of Hameln, with her solid old buildings of stone and timber, her "rat-catcher's house" and her Hochzeitshaus where Tilly is said to have garrisoned himself and his generals the night before they marched against Magdeburg. My own ancestor, my namesake, fought with Tilly on that occasion, to our family's shame.

We turned a tight corner in the road and without warning encountered our first roadblock. These were SA. Bastable knew if we were inspected, they would soon realise we were not what we seemed. We had to keep going. So I raised my arm in the Nazi salute as our car slowed, barked out a series of commands, referring to urgent business and escaped traitors while Bastable did his best to look like an SS driver. The confused storm troopers let us pass. I hoped they were not in regular communication with anyone else on our route.

With no way of bypassing Hameln—and I even doubted that an old bridge could take as large a car as ours across the Weser—we had no choice. Bastable slowed his speed, put on his cap and became stately. I was an honoured civilian, perhaps with his mother. We reached the ferry without incident but it was obvious that nothing could take the weight of our car. Bastable drove the machine back to the nearest point to the bridge and led us over on foot. We had no weapons apart from the woman's bow and the black sword I held on my shoulder as I limped in the rear.

We crossed the bridge and soon Bastable was leading us along a footpath barely visible in the misty moonshine. I caught glimpses of the river, of the lights of Hameln, clumps of tall trees, banks of forest. Perhaps the distant headlamps of cars. We seemed to be pursued by a small army. Bastable increased his pace, and I was finding it difficult to keep up. He knew exactly where he was going but also was becoming increasingly anxious.

From somewhere we heard the roar of motor engines, the scream of klaxons, and we knew that Gaynor and Klosterheim had anticipated our destination. Was there a route by road to where Bastable led us? Or would they have to follow us on foot? I panted some of these questions to Bastable.

He replied evenly. "They'll have split into two parties, is my guess. One coming from Hildesheim and the other from Detmold. They won't have our trouble with the river. But the roads are pretty bad and I don't know how good their cars are. If they get hold of a Dornier-Ford-Yates, for instance, we're outclassed. Those monsters will roll over anything. We're almost at the gorge now. We can just pray they haven't anticipated us. But Gaynor really can't be underestimated."

"You know him?"

"Not here," was Bastable's cryptic reply.

We were stumbling into a narrow gorge which appeared to have a dead end. I'd become suspicious. I thought for a moment that Bastable had brought us into a trap, but he cautioned us to silence and led us slowly along the side of the canyon, keeping to the blackest shadows. We had almost reached the sheer slab of granite which closed us in when from above and to the sides voices suddenly sounded. There was some confusion. Headlamps came on and went out again. A badly prepared trap.

"The sword!" Bastable shouted to me, flinging his body against the rock as the beams of flashlights sought us out. "Von Bek. You must strike with the sword."

I didn't know what he meant.

"Strike what?"

"This, man. This wall. This rock!"

We again heard the roar of engines. Suddenly powerful headlamps carved through the darkness. I heard Gaynor's voice, urging the car forward. But the driver was having difficulty. With an appalling scraping of gears, whining and coughing, the car rolled forward.

"Give yourselves up!" This was Klosterheim from above, shouting through a loud-hailer. "You have no way of escape!"

"The sword!" hissed Bastable. The young woman put her quiver over her shoulder and strung her oddly carved bow.

Did he expect me to chop my way through solid granite? The man was mad. Maybe they were all mad and my own disorientation had allowed me to believe they were my saviours?

"Strike at the rock," said the young woman. "It must be done. It is all that will save us."

I simply could not summon enough belief, yet dutifully I tried to lift the great sword over my shoulders. There was a moment when I was sure I would fail and then, again, my doppelgänger stood before me. Indistinct and in some evident pain, he signed to me to follow him. Then he stepped into the rock and vanished.

I screamed and with all my strength brought the great black battle-blade against the granite wall. There was a strange sound, as if ice cracked, but the wall held. To my astonishment, so did the sword. It seemed unmarked.

From somewhere behind me a machine gun rattled.

I swung the blade again. And again it struck the rock.

This time there was a deep, groaning snap from within the depths of the granite and a thin crack appeared down the length of the slab. I staggered back. If the sword had not been so perfectly balanced I could not have swung it for a third time. But swing it I did.

And suddenly the sword was singing—somehow the vibrating metal connected with the vibrating rock and produced an astonishing harmony. It bit deep into my being, swelling louder and louder until I could hear nothing else. I tried to raise the sword for a fourth time but failed.

With a deafening crack, the great slab parted. It split like a plank, with a sharp crunching noise, and something cold and ancient poured out of the fissure, engulfing us. Bastable was panting. The young woman had paused to send several arrows back into the Nazi ranks, but it was impossible to see if she had hit anyone. Bastable stumbled forward and we followed, into a gigantic cave whose floor, at the entrance, was as smooth as marble. We heard echoes. Sounds like human voices. Distant bells. The cry of a cat.

I was terrified.

Did I actually stand at Hell's gates? I knew that if somehow that wall of rock closed behind me, just as it had in the Hameln legend, I would be buried alive, cut off for ever from all I had loved or valued. The enormity of what had happened—that I had somehow created a resonance with the blade which had cracked open solid rock to reveal a cave—supported a bizarre legend which everyone knew had grown out of the thirteenth century and the Children's Crusade. I think I was close to losing consciousness. Then I felt the young woman at my elbow and I was staggering forward, every bruise, fracture and break giving me almost unbearable pain. Into the darkness.

Bastable had plunged on and was already lost from sight. I called out to him and he replied. "We must get into the stalagmite forest. Hurry, man. That wall won't close for a while and Gaynor has the courage to follow us!"

A great shriek. Blazing white light as Gaynor's car actually reached the entrance of the cave and drove inside. He was like a mad huntsman in pursuit of his prey. The car was a living steed. No obstacle, no consideration was important as long as he held to our trail.

I heard guns sound again. Something began to ring like bells, then tinkle like glass. A heavy weight came whistling down out of the darkness and smashed a short distance from me. Fragments powdered my body.

The shots were disturbing the rock formations typical of such caves. In the light from Gaynor's car I looked upwards. Something black flew across my field of vision. I saw that Bastable and the young archer were also watching the ceiling, just as concerned for what the gunfire might dislodge.

Another spear of rock came swiftly downwards and bits of it struck my face and hands. I looked up again, lost my footing and suddenly was sliding downwards on what appeared to be a rattling slope of loose shale.

Above me I heard Bastable yelling. "Hang on to the sword, Count Ulric. If we're separated, get to Morn, seek the Off-Moo."

The names were meaningless, almost ludicrous. But I had no time to think about it as I did my best to stop my slide and hold on to Ravenbrand at the same time. I was not about to let go of that sword.

We had become one creature.

Man and sword, we existed in some unholy union, each dependent upon the other. I thought that if one were destroyed the other would immediately cease to exist. A prospect which seemed increasingly likely as the slope became steeper and steeper and my speed became a sickening fall, down and down into impossible depths.

6

Profundities of Nature

I was weeping with anguish as my body came to rest at last. Somehow I had
bonded my hand to the hilt of the sword. Instinctively I knew that the black
blade was my only chance of survival. I could not believe I had an unbroken
bone. I had no real business being alive at all. The tough, padded deerstalker had
saved my head from serious injury. The peak had come down over my eyes but
when I at last pushed it up I lay on my back looking into total darkness. Shouts
and the occasional shot were far distant, high above. Yet they were my only contact with humanity. I was tempted to shout out, to tell them where I was, even
though I knew they would kill me and steal my sword.

Not that I could have shouted. I was lucky still to have my sight. I watched
their lights appear on the distant rim. This gave me some hint of the height
of the cliff. I could not be sure I was at the bottom. For all I knew I would
walk a foot or two and step into a cold, bottomless abyss and fall for ever in
limbo, held always in that eternal moment between life and death, between
consciousness and bleak oblivion. A fate hinted at in those terrible dreams.
Dreams which now seemed to have predicted this increasingly grotesque adventure.

But now, with some relief, I could see an end to it. None would find me here.
I would soon sleep and then I would die. I would have done what I could against
the Nazis and given my life in a decent cause. Dying, moreover, with my sword,
my duty and my defender, unsurrendered, as I had always hoped I would die, if
die I must. Few men could hope for more in these times.

Then something touched my face. A moth?

I heard the young woman's voice. A murmur, close to my ear. "Stay silent until they're gone."

Her hand found mine. I was surprised how much this comforted me. I took shuddering, painful breaths. There was not a centimetre of my body which did not in some way hurt, but her action allowed the pain no effect. I was instantly heartened. I sensed feelings towards this half-child which were hard for me to identify—feelings of comradeship, perhaps. Only mildly did I feel sexually attracted towards her. This surprised me, for she had a sensuality and grace which would have drawn the attention of most men. Perhaps I was beyond passion or lust. In circumstances like mine, such needs become neurotic and self-destructive, or so it has always seemed to me by observing the erotomanes in my own family. For them the stink of gunpowder was always something a little delicious.

I asked her if, under the circumstances, she would mind telling me her name. Was it really "Gertie"? I heard her laugh. "I was never Gertie. Does the name Oona sound familiar to you?"

"Only from Spenser. The Lady of Truth."

"Well, perhaps. And my mother? Do you not remember her?"

"Your mother? Should I have known her? In Bek? In Berlin? Mirenburg?" Ridiculously, I felt as if I had made a social faux pas. "Forgive me . . ."

"In Quarzhasaat," she said, rolling the exotic vowels in a way that showed some familiarity with Arabic. It was not a place I recognised and I said so. I sensed that she did not entirely believe me.

"Well, I thank you, Fräulein Oona," I said, with all my old, rather stiff courtesy. "You have brought me many blessings."

"I hope so." Her voice from the darkness had grown a little abstracted, as if she gave her attention to something else.

"I wonder what's happened to Bastable?" I said.

"Oh, that's not a problem. He can look after himself. Even if they capture him, he'll get free one way or another. For a while at least his part in this is over. But I have only his instructions for finding the river which he promises will lead us eventually to the city of Mu-Ooria."

The name was faintly familiar. I remembered a book from my library. One of those unlikely memoirs which enterprising hacks turned out in the wake of Grimmelshausen's *Simplicissimus* and Raspe's *Münchhausen*. The author, perhaps the pseudonym for an ancestor, claimed to have visited an underground kingdom, a refuge for the dispossessed, whose natives were more stone than flesh. I'd enjoyed the tale as a boy, but it had become repetitive and self-referencing, like so much of that fantastic stuff, and I had grown bored with it.

I pointed out that I was in rather poor shape for a long walk. I was already surprised by the immensity of the cave system. Did she know how far it extended?

This seemed to amuse her. "Some think it extends for ever," she replied. "But it has never been successfully mapped." She told me to wait and went off into that cold darkness. I was astonished by the ease with which she seemed to find her way. When she came back I heard her working at something. At length, I felt her lift me under the shoulders and drag me a few feet until I was lying on cloth. She placed my sword beside me.

"Thank the Nazis for starving you," she said, "or I wouldn't have the strength for this." I felt the cloth rise and tauten under me. I could now feel the sides, like long, smooth saplings, but not wood. And then we were moving forward. Oona the Bow-woman was actually dragging me on a kind of travois.

I noticed with a certain dismay that we were still going downwards, rather than back up towards the crevice I had created with the sword's harmonics. Although never very conscious of it before, even in the dugouts of Flanders, my tendency to claustrophobia was growing. Yet I knew even Oona wasn't strong enough to drag me back to the surface. She seemed to have some sense of what lay ahead. Trying to reach a place of safety which she knew of either from her own experience or from what Bastable had told her. I hoped that Bastable himself had not been captured. No civilised man can imagine the tortures those brutes invented. I shuddered at the thought of Gaynor finding me in this condition. I tried to speak to Oona but became dizzy just from the effort. Soon it scarcely mattered to me, for I passed out at last.

I awoke with a sense that something had changed. The silence around me had become peaceful rather than sinister. There was a whispering, as of a wind through leaves, and I realised that I could see a dim band of light in the distance, as if we faced a horizon.

Oona was faintly visible to me as a dark shape against a darker background. She had prepared food. Something which smelled like turnip, tasted like mashed ginger root and had an unpleasant slimy texture; but I felt invigorated by it. She told me our breakfast was made from local food. She was used to foraging down here.

I asked her if this cave system was like the famous catacombs of Rome and elsewhere, where victims of religious persecution had hidden, sometimes developing whole communities.

"The victimised do sometimes arrive here," she said, "and find a certain sanctuary, I suppose. But there is a native race, who never venture close to the surface, who are the dominant people."

"Do you mean an entire civilisation dwells in this cave system?"

"Believe me, Count Ulric, you will find much more than one civilisation down here."

Rationally, I refused to accept this fantastic claim. Even the recently explored caverns of Carlsbad in New Mexico were not so vast.

And yet something in me was prepared to believe her. I sensed an echo of a mysterious truth, something that perhaps I had once known, or that an ancestor had experienced and which was imprinted in my race memory. I knew of the fashionable fascination amongst German bohemians who spoke of a world within the world, whose entrance lay at the North Pole, and I knew some of this nonsense had been given credence by Nazis like the vegetarian crank Hess, but I had never suspected that such an underworld existed beyond the fantasies. Probably it did not. This system, though vast, was bound to be finite and so far there had been no evidence of it being populated by any kind of human settlement. Perhaps Oona herself was one of those who believed the myth. I had no choice but to trust her judgement. She had, after all, saved my life more than once.

I was convinced that Gaynor and Klosterheim were still in pursuit, that my sword meant too much to them. They would follow it, if necessary, into Hell.

As the light grew less faint, I could make little of my surroundings. The echoes told me that the roof of the cavern was very distant, and I began to wonder how much farther we could go down before gravity began to crush us. Mostly what I saw was a kind of reflected glow from stalactites and stalagmites. We seemed to be following a smooth road of igneous rock, perhaps some ancient lava path, which wound down towards the shining horizon. As we got nearer, we became aware of a rushing sound which grew louder until it was a distant roar. I could not imagine what was causing the sound. Neither could I guess the source of the light.

We made increasing stops as Oona rested. She was growing tired and the roaring was so loud, so unbroken that we could hardly hear each other. Yet she was determined to continue. Fifteen minutes and she was up again, dragging me and the travois down the gleaming slope until at last the ground levelled out and we were standing on a kind of hillock, looking towards a band of pale pewter light which danced forever ahead of us.

I had tried to ask her what it was, but she couldn't hear me. She was almost as exhausted as I was. I could tell by the way she moved the poles onto her shoulders, settled the makeshift harness around her, and plodded on.

My strength had hardly returned. If I did not see a doctor soon, many of my broken bones would not heal properly and a split rib might pierce some internal organ. I had no special fear for myself, but I acknowledged this reality. I was already reconciled to death. It would give me great satisfaction if I and the sword were lost for ever to my enemies.

We kept moving, metre by painful metre, towards the source of the light and the sound. Now, every hour or so, Oona would pause and take a drink from the flask she carried. Then she would force me to swallow some of the ill-smelling stuff. A witch's brew, I said. If you like, she replied.

I had no idea how far or for how long we travelled. The sound grew louder and louder until it pounded like blood in my eardrums. My own skull seemed to have become a vast auditorium. I was aware of nothing else. And, though still dim by ordinary standards, the light was growing so bright it had begun to hurt my eyes. I found it hard to turn my head, but when I did so I saw that the band of sparkling brilliance had grown much higher and was rising into the darkness, illuminating every kind of grotesque shape. I saw frozen rock that seemed organic, that assumed the shapes of fabulous beasts and buildings, of people and plants. Etiolated crags. A silvery light contrasting with the utter blackness of the farther reaches. A place of deep, alarming shadows. A monochrome world in extremes of black and white. A mysterious spectacle. I could not believe it had not been discovered or written about before now. I had no idea of its history or geography. It seemed somehow obscene that the Nazis should be obsessed with exploring and no doubt conquering this weird unspoiled territory. They had a natural affinity, I suppose, for darkness. They sought it out.

For my own part, though it was a wonderful revelation to know that such a world existed, I longed to be free of it. Half-dead as I was, this world shared too much with the grave.

Yet it was clear I was in some ways restored. Whatever remedy Oona had forced me to drink had reinvigorated me in a way that the sword could not. Even the pain of broken bones and torn muscles and flesh was reduced to a single, dull, acceptable ache. I felt fresher and cleaner, as I used to feel when I took an early swim in the river at home.

I wondered if I still had a home. Had Cousin Gaynor fulfilled his promise to pull the place down stone by stone?

Perhaps he now thought me in possession of both cup and sword and would do no further damage to Bek or its inhabitants. But that meant he would be here, somewhere, determined to claim the sword for himself, certain in his madness that I knew the whereabouts of a mythical and probably non-existent Holy Grail.

The roar seemed to absorb us. We became part of it, drawn closer and closer to its source as if hypnotised. We made no resistance, since this was our only possible destination.

Using the poles of the travois and with the sword slung over my back on a piece of queerly tough fibre Oona had given me, I was now able to hobble forward beside her. The light had the brilliance of the flash-powder that cameramen use. It blinded and dazzled, so that Oona soon replaced her smoked glasses and I drew the peak of my deerstalker down over my eyes. Effectively we were blind and deaf and so moved even more slowly and carefully.

The phosphorescence curved in a wide ribbon that stretched across our horizon and fell, almost like a rainbow, downwards into sparking blackness. Farther away one could just make out another glowing area, much wider than the great band of light which pierced the darkness of the vast cavern. None of this light revealed a roof. Only the depth of the echo gave any notion of height. It might have been a mile or two up. The roar, of course, was coming from the same source as the light. And so, I now began to notice, was the heat.

If complex life did exist so far below the surface of the earth, I now knew at least how it survived without the sun.

From the humidity I guessed us to be approaching the river Bastable had mentioned. I was unprepared for the first sign that we were near. Like winking fireflies at first, the rocks soon became alive with the same silvery blaze we could see ahead. Little stars blossomed and faded in the air and began to fall on our bodies.

Liquid. I thought at first it must be mercury but realised it was ordinary water carrying an intense phosphorescence, no doubt drawn from a source closer to the surface, perhaps under the sea. Oona was more familiar with the stuff. When she found a pool, she cupped her hands and offered some to me. The water was fresh. Her hands now glowed, so that she resembled some garish saint from a commercial Bible. Where she pushed back her hair, her head was briefly surrounded by a halo. Wherever the water clung to us, we were jewelled in pewter and glinting quicksilver. She signed that I could drink if I wished. She bent to her hands and sipped a little. For an instant, her lips glowed silver and her ruby eyes regarded me with enthusiastic glee. She was enjoying my astonishment. For a few seconds the water passing down her throat illuminated veins and organs so that she seemed translucent.

I was entranced by these effects. I longed to know more about them, but the roar continued to deafen us and it was still hard to look directly at the horizon.

As the phosphorescent water fell on our heads and bodies, covering us with tiny fragments of stars, we ascended smooth, slippery rocks at the point where the great wall of light began its gentle downward curve.

At last we could see the reason for the roaring. A sight which defied anything I had witnessed in all my travels. A wonder greater than the seven which continue to astonish surface dwellers. I have often said that the wonders of the world are properly named. They cannot be photographed or filmed or in any way reproduced to give the sense of grandeur which fills you when you stand before them, whether it be Egypt's pyramids or the Grand Canyon. These unknown, unnamed falls were like something you might discover in Heaven but never on our planet. I was both strengthened and weakened by what I observed. To describe it is beyond me, but imagine a great glowing river widening across a falls vaster than Victoria or Niagara. Under the roof of a cavern of unguessable height, whose perimeters disappear into total darkness.

A vast tonnage of that eery water crashed and thundered, shaking the ground on which we stood, rushing down and down and down, a mighty mass of yelling light and wild harmonies that sounded like human music. Throwing monstrous shadows everywhere. Revealing galleries and towers and roads and forests of rock, themselves throwing out soft illuminating silver rays like moonbeams. Relentlessly carrying the waters of the world down to the heart of creation, to renew and be renewed.

Something about that vision confirmed my growing belief in the existence of the supernatural.

I felt privileged to stand at the edge of the mighty cataract, watching that fiery weight of water tossing and swirling and sparking and foaming its way down a cliff whose base was invisible, yet which became a river again. We could see it far below, winding across a shallow valley and forming at last the main mass of shining water which I now realised was a wide underground sea. At least this geography followed surface principles. On both sides of the river, on the rising banks of the valley, were slender towers of white and grey light so varied they might have been the many-storeyed apartment blocks of the New York skyline. The formations were the strangest I'd ever experienced. My geologist brother, who died at Ypres, would have been astonished and delighted by everything around us. I longed to be able to record what I was seeing. It was easy to understand why no explorer had brought back pictures, why the only record of this place should be in a book by a known fantast, why sights such as these were incredible—until witnessed.

In the general yelling turbulence and showering silver mist, I had not considered what we would do next and was alarmed when Oona began to point down and enquire, through signs, if I had enough energy to begin a descent. Or should we sleep the night at the top?

Although weak, I did everything I could to move under my own volition. I still felt Gaynor had a chance of catching us. I knew I would feel more secure when I had put a few more miles between us. On the other hand, I was deeply uncomfortable with my circumstances and longed to begin the climb back to the surface, to get to a place where I could continue the common fight against Adolf Hitler and his predatory psychopathic hooligans.

I didn't want to continue that descent, but if it was the only way, I was prepared to try. Oona pointed through the glittering haze to a place about halfway down the gorge, where I saw the outlines of a great natural stone bridge curving out over the water, apparently from bank to bank. That was evidently our destination. I nodded to her and prepared to follow as she began to make her way carefully down a rough pathway which appeared to have been covered with droplets of mercury. The roaring vibrations, the long fingers of stone which descended from the roof or rose from the ground, the light, the massive weight of water, all combined to half-mesmerise me. I felt I had left the real world altogether and was in a fantastic adventure which would have defeated the imagination of a Schiller.

In all directions the rock flowed in frozen, organic cascades. Every living thing on Earth seemed to have come here and fused into one writhing chimera so that trees turned into ranks of bishops and bishops into grinning gnomes. Ancient turtle heads rose from amongst nests of crayfish and their eyes were the eyes of basilisks. You felt they could still reach you. Gods and goddesses like those intricate carvings on the pillars of Hindu temples or Burmese pagodas. I found it impossible to believe at times that this was not the work of some intelligence. It reproduced every aspect of the surface, every human type and every animal, plant and insect, sometimes in grotesque perspective or magnified twenty times. As if the stuff of Chaos, not yet fully formed, had been frozen in the moment of its conception. As if an imagination had begun the process of creating an entire world in all its variety—and been interrupted.

This vision of a not-quite-born world made me long for a return to the darkness which had hidden it from me. I was beginning to go mad. I was coming to realise that I did not have the character for this kind of experience. But something in me pushed me on, mocked me to make me continue. This is what they had tried to reproduce in Egypt and in Mexico. This is what they remembered in their Books of the Dead. Here were the beast-headed deities, the heroes, the heroines, angels and demons and all the stories of the world. There was no evident limit to these statues and friezes and fields of crystal looming over us, no far wall which might help us get our bearings. I had begun to understand that we had passed beyond any point where a compass could help us. There were no conventional bearings here. Only the river.

Perhaps those Nazi pseudoscientists had been right and our world *was* a convex sphere trapped in an infinity of rock and what we perceived as stars were points of light gleaming through from the cold fires which burned within the enveloping stone.

That I was experiencing full proof of their theory was no comfort. Without question we explored an infinity of rock. But had that rock once lived? Or did it merely mock life? Had it been made up of organic creatures like us? Did it strive to shape itself into the life of the surface as, in a less complex way, a flower or a tree might strive through the earth to reach the light? I found it easy to believe this. Anyone who has not had my experience need only find a picture of the Carlsbad Caverns to know exactly what I mean.

Pillars looked as if they had been carved by inspired lunatics so that you saw every possible shape and face and monster within them, and each rock flowed into another and they were endless in their variety, marching into the far darkness, their outlines flickering into sharp relief and dark shadow from the white fire flung up by that enormous phosphorescent river as she heaved herself endlessly into the heart of the world. Like Niagara turned into moonlit Elfland, an opium-eater's dream, a glorious vision of the Underworld. Did I witness the landscapes and the comforts of the damned? I began to feel that at any moment those snaking rocks would come alive and touch me and make me one of themselves, frozen again for a thousand years until brought to predatory movement only when they sensed the stray scuttling of creatures like ourselves, blind and deaf and lost for ever.

The beauty which the river illuminated inspired wonder as well as terror. High above us, like the delicate pipes of fairy organs, were thousands and thousands of hanging crystal chandeliers, all aflame with cool, silvery light. Occasionally one of the crystals would catch a reflection and turn whatever colour there was to brilliant, dazzling displays which seemed to travel with the water, flickering, through the haze, following the currents as that huge torrent endlessly roared, flinging its voice to the arches and domes above even as it fell.

I could not believe that the system could go so deep or, indeed, be so wide. It seemed infinite. Were there monsters lurking there? I remembered an engraving from Verne. Great serpents? Gigantic crocodiles? Descendants of dinosaurs?

I reminded myself that the real brutes were still somewhere behind us. Even Verne, or indeed Wells, had failed to anticipate the Nazi Party and all its complex evil.

No doubt Gaynor and his ally, Klosterheim, had more ambitious motives than helping the Nazi cause. My guess was that if the Nazis were no longer useful to them, the two men would no longer be Nazis. This made them, of course, an even greater threat to us. They believed in no cause but their own and thus could appear to believe in all causes. Gaynor had already showed me both his charming and his vicious side. I suspected there were many shades of charm and, indeed, viciousness which others had seen. A man of many faces. In that, he reflected some of Hitler's qualities.

I cannot explain how I inched down that long, slippery pathway, much of it with Oona's help, constantly aware of the broken bones in my foot but, thanks to her potion, in no severe pain. I knew my ruined body couldn't support me for much longer.

We at last reached the extraordinary bridge. It rose from the surrounding rock with that same sinuous dynamic as if something living had been frozen only moments before. Against the glowing spray its pale stone columns were outlined before us in all their cathedral-like beauty. It reminded me of a fantasy by the mad Catalan architect Gaudí or our own Ludwig of Bavaria, but far more elaborate, more delicate. Flanked on both sides by tall spires and turrets, all formed by the natural action of the caverns and again bearing that peculiarly organic quality, its floor had not been naturally worn but smoothed to accommodate human feet. The delicate silvery towers marched across the gorge through which the glowing river ran in "caverns measureless to man, down to a sunless sea." Had the opium poets of the English Enlightenment seen what I was now seeing? Had their imaginations actually created it? This disturbing thought came more than once. My brain could scarcely understand the exact nature of what my eyes witnessed and so I was inclined, like any ordinary lunatic, to invent some sort of logic, to sustain myself, to stop myself from simply stepping to one unguarded edge of that great bridge and leaping to my inevitable death.

But I was not by nature suicidal. I still had some faint hope of getting medical assistance and a guide back to the surface where I could do useful work. The roar of the water in the chasm below made it impossible to ask Oona questions and I could only be patient. Having rested, we began to hobble slowly across the bridge, I using my sword as a rough crutch and Oona using her carved bowstaff.

The foam from the torrent below engulfed the bridge in bright mist. I slowly became aware of a figure, roughly my height, standing in my path. The fellow was a little oddly shaped and also seemed to support himself on a staff. Oona pressed forward, clearly expecting to be met.

When I drew close, however, I realised the figure who waited to greet us was a gigantic red fox, standing on his hind legs, supporting himself with a long, ornamental "dandy pole" and dressed elaborately in the costume of a seventeenth-century French nobleman, all lace and elaborate embroidery. Awkwardly removing his wide-brimmed feathered hat with one delicate paw, the fox mouthed a few words of greeting and bowed.

With some relief, as if escaping a nightmare, I lost consciousness and fell in a heap to the causeway's quivering floor.

7

People of the Depths

Unable to accept any further assault on my training and experience, my mind did the only thing it could to save itself. It had retreated into dreams as fantastic as the reality, but dreams where I appeared at least to have some control. Again I experienced the exultation of guiding not just one great sinuous flying reptile but an entire squadron of them. Racing up into cold, winter skies with someone held tight against me in my saddle, sharing my delight. Someone I loved.

And there stood my doppelgänger again. Reaching towards me. The woman had vanished. I was no longer riding the dragon. My double came closer and I saw that his face was contracted with pain. His red eyes were weeping pale blood. At that instant I no longer feared him. Instead I felt sympathy for him. He did not threaten me. Perhaps he tried to warn me?

Slowly the vision faded and I knew a sense of extraordinary, floating well-being. As if I was being reborn painlessly from the womb. And as I relaxed, my rational mind slowly came awake again.

I could accept the existence of an underground kingdom so vast as to seem infinite. I could accept and understand the effects of its weird formations on my imagination. But a fox out of a fairy tale was too much! In my feverish attempts to absorb all those alien sights, it was quite possible I'd imagined the fellow. Or else had become so used to the fantastic that I had failed to recognise an actor dressed up for a performance of *Volpone*.

Certainly the fox was nowhere to be seen when I opened my eyes. Instead, looming over me was the figure of a giant, whose head resembled a sensitive version of an Easter Island god. He looked down on me with almost paradoxical concern. His uniform alarmed me until I realised it was not German. I hardly found it extraordinary that he was wearing the carefully repaired livery of an officer in the French Foreign Legion. An army doctor, perhaps? Had our journey brought us up into France? Or Morocco? My prosaic brain jumped at ordinary explanations like a cat at a bird.

The large legionnaire was helping me to raise myself in the bed.

"You are feeling well now?"

I had answered, rather haltingly, in the same language before I realised we were speaking classical Greek. "Do you not speak French?" I asked.

"Of course, my friend. But the common tongue here is Greek and it's considered impolite to speak anything else, though our hosts are familiar with most of our earthly languages."

"And our hosts are what? Large, overdressed foxes?"

The legionnaire laughed. It was as if granite cracked open. "You have met Milord Renyard, of course. He was eager to be the first to greet you. He thought you would know him. I believe he was friendly with an ancestor of yours. He and your companion, Mademoiselle Oona, have continued on urgently to Mu-Ooria, where they consult with the people there. I understand, my friend, that I have the honour to address Count Ulric von Bek. I am your humble J.-L. Fromental, lieutenant of France's Foreign Legion."

"And how did you come here?"

"By accident, no doubt. The same as M'sieur le Comte, eh?" Fromental helped me sit upright in the long, narrow bed, whose shallow sides tightly gripped even my half-starved body. "On the run from some unfriendly Rif, in my case. Looking for the site of ancient Ton-al-Oorn. My companion died. Close to death myself I found an old temple. Went deeper than I suspected. Arrived here."

Everything in the room seemed etiolated. The place felt like certain Egyptian tombs I had seen during that youthful trip with my school to the ancient world and the Holy Land. I half expected to see cartouches painted on the pale walls. I was dressed in a long garment, a little on the tight side, rather like a nightshirt, which they call a djellabah in Egypt. The room was long and narrow, like a corridor, lit by slim glasses of glowing water. Everything was thin and tall as if extended like a piece of liquid glass. I felt as if I was in one of those "Owl Glass Halls" of mirrors which were such a rage in Vienna a few years ago. Even the massive Frenchman seemed vaguely short and squat in such surroundings. Yet strange as everything was, I had begun to realise how well I felt. I had not been so fit and at one with myself since the days of my lessons with old von Asch.

The silence added to my sense of well-being. The sound of water was distant enough to be soothing. I was reluctant to speak, but my curiosity drove me.

"If this is not Mu-Ooria, then where are we?" I asked.

"Strictly speaking this is not a city at all, but a university, though it functions rather more variously than most universities. It is built on both sides of the glowing torrent. So that scientists can study the waters and understand their language."

"Language?"

That was the nearest translation. "These people do not believe that water is sentient as animals are sentient. They believe everything has a certain specific nature which, if understood, allows them to live in greater harmony with their surroundings. It's the purpose of their study. They are not very mechanically minded, but they use what power they discover to their advantage."

I imagined some lost oriental land, similar to Thibet, whose peoples spent their lives in spiritual contemplation. They had probably come here, much as we had come, hunted by some enemy, then grown increasingly decadent, at least by my own rather puritanical standards.

"The people here brought you back to health," Fromental told me. "They thought you would rather wake to a more familiar type of face. You will meet them soon." He guessed what I had been thinking. "There are practical advantages to their studies. You have been sleeping in the curing ponds for some long time. Their bone-setters and muscle-soothers work mostly in the ponds." At my expression he smiled and explained further. "They have pools of river water, to which they have added certain other properties. No matter what your ailment, be it a broken bone or a cancerous organ, it can be healed in the curing ponds, with the application of certain other processes specific to your complaint. Music, for instance. And colour. Consequently, timeless as this place is, we are even less aware of the familiar action of time as we know it on the surface."

"You do not age?"

"I do not know."

I was not ready for further mysteries. "Why did Oona go on without me?"

"A matter of great urgency, I gather. She expects you to follow. A number of us are leaving for the main city, which lies on the edge of the underground ocean you saw from above."

"You travel together for security?"

"From a habit of garrulousness, no more. Expect no horrid supernatural terrors here, my friend. Though you might think you've fallen down a gigantic rabbit burrow, you're not in Wonderland. As on the surface, we are at the dominant end of the food chain. But here there is no hot blood. No conflicts, save intellectual and formal. No real weapons. Nothing like that sword of yours. Here everything has the quiet dignity of the grave."

I looked at him sharply, looking for irony, but he was smiling gently. He seemed happy.

"Well," I admitted, "bizarre as their medicine might be, it seems to work."

Fromental poured me a colourless drink. "I have learned, my friend, that we all see the practice of medicine a little differently. The French are as appalled by English or American doctoring as the Germans are by the Italians and the Italians by the Swedes. And we need not mention the Chinese. Or voodoo. I would say that the efficacy of the cure has as much to do with the analysis and treatment as it does with certain ways of imagining our bodies. What's more, I know that if the cobra strikes at my hand, he kills me in minutes. If he strikes at my cat's neck, my cat might feel a little sleepy. Yet cyanide will kill us both. So what is poison? What is medicine?"

I let his questions hang and asked another. "Where is my sword? Did Oona take it with her?"

"The scholars have it here. I'm certain they intend to return it to you now that you are well, They found it an admirable artefact, apparently. They were all interested in it."

I asked him if this "university" was the group of slender pillars I had seen from the distance and he explained that while the Off-Moo did not build cities in the ordinary sense, these two groups of pillars had been adapted as living quarters, offices and all the usual accommodation of an active settlement, though commerce as such was not much practised by them.

"So who are these utopians? Ancient Greeks who missed their way? Descendants of some Orpheus? The lost tribe of Israel?"

"None of those, though they might have put a story or two into the world's mythologies. They're not from the surface at all. They are native to this cavernous region. They have little practical interest in what lies beyond their world but they have a profound curiosity, coupled with habitual caution, which makes them students of our world but instinctively unwilling to have intercourse with it. When you have lived here for a while you'll understand what happens. Knowledge and imagination are enough. Something about this dark sphere sets people to dreaming. Because death and discomfort are rare, because there is little to fear from the environment, we can cultivate dreaming as an art. The Off-Moo themselves have little desire to leave here and it's a rare visitor who is willing to return to the upper world. This environment makes intellectuals and dreamers of us all."

"You speak of these people as if they were monks. As if they believed there was purpose to their dreaming. As if their settlements were great monasteries."

"So they are, in a way."

"No children?"

"It depends what you mean. The Off-Moo are parthenogenetic. While they often form lasting unions, they do not need to marry to reproduce. Their death is also their birth. A rather more efficient species than our own, my friend." He paused, putting a gentle hand on my shoulder. "You'd best prepare yourself for many surprises. Unless you decide to jump in the river or go so far you fall into the lands that are called Uria-Ne by the Mu-Oorians. The Lands Beyond the Light is what we would call them, I suppose. Or perhaps just the Dark World. These people do not fear that world as much as we do. But only a desire for painful death would take you there."

"Is that not our own world they describe?"

"It could be, my friend. There are few simplicities in this apparently black-and-white environment. You and I do not have the eyes to see the beauties they perceive, nor the subtleties of tone and shade which to them are as vivid as our surface roses or sunsets. Soon you could become as obsessed as I with understanding the sensibilities of this gentle and complex people."

"Perhaps," I said, "when the time comes for me to want peace. But meanwhile in my own country there is a ruthless enemy to be fought, and fight him I must."

"Well, every man must be able to look his best friend in the eye," said Fromental, "and I will not dissuade you. Can you walk? Come, we'll seek what advice we can from Scholar Fi, who has taken a strong interest in your welfare."

I found that I could walk easily with a great sense of energy. I followed Fromental, who had to squeeze his massive body through some of the doors, down a sinuous spiral walkway and at last into the street. I was almost running as I reached the cool, damp outside air. Yet the nature of that dreaming town, apparently bathed in perpetual moonlight, with spires so slender you would think the slightest sound would shatter them, with its basalt pathways and complex gardens of pale fungi whose shapes echoed those of the rocks, made me walk slowly and with respect. As we left our elongated Gothic doorway behind, I smelled a dozen delicious, delicate, warm scents, perhaps of prepared food. And the plants had a musty perfume you sometimes find above ground. The delicate aroma you associate with certain truffles.

The towers themselves were of basalt fused with other kinds of rock to produce the effect of creatures trapped behind thick glass, perpetually staring out at us. This natural architecture, which intelligent creatures had fashioned to their own use, was of extraordinary beauty and delicacy and sometimes, when a faint shudder from the river shook the ground, it would sway and murmur. Buildings suddenly brought to life. All this pale wonder framed against the shifting glow of the blazing river and the more distant light from the lake. I suddenly saw the river as their version of the Nile, the mother of all civilisations. Was that why I made that instinctive connection with the builders of the pyramids?

As we walked I asked Fromental if he knew Bastable. Fromental had met him once at this very university. He understood that Bastable regularly visited the main city of Mu-Ooria.

"So it is possible to come and go?"

Fromental was amused. "Certainly, my friend. If you're Bastable. That Englishman belongs to a somewhat exclusive group of people who are able to travel what some call the moonbeam roads. It's a talent denied me. He can move from one sphere to another at will. I understand he believes you to be a very important fellow."

"How could you know that?"

"From Ma'm'selle Oona. Who else?"

"I think he values my sword more than he values me."

"Scholar Gou knows him. I've heard him speak about it. I think Bastable values both."

And then we had stepped through another archway and entered a house that seemed made of flesh-and-blood internal organs yet was cold marble to the touch.

We were in a very high chamber lit by a chandelier containing dozens and dozens of the same long, slender light bottles I had seen earlier. Around the walls of the chamber were charts, diagrams, pictures in many languages. The dominant script reminded me of the most beautiful Arabic in its flowing, elaborate purity. Clearly the written speech of the Off-Moo. All in what to my eye was monochrome, as if I had entered a film set and was trapped in a wild adventure serial.

Fromental's voice seemed even deeper and more resonant. "Count von Bek, may I present my good friend and mentor Scholar Fi, who directed the team which healed you."

My voice sounded coarse and heavy in my own ears. I could scarcely open my mouth and not gape. At first I thought I had come upon my doppelgänger, but this figure was far taller and thinner, even though his long, thin triangular features were an exaggerated version of my own. He too was an albino. But his skull must have been at least twice the length of mine and about half the width and was framed by a conical headdress that went to a point, exactly mirroring the length and shape of the scholar's face. The hat fanned over his shoulders across a garment identical to my own, with long "mandarin" sleeves and a hem that trailed the floor. I could not make out the size or shape of his feet. His robe, however, was woven from the same fine silk as the one I wore. His slanting ruby eyes, his long ears and strangely shaped brows all made his face a parody of my own. Were people like this my ancestors? Was it Off-Moo genes which made me an earthly outcast? Had I found my own people? The sudden sense of belonging was overwhelming and I almost wept. I recovered myself and thanked him gravely for his hospitality. And for bringing me back to life.

"You are most welcome." As soon as the creature spoke in the beautiful, liquid formality of Greek, I knew that my preconceptions had been nonsense. "It's only rarely I have the privilege of serving one of your particular physiology, which has much in common with our own." His voice was gentle, precise, lilting—almost a song. His skin was if anything paler than my own and much thinner. His eyes were a kind of rosy amber, and his ears slanted back from his head, ending in points. My own ears, though not as exaggerated, were similar to his. They were called "devil's ears" in my part of the world.

Scholar Fi seemed an enthusiastic host. He asked after my well-being and said if I had any questions he would answer them as best his poor powers allowed. I had a feeling Fi spoke with the modesty of genius. First he took me to an alcove and showed me my sword resting there. Fromental, perhaps discreetly, said he had some business on the outskirts of the city and would rejoin us later.

Scholar Fi suggested we stroll in the shade-flower forest, which was restful and aromatic, he said. Gently he led me from his house through serpentine streets where orderly natural rows of gigantic pagoda stalagmites marched into the distance, all illuminated by the glow from the river. As I looked closer I realised the vast pillars were thoroughly occupied. Such glorious architecture would touch a chord in any romantic, finding that authentic frisson the poets entreated us to seek. What would Goethe, for instance, make of all this extraordinary, pale beauty? Would he be as overwhelmed, both aesthetically and intellectually, as I?

Scholar Fi led me through a series of twittens to a wall and a gateway. We passed into an organic world of pale grey and silver—an astonishing spectacle of huge plants which grew from a single massive stem and opened like umbrellas to form a canopy displaying delicately shaded membranes. The giant plants also resembled living organs, like a cross-section in a medical book. They gave off a heavy, narcotic scent which did not so much sedate as excite. My vision seemed to improve. I noticed more detail, more shades. Fi told me that in Mu-Ooria there were gardens like this as large as earthly countries. The flowers and their stalks were important sources of nutrients and remedies, as well as materials from which to make their furniture and so on. They grew in rich silt which the river brought from the surface. "The river brings us everything we need. Food, heat, light. Originally we lived in towers and galleries already hollowed by the water's action but gradually, as our numbers expanded—we occasionally give birth to twins—we learned to fashion houses from within, using chiefly elemental methods."

Although not entirely understanding some of his answers, I asked him how old their civilisation was. I could not believe a human traveller had never visited this place and returned with his story. Scholar Fi was regretful. He was not an expert in time, he said. But he would find someone who could probably translate for me. He thought his people had probably existed for about as long as our own. The journey between one world and the other was a matter of luck, since it involved crossing the Lands Beyond the Light, and the methods we used on the surface to measure space were less than helpful there. That is why they never felt curious enough to visit what Scholar Fi called "the Chaos side," presumably the surface. Their notions of the natural universe were as alien as their ideas of medicine. I could only respect them. I was getting a glimmering of their logic, beginning to understand the way the Off-Moo perceived reality. I could understand Fromental's fascination. As I walked in that narcotic mist, the huge veins and sinews of the plate plants vibrating overhead, I casually considered the idea of forgetting Hitler and staying here, where life was everything it should be.

"Fromental and a party of others leave for Mu-Ooria when the current turns to the fourth harmony. You will be wanting to go with them? Can you hear the harmonies, Count Ulric? Are you familiar with"—a glint of dry humour—"our aural weather?"

"I fear not," I said.

He produced a small piece of metal from his sleeve, holding it in those incredibly long fingers that seemed too delicate to grasp a bird feather. He then blew on the metal, producing a sweet vibration.

"That is the sound," he said.

I think he expected me to remember it after hearing it only once. I decided that my best chance was to stay with Fromental at all times and depend upon his experience and wisdom.

"I am hoping to get help in Mu-Ooria," I said. "I need to return to my own world. I have a duty to perform."

"There you will find our wisest people who will help you if they can."

I remembered to ask him more about the creature who had met us on the bridge. Lord Renyard was an explorer and a philosopher, said Scholar Fi. His old home had been destroyed in a supernatural battle and his current home was under threat, but he was a regular visitor. "He has never known others of his own kind. You are probably lucky that he wasn't able to pump you on your knowledge of the thinkers and scholars he admires. He has a great enthusiasm for one of your philosophers. Do you know Voltaire?"

"Only as well as the average educated man."

"Then you are probably fortunate."

I had not expected sarcastic humour from such a being as Scholar Fi and again I was charmed. There were more and more reasons why I should stay here.

"He wanted to greet you so badly." Scholar Fi led me around a great piece of bulbous root that seemed to rise and fall like a creature breathing. "He was acquainted apparently with one of your ancestors, a namesake, whom he had known before his fiefdom was destroyed by warfare. He had considerable praise for this Count Manfred."

"Manfred!" The family had always considered him an embarrassment. A liar on the scale of Münchhausen. A scapegrace and turncoat. A spy. A Jacobin. A servant of foreign kings. An adventurer with women. "His name is never mentioned."

"Well, Lord Renyard seemed to think he was a fair scholar of the French Enlightenment, by which he sets great store."

"My ancestor Manfred was a scholar only of the street song, the beer stein and the good-natured strumpet." He had brought such shame to the family that a later ancestor of mine destroyed many of his accounts and suppressed others. Manfred had been the hero of a famous burlesque opera: *Manfred; or, The Gentleman Houri*. There had been some attempt by his contemporaries to have him declared insane but after escaping the French Assembly, of which he had briefly been a member, he kept his head and disappeared into Switzerland. The last anyone heard, he had appeared in Mirenburg in the company of a Scottish aerial engineer by the name of St Odhran. They had made claims for an airship which they could not substantiate. Eventually they escaped from angry investors in their vessel. Apparently they turned up again later in Paris selling a similar scheme. By that time, to our family's intense relief, the name von Bek was no longer used. He was also known as the Count of Crete, and rumour had it that he was hanged as a horse thief in the English town of York. Other stories claimed he had lived near Bristol as a woman for the rest of his life, broken by love. And another story told how he had tracked a piper out of Hameln, never to be seen again. I became disturbed. Was I following in the footsteps of legendary ancestors whose lives had been so secret even their nearest and dearest did not know who they really were? And was it my destiny to be destroyed by the knowledge which had almost certainly destroyed them?

Scholar Fi was baffled by my opinion of Manfred. "But I am learning more and more about your perceptions."

I tried to explain how we no longer believed the old myths and folktales of our ancestors and he continued to be mystified. Why, he wondered, would one idea have to be rejected in favour of another? Did we only have room in our heads for one idea at a time?

Scholar Fi trembled all over with laughter. He trilled appreciatively at his own wit. This was completely charming and I found myself joining in. Even in motion there was a quality about the Mu-Oorian which made it seem a delicate stone figure had become animated.

Suddenly my host cocked his head to one side. His hearing was far more acute than mine. He began to turn.

In time to see Fromental walking rapidly towards us.

"Scholar Fi, Count Ulric. Citizens reported their approach. I went to verify it. I can now tell you that a party of about a hundred armed men, equipped with the latest technical help, have crossed the bridge and now wait at the outskirts. They're demanding to speak to our 'leader.' "

I had no time to explain the notion to the bewildered scholar. Fromental turned to me. "I think it's your particular nemesis, my friend. His name is Major von Minct and he seems to believe you are a criminal of some kind. You stole a national treasure, is that it?"

"Do you believe him?"

"He seems a man used to power. And used to lies, eh?"

"Did he threaten you?"

"His language was relatively diplomatic. But the threats were implicit. He's used to getting his way with them. He wants to speak to you. To persuade you to do your duty and turn yourself over to the forces of law and order. He says he has not much time and will only use enough violence to demonstrate his power."

Clearly Fromental had not believed a word of Cousin Gaynor's story. But a hundred swaggering storm troopers could do considerable damage to creatures with no understanding of war or any other form of aggression. I feared for Scholar Fi's people more than I feared for myself.

"Do you wish to speak to this man?" asked Scholar Fi.

I did my best to explain what had happened and in the end he raised one long-fingered palm. Did I mind, he asked, if he came with me to meet Gaynor? Uncertainly, I agreed.

Gaynor and his army of uniformed ruffians were lounging about near the bottom of the bridge. The sound of the water was louder here, but Scholar Fi's voice carried through it. He made a small speech of welcome and asked Gaynor their business. Gaynor uttered the same nonsensical claims. And Scholar Fi laughed in his face.

Klosterheim, beside Gaynor, instantly drew his Walther PPK from its holster and pointed it at Scholar Fi. "Your creature had best show more respect for an officer of the Third Reich. Tell him to be careful or I'll make an example of him. To quote the Führer—Nothing is so persuasive as the sudden overwhelming fear of extinction."

"I am serious about the sword." Gaynor's terrible eyes looked straight into mine. The little sanity he had when he entered the caverns had been driven out of him by what he had experienced here. "I will kill anyone who stops me from holding her. Where have you hidden her, cousin? My love. My desire. Where's my Ravenbrand?"

"She's hidden herself," I said. "You'll never find her here and I'll never tell you where she is."

"Then you are responsible for this monster's death," said Klosterheim. He levelled his pistol straight at the gentle scholar's domed forehead and pulled the trigger.

BOOK TWO

Gone to the world beyond the world,
Gone to the sea beyond the sea.
Orpheus and his brothers
Seek wives amongst the dead.

—Lobkowitz,
Orpheus in Auschwitz, 1949

8

The Arms of Morpheus

At that moment, as Klosterheim squeezed his automatic's trigger, I understood profoundly how I'd left my familiar world far behind and was now in the realm of the supernatural.

Klosterheim's gun barked for the briefest moment and there was no echo. The sound was somehow absorbed into the surrounding atmosphere. Then I watched as the bullet stopped a few inches from the barrel, and was *swallowed* in the air.

Klosterheim, an oddly fatalistic expression on his face, lowered his arm and holstered his useless weapon. He glanced meaningfully at his master.

Gaynor swore. "God be damned—we're in the Middle March!"

Klosterheim understood him. And so did I. A memory as ancient and mysterious as my family's blood.

The surrounding landscape, alien as it was, felt far too solid for me to believe myself dreaming. The only other conclusion had been edging at the corners of my mind for some time. It was as logical as it was absurd.

As Gaynor had guessed, we had entered the mythical Mittelmarch, the borderlands between the human world and Faery. According to old tales, my own ancestors had occasionally visited this place. I'd always assumed that realm to be as real as the storybook world of Grimm, but now I was beginning to wonder if Grimm was no more than a recollection of my present reality. Hades, too, and all the other tales of underworlds and other worlds? Was Mu-Ooria the original of Alfheim? Or Trollheim? Or the caverns where the dwarves forged their magic swords?

As the strange scene unfolded before me, all these images and thoughts passed through my mind. Time really did seem to have an indescribably different quality in this twilight realm. A foreign *texture*, a sense of richness, even a slight instability. I was sensing a way of living simultaneously at different speeds, some of which I could actually manipulate. I'd already experienced a hint of this quality in my recent dreams, but now I was certain that I was more awake than I had ever been. I was beginning to sense the multiverse in all her rich complexity.

Now that he had an idea of his geography, Klosterheim seemed more at ease than any of us. "I have always preferred the night," he murmured. "It is my natural element. When I am at my predatory best." A long, dry tongue licked thin lips.

Scholar Fi offered Klosterheim a shadowed smile. "You could try to kill me by some other means, but I can defend myself. It would be unwise to pursue your present aggression. We have countered violence before in our history. We have learned to respect all who respect life. We do not show the same respect for those who would destroy life and take all with them into the oblivion they crave. Their craving we are able to satisfy. Though it is a journey that can only be made alone."

I cast my eye over the Nazi ranks to see if any of them but their leaders understood the scholar's Greek, but it was clear all they heard were threatening foreign sounds. My attention was caught by a figure at the back of the party and to the right, standing beside a tall stalagmite, like a set of giant dishes stacked one on top of the other. The figure's face was obscured by an elaborate helmet and its body was clad in what appeared to be armour of coppery silver, gleaming like dull gold in the semi-darkness. The baroque armour was almost theatrical, like something designed by Bakst for a fantastic Diaghilevian extravaganza. I felt I had glimpsed Oberon in Elfland. I turned to ask Fromental if he had seen the figure, but the Frenchman's attention was on Gaynor again.

My cousin had scarcely been listening to Scholar Fi. He drew the ornamental Nazi dagger from its scabbard at his belt. Pale steel and polished ebony, the hilt reflected the dancing, misty light. The blade's gleam seemed to pierce the atmosphere, challenging the whole organic world around us.

Balancing the dagger on the flat of his hand, Gaynor thrust it out to his side. His eyes challenged mine. Without turning his head he called behind him in German. "Lieutenant Lukenbach, if you please."

Proud of his master's recognition, a tall brute in SS black stepped forward and closed his fingers almost voluptuously around the dagger. He waited like an eager hound for his orders.

"You have the temerity to speak of aggression." Gaynor took a cigarette from his case. "You shall know that you challenge the authority of the Reich. Whether you realise it or not, my undernourished friend, you are now citizens of the Greater Germany and bound by the laws of our Fatherland." This speech was spoiled by his failure to ignite his cigarette. He threw both lighter and cigarette to the ground. "And some of your own laws, too, it seems . . ."

He was mocking himself. I admired his coolness, if not his folly, as he signed Lieutenant Lukenbach forward. "Show this fellow how sharp our old-fashioned Ruhr steel can be."

I became increasingly fearful for Scholar Fi, who lacked the physical strength to defend himself against the Nazi. Fromental, too, was looking a little worried, but motioned me back. He was prepared to trust the Off-Moo's sense of survival.

Neither Scholar Fi's expression nor his stance had changed as he watched this threatening drama. He seemed completely unmoved, murmuring in Greek as the SS man approached.

I would have been terrified by what I saw in Lukenbach's eyes alone. They held that familiar dreaming glaze I had seen so many times in recent months—the look of the sadist, of a creature allowed to fulfil its most vicious yearnings in the name of a higher authority. What had the Nazis awakened in the world? Between relativism and bigotry, there is no room for the human conscience. Perhaps without conscience, I thought, there could only be appetite and ultimate oblivion—an eternity of unformed Chaos or petrified Law, which found such excellent expression in the lunacy of communism and fascism whose grim simplifications could only lead to sterility and death and whose laissez-faire capitalist alternative also brought us ultimately to the same end. Only when the forces were in balance could life flourish at its finest. The Nazi "order," however, was a pretence at balance, a simplified imposition on a complex world—the kind of action which always brought the most destruction. The fundamental logic of reaction. I was about to witness another example of that destructive power as the SS officer came slowly on.

Lukenbach's eyes were greedy for butchery. He drew back his arm and began to take the last few paces towards us, grinning into Scholar Fi's extinction.

Unable to restrain myself as the Off-Moo's life was threatened, I sprang forward, ignoring Fromental and the scholar. But before I could reach Lukenbach, another man appeared between us. This figure was also clad from head to foot in armour as baroque as the other I had seen, but his was jet-black. Unfamiliar as his costume was, the face was all too familiar. Gaunt, white, with blazing eyes hard as rubies. It was my own. It was the creature I had already seen in my dreams and later in the concentration camp.

I was so shocked by this that I was stopped in my tracks, too late to grapple with the Nazi. "Who are you?" I asked.

My doppelgänger was prepared to reply. He mouthed some words, though I heard nothing. Then he moved to one side. I tried to see where he went, but he had vanished.

Lukenbach was almost on his victim. I could not reach him in time.

Slowly Scholar Fi raised a long, slender arm, perhaps in warning. Lukenbach continued to advance, as if he were himself entranced. His grip on the swastika dagger tightened as he prepared to aim his first blow.

This time both Fromental and I instinctively moved to defend the scholar but he gestured us back. As Lukenbach came within striking distance the Off-Moo opened his mouth wider than any human's, almost as if he unhinged his jaw like a snake, and shrieked.

The sound was at once hideous and harmonious. A ululation, it seemed to weave its way through the quivering stalactites overhead, threatening to bring them all down on us. Yet I had the impression the shriek was directed very precisely and pitched in a specific way.

Overhead crystal began to tinkle and murmur in sympathetic vibration. Yet none broke free.

The shriek seemed endless, as melodic as it was controlled. High above, the crystals continued to rustle and chime until gradually they formed a single sweet harmonic whose note, surprisingly harsh, ended with a sudden *snap*.

A single slender spear had broken clear of its companions, as if the Off-Moo had selected it, and was dropping down towards the threatening Nazi whose grin broadened as he anticipated his pleasure. Clearly he thought Scholar Fi was shrieking with fear.

The crystal shaft hesitated a short distance above Lukenbach's head. The Off-Moo was controlling the thing with sound alone.

The shriek ended. Scholar Fi made a tiny movement of his lips. In response to a murmured command, the crystal lance changed its angle and rate of descent. Then the scholar gestured very carefully. The stalactite described a gentle arc and then, with an almost elegant impact, struck deep, precisely into the Nazi's heart.

That shriek continued to echo through the endless caverns while Lukenbach's death throes took their rapid course.

He lay still on the rocky surface, his blood welling up around the crystal spear jutting from his chest. Fromental and I were shocked by this death as much as we welcomed it. Gaynor was clearly revising his strategy.

My cousin bent forward and retrieved his dagger from Lukenbach's stiffening fingers. With some distaste he stepped back, straightening and looking directly into my eyes.

"I'm learning not to underestimate you, cousin. Or your comrades. Are you sure you won't throw in with us? Or, failing that, give me the Raven Sword and I'll promise to harass you no further."

I allowed myself to smile at his knowing effrontery while Fromental declared, "You're in a rather weak bargaining position at the moment, my friend."

"I have a habit of strengthening my position." Gaynor was still looking directly at me. "What d'you say, cousin? Stay here with your new friends and I'll take the sword back to the real world to carry on the fight against the forces of Chaos."

"You're *not* the forces of Chaos?" My amusement grew.

"They are exactly what I fight. Which is why I must have the Black Sword. If you return with me, you'll have honours, power—power to make the kind of justice the world is crying out for! Hitler is merely a means to this end, believe me."

"Gaynor," I said, "you've given yourself in service to the Beast. You'll bring nothing but chaos to the world."

It was my cousin's turn to laugh in my face. "Fool. Have you no idea how wrong you are? You're duped if you believe I serve Chaos. Law's my master and ever will be! What I do, I do for a better, more stable, predictable future. If you also believe in such a future, come over to our side while you can, Ulric. It's you who serves the cause of Chaos, believe me."

"This sophistry's unworthy of a Mirenburger," I said. "You have demonstrated your loyalty to evil. You are wholly selfish, I've witnessed your cruelty, heard your callousness too often, to be persuaded of any sincerity you protest, other than a sincere need to devour us all. Your love of Law's no more than a madman's obsession with tidiness, Gaynor. That's not harmony. Not true order.

A strange expression crossed Gaynor's handsome features as if he recalled memories of better times. "Ah, well, cousin. Ah, well."

"They're dupes, my lord," said Klosterheim suddenly. He looked troubled. "There's no convincing them."

"And do you, Herr Klosterheim, regard yourself a noble servant of Law?" asked Fromental.

Klosterheim turned his barren eyes on the Frenchman. He smiled his bleak, loveless smile. "I serve my own master. And I serve the Grail, whose guardian I shall again become. We shall meet again, gentlemen. As I told you, I am at last in my element. I have no fear of this place and shall eventually conquer it." He paused and looked around him in joy. "How often I have yearned for the night and resented the interruption of day. Sunrise is my enemy. Here I can come into my own. I am not defeated by you."

Gaynor seemed surprised by this outburst.

"A somewhat old-fashioned view," I said. "You sound as if you've been reading far too much romantic poetry, Herr Captain."

He levelled glowering eyes at me and said flatly: "I am an old-fashioned man, a cruel and vengeful man." For a moment his voice was filled with poisoned dust.

"You must go now," said Scholar Fi suddenly. "If you are found in the light, our guards will kill you."

"Go? Go where? What guards?"

"Go into the dark. Beyond the light. Our guards are many." Scholar Fi gestured and it seemed the pointed rocks all around moved slightly. In each one I saw the face of an Off-Moo. "Time is not our master, the way it is yours, Prince Gaynor."

Gaynor and Klosterheim had underestimated us. I don't believe we underestimated them. Gaynor von Minct had become a handsome, watchful snake. "If we go back, we can return with an army."

"More than one army has been lost here," said the scholar casually. "Besides, you are unlikely to get back to the place you left and equally unlikely to find an entrance to our world again. No, you will journey to the darkness, beyond the river, and there you will learn to survive or perish, as fate decides. There are many others of your kind out there. Remnants of those same armies. Whole tribes and nations of them. Men as resourceful as yourselves should survive well and no doubt discover some means of flourishing."

Gaynor was contemptuous, disbelieving. "Whole nations? What do they live on?"

Scholar Fi began to turn towards the settlement. His patience had expired. "They are primarily cannibals, I understand."

He paused as we joined him. He looked back. Gaynor and the Nazis had not moved.

"Go!"

He gestured.

Gaynor continued to defy him.

Scholar Fi moved his mouth again, this time in a kind of echoing whisper. About a dozen crystal spears came crashing down a foot or two from the Nazis. We stood there and watched as Gaynor gave the command to retreat. Slowly the party disappeared into the darkness.

"We are unlikely to see them again," said the Off-Moo. "Their time will be taken up with defending themselves rather than attacking us."

Fromental's eyes met mine. Like me, he did not share the scholar's confidence.

"It's perhaps as well we're travelling to Mu-Ooria," he said. "We should at least report this."

"I agree," said the scholar. "And because of the circumstances, I suggest you take the *voluk*, rather than go on foot. We have no clear idea how closely the time-flows coincide in this season, so it is as well to be cautious." He was not expressing anxiety, rather common sense.

Fromental nodded his huge head. "It will be interesting," he said.

"What is the *voluk*?" I asked him, after we had parted from Scholar Fi.

"I have never seen it," he said.

When he returned me to my quarters, Ravenbrand was waiting for me. My hosts were telling me to be prepared for the worst.

I slept fitfully for what seemed a few hours, but my dreams were confused. I saw a white hare running across the underground landscape, running through sharp crags and looming inverted pillars, running towards the towers of Mu-Ooria, pursued by a red-tongued, jet-black panther. I saw two horsemen riding across a frozen lake. One horseman wore armour of silvered copper, glaring in the light from a pale blue sky. The other, who challenged him, wore armour of black iron, fashioned in fantastic forms, with a helm on his head that resembled a dragon about to take flight. The face of the black-clad horseman was my twin. I could not see the face of the other horseman, but I imagined it to be Gaynor, perhaps because I had encountered him most recently. As I fell in and out of these dreams, I wondered about my doppelgänger, who had clearly not wanted me to interfere in the Off-Moo's defence. Was I deluded? Was it only I who could see him? Was there some Freudian explanation to my dreams and visions? And if what I saw was real, how was it possible? I consoled myself that in Mu-Ooria I might learn a little more of the truth. Oona, for instance, would be glad to educate me. And there, I decided, I would ask for help in returning to my own Germany, to join in the fight against an evil which must soon engulf the whole of Europe and perhaps the world.

I had been awake for only a short time when Fromental called for me. I was surprised to see that he was carrying a sword at his hip and a bow and quiver of arrows on his back.

"You're expecting attack?" I asked.

"I see no point in not being ready for trouble. But I believe Scholar Fi's optimism is probably well founded. Your cousin and his band will have much to occupy them in the Lands Beyond the Light."

"And why do you travel to Mu-Ooria?" I asked him.

"I hope to meet with some friends of Lord Renyard's," he said. And would not be drawn further.

I had wrapped my sword in a cloth and bound it up so that I, too, could sling it over my back. I had a few provisions and changes of clothing and was now wearing my own familiar outfit, complete with deerstalker, which looked even more incongruous than Fromental's kepi.

After we had breakfasted on some rather bland broth, he led me through the twisting streets until we stood at last on the banks of the river, in a kind of cut where the waters were calmer. Scholar Fi and a group of Off-Moo were already on the harbourside, apparently in light-hearted conference.

My own astonished attention was drawn to what was moored there. At first I thought the thing alive, but then I guessed it to be cunningly fashioned from some kind of crystalline stone, predominantly of dark maroon and crimson. The massive vessel seemed to have been carved from a single ruby. Yet the stone was light as glass and sat easily in the waters like a ship. The *voluk* looked like some mythical sea-beast drawn up from the depths where it had long since petrified. As I regarded its fishy, reptilian face, all flared nostrils and jowls and coiling tendrils, I imagined that it looked at me. Was it alive? I had a nagging memory . . .

On the *voluk*'s back was a large, flat area, created by a kind of enormous saddle, making a platform, a raft large enough to take fifteen or twenty passengers and steered by two massive sweeps, one on each side.

I was impressed by the size as well as the complexity of the carving and remarked on it to Fromental as we followed the Off-Moo crew up the gangplank to where they took their places at the oars.

The Frenchman was amused by this. "It's nature's hand, not the Off-Moo's, you must blame for this monster. They draw these remains from their lake and find that with only minor modification, they can employ them as rafts. But, of course, they're rarely used, since they have to be dragged back upstream. Clearly, by putting a *voluk* at our disposal, our hosts are showing they believe the situation to be serious."

"They expect attack from Gaynor, when they are so easily able to defend themselves? Have they a means of seeing into the future?"

"They can see a million futures. Which in some ways is the same as not seeing any. They trust their instincts, I suspect, and know Gaynor's type. They know he will scarcely sleep until he has been revenged for what happened out there. They have survived for so long, my friend, because they anticipate danger and are ready to counter it. They will not underestimate men such as Gaynor. Whatever lives out there in the Lands Beyond the Light seems dangerous enough, from what I've learned. But the Off-Moo know that periodically one of the creatures unites the others in a truce, long enough to try to attack Mu-Ooria. They can see that Gaynor and Klosterheim have the intelligence and motive to succeed in creating some kind of alliance of the darklands tribes. All hate Mu-Ooria because at some stage Mu-Ooria has welcomed them and then banished them to the outer darkness."

"Are we all eventually banished there?"

"By no means. Wait until you get to Mu-Ooria herself!" Fromental clapped me on the back, clearly relishing the wonders he would soon be showing me.

Scholar Fi approached us as we settled into the shallow seats at the centre of the raft. He was gracious. He hoped we would return, he said, and let them all know how we fared. Then he went ashore, the gangplank was raised, and the slender Off-Moo, in their nodding conical cowls and their flowing pale robes, lent their strength and experience to the sweeps, guiding us out of the calm water and into the black, star-studded channel of the main river.

At once the current caught us. The crew had little to do but keep the monstrous hull on course. We moved with alarming speed, sometimes striking white water as the river narrowed between high banks and seemed to pour even deeper into the core of the planet.

Not, of course, that we were any longer on the planet, as we knew it. This was the Mittelmarch, which obeyed the laws of Elfland.

The dark waters were surprisingly clear and it was often possible to see to the bottom, where the rock had been worn to an artificial smoothness. I wouldn't have been surprised to learn that we were actually moving along a man-made canal. The light grew increasingly bright as we neared the lake and the temperature also grew warmer, suggesting that this inland sea was the source of the Off-Moo civilisation. It was to them what the sun and the Nile were to Egypt.

Although both banks were visible most of the time, the shadows and strange shapes of the rocks, the way the light from the water constantly varied, made it seem that the river course was populated with all kinds of monsters. Gradually I became used to the phantasmagoric nature of the swiftly passing landscape. But then, as I admired a grove of slender stalagmites which grew just on the edge of the water, like earthly reeds, I was sure I saw an animal of some kind.

It was not a small animal. The light had caught its eyes, emerald green, glaring at me from the darkness. I turned to Fromental, asking him if he knew what creature it might be. He was surprised. There were usually no animals about larger than the Off-Moo themselves. Then, in a length of bank where the light flickered strongly, I saw it again.

I'd seen it once before. In my dream. A gigantic cat, far larger than the largest tiger, jet-black, its red tongue lolling from a jaw filled with sharp, white fangs, and two enormous curving canines. A sabre-toothed panther, its long tail lashing even as it ran, was keeping pace with us. A creature of my dreams. Running beside the raft as the current bore us towards the Off-Moo capital!

Now Fromental could see the beast. He knew what it was. "Those cats are never normally found this close to the river, as they loathe and fear it. They hunt the Lands Beyond the Light. The cannibals are their natural prey. They're greatly feared because they can see in the dark, if not in the conventional sense. Though it seems those eyes look at you, in fact the beasts are completely blind."

"How do they hunt? How is that beast able to follow us?"

"The Off-Moo tell me it is heat. Somehow the eyes see heat rather than light. And their sense of smell is extraordinary. They can pick up certain scents that are a mile or more away. The darklanders live in terror of them. The Off-Moo believe the cats are their greatest single protection against threats from the cannibals."

"The cannibals don't hunt the panther?"

"They can hardly protect themselves against it. Superstition and fire are about all they have in their defence, for they, too, are largely blind. They instinctively fear the creatures, for whom they are relatively easy prey."

But the Off-Moo were alarmed now that they could see the cat. They spoke in high-pitched Greek which was almost impossible for me to understand. Fromental told me that this sign increased their anxiety, their sense of danger. Why had the cat come so close to the river?

"Perhaps nothing more than curiosity," suggested my friend.

He signalled to Scholar Brem, an acquaintance, and went to talk to him. When he came back he seemed disturbed. "They fear that some powerful force drives the cats away from their usual hunting grounds. But there again it might just be an isolated young male looking for a mate." I didn't see the great, black sabretooth again. We were already slowing as the thrust of the river met the embrace of the blazing lake, whose further shores were lost in the pitch-darkness beyond.

Gradually, just as one might from a ship or a train entering the outskirts of a mighty city, we began to notice that the formations around us had given way to the slender living towers of the Off-Moo. These towers often reflected soft shades, the merest wash of colour, which added to their mysterious beauty. Curious Off-Moo began to appear on the banks and on their balconies while our steersmen strained against their sweeps, catching the current which bore us gracefully in towards a harbour, where several similar petrified sea monsters were moored.

With considerable skill, the sweepsmen brought the raft alongside a quay of elaborately carved rock. On it a small crowd waited to greet us. For the most part they were Off-Moo, subtly individual in their conical hoods, but then I recognised a shorter figure standing to one side and knew such pleasure, such relief, that I was surprised by the depth of my own emotion. I had come to care very much for Oona. Her pale, albino beauty gave her an even more ethereal quality in this world than it had in my own. But that was not what gladdened my heart. It was a feeling far more subtle. A sense of recognition, perhaps? I hurried off the bizarre raft and onto the basalt of the quayside, running to greet her, to embrace her, to feel the warmth, the reality, the profound familiarity of her.

"I am glad you are here," she murmured. She embraced Fromental. "You have arrived in time to meet Lord Renyard's friends. They bring desperate news. As we suspected, our foes attack three realms at least, all of them strategic. Your own world is in mortal peril. Tanelorn herself is again under deep siege, this time from Law, and could fall at any moment. And now, it seems, Mu-Ooria herself faces her greatest threat. This is not coincidence, gentlemen. We have a very powerful opponent." She was already leading us away from the docked raft, through twisting, narrow streets.

"But Tanelorn can't be conquered," said Fromental. "Tanelorn is eternal."

Oona turned serious eyes up towards his distant face. "Eternity as we understand it is in jeopardy. All that we take for granted. All that is permanent and inviolable. *Everything* is under attack. Gaynor's ambitions could bring about the destruction of sentience. The end of consciousness. Our own extinction. And possibly the extinction of the multiverse herself."

"Perhaps we should have killed him when he first threatened us," said Fromental.

The young huntress shrugged her shoulders as she led us into one of the slender buildings. "You could not kill him then," she said. "It would be morally impossible."

"How so?" I asked.

Her tone was matter-of-fact, as if I had missed the most obvious answer in the world.

"Because," she said, "at that point in your mutual histories he had yet to commit his great crime."

9

A Conference of Spheres

I was having difficulties with Mittelmarch notions of time. It seems we were all fated to live identical lives in billions of counter-realities, rarely able to change our stories, yet constantly striving to do so. Occasionally, one of us was successful, and it was the effort to change that story which somehow helped maintain the balance of the universe—or rather the multitude of alternate universes Oona called "the multiverse," where all our stories were being played out in some form.

Oona was patient with me but I was of a prosaic disposition and such notions didn't sit easily with my ideas of common sense. Gradually I began to see the broader vision, which helped me understand how our dreams were simply glimpses of other lives, often at their most dramatic, and how it was possible for some of us to move between these dreams, these other lives, and even sometimes change them.

She spoke of these matters after she had taken me to my quarters and allowed me to refresh myself. Then, when I was reinvigorated, she led me out into the sinuous streets of Mu-Ooria, a vital, crowded city which was far more cosmopolitan than I had anticipated. Clearly not all humans were banished into the darkness. Entire quarters were filled with people of many different races and creeds, evidence of a great mingling of cultures, including that of the Off-Moo. We passed through street markets which might have flourished in modern Cologne, between houses which would not have been out of place in medieval France. Clearly the Off-Moo had a long history of welcoming refugees from the surface, and these people had kept their habits and customs, blending happily with the others.

As well as the familiar, there was also the exotic. Oona led me past reflective jet and basalt terraces festooned with pale lichens and fungi, balconies of sinuous limestone whose occupants were sometimes indistinguishable from the rock. This eternal, sparkling night had a luring beauty of its own. I could understand how so many chose to settle here. While you might never know sunlight and fields of spring flowers, neither would you know the kind of conflict which could rob you of both in an instant.

I understood and sympathised with the people who had chosen to live here, but I longed to see again the familiar, robust, cherry cheeks of our honest Bek peasantry. Not one of the inhabitants of this place looked entirely alive, though they obviously took pleasure in their existence and enjoyed a high level of complex civilisation, despite the sense of the crushing weight of rock overhead, the knowledge of this land's dark boundaries, the hush which seemed to settle everywhere, the slightly exaggerated courtesy you didn't expect to find in a busy metropolis. I had every admiration for it but would never choose to settle here myself. Would I ever now find my way back to my fatherland?

Again I was filled with a sense of desperate frustration. I loved my country and my world. All I wanted was the opportunity to fight for what was decent and honourable in both. I needed to take my place with those who resisted a cowardly terror. Who encountered cruelly philistine forces wishing to destroy everything that had ever been valuable in our culture. I told Oona this, as we continued to stroll through the winding canyons of the city, admiring gardens and architecture, exchanging pleasantries with passers-by.

"Believe me, Count Ulric," she assured me, "if we are successful, you will have every opportunity to fight the Nazis again. But there is much to be done. The same battle lines are being drawn on at least three separate planes and at this stage it looks as if our enemies are stronger."

"You're suggesting I fight for the same cause by taking part in your struggle?"

"I am saying that the cause is the same. How you serve it will ultimately be your decision. But it will be simultaneous with other decisions." She smiled at me and put her delicate hand into mine, leading me eventually into a great, natural circle, slightly concave, close to the city's centre. Here there were no stalagmites, and the stalactites in the roof were hidden by the deep shadow created by the lake's glare.

I thought at first this was an amphitheatre, but there was no evidence that it accommodated any kind of audience. Leading out of the circle was one wide main thoroughfare which seemed to go directly to the lake. If the Off-Moo were a different people I would have assumed it was designed to display some kind of military triumph—a returning navy might parade up this avenue and its victorious forces present themselves to the people in the great, shallow bowl.

Oona was amused by my stumbling suggestions, my noticing that the floor seemed to have been worn smooth by thousands of feet, that there was a faint, familiar smell to the place.

"This is the only chance you will have to come here," she said. "Assuming the tenant returns."

"Tenant?"

"Yes. He has lived with the Off-Moo for as long as their history. Some think they came to this world together. There is even evidence that the city was created around him. He is very old indeed and sleeps a great deal. Periodically, perhaps when he is hungry, he leaves this place and travels down there"—she pointed to the broad avenue—"to the lake. The times of his disappearances vary, but he has always returned."

I looked around for some kind of dwelling. "He lives here without furniture or shelter?"

She was enjoying my mystification.

"He is a gigantic serpent," she said. "In appearance not unlike the *voluk*, but much bigger. He sleeps here and offers no harm to the Off-Moo. He has been known to protect them in the past. They believe that he goes into the lake to hunt. A strange beast, with long side fins, almost like the wings of a ray, but primarily reptilian. Some believe he has vestigial limbs secreted within his body, that he is in fact more lizard than snake. Not unlike those resurrected husks they turn into rafts, though much larger, of course."

"The World Serpent?" Half amused, half in awe, I referred to the mythical Worm Ouroboros, said by our ancestors to guard the roots of the World Tree.

Surprisingly her tone was sober when she replied. "Perhaps," she said. Then, deliberately, she lightened her mood and took my hand again.

I was suddenly conscious that I was trespassing and was glad to let her laugh and lead me through another series of winding twittens to show me the pastel glories of the water gardens, fashioned from natural stone and cultivated fungi. Glimmering points of light from the misty miniature falls reflected all the subtle colours of the bizarre underground flora. My guide was delighted at my enchantment, taking proprietorial pride in the wonders of Mu-Ooria.

"Could you not learn to love this place?" she asked me, linking her arm in mine. With her I felt a friendliness, a comfortable closeness which I had never experienced with another woman. I found it relaxing.

"I love it already," I told her, "and I think the Off-Moo a civil and cultivated race. An exemplary people. I could stay here for a year and never experience all the city has to offer. But it isn't in my nature, Fraülein Oona, to take exotic holidays while my nation is threatened by a monster far more dangerous than Mu-Ooria's adopted serpent!"

She murmured that she understood my concern and that she would do everything she could for me. I asked after Captain Bastable, the mysterious Englishman, but she shook her head. "I believe he's engaged elsewhere."

"So will you, who clearly can come and go at will, lead me out of here?"

"There are dream roads," she said. "Finding them isn't difficult. But getting you back to where you came from can sometimes prove impossible." She raised a hand to forestall my anger. "I have promised you that you'll have the chance to fight your enemies. Presumably you would like to be as successful as possible?"

"You are telling me to be patient. What else can I be?" I knew she was sincere. I gave her arm an affectionate squeeze. I felt I had known her all my life. She might have been one of my more attractive relatives, a niece perhaps. I recalled her rather odd expectation that I would know her. Now I understood that, in the conflicting time streams of the multiverse, it was possible for something to be both mysterious and familiar. She had no doubt mistaken me for someone else, even one of my myriad "other selves" who, if she and the Off-Moo were to be believed, proliferated throughout a continuously branching multiverse.

I was not comforted by her assurance that I had not one doppelgänger but an infinite number. Which reminded me to ask her about the two bizarre figures I had seen earlier. One of them had been my double.

She found my news disturbing, rather than surprising. She asked me precise questions and I did my best to answer. She shook her head. "I did not know there were such forces at work," she said. "Not such great forces. I pray some of them choose to ally their cause with our own. I might have misused or misunderstood my mother's skills."

"Who were those armoured men?"

"Gaynor, if he wears the armour you describe. The other is his mortal enemy, one of the greatest of your avatars, whose destiny is to change the very nature of the multiverse."

"Not an ancestor, then, but an alter ego?"

"If you like. You say he was asking you for something?"

"My guess."

"He is desperate." She spoke affectionately, as if of a very familiar friend. "What did Fromental see?"

"Nothing. These were glimpses only. But not illusions. At least, not in any sense I understand."

"Not illusions," she confirmed. "Come, we'll confer with Fromental and his friends. They've had long enough without us."

We crossed a series of canals rather like those of Venice, one narrow bridge after another, following natural gullies and fissures employed as part of the city's water system. I was impressed by how the Off-Moo adapted to the natural formations of the earth. Goethe, for instance, would have been impressed by their evident respect for their surroundings. Ironically, those surroundings, if described in my own world, would have been taken for the fantasies of some opium-addicted Coleridge or Poe. A tribute to the majority's capacity to deny any truth, no matter how monumental, which challenges its narrow understanding of reality.

Eventually we entered a small square and Oona led me into a doorway and up a twisting, asymmetrical staircase until we came into a large room, surprisingly wide for an Off-Moo apartment. The place was furnished more to human taste, with large couches and comfortable chairs, a long table loaded with food and wine. Evidently a meal had been eaten while Fromental conferred with Lord Renyard and the three strangers who rose to greet us as we entered the room.

I had never, outside of a comic opera, seen such a collection of swaggering fantasticos. Lord Renyard wore the lace and embroidery of a mid-seventeenth-century fop, balancing his slightly unsteady frame on an ornamental dandy pole. A scarlet silk sash over his shoulder held the scabbard of a slender sword. His eyes narrowed in pleasure as he recognised us. "My dear friends, you are most welcome." He bowed with an awkward grace. "May I introduce my fellow citizens of Tanelorn—Lord Blare, Lord Bragg and Lord Bray. They seek to join forces against the common enemy."

These three were all dressed in the exaggerated uniforms of Napoleonic cavalry officers. Lord Blare had huge side-whiskers and a wide, horsey grin displaying large, uneven teeth. Lord Bragg was a glowering, self-important cockerel, all blazing wattles and comb, while Lord Bray had a solemn, mulish look to his huge face. Although not as distinctly animal-like as Lord Renyard, they all three had a slight air of the farmyard about them. But they were cordial enough.

"These gentlemen have come by a hard and circuitous route to be with us," Fromental explained. "They have walked the moonbeam roads between the worlds."

"Walked?" I thought I had misheard him.

"It's a skill denied to many." Lord Renyard's voice was a sharp, yapping bark. He spoke perfect classical French but he had to twist his mouth and vocal cords to get some of his pronunciations. "Those of us who learn it, however, would travel no other way. These are my good friends. When we understood the danger, we all left Tanelorn together. Our Tanelorn, of course. We were separated some while ago, during an alarming adventure. But they came here at last and brought fresh news of Tanelorn's plight."

"The city is under siege," said Fromental. "Gaynor, in another guise, attacks it. He has the Higher Worlds on his side. We fear it will soon fall."

"If Tanelorn falls, then all falls." Oona was pacing. She had not expected such dramatic news. "The doom of the multiverse."

"Without help Tanelorn will most certainly perish," said Lord Bragg. His flat, cold voice held little hope. "The rest of our world is already conquered. Gaynor rules there now in the name of Law. His patron is Lady Miggea the Mad. And he draws on the power of more than one avatar."

"We came here," said Lord Bray, "searching for those avatars in the hope that we could stop them combining. In our world it has happened already. Here, Gaynor has barely begun to test his power."

I didn't understand. Oona explained. "Sometimes it is possible, with immortal help, for two or more avatars of one person to be combined. This gives them considerably greater power, but they lose sanity. Indeed, such an unnatural blending threatens the stability of the entire multiverse! The one who draws on the souls of his avatars in this way takes terrible risks and can pay a very great price for the action."

Something in the way she glanced at me caused me to shudder. The chill went deep into my bones and would not leave me.

"We can't let Mu-Ooria be attacked because of us," I said. "Why don't we lead an expedition into the Dark Land and strike at them first? It will take Gaynor months to marshal a force."

Oona smiled grimly. "We cannot anticipate the rate at which time passes for him."

"But we know we can defeat him."

"That depends," said Lord Renyard, apologetic for interrupting.

"On what?"

"On the quality of help we can summon. I would remind you, dear Count von Bek, that in our world all that remains unconquered is Tanelorn herself. Gaynor has mighty help. The help of at least one goddess."

"How has Tanelorn resisted up to now?" I asked.

"She is Tanelorn. She is the city of eternal sanctuary. Usually neither Chaos nor Law dare attack her. She is the embodiment of the Grey Fees."

Oona came to my rescue. "The Grey Fees are the lifestuff of the multiverse— you could call them the sinews, muscles, bones and sap of the multiverse—the original matter from which all else derives. The original home of the Holy Grail. Although creatures can meet in the Grey Fees, even dwell there if they choose, any attack on them, any fight that takes place within the Fees, is an affront to the very basis of existence. Some would call it an affront to God. Some believe the Grey Fees to be God, if the multiverse itself is not God. I prefer to take a more prosaic view. If the multiverse is a great tree, forever growing, shedding limbs, extending roots and branches in all directions, each root and branch a new reality, a new story being told, then the Fees are something like the soul of the entity. However crucial the struggle, we never attack the Grey Fees."

"Is attacking Tanelorn the same as attacking the Grey Fees?" I asked.

"Simply call it an alarming precedent," said Lord Bray, showing more irony than I first suspected in him.

"So Gaynor threatens the fundamental fabric of existence. And if he succeeds?"

"Oblivion. The end of sentience."

"How might he succeed?" My habits of logic and strategy were returning. Old von Asch had taught me how to reason.

"By recruiting the help of a powerful Duke of Law or Chaos. There are elements in either camp who believe that if they control everything, the multiverse will accord better with their own vision and temperament. The lives of the gods have cycles when senility and bigotry replace sense and responsibility. Such is the case with Gaynor's ally in our realm."

"A god, you said?"

"A goddess, as it happens." Lord Blare uttered an unruly laugh. "The famous Duchess Miggea of Dolwic. One of the most ancient of Law's aristocrats."

"Law? Surely Law resists such injustice?"

"Aggressive senility isn't only a characteristic of Chaos in its decline. Both forces obey the laws of the multiverse. They grow strong and virile, then decline and die. And, in their dying, they are often desperate for life. At any price. All past loyalties and understanding disappear, and they become little more than appetites, preying upon the living in order to sustain their own corrupted souls. Even the noblest Lords and Ladies of Law can suffer this corruption, often when Chaos is at her most vigorous and dynamic."

"Don't make my mistake," murmured Fromental to me, "and confuse Law and Chaos with Good and Evil. Both have their virtues and vices, their heroes and villains. They represent the warring temperaments of mankind as well as the best we might become, when the virtues of both camps are combined in a single individual."

"Are there such individuals?"

"A few," said Lord Bray. "They tend to arise as the occasion demands."

"Gaynor's not one of those?"

"He's the opposite!" Lord Renyard yapped indignantly. "He combines the vices of both sides. He damns himself to eternal despair and hatred. But it's in his nature to believe he acts from practical necessity."

"And he has supernatural help?"

"In our world, yes." Lord Bragg's long face became briefly animated. "At his side rides Lady Miggea. The Duchess of Law has all the powers of her great constituency at her command. She could destroy whole planets if she wished. The hand of Law is deadly when it serves unthinking destruction rather than justice and creativity. We had hoped Lord Elric . . ."

Lord Blare had begun to pace about the room. He was all urgent blue eyes, rattling spurs and jingling harness. "Much as I enjoy a good chin-wag, gents, I'd remind ye that we're all in immediate danger and our journey here was to seek the help of the Grey Lords, whom we understood these Off-Moo fellers to be."

"But they can't offer much in the way of practical help, I gather. Gaynor threatens your world, too." Lord Bragg fingered his muttonchops. "So we must look elsewhere for salvation."

"Where would you go?" asked Fromental.

"Wherever the moonbeam roads lead us. They are the only way we know to travel between the realms." Lord Bray seemed almost apologetic. "With Elric duped and charmed . . ."

"Would you teach me to walk those roads if I came with you?" Fromental asked quietly.

"Of course, my friend!" Lord Renyard responded with a generous yap. A clap of his paw upon Fromental's vast arm. "I for one would be proud to have the company of a fellow citizen of France!"

"Then I'm your man, monsieur!" The legionnaire straightened his cap and saluted. He turned to me. "I hope, my friend, that you don't feel I desert you. My quest was always for Tanelorn. Perhaps in my search I will learn something that will help us all fight Gaynor. Be assured, my friend, if you are ever in danger, I will help you if I can."

I told him much the same. We shook hands. "I'd go with you," I said, "only I have sworn to return home as soon as possible. So much is threatened at this moment."

"We have our separate destinies," said Lord Renyard, as if to console us. "All are threads in the same tapestry. I suspect we shall all meet again. Perhaps in happier circumstances."

"The Off-Moo are populous and resourceful, even when supernatural forces are brought against them." Oona stepped amongst the huge, beastlike military dandies to make her own farewells. "We each serve the Balance best by serving our own realms." She, too, shook Fromental's hand.

"Do you think Gaynor will attack the city?" asked the big legionnaire.

"This is his story," she said a little mysteriously, "his dream. I would not be entirely surprised if his great campaign has already begun. This is the adventure which will earn him his best-known sobriquet."

"And what is that?" asked Fromental, trying to smile.

"The Damned," she said.

When we had parted from the Tanelornians (of whom I could not help thinking in my own mind as "the Three Hussars"), I asked Oona how she understood so much.

She smiled and again settled her small body comfortably against mine as we walked through the twilight canyons in which so many commonplace activities were no doubt taking place.

"I am a dreamthief's daughter," she said. "My mother was a famous one. She stole some mighty dreams."

"And how are dreams stolen?"

"Only a dreamthief knows how. And only a dreamthief can safely carry one dream into another. Use one dream against another. But that is how she earned her riches."

"You could steal a dream in which I was emperor and place me in another where I was a pauper?"

"It's a little more complicated than that, I understand. But I did not receive my mother's training. The great school in Cairo was closed during my time in the city. Besides, I lacked the patience."

She paused in her step, bringing me to a halt. She said nothing, merely stared up into my face. Ruby eyes met my own. I smiled at her and she smiled back. But she seemed a little disappointed.

"So you are not the thief your mother was?"

"I didn't say I was a thief at all. I inherited some of her gifts, not her vocation."

"And your father?"

"Ah," she said, and began to laugh to herself, looking down at the jade-green street which reflected our shadowy figures. "Ah, my father."

She'd not be drawn further on that matter, so instead I asked her about her journeyings in other worlds.

"I've travelled very little compared to Mother," she said. "I spent some while in England and Germany, though not in your history. I must say I have something of a fascination with the worlds that would be most familiar to you, perhaps because my mother had such affection for them. And you, Count von Bek, do you miss your own family?"

"My mother died giving birth to me. I was her last child. Her hardest to bear."

"And your father?"

"A scholar. A student of Kierkegaard. I think he blamed me for my mother's death. Spent most of his time in the old tower of our house. He had a huge library. He died in the fire which destroyed it. Dark hints of madness and worse. I was away at school, but there were some strange tales told of that night and what the people of Bek believed they witnessed. There was a grotesque and sensational story spread about my father's refusing to honour some family "pact with the devil" and losing an heirloom that was his trust."

I laughed, but not with my companion's spontaneity. I found it difficult to grieve for a man so remote from me, who would not, I suspect, have grieved if I had died in that fire. He found my albinism repulsive. Disturbing, at least. Yet my attempts to distance myself from my parents and their problems had never been wholly successful. He expected me to carry the family duty but could not love me as he loved my brothers. Oona did not press me further. I was always surprised by the levels of emotion such memories revealed.

"We share a complicated family life," she murmured sympathetically.

"For all that," I insisted, "I still intend to return to Bek. Is there no way you can get me home soon?"

She was regretful. "I journey between dreams. I inhabit the stories, they say, which ensure the growth and regeneration of the multiverse. Some believe we dream ourselves into reality. That we are yearnings, desires, ideals and appetites made concrete. Another theory suggests the multiverse dreams us. Another that we dream it. Do you have a theory, Count von Bek?"

"I fear I'm too new to these ideas. I'm having some trouble believing the basic notions behind them." I put my arm around her because I sensed a kind of desperation in her. "If I have a faith, it's in humankind. In our ultimate capacity to pull ourselves from the mud of unchecked appetite and careless cruelty. In a positive will to good which will create a harmony not easily destroyed by the brutes."

Oona shrugged. "Anxious dogs overeat," she said. "And then they usually vomit."

"You are a cynic?"

"No. But we have a long battle, we Knights of the Balance, to achieve that harmony."

I'd heard a similar phrase earlier. I asked her what it meant.

"A term some use to describe those of us who work for justice and equity in the world," she explained.

"And am I one of those knights?" I asked.

"I believe you know," she said. Then she changed the subject, pointing out the flowing cascades of what she called moonflowers, pouring down the slender terraces of Mu-Ooria's spires.

In spite of all the dangers and mysteries I had known, it was a privilege to witness such beauty. It defied anything I had ever anticipated. It had an intensity, a tactile and ambient reality, that even an opium-eater could not understand. I knew that, whatever I experienced, I was not dreaming. There was no denying the absolute reality of this gloomy, rocky world.

Oona clearly wished to answer no further questions, so we spent the next while in silence, admiring the skills of the Off-Moo architects who blended their own creations with the natural, giving the city an organic wholeness I had never seen in a place of that size before.

As we turned from admiring a fluted curtain of transparent rock appearing to undulate in the light from the lake, I saw a man standing not four feet from me. I felt sick and silenced by the shock. Again this was my doppelgänger, still clad in the baroque black armour, his face an exaggerated likeness of my own, with high cheekbones, slightly slanting brows and glaring red eyes, his skin the colour of fresh ivory. Screaming at me. Screaming at me and understanding that I could not hear a word.

Oona saw him, too, and recognised him. She began to approach him, but he moved away down an alley, signalling me to follow. His pace increased and we were forced to run to keep up with him. Twisting, turning, dipping down into narrow tunnels, ascending steps, crossing bridges, we followed the armoured man to the outskirts of the city, until we were some distance inland. He remained ahead of us, moving steadily up the bank of the river, in and out of the constantly changing shadows, the flickering, silvery light. Every so often he glanced back and the black metal helmet framed a face filled with urgency. I was certain that he wished us to follow him.

Momentarily blinded, I lost track of him. Oona began to run ahead of me. I think she could still see him. I hurried in her wake.

Then, from ahead, I heard a sudden, agonised scream, a wail of grief and terror combined. Rushing forward I found the young woman kneeling on the ground beside what I took at first for the corpse of the black-armoured stranger.

But the stranger had vanished. The carcass was that of the great sabre-toothed panther who had kept pace with our raft as we sailed towards the city.

Oona raised her weeping eyes to mine.

"This can only be Gaynor," she said. "Murdering for pleasure."

I looked up, hoping to see the stranger, wondering if he had killed the cat. I thought I caught a glimpse of coppery silver, heard a mocking note in the current of the river, but there was no sign of my doppelgänger.

"Did you know the animal?" I asked Oona, kneeling beside her as she wrapped her arms around its huge body.

"Know her?" Oona's slender frame shivered with unbearable emotion. "Oh, yes, Count von Bek, I know her." She paused, trying to take control of her grief. "We are more than sisters." The tears began to come now, streaming silver against her bone-white skin.

I thought I'd misheard her.

"Only Gaynor," she whispered, rising and looking about her. "Only he would have the cruel courage and cleverness to attack our cats first. They are crucial to Mu-Ooria's defence."

"You say she's your sister?" I looked wonderingly down at the massive black cat, her curved, white tusks the length of swords. "This beast?"

"Well," she said abstractedly, still trying to recover herself. "I am, after all, a dreamthief's daughter. I have some choice in the matter."

Then Gaynor, still in his SS uniform, stepped from behind a pillar. Incongruously he had a short, bone bow in one hand. With the other, he was drawing back a string. Nocked to it was a slender silver arrow aimed directly at Oona's heart.

She reached for her own weapon but then froze, realising that Gaynor had the complete advantage.

"I've been having some interesting adventures and encounters, cousin," he said. "Learning some good lessons. Time's simply zipped by. How has it been for you?"

IO

Rippling Time

My Raven Sword was where I had left it in my new lodgings. Oona could not use her bow and was otherwise without arms. Gaynor was choosing which one of us to shoot. His aim wavered, but he was too far distant for me to be able to attack him.

Then reason reminded me that he could not afford to kill us. He wanted my sword. He also seemed to have forgotten the still, slow-time Off-Moo sentinels.

"You'll recall, cousin, that not all who guard this place are immediately detectable," I said.

His smile was dismissive. "They're no danger to me. I've had many ordeals, many adventures and encounters since we last met. I have more powerful help now, cousin. Supernatural help. We already lay siege to Tanelorn. The Off-Moo's defences are unsophisticated in comparison. This is a wonderful realm, once you find your way around in it. I have learned much that will be useful when I have the Grail."

"You think that it will be easy for you to return?"

"For me, cousin, yes. You see, I've made some fine new friends since we parted on such bad terms. Once you meet them, you'll soon be enthusiastically apologising to me. And only too pleased to run home to fetch the Raven Sword while I entertain your pretty young friend, eh?"

I recognised an element of bravado in him, an unsteadiness about his eyes. I replied contemptuously. "If I had the sword with me, cousin, I suspect you'd be a little more civil. Lower your bow. Was it you who killed the panther?"

"I'll keep the bow strung and maintain our equilibrium for the moment, cousin. Is the big cat dead? An epidemic, no doubt? One of those dreadful plagues which sometimes attacks the feline world . . ." His arrow was still level with my heart, but the verbal barb was intended for Oona.

Oona did not respond. What was meant to goad her only drove her to take further charge of herself. "Your claims are illegitimate, Prince Gaynor. Your own cynicism will defeat you. All the future holds for you is an eternity of despair."

His amusement increased. Then he frowned, as if he brought himself back to business. "True, I'd hoped to find you here with your sword, Ulric. So I'll strike that bargain—bring me the blade and I'll spare the girl's life in exchange."

"The sword is my charge," I said. "I can't give it up. My honour depends upon my stewardship . . ."

"Bah! Your father's honour also depended upon a stewardship—and we know how thoroughly he defended his trust!" Now he was contemptuous.

"Stewardship?"

"Fool! The von Beks had the most powerful combination of supernatural artefacts in the multiverse. Your weakling father, degenerated to mumbling voodoo spells and other witcheries, let one fall from your possession. Because he feared it would be stolen! Your family doesn't deserve its destiny. From now on, I and mine will keep those objects of power together. For ever."

I was baffled. Had he gone mad? Though he seemed to think I understood him, I could scarcely make sense of a word he said.

"Quickly." He drew the bowstring back a little farther. "Which one will get the sword, which one will stay here as hostage for it?"

Oona suddenly clutched her head and staggered. Gaynor turned the bow on her.

At Oona's feet, the shining black body quivered. Huge muscles flexed. A tail lashed. Vast whiskers twitched. Jade eyes gleamed. A great, black nose made a single, searching snort.

Oona was disbelieving, but Gaynor was cursing as the sabretooth climbed slowly to its feet, its glaring eyes casting around for an enemy, its huge ivory tusks glinting in the riverlight. And then, standing shoulder to shoulder with the gigantic cat, I saw another human figure.

My doppelgänger.

Had he brought the cat back to life? Gaynor barely disguised his own terror.

Oona had the common sense to drag us behind the shelter of a nearby stalagmite so we could watch from cover.

The other albino seemed to be talking to Gaynor. He gestured. Suddenly both he and the cat vanished. Gaynor unnocked the arrow, stuck it in his belt and ran into the darkness.

I was completely mystified by the exchange. I tried to ask Oona if she understood any better, but she was grim, hurrying back to the interior of the city. "We must warn them of what's happening. This will take all their resources."

"What does it mean? Who is that bizarre version of myself?"

"Fairer to say that you are a version of him," she said. "He's called Elric of Melniboné and he carries the greatest burden of us all."

"And he's from another—what—? One of these alternatives to our own reality?"

"Some call them 'branches' or 'branes.' Or 'the realms,' or 'the scales,' but they are all versions of our universe." She was still intent on negotiating the winding lanes of Mu-Ooria, heading deeper and deeper into the city.

"And like you, this doppelgänger of mine travels between these worlds? And he knows you?"

"Only in his dreams," she said.

We were both out of breath. I had no idea where she was leading us, but she would not rest. While the immediate danger was in the forefront of my mind, I still seethed with a thousand unanswered questions. Questions so numinous I could not begin to frame them in words.

She had led us through a high doorway, down a long corridor and up a short winding ramp until we stood in a low-ceilinged hall full of long benches of carved stone arranged around a large, glassy circular area.

I was reminded of monks' communal quarters. The hall was lit by the tall, watery glasses. An air of tranquillity hung about the place. The shadows were soft. The circular area at the centre stirred occasionally, its shades shifting from jet-black to dark grey.

Oona led me behind the main rank of benches. As she did so, the first Off-Moo began to arrive, their long faces grave, their odd eyes questioning. I hadn't seen the young woman give any signal. Our presence in the room must have been enough to bring the Off-Moo elders there immediately. Some had the air of people interrupted in important tasks. Clearly they believed the matter serious. How had she summoned them? Was she in telepathic communication with their group intelligence? Her face had a beautiful, open quality when she communicated with them. The gracious unhumanity of these creatures made me feel I was in the company of angels.

With murmured acknowledgement to us, they assembled around the obsidian circle and listened gravely as Oona told them what she had seen and what we had learned.

"Could be an army already marches against Mu-Ooria." She spoke a little hesitantly.

Again, she was acknowledged. But the Off-Moo's concentration had begun to focus on the reflective, glossy circle of rock around which they had gathered. I wondered what they saw there, if this were their version of a crystal ball? Some means of focusing their group consciousness?

Then I fell back, dazzled, throwing up my hands to protect my eyes. I thought the Off-Moo would be equally affected, but they calmly held their ground. Still guarding my eyes, I found Oona. She held her own hands before her face. "What's happening?" I asked.

"I think they have a way of bending light," was all she could tell me. Then the worst of the white-gold glare had gone and my eyes had become accustomed to what remained. I could see the source of the radiance. At the centre of the circle, it was three-dimensional and thoroughly real—an ordinary block of stone suspended in space and giving off a faint, sweet-sounding vibration which brought strange memories, recollected moments of purity. When thought, deed and idea were all in harmony. I half expected Sir Parsifal, the pure knight, to appear kneeling before it. For the stone had changed before my eyes.

I was now looking in absolute awe at what I had always assumed to be nothing more than a beautiful legend. A great, golden bowl, set with crystal and precious jewels and brimming with thick, crimson wine which poured down the sides to be absorbed by the light which darkened to deep gold and showed the whole Off-Moo conference chamber in dramatic, organic contrast, alive with dark, swirling colour. My senses were barely capable of registering so much at once. I felt oddly weak and found myself, for no clear reason, longing to be united with my Raven Sword. I felt that if only I could grasp the hilt, I would be able to draw strength from the black blade. But the sword was still in my chambers and I could not bear to leave the presence of that extraordinary vessel. The bowl, this Grail, grew larger. Everywhere the tall, conical hoods of the Off-Moo waved and nodded, as if this sight was unusual, even to them. Angular shadows were softened by the rounded rock over which they fell.

The Off-Moo's voices began a single low note which became a chant, a word, a mantra threatening to set the entire world vibrating. Light and dark were shaken together and mingled. The bowl then re-formed, rolling into itself until it was a golden, jewelled staff, rotating slowly in the air above the obsidian disc.

The Off-Moo chant changed and the staff expanded, grew. Just for an instant it became the shape of a small child with a round, beatific face. Then the staff returned, and slowly changed shape again until it was a single arrow. The Sign of Law. Then it became a sheaf of arrows, fanning out and upwards above the glassy circle. Eight golden, jewelled arrows, spinning slowly overhead. Chaos.

The Off-Moo were concentrating on the field of glistening obsidian. Very quickly a three-dimensional picture began to form there. Riders seemed to be emerging from the rock and galloping towards us. The illusion was not unlike a very realistic cinema experience. But it was also a terrifying reality. Gaynor, in his bizarre armour, rode a great white stallion whose blind eyes stared upwards, yet whose footing was unconsciously sure. Behind him, also on pale, blind horses, still in their black-and-silver uniforms, came the majority of his SS followers, Klosterheim at their head. All were cloaked and armed with miscellaneous antique weaponry.

Behind these was as bizarre a collection of monsters and grotesques as ever came shuffling and hopping out of a picture by Bosch. Perhaps, after all, the painter had been drawing from experience rather than imagination? They were long-limbed, long-headed, with huge myopic eyes. They had snuffling, exaggerated snouts, showing that they used scent more than sight. These loose-limbed travesties were much larger than the men who rode ahead of them, like toy soldiers modelled to two different scales. They were clearly savages, armed with maces and axes. Archers were in their ranks, and swordsmen. A mob rather than a disciplined army. But there were thousands of them.

"Troogs," said Oona.

I could see why the Off-Moo had known they had little to fear from these denizens of the borderlands. The giants had neither the intelligence nor the ambition to attack Mu-Ooria on their own accord.

One of the Off-Moo murmured something and Oona nodded. "All the panthers have disappeared," she told me. "They no longer control the troogs. We don't know if the cats are dead, charmed or have simply vanished."

"How could they vanish?"

"The workings of a powerful spell."

"Spell?" I was thoroughly sceptical. "Spell, fräulein? Are we so desperate we rely on sorcery?"

She showed some impatience with me. "Call it what you like, Count von Bek, but that is the best description. They sense a Summoning. A being far more powerful than the kind which usually walks these caverns. Perhaps a Lord of the Higher Worlds. Which means that Gaynor has somehow brought them out of their own realm and has given his allegiance. If they are able to bring all their power with them, they will be almost impossible to defeat. But some need the medium of a human creature like Gaynor and his army."

"Those 'troogs' are huge."

"Only here," she said. "In certain configurations of the branches, they are tiny. They're just the creatures who inhabit the borderland between Mu-Ooria and the Grey Fees. They are not of the Higher Planes but exactly what you know them to be, creatures of the lower depths. They're Gaynor's cannon fodder. If Gaynor's sorcery is successful against us, they will do the routine slaughtering."

"You seem to have experienced such an invasion before," I said.

"Oh, more than once," she said. "This struggle is constant, believe me. You cannot imagine what is beginning to happen in your own world."

Increasingly, I was feeling the need to have the Raven Sword at my side. While Oona continued to confer with the Off-Moo, I told them I would return soon.

I ran through serpentine streets, through the shifting light, finding my way as much by the muted colours as by the shape of the buildings, until I reached my quarters. I went to where I had left the sword. To my enormous relief it was still in the alcove near my bed. I unwrapped it, just to make sure it was my own beloved blade, and the dark, vibrating steel murmured to me in recognition.

Settling Ravenbrand in its makeshift scabbard, I left the room with it over my shoulder and once again made my way through the winding streets, recognising how a shaft of silvery light fell here, how the shadows moved there, how the colours changed in a particular stretch of wall, what was contained in those weird gardens.

I crossed the central plaza again and was approaching the streets on the other side when I heard a mocking sound from behind me. Turning, I stared into the triumphant eyes of my cousin Gaynor. He was aiming an arrow directly at me.

It hadn't occurred to me that he would have the audacity to follow us all the way into the heart of Mu-Ooria. I was still not used to seeing two versions of the same person—one leading a hideous army against a great city and the other already in the city.

Gaynor had a happy cruelty about him. "Surprised, I see, cousin. I have an alter ego taking care of one front, while I'm free to attack on another. Every general's greatest desire, eh?" He was salivating and his eyes kept moving towards the sword. He was fascinated—almost enraptured—by it.

Without thinking, I shifted my grip on the hilt and held it with the point down, against the counterweight of the pommel, so that it could come up rapidly, almost without any effort on my part, and send Gaynor's bow flying from his grasp. I only had to bring him in a little closer.

But he was wary. He stayed some distance off, the arrow still nocked against the string. He was clearly new to the art of archery but seemed to have mastered it well enough.

There was nothing else for it. I would have to close with him.

I began to move, very gradually, talking as I attempted to shorten the distance between us. But Gaynor was grinning and shaking his head from side to side. "Why on earth would you think I had any reason to keep you alive now, cousin. You have what I need. All I have to do is kill you and take it from you."

"You could have shot me in the back to do that," I said, just as he loosed an arrow which caught me high in my left arm. I was surprised that I felt no pain, then I realised my sturdy Norfolk jacket's tweed had taken the arrow. I was untouched. Before he could fit another shaft to his bowstring, I took a few swift steps towards him and held the sword's needle-sharp point to his throat.

"Drop your weapon, cousin," I demanded.

I felt a sharp pain in my side, looked down and saw the blade of a Nazi dagger pressed against my rib cage. Looking up I stared into the lifeless eyes of the gaunt Klosterheim.

"So, you also have a twin." I shuddered.

"We are all the same," murmured Klosterheim. "All of us. Millions of us." He seemed feverish, abstracted. Even nervous.

We were now in a stalemate, with my blade at Gaynor's throat and Klosterheim's at my ribs.

"Lower your sword, sir," he said. "And place it on the ground before you."

I laughed in his face. "I'm sworn to die before I give up Ravenbrand."

Gaynor was impatient. "Your father, too, was sworn to die to protect your family's inheritance. And die he did, sir. Ulric. Dear cousin. Give me the Black Sword and I guarantee that you will be allowed to live on at Bek, with all your villagers, your castle and everything back the way you're used to. No-one will bother you. Believe me, cousin, there are those of us, quite as idealistic as you, who are prepared to get their hands dirty in order to plant the seeds of paradise. If you choose to keep clean hands, that is your decision. But I do not make that choice. I'm ready to accept the necessity, to establish order throughout the multiverse. Do you understand?"

"I understand that you're mad," I said.

He laughed aloud at this. "Mad? We're all that, cousin. The multiverse is mad. But we shall make it sane again. We shall make it whatever we wish it to be. Can't you feel yourself changing? It is the only way you'll survive. It's how I've survived. But no human brain can accept so much intellectual and sensory overload without radically adapting. Do you really believe you're the same person who so recently fled a concentration camp?"

He spoke the truth. I could never be the same man. Yet he was still trying to confuse me.

"Herr Klosterheim will have to kill me," I said, "because I am not going to volunteer you my services or my sword."

We had reached a rough-and-ready stalemate. I looked past Gaynor. Over his shoulder a familiar figure raced towards me across the smooth floor of the plaza. It wore ornate black armour, a complicated helm. Its red eyes blazed as its pale hands reached out. It ran straight through the unaware Gaynor. A mirror-ghost. It radiated a terrible, desperate urgency. My instinct was to pull back, but my intellect told me to hold my ground.

The figure charged at enormous speed. It must surely knock me down. But he did not stop. Neither did he run through me. Instead he ran directly *into* me. Armoured body, helmed head, everything passed into my sensibly dressed twentieth-century person and was absorbed! A moment earlier I had been one individual. Now I was two.

I was two men in a single body. I did not for a second question this fact. How could I?

Suddenly I had two sets of memories. Two identities, each very distinct. Two futures. Two sets of emotions. But I also shared much with my doppelgänger. An overweening hatred for Gaynor, his brutal pack and all that it represented both here and in my own world. My double's resolve combined to strengthen my own, to complement my own anger. I knew at once that this was his intention. He had deliberately set out to achieve a combination of our power. And, because he was in so many ways myself, I could only trust him. He could not lie to me. Only to himself.

Now the Black Sword began to pulse and murmur, the red runes running like veins up and down her throbbing length. I felt her writhe in my hand. She rose under her own volition, rose in my fist until I held her shoulder-high. I cried out some savage battle-shout as the sword set my body thrilling with power, with a thousand conflicting notions and feelings, with a cruel, unfamiliar death-lust. I could taste the sweet blood and bitter souls my sword would soon devour. I licked my long lips. I was coming alive!

The beast will return to the fold, the sparrow to the field. Swords to marry, souls to heal.

I was speaking. A mantra. The end of some longer chant? A spell. In a language which one half of me did not understand at all, but the other half knew perfectly. It was not the language either of us habitually spoke. I could understand my thoughts in both languages and they were almost the same, save that the older tongue was full of throat-twisting glottal stops, clicks and hisses.

This other speech was far more liquid, immeasurably more ancient. Not human at all. Something that had to be learned, sound by sound, meaning by meaning. Something that had taken me many tortured years to come by.

THE DREAMTHIEF'S DAUGHTER

Two cups for justice. Two swords for harmony. Twin souls for victory. Lords and ladies walk on moonshine. Twins command the serpentine. Flows the blood and flows the wine. Flows the river to the sign. Twins in harlequin combine.

My alter ego was concentrating on the mantra. It had enabled him to perform this astonishing magic. Of course, I understood everything at once, for we were now the same creature. And being two identities in a single body, I saw how it was possible to be many people. To be sane and conscious of many other identities all at the same time. So many decisions, choices, obstacles. To understand that, at every moment, a million other selves were determining a million subtly or radically different paths. To be able to see the multiverse in whole, to have no worlds hidden, no possibilities denied! A glorious gift. All you had to do was find the roads. Now I understood the lure of such a life and why Oona and her mother and her mother's mother had inevitably chosen it.

The immediacy of the moment was in no way lessened by this experience of infinity. I was able to defend myself, indeed to carry the attack if I so desired, for I had combined Elric's training with my own. I knew how to act in battle and concentrate on a spell at the same time, for I was of the pure, old blood of Melniboné and we nurtured such gifts in ourselves. Our ancient folk had forged many compacts with the elementals of the multiverse. With the powers of earth, air, water and fire. And many of those compacts remained unbroken. I could call on all the powers of nature, though not all nature's power. To sense one's control of the wind, fire, the very form of the earth and flow of the water, to have conversed with the great beast-gods, those archetypes from whom all other animals came and who could command legions should they desire: all this was indescribably marvellous. Few of these allies had more than a healthy beast's need for a sufficiency of things and so had few ambitions in the affairs of men or gods, though the Lords of the Higher Worlds respected them. Only when called would the elementals agree, occasionally, to concern themselves in mortal conflicts. And now I had all these powers, understood the price to be paid for exercising them and the need for a psychic and physical sustenance far greater than anything I had required in the world of Bek. The reality was more intense, the stakes far higher than anything I had ever guessed possible.

But it required fuel for my flexing muscles, my heaving lungs, fuel to power my warrior's body as well as my warlock's wisdom. Only two sources for that fuel existed. One was a combination of herbs and other ingredients which allowed me to lead an active life. The other was the sword. Understanding what the sword did, my ordinary human self was thoroughly repulsed. Yet I also understood that survival depended upon my using her and that she would not allow me to act against my own interest. My affection for Ravenbrand remained, but I had a new respect for her. Clearly this sword chose who would wield her.

All my lessons of swordsmanship came back to me as I prepared to do battle. I was not reluctant to fight. I panted to fight, I yearned to draw blood.

"Prince Gaynor." Elric's haughty formality made my Saxon manners seem loose. "Has your death time come so soon?"

The Hungarian's damaged face had a demented look. "What are you? Do you control that human?"

"You're impertinent, Prince Gaynor. Your questions are offensive and coarsely put. I am of the royal line of Melniboné and your superior. Throw down that bow. Or my sword drinks your soul."

Gaynor was frightened by the changes in me, even though he guessed the reason. He had not been prepared for anything like this. Klosterheim's knife no longer pressed against my side. Gaynor's cadaverous colleague was staring with dawning intelligence. He had seen Elric run through his master and be absorbed by my body. He knew what I was, and I frightened him.

The sword was hungry for their souls. I could feel her needs speeding from her hilt to my hands. I did all I could to resist, but she became increasingly demanding.

"Arioch!" The name formed on my lips. "Arioch!" It tasted like the most exquisite wine. I was one with a being for whom words had specific flavours and for whom music was also colour.

"He'll not empower you here." Gaynor was recovering himself. He unstrung his bow. "Not in Mu-Ooria. Law rules here now."

I took charge of the quivering blade. I replaced it firmly in the rough sheath I had made. Gaynor had revealed something. Perhaps a weakness. Were his own supernatural allies also unable to enter Mu-Ooria herself? Did she have subtler defences?

"Only when the city's taken," I said on a hunch.

And then he realised what he had revealed to me and smiled a wry acknowledgement. I now thought he had slipped into the city with a few men, but could not draw on his ally's powers. It was a tribute to his daring that he came here with only Klosterheim to help him steal the Raven Sword.

"You understand much of the multiverse, cousin," said Gaynor.

"Only in my studies and dreams," I told him. "I am here at the request of my blood-kin. Otherwise I'd have no part of this business."

"Blood-kin?"

I became circumspect. I now knew what Ulric had previously not known.

I could scent familiar, ancient perfumes, traces of mustier smells. I began to take an interest in my surroundings.

With my attention off him, Gaynor made several rapid steps backwards, believing himself out of range of my sword. He yelled and gestured. Klosterheim drew his own sword and ran to join him. I began to smile. This promised tasty sport. My left hand closed over the scabbard and held it firmly so I could draw the sword rapidly if I had to. She was murmuring and quivering again. She echoed my own rapidly changing moods.

My ears were far sharper than when they belonged only to von Bek. I heard swift, slithering movements from the shadows. While Gaynor's most powerful allies might not be able to help him here, his lowlier troops were all too evident. He had not, after all, braved the city with only Klosterheim's support. I could see them, closing in from all sides. Their fear of cats dispelled, they had gathered enough courage to obey Gaynor and follow him. The gigantic grotesques Oona had called troogs. They snuffled and grunted in anticipation of a flesh feast. I recalled that the Off-Moo had called them cannibals.

I began to laugh. "Here's an irony, gentlemen," I said. I made a fluid movement, and the black blade was loose again. The runes ran crimson up and down her length. The iron pulsed and crooned. I began to pad like a cat towards Gaynor and Klosterheim. I broke into a trot as I closed the distance between us. The dark iron lifted higher. At one with my blade and my doppelgänger I knew a sense of boundless power. My laughter filled those immeasurable caverns!

Gaynor shrieked for his followers to attack. I defended myself against a blizzard of iron. Maces and swords swung at me from all sides. I dodged them with preternatural instincts and reflexes. I had soon cleared a space around me, but they scarcely feared me. I saw their nostrils dilating as they sniffed. I suspected they could hardly see me. Even here, they had no need of eyes. They had numbers. They had my scent. They were waiting only for Gaynor's signal before moving in again. This time it seemed they must surely crush me.

Now the black blade was howling. The sword which I called Ravenbrand and my alter ego called Stormbringer would not let me sheathe her again until she had been blooded. Her song blended with the delicate chimes of the crystal above. Her song was a hungry one. In her time, she had slain whole armies. She demanded her feast. She had moaned and lusted so long for satisfaction.

At last she could take her pleasure. At last she could feed. And deliver to me the energy I would need for my next Summoning.

II

The Power of Two

Gaynor shouted an order and the monsters were upon me. Seconds later I was carrying the attack. The sword was alive. She possessed an intelligence of her own. She slashed red gouting trails into the surrounding air, slid through flesh and bone and sinew and drew deep of this crude lifestuff, the souls of the slain. Every soul went to satisfy my own flagging substance. I had a taste for the work. I hacked my way through to where Gaynor and Klosterheim stood, on the edge of the square, goading the troogs and savages to kill me. I cleared a path towards the two leaders as another might clear his way through tall grass. They began to be afraid of me.

I was used to that fear. I expected little else. All humans had it. I despised it. No such weakness was allowed to infect the blood of a Melnibonéan. My folk had ruled the world for ten thousand years. They had determined the histories of the Young Kingdoms, those nations of humankind. My race was older, wiser and infinitely crueller than men. We knew nothing of the softer ways, the cruder ways of creatures we regarded as scarcely higher than apes. In my bones I had only contempt for them.

I was a Melnibonéan aristocrat. I had known more terror in the training for my sorcerous powers than these creatures had capacity or senses to experience. I had earned my alliances with the elementals and the lesser Lords of Chaos. I could raise the dead. I could force my will on any natural creature and could destroy an enemy with nothing but my black runeblade.

I was Elric of Melniboné, Last of the Sorcerer Emperors, Prince of Ruins, Lord of the Lost. Called Traitor and Womanslayer. Wherever I went I was feared and courted, even by those who hated me, for I had a power no human could begin to control.

Even amongst my own people, I had only ever had one living rival. My family had kept its power down the millennia by cultivating its traditional learning and constantly making new alliances with Chaos. Our household gods were Dukes of Hell. Our patron was Lord Arioch of Chaos, whose fiefdom included a million supernatural realms. Whose power was vast enough to destroy them all. Those of my blood could call casually upon such forces for help. A handful of us had controlled the world for ten thousand years. We might have continued to rule, had I not betrayed that blood and made myself an outlaw everywhere.

"Arioch!" Again the name came readily to my lips. Arioch was my own patron Lord of Chaos, whose power was shared by the Black Sword, who fed from the same souls which fed me and the sword. Were we one creature—sword, god and mortal—truly potent only when all parts came together? These were easy, casual thoughts for a Melnibonéan. What were less familiar were the notions of morality, of right and wrong, which now contaminated my brain and had done, it seemed, from childhood. A burden I had as yet not managed to abandon. My father had loathed me for this. My other relatives had been embarrassed. Many supported my cousin Yyrkoon's desire to replace me.

"Arioch!"

He could not or would not manifest himself here.

I heard a murmur in the back of my brain, as if that great Duke of Hell tried to speak, but then even that became faint.

Gaynor was growing more confident.

Recklessly he yelled for his remaining forces to attack me.

There was every chance I could be borne down under the weight of their numbers. Even the sword, which seemed to have a life of its own, could not kill them all. With desperate clarity my mind began to project a different quality of thought, like rapidly growing tendrils, into the surrounding supernatural realms, those infinite worlds the Off-Moo called the multiverse.

I was not sure I would be answered. I knew Duke Arioch could not aid me. But I had considered all the likely dangers I would have to face when I accepted the dreamthief's help. And while this human brain might lack some of the subtlety of my own, it was a good one. There was every chance I would be successful.

I began to murmur the deceptively simple mantra which helped my mind follow certain paths, engage with the stuff of the supernatural, speak a language which no living creature on the earth could understand. The verses were plain enough. They connected me to the complexities of the elemental spheres, where I might, if luck was on my side, find the means of escaping an increasingly likely fate.

I fought on, pushing back first one wall of battling flesh and then another. Yet I never gained ground, was always threatened with losing the last few metres I had cleared. The bodies became a barrier which I could use to my advantage. Never once did I lose that special concentration which continued to send tentacles of thought through all planes of the multiverse until, just for a second, I seemed to touch an alien intellect. One that recognised me.

And one I, too, recognised.

I sensed a world of water. Universe upon universe of water. Populated water. Water that coursed from one plane of existence to another. Ancient water. Newborn water. Swirling and still, wild and tranquil. Water lapped my face, even as a score of monsters fell to my hungry sword.

I began to sing—

King of all oceans; king of all the waters of the worlds;
King of the deep darkness, king of silence, king of pearls;
King of washed bones, king of all our drowned;
King of sadness, of sinking souls unfound,
Revive our ancient friendship, our enemies confound.
As your old tides curl their currents like woven threads,
Recollect our bargains. Recall our sacrificial dead.
Bring honour to those compacts, and bind them fresh around,
Tie stronger still the white knots and the red,
Two kingdoms and two wounds. A mutual victory.
A memory, a means to meet our double destiny.

A tide suddenly swirled around me, passed and was gone. I looked for water but saw only the glittering faraway lake, the long prospect which stretched towards it from the square said by Oona to be the lair of the great World Worm.

All of this I took for granted, for I had seen more monsters and miracles than most mortals. But, as the cannibals formed a circle around me and began to press in again, I knew I was lost if King Straasha, my old ally, avatar of all the gods of all the oceans of the multiverse, could not hear me, or did not wish to hear me.

Gaynor saw the thing first. My cousin whirled and pointed, as he signalled Klosterheim to flee. Gaynor had no disrespect for my powers of sorcery. He had counted on my not being able to use them here.

Beyond the quays and the tethered boats, the water was rising. It formed a towering wall, did not move like a tidal wave, but stayed in place, quivering, threatening. The wall grew higher. If it fell, it would extinguish the whole city.

Now the help I had summoned threatened to kill my friends as well as my enemies. I knew a sardonic moment. This seemed to be my perpetual destiny.

Yet I was sure the Off-Moo were not as vulnerable as they appeared. They must know by now that I fought Gaynor and his minions in the square. Had they fled? Or were they preparing defences?

The wall of water began to move. It gathered itself together. It started to form a shape. And soon, in shimmering outline, I distinguished the bulky figure of a giant. He was all shifting, swirling pale green water, never stable, never completely still, with pale blue eyes that searched the city and, at length, found mine.

Gaynor's followers fell back screaming for orders. Gaynor knew he could not possibly begin to fight King Straasha. A heavy, wet movement brought water running around our feet. King Straasha stepped ashore. His huge body walked, step by liquid step, up the great prospect towards us. If that weight of water should lose its form, it would drown us entirely.

As Gaynor searched for the swiftest escape route, another human figure appeared on the far side of the square and ran towards me.

Oona, the dreamthief's daughter.

"Warn the Off-Moo," I said. "They are in danger."

"They know of their danger," she said.

"Then save yourself"

"I'm safe enough, Lord Elric." She addressed me casually by this name, as if she had always known it. "But you must go. You have achieved your purpose here. The rest is work for me and the others to do. At least for now."

I began to suggest she stay with me for safety, but Klosterheim flung a dagger at me. I was distracted by its clattering to the ground a few metres away. When I looked up again, Oona had gone.

King Straasha was still wading towards me. I could tell the action was painful to him, but he was genial enough. "Well, little mortal, I am here because I have never yet broken a bargain and I have a certain affection for your kind. What would you have me do? Does this city have to be destroyed?"

"I need your help, sire. I need to move through the realms of water. I need to find the realm I left—the realm where my mortal form remains."

He understood.

"Water to water," he said, "and fire to fire. For the respect your ancestors showed my folk, I will do, Prince Elric, as you desire."

A vast watery hand descended towards me. I gasped, sensing that I was drowning as I struggled in King Straasha's grip. I feared he would kill me by accident.

Then I was engulfed in a bubble of air, held by a gigantic hand. I knew a sudden sense of peace, of absolute security. I was in the safe-keeping of the king of water elementals. We flew over the crags and spires of Mu-Ooria, until all I could see was the glowing lake surrounded by a mighty darkness. That part of me which was von Bek would have been incredulous, had not that part of me which was Elric shown such familiarity with the supernatural. Within me, even as I experienced the impossible, I could sense that von Bek believed in a world where all was Law, save for occasional upheavals of Chaos, and I believed in a multiverse where all was Chaos, where Law was something carved from that stuff and maintained by the will of mortals and the designs of the Lords of the Higher Worlds. Chaos was clearly the dominant force in all the realms, natural and supernatural. Two fundamentally opposed views of existence, yet in balance within the single body, the only mind. The harmony of opposites, indeed!

Von Bek neither hesitated nor questioned what I as Elric determined. For this was a world I understood and which had been a total mystery to him. Of course, he had all my memories, as I had all of his. For the moment the dominant "me" was the sorcerer-king, calling upon a great manifestation of an elemental, who served neither Law nor Chaos, nor any other thing, but lived to exist and perpetuate that existence endlessly.

The city was lost to sight. King Straasha hesitated, contemplating what he must do next. He and I had already communicated something which could not be represented by spoken language.

Unlike most sorcerer races, Melnibonéans had deliberately cultivated alliances with the elementals. With those great, old beings who were the embodiment of familiar and unfamiliar animals—with Meerclar of the Cats and even Ap-yss-Alara, Queen of the Swine, who was said to refuse all mortal advances and would continue to do so while one of them still ate pork.

Since pork was not eaten by any Melnibonéan of the higher castes, my folk had first made their accommodation with the queen.

The blood fever was dying away in me. For the moment Stormbringer was satiated. The energy we had acquired was crude and would not last long, but it enabled me to do what I must. I delighted in the knowledge that I was thwarting Gaynor not on one plane, but on two or more.

We came to rest in the centre of the lake. For a second I looked on a placid stretch of sparkling water: moonlight illuminating a Mediterranean idyll. Then King Straasha made a gesture with his other watery hand. He was laughing. Instantly I stared down into the wide mouth of a raging maelstrom. It sent clutching, foamy tendrils up towards me. It roared and lusted for my life and soul. It swirled and eddied and whispered for me to jump from King Straasha's protecting hand, down into the sublime rapture of its heart. That hypnotic sound, at once shriek and murmur, drew me helplessly towards it. My animal instinct was to resist, but I knew I must not.

The surrounding bubble had burst. I stood there on the sea-king's palm. Without further thought, I secured the runesword and dived into the howling vortex.

I was caught like a speck of dust and drawn deeper and deeper towards the infinite. I knew that I was whirling to my death, but I had no fear.

I knew what I was doing, where I was going, just as had King Straasha. There was still a chance I could lose my way and be carried off by my enemies. Both Chaos and Law, in this current battle, had much at stake and could be ruthless in their self-protection.

I heard the sea-king's roaring voice fade into the shout of the great maelstrom and I gathered all my resources, attempting to make my way through, to find the one pathway I needed.

It became almost impossible to breathe. The water began to fill my lungs. I wondered how much longer I could survive before I drowned. Then the sword stirred at my belt. Some instinct made me reach for her blindly, drag her free of her scabbard and then let her pull me through the wild swell. Her course took me first up, then down, then deep within those watery walls.

Whole cities, continents, races swirled around me. All the oceans of all the worlds had combined into one. I passed through universes of water. Blind instinct guided me while the sword pointed like a lodestone, pulling me deeper and deeper down into the maelstrom.

My feet touched something solid. I could stand upright, though water still flowed. I could feel its pressure on my legs and torso. The great underground ocean stopped its agitation. Overhead was blackness, before me was more water. I was standing waist-high in it.

Warily I sheathed my sword. I began to move forward, expecting at any moment to find the ground give way beneath my feet. At last I trod on fine gravel. There was a cool, steady breeze on my cheek. Somewhere, in the distance, a fox barked.

I was no longer in Mu-Ooria but did not know if I had found my destination. As I emerged completely from the water, I looked up at a familiar sky, at familiar stars. Near the horizon was the thin outline of a gibbous moon. Growing accustomed to the faint light, I made out the steep roofs and spires of a city I recognised. A quiet place, with few monumental buildings, no great architecture. Like one of the more ordinary medieval German towns I had seen on our dash towards Hameln. I hoped I had returned to the right time as well as place.

A wide moat surrounded the island on which the city was built. The island had not always been there. I had created the moat in one of my first attempts to defend the city, which no longer existed in exactly the same position as when I had first arrived there. I had used all the forms of sorcery I knew to save her from conquest, but every spell had been countered. And he had defeated me.

Elric's personality was now paramount. As I waded ashore, I hoped no-one had guessed my strategy, though it was clear Gaynor had been able to manifest himself concurrently on at least three different planes, no doubt with the help of his supernatural mistress. Miggea, Duchess of Law. Lady Miggea.

In Mu-Ooria she had been unable to break through, but here she dominated the world. Only here, beyond the moat, was there any safety from Miggea's cold, relentless rule, and that safety was already threatened.

I was soaked and shivering. My clothing made movement difficult. I pulled off the cap and squeezed water from my long hair. I moved warily up the bank, my senses alert, my hand ready to pull my sword free in an instant.

Only now did I realise how weary I was. I found it difficult to put one heavy foot in front of another. I still did not know if I had reached my desired destination. Everything looked right. But a fundamental of the illusionist's art is that everything *should* look right . . .

I had become too used to deception. For all I knew I was quite alone in a world bereft of men and gods. Or did a thousand eyes even now watch me from the darkness?

I thought I heard a footfall. I paused. I could see very little. Just the outlines of shrubs and trees, the silhouette of the city ahead of me. Automatically I brought up my sword. All the energy we had stolen together, all the souls we had eaten, had dissipated in that journey through the vortex. I felt weak again. I was dizzy.

Voices. I prepared myself for battle.

I think I fell backwards. I still had some hold on my senses. I was aware of faces looking down at me. I heard my name spoken.

"It can't be him. We were told nothing could lift the enchantment. Look at its bizarre garments. This is a demon, a shape-changer. We should kill it."

I tried to join in the argument, to assure them that despite my costume I was truly Elric of Melniboné. Then my senses completely failed me. I fell into dreaming, urgent shadows. I struggled to get back. But it was useless. I was too weak to resist or to flee.

I thought I heard mocking laughter. The laughter of my enemies.

Had I been captured? After all my efforts, was I doomed never to reach my city again?

Darkness encircled my brain. I heard the whispering of my captors. Consciousness began to fade.

I knew I had failed.

I tried to lift my sword. Then I was engulfed.

Dreams fled away from me. Important dreams. Dreams which could save me. A white hare on a white road.

I tried to follow. I woke up in a clean bed, looking around at a familiar room. In front of me stood a stocky red-headed fellow with a wide mouth and freckled skin, dressed simply but with a certain style, in green and brown.

"Moonglum?"

The red-headed man grinned.

"So, Prince Elric, you know who I am?"

"It would be strange if I did not." I was weeping with relief. I had managed to return. And Moonglum, who had accompanied me on more than one recent adventure, was waiting for me. Foolish as it was, I felt more than comradeship for the loyal swordsman.

"True, my lord." He grinned and swaggered forward, a little puzzled. "But I wonder what exotic creature you robbed for your clothes."

"They're conventional," said von Bek, "in my time. His time."

I knew exactly where I was. In the Tower of the Hand in Tanelorn. A Tanelorn whose ruin was almost certain. And if she perished, all that she stood for would perish, too. It was for her that I had risked so much and had accepted the dreamthief's help. Not, she insisted, that Oona was a dreamthief. She was merely a dreamthief's daughter.

"And my body?" I asked, rising.

His face darkened and his eyes took on a certain expression, familiar to me when he believed sorcery to be involved. "Still in its place," he said. He grinned, but refused to meet my gaze. "Still sleeping. Still breathing." He paused. "Where, might I ask, my lord, did you acquire this new body? Is it something fashioned of sorcery?"

"Only of dreams," I said, and promised to answer him further when I knew more.

He led me from that simple bedroom to another. There in the gloom lay a sleeping man. I was not prepared for the sight of my own body lying stretched out before me, hands folded across my chest, which rose and fell with slow regularity. My eyes were open. Twin rubies staring into the void. I slept. I was not dead. But neither could I be awakened. I was, after all, dreaming this dream. I reached to close my eyes.

Gaynor had brought great power against me. I knew the enchantment. I had used it myself, to ill effect. It threatened all I loved.

Now he gathered his strength to finish us. And if he finished Tanelorn, then all the worlds of all the realms were in danger.

I looked up from my sleeping self. Through the window, the sun was beginning to rise. Its first golden light slipped above the horizon. I held up my hand in the faint rays and compared it to that of the sleeping man. Essentially we seemed to be the same creature. It had taken great sorcery and the work of a dreamthief to achieve this, but now both my body and my sword were restored to me.

There might yet be time to rescue Tanelorn.

12

The Word of Law

A few weeks earlier, Moonglum and I had come down out of the hills on the other side of Cesh, following any goat trail we could, having left the employ of the Cesh of Cesh in bad faith. In return for the destruction of a small supernatural army, we had been promised a treasure hoard. The army destroyed, the hoard was found to be two coins, one of them forged. I had left the Cesh on display at the city gates, as a warning to others not to waste our time or our good will. I had been weak before I left the place and in no condition to confront the war party sent to pursue us by the Cesh's blood relatives, duty-bound to kill us.

With imperfect maps we lost ourselves in the rocky terrain but lost our pursuers as well. We had certainly not expected to come upon Tanelorn so soon after finding our way down from the hills. We had expected to cross a desert before we found any form of civilisation. We knew that it was in the nature of this city to manifest herself occasionally in another place, so we did not challenge our luck. Without hesitation, we led our exhausted horses down towards the city walls. We were grateful for sight of the ancient, welcoming buildings, the gardens and tall trees, the red brick, black beams and thatch, the orchards and fountains, the twisting timbers of the gables. I, for one, had become weary of the fantastic and looked forward to the common human comforts I'd become used to.

Our habit, when our travels took us here, was for Moonglum and myself to rest until we were ready to wander on, seeking fresh employment, new masters. Ours were the lives of mercenary swordsmen and, if sometimes short of wages, we were rarely short of work. Tanelorn, we consoled ourselves, would give us credit. We had acquaintances in the city. We occasionally met enemies there. But there was no conflict. Tanelorn was the haven to which all weary people could come, to rest, to stand outside the wars of men and gods. Here, with the necessary drugs, I could enjoy a certain peace.

I had hoped to lodge with my old friend Rackhir of Phum, the Red Archer, but he was gone on an adventure of his own. And he had left something in his house he did not want disturbed.

An acquaintance of mine, Brut of Lashmar, who had been a professional soldier, was the first familiar face to greet us. He was tall with close-cropped hair and scarred, handsome features. He wore dark linen and wool, seeming more monkish than soldierly, as a sign of his retirement. He seemed troubled. He was not an eloquent man, and it was difficult for him to find appropriate words to describe his feelings. He took us to his rambling house, gave us rooms there, an entire wing, and made us welcome. As we ate, he told us that there seemed to be sorcerous currents in the air. "Wizardry buzzing everywhere. Strange, powerful magic, my friends. Perilous magic."

I asked him to be specific, but he could not. I told him that I always knew when Chaos was present. I assured him there was no smell of Chaos here, unless about my own person. He was not happy, he said, that the city had moved. Usually moving was something she did to save herself only when in the worst danger.

I told him that he had become timid in his retirement. Tanelorn was safe. We had already fought for and won her security. Perhaps we should have to do so again some day, for Tanelorn, like all fragile ideas, had to be perpetually defended. Still, it was highly unlikely that Chaos would attack her again.

In good faith I was not as certain as I sounded. I told Brut that no being in all creation would be foolish enough to risk the destruction of the Balance itself. But in my heart I knew there were always such beings. We had already defended the city against them once. But it would be madness to assume Chaos would attack again, so soon after we had driven her back. I refused to become anxious. I intended to make the most of my stay, I said, and restore myself as best I could.

Most of our talk was reminiscence. It was the nature of the place. We discussed old fights, old threats, legendary battles of the past and speculated upon the nature of our sanctuary.

We were in Tanelorn less than a week, however, before the city came under direct threat. And, of course, I had not sniffed Chaos. I had never anticipated that Law would be taking her turn as aggressor. My world had little stability. Did it go back to that one moment in my past, that moment when I killed the only woman I truly loved? Had I set these events in motion, all that long time ago?

Meanwhile, again Tanelorn was threatened. And by Law gone mad. That these besieging powers must be particularly corrupt and manipulated by a creature whose ambitions were unusually determined was no comfort. Such mindlessness was always the most destructive. It had nothing to lose but its own threatened oblivion.

I knew we were being challenged by unusual wizardry one afternoon when the whole surrounding landscape melted even as we watched from the battlements and old walls. The land turned to glaring ash flats studded with wind-carved limestone crags—a world of crystalline whiteness. The inhabitants of Tanelorn were astonished and alarmed. This was the work of the gods. Or demons. Even I was not capable of such sorcery.

What fresh interest did the Lords of the Higher Worlds have in Tanelorn? Everything but Tanelorn was now the colour of wind-scarred bone. Her gentle trees and pretty houses were made vulgar by all that starkness.

The moon must look like this, I said. Everything scoured away. Was that where we were now? Tanelorn's wise men thought we had merely been shifted to an alternative world from our own, which had already been conquered.

I was capable of one last Summoning. I begged the earth elementals to dig a defensive moat around the city walls. It was the best I could do and it exhausted me.

We could not imagine the madness of a creature capable of reducing a world to such barren horror.

There were scholars of every kind in Tanelorn. I sought their best wisdom. Who had moved us to this world?

"My Lady Miggea of Law," I was told. "Almost certainly. She has already reduced several more realms to similar nothingness." She had immense supernatural resources and commanded more. I knew my gods and goddesses. I knew she had her own cycle of myth and legend which empowered her on Earth, but she had to have mortal agents or she could not break through into these spheres.

At least one mortal was serving her here. My Lord Arioch of Chaos was equally helpless without mortal compliance. My patron, impulsive as he could be, had learned never to attempt the conquest of Tanelorn.

Our first attackers were mostly half-armoured foot soldiers, oddly identical. They marched out of nowhere and did not stop marching until they reached our moat and then did not stop marching, over the backs of drowning comrades, until they were at our walls. Thousands and thousands were thrown against us daily and were so incapable of individual decision that we killed them effortlessly with few losses to our side.

The soldiers attacked again. We defended Tanelorn. We debated plans for her salvation. But we hardly knew what we were defending against, who our enemy really was. None knew how far the ash desert extended. A manifestation of Lady Miggea had been seen by some who recognised it, confirming that she was indeed in this realm now and watching from afar. At least this is what I was told. Some of our newer inhabitants had fled realms where she already ruled, had come here because of the terror they had left behind. But we still did not know the name of the mortal who served the Lady Miggea. And we wondered why the city did not shift herself away from danger, as we thought she could.

The marching minions of Law were easy enough to defeat. They had no true will and seemed almost drugged. They were mechanically predictable. They used identical tactics every time they tried to take the city. It was nothing to slaughter them in hundreds as they swam over or attempted to bridge the moat. I began to believe that their only function was to distract us while larger plans were hatched.

Warfare at its most boring.

Then Lady Miggea herself came to look at Tanelorn.

At first even I didn't understand the significance of the visit.

One morning I took my usual walk around the wall and to my astonishment saw that the surrounding horizon was filled with the pennants and lances of a vast mounted army. Everywhere their outlines signified our annihilation. These were not Law's cannon fodder, but her finest knights, drawn from all over the multiverse.

I threw up my hand to defend my eyes and saw, as if emerging from a shimmering mirage, a massive she-wolf, the size of a large mare, all caparisoned with pretty silks and beaded leather, with painted leather saddle, with brass and silver and glinting diamonds in her harness. Her deep-set eyes were mysterious as she came racing towards the city at the head of a pack of human knights. Her white, fanged muzzle twitched a little, as if she scented prey. Perhaps the wolf had been caught in Melniboné, I thought, for like me she was a pure albino. Her red eyes glared from bone-white fur, streaming behind her as she ran.

Even more bizarre was her rider. An armoured man whose glittering silver helm completely hid his face. Whose lance shimmered the colour of pewter. Whose metal was festooned with fluttering silks, with cloaks and scarves of a thousand colours.

I saw him turn, stand in his stirrups, and raise something to his helm. I heard the sound of his horn.

They came on and on. Thousands of white horses and their silver-armoured riders. Surely they meant to trample Tanelorn beneath their hoofs.

Then I saw what the wolf pursued.

A hare, as white as winter, raced over the pale ash ahead of that whole thundering army. Racing for our gates. A thousand spears poised to pierce her.

Too late.

The hare reached the moat and plunged into the water. She swam to the city gates and sped through a narrow gap, disappearing at once into the streets.

Only when the little animal found the safety of the city did the hunt quickly disperse, fanning to both sides around Tanelorn's wide moat. They had lost their prey. A distant horn called them away.

But they had impressed us with their armour. Their shining armour. Their faceless, enigmatic helms. And their numbers.

I knew their kind. The Knights of Law served a holy cause. Summoned to the standard of their mistress, the Lady Miggea, I knew they would fight to the death for her. They did not and could not question her. Their nature was to serve the office, no matter how warped it had become. They clung to a single idea, just as she did, unable to imagine more than one thing, one future, which they must create. They disguised their natural rapacity as their quest for Order.

But it had been the hare they intended to destroy that morning, not us. Their horses' hoofs churned the ashy desert as from her huge pale throat, the white she-wolf voiced her angry frustration at losing her quarry. A chilling growl.

Again the horn sounded.

The mounted knights began to reorder themselves, turning and moving back towards the horizon.

Moonglum stepped up beside me. He had been commanding a group of fighters farther along the wall.

"What's this?" He sniffed and rubbed at his sleeve, as if to remove a stain. "Were they simply out for a gallop? Did you see the quarry they followed, my lord? The little hare?"

I had seen her and I wondered why she was so important to a Duchess of Law. What had held them back from pursuing her into the city? Some understanding that by entering eternal Tanelorn they threatened the fundamental order of all our realms?

Madness is what I witnessed. I had seen it more than once when Law became corrupted and decadent. For that reason alone my people preferred the uncertainties and wildness of Chaos. Law gone rotten was a far more perilous prospect. Chaos did not pretend to logic, save the logic of temperament, of feeling.

The she-wolf had turned and was loping back towards us, bearing her arrogant rider, who now, apparently relaxed, held his lance easily in its stirrup.

I heard a noise from within the helm. I heard a voice. I heard my own name.

"Prince Elric, called Traitor. Is that you?"

"You have me at a disadvantage, sir."

"Oh, you'll soon be familiar enough with one or another of my names, sir."

"Why," I asked, "do you attack our Tanelorn? What do you want from it?"

"What, my lord, do you defend? Do you know? Have you never questioned your actions? You defend nothing. You defend an innocent idea. Not a reality."

"I have seen many an idea made reality," I replied. "I'll defend Tanelorn or sack her, should I feel the urge. I have nothing better to do, sir. And I would like a chance to kill you."

He laughed within his helm. An easy laugh. A familiar laugh. He ignored my taunt. "Prince Elric, I have a bargain to make with you. All in Tanelorn will be saved if you simply give me your sword. Upon my word, I will then leave you in peace. All of you. There's enough physic in the city to keep you alive and well. It's a fair bargain, Prince Elric. You save all your comrades and lose nothing but a useless blade."

"I have more care for my sword than for most of my comrades, sir. So the offer has no attraction for me. You are welcome to the city. I shall enjoy killing a vast number of you before you take it. If you know me well, sir, you know that I am only replenished by the work of slaughter. Sir, if you'll forgive me for repeating myself, have you the courage to accept a challenge? I would enjoy the pleasure of killing you. And the overlarge beast you ride."

At this the beast turned her head and her red eyes met my own. There was a kind of threatening mockery in her expression.

"You will have considerable difficulty killing a Duchess of Law, Prince Elric," she said. She grinned, her pale tongue lolling amongst her sharp, yellow teeth.

I returned her stare. I said, "But a wolf might kill a wolf."

She made no answer, though it seemed she was off before her rider was ready. It amused me that she chose that particular form and pretended that the man on her back was her master. Another sign of her monstrous delusion. I had ventured into supernatural realms where logic of her sort ruled. Nothing was more hideous. Even a Melnibonéan could not take pleasure in the wretchedness which the likes of Miggea created. Her half-dreaming mind was scarcely aware of the consequences of her actions. She believed that she ordered and protected, that she sacrificed herself to the common good. Her knights, of course, would obey her without question. Duty and loyalty were all. Virtues unto themselves. They were as mad as she.

I began to wonder if, after all, the object of their assault was not the city? What if they only wanted my sword? What if they directed all this vast sorcery upon Tanelorn merely in order to strike a bargain with me? A bargain I had refused. And would continue to refuse.

They would never compromise me. I would hold firm against them. And ultimately I would overcome them.

For the next few days the whole besieging army withdrew to below the horizon. Life in Tanelorn returned to something approaching normal. Not a single citizen attempted to leave as there was nowhere to go. The armies of Law had retreated, but the surrounding landscape had not returned to its natural state. For as far as the eye could see were bleak ash flats relieved by grotesque columns of clinkered limestone. A landscape of petrified death. I grew increasingly miserable with just that glinting desert for a view. I began to consider taking a horse and riding out to explore this world.

At night I began to dream again of different worlds. Worlds hardly distinguishable from my own. Worlds hideously or beautifully or subtly different. I dreamed of Bek, though I did not recognise it. I dreamed of uniformed men who stole my sword and tortured me. I dreamed of battles won and lost loves, of loves won and battles lost. I dreamed of terrifying landscapes and breathtaking natural visions. I dreamed of impossible futures and possible pasts. I dreamed of Cymoril, my murdered betrothed, pleading with me as her soul-stuff poured into mine. I woke sobbing.

Moonglum, in the next room, took to wrapping his bedclothes around his ears.

I was dreaming, of course, of my past as well as my near future. I dreamed of the world I would find. The world of my nightmares made reality.

This strategy of Law's was probably merely a pause while our enemies gathered strength to crush us. We discussed the nature of our predicament but had no precedents for it. I failed in my attempts to summon any further supernatural aid. Lady Miggea obviously controlled almost everything in this realm. We were dumbfounded. We hardly knew how to counter Law. Chaos had attempted to take Tanelorn more than once, but never, as far as we knew, the forces of Order.

For some reason not one of us believed we would all die. Perhaps Tanelorn had already demonstrated her invulnerability, when the White Hunt had divided around the city. Perhaps they could not enter. Some greater force prevented them. Or, perhaps like many gods and elementals, they needed to be invited by mortal agents into mortal realms? And, strictly, Tanelorn was not in this realm.

Our speculation was of little use to us. It was impossible to anticipate Law's next move. Impossible to understand their intentions.

We made some attempt to discover the white hare, but clearly she had waited for the hullabaloo to die down and gone back to her own territory.

I confided to Moonglum that I was growing bored. If no attempt was made on the city soon, I had it in mind to ride on. He did not offer to join me. I think he had some notion that I planned to betray Tanelorn.

Then one afternoon when the sun stained the ash flats scarlet, an armoured rider on a white wolf came down the hills towards Tanelorn and sat yelling before our causeway gates, demanding that I be summoned.

The swaggering silver knight had draped himself in even more gaudy silk, as if in defiance of Law's cold taste. He sat arrogantly in his saddle. The water of the moat reflected his armour. He seemed made of mercury.

Still nameless.

He recognised me the moment I appeared on the eastern keep and stepped up to the battlements. He gestured elaborately. Some unknown form of greeting.

"Good morning, Prince Elric."

"Good morning, Sir No-Name."

Easy laughter came out of that helm, as if I'd made a rich joke. This creature used every weapon in his arsenal, including subtle flattery and charm.

This morning he presented himself as being in a bluff, commonsensical kind of mood.

"I'll not waste your time, my lord," he said, "but as a Knight of the Balance and a servant of Law, I have come to take you up on a challenge. Hand-to-hand combat, as you said. And what's more I offer you a bargain." He had that half-belligerent tone you often hear amongst merchants and office-seekers, forever trying to sell you something you don't want or need.

"I understand those roles to be contradictory," I said mildly. While I exulted at the chance to fight him, I had, of course, become immediately suspicious of his motives. "A Knight of the Balance serves only the Balance."

"Aye," says he, almost impatiently, "that's the old thinking on it. But Chaos threatens and will engulf all unless we guard against her."

"Well," says I, "as one who serves Chaos, I can only speak for myself: I have no plans to engulf anything or anyone."

"Then you're a liar or a dupe, sir," says he.

"I've often wondered the same," I admitted easily. I knew he attempted to goad me, but there were few who could match the cruel wit of the average Melnibonéan aristocrat. "What would you sell me this morning, sir?"

"If you'll grant me a little hospitality, I'll tell you over breakfast. It's not my way to speak of private matters so publicly."

"We do not have private matters here in Tanelorn, sir. It's a communal place. We bother neither with secrets nor post-mortems. It is part of our way of life."

"I have no wish to disturb that way of life, sir." The wolf moved suddenly as if not entirely in agreement with her rider. "And you can easily ensure your tranquillity. I came, after all, to accept your challenge. A duel. One to one. To decide the issue. Or, if you no longer feel you wish to settle this as a matter of honour, I'll take token tribute. All I seek is that old sword you carry. Give me the runeblade and I'll take my men away. You have seen the weight of armour we can bring against you. You know you would be crushed in an hour. Wiped out of existence. A few forgotten whispers on an ancient wind. Give me the sword and you'll all be immortal. Tanelorn will remain something more than a memory."

"Metaphysical threats," I said. "I've heard them echoing out of steel helmets all my life, sir. They always have the same apocalyptic ring to them. And they're exceedingly hard to prove . . ."

"There's nothing vague about *my* threats, sir," says the Knight of the Balance, shifting impatiently and pushing almost fussily at his errant silks. "Nothing insubstantial. They are backed by a hundred thousand lances."

"Not one of which can enter this city, I'd guess." I began to turn away. "Without being invited. You have nothing to offer me, sir, except the boredom I seek to escape. Even your unsavoury, near-senile mistress Miggea cannot stride unasked into Tanelorn. Those mortal soldiers we fought were recruited here. Most are dead. Anything supernatural still must beg to be admitted. And you, sir, have already demonstrated your belligerence. I do not believe you have any intention of fighting me fairly."

"My tone was a mistake, I'll grant you, Prince Elric. But you will find me a more reasonable Champion of Law today. Willing to meet you man to man. Here's what I offer: I'll fight you fairly for the sword. Should you defeat me, all Law retreats from Tanelorn and you are returned to your natural condition, the city untouched. Should I defeat you, I take the sword. And leave you to defend yourselves as best you can."

"My sword and I are bonded," I said simply, "we are one. If you held the sword she could destroy you. And eventually she would return to me. Believe me, Sir Secret, I would not have it thus by choice. But it is so. And we are full of energy now. We have feasted well on your opposition. You have made us strong."

"Then let's test the strength. You have nothing to lose. Let me in and we'll fight for all to see—in the public square."

"Fighting is forbidden in Tanelorn." I said only what he already knew.

His voice was all mellow mockery. "What forces threaten your right to fight?" The knight's tone became openly challenging. "What power nursemaids an entire metropolis? Surely you are not going to let yourself be dictated to by meaningless custom? No free man should be forbidden the right to defend his life. To carry his weapons with pride and use them when he has to. That is how we of Law think now. We have rejected the great weight of ritual and look to a cleaner, fresher, more youthful future. Your rituals and customs are rules that have lost their meaning. They are no longer connected to the harsh realities of survival. Today the battle is to the strong. To the cunning. Those who do not resist Chaos are doomed to be destroyed by it."

"But if you destroy Chaos?" I asked. "What then?"

"Then Law can control everything. The unpredictable will be banished. The numinous will no longer exist. We shall produce an ordered world, with every- thing in its place, and everyone in their place. We will know at last what the future brings. It is man's destiny to finish the gods' work and complete the divine symphony in which we shall all play an instrument."

In my mind I was thinking I had rarely heard such pious lunacy expressed so perfectly. Perhaps my overfondness for reading, as a child, had made me too familiar with all the old arguments used to justify the mortal lust for power. The moment the moral authority of the supernatural was invoked, you knew you were in conflict with the monumentally self-deceiving, who should not be trusted at any level.

"Man's destiny? *Your* destiny, I think you mean!" I leaned on the battle- ments like a householder enjoying a chat across the fence with his neighbour. "You have a strong sense of what is righteous, eh? You know there is only one path to virtue? One clean, straight path to infinity? We of Chaos have a less tidy vision of existence."

"You mock me, sir. But I have the means of making my vision real. I suspect that you do not."

"Neither the means nor the desire to do so, sir. I drift as the world drifts. We have no other choice. I don't doubt your power, sir. Law has driven my own allies away from this realm. All that stands between us and your total conquest of us is my sword and this city. But somehow, I know, we can defeat you. It's in the nature of those of us who serve Chaos to trust a little more to luck than you do. Luck can often be no more than the mood of a mob, running in your favour. Whatever it is, we trust to it. And in trusting to luck, we trust ourselves."

"I'm not one to argue with Melnibonéan sophistry," said the Silver Knight, fussing with his fluttering scarves and flags. "The ambitions of your own patron,

Duke Arioch, are well known. He would gobble the worlds, if he could." A cool morning breeze stirred the surrounding desert. Our visitor seemed almost bound up by those long scarves. Hampered by them, yet unwilling to be rid of them. As if he could not bear the idea of wearing undecorated steel. As if he yearned for colour. As if he had been denied it for an eternity. As if he clutched at it for his life. Sometimes when the sun caught his armour and the fluttering silk, he seemed to be on fire.

I knew I could defeat him in a level fight. But if the Lady Miggea helped him, it would be more difficult, perhaps impossible. She still had enormous powers, many of which I could not even predict.

There was no doubt, when I looked back on that morning, that my enemies knew me in some ways better than I knew myself. For they were playing on my impatience, on my natural boredom. I had very little to lose. Tanelorn was tired. I did not believe she could be defeated by this beribboned knight, nor even by Miggea of Law. I was anxious for the siege to end, so that I could continue about my restless and, admittedly, pointless business. I was constantly reminded of my beloved cousin Cymoril, who had died by accident as Yyrkoon and I fought. All I had wanted was Cymoril. The rest I was willing to give up to my cousin. But because Cymoril loved me, Yyrkoon needed also to possess her. And as a result of my own pride, my folly and passion, and of Yyrkoon's overweening greed, she had died. Yyrkoon, too, had died, as he deserved. She had never deserved such awful violence. My instincts were to protect her. I had lost control of my sword.

I had sworn never to lose that control again. The sword's will seemed as powerful as my own sometimes. Even now, I could not be entirely sure whether the energy I felt coursing through me was mine or the blade's.

Grief, anger and desperate sadness threatened to take hold of me. Every habit of self-discipline was strained. My will battled that of the sword and won. Yet I became determined to fight this stranger.

Perhaps my mood was encouraged by a clever enemy. But it seemed that I was offering to fight him on my terms.

"The she-wolf must leave," I said. "The realm—"

"She cannot leave the realm."

"She can have no hand in this. She must give me the word, the holy word of Law, that the wolf will not fight me."

"Agreed," he said. "The wolf shall have no part in our fight."

I looked at the wolf. She lowered her eyes in reluctant compromise.

"What guarantee is there that you and she will keep your word?"

"The firm word of Law cannot be broken," he said. "Our entire philosophy is based on that idea. I'll not change the terms of the bargain. If you defeat me, we all leave this realm. If I defeat you, I get the sword."

"You're confident you can defeat me."

"Stormbringer will be mine before sunset. Will you fight me here? Where I stand now?" He pointed back behind him. "Or there, on the other side?"

At this I began to laugh. The old blood-madness was gripping me again. Moonglum recognised it. He came running up the steps. "My lord—this has to be a trick. It stinks of a trap. Law grows untrustworthy. Everything decays. You are too wise to let them deceive you . . ."

I was grave when I put my hand on his shoulder. "Law is rigid and aggressive. Orthodoxy in its final stages of degeneration. She clings to her old ways, even as she rejects what is no longer useful to her. She'll keep her word, I'm sure."

"My lord, there is no point to this duel!"

"It might save your life, my friend. And yours is the only life I care for."

"It could bring me torment, and the same to all others in Tanelorn."

I shook my head. "If they break their word, they can no longer be representatives of Law."

"What kind of Law do they represent, even now? A Law willing to sacrifice justice for ambition." Moonglum dragged at my arm as I began to descend the steps back to the ground. "And that's what makes me doubt everything they promise. Be wary of them, my lord." He gave up trying to persuade me and fell back. "I'll be watching for any signs of their treachery and I'll do what I can to ensure the duel's fair. But I say again—it's folly, my friend. Your mad, old blood has seized your brain again."

I was amused by this. "That mad blood has found us many ways out of trouble, friend Moonglum. Sometimes I trust it better than any logic." But I could not raise his spirits.

A dozen others, including Brut of Lashmar, begged me to be cautious. But something in me was determined to break this stalemate, to follow my blind instincts and embrace a story that was not inevitable, that took a fresh direction. I wanted to prove that it was not the working-out of some prefigured destiny. As I'd told Moonglum, this was by no means the first time I had let the old blood blaze through my veins, sing its song in me and fill my being with wild joy. If I lived, I swore it would not be the last time I felt that thrill.

I was entirely alive again. I was taking risks. My life and soul were the stakes.

I marched down the steps, shouted for the gates to be raised. Demanded that the she-wolf be gone. That the faceless knight meet me alone.

When I had put Tanelorn's walls at my back and stepped across the causeway out into that barren world, the she-wolf had vanished. I looked into a mirror. I saw my own blazing features, my glaring ruby eyes, my fine, white hair whipping about my shoulders as the wind continued to blow across the ash desert.

The dismounted knight's helm and breastplate reflected everything they faced. Seemingly an advantage in battle. It would feel as if you were fighting yourself!

The knight stood with a silvery steel broadsword in his gauntleted hands. I was disturbed by the sight of it. He had not carried it earlier. This sword was a mirror of Stormbringer in everything but colour. A negative image. I could easily recognise the symbols of sorcery, and that silver sword had no magical properties to speak of. I would have smelled them. Instead it exuded a deadness, a negativity.

No sorcery. Or sorcery so subtle even I couldn't detect it? A slow chill passed through me, leaving me wary and briefly weaker. I felt a frisson of déjà vu.

Something chuckled from within the silver helm. A different note, almost a whisper.

"We act out our stories many times, Prince Elric. And occasionally we are granted the means to change them. You will understand, I hope, that in some of those stories, in some of those incarnations, you lose. In some, you die. In others, you suffer more than death."

Again that mysterious chill.

"I think this will be one of those other stories, my lord."

Then the gleaming blade was rushing down on me.

I barely blocked it in time. Stormbringer growled as she clashed with that white steel. She was expressing hatred. Or was it fear? Not a sound I had heard from her before.

I felt energy flowing out of me. With every countered blow, I found it harder to lift my sword. I peered into the silver helm as we fought but could see no hint of the features within.

I was horrified. I relied on my sword's strength to sustain my own. And now instead Stormbringer was sapping my strength. What aided this mysterious warrior? Why had I not smelled sorcery? I was clearly the victim of some super-natural force.

The knight was not an expert swordsman, as I had expected. He was rather clumsy. Yet every blow of mine was met. Only rarely did the knight feint back at me. He seemed to be playing an entirely defensive role, This, too, made me suspicious. If I had not agreed to the fight, I would have ended it there and then and returned to the city.

I was used to the wild song of my sword as I fought, but now Stormbringer merely vibrated with her blows. And those vibrations seemed feebler for every passing moment.

Moonglum had been right. I was the victim of a trap. I had no choice but to fight on.

Two more blows of mine were met by two of the knight's and then I was staggering, my knees buckling. I could barely lift my sword, which increasingly became a dead weight in my hands. I was baffled. The urgency of my movements tired me further. I had been completely outmanoeuvred.

Again a low unfamiliar chuckle came from the depths of that helm.

I rallied everything I had. I tried to call on Arioch for help, but I was over-whelmed with tiredness. An unnatural tiredness. I used all my sorcerer's disci-plines to bring my mind back into control over my body, but it was no use. The heavy pall of enchantment seeped through my being.

Within a few minutes of that fight beginning I lost my footing, and fell backwards onto the harsh, white ground. I saw the armoured figure stoop and take Stormbringer and I was horrified. I had no means of resistance. I tried to struggle up and failed. Few could handle that sword without evil consequences, yet my opponent was casually able to pick her up. My certainties were collaps-ing around me. I feared I was going mad.

As my vision began to blur, I grew aware of the armoured figure looking down on me, still laughing.

"Well, Prince Elric. Our bargain and our duel are settled and you are free to return to Tanelorn. We'll not harm the city, have no fear. I have what we came for."

The knight then lifted the helm for the first time. A woman looked down at me. A woman with pale, radiant features, with blonde hair and glaring black eyes. A woman whose teeth were pointed, whose lips were on fire.

I knew immediately how I had been deceived.

"Lady Miggea, I presume." I could barely whisper. "You gave your word. The word of Law."

"You didn't listen carefully enough. It was the wolf who swore not to fight. Your blood is wise," she said softly, "but it informs your heart, not your mind. These are urgent times. There is much at stake. Sometimes the old rules no longer sustain the reality."

"You'll not keep your word? You said you'd leave the city in peace!"

"Of course I shall. I'll let it die of natural causes."

"What do you mean?" My words were a dry gasp. I was beginning to realise the folly of my decision. Moonglum was right. I had brought untold disaster both to myself and my world. All because I had followed wild "instinct" rather than logic. There are times when faith provides only further catastrophe.

"There's no more water in this realm. Only what you see. Nothing to sustain your gardens. Nothing for you to drink." She smiled to herself as she held up Stormbringer by the blade, clutching it in a fist which seemed to grow larger as she spoke. "Nothing to help you. No supernatural aid. You cannot return to your own realm. It took my power to bring you here and keep you here. Few are as powerful as Miggea of Law. No human aid will save you. In time you'll wither away and that will be the end of you and your stories. But I have been merciful. You'll know none of this, Prince Elric, for you will be asleep."

As my sight faded and the last of my strength went out of me, I made one last attempt to rise. "Sleep?"

Her horrid crazed face came close to mine. She pursed her lips and blew into my eyes.

And then I descended into dreaming darkness.

13

The Dreamthief's Daughter

I became dimly aware of my friends from the city carrying me back. I was entirely incapable of movement, drifting in and out of an enchanted sleep, only vaguely conscious of the surrounding world, sometimes completely oblivious to it. I knew my friends, especially Moonglum, were concerned. I tried to rouse myself, to speak, but every effort took me deeper into my dreamworld.

I did not want to go deeper. I feared something there. Something which Miggea had prepared for me.

The only course open to me was the interior. Incapable of movement or communication, yet aware of my own condition, I finally let myself slip slowly down, afraid that I might never emerge again from the pit of my own complex psyche. Drowning in my own dark dreams.

The last of my will deserted me. I began to fall. Away from Tanelorn. Away from all the fresh dangers of the future. Dangers I would not be able to face without my sword. And how would the sword be used? To destroy the Balance itself? My mind was in a turmoil. Falling at last into oblivion was a relief.

I was unconscious for seconds, and then I began to dream. In my dream I saw a man clothed in rags, standing with his face turned from his own house, a book in his hand and a great bundle on his back. I wanted to ask him his name, but his eyes were filled with tears and he could not see me. For a moment I thought when he turned towards me his face would be mine, but it was a plain, round human head. He hesitated and then began to return to his house where his wife and children waited for him, glad he had not left them. They had not seen how distressed he was. For one of my kind to feel sympathy for such ordinary souls was almost disgusting, yet I longed to help these people in their misery.

Time passed. At last I saw the man leave his house with his burden and walk away until he was out of sight. I began to follow him, but when I reached the crest of the hill he had gone. I saw a valley and in that valley a number of different battles were being fought. Men burned castles, villages and towns. They slaughtered women and children. They killed everything that lived, and then they turned on one another and began to kill again. The only road took me through this valley. Reconciled, I began my descent.

I had not gone very far, however, before a small, hunched figure jumped from a rock onto the path in front of me and, grinning, offered me an elaborate bow. He spoke to me, but I could not hear him. He became frustrated, signing and gesturing, but still I could not understand him. Eventually he took me by the hand and led me around a corner of the rock. There ahead was what seemed like an ocean, rising vertically to form a wall in front of me. Through the ocean ran a gleaming road of dappled light, like one ray of sunshine falling on water.

So strange was the perspective that I felt almost ill. Yet the crooked little man continued to lead me until we had stepped onto that dappled road and were walking up its steep surface. I had the strong smell of ozone in my nostrils. The road then straightened and became a silver moonbeam in a complex lattice of moonbeams, like the roadways through the realms. My guide was gone.

I was alarmed. At the same time I realised I had a feeling of physical well-being. I had never known it before. I had only ever experienced pain or relief from pain, but never a body that did not know pain at all. All my life I had had to deal with some weakness, either physical or moral. Now I began to feel fresh, elated, even relaxed. Yet I knew that in reality I had no physical body at all, that it was only my dreaming soul which wandered these worlds of enchantment.

The conflicting emotions within me did nothing to help my condition. I did not know if this was part of Miggea's trap. I did not know which path to choose. I looked up into all that vast complexity and I saw a million roads, each one like a ray of light, on which creatures of every kind walked. I knew that there was no such thing as a multiversal vacuum, that every apparently empty space was populated. I saw the roadways as branches of a great silver tree, whose roots somehow went deep down into my own brain. I knew that this was the fundamental structure of the multiverse. I decided, in spite of recent experience, to trust my instincts and to follow a small branch running off a more substantial limb.

I set foot on the pale road and it gave slightly to my step. It made walking a pleasure. In no time I had passed half a dozen branches, heading for my chosen path. But as I did so, I realised that the weave of the branches was more complicated than I had originally seen. I found myself in a tangle of minor brambles, which blocked my way and which I could not easily push aside. My body felt so light, so insubstantial that there was no danger of my breaking the branches. It seemed to me that tiny figures moved along other branches, just as I moved along mine.

Eventually I found ways of passing through the branches so that I disturbed very little. I had the impression that somewhere up there might be another creature, far bigger than myself, perhaps a version of myself, who was carefully trying to avoid knocking me from my branch.

At one point I paused. I was no longer dressed in my ordinary clothes but wore full Melnibonéan war armour. Not the elaborate baroque of ceremonial plate, but the efficient, blade-turning protection a man needed in battle. I had no sense of weight to the armour, any more than there was to my body. I half assumed I had died and become some kind of wandering ghost. If I remained here for a long time, I would gradually grow amorphous and merge with the atmosphere, breathed in like dust by the living.

Having lost my original direction, I found myself wandering down increasingly narrow and twisting branches. I thought I must soon step upon the last twig at the farthest edge of the multiversal tree. I was beginning to despair when I saw that the track led through a tunnel formed of willow boughs. On the other side of that tunnel was a weirdly shaped cottage, thatched with the straw of centuries, its bricks apparently borrowed from every source in existence, its windows at peculiar angles and of odd sizes, its door narrow and tall, its chimneys fantastically curled. From the roof of the small porch hung several baskets of blooming flowers and a birdcage. Under the birdcage sat a black-and-white sheepdog, her tongue lolling as if she had just come in from a day's work.

The pleasant pastoral scene made me oddly wary. I had become used to traps and delusions. My enemies seemed to enjoy making promises they had no intention of keeping, as if they had just discovered the power of the lie. If this image were a lie, it was a clever one. Everything looked perfect, including the plume of smoke coming from the chimney, the smell of baking, the domestic clatter from within.

I glanced back. Behind me, dwarfing everything, was the multiverse. Its great lattice filled all the myriad dimensions, its branches stretched into infinity. And its light shone down on this little cottage which sat exactly on the edge of the abyss, a great dark wood behind it. I tried to move forward and to my astonishment had some difficulty. The armour was heavy. My body, though feeling fit, was weary. In an instant I had become full corporeal!

I opened the gate of the cottage and dragged myself up the slate path to knock on the door. I remembered to remove my helmet. It was an awkward thing to carry under one's arm, all angles and filigree.

"Come in, Prince Elric," called a cheerful young voice. "You have trustworthy instincts, it seems."

"Sometimes, madam." I passed through the narrow doorway and found myself in a low-ceilinged room with black beams and white plaster. On the floor was luxurious carpet and on the walls were tapestries, living masterpieces showing every manner of human experience. I was astonished at the opulence, which seemed in contrast to the domestic atmosphere.

A young woman came from the next room, evidently the kitchen, wiping flour from her hands and arms. The powder fell in a silvery shower to the rich maroon carpet. She sniffed and then sneezed, apologising. "I have waited for you for what seems an eternity, my lord."

I could not speak. I looked at one of my own kind. She had extraordinary, aquiline beauty, with slanting eyes and delicate, small, slightly pointed ears. Her eyes were red as fresh strawberries in a skin the colour of bleached ivory. Her long, bone-white hair fell in soft folds down over her shoulders. She wore a simple shirt and breeches, over which she had thrown a rough linen apron. And she was laughing at me.

"My friend Jermays put you on the right road, I see."

"Who was that little man?"

"You'll meet him again in time, perhaps."

"Perhaps."

"We all do. Often when our stories start to alter. Sometimes one's destiny changes radically. A new tale is born. A new myth to weave in with the old. A new dream."

"I am dreaming this. I am dreaming you. Therefore I am dreaming this conversation. Does this mean that I am mad? Has the enchantment which holds me in sleep also attacked my brain?"

"Oh, we all dream one another, Prince Elric, in some ways. It is our dreams and our demands upon them which have made us so various and at odds with so much and so many."

The young woman even had gestures which I recognised.

"Would you do me the honour, madam, of telling me your name."

"I'm called White Hare Sister by the dreamthieves and shape-changers amongst whom I was raised. But my mother calls me Oona, after the custom of her folk."

"Her name is Oone?"

"Oone the Dreamthief. And I am Oona, the dreamthief's daughter. And in time, further down the line, there will no doubt be an Oonagh."

"Oone's daughter?" I hesitated. "And mine?"

She was laughing openly now as she came towards me. "I think it likely, don't you?"

"I did not know there was—issue."

"Oh, quite spectacular 'issue,' I assure you, Father."

The word struck at me with the force of a tidal wave. Father! An emotional blow worse than any sword stroke. I wanted to deny it, to say anything which would prove me to be dreaming. To make this fact disappear. But my eyes could not deceive me. Everything about her showed that she was my daughter and Oone's. I had loved Oone briefly. We had sought the Fortress of the Pearl together. But as I remembered this, another thought occurred to me. More deception!

"Not enough time has passed," I said. "You are too old to be my daughter."

"In your plane, perhaps, my lord, but not on this one. Time is not a road. It's an ocean. I believe you and my mother celebrated your friendship here in this realm."

I liked her irony.

"Your mother—?" I began.

"Her interests are no longer in these worlds, although she occasionally visits the End of Time, I understand."

"She gave birth to you here?"

"I was one of twins, she said."

"Twins?"

"So she told me."

"Your sibling died?"

"My twin didn't die when we were born. But something happened which Mother could not explain, and I was soon separated from my sibling. Gone. Gone. My mother's words. I know nothing else."

"You seem very casual about your twin's fate."

"Reconciled, my lord. I thought, until recently, you had found that twin to raise as your own, but, of course, I now know that is not the case." She turned urgently, disappearing back into the kitchen. The smell of greenberry pie came to me in a single, delicious wave. I had forgotten the simple pleasures of human life.

Because this was a dream I saw nothing strange about being invited to sit down at a kitchen table and enjoy a meal of good, new bread, fresh-churned butter, some chandra and a bottle of goldfish sauce, with the prospect of the pie, and perhaps a puff of glas to complete my pleasure.

Not once, for all the trickeries of Law, did I further suspect this young woman. Nor the sense of sanctuary which came from her cottage. It was impossible. I knew she was of my blood. If she had been a lie, a shape-changing creature of Chaos, I should have guessed it immediately.

Yet a voice in the back of my mind told me I had not smelled sorcery when Law had so successfully defeated me and essentially committed me to my present fate. Had I lost my powers? Was I only now beginning to realise it? Was this another illusion to steal what was left of my soul?

My temperament was such that I could not go cautiously. Nothing was to be gained from caution. I had few choices in this extraordinary cottage at the centre of the silvery matrix of moonbeams.

"So you have no idea what became of your sister?"

"My sister?" She smiled. "Oh, no, my dear father. It was not my sister. It was my brother we lost."

"Brother?" Something in me shuddered. Something else exulted. "My son?"

"Maybe it's as well you did not know, my lord. For if he is dead, as I suspect, then you would be grieving now"

I reflected that I had only known I had a son for a few seconds. I was in shock. It would be a moment or two before I came to the grieving stage!

I looked wonderingly at my daughter. My feelings were both direct and complex. On an impulse which would have shocked and disgusted a Melnibonéan, I stepped forward and embraced her. She returned my embrace awkwardly, as if she, too, was not used to such customs. She seemed pleased.

"So you are a dreamthief," I said.

She shook her head fiercely. I saw a dozen honest emotions flit across her features. "No. I am a dreamthief's child. I have the experience and some of the skills, but not the vocation. In fact, to tell you the truth, Father, I'm somewhat divided. Part of my character vaguely disagrees with the morality of Mother's profession."

"Well, your mother was of great help to me when we sought the Fortress of the Pearl together." I myself was over-familiar with matters of moral and emotional division.

"It is one of the few adventures she retold. She was unusually fond of you, given the number of lovers she has known down the centuries and over the whole of the time field. I suspect you are the only one by whom she had children."

"Special affection or special resentment?"

"She bore you no ill will, sir. Far from it. She spoke of you with pleasure. She spoke of you as a great warrior. As a brave and courteous knight of the limits. She told me you would have made the most gorgeous dreamthief of them all. That was her own special dream, I think. What do you think dreamthieves dream of most, Father?"

"Perhaps of dreamless sleep," I said. I was still surprised by the discovery of my child. A child whose beauty was stunning and whose character seemed, as far as I could tell, complex and full of intelligence. A child who had brought me here to her little hearth on the very edge of time. Her birthplace, she told me as we ate.

The forest, which looked threatening to me, she assured me was full of amiable wonders. She had enjoyed a perfect childhood, she said. The forest and the cottage were protected in some way, much as Tanelorn was protected, from the rapacity of either Law or Chaos. The place was far from lonely. Many of her mother's friends travelled between the worlds, as she did, and they loved nothing better than bringing back stories to tell in the evening around the fire.

When she was fifteen, she had gone with her mother to those worlds where Oone intended to retire, but she had not liked them. She decided to find her own vocation. Meanwhile she, too, would wander the myriad realms of the multiverse for a time. To give her travels some purpose, she tried to discover if her brother were still alive, but the only albino she heard of was her father, the feared and hated Elric of Melniboné. She had felt no great desire to meet him.

Then, later, she had discovered others. A bloodline, of sorts, which she was still trying to trace. She hoped this might provide a better means of finding her brother. She believed he had settled in one particular realm, similar to the kind her mother favoured. Not only had he settled there, he had absorbed himself in his host culture, married and produced offspring.

I was feeling older by the moment. While I could grasp the notion of time having passed in different ways in different realms, it was still hard for me, a relatively young man, to see myself as the patriarch of generations. The responsibility alone made me uncomfortable. I felt a certain wariness overcome me, and I wondered if this were not part of Law's complicated deception, part of some greater cosmic plot in which I played a minor role. I again began to feel like a pawn in a game. A game the gods played merely to while away their boredom.

This thought fired me to quiet anger. If that were the case, I would do everything I could to defeat their plans.

"I called you here, Father, not from curiosity, but out of urgency. I know how you were duped. And why." She seemed to sense my mood. "Miggea and her minions threaten Tanelorn and several other realms, including the one inhabited by your descendants."

"A race resembling Melniboné's?"

"Resembling their last emperor, at any rate. Fighting the same forces we both fight, sir. They are our natural allies. And there is one who can help us defeat Law."

"Madam," I said with every courtesy, "you are aware perhaps that beyond this realm I have no true physical form. I am a shade. A ghost. Outside this environment I am a spirit. I am, madam, as good as dead. I could not hold a cup if it were not for whatever temporary physicality you or this place has bestowed on me. My body lies in a deep, unwakeable slumber in the doomed city of Tanelorn, while Miggea, Duchess of Law, now holds the Black Sword and can do with it whatever she likes. I am defeated, madam. I have failed in every venture. I am a dream within a dream. All this can be nothing but dream. A useless, pointless dream."

"Well," she said, picking up the dishes, "one person's dream is another's reality."

"Platitudes, madam."

"But truths, too," she said. A kind of confident stillness had come upon her as she undid her apron and hung it up. "Well, Father, are you pleased to see me?"

Her eyes, humorous and enquiring, looked frankly into mine.

I began to smile. "I believe I must be," I said. "Though no royal Melnibonéan would admit it."

"Well," she said, "I am glad I am not a royal Melnibonéan."

"I'm the last of those," I said, "or so I understand."

"Aye," she said, "that seems to be the truth. Melniboné falls, but the blood continues. Ancient blood. Ancient memory."

"Forgive me if I seem brusque," I said, "but I understood you to say, Lady Oona, that you guided me here as a matter of some urgency." I could not bring myself to address her informally.

"With my skill I can help you, Father," she said. "I can help you get your sword back and possibly even be revenged on the one who stole it from you."

Again, I should have suspected a trick, but my daughter convinced me completely. I knew that this entire episode could be a development of the same enchantment under which Law had put me. But it seemed I had no other course of action to take. I had to trust her or remain frozen on my couch in Tanelorn, unable to retrieve my sword or claim vengeance on the one who had stolen it.

"You know the future?" I challenged.

She replied quietly, "I know more than one."

She explained how the multiverse is made up of millions of worlds, each only a shade different from our own. In each of those worlds certain people struggle eternally for justice. Sometimes for Law. Sometimes for Chaos. Sometimes simply for equilibrium. Most people do not know that other versions of themselves are struggling, too. Each story is a little different. And very occasionally a major change can be made to the story. Sometimes their strengths can be combined. Which was exactly what we hoped to achieve through my daughter's extraordinary strategy.

She believed it was possible for two or more avatars to occupy the same body, if the body was of like blood. I needed a physical body and a physical sword. She believed she had found both.

She told me of von Bek, of his blade and his own fight against corrupted authority. She said she believed our fates were intertwined at this particular configuration of the cosmic realms. He and I were both avatars of the same being. I could help him, and he could help me, by lending me his body and his sword.

I said that I had to think.

Dreamlessly, perhaps because I now lived a dream, I rested at Oona's cottage on time's borderlands in the so-called Mittelmarch. While I rested, my daughter taught me more of the dreamthief's secrets. How to travel the roads between the realms. The realms we thought supernatural but which were perfectly mundane to their inhabitants. She had her mother's library and was able to show me old tales, current scientific ideas, the theories of philosophers, all of which spoke of dreams as being glimpses of other times and places. Some of them understood what Oona understood—that the worlds of our dreams have physical reality and cannot be easily manipulated, that each one of us has a version of themselves in all these billions of alternative worlds and that somehow all our actions are interlinked to make a grander cosmic whole whose scale is inconceivable, a pattern of order which we either support or threaten, depending on our loyalties and ambitions.

One morning, looking at a book of watercolours done by an ancestor of Oona's, I asked my daughter if she really believed that somehow we might dream one another. Did we exist entirely as a result of our own wills? Did we bring ourselves and our worlds into reality because of some mighty desire, stronger than the physical universe? Or was it possible we had already created the universe? The multiverse, even. Was the great tree something which mortals had nurtured until it was no longer in their control?

If so, had we also created the gods, the Cosmic Balance, the elementals? I could not bring myself to believe that. It would suggest we had forged our own chains, as well as creating the means of our salvation! It would mean that the gods were just symbols of our own strengths, weaknesses and desires!

I offered this speculation to my daughter, but she dismissed it. She had heard it all too often. There was little point to it, she seemed to say. We are here. Whatever the causes or the reasons, we now exist and have to make the best of it. She reminded me of her purpose in bringing me here.

"Once you are free," she said, "you will be able to do everything you could do before. In Mu-Ooria you will not be blocked from your elemental allies. Von Bek has one of Stormbringer's manifestations. He is the only way you can recover your own blade. With von Bek's help, you might get your sword back and save Tanelorn. I will help you as best I can, but my powers are limited. I have my mother's skills, but not her temperament."

The next morning I stood beside her as she locked her door and gave last instructions to her dog and bird, who listened intelligently.

"Now." She turned to me as if we were going on a family outing to the country. "We'll take the moonbeam roads which will lead us to the heart of the multiverse. To the Grey Fees. And thence to Mu-Ooria, dear Father, and your continuing destiny."

The Grey Fees? I shall not attempt to describe that place which is, most believe, the origin of all things, the fundamental stuff of the multiverse, misty fields where you glimpse ribbons of basic matter creating cryptic arabesques, perpetually writhing and pulsing, forming and re-forming, becoming whole worlds, dissipating again, and, perhaps most bizarrely, inhabited by mad adventurers with loyalty neither to Law nor to Chaos, only to their own idiosyncratic mathematics. Amiable enough fellows, and magnificently intelligent, able to sail anywhere in the multiverse by means of "scale ships" but warped by their environment in mind and body. We avoided these Lords and Ladies of Sublime Disorder whenever possible. Even they were aware that some great disaster threatened us all. That Law had gone mad.

The Chaos Engineers guided us through the bewildering Grey Fees to the terrifying world of the Nazis. Thereafter, I was with von Bek most of the time, though he could rarely see me. I became his guardian angel; his life was very important to me. By following Oona's instructions I was able to help my doppelgänger von Bek in the camps and later in the caverns of Mu-Ooria, where I discovered that what my daughter had said was true. It was possible to blend my own substance with von Bek's.

My powers had some small potency even before I bonded with von Bek. But with von Bek to help, they were now completely restored. We were more than the sum of our parts. We were stronger when we came together although it was not easy to achieve the bonding or to make it last.

I tried more than once to merge with him but either he had resisted or the time had not been right. Twice I almost succeeded, but lost him again. Eventually, when he needed my help most and was prepared to accept what I could offer him, I stepped into his body, just as Oona had taught me, and immediately we became the single creature I have already described. I merged with him, blending his skills and character with my own. And now I had the benefit of von Bek's wisdom and swordsmanship. That was how I had been able to return to Tanelorn. That was the only possible way to thwart the enchantment put upon me.

There was precious little time. Although we had returned rapidly, Lady Miggea and her knights could have left this world and, with Stormbringer to help them, even now be conquering Mu-Ooria.

Brut gave us his best horses. Moonglum and I rode out of Tanelorn onto those unforgiving ash flats whose sentinels of limestone were a constant reminder of our mortality. On Oona's advice and my own impulse, determined to achieve the impossible, we were going hunting.

Hunting for a goddess.

14

Fresh Treacheries

A deep chill had settled on this world. Nothing was alive. When the breeze stirred the ash drifts or flaked the crags so it seemed to snow, a complete absence of vitality was evident in the landscape.

Miggea's was no ordinary desert. It was all that remained of a world destroyed by Law. Barren. No hawks soared in the pale blue sky. There were no signs of animal life. Not an insect. Not a reptile. No water. No lichen. No plants of any kind. Just tall spikes of crystallised ash and limestone, crumbling and turned into crazy shapes by the wind, like so many grotesque gravestones.

Law's cold hand had fallen on everything. Law achieved this desolation at her worst. This tidiness of death. Mankind inevitably achieves the same when it seeks to control too much.

Moonglum had insisted on accompanying me and I had not refused. Unusually, I felt the need for company. Moonglum's comradeship was something I valued. He recognised when I was at my most negative, my most self-pitying, and would say something sardonic to remind me of my stupidity. He was also a brilliant swordsman, who had fought sorcerers as well as soldiers, the steadiest man to have at one's side in any kind of fight.

As we rode, I tried to explain to my somewhat repulsed friend how I was now two people—two entirely different identities but of the same blood, locked together in one near-identical body. By this combination we had thwarted Lady Miggea's enchantment. By entering the world of dreams and finding an alternative version of myself.

All this made my friend very uncomfortable. "Two people warring inside you?" He shuddered. "To be joined physically, by the head, say, is one thing. But to be joined in the mind! Forever in conflict . . ."

"We are not in conflict," I explained. "We are one. Just as, say, a playwright will invent a character and that character will live within him, quite comfortably. So it is with von Bek and myself. Where his world is the most familiar, he will take the ascendancy, but here, within an environment I understand a little better, I am in command. We have shared memories also—the entire creature from birth to present. And believe me, my friend, there is less conflict between von Bek and myself than there is between me and myself!"

"That's easy enough to believe, my lord," said Moonglum, staring with half-seeing eyes out at the forest of stones.

We could ride only so far without water. We had large canteens, enough to last for several days, but no certainty that any of our enemies were still here. Indeed, Lady Miggea had a use for the sword, no doubt as part of her plans for further conquest. All we could do was follow the faint trails marked by her army, hoping they had left some clue behind that would lead us to discover where she had gone with my sword.

The sky was a stark eggshell-blue. We had no means of keeping our direction except by noting the shapes of the different rocks we passed, hoping to recognise them on our return.

Less than a day from the city we began to descend into a wide shallow valley which stretched for several miles on all sides. When we were halfway down and rounding a great bulk of tattered rock, we saw some distance ahead of us a grotesque building, clearly the work of intelligent beings, but reeking of mad cruelty.

Dry wind whispered through a palace built of bones. Many of those bones still had rotting flesh clinging to them. The bones of horses. The bones of men. From the evidence, the bones of all those Knights of Law who had so recently threatened us. Who had thundered so forcefully past us in pursuit of the little white hare. Their silver armour was scattered around the building, thousands of breastplates, helmets, greaves, gauntlets. Their lances and swords lay half-buried in the pale ash. Miggea had expected the ultimate sacrifice from her loyal followers, and she had received it.

But what had she built her fortress against?

Or was it a fortress? Did it now function as a prison?

As we drew nearer, the wind began to sough more miserably than ever through those half-picked bones, turning to a mournful howling that filled the world with despair. We slowed our horses and moved more cautiously, searching the low surrounding hills for the sight of wolves. There was none.

We moved closer to the towering palace of bones. Keeps and domes and battlements and buttresses were shaped from the recently living bodies of men and horses from which strips of flesh and fur and linen fluttered like banners in the erratic wind. And the terrible howling continued. All the grief in all the realms of the multiverse. All the frustration. All the despair. All the wounded ambition.

So dense were the bones packed to form the walls of the palace that we could not see inside. But we thought we saw a movement behind the palace. A solitary figure. Perhaps an illusion.

"The howling's coming from inside the bones, my lord." Moonglum cocked his head to one side. "From deep within that house of bones. Listen."

He was better able to locate the source of sounds than I, though my hearing was more acute. I had no reason to disbelieve him.

Whatever was howling was either trapped in the bone palace or was defending it. Was Miggea still here, still in the shape of a wolf? That would explain the howling and also the frustration. What could have thwarted her plans?

Again we glimpsed movement, this time from within the palace, as if something paced back and forth. We moved closer still until the vast construction loomed over us. And now we could smell it. Sweet, cloying, horrible, It stank of rotting flesh.

We hesitated before the great central entrance. Neither of us had any desire to confront what was within.

Then, as we made up our minds to dismount and enter, another human figure came around one of the bone buttresses. Coloured rags still clung to him. He carried a sword in either hand. Leaf-bladed broadswords. One was a shade of diseased ivory with black runes running its length. The other was Stormbringer, all pulsing black iron and scarlet runes.

The man who bore them was Prince Gaynor of Mirenburg. He was wearing a mirror breastplate over the torn remains of his SS uniform.

He was laughing heartily.

Until I drew my Ravenbrand.

Then his breath hissed from him. He looked about, as if for allies or enemies, then he faced me again. He forced a grin.

"I did not know there was a *third* sword," he said. I could see from his eyes that he was attempting a new calculation.

"There is no third sword," I told him, "or second sword. You are disingenuous, cousin. There is only one sword. And you have stolen it. From your mistress, eh?"

He looked down at both hands. "I seem to have two swords, cousin."

"One, as you know, is a *farun*, a false sword, forged to attract the properties of the original and absorb them. It can steal the souls of men as well as swords. It's a kind of mirror, which absorbs the essence of the thing it most resembles. No doubt Miggea made it for you. Only a noble of the Higher Worlds can forge such a thing. Foolishly I did not anticipate such elaborate conjuring.

"That was how you two tricked Elric. And were able to capture first my energy, then the power of my blade and then the blade itself. I name your second sword 'Deceiver' and demand you return its stolen power. You defeated me by trickery, cousin, with words and illusions."

"You always were too wild-blooded, cousin. I relied on you being unable to resist a challenge."

"I shall not be so foolish again," I said.

"We'll see, cousin. We'll see." He was eyeing Ravenbrand. Looking from it to Stormbringer, as if alarmed by what might happen if the two should meet in battle. "You say there's only one sword, yet—"

"Only one," I agreed.

He understood the implications of my words. While he had not studied as I had and did not possess my skills or learning, he had masters whose casual knowledge was far more profound than all my wisdom. Yet he was impressed. His answering grimace was almost admiring. "Powerful sorcery," he said. "And clever strategy. You've had unanticipated help, eh?"

"If you say so, cousin." I was reluctant to use the blade. I had no idea what the consequences might be. I had a sense of extraordinary supernatural movement all around me, unseen, not yet expressed. An imminence of sorcery. It was easy, in that atmosphere, to feel little more than a desperate pawn in a vast game played by the Lords of the Higher Worlds, who some said were also ourselves at our most powerful and least sane. I took control of myself. Slowly, with all the habits of discipline learned from Bek as well as Melniboné, I extended my mind to include as many of the supernatural realms as I could, sensing unexpected friends as well as mighty enemies.

Gaynor's answer was drowned by a vast, mournful howl from within the palace of bones. He laughed richly in response. "Oh, she is an unhappy goddess," he said jubilantly. "Such a sad old she-wolf. A prisoner of her own forces. A pretty irony, eh, cousin?"

"You did this to her?"

"I arranged it, cousin. Even I cannot control a Duchess of the Distance, a Denizen of the Higher Worlds." He paused, as if with modesty. "I only helped. In a small way."

"Helped what? Whom?"

"Her old enemy," he said. "Duke Arioch of Chaos."

"You serve Law! Arioch is my patron!"

"Sometimes these alliances are convenient," he said, shrugging. "Duke Arioch is a reasonable fellow, for a Lord of Hell. When it became evident that my patroness was no longer in charge of her sanity, I simply made a bargain with that Master of Entropy to deliver my erstwhile mistress into his keeping. Which I shall do as soon as I can deliver her to him. Tricking her, Prince Elric, was even easier than tricking you. The poor creature is senile. She has lost all judgement. She brought no honour to her cause. Only defeat. I had to save the good name of Law. It was time she sought dignified retirement. Her followers were no longer useful to her. And so they became her home. She believed she was going to the Isle of Morn . . ."

"She doesn't seem to appreciate it greatly," said Moonglum. "Indeed she appears to be acting as if you have imprisoned her."

"It's for her own good," said Gaynor. "She was becoming a danger to herself, as well as to others."

"Such a high moral purpose," I said. "And meanwhile you steal from her the sword she fought me for."

"The plan was mine and the sword is mine," he said. "Only the magic was hers."

He held the white sword by the hilt and stripped off the last of his coloured scarves, as if he had no further need of them.

"Her ambitions were unrealistic. I, on the other hand, am the ultimate realist. And soon I shall have everything I have sought. All the old, mystic treasures of our ancestors. All the great objects of power. All the legendary treasures of our race. Everything that guarantees us victory and security for the next thousand years. Herr Hitler's time will soon be over. He'll be recognised as the flawed knight, my precursor."

He gave me a mad, knowing look, as if I were the only creature who could possibly understand his intelligence and the logic of his ambition.

"I shall prove their Parsifal. Their true Führer. For by then I will have the sword and the cup, and I will be able to show the world proof of my destiny to rule. All Christendom, East and West, will rally to my banner. Arioch has promised me this. I shall have no challengers, for my power shall be both temporal and spiritual. I will become the true blood-leader of the Teutonic peoples, cleansing the world in the name of our holy discipline. Then the Golden Age will begin. The Age of the Greater Reich."

I was familiar with such nonsense. I had heard a hundred like him in those years before and after Hitler ascended to the chancellorship. For all his bombast, he seemed to be playing a tyro's game. Such games often progress rapidly, whether in chess or with worlds for stakes, because of the very lack of sense behind their strategies. They can't be anticipated or countered logically. They eventually doom themselves and are always overcome. I was far more interested in what he had said earlier. "How," I asked him, "did you strike a bargain with my own patron, Arioch of Chaos?"

"Miggea was no longer trustworthy and therefore no longer useful to my plans. For an eternity Arioch has yearned for vengeance on his old enemy. I sought him out and offered to help him reach this plane. He could do so only with human agency. He agreed happily to the bargain and trapped her here. She cannot leave. For she has no-one left to help her. Should you attempt to free her, you will be betraying your trust, flaunting the will of your patron demon." He raised his voice in malevolent glee, to be heard by his prisoner as well as by me.

Once more the air was filled with that terrible howling.

Furious, I raised my black sword and spurred my horse towards my cousin. He began to laugh at me again. Standing his ground as I rode down on him. "One other thing I forgot to mention, cousin." He crossed the two blades in front of him, as if for protection against me. "I am no longer part of your dream."

The blades formed an "X" as a strange yellow-and-black light began to pulse from them, half blinding me so that I could no longer see Gaynor clearly. I held up one hand to shade my eyes, my sword ready. But he had become a rapidly moving shadow, racing away from me with violent light flickering all around him. He passed between two great crags and disappeared.

I spurred after him around the great bone palace while the she-wolf kept up her perpetual howling, and I almost caught him. Again the two swords were crossed and again they fluttered with that confusing black-and-yellow light.

Blinded by the light, deafened by the howling, I once more lost sight of Gaynor. I heard Moonglum yelling something. I looked around for my friend but could not see him. More shadows ran back and forth in front of me.

The horse baulked, reared and began to whinny. I tried to control him but only barely managed to get him steadied. He was still uneasy, shifting his feet and snorting. Then there was an explosion of silver—soft, all-engulfing, narcotic. And a sudden silence.

I knew Gaynor was gone.

After a while, the she-wolf began her howling again.

Moonglum suggested that I summon Arioch. "It is the one move you can make to allow us to pursue Gaynor. Arioch can come and go as he pleases here now. Miggea's power no longer opposes his."

When I pointed out that Arioch habitually demanded a blood sacrifice as the price of his summoning and that he, Moonglum, was the only other living mortal soul in the vicinity, my friend put his mind to alternative schemes for our salvation.

I suggested that rather than remain and listen to Miggea's eternal lament, we should return to Tanelorn and seek the advice of the citizens. Should a blood sacrifice still be necessary, at least I could kill an exiled witch-lawyer and win easy popularity with the majority.

So we turned our horses, hoping to reach the city by dark.

By nightfall, however, we were hopelessly lost. As we feared, it had been impossible to tell one pillar of ash from another. The wind recarved them by the moment.

With some relief, therefore, a few hours later, with the stars our only light, we heard someone calling our names. I recognised it at once. My daughter's voice. Oona had found us. I congratulated myself on the intelligence of my relatives.

Then I thought again. This could be another deception. I cautioned Moonglum to ride forward carefully in case of a trap.

In the starlight, reflecting the glittering desert, I saw the silhouette of a woman on foot, bow and arrows slung over her shoulder. I had begun to guess that Oona had a more supernatural means of travelling than by horseback.

Once again I was looking at her intensely.

Her white skin had a warmth to it which my own lacked. Her soft hair glowed. She had much of her mother in her, a natural vitality I had never enjoyed. I had admired, respected and loved Oone the Dreamthief for a brief time when our paths had crossed. We had risked our lives and our souls in a common cause. And we had grown to love and ultimately lust for each other. But this feeling for my daughter was a different, deeper emotion.

I felt a peculiar pride in Oona, a gladness that she so resembled her mother. I imagined that her human characteristics sat better than those of her Melnibonéan ancestry. I hoped she had less conflict in her than did I. I suppose I envied her, too. It could be, of course, that all of us were doomed eternally to conflict, but maybe Fate granted a few a little more tranquillity than others. What I chiefly felt, even in these dangerous circumstances, was a quiet affection, a sense that whatever virtues I had were being passed by my blood from one soul to another. That perhaps my vices had atrophied and been lost from the blood.

Surging up from the ancient layers of my breeding came the utterly Melnibonéan response to one's children, to cut off all feelings of affection lest they weaken us both, to turn away from them. I resisted both impulses. My self-discipline was constantly being tested, constantly being tempered and retempered.

"I thought you had again fallen prey to Gaynor." She sounded relieved. "I know he was here until a short while ago."

I told her what had happened to Miggea. I spoke grimly of Gaynor's trick with the swords, his escape. I cursed him for a traitor, betraying his mistress to my patron, Duke Arioch. Whom he would doubtless betray as well, should it suit him.

At this Oona began to laugh heartily. "How thoroughly he behaves according to type," she said. "There is no hope for that poor soul. No redemption. He races towards his damnation. He embraces it. Betrayal is becoming a habit with him. Soon it will become an addiction and he will be wholly lost. Declaring it mere common sense, he betrays Law in the name of the Balance and betrays the Balance in the name of Entropy. Inevitably he will betray Arioch. And then what a sad renegade he will be. For the moment, admittedly, he achieves a certain power."

"Then there is no defeating him," I said. "He will destroy Mu-Ooria and then his own world."

She held my reins as I dismounted. Somewhat awkwardly, I embraced her. She seemed in good spirits. "Oh," she said, "I think we still have a good chance of thwarting Gaynor's ambition."

Moonglum began to grin. "You're an optimist, my lady, I'll say that. You must own a strong belief in the power of luck."

"Indeed I do," she agreed, "but I think we'd be wiser for the moment to rely upon the power of dreams. I shall visit the imprisoned goddess while you make haste for Tanelorn. You are free to inhabit your own form now, Father, and leave poor Count von Bek the privacy and sanctity of his overworked body."

With that she loped off the way we had come and was soon out of sight. The sun began to pour its scarlet light over the forlorn horizon. It revealed in the distance the gables and turrets of our doomed, beloved Tanelorn.

Riding out to greet us was as odd a group of warriors as I had seen. The leader was Fromental, still in his Foreign Legion uniform. Behind him rode the three beastly lords, Bragg, Blare and Bray, while on all fours, and looking a little odd in all his fineries, trotted Lord Renyard. He was the first to greet us. They had heard of our quest and had come to aid us.

I told them of our adventures and suggested we all turn back to Tanelorn for some food and rest, but the members of that motley party were adamant. They had come all the way from the Stones of Morn to settle with Gaynor. They could find a way to follow him. Perhaps Miggea would help them.

Resignedly I gave them directions and wished them good fortune. My purpose was to save Tanelorn, not pursue Gaynor, but I had no objection if they wished to take their revenge on him. My thoughts were elsewhere.

Soon it would be time for me to return to my own body and allow von Bek to make what he could of his destiny in our fight against the common enemy.

BOOK THREE

Two long songs for the pale lord's brood
Two short lies disguise them,
    Sing true, true, true for the snow-white bird.
Dead now lies my ivory child,
Emptied of sadness, his eyes defiled;
    Sing lie, lie, lie for the ivory child.
The white hare's fleet against the falling sun.
Two dark shadows she'll embrace;
One in shoddy, one in lace.
She speeds the lost old river's course,
Fleet against the falling sun,
The sweet beast runs
Where the ashy wastelands toss,
    To where the wasteland's ashes flow.
    Wild against the fallen sun.

                —Wheldrake,
                The Wild Hare

BOOK THREE

15

Where the Multiverse Begins

Tanelorn was a triumphant stain of warm life upon the endless ash. I wondered how long she would be trapped in this dead realm, conquered by Law, all traces of Chaos thoroughly extinguished. Eventually Miggea's spell would fade and the city must return to her natural place. My feelings were mixed as Moonglum and I rode through the low gates to be greeted by our friends. We told them we believed Tanelorn no longer to be in danger. But the dangers to other places to which we'd given our love and loyalty were considerable. Mu-Ooria was still threatened, perhaps conquered by now. And my Germany was still in the grip of a mad tyrant. It was hard to retain one's focus when so many issues remained unresolved.

With deep anxiety I dismounted outside Brut of Lashmar's house and gave my reins to his ostler. I hoped Fromental and his strange band would be successful, but I doubted it. Gaynor was playing a far more ambitious game than I had guessed. It was never wise, as we of Melniboné had discovered to our cost, to set Law against Chaos in the hope of achieving one's mortal ends.

No creature, human or Melnibonéan, could ever command or contain the kind of power the gods commanded. To become involved in their struggles in this way was certain destruction. Part of me cared little if these inferior beings lived or died, but another part of me understood that there was a common bond, a common threat, and that my fate was closely bound up with the fate of the race which had founded the Young Kingdoms. I also understood that commonality was not a matter of race, but of intellect and disposition, that, while my own culture was so alien to these humans, yet as an individual I made more friendships with them than I did with my own kind.

Melniboné's isolation and arrogance created within me a perpetual conflict. Like the multiverse itself, my mind was rarely at rest. I felt torn constantly between the opposing forces which bound reality, the eternal paradoxes of life and death, of war and peace. Yet if peace was all I sought, then why had I never settled in beguiling Tanelorn, where I had friends, books, music and memories? Why did I lust sometimes for the next conflict and the next? For the dreaming violence, the bitter oblivion of the battlefield?

We were greeted by Brut, ill at ease but glad to see us. "How long must we suffer this damned enchantment?"

"Miggea's power's defeated. Or at least contained. It should not be long before you see your familiar surroundings once more." Brut's question seemed a minor problem, given Gaynor's growing power.

We stayed long enough at Brut's to refresh ourselves, then Oona came back, hard-faced and speaking little. "We must begin this at once," was all she would say. We went with somewhat mixed feelings to the Tower of the Hand, that queer red building whose battlements resembled a palm held outward in a gesture of peace. Where my body still lay in conjured slumber.

Acknowledged by the guard, we entered the low doorway and began to climb a steep staircase which let onto a warren of corridors. Oona led the way, her step light and sure. I came behind, a little less speedily, and Moonglum brought up the rear. He had the air of a man who had seen far too much sorcery and was not looking forward to witnessing any more. He was babbling about our need to leave Tanelorn as soon as possible, to get back on our original course, to put all this behind us and return to the solid realities of the Young Kingdoms, whose sorcery, by and large, was of human proportions.

Oona was grim. "There will be precious few solid realities if Gaynor brings Arioch to the Stones of Morn." Again she fell into an unresponsive silence. I had heard her and Fromental refer earlier to the Stones of Morn but had no clear idea what they were.

At the end of a narrow passage we found another guarded door. I stopped to draw breath while Moonglum exchanged a conventional word or two with the man on duty.

Pretending to have trouble with the door lock, I continued to hesitate. I felt Moonglum's hand on my arm. Oona smiled at me with diffident encouragement.

I pushed open the door.

The long body of a Melnibonéan noble lay before me. Aside from its co-lourless skin, it could have been one of a hundred ancestors. The refined features were in contrast to the vulgarity of the costume. The hands were longer and more slender than von Bek's, the bones of the face more sharply defined, the ears tapering slightly, the mouth sensitive, sardonic. The clothing was that of a bar-barian from the South; that alone identified it as mine. For some time I had cho-sen not to wear my traditional costume. Even the milky hair, pinned at the nape of the neck, was a barbarian fashion. The figure lay dressed just as it had fallen. Nobody had wished, Oona said, to disturb anything, in case I should awaken suddenly. The knee-length boots of doeskin, the baroque silver breastplate, the chequered jerkin of blue and white, scarlet leggings, heavy green cloak. Even the empty scabbard lay beside him. A far better scabbard than the rough-and-ready thing I had made for Ravenbrand.

Though the figure was mine and familiar to the half of me which was Elric, I observed it with a certain detachment, until suddenly I was filled with a surge of emotion and, darting forward, kneeled beside the bed, mutely grasping the limp, corpselike hand, unable to express the feeling of intense sympathy which consumed me. I was weeping for my own tormented soul.

I tried to pull myself together, embarrassed by my unseemly response. I took Ravenbrand and placed it in the cold hand. I began to rise, to say something to my friends, when suddenly the sleeping man's other hand closed on my own and kept me firmly where I was. He was still, as far as I could tell, in a deep, enchanted slumber. Yet there was no denying the power of his grip.

As I struggled to free myself, my eyelids grew heavier and what remained of my energy seeped away. I wanted only to sleep. This feeling was unnatural. I could not afford to sleep. What enchantment had Gaynor left behind for me?

I could not see that it mattered now whether I continued or whether I rested. It seemed perfectly logical, in the circumstances, to lie down beside the bed and join my other self in a much-needed slumber. I heard Moonglum's anxious voice in the deep distance. I heard Oona say something about our safety and the Stones of Morn.

And then I slept.

I was naked.

I stood with my feet planted in blackness. Filling the horizon ahead was a tall silver tree, its roots twisting about itself, the tips of its branches lost in the distance. I had never seen anything so delicate, so intricate. I stood outside existence and looked upon all the branes of all the branches of the multiverse, constantly growing, constantly dying. Like a piece of the most intricate filigree, that silver tree, the complexity so great that it was impossible to see and understand the whole. I knew that what I looked upon was immeasurable, infinite. And what if this were only one of many such trees? I began to move towards it until I could no longer see the tree itself, but only the nearest branches, on which figures moved, back and forth, walking between the worlds.

At last I was standing on a branch, and I felt the comfort of familiarity. I had no memory, either as Elric or Ulric, of these roads. Instead I had a sense of connection with countless other selves with endless pain, with indescribable joy, and I felt that I was walking home.

One branch met a wider branch and then wider still and I met more and more people walking, like me, on the silver roads between the worlds, seeking, like me, some desperate goal, some lost reality. Our greetings were brief. Few lasting friendships were ever made on the silver roads.

After walking a while, I began to notice a certain familiarity about those I passed. In some it was striking, in others subtle. Every one of these solitary men and women was myself. Thousands upon thousands of versions of myself. As if I were drawing in the vast single personality that was the sum of our parts, swiftly losing my own identity to the greater whole, performing some mysterious dance or ritual, making patterns which would ultimately determine the fate of all.

In this second journey, my dream-quest did not take me to Oona's cottage on the borderland. It took me step by step towards a number of circular branches curving around one upon the other, evidently in an agitated condition.

Using the disciplines I had learned in the art of sorcery, I made myself advance.

The silver threads broadened to ribbons and then to wide roads so complicated in their design that it was impossible to guess which direction they would take. All seemed ultimately to return to wherever I happened to pause. I was glad, therefore, to find a fellow traveller, but a little astonished to look on a face that bore no resemblance to my own yet which was familiar.

As happens in dreams, I felt no special surprise at meeting Prince Lobkowitz here. The distinguished older man, who used the *nom de guerre* of Herr El,
gravely shook hands with me, as if we had met on a country road. He seemed
comfortable in his natural environment. I remember the warmth and firmness of
his grip, his reassuring presence.

– My dear Count! Lobkowitz seemed casually delighted. – I was told I might
run across you out here. Are you familiar with these crossroads?

– Not at all, Prince Lobkowitz. And I'll admit I don't seek to become familiar with them. I am merely trying to get home. I have, as I'm sure you're aware,
many reasons for returning to Germany.

– But you cannot return, can you, without the sword?

– The sword is in better hands than mine now. I shall not have any particular need of it, I suspect, in my fight against Hitlerism, which is why I wish to
return home.

Lobkowitz's sad, wise eyes took on an ironic glint. – I think we are all wishing that, my lord. Here, on the moonbeam roads, we occasionally encounter this
phenomenon, where branches appear to curve in on themselves, swallow themselves, reproduce themselves in peculiar ways and grow increasingly complex
and dysfunctional. The theory goes that such places are a kind of cancer, where
Law and Chaos are no longer in equilibrium but maintain form in their mutually
destructive conflict. They can be dangerous to us—their paradoxes are perverse,
unnatural and have age, not wisdom. They only lead towards further confusion.

– But my path takes me this way. How can I avoid it?

– You can't—but I can help you, if you wish.

Quite naturally, I accepted his offer and he fell in beside me, staring up at
the lattice of silvery roads all around us and remarking on their beauty. I asked
him if these were the Grey Fees. He shook his head.

– These are roads we ourselves make between the realms. Just as generations
tread footpaths across familiar countryside until those footpaths turn to high-
ways, so do our desires and inventions create familiar paths through the multiverse. You could say we create a linear way of travelling through non-linearity,
that our roads are entirely imaginary, that any form we believe we see is simply an illusion or a partial vision of the whole. The human psyche organises
Time, for instance, to make it navigably linear. They say human intelligence and

human dreams are the true creators of what we see. I have great faith in the benign power of dreams and am myself partial to that notion—that in effect we create ourselves and our surroundings. Another of the paradoxes which bring us closer to an understanding of our condition.

The maze of roads had tangled all around us now and I knew a slight sense of alarm.

– Then what does this nest of silver threads represent?

– Linearity turned in on itself? Law gone mad? Chaos unchecked? At this stage it scarcely matters. Or perhaps these shapes are like blossoms on a tree, creating in turn whole new dimensions? I believe some call this junction *The Chrysanthemum* and avoid it.

– Why so?

– Because you become truly lost, truly cut off from any familiar reality. Or perhaps if they are cancers . . . ?

– Does no-one know their true origin or function?

– Who can? They could be all of those things or none of those things.

– So we could be trapped. Is that what you're saying?

– I did not insist on it as a certainty. Here the philosophical idea can turn out to be a concrete reality. And vice versa . . .

Lobkowitz smiled a thin smile.

– Here it is best to have only informed theories—realities and certainties are unreliable at best. It is harder to be betrayed by a theory. They say that if you would understand the multiverse, you must change from the conceptual state to the perceptual—from manipulation to understanding, and from understanding to action.

I was taught something similar as a young student of sorcery. Yet I feared to let this silvery tangle of roads absorb me. The Austrian seemed almost amused.

– What were you hoping to find here?

I laughed. – Myself, I said.

– Look. Lobkowitz pointed. A small straight branch led out of the tangle into glinting blackness. – Would you go this way?

– Where does it lead?

– Where you have the will and the courage to go. Whatever you have the will and the courage to make.

I had hoped for rather more specific advice, but understood why it was not possible in a multiverse so malleable, so susceptible to mortal demands and so treacherously unstable. Nonetheless I had an uneasy feeling I had become trapped in some peculiar parable.

These dreams I dreamed as both von Bek and Elric. They were profound dreams, hard to recollect. Elric's dreams were the deepest and he would come to remember them only as nightmares amongst other, equally disturbing, nightmares. The kind that made him wake screaming in the night. That drove him to more and more desperate adventuring as he sought to escape the faintest memory of them.

Now, however, links with von Bek seemed increasingly tenuous as I stepped onto the new straight road. "You ultimately need to reach the Isle of Morn." Prince Lobkowitz wished me goodbye and turned back towards the dense tangle of paths.

I drew further away and looked over my shoulder. "Morn?" I could no longer see the mysterious Prince Lobkowitz, Herr El. The great complex now resembled an impeccably carved ivory chrysanthemum, so perfect it was possible to imagine it made by a mortal craftsman. I understood why it had acquired the name. Were there people who actually mapped these routes? Who could make identical journeys over and over again?

Why had Lobkowitz set me on this path to risk the danger he had described? Why had he, too, mentioned Morn? For a moment it occurred to me to wonder if he had deceived me, but I put the thought aside. I must trust the few I had learned to trust or I would be truly lost.

My road joined with another and another until I was again on a main branch of the multiverse, approaching a place where a silvery bough had turned upwards and then down to form a rough arch.

I had no choice but to go under this and find myself staring upwards into a glowing cauldron of white fire, which turned suddenly to shower me with flames the colour of bone and pewter, absorbing me even as they fell and I fell with them—down for a thousand years, falling, falling for a thousand years. When I looked down I saw a vast field of ivory and silver flowers—of roses and chrysanthemums, marigolds and magnolias—each one representing a different universe.

I feared that I would be drawn into one of the densely woven universes, but gradually they began to form a simple field of white in which two spots of ruby-red glowed, until I realised I was staring into my own gigantic image and then instantly I was staring up at the anxious faces of Moonglum and my daughter, Oona. I turned my head. On the floor beside me was the stirring body of Ulric von Bek. But there had been a fundamental change. Everything was most definitely not what it had been . . .

As von Bek, however isolated I was from Elric and while he would scarcely remember me once this dream was ended, I could not rid myself of him. I remain both men. His story continues within me. I shall never be free of him. I have no reason to believe I was singled out for this fate and every reason to think it a mere accident, for if I've learned nothing else from my experiences, it is that luck has far more to do with one's fortune than any kind of judgement and that to believe oneself in control of the multiverse is to suffer the greatest delusion of all.

Since then I have heard of others who carry the identities of a thousand souls within them, but at that moment I was horrified by the notion. A simple Saxon landowner, I was bound by supernatural ties to the soul of a non-human creature separated from me by untold distances of time and space. Even as I looked on his face, I saw my own face looking back at me. It felt for a moment as if I stared down an endless corridor of mirrors—thousands upon thousands of selves reflected back at me. I rose with some difficulty from where I had fallen. I had the impression everything had happened simultaneously. Moonglum was overjoyed by his friend's restoration, and Oona took her father's hand as he stared with disbelieving eyes at the scene before him.

Only I retained a conscious memory of the journey through the moonbeam roads.

Elric looked at me. "I believe I have you to thank, sir, for waking me from that enchanted slumber?"

"I think the Lady Oona is to be thanked by both of us," I said. "She has her mother's skills if not her inclinations."

He frowned. "Ah, yes. I remember something." Then a shudder ran through him. "My sword—?"

"Gaynor has Stormbringer, still," said Moonglum quickly. "But your—this gentleman—has brought you another."

"I remember." Elric frowned. He looked down at Ravenbrand, which I had placed in his grasp. "Fragments. Gaynor won my sword, then I fell asleep, then I dreamed I found Gaynor and lost him again." He became agitated. "And he threatens—he threatens . . . No, Tanelorn is safe. Miggea's imprisoned. The Stones of Morn! Other friends are in danger. Arioch—my Lord Arioch—where is he?"

"Your Duke of Hell was here," said Moonglum. "In this realm. But we did not know it. Perhaps Gaynor went with him."

Elric clutched his head, groaning. "The sorcery is too much, even for me. No mortal can sustain sanity or life if exposed to it for long. Oh! I remember! The dream! The cottage! Those white faces. Caverns. The young woman . . ."

"You remember enough, Father," she said quietly. He looked up at her again. Startled. Baffled. Alarmed.

"Probably more than enough," I suggested. I was beginning to yearn for some natural, dreamless sleep.

Oona said quietly, "All is not over. Nor will it be until we have succeeded in getting rid of Gaynor. His strategy isn't clear. He still attacks on two fronts and becomes increasingly reckless—careless of all life, including his own."

"Where shall we seek him?" Elric made a careful inspection of the runesword. He seemed suspicious of it, yet the blade itself was clearly the one he was familiar with.

"Oh, there's no doubt," she said, "about where to find him. This Gaynor? He'll choose one of two places of power—Bek or Morn. How to fight him is the problem. If you are ready, Father, we should return as soon as we can to Mu-Ooria, where there's still a great deal of work for us."

"How do you propose to get there?" I asked her. "I doubt if King Straasha can be prevailed upon to help me twice."

She smiled. "There are less dramatic means of travel. Besides, I think Miggea's spell has lifted. Now only she is trapped in the barren world she created for herself. Without human aid, there she stays. But while we can journey fairly easily between the worlds, Master Moonglum cannot. You must wait here, Moonglum, in Tanelorn, until Elric returns."

Moonglum seemed partially relieved at this news but he grumbled. "I've chosen to travel with you, Elric—to hell, if necessary."

Elric stretched out his long, pale hand and placed it on Moonglum's shoulder. "It will not be necessary yet, old friend."

Moonglum took this well, but he was clearly saddened. "I'll wait a few weeks," he said. "And if you don't return by then, I might head back towards Elwher. I, too, have unfinished business. If I'm not here when you return, you'll find me there."

We left the little red-headed outlander in that room. He preferred, he said, to stay there until we had gone. He wished us luck. He was sure our paths would cross again.

Oona led us out of the Tower of the Hand into cheering streets and gentle sunlight. There, all around the city's walls, were familiar gentle green hills. Tanelorn had returned to her natural position in the multiverse.

Oona led us swiftly through the twittens and lanes of Tanelorn's most ancient districts until we entered a low house which had, by its condition, been abandoned years earlier. The upper floors were ruined but the basement was in good repair, its main room guarded by an iron-bound door which Oona, after checking that we weren't observed, opened with a surprisingly small key.

There seemed to be nothing especially valuable on the other side of the door. The room was furnished with a bed, working and cooking facilities, a desk, chair and several shelves of books and scrolls. It had the neat, well-used air of a nun's cell.

I didn't question her. This was one of her smaller surprises, after all.

Only when Elric was physically nearby did I not strongly sense his mind. The albino seemed more ill at ease than anyone else, and I had no clear idea why. I think I assumed a sophistication in him. After all, my experience of the inventive twentieth century was not his. Indeed, he was often awkward in my presence, avoiding my eye and rarely addressing me directly. Clearly I made him deeply uncomfortable and would have left him, if I could. He had something of the air of a somnambulist. I began to wonder if he thought he dreamed all that was happening.

Perhaps he did dream? Perhaps he dreamed us all?

Now Oona crossed to the far wall and pushed back a tapestry hanging to reveal another door.

"Where does this lead?" I asked.

"It depends." She was smiling a little grimly.

"Upon what?"

"On whether Law or Chaos has control of certain realms."

"And how do you know?"

"You find out," she said, "by going through."

Elric was impatient. "Then let's go through," he said. "I've a mind to confront Cousin Gaynor on a number of issues." His hand was on the hilt of Ravenbrand. I admired his wild courage. We might have the same blood and some of the same dilemmas, but we were temperamentally very different. He sought oblivion in action, while I sought it in philosophy. I was reluctant to take decisions, whereas for Elric decisions were everything. He took them, as he took risks, habitually.

If he'd lived a prosaic life, with prosaic considerations, then prosaic things would chiefly have happened to him. But he was in no way prosaic, this wolfish whiteface, who relied on sorcery for his very sustenance.

Would I have been like him in his circumstances? I doubted it. But I had not known a childhood of sorcerous schooling and overbearing tradition. I had not, as a youth, stared into the most profound horror, and learned the skills of the Dragon Masters, learned how magically I could manipulate the world. I knew everything about his past, of course, for his memories remained my memories, while he recalled nothing at all of me. In some ways I envied him his lack of consciousness.

With an air of impatience, Elric flung himself through the door and I followed. Oona closed the door behind us.

The three of us stood in a pleasant sunken garden. The kind of place one might seek rest and contemplation and exactly what one would have expected to find on the other side of that door. A comforting domesticity. The garden was surrounded by a high wall which was surrounded in turn by tall buildings, all of which had the effect of making it seem smaller than it was. Herbs and flowers, all sweet-scented, were laid out in formal beds. Peacocks and ornamental roosters strutted between the shrubs. At the centre was a pool with a fountain. The fountain was ornate, of some dark, gleaming rock, and its sound added to the garden's sense of tranquillity.

Although pleasant, the scene was an anticlimax. We had expected something much more dramatic. Elric hesitated. He looked around him, suspiciously. I think he was trying to find something to kill.

Oona was relieved. She had clearly expected some less attractive scene. The garden had no exterior gate. The only way to get in or out was through the door we had just used.

"What now?" Elric glanced impatiently about. "Where do we go?"

"From Tanelorn to Mu-Ooria and from Mu-Ooria to Tanelorn," she said, "the way is always by water."

Elric dipped his hand into the ornamental pool. "By water? How? There's no room for a ship on this, madam." He stared with interest at the unusual fish swimming there, as if he expected to find some secret in the pool.

Smiling, Oona reached down with her curved bow and drew it gently across the surface, describing a circle. The circle remained visible. Within, the water became gradually more agitated, full of colour and lilting ripples. Suddenly it began to funnel upwards, red and shining, like a fresh wound, a pillar of pulsing ruby light. The colour was reflected in our three pale faces, giving our skin the appearance of bone stained with old blood.

Elric grinned his wolf's grin—the red light dancing in his eyes. "Is this the way?" he asked Oona.

She nodded.

Without a word or any further hesitation, the Melnibonéan flattened his body against the pillar. For a moment he jerked, like a frog on an electric fence, and then was absorbed.

I didn't move quite so readily and Oona laughed at me, taking my hand and stepping forward, leading me into the yielding, fiery light.

I felt something tugging at my body, pulling me away from her. I tried to hold on, but lost my grip. I was swimming through roaring, fluttering flames, down into a scarlet abyss which threatened to drown me in all the spilled blood of the multiverse. Fire which did not burn, but licked at the secret places of the soul. Fire which revealed gibbering faces, like the faces of the damned in Hell. Obscenely tortured bodies, a writhing ballet of torment. But I was not burned.

The fire had the quality of water, for I could swim through it easily. I hadn't drawn a single breath and felt no need for air. I was reminded of the thick, sluggish waters of the Heavy Sea which lay beyond Melniboné.

As I swam, I looked about for the others, but they had disappeared. Had this been a plan on the part of Elric and Oona to get rid of me now that I'd served my turn?

Behind me I had the sense of a malignant, monstrous presence. I swam faster than ever, even as the creature gathered speed. When I glanced back, seeking a glimpse of what pursued me, all I could see was a huge, shadowy white bulk, like the body of a shark seen through twilight seas. It seemed to carry the weight of the ages. It moved as in great pain. I heard it utter a peculiar groan. I felt something brush by me and then fall away back into the depths, as if it had attempted to attack me and failed.

I swam on through forests of identical ruby pillars. I swam between banks of blue flame and over fields of emerald and pearl. And I still had no need to draw breath, no need to defend myself.

I swam through cities in flames. I swam over battles between whole peoples and I swam over the destruction of worlds. I swam through tranquil woods and flowering fields and then, quite unexpectedly, I was inhaling liquid.

I coughed, flung myself upwards, and emerged into blazing blackness.

From somewhere in the darkness I heard an exultant voice. Oona was speaking to my doppelgänger. "Welcome, Father," she said. "Welcome to Mu-Ooria. Welcome to your destiny."

16

The Greater Blasphemy

The other two were waiting for me as I waded to shore. It was bitterly cold. In that weird phosphorescent light from the lake, I saw the by now familiar outlines of Mu-Ooria, but they seemed more ragged than before. Every so often a column of pale fire would rise for a moment, flutter into fragments and subside. While I had no idea of the cause, there was an ominous quality to the fire which made me fear the worst. I heard distant sounds, like the thin striking of a clock, *pnin, pnin, pnin*, a roar like a landslide, then laughter in the darkness. A crash. A panting noise, like the ardour of coupling dogs. The echo of what might have been a scream. A sense that something terrible was taking place, something obscene.

I did my best to keep my fears to myself. "On the evidence," I said, "Gaynor has been successful in his ambitions here."

As was his unconscious habit when disturbed, Elric put his hand on the pommel of Ravenbrand. "Then we had best go to see him at once."

I was beginning to understand that my near-twin was incautious by nature. What would seem insanity to an ordinary man was for Elric the logical course of action.

Oona smiled at this. "Perhaps we should first find out what his strength is. Remember, Father, that your sorcery could be limited here. Even the sword might lack her normal powers."

Elric shrugged at this but seemed willing to trust her judgement. After all, we were here largely at her volition and she knew far more about this world than either of us.

Making no effort to hide himself, Elric began to stride towards the city, following the curve of the shoreline. We could only continue in his wake.

Soon the signs of Gaynor's ambitions could be seen everywhere in that haunted, unsteady darkness. More than once we stumbled over the prone body of a giant black cat which had previously hunted this territory. Twice we found what were Off-Moo remains—crumpled corpses, hacked cartilage, but no bones. Did the Off-Moo have bones, in the conventional sense? We found one of their long, conical headdresses and still could not tell if they fitted the shape of the head or exaggerated it. We found signs of fires made from Off-Moo artefacts. We found the bodies of troogs and savages everywhere. Evidently some had fought amongst themselves for whatever prizes they discovered in Mu-Ooria. I guessed there was little here they would value, which would make their destructiveness all the more frenzied.

How had they defeated the Off-Moo, who had been so well and cleverly protected? The dormant Off-Moo, those who had resembled statues and who guarded their borders, had clearly been caught unawares. They had never had a chance to wake. The Off-Moo's ability to direct deadly stalactites against their enemies had somehow been impaired. Initially knowing nothing of the Off-Moo, Gaynor had somehow learned much since I last visited their city.

Signs of savage, mindless cruel destruction were everywhere.

What had become of the Off-Moo? Had they fled? Were they in hiding in the city? Had they all been killed? Or captured? It was hard for me to remember that Gaynor had gathered supernatural allies since I had last visited this realm.

We saw a few silhouettes moving in the ruins. They had the shambling walk of the troogs or the swagger of the half-blind savages who fought beside them.

As we drew nearer to them, even Elric began to keep to the shadows, watching to see what they were doing. But it was clear they were doing very little, save sifting through the ruins for the loot they had hoped to find. I couldn't imagine what possessions of the Off-Moo would be valuable to these semi-brutes. Where was Gaynor's main army?

We were coming close to the great plaza of the city. Everywhere the mysterious towers of the Off-Moo burned with that strange fluttering white fire. What I had mistaken for their screaming was the noise the towers made as they burned. The sound of a mortal voice.

Where the towers burned, neither the conquerors nor the conquered were in evidence.

We decided we would have to capture one of the savages and interrogate him. Oona cocked her head, listening. She walked rapidly towards a burning tower and peered in.

Seconds later a dark shape appeared in the doorway. Its own robes flickered as the fire flickered and its eyes glittered. I saw no welcome in them.

Oona exchanged a few words with the figure. Cautiously he came out of the tower and glided towards us. It was hard to tell from the long, stony face if we were recognised or not. The Off-Moo spoke slowly, in Greek:

"Gaynor did this to us. He feared we would try to stop him in his ambitions. And he feared rightly. But he has made exceptional alliances with certain of the Lords of the Higher Worlds and so gained the knowledge of how to defeat us and with what."

"How many of you has he killed?" Elric spoke with the direct bluntness of a professional soldier.

"That remains to be seen, sir. I am Scholar Crina. I was not here when Gaynor attacked. When I returned I found our city much as you find it now. My departing colleagues were able to inform me that the weight of barbarians overwhelmed them. But before that something else occurred."

"Where are the barbarians now?" I asked. I was shivering, still soaked through. "Do you know?"

"They marched away," was all he would say.

"Where's this Gaynor?" Elric asked brusquely. "Presumably his will is what it always was?"

"He has done what he needed to do here."

"And what was that?"

"He has stolen our Great Staff and now marches against the Grey Fees."

"Impossible," said Oona. "The Staff is useless in his blood-soaked hands. It could as easily destroy him as aid him. No-one would take such a risk. Nobody would be so foolish as to chance such destruction."

"No-one except Gaynor," said Elric.

"What does he expect to gain from invading the Grey Fees?" I asked.

Scholar Crina answered that question. "Enormous power. Power over the forces of creation themselves. This was what he first offered us, if we would help him. Naturally we refused him."

"The gods would never allow it."

Scholar Crina seemed amused. "No sane being would. But there is a theory that the Lords of the Higher Worlds themselves are no longer entirely sane, as disturbing changes take place throughout the multiverse. A conjunction comes. All the realms will realign within the great field of Time. New destinies will be decided. New realities. Yours is not the only story. There are others. Other lives. Other dreams. All lead to the same great supernatural moment. Nothing is as certain as it was. Even loyalties to Law and Chaos are no longer permanent. Look at Gaynor. He employs both Law and Chaos in his attempt to make himself the ruler of worlds. Once such things were impossible for mortals. But now, it seems, even mortal power increases and becomes less stable."

"Gaynor does not mean to destroy himself," said Oona. "He no doubt believes he is invulnerable now that he bears your Great Staff."

"He claims to be king of the world. And it is true that his possession of our Great Staff gives him the confidence to march upon the Grey Fees. But to what end? What can he hope to achieve, save complete destruction of the multiverse?"

"He reminds me of a certain dictator in my own country," I said mildly. "His madness, his poor grasp on reality seems to be what drives him. His addiction to power is so great, he will destroy whole realms in order to satisfy his craving."

Scholar Crina lowered his eyes. "He has no ordinary sense of self-interest. Those are the most dangerous people of all to gain control of a civilisation."

"Echoes," said Oona thoughtfully to herself. "On how many planes, do you think, is a version of this story being played out? We believe we have volition, but we can do little to change the consequences or the direction of our actions, because those consequences and actions are taking place, with minuscule differences expanding to vast differences, on countless levels of the multiverse."

Elric showed no interest in her philosophy. "If Gaynor can be stopped on this plane," he said, "then presumably his defeat will be echoed, as his victories are?"

She smiled at him. "Well, Father, if anyone was best fitted to change his own destiny, then it is you."

Neither Elric nor I knew exactly what she meant, but I shared his sense of determination.

"Gaynor's power was too great for us," said Scholar Crina.

"But your Staff," said Oona. "How could he have taken that from you?"

"The Staff itself appears to have allowed it," said Scholar Crina simply. "We have always known it had volition. That is how it came to us."

They were referring to the malleable artefact—bowl, child, staff—I had witnessed the Off-Moo manipulating in that first ceremony. Or *had* they been the manipulators? Were they perhaps the manipulated? I remembered how it had changed shape. At whose volition?

"Does it always take the form of a staff?" I asked him. I recalled all the shapes it had made.

"We know it as the Runestaff," he said. "But it takes several forms. It is a staff and a cup and a stone and is one of the great regulators of our realities."

"Is that what my people know as the Grail?" I remembered von Eschenbach and some of our own family legends. "Were you its guardians?"

"In this realm," he said. "And in this realm we have failed."

"You mean various versions of the Grail inhabit other realms?"

Scholar Crina was regretful. "Only one Great Staff exists," he said. "It represents the Balance itself. Some say it *is* the Balance. Its influence extends far beyond any realm in which it is kept."

"My family was once said to guard the Grail," I told him. "But it was removed from our keeping. Presumably we also failed in our trust."

"The Runestaff has the power to change form and to move of its own volition," Scholar Crina told me. "Some say it can take the shape of a child. Why should it not, since it can presumably assume any form it likes? In this way it preserves and defends itself. And thus preserves those who respect and defend it. It is not always obvious what form it has taken."

"In what form does Gaynor possess it?" Oona wanted to know.

"The form of a cup," he said. "Of a fine drinking vessel. With that and the two swords he now carries, he has more power to change the destiny of worlds than any other mortal before him. And because the gods themselves hardly understand what is happening, he could succeed. For it is well known that a mortal will eventually bring about the destruction of the gods."

I paid little attention to this last. It had the smack of legend and superstition about it, yet at the same time a frisson of recognition went through my body. I tried to recall where I had heard a similar story, one which was couched in the mythology of my own age and people, the story of the Holy Grail and its ability to cure the world's pain. That legend also had a mortal changing the destiny of his world. I checked myself. I felt as if I was receiving an overdose of Wagner. My own tastes were for the clearer waters of Mozart or Liszt, whose appeal was as much to the intellect as to the emotions. Was that what I recognised? Had I somehow found myself in a very complicated Wagnerian opera? I shuddered at the thought. Yet even the momentous events of the Ring Cycle were as nothing compared to what I had already witnessed.

I turned to Oona. "You said something of my particular relationship with the Grail. What did you mean?"

"Not everyone is privileged to serve it," she said.

Her manner was grim. She did not seem optimistic. I think she had not expected Gaynor to get this far.

A strange stink filled the air. A mixture of a thousand different odours, none of them pleasant. The smell of evil.

I still could not see how Gaynor had so thoroughly defeated the Off-Moo and said as much to the scholar.

"You do not yet know," he said, "if Gaynor has defeated us. The game, after all, is not over."

I kept my own counsel, but as far as I could see this aspect of the game at least was well and truly won.

Elric wanted to know where Gaynor was, whether it was possible to catch up with him on foot.

"He moves towards the Grey Fees with his army. He believes he can take the power of the multiverse for himself. It is a delusion. But his delusion will destroy us all, unless someone challenges him." Scholar Crina seemed to glance enquiringly at me.

But it was Prince Elric who answered. "I have been insulted and humiliated by that creature. I have been deceived. Whatever power he now has, he will not escape my vengeance."

"You think not?" Oona stooped to run her hand through the sleek fur of one of the big cats, then drew it away again quickly, as if she did not wish to contemplate what had happened to the animal. Was it dead, or enchanted?

"Dream or no dream," said Elric quietly, "he shall be punished for what he has done."

I would not have believed another. Elric, however, was beginning to convince me that we might yet, somehow, defeat an entity who had become probably the greatest single force for evil in the multiverse. As often happened between us, Elric replied to my unvoiced ideas. "Melnibonéans believe that fate cannot be altered. That each of us has a settled destiny. That to break free of it—or attempt to break free of it—is an act of blasphemy. A blasphemy I am prepared to commit. To prevent, perhaps, a greater blasphemy."

He had the air of a man who wrestled with his own soul as well as his conscience and background. I had the impression that he might have spoken more, had he been able to put into words the huge conflicts taking place within him.

We spent little time in Mu-Ooria. The flames were already beginning to die down and serious damage had been done. We found no more Off-Moo. No sign of them. No piece of writing. No clue. They had fled in defeat. I was disappointed in them. They had no doubt become decadent, overconfident of their ability to resist attack, relying, as Byzantium had done for so many decades, on their ancient reputation. I had assumed them to be both courageous and resourceful. Perhaps they had been once. Now, it seemed, they had no capacity to resist Gaynor or anyone else who chose to take their wealth and secrets.

"There is only one possible course of action," said Prince Elric.

"Pursue Gaynor?" I asked.

"And hope to defeat him before he can reach the Grey Fees."

"He is almost there," said Scholar Crina. "He and his army must even now be close to the borderland." For the first time he appeared to show some kind of emotion. "The end for us," he said. He lowered his cowled head. "The end for everyone. The end of everything."

Oona was impatient with this. "Well, gentlemen, unless you welcome the end as thoroughly as Scholar Crina, who seems to derive some form of gloomy satisfaction from the situation, I suggest we rest for a while, eat well and then continue our pursuit."

"There's no time," said Elric, almost to himself. "We must eat on the move. And we must begin soon, for we have no mounts and must pursue Gaynor on foot."

"And when we catch up with him?" I said. "What will we do?"

"Punish him," said Elric simply. "Take back the sword he has stolen." He touched his hilt. He stroked it with his long fingers. He was beginning to grin. I found his humour alarming. "Use his own methods against him. Kill him."

A kind of lust smouldered in the Melnibonéan. He was longing for a blood-letting and did not much care how it was achieved. I began to fear for the safety of myself and his daughter. Scholar Crina sensed it, too. When I looked for him again, he was slipping back into the burning building. He seemed untroubled by the flames.

Wrapping my damp clothing about me and feeling the need for movement, I trudged towards the outskirts of the city, my companions behind me. I was convinced that I was likely to die in this adventure. I consoled myself that if Elric and Oona had not helped me escape the concentration camp, I would be dead by now anyway. At least I had had the chance to observe the supra-reality that constituted the interlinked worlds of the multiverse.

We had retreated to the outer reaches of the city when suddenly the ground underfoot began to shudder. Pieces of stone whistled from above and crashed to the cavern's floor. Did an earthquake grip Mu-Ooria? The rumbling staccato sound which followed the shock had the quality of mocking laughter.

I glanced a question to Oona, who shook her head. Elric, also, was baffled. Another shock. More falling rock. As if a giant strode in our wake.

If I had not known better, I would have guessed that high explosives were being set off. I had experienced similar sensations and sounds when visiting the site of a new railway tunnel with my engineer brother, who had died while digging a trench three days after the outbreak of war.

I peered into the distance, between those vast columns of rock. It was impossible to see very far into that cavern or guess its dimensions. But now, far away, I caught glimpses of a flickering, raging fire. The phosphor from the lake had combined to form a whirlwind.

Several of these slender tornadoes were approaching us. Shrieking whirlwinds of whistling white light touched the ruins of the city and swirled them into new, even crazier patterns. Something about those thin twisters suggested they were sentient, or that they were at least controlled by a thinking creature.

We knew enough to run, seeking some kind of ditch or fissure into which we could climb in the hope that the tornadoes would bounce over us like their earthly counterparts, but it was a faint enough hope.

It was clear now what force Gaynor had used against our friends. Some fresh supernatural alliance, no doubt, brought him the strength of the *ishass*. Wind demons. Even in my earthly mythology I had heard of them. They figured largely in the folktales of desert peoples, usually as *ifrits*.

"Can they be harnessed by the likes of Gaynor?" Oona was asking Elric.

"Clearly," replied the albino laconically as he ran.

I brought up the rear, gasping for breath and unable to voice any of the questions rushing through my mind.

Oona signalled to us. She stopped and pointed. Ahead was the even darker mouth of a small cave. Hearing the advance of the *ishass* and not daring to look, without hesitation we squeezed into the hole, which was barely large enough to contain all three of us. The closeness of our bodies was a comfort to me. I felt as if the three of us had returned to some safe, defendable womb. Outside the shrieks and crashing grew louder and louder as the whirlwinds passed directly over us. Then came a lull. More twisters could be heard far away, but their sound was distant.

"This is a powerful force," Elric mused. "It requires enormous skill to summon it. Important bargains. I do not believe even your cousin, Count Ulric, with all his cleverness, could physically contain it. These demons are famous in the netherworlds. They are called the Ten Sons, the *ishass*. This means he keeps his alliances with Chaos, for the *ishass* will not serve Law and Law, save at its most unstable, would never employ them."

I felt guilty for judging the Off-Moo. No mortal creature could stand against such power. It would be like trying to confront an American twister with courage and moral integrity as your only weapons. And the Off-Moo, for all their sophistication, had nothing which would defend them against these *ishass*.

The wind demons were passing close by now. Yelping and shrieking and yapping like wild dogs, bringing ancient stones crashing down, uprooting columns which had taken a million years to grow. My fear took second place to my sense of outrage. What purpose could there be to such wild destruction? And why had Gaynor bothered to unleash the Ten Sons again upon a clearly defeated city? What was it in some mortals that gave them satisfaction in destruction?

What terrible need did they satisfy by destroying the work and beauty of the centuries? Did they think they cleansed the world of something?

Only long after they passed, and we climbed out of our cramped little cave, did it occur to me that perhaps Gaynor did not command the Ten Sons. Perhaps they had escaped his control and now contented themselves with wreaking wholesale mayhem upon that once peaceful world? Or was this their reward for aiding him? They destroyed indiscriminately, not even sparing the few savages left rooting in the ruins who came into their path. They were caught up, arms and legs desperately flailing, swallowed, stripped of clothing and flesh, which was flung in all directions, their bones scattered. The bones fell like rain on a rooftop.

The Ten Sons were ahead of us now, forming a ragged line which could be followed easily. We came in their wake, stumbling along the wide path they had created and wondering what could lie before us that would be any more terrifying than what we had already witnessed.

Oona was frowning, She had had an idea, she said. "Perhaps they hurry to join Gaynor's army? Perhaps he has already reached the Grey Fees and summons them to his service once more. Does he think he can conquer Creation with a few wind demons?"

"I would imagine," I said, "that he has planned rather more thoroughly. What we can be sure of, I think, is that his power is the greatest granted to any human being before him."

"I think he will be hard to defeat," mused the Lord of Melniboné. "It's as well there are three of us. I am not sure I could do it alone."

We moved farther away from the city and into darkness which we illuminated with the barbarians' fallen brands. We had little chance of catching Gaynor's army quickly, but at least we were now safe from the Ten Sons, who leaped ahead of us, tiny now, glimpsed rarely amongst the massive tall stones which formed in this area a series of arches, like a huge rose arbour. We were grateful to them. They brought light to that aching distance. They gave us a clue to Gaynor's whereabouts. But it would be some time before we were able to get closer to them.

And, when we did, I was not at all sure we wouldn't be instantly killed. I had every reason to suspect Elric's determined optimism had much to do with his knowledge of sorcery but not a great deal to do with the vast numbers of soldiers Gaynor commanded, not to mention his evident supernatural allies.

We were lucky to come across the slaughtered corpse of a troog. The huge half-human still had its crude pouch on a belt about its misshapen waist. The pouch was full of miscellaneous and generally useless loot salvaged from Mu-Ooria. But there was also food. Two solid loaves of bread, a couple of pots of preserved meats and bottles of pickled vegetables. He had also found from somewhere a leather bottle of wine. We had to prise it from his gigantic, scabby hand. An unpleasant task, but worth it in the end, for the wine was of good quality. I had a feeling it had originally belonged to one of Fromental's colleagues, perhaps even his friend the talking beast. This led me to wondering about the Frenchman's fate. I hoped he and his strange companions had been successful in finding the Tanelorn they sought.

We moved rapidly and eventually caught our first sight of Gaynor's terrible army.

In the far distance a band of grey formed a kind of horizon. Were we nearing the beginning of the mysterious Fees?

I turned enquiringly to Oona.

"The Forbidden Marches," she confirmed. "And beyond them, the Grey Fees."

17

Careless Angels

"Some peoples believe," said Oona conversationally, "that each of us has a guardian angel who discreetly looks after our interests, perhaps in the way we care for and protect a pet. The pet is barely conscious of what we do for it, just as we are hardly conscious of our guardian angel. And just as some pet animals have conscientious owners, others have bad owners. Therefore, though we are all assigned such an angel, the unlucky ones have careless angels."

We lay upon a broad terrace looking down into a valley that had probably never seen light before. It was illuminated by the marching twisters, the Ten Sons, which formed a loose line of whirling, shrieking light. They were clearly disciplined by something as they followed behind the brands of the blind cannibals with Gaynor. The torches were not for them, but for Gaynor and his Nazis, whose horses were equally blind. Every so often a vast shadow would be thrown upon a wall of ancient, fleshy rock. The gigantic troogs, the sightless savages, the Nazis in the remains of their black-and-silver uniforms. A foul alliance indeed. Beasts and men. Half-men and half-beasts. Shambling and lolloping, trudging and dancing, striding and riding. Some of them stumbling. Ironically, while they had learned to adapt themselves to the dark, they were often blinded by the light. A ragged army. An ugly army. A monstrous army, marching relentlessly towards the Grey Fees.

"Could be," I said, "that we're already deserted by our angels. Have you ever witnessed such grotesquerie?" I indicated Gaynor's army.

"Rarely," said Oona. Her sweet, beautiful face, framed by her long white hair, looked up at me with sardonic intelligence. For a moment I felt an extraordinary sensation as she glanced away. I believe I was falling in love with her. And already, of course, I was debating the morality of this.

Oona was not my daughter. She was Elric's. But at what point did a being conscious of its place in the multiverse choose to ignore the relationship it had in common with a million other beings? I could easily see the drawbacks of being fully conscious. Perhaps, years before, in his early sorcerous training Elric had been given the choice of being knowing or unknowing and had chosen to become unconscious of the multiverse. Otherwise he might never have been able to act at all.

What can it be like to be conscious that every action one performs has a consequence throughout time and space? One would become very circumspect about the company one kept. About the things one did or said. One could be frozen into complete inaction. Or returned to a state of absolute ignorance as the mind refused all information.

Or it could make one entirely reckless, willing, like Elric, to risk everything. For if one risked and lost, the reward was, after all, complete oblivion. And oblivion was what that poor, tortured soul longed for so frequently. This quality made him an unreliable ally. Not all of us sought or found oblivion in battle. Something in me still looked forward to a restoration of the tranquillity of my old estate, a return to the quiet pleasures of rural life. Not that the prospect seemed especially close at this particular moment.

Elric frowned to himself. He seemed to be calculating something. I looked at him nervously, hoping he would not decide on one of his reckless moves. We three could not stand alone against those strange forces.

Cautiously, using all the cover available, we gradually drew closer to Gaynor's horrible army. The wind demons seemed positioned to protect the flanks and rear. I could not guess how my cousin controlled them.

"How do you know these sentient tornadoes?" I whispered. "Have you encountered them before?"

"Not all ten," he said. He was impatient with my interruption. "I once summoned their father. They all command different aspects of the elements, these wind-beings. They are protective of their separate domains. They know strong rivalries. And they can be fickle. This is not work for the *sharnahs*, makers of gales, but for the *h'Haarshanns*, builders of whirlwinds."

I fell silent again. My instinct was to turn, to go back, to find the falls, the way through to Hameln. I would rather risk the horrors of a Nazi concentration camp than confront any more supernatural threats.

The marching army stopped. They pitched camp. Perhaps Gaynor needed to consider his next action? The Ten Sons became guardians of that vast horde by forming a rough circle around it. I studied the blazing whiteness as best I could, trying to see what really constituted the Ten Sons, but my vision began to blur immediately. I found it impossible to look at the wind demons for more than a few seconds.

I wondered if I tied a piece of gauze about my face it would be easier to make out whatever fundamental shape lay at the core of the Ten Sons. But perhaps I was deceiving myself. Perhaps there was no fundamental shape.

Elric murmured, "First the Ten, then my lady M."

He was speaking in rhyme. Indeed, even his breathing had a rhythmic quality I had not previously noticed. His movements took on a balletic air. He was scarcely aware of either Oona or myself. His eyes had a distant glaze.

I frowned and moved forward to touch him on the shoulder and ask him if he was all right, but Oona lifted a finger to her lips and motioned me away. She gave her father an expectant look, then, when she glanced back at me, she seemed to have a proud, proprietorial gleam in her eyes, as if to say "Wait. My father is a genius. Watch."

I had known him as intimately as it is possible to know another human being, from deep within, soul sharing soul. I had considerable respect and great sympathy for him. But only now did it occur to me that he might be a genius.

Elric warned us to speak softly, if we spoke at all. The Ten Sons had acute hearing.

All at once Elric was moving, climbing down the rocks nearby and, perhaps in answer to my unspoken question, muttering, "Oldfather. Oldfather needs a little fresh blood."

He disappeared for a moment. I heard a musical sound. Soft, menacing. I saw him below, walking cautiously towards Gaynor's camp. Ravenbrand was unscabbarded in his right hand.

Time passed. The camp slept. I continued to watch. Waiting for Elric to return. Oona, however, curled up and told me to wake her if I became sleepy.

Eventually I heard a noise below and saw the familiar outline. Elric was dragging something behind him. Something which grunted and groaned as it bumped over the rocky floor.

Next I saw him on the other side, still below me. Here the rocks formed a small natural amphitheatre at the centre of which Elric dumped his prize. It wriggled for a moment until he kicked it. I saw his face then. His eyes were glassy, blazing rubies. They looked into a world I could not begin to imagine. They looked into Hell itself. And his mouth was moving, his sword describing complicated geometries in the air, his whole body beginning to turn in ritual movements, a ghostly dance.

Oona awakened and lay beside me, watching Elric as he cut through the material binding his victim. I recognised the terrified human being. One of the Nazis who had originally come here with Gaynor. He was snarling like a trapped dog, but there was stark horror in his eyes and he could not control his trembling. He tried to strike out at Elric. Ravenbrand licked him. He pulled back his bleeding hand. Ravenbrand licked him again. His face carried a thin line of blood. And again. The ragged shirt covering his chest fell away to reveal another line from neck to navel.

The Nazi was whimpering, trying to find escape, allies, God, anything. The sword tasted him. Savoured him. Relished his blood drop by drop. And while he played with the snivelling wretch, Elric crooned a haunting wordless song. The cadences rose and fell. I was astonished that they issued from a mortal throat. All the time they grew in intensity and bit by bit the Nazi died, pieces of his flesh falling away as he watched. The sword continued its delicate, terrible work.

Oona craned to see, fascinated. In this she was her father's child. She had the look of a cat. I, however, was forced to turn away more than once. Forced by the sound of that voice, rising and falling, growing stronger and stronger, by the sight of Elric himself, his wild, crimson eyes raised towards the upper darkness, his mouth open in something between a melody and a scream, his white flesh glinting and his great black runesword turning a human being to slivers before his own eyes.

The Nazi was still fully conscious, such was Elric's appalling artistry. The man still wore his black SS boots. He knelt before my doppelgänger and tears

THE DREAMTHIEF'S DAUGHTER

mingled with the blood from his eyes as Elric's blade teased them out until they hung by a few strands of muscle on his own cheeks.

Most of the time Elric's voice drowned the hideous screaming of the Nazi, his pleadings to spare him or kill him, and I was thankful for that.

Sword and man acted in unison—two intelligences in an unholy pact. I had never felt this of Ravenbrand before. Elric's use of the blade seemed to have awakened an evil in the very iron. Red runes slithered up and down its length, pulsing like veins. The sword seemed to relish the subtle, disgusting wounds which it now inflicted upon the Nazi's bloody flesh. It was without doubt the most loathsome sight I had ever seen.

Again I turned away. Then I heard Oona gasp and I looked back.

Another shape formed itself around the Nazi's tormented body. It twisted in and out, growing like something organic. Gradually, snakelike, it swallowed Elric's victim, then became increasingly agitated and gouted up out of what remained of the corpse. Gushing towards the cavern's roof. Swirling like a cloud overhead. A cloud in which tiny strands of lightning seemed to flash and writhe, taking on the colour of the Nazi's blood as the man squealed like a bled pig, realising that there were worse fates than the one he had just endured. He finally gave himself up to the cloud.

I heard Elric's voice above all the other sounds. "Father of Winds. Father of Dust. Father of Air. Father of Thunder. h'Haarshann Oldfather. Oldest of fathers. h'Haarshann Oldfather, father of the first." I knew the language he spoke, because I knew all such things now, and I knew that he was delivering the wretched mortal up to the one he summoned.

"Oldfather! Oldfather! I bring you what the lord of the h'Haarshann demands. I bring thee the exotic meat thou craveth."

The cloud grunted. It was satisfied. It uttered a kind of soft whistle.

Now the scarlet lightning began to dance and skip again, forming a shape. I thought I saw the wizened face of a vindictive old man, long strands of lank hair hanging to his shrunken shoulders. A toothless mouth smacking lips as the last of the sacrifice was absorbed. Then the mouth grinned.

"You know how to feed an old friend, Prince Elric." The voice was a sighing breeze, a gale, a fluttering wind.

"As you have fed before, h'Haarshann Oldfather." My near-twin had sheathed the bloody black blade and now stood with arms outstretched in an attitude of respect. "As you will feed again, while I live. That is our bargain. Made with my ancestors a million years since."

"Ahaaaa . . ." A deep sigh. "So few remember. I have a mind to grant you my aid in return for that exquisite moment. What is it that you desire of me?"

"Someone has summoned your sons to this plane. They have misbehaved themselves. They have done great damage."

"It is in their nature. It is what they must do. They are so young, my Ten Sons. They are the ten great *h'Haarshanns* that stride the worlds."

"That is so, Oldfather." Elric glanced down at the remains of the Nazi. As a hawk takes every part of the bird save the feathers, so Oldfather had taken the mortal, leaving nothing but the blood-soaked remains of his SS uniform. "They have been brought by my enemies from their place amongst the worlds. To threaten the lives of me and mine."

Oldfather quivered. "But without you I cannot know the exquisite taste of flesh. And my Ten Sons have business about the worlds, to breathe my will upon them."

"That is so, great Oldfather."

"None is left save you, sweet mortal. None who knows what Oldfather likes to eat."

At that moment Elric looked up. His eyes met mine. The sardonic mockery in his expression made me turn my head in disgust. I knew that Elric of Melniboné only resembled a man, that his blood was of an older, crueller kind than mine. In my own world such savage and sadistic sacrifice was only performed by the mentally ill. For Elric and his kind, those practices were a way of life, refined to an art and enjoyed as spectacle. In Melniboné praise was given to the victim who died with style and who best entertained his audience with his dying. What Elric had just done caused him no troubled conscience. The actions had been necessary and were natural to him.

Oldfather seemed to be debating the value of the sacrifice.

"Would you feast again, noble Oldfather?" Elric's voice was soft, coaxing. There was no threat in it, but Oldfather was remembering the taste of mortal flesh and was already yearning for more.

"I will see to my sons," said the apparition. "They, too, have eaten well."

The whirling scarlet fire swelled until it resembled circling cloud, sweeping up towards the cavern's faraway roof and then down into the darkness until it had disappeared, leaving the faintest of pink, dissipating light.

I looked towards Gaynor's camp. They had become aware of something. I saw troogs peering in our direction. One of them ran towards the centre of the camp where Gaynor had pitched an ostentatious tent, its guy ropes secured by pegs hammered into the living rock.

I guessed the Nazi's death to have been pointless after all. Oldfather had gone. The ten whirling inverted cones of phosphorescent light still guarded the camp. Elric's filthy ritual had done nothing but attract the attention of Gaynor's horde.

A party of troogs lumbered in our direction. They had not seen us, but it would not take them long to find where we were. I looked around for some way of escape. Only Oona had a weapon. My sword was in the hands of my doppelgänger. I was not sure I would feel quite the same emotions towards the blade in the future. If I had a future to contemplate.

The troogs were beginning to climb the rocks towards us. They could smell us.

I looked around for something to throw. The rocks were the only weapons available to me.

Glancing back, I saw that Elric had sunk to his knees totally exhausted. I wondered if I could get to the sword before the troogs reached us. If I could ever handle that blade again.

Oona nocked an arrow to her bow and took aim.

She looked once or twice over her shoulder, unable to believe that Elric had failed, that Oldfather had taken his offering and left without giving us any of the help he had seemed to promise.

I caught a glimpse of something not far from the grey horizon. A scarlet flash which began to speed towards us, coming faster and faster and making a mighty thrum, as if someone plucked the strings of an enormous guitar whose sound was amplified through all creation.

Elric scrambled up to join us. He was grinning. He panted like a wolf. He had a look of wild lust in his eyes. A look of triumph, of hunger.

He said nothing to us but looked to where the scarlet cloud was approaching. To where the Ten Sons danced at the edges of Gaynor's camp.

Then he lifted his head, raised the black runesword in a victorious gesture and began to sing.

I knew the song. I knew Elric. I had been Elric. I knew what it meant. I knew what it said. But I could not know its effect. I do not believe I ever, in all my life of concert-going, heard such extraordinary beauty. If there was menace in it, if there was triumph in it, if there was cruel exultation in it, still, it was beautiful. I felt I heard an angel sing. More than one tune, many harmonies, were all carried on that strange voice. It brought tears to my eyes. It brought grief and mourning. I was mourning the death of the man I had seen killed. I was hearing the voice of a grief which had never filled the world before.

For a moment Elric's song stopped the troogs in their tracks.

I looked at Oona. She was weeping. She understood something in her father which mystified me and perhaps, therefore, him as well.

The song swelled and I realised Ravenbrand had joined with Elric. An almost tangible sound. I felt it embracing me. I felt the complexity of it, a thousand different sensations passing through my blood and nerves all at the same time. Something in me was strengthened by that song, but physically it weakened me, and I could barely stand.

Then another song joined in, from far away, near the grey horizon. I saw shreds of scarlet light radiating from a hidden source. Fingers of scarlet, like ropes, twisting around the rocky columns, reaching across the ranks of that vast army. A gigantic hand was stretching through the cavern. The hand of God. Or the hand of Satan. The flaming hand made a fist and that fist drew in each of the Ten Sons, who whirled and buzzed in sudden fury, resisting Oldfather's discipline. The white fire scattered and raced, but the hand extended to enfold it.

All the while Gaynor's camp was in uproar. I saw a figure emerge from his tent and mount one of the blind horses. I heard bugles sounding, drums beating. Confusion reigned as partially clothed men tried to control their mounts. The blind cannibals milled around gathering their weapons. Only the troogs were wide awake. Many of them were running back into the darkness, away from the Grey Fees, while the red hand of Oldfather gathered in his wild, squealing sons. The destruction they caused as they sought to avoid him brought more rocks crashing to the cavern floor, more stones whirling into the air.

A sea of brands moved chaotically in all directions as Gaynor demanded more light.

We could see him now, on his great albino horse, its blind red eyes rolling as it snorted and scented, its ears frantic as it tried to catch the source of the sounds. Yet Gaynor controlled the stallion with one hand and his knees. The other hand held the ivory sword—the sword Miggea's magic had made. He spurred in our direction, though I doubted he had any clear idea of what was happening. His main object was to turn the fleeing troogs and savages back to the camp. His men followed on their own horses, lashing out at the foot soldiers, yelling at them and causing further panic. Two of the Nazis rode up behind the troogs who were preparing to attack us.

They had no common language. The Nazis bellowed. The troogs bellowed back.

Elric suddenly rose from cover and began running at tremendous speed down the slope towards the Nazis.

Ravenbrand was still in his right hand. The sword howled with triumphant glee as it sliced into the neck of the first SS man. Elric dragged the corpse from its saddle and took the Nazi's place, spurring the blind horse directly at the other Nazi, who was already trying to flee the way he had come. Too late.

Elric swung Ravenbrand sideways, using the sword's wonderful balance to carry the weight of a blow which neatly took the Nazi's head from its shoulders as if it had been a cabbage on a stalk. He reached down to gather up the horse's reins and then rode back, scattering troogs as he came towards us.

"Here's a mount for one of you," he said. "The other must get their own."

I held the horse for Oona. She shook her head, grinning. "I can't ride," she said. "I've never had to learn." She replaced the arrow in her quiver. The troogs had given up any idea of attacking us.

I got into the saddle. It was a good, responsive horse. I told her to climb behind me, but she laughed. "I have my own ways of travelling," she said. "Though I thank you for the courtesy."

Gaynor had seen something and was charging towards us, his men at his back, Klosterheim by his side.

I looked forward at last to confronting him man to man.

Elric turned his horse, signalling that we should ride back the way we had come. He leaned down in his saddle and picked up one of the guttering brands. He handed it to me, then sought another for himself. The horses were excited. They wanted to gallop. I knew it would be dangerous in this darkness, but my cousin was gaining on us. He had become a far more expert rider in this bizarre landscape than I could hope to be.

I looked around for Oona. She had vanished.

Elric yelled for me to follow. I had no choice.

I cried out for him to stop, to wait for his daughter, but he laughed when he heard me and signalled me on.

He did not fear for her. I could only trust him.

We plunged into the booming darkness as the Ten Sons whirled their last ahead of us. All had been taken up in that one great red fist and were buzzing and whirring like wasps as the fingers moulded and moulded, turning the powerful, white light into something resembling a ball and hurling it upwards, higher and higher, until a moon hung overhead. Then it became a star. A point of light. And then it was gone.

A grumbling growl from the red cloud and Oldfather, too, vanished. Only Elric and myself remained, urging our horses into the blackness towards Mu-Ooria, while Gaynor and his men, howling for our blood, came thundering behind us.

We followed the rough road the Ten Sons had carved, leaping broken columns, weaving between piles of rubble. Had I not known otherwise, I would have sworn the horses were sighted, they were so sure-footed. Perhaps they had developed some of the qualities of bats. In a moment of humour I wished they had developed bat wings.

I was distracted by something white moving ahead of me along the broad road. The white hare raced as fast as it was possible to go. Towards the distant towers of Mu-Ooria. I refused to let myself believe the obvious. I told myself that the white hare had found us again, that it had followed us from Tanelorn, when Miggea's hunt had chased it into our territory.

But Elric was grinning as he pursued it. For a moment I thought he was hunting it, but he kept behind it. He was following the beast.

Behind us came Gaynor, shouting like an angry ape, his own voice echoing in that mysterious helm, his cloak swirling about him like an agitated ocean, his horse's red eyes glaring sightlessly forward. He held up the ivory sword like a flag. The ragged remains of his SS guard were close behind him. Only Klosterheim, gaunt and hollow-eyed as ever, showed no emotion. At one moment, even that far away, I caught his grim, sardonic eye. In his own dark way, he was enjoying his master's discomfort.

"There's more to do yet," said Elric.

He looked back at the furious Gaynor and laughed.

For the first time I began to believe that perhaps he was not mad. At least, not in the way I had thought. His daughter thought him a genius. Presumably she believed him greater than most other sorcerers. His reckless courage might have been madness in another, but not in him. He could command power as no other mortal being could. And what was more, as I had witnessed, his alliances went back through generations upon generations, blood upon blood, when his own ancient people had been young and the world was not entirely formed.

For all his predatory skills, Elric was not by nature a predator. That differentiated him from his own people. Perhaps this was the bond all three of us shared.

"Fool!" Elric cried, dropping back to let my cousin gain on him. "Did you think I would allow an amateur sorcerer to invade the Grey Fees? I am Elric, last emperor of Melniboné, and I accept no insult from a mere man-beast. Everything you believe you have gained I will take from you. Everything you believe you have destroyed will be restored. Every victory will become defeat."

"And I am Gaynor, who has mastered the Lords of Law and Chaos! You cannot defeat me!"

"You are deluded," shouted my doppelgänger almost merrily. "I care not what a man-beast calls itself. You have known a lucky moment. You should have made better use of it while you had it."

Elric turned his back on Gaynor and urged his horse to a faster pace. I was barely able to keep up with him but was astonished at the agility of my mount. It sensed all obstacles ahead. Our brands guttered in a sudden current and threatened to go out altogether, but the horses galloped on. Gaynor was fast catching up with us, following the light we made. When the torches flared back to life, I caught a sudden glimpse of Oona. The dreamthief's daughter was standing to one side, gesturing to us. Elric extinguished his torch and gestured for me to do the same.

We heard Gaynor and his men galloping behind us. We saw the ragged light of their torches. They were almost on us and I was not sure Elric still had enough energy to engage so many. Without a sword, I would be killed or captured immediately.

I saw the faintest circle of light ahead. I could still hear Gaynor and his Nazi band. They were closer. Then, quite suddenly, the sound dropped away, distant, faint, and the light ahead grew a little brighter. We were riding down a kind of natural tunnel, following the swift-footed white hare. The roof of the tunnel reflected the light. It was mottled, like a book's marbling, like mother-of-pearl. The noise of Gaynor and his army was gone completely.

We had not come this way. I realised that Elric—or the white hare—did not intend to return to Mu-Ooria, at least not immediately. After a while, the Prince of Melniboné lit his torch again. I lit my own. We were reaching the end of the tunnel.

The tunnel led downwards, opening into a great circular cavern which had clearly once been inhabited by human beings. Rotting remains of clothing and old utensils suggested that the occupants had been killed while away from their home. It looked as if a whole tribe had lived here. Everything spoke of sudden disaster. But Elric was not interested in the previous tenants. He lifted his torch to inspect the cavern, seemed satisfied enough and dismounted.

I heard a movement behind me and looked back. Oona stood there, leaning upon her bowstaff. I did not ask what magic had brought her here. Or what magic she had used to bring us here. I did not believe I needed to ask or to know.

Leaving the brands burning in the wall holes clearly designed for the purpose, Elric signalled for me to dismount and follow him back to the entrance of the tunnel. He wanted to be certain Gaynor had not found us. We moved cautiously, expecting to see our pursuers, but we had evaded them. Outside it was pitch-black. I heard Elric sniff. I felt his hand tugging me to go with him.

We moved through utter darkness, but Elric was sure-footed, using his ears as well as his nose. I was again struck by our differences. He was Melnibonéan. His senses were far sharper than my own.

When he was entirely satisfied that Gaynor and his men had ridden on, with no idea of where we had hidden ourselves, he led me back to the tunnel and into the huge cave, where Oona was already busying herself with a fire and the food we had taken from the troog.

We ate sparingly. Elric sat some distance away. Frowning, wolfish. Clearly deep in thought, he did not wish to be disturbed. Oona and I exchanged a few words. She reassured me. We were not merely hiding, she said. We needed a place such as this. More sorcery was required. She was not sure how long her father could continue to find energy, from whatever source, to carry on. There was too much to be done, she murmured. She was careful to make sure that her father could not hear us.

When we had finished, Elric signed for us to get up and go outside. When he was sure Gaynor was no longer in the region, he told me to bring the horses. The three of us set off into the darkness, following a small, slow-burning taper which Elric held to guide us. We rode for miles over the rocky cavern floor until he stopped. Another cautious pause, then he took out one of our brands and lit it. This part of the underground world had not seen the movement of Gaynor's army. It was as still, as untouched, as it had always been. But where a group of stalagmites formed what looked like a circle of Off-Moo heads bent in prayer, I saw a body.

One of the big black cats the troogs feared, which Gaynor had somehow enchanted.

The thing was huge. Elric went up to it and attempted to lift it. Oona joined him, and then I. We were just able to get the beast off the floor of the cavern.

"We must take it back with us," the Melnibonéan said. "We'll use the horses."

The horses were not happy being so close to one of the panthers, let alone being used to transport it. We managed to make a sling and, with many minor pitfalls, finally succeeded in getting the huge body back to our hiding place.

Oona and I were exhausted, but Elric was filled with an edgy excitement. He anticipated with some pleasure what he had to do.

"Why have we brought this beast here?" I ventured.

His answer was dismissive.

"A further Summoning," he said. "But first we shall need an appropriate sacrifice."

I looked at Oona.

Did he intend to kill one of us?

18

Old Debts and New Dreams

Oona nodded briefly and ran from the cave. Elric let her go. He paid no attention to me. I wondered if this was because he did not wish to improve his relationship with one whom he might soon need to kill. Ironic, I thought, if my own sword drank my soul.

After a time, he got up, took a horse, and began to walk back towards the entrance.

"Do you wish me to stay here?" I asked him.

"As you please," he said.

So I followed him. My curiosity was far stronger than any fear that he might turn on me.

He had mounted and urged the horse forward through the darkness. Happily my own beast was inclined to follow its companion. By this means, I kept pace with the Melnibonéan.

At last the lights of Gaynor's camp could be seen again. It was still in confusion. We heard shouts and curses. Elric dismounted, handed me his reins and told me to wait. Then he made his way cautiously down towards the camp.

Fires had been extinguished and it was by no means as easy to see as it had been. But soon I began to hear shouts and the wild, pleading cries, and I knew that Elric was replenishing his energy.

Some while later, his white face suddenly appeared from the darkness. His glittering, ruby eyes had a hot, satisfied look, and his lips were partly open as he panted like a well-fed wolf. I could see the blood on his lips.

Blood caked the black blade he held in his right hand. I knew it had taken a score of souls to satisfy both flesh and iron.

We rode back in silence and were not followed. I had the impression that Gaynor and his men were still riding the vast caverns of Mu-Ooria, perhaps believing the last lord of Melniboné to have returned to the ruined city.

Elric said nothing as he led the way through the blackness. He hunched over his saddle, still breathing slowly, a sated predator. As close as we were, both in mind and blood, I found myself shuddering at this obscenity. Too much of my own blood was human, not enough Melnibonéan, for me to relish the sight of my kinsman or ancestor or whatever he was absorbing the souls he had stolen.

But what black souls they had been! I heard myself saying. Did they not serve some better purpose now? Did they not deserve to die in this perverse and terrible way, given the crimes they had already committed, the blasphemies they had performed?

It was not in my civilised Christian soul to rejoice. I could only mourn the destruction of so many in such an ungodly cause.

Once I thought I had lost Elric and lit my taper. Then I saw the creature's demonic face, his glaring red eyes, his disgusted mouth telling me to put the light out. He was irritated by me in the way a man might be irritated by a badly trained dog. I saw nothing human in that face. I had been stupid, nonetheless. Gaynor must even now be returning from the city, having failed to find us. A tiny light in this blackness would be seen for miles.

Only when we had found the tunnel again did Elric allow me to light my way.

Oona had clearly been sleeping when we returned. She darted a mysterious, concerned look at her father and another at me. I could say nothing to her. I could tell her nothing. A vampiric symbiosis existed between man and blade. Who could tell which fed the other? I guessed she was already familiar with these characteristics. Her mother would have told her, if she had not observed them for herself by now.

Elric stumbled to the centre of the cave where we had arranged the huge bulk of the black cat. He pressed his head against the body, against the thing's gigantic skull. He muttered and busied himself. Oona could not answer my unspoken question. She watched in fascination as her father walked around the great beast, muttering, making passages in the air with his hand, as if trying to remember a spell.

Perhaps he was doing exactly that.

After a while he looked up, directly into our faces. "I shall need your help in this." He spoke almost impatiently, in self-disgust. He must have been surprised by his own continuing weakness. Perhaps the kind of sorcery he had already performed drained him more than he expected.

I knew I had no choice in the matter. "What do you want?"

"Nothing yet. I'll tell you when it's time." His expression, when he looked at his daughter, was almost pitying. I'm not sure if I imagined it, but I thought she moved a little closer to me for comfort.

Elric seemed to be in pain. Every muscle on his body appeared independently alive for a moment. Then he subsided into sweating stillness. His eyes glared up into worlds—and their creatures—far beyond my understanding. The words, as I heard them, meant little, even though another part of me knew their meaning all too well.

One word had special resonance—*Meerclar*—*Meerclar*—*Meerclar*—he repeated it over and over. A name. It meant more than that. It meant a friend. A bond. Something resembling affection. Old blood. Ancient ties . . . And more. It meant bargains. Bargains struck to last for eternity. Bargains struck in blood and souls. Bargains between one unhuman creature and another.

Meerclar! The word was louder, sharper.

MEERCLAR! His face blazed like burning ivory. His eyes were living coals. His long, wild hair seethed about him like a living thing. One hand held Ravenbrand on high. The other clutched at the air, describing geometries which existed in a thousand dimensions.

MEERCLAR! GREAT LORD OF FANG AND CLAW! *MEERCLAR!* YOUR CHILDREN SUFFER. AID THEM, MEERCLAR! AID THEM IN THE NAME OF OUR ANCIENT COMPACT!

MEERCLAR! The vocal cords strained and twisted to pronounce the name. His body pitched and shook like a ship in a typhoon. He was hardly in control of it. Yet all the while he spoke and kept his grip on the black sword.

A yowl from somewhere. A deep animal stink. The thrumming of breath. A swish, as of a feline tail.

MEERCLAR! SEKHMET'S FAVOURITE SON! BORN OF OUR UNION. BORN OF THE COMING TOGETHER OF LIFE AND DEATH. *MEERCLAR*, LORD OF THE CATS, HONOUR OUR COVENANT!

The body of the huge panther in the centre of the cavern twitched and stretched. A massive puff rolled from its chest. The whiskers straightened. But the eyes did not open and soon the cat was prone again, as if something had sought to animate it and failed.

MEERCLAR!

He summoned that most conservative of creatures, that least tractable of elementals, Meerclar, Son of Sekhmet, the archetype of all cats.

My doppelgänger howled like a gale. His voice rose and fell in a series of shrieks and groans which shook the walls of our cave and must surely be heard outside, where Gaynor searched for us.

I realised Oona had vanished. Had Elric taken his own daughter for a sacrifice? I would have believed anything at that moment.

The horses, already frightened, began to buck and whinny, retreating as far as they could from a dark shadow forming near the distant wall. A shadow that moved back and forth, like a pacing beast. A shadow that lifted a great head, gave voice, quintessentially feline, and began to harmonise with Elric.

A great black figure, tall and broad, but standing on two legs and looking down at us as it materialised, uttered a huge, growling purr and dropped to all fours. The eyes bore an intelligence older than Elric's. The handsome, wedge-shaped head was fierce with jutting whiskers, fangs and glowing yellow-and-black eyes. The monstrous tail lashed and threatened to destroy the remains of the abandoned living quarters. The huge claws flexed and withdrew, flexed and withdrew. I wondered if this mighty supernatural cat had eaten. For all my own natural affinity with the species, I was nervous. I knew that cats had little sense of regret or of consequence, and this one might eat us casually, without malice or even hunger.

This was Meerclar, Lord of the Cats. His image flickered a little, in and out of the various realities he inhabited. I had become used to witnessing this phenomenon in creatures which lived in more than one of time's dimensions.

I feared for Oona. She was nowhere to be seen. Lord Meerclar had the air of a cat which had recently feasted.

Had Oona not told me earlier that one of the great panthers was her avatar in this world? But what was the white hare?

How many avatars could a dreamthief possess?

How many lives?

Elric addressed Lord Meerclar. The great elemental's deep voice rumbled in response as Elric recounted what had happened. How Lord Meerclar's own kin had been entranced and put into a slumber that must ultimately kill them as they starved.

At this the mighty cat began to show some agitation. It paced on all fours, tail lashing, breath grumbling. Then it sat, in thought, claws flexing.

In the far corner, the terrified horses no longer snorted and dilated their eyes. They stood frozen, perhaps certain that they must soon become Lord Meerclar's prey.

I was scarcely more active. I watched as Elric reversed the sword. He placed his two hands on the hilt and stood with his legs wide apart staring up into the cat elemental's huge face, still speaking in those same strange tones.

I was shocked, therefore, when I felt something warm and damp upon my neck. Turning, I looked straight into the muzzle of the panther, which I had assumed was dead. The big cat narrowed his eyes and a vast purr vibrated from his chest. I felt his spittle on my face, felt the heat of him against my body.

In an extraordinary gesture of submission, the great panther crossed to Meerclar and Elric, laid his head between his paws, and looked up into Meerclar's face.

A mighty purr escaped the Lord of the Cats, as of profound satisfaction, and the panther rose, stretched, turned and trotted from the chamber. The beast looked as if it had just risen from a quick nap.

Oona was still nowhere to be seen. I had an impulse to follow the panther. Meerclar then stretched his huge muscles, his eyes narrowed, and he said something in his own language which I could not hear.

Elric was showing signs of considerable strain. His limbs shook. He could barely stand up. His eyes had begun to take on a glazed look. His face was harrowed. I moved towards him, to help him, but he saw me and signed me back.

The huge yellow eyes turned on me. They regarded me with dispassionate curiosity. I knew what it must be like to be a mouse in such a situation. All I could do was make a courteous bow and retreat.

This seemed to satisfy Lord Meerclar, who returned his attention to Elric. He was purring again, his pleasure the result of whatever it was Elric had done. He praised my doppelgänger. He expressed a kind of gratitude. Something seemed to embrace the Melnibonéan. And then the Lord of the Cats became smoke. And vanished.

"Where is Oona?" I wanted to know. Elric tried to speak. His eyes lost focus. I caught him as he fell, the great iron sword clattering to the floor. I thought the spell-making had taken too much. I thought it had killed him.

But I found a pulse. I checked his eyes. He was in a swoon, perhaps a supernatural trance brought about by his contact with the elementals. He was breathing heavily, as if drugged. I had seen men in alcoholic stupor, and others who had imbibed the famous Mickey Finn, who seemed more lively. However, I was convinced he would not die immediately.

I considered going out of the cave again and seeking Oona, but common sense told me she was better able to look after herself. And if, as I suspected, she could change her shape—to that, specifically, of a white hare—she was out there somewhere. Unless she had, indeed, been given as hostage to Meerclar. He might regard her, after all, as one of his own. And he might have demanded that she return home with him.

A noise came from the tunnel. At first I assumed the panther had made it. Then I identified it more clearly. The sound of horses' hoofs, the clatter of harness and weaponry, of metal and leather. Warriors riding towards us. Could they be the original inhabitants, come to reclaim their own quarters? It did not seem likely.

We had no other way out of the cave and the man who might have saved us lay in an exhausted slumber on the rocky floor. Oona, who could have defended us with her bow, was also gone. I had no weapon.

I knelt beside Elric, trying to wake him, but he would not stir. His breathing was long, like that of a hibernating animal, and I could not see his eyes. He was completely unconscious.

I reached reluctantly towards the Raven Sword, still lying near his right hand. Even as the tips of my fingers touched that strange, living iron, light came brawling into the cave. A mounted man with a brand. Another behind him. And another.

Our own horses whinnied and pranced in recognition. The other horses snorted and stamped on the floor of the cave. A coarse voice said something in German.

My fingers closed on the sword's familiar hilt. The torchlight half blinded me, but I climbed to my feet, using the sword to help me. I looked up and recognised the armoured outline. Gaynor, of course, had found us. No doubt he or one of his men had seen my foolish light or the panther leaving the cave entrance and investigated.

Gaynor's unhappy laughter boomed in his helm. "This will make a splendid tomb for the pair of you. A shame you will lie here unknown and forgotten for the rest of eternity."

He was a splendid figure in his silvery armour, a black sword on his left hip and the mysterious ivory sword on his right. He had a glow about him that I could only believe was supernatural. His flesh had a look of exaggerated health. He swaggered in the joy of it all and mocked the feeble thing I was.

Or had been.

My anger outweighed my fear. I reached and drew Ravenbrand to me. I held my old sword in my two hands. I felt its familiar balance, coupled with an unfamiliar power. I snarled at him. As I gripped the sword, some of that filthy, stolen vitality coursed into me. It filled my veins with dark energy. It filled them with evil strength. Now I was laughing, also. Laughing back at my cousin Gaynor Paul von Minct and relishing his doom.

Part of me was troubled by how I was behaving, but something of Elric was in me now and the sword responded to that.

"Greetings, Gaynor," I found myself saying. "I thank you for your courtesy in saving me the trouble of tracking you down. Now I shall kill you."

Gaynor laughed in turn as he saw the prone Melnibonéan. I suppose I must have looked a little odd, dressed in my tattered twentieth-century clothes, holding the great iron battle-blade in two hands. But his laughter wasn't as confident as it might have been and Klosterheim, beside him, was not at all amused. He had not expected to find two of us.

"Well, cousin," Gaynor said, leaning on his pommel, "you've come to prefer the darkness to the light, I see. Selective ignorance was always a trait of your side of the family, eh?"

I ignored this. "You have done a great deal of killing since we last met, Prince Gaynor. You appear to have slaughtered an entire race."

"Oh, the Off-Moo! Who's to tell, cousin? Who's to tell? They suffered the delusion common to all isolated peoples. They decided that because they had never been conquered, they were invulnerable. The British have the same delusion in your world, do they not?"

I was not here to discuss imperial delusions or the philosophy of isolationism. I was here to kill him. A completely unfamiliar bloodlust was rising in me. I felt it take me in its grip. Not a pleasant sensation for one of my basic disposition. Was it a response to Gaynor's threats? Or was the sword transferring to me what it had earlier transferred to Elric?

I trembled with the excess energy which pulsed through me. Now came unexpected desires of all kinds, all forming one single directive in my mind— kill Gaynor and any who rode with him. I anticipated the sweet slicing of the sword into flesh, the impact of the bone as it shattered under sharpened steel which slipped through muscles and sinew as smoothly as a spoon through soup, leaving red ruin behind. I anticipated the relish I would know as a human life was taken to feed my own greedy soul. I licked my lips. I regarded Gaynor's followers as so much food and Gaynor himself the tastiest choice of all. I could feel my own hot breath panting in my throat, the saliva, blood as salt, on my tongue and I had begun to scent at the men and beasts before me, recognising each individual by their specific smell. I could smell their blood, their flesh, their sweat. I could even smell the tears as I took my first Nazi and he wept briefly for his mortal soul as I sucked it from him.

The yelling in the cave, the stamp of the horses and the clash of metal, echoed everywhere. It was impossible to tell where all my enemies were. I killed two before I realised it and their souls went to strengthen me, so that I moved with even greater speed, the sword writhing and turning in my hands like a living creature, killing, killing, killing. Killing, while I laughed my wolf's laugh and dedicated my victims to eternal service with Duke Arioch of Chaos.

Gaynor, typically, had thrown his men to the front. Within the confines of that cavern I could not easily reach either him or Klosterheim. I had to hack my way through men and horses.

I saw my cousin pull something from within his clothing. A golden staff, raging with fiery light, as if all the life of all the worlds was contained within. He held it before him as one might hold a weapon and then, from his scabbard, he drew Stormbringer, the blade he had stolen from my doppelgänger, brother to the Raven Sword I now held.

It did not alarm me. I leaped and sliced and was almost upon my cousin as he took in his reins, cursing at me, the Runestaff returned to his shirt, the black blade howling. I knew that the blade could not be resheathed until it had taken souls. That was the bargain one always made with such a sword.

Urging his men forward, the Knight of the Balance turned his great pale horse back into the tunnel and yelled for Klosterheim to follow. But I was between him and Klosterheim, who was grappling at his horse's reins. I swung my sword upwards, trying to get through his guard. Every time I struck, the Raven Sword was countered by Stormbringer. By now both swords were howling like wolves and shrieking as they clashed, their red runes rippling up and down the black iron like static electricity. And that hideous strength still flowed into my veins.

Gaynor was neither laughing nor cursing. He was screaming.

Something happened to him every time the two swords crossed.

He began to blaze with an eery crimson fire. The fire burned only briefly, and when it went out, Gaynor looked even more drawn.

Metal met metal with a terrible clang and every time the same fire raged through Gaynor.

I did not understand what was happening, but I pressed my advantage.

Then, to my astonishment, my cousin let go of the black sword and his left hand reached for the ivory blade, scabbarded on his opposite hip.

For some reason this amused me. I swung a further arc of iron and he bent backwards, barely avoiding it. The ivory sword met the black and for a moment it was as if I had hit a wall at sixty miles an hour. I was instantly stopped. The black sword continued to moan and its remaining energy still passed into me, but the white sword had countered it. I swung again. Gaynor, untriumphant but clearly glad enough to survive, spurred his horse into the darkness of the passage, Klosterheim and the remains of his band fast behind him.

I was suddenly too weak to continue after them. My own legs buckled. I was paying the price for all that unexpected power.

I tried to keep my senses, knowing that Gaynor would immediately take advantage of me if he knew that I, like Elric, had collapsed.

I could do nothing to save myself.

I stumbled deeper into the cavern, now a charnel house of dead horses and human corpses, and tried to reach Elric, to revive him, to warn him of what was happening.

My pale hand reached out towards his white, unresponsive face, and then I was absorbed by darkness, vulnerable to anything that now desired my life.

I heard my name being called. I guessed it was Gaynor, returning to have his revenge upon me.

I took a fresh grip on the sword, but the energy no longer filled me. I had paid my price for what it had given me. It had paid its price to me.

I remember thinking, sardonically, that the account was now fully closed.

But I looked up into Oona's face, not Gaynor's. Had any time passed? I could still smell the blood and torn flesh, the ordure of savage battling. I could feel cold iron against my hand. But I was too weak to rise. She lifted me. She gave me water and some kind of drug which set my veins to shaking before I drew a long, deep breath and was able to get to my feet.

"Gaynor?"

"Already witnessing the destruction of his army," she said. She had an air of satisfaction. I had the impression her lips were bloody. Then she licked them, like a cat, and they were clean.

"How so? The Off-Moo?"

"Meerclar's children," she said. "All the panthers were revived. They wasted no time hunting down their favourite prey. The troogs are dead or fled and most of the savages have gone back to their old territories. Gaynor can no longer protect them against their traditional enemies. They would be going to their instant doom if they followed him into the Grey Fees."

"So he cannot conquer the Grey Fees?"

"He believes he has the power to do it without his army. For he has the white sword and he has the cup. These he believes contain the power of Law, and he believes the power of Law will give him the Grey Fees."

"Even I know that's madness!" I began to walk unsteadily to where the Melnibonéan was still lying. Now, however, he had the air of a man experiencing ordinary sleep. "What can we do to stop him?"

"There's a chance," she said quietly, "that he cannot be stopped. Just by introducing those two great objects of power into the Grey Fees he could unbalance the entire multiverse, sending it spinning to its eternal destruction and all living, feeling creatures with it."

"One man?" I said. "One mortal?"

"Whatever happens," she said, "it is predicted that the fate of the multiverse shall depend upon the actions of one mortal man. That encourages Gaynor. He thinks he is the mortal chosen for that honour."

"Why should he not be?"

"Because another has already been chosen," she said.

"Do you know who it is?"

"Yes."

I waited, but she said no more. She leaned over her father, testing for his pulse, checking his eyes, just as I had earlier. She shook her head. "Exhausted," she said. "Nothing else. Too much sorcery, even for him." She rolled up a cloak and put it under his head. It was a strange, rather touching gesture. All around us was death and destruction. Spilled blood was everywhere, yet Elric's daughter behaved almost as if she kissed a child goodnight in its own bed.

She picked up Stormbringer and resheathed it for him. Only then did I realise I still held Ravenbrand in my hand. Oona had found Elric's sword where Gaynor had hurled it when it turned on him and instead of giving him strength burned up what remained of his energy.

"Well," I said, "at least we have the stolen sword back."

Oona nodded reflectively. "Yes," she said, "Gaynor must change his plans."

"Why didn't Stormbringer feed off him earlier?"

"By betraying Miggea, he also lost her help. He seemed to think he would be able to keep it, in spite of her being a prisoner. She has to be able to exert her will in order to aid him, and he ensured that she could not."

I heard a mumble and looked to where Elric lay. He stirred. His lips formed words, tiny sounds. Troubled sounds. The sounds of a distant nightmare.

Oona laid her cool hand upon her father's forehead. The Melnibonéan immediately breathed more regularly and his body no longer twitched and trembled.

When, eventually, he opened his eyes, they were full of wise intelligence.

"At last," he said. "The tide can be turned." His hand went to the handle of his runesword and caressed it. I had the feeling she had somehow communicated everything that had happened to him. Or did he get it telepathically from me?

"Perhaps it can be, Father." Oona looked around her, as if seeing the signs of battle for the first time. "But I fear it will take more resources than we can summon now."

The Prince of Melniboné began to rise. I offered him my arm. He hesitated, then took it with an expression of profound irony on his face.

"So now we are both whole men again," he said.

I was impatient with this. "I need to know what unique qualities that staff or cup—or whatever it is—and that white sword have. Why are we fighting for possession of them? What do they represent to Gaynor?"

Elric and Oona stared at me in some surprise. They had concealed nothing deliberately from me. They had simply not thought to tell me.

"They exist in your own legends," said Oona. "Your family protected them on your plane. That is your traditional duty. According to your legends the Grail is a cup with magical properties, which can restore life and can only be beheld in its true, pure form by a knight of equally true and pure soul. The sword is the traditional sword which bestows great nobility upon its wielder, if used in a noble cause. It has been called many names. It was lost and Gaynor sought it. Klosterheim got it from Bek. Miggea told him that if he bore both the black sword and the white and took them, together with the Grail, into the Grey Fees, he would be able to set his will upon existence. He could re-create the multiverse."

I found this incredible. "He believed such nonsense?"

Oona hesitated. Then she said: "He believed it."

I thought for a moment. I was a twentieth-century man. How could I give any credibility to such mythical tomfoolery? Perhaps all I was doing was dreaming after hearing some overblown piece of Sturm und Drang. Was I trapped in the story of *Parsifal*, *The Flying Dutchman* and *Götterdämmerung* all at the same time? Of course it was impossible to pursue such logic. Not only had I been party to Elric's past, his entire experience of the sorcerous realms, but I recollected everything I had seen since escaping from the Nazi concentration camp. From the moment my sword clove the cliff of Hameln, I had accepted the laws of wizardry.

I began to laugh. Not the mad laughter I'd offered Gaynor, but natural, good-humoured self-mockery.

"And why should he not have done?" I said. "Why should he not believe anything he chooses?"

19

Beyond the Grey Fees

"We must follow Gaynor," said Oona. "Somehow we must stop him."

"His soldiers are scattered or destroyed," I said. "What harm can he do?"

"A great deal," she said. "He still has a sword and the Grail."

Elric confirmed this. "If we are swift, we could stop him reaching the Grey Fees. If we do that, we shall all be free of his ambitions. But the Fees are malleable—subject to human will, it's said. If that will is complemented with Gaynor's new power . . ."

Oona was striding for the tunnel. She disappeared into the shadows. "Follow me," she said. "I'll find him."

We mounted wearily, Elric and I. Each of us had a black runesword at his belt. For the first time since this affair started, there was real hope we could capture Gaynor before he did further damage. Perhaps I was stupid to believe that the ownership of a sword conferred a sense of self-respect upon me, but I now felt Elric's equal. Not just the sword, but what I had done with it made me proud to ride beside the gloomy prince of ruins in pursuit of a kinsman still capable of destroying the fundamental matter of existence.

That I should feel self-respect as a result of killing almost half a score of my fellow human beings was a mark of what I had become since my capture by the Nazis. I, who in common with most of my family, abhorred war and was disgusted by mankind's willingness to kill their own so readily, in such numbers and with such abandon, was now as thoroughly blooded as any of the Nazis we fought here in the world of Mu-Ooria. And the strongest thing I felt was satisfaction. I looked forward to killing the rest.

In a way the Nazis' rejection of traditional humanism led to their appalling fates. It is one thing to mock the subtle infrastructures of a civil society, to claim they serve no purpose, but quite another to tear them down. Only when they were gone did we realise how much our safety and sanity and civic well-being depended on them. This fascist lesson is learned over and over again, even into modern times.

Emerging from the tunnel with guttering torches we saw ahead of us one of the panthers awakened by Elric's sorcery. The beast turned bright knowing eyes on us. It was leading us through the caverns, searching, I was certain, for my cousin Gaynor.

Was the panther Oona? Or was the beast mentally controlled by my doppelgänger's daughter? Mystified, we could do nothing save trust the beast as it padded ahead of us, occasionally looking back to make sure we followed.

I was half expecting another ambush from a furious Gaynor. My cousin would be considering his revenge on us already. But I soon realised he would no longer be flinging an army into the Grey Fees. His army had been destroyed.

As if to demonstrate this destruction, the panther led us straight through Gaynor's camp. The big cats had done their work swiftly and efficiently. Ruined troog bodies lay everywhere, most with their throats torn out. The savages had also been attacked, but clearly a great many of them had fled back to their own territories. I doubted if Gaynor would be able to raise another army from their ranks.

A weird howling came from behind us, as if jackals mourned their own kind, and then from around a huge stalagmite rode Gaynor. Klosterheim and the remains of his men followed him, though not with enthusiasm. Gaynor whirled the great ivory runesword around his head, bearing down on us with single-minded hatred. I could not tell if the sounds came from him or the blade.

Elric and I acted as one.

Our swords were in our hands. Their murmuring became a shrill whine modifying to a full-throated howl which made the white blade's sound seem feeble.

Gaynor had become used to unchallenged power. He seemed surprised by this resistance, in spite of his recent experience. He tugged on his reins, bringing his horse to a skidding turn and urged his men towards us.

Once again I felt the battle-frenzy in my veins. I felt it threatening to take over my entire being. Beside me Elric was laughing as he spurred towards the leading rider. The howling of his sword changed, first to triumph as it bit into its victim's breast, then to a satiated murmur as it drank the man's soul.

My own black battle-blade twisted in my hand, thrusting forward before I could react, taking the next rider in the head, shearing off half his skull in the process. And again the sword drank, uttering a thirsty croon as the Nazi's life-essence poured into it and mixed with mine. Those who lived by the sword, I thought . . . The idea took on an entirely new meaning. I saw Klosterheim and urged my horse towards him. Elric and Gaynor were fighting on horseback, sword against sword. Two more of Gaynor's men came at me. I swung the heavy sword—it moved like a pendulum—and took the first rider in the side, the second, as I swung back behind me, in the thigh. As the first died, I finished the second. Their soulless remains slumped like so much butcher's meat in their saddles. I found myself laughing at this. I turned again and met the crazed ruby blaze of Elric's own eyes, my eyes, glaring back at me.

Gaynor jumped his horse over a pile of bodies and turned, the Runestaff held in his gauntleted hand. "You cannot kill me while I hold this. You are fools to try. And while I hold this—I hold the key to all Creation!"

Elric and I did not have horses capable of jumping so high. We were forced to ride around the pile of corpses while Klosterheim and the three remaining Nazis interposed themselves between us and our quarry.

"I'm no longer Knight of the Balance," Gaynor raved, "I am Creator of All Existence!" Lifting the white sword and the Runestaff over his head, he spurred his horse, galloping off into the misty blackness, leaving his followers to slow our pursuit.

I took no pleasure in that killing. Only Klosterheim escaped, disappearing soundlessly amongst the great pillars. I made to go after him, but Elric stopped me. "Gaynor must be our only prey." He pointed. "Let her guide us. She can follow his scent."

The panther padded on without pause and our tireless blind horses trotted behind it.

Once I thought I heard Gaynor's laughter, the galloping of hoofs, and then I saw a blaze of golden light as if the Grail signalled its own abduction. The pearly grey of the horizon grew wider and taller ahead of us until its light spread like a gentle blanket of mist over the whole vast forest of stone. The air had grown noticeably cooler and there was a clean quality to it I could not identify. For a while that featureless grey field filled me with utter terror. I looked upon endless nothingness. The finale of the multiverse. Limbo.

The calmness of it frightened me. But the fear began to disappear and was replaced by an equally strong sense of reconciliation, of peace. I had been here before, after all. None of these emotions affected the course of our actions, however, for the blind horses bore us relentlessly on. The panther continued to lead us and gradually, without any dramatic event, we found ourselves slowly absorbed into the gentle grey mist.

The mist had a substantial quality to it. I could not rid myself of the sense that Gaynor and Klosterheim might rush on us suddenly from ambush. Even when, for a few brief moments, the air ahead of us was filled with the brilliant scarlet and green of huge, delicate amaryllis blooms and creamy iris, I did not drop my guard.

"What was that?" I asked Elric.

The sorcerer offered me a crooked smile. "I don't know. Someone's sudden thought?"

Had those shapes been formed spontaneously by the strange, rich mist? I felt the stuff could create recognisable shapes at any moment. While I had expected something more spectacular from the legendary Grey Fees, I was relieved that it was not the roiling tangled strands of Chaos others had led me to expect. I had the feeling I would only have to concentrate to see my own most bizarre imaginings made concrete. I scarcely dared think of Gaynor and Klosterheim for fear of conjuring them into being!

The sound of our horses, of our harness, of our very breathing, seemed amplified by the mist. The panther's outline was half-hidden by it, but remained just in view, a shadow. Whether we rode on rock or hard earth was impossible to tell now, for the pewter-coloured fog engulfed the horses to their bellies, washing around them like quicksilver.

The ground beneath us became softer, a turf, and the sounds were more muffled. A silence was gradually dominating us. The tension was still considerable. I spoke briefly to Elric. My voice seemed to be snatched away, deadened.

"We've lost him, eh? He's escaped into the Fees. And that, I understand, is a disaster."

When he replied I was not sure if he spoke or if I read his mind. "It makes the task more difficult."

Everything was becoming less certain, less defined, no doubt a quality of the Grey Fees. It was supposed to be, after all, the unformed fundamental stuff of the multiverse. But no matter how obscured, the panther remained in sight. Our path remained constant. Gaynor remained a threat.

The panther stopped without warning. It lifted its handsome face, sniffing, listening, one paw raised. The tail lashed. The eyes narrowed. Something perturbed the great black cat. It hesitated.

Elric dismounted, wading chest-high through the mist to where the panther stood. The mist thickened and I lost sight of him for a moment. When I next saw him he was talking to a human figure. I thought at first we had found Gaynor.

The figure turned and came back with him. Oona carried her bow and her quiver over her shoulder. She might have been taking a casual stroll. Her grin was challenging and told me to ask no questions.

I still did not know if she was a sorceress, an illusionist, or if she merely controlled the movements of the panther or the hare. I had no clear idea of the magic involved. I was now perfectly prepared to accept that it was indeed magic that I witnessed. These people manipulated the multiverse in ways which were normal for them but which were totally mystifying to me. Once I realised that my own familiar twentieth century seemed a world of bizarre, chaotic mechanical invention to others, as mysterious to them as theirs was to me, that it still represented a terrifying conundrum to demigods able to manipulate worlds with their own mental powers, I began to accept for its own sake everything I experienced. I did not attempt, as some lunatic map-maker might, to impose the grid of my own limited experience and imagination upon all this complexity. I had no wish, indeed, to make *any* mark on it. I preferred to explore and watch and feel. The only way to understand it at all was to experience it.

The pearly mist continued to swirl around us as I joined Oona and Elric. The Grey Fees I had crossed before had been more populous. She frowned, puzzled. "This is not," she said almost disapprovingly, "my natural element."

"Which way have they gone?" I asked. "Do you still have their scent, Lady Oona?"

"Too much of it," she said. She dropped to one knee and made a sweep with her left hand, as if clearing a window. Her gesture revealed a bright, sunny scene. "See!"

A scene I immediately recognised.

I gasped and moved forward, reaching towards that gap in the mist. I felt I'd been given my childhood back. But she restrained me. "I know," she said. "It is Bek. But I do not think it is your salvation, Count Ulric."

"What do you mean?"

She turned to her right and cleared another space in the mist. All was red and black turmoil. Beast-headed men and man-headed beasts in bloody conflict. Churned mud almost as far as the eye could see. On the horizon the ragged outline of a tall-towered city. Towards it, in triumph, rode the figure of Prince Gaynor von Minct—the one who would come to be called Gaynor the Damned.

Elric craned forward this time. He recognised the city. It was as familiar to him as Bek was to me. Familiar to me, too, now that our memories and minds had bonded. Imrryr, the Dreaming City, capital of Melniboné, the Isle of the Dragon Lords. Flames fluttered like flags from the topmost windows of her towers.

I looked back. Bek was still there. The green, gentle hills, the thick, welcoming woods, the old stones of the fortified manor farm. But now I saw that there was barbed wire around the walls. Machine-gun emplacements at the gates. Guard dogs prowling the grounds. SS uniforms everywhere. A big Mercedes staff car drove into view, speeding down the road to my old home. The driver was Klosterheim.

"How—?" I began.

"Exactly," said Oona. "Too much spoor, as I said. He took two paths and there he is in two different worlds. He has learned more than most of us can ever know about existing in the timeless infinity of the multiverse. He still fights on at least two fronts. Which could be his weakness . . ."

"It seems to be his strength," said Elric with his usual dry irony. "He is breaking every rule. It's the secret of his power. But if those rules no longer have meaning . . ."

"He has won already?"

"Not everywhere," said Oona. But it was clear she had no idea what to do next.

Elric took the initiative.

"He is in two places—and we can be in two places. We have two swords now and sword can call to sword. I must follow Gaynor to Melniboné and you must follow him to Bek."

"How can you see these places?" I asked her. "How do you select them?"

"Because I desire it?" She lowered her eyes. "We are not told," she said. "What if the Grey Fees are created by the will and imaginations of mortals and immortals? What they most wish for and most fear are therefore created here. Created over and over again. Through the extraordinary power of human memory and desire."

"Created and re-created throughout eternity," mused Elric. He laid his gauntleted hand on the pommel of his runeblade. "Always a little different. Sometimes dramatically so. Memory and desire. Altered memories. Changing desires. The multiverse proliferates, growing like the veins in a leaf, the branches in a tree."

"What we must not forget," said Oona, "is that Gaynor has in his hands the power to create almost any desired reality. The power of the Grail, which is rightfully yours to protect but never directly use."

In spite of our bizarre circumstances, I found myself laughing. "Rightfully mine? I would have thought such power was rightfully Christ's or God's. If God exists. Or is He the Balance, the great mediator of our creativity?"

"That's the cause of much theological discussion," said Oona, "especially amongst dreamthieves. After all, they live by stolen dreams. In the Grey Fees, they say, all dreams come true. And all nightmares."

I felt helpless, staring around me in that void, my eyes constantly returning to those two scenes. They only reminded me of our quandary. They, too, could be an illusion—perhaps created by Oona herself, using the arts she had learned from her mother? I had no reason to trust her, or to believe she acted from altruism, but no reason not to either.

I felt a frustrated fury building in me. I wanted to draw my sword and cut through the mist, cut my way through to Bek, to my home, to the more peaceful past.

But there was a swastika flag flying over Bek. I knew that scene was no lie. Elric was smiling his old, wan smile. "Difficult," he said, "to follow a man who travels in two directions at once. Reluctant as we are to accept this, I do not believe we can continue this adventure together, my friends. You two must follow him one way—I'll seek to stop him the other."

"Surely we weaken our power by doing that?" We knew we fought against the Lords of the Higher Worlds as well as Gaynor and Klosterheim.

"We weaken our power significantly," agreed Elric, "perhaps impossibly. But we have little choice. I shall go back to Imrryr to fight Gaynor there. You must go to your own realm and do the same. He cannot have the Grail in two places at once. That is a certain impossibility. He will have it, therefore, where it will serve him best. Whoever finds it first must somehow warn the others."

"And where might such a place be?" I asked.

He shook his head. "Anywhere," he said.

Oona was less uncertain. "That is one of many things we do not know," she said. "There are two places he might go. Morn, whose stones he needs to harness the power of Chaos, or Bek."

Elric remounted his blind horse. The beast whinnied and snorted, stamping at the mist. He urged it forward, towards the scene of turmoil which opened to absorb him. He turned, drawing his great blade, and saluted me. It was a farewell. It was a promise. He then rode into the battling beasts, his black sword blazing in his right hand as he urged the horse towards Imrryr.

With a touch of her staff Oona sent my horse racing back into the mist. The beast would have no trouble getting home. Taking my arm Oona led me forward until we stood smelling the summer grass of Bek, looking down at my ancient home and realising, for the first time, that it had been turned into a fortress. Some kind of important SS operations centre, I guessed.

We dropped to the ground. I prayed we had not been seen. SS people were everywhere. This was no ordinary establishment. It was thoroughly guarded, with machine-gun posts and heavy barbed wire. Two crude barbicans of wire surrounded the moat.

We crept down the hills away from Bek's towers. I was easily able to guide Oona through the dense undergrowth of our forestland. I knew as many trails as the foxes or rabbits who inhabited these woods when Beks had cleared the land to build their first house. We had lived in harmony, for the most part, down all those centuries.

My home had become an obscenity, a shameful outrage. Once it had stood for everything Germans held to be of value—prudent social progress, tradition, culture, kindness, learning, love of the land—and now it stood for everything we had once loathed; intolerance, disrespect, intemperate power and harsh cruelty. I felt as if I and my entire family had been violated. I knew full well how Germany had already been violated. I knew the nature of that evil and I knew it had not been spawned from German soil alone, but from the soil of all those warring nations, the greed and fear of all those petty, self-serving politicians who had ignored the real desires of their voters, all those opposing political formulae, all those ordinary citizens who had failed to examine what their leaders told them, who had let themselves be led into war and ultimate damnation and who still followed leaders whose policies could only end in their destruction.

What was this will to death which seemed to have engulfed Europe? A universal guilt? Its utter failure to live up to its Christian ideals? A kind of madness in which sentiment was contrasted by action at every turn?

Night came at last. Nobody hunted us. Oona found some old newspapers in a ditch. Someone had slept on them. They were yellow, muddy. She read them carefully. And, when she had finished, she had a plan. "We must find Herr El," she said. "Prince Lobkowitz. If I am right, he's living quietly under an assumed name in Hensau. Time has passed here. We are several years further on than when you left Germany. Hensau is where he will be. Or was, the last time I was in 1940."

"What do you mean? You are a time traveller, too?"

"I once thought so, until I understood that time is a field, and the same event takes place over and over again within that field, all at the same time. How we select from that field gives us a sense of the multiverse's mortality. We are not really time-travelling but shifting from one reality to another.

"Time is relative. Time is subjective. Time alters its qualities. It can be unstable. It can be too stable. Time varies from realm to realm. We can leave this realm and find ourselves in a similar one, only separated by centuries. By this same process people sometimes believe they have discovered time travel. We escaped from Hameln in 1935, I believe. Five years ago. It is now the summer of 1940 and your country is at war. She appears to have conquered most of Europe."

The old newspapers gave no idea of what events had led to the current situation, but "brave little Germany" was now fighting alone against a dozen aggressive nations bent on taking back what little they had not already looted. According to the Nazi press, Germany for her part was merely demanding the land she needed for her peoples to expand—a region she was calling Greater Germany. A bastion against the Communist Goliath. Some European nations were already described as "provinces" of Germany while others were included in the German "family." France had reached a compromise, while Italy under Mussolini was an ally. Poland, Denmark, Belgium, Holland. All defeated. I was horrified. Hitler had come to power promising the German people peace. We had yearned for it. Honest, tolerant people had voted for anyone who would restore civil order and avert the threat of war. Adolf Hitler had now taken us into a worse war than any previous one. I wondered if his admirers were cheering him quite so enthusiastically now. For all our self-destructive Prussian rhetoric, we were fundamentally a peaceful people. What mad dream had Hitler invented to induce my fellow Germans to march again?

At last I slept. Immediately my head was filled with dreams. With violent battle and bizarre apparitions. I was experiencing everything my doppelgänger was experiencing. Only while awake could I keep him out of my mind, and even then it was difficult. I had no idea what he did, save that he had returned to Imrryr and from there gone under ground. A scent of reptiles . . .

Awake again, I continued to read all I could. Most of what I read produced fresh questions. I could not believe how easily Hitler had come to power and why more people were not resisting, though the blanket of lies issued by the newspapers stopped many decent people from having a clear idea of how they could challenge the Nazi stranglehold. Otherwise, I had to piece together the picture for myself. It left many questions.

I learned most of the answers when we eventually found our way to Lobkowitz's apartment in Hensau, travelling at night for almost a week, scarcely daring the woodland trails, let alone the main roads. I was glad to sleep during daylight hours. It made my dreams a little easier. The newspapers, once read, were used to wrap around Ravenbrand. Our weapons seemed scarcely adequate to challenge the armaments of the Third Reich.

Everywhere we saw signs of a nation at war. Long trains carrying munitions, guns, soldiers. Convoys of trucks. Droning squadrons of bombers. Screaming fighters. Large movements of marching men. Sometimes we saw more sinister things. Cattle trucks full of wailing human beings. We had no idea at that time the scale of the murders Hitler practised on his own people and the conquered citizens of Europe.

We travelled extremely cautiously, anxious not to draw the attention of even the most minor authority, but Oona risked stealing a dress from a clothes line. "The gypsies will be blamed, I suppose."

Hensau, having no railway station and no main road, was relatively quiet. The usual Nazi flags flew everywhere and the SS had a barracks nearby, but the town was mostly free of military people. We could see why Lobkowitz had chosen it.

When we eventually stood before him, Oona in her rather flimsy stolen dress, we must have looked a wretched sight. We were half-starved. I was in rags. We bore incongruous weapons. I had not changed clothes for days and was desperately tired.

Lobkowitz laughed as he offered us drinks and told us to seat ourselves in his comfortable easy chairs. "I can get you out of Germany," he said. "Probably to Sweden. But that's about the limit of the help I can give you at present."

It emerged that he was running a kind of "underground railway" for those who had aroused Nazi displeasure. Most went to Sweden, while others went through Spain. He regretted, he said, that he had no magical powers. No way of opening the moonbeam roads to those who sought freedom. "The best I can promise them is America or Britain," he said. "Even the British Empire can't stand against the Luftwaffe much longer. I have soldier friends. Another few months and Britain will seek an armistice. I suspect she will fall. And with the capitulation of the empire, Germans need not fear American involvement. It's the triumph of evil, my dears."

He apologised for making such melodramatic statements. "But these are melodramatic times.

"The irony," he continued, "is that what you seek is already at Bek."

"But Bek is too heavily guarded for us to attack her," said Oona.

"What is it that we seek?" I asked wearily. "A staff? A cup? Isn't there another one that will do?"

"These are unique objects," Prince Lobkowitz said. "They take different forms. They have some sort of will, though it is not conscious in the same way as ours. You call one object the Holy Grail. Your family was entrusted to guard it. Wolfram von Eschenbach speaks of such a trust. Your father, half-mad, had not easily accepted this story. When he lost the Grail, he felt obliged to get it back and in so doing he killed himself."

"Killed himself? Then Gaynor's accusations were true! I had no idea—"

"Clearly the family wished to avoid scandal," Prince Lobkowitz continued. "They said he died in the subsequent fire, but the truth is, Count von Bek, your father was racked by guilt—every kind of guilt—for your mother's death, his own failings, his inability to shoulder the family responsibilities. Indeed, as you know, he found it difficult to communicate with his own children. But he was neither a coward nor one to escape the inevitable. He did his best and he died in the attempt."

"Why should he place such importance on the Grail?" I asked.

"Such objects have great power in Teutonic mythology, too, which is why Hitler and his disciples are so greedy to possess them. They believe that with the Grail and Charlemagne's sword in their hands, they will have the supernatural means, as well as the military means, of defeating Britain. Britain is all that stands in the way of the triumph of the German Empire. The cup is more important than the sword, in this case. The sword is an arm. It has no independent life. There should, in truth, be two swords on either side of the cup for the magic to work at its fullest. Or so I'm told. What Gaynor thinks he will achieve, I do not entirely know, but Hitler and his friends are convinced that something monumental will happen. I've heard a rumour about a ritual called Blood-in-the-Bowl. Sounds like a fairy story, eh? Virgins and magic swords."

"We must try to get the Grail back," I said. "That is what we are here to do."

Lobkowitz spoke softly, almost by way of confirmation. "Your father feared Bek would perish once the Grail left your family's safe-keeping. He feared the entire family would perish. You, of course, are his last remaining son."

This was not something I needed to be reminded of. The waste of my brothers' lives in the Great War still made me despair. "Did my father start the fire which killed him?"

"No. The fire was a result of the demon who volunteered his assistance in fulfilling your family trust. A reasonable thought, I suppose, in the circumstances. But your father was at best an amateur sorcerer. The creature was not properly contained within the pentagram. Rather than defend the Grail, it stole it!"

"The demon was Arioch?"

"The 'demon' was our friend Klosterheim, then in the service of Miggea of Law. She was drooling crazy and feeling her power wane. Klosterheim served Satan until Satan proved insufficiently committed to the cause of evil and sought a reconciliation with God through the medium of your Bek ancestors. Through your namesake, as a matter of fact. Your ancestor was charged by Satan himself to find the Grail and keep it, until such time as God and Satan shall be reconciled."

"Fanciful old stories," I said. "They do not even have the authenticity of myth!"

"Stories our immediate ancestors chose to forget," said the Austrian quietly. "But you have more than one dark legend attached to your family name—even into recent times with the Mirenburg legend of Crimson Eyes."

"Another peasant fireside tale," I said. "The invention of the under-educated. You know that Uncle Bertie is now doing a perfectly respectable job in Washington."

"Actually, he's in Australia now. But I take your point. You must admit, my dear Count Ulric, that your family's history was never as uneventful as they pretended. More than one of your kinsmen or ancestors has reason to agree."

I shrugged. "If you will, Prince Lobkowitz. But that history has little to do with our current problems. We must find the Grail and the Sword but need your suggestions as to how we might get them back."

"Where else?" he said. "I have told you. Where the Grail has been for so many centuries. At Bek. That is why the place is so heavily fortified and guarded, why Klosterheim keeps permanent guard over the Grail chamber, as he calls it. You know it as your old armoury."

That place had always possessed an atmosphere. I cursed myself. "We saw Klosterheim go to Bek. Are we too late? Has he removed the Grail?"

"I doubt he would wish to do that. I have it on the best authority that Hitler himself, together with Hess, Göring, Goebbels, Himmler and company, are all making plans to meet at Bek. They can hardly believe their luck, I'd guess. But they wish to ensure it! France has fallen and only Britain, already half-defeated, stands in their way. German planes have attacked British shipping, lured fighters into combat and weakened an already weak RAF. Before they invade by sea and land, they intend to destroy all main cities, especially London. They are preparing a vast aerial armada at this very moment. For all I know it is on its way. There is very little time. This meeting at Bek involves some ritual they believe will strengthen their hand even more and ensure that their invasion of Britain is completely successful."

I was disbelieving. "They are insane."

He nodded his head. "Oh, indeed. And something within them must understand that. But they have had total success so far. Perhaps they believe these spells are the reason for it. Clearly whatever supernatural aid they have called upon is not disappointing them. Yet it is unstable magic—in unstable hands. And it could result in the death of everything. Like Gaynor and the rest of their kind, their ignorance and disdain for reality will eventually destroy them. They relish the notion of Götterdämmerung. These people seek oblivion by any means. They are the worst kind of self-deceiving cowards and everything they build is a ramshackle sham. They have the taste of the worst Hollywood producers and the egos of the worst Hollywood actors. We have come to an ironic moment in history, I think, when actors and entertainers determine the fate of the real world. You can see how quickly the gap between action and affect widens . . . Of course they are expert illusionists, like Mussolini for instance, but illusion is all they offer—that and a vast amount of unearned power. The power to fake reality, the power to deceive the world and destroy it under the weight of so much falsification. The less the world responds to their lies and fancies, the more rigorously do they enforce them."

I began to realise that Prince Lobkowitz, for all his practicality, was a discursive conversationalist. At length I interrupted him. "What must I do when I have the Grail?"

"Very little," he said. "It is yours to defend, after all. And circumstances will change. Perhaps you'll take it back to its home in what the East Franconians called the Grail Fields. You know them by their corrupted name of the Grey Fees. Oh, yes, we've heard of them in Germany! There's a reference to them in Wolfram von Eschenbach, who cites Kyot de Provenzal. But your chances of getting to those *Graalfelden* again are also very slim."

I had the advantage, he said, of knowing Bek. The old armoury, where the Grail was held, where I had received my first lessons from von Asch.

"Guarded presumably by these SS men," I said. "So there isn't much chance of my strolling in, calling 'I'm home,' saying I've just dropped in to pop up to the armoury, then tucking the Holy Grail under my jacket and walking out whistling."

I was surprised by my host's response.

"Well," he said with evident embarrassment, "I did have something like that in mind, yes."

20

Traditional Values

Which was how I came to be wearing the full uniform of a Standartenführer, a colonel in the SS, including near-regulation smoked glasses, sitting in the back of an open Mercedes staff car driven by a chauffeuse in the natty uniform of the NSDAP Women's Auxiliary (First Class) who, with her bow and arrows in the trunk, took the car out of its hidden garage into the dawn streets of Hensau and into some of the loveliest scenery in the whole of Germany—rolling, wooded hills and distant mountains, the pale gold of the sky, the sun a flash of scarlet on the horizon. I was filled with longing for those lost times, the years of my childhood when I had ridden alone across such scenery. The love of my land ran deep in my blood.

Somehow we had gone from that pre-1914 idyll to the present horror in a few short bloody years. And now here I was riding in a car far too large for the winding roads and wearing the uniform which stood for everything I had learned to loathe. Ravenbrand was now carried in a modified gun case and lay at my feet on the car's floor. I could not help reflecting on this irony. I found myself in a future which few could have predicted in 1917. Now, in 1940, I remembered all the warnings that had been given since 1920. Years of anti-war films, songs, novels and plays—years of analysis and oracular pronouncements. Too many, perhaps? Had the predictions actually created the situation they hoped most to avert?

Was anarchy so terrible, compared to the deadly discipline of fascism? As much democracy and social justice had emerged from chaos as from tyranny. Who had been able to predict the total madness that would come upon our world in the name of "order"?

For a while we followed the main autoroute to Hamburg. We saw how busy the roads, rail-lines and waterways had become. We travelled for a short while on an excellent new autobahn with several lanes of traffic moving in both directions, but Oona soon found the back roads to Bek again. We were only fifty kilometres from my home when we turned a sharp bend in a wooded lane and Oona stamped quickly on the brake to stop us crashing into another car, quite as ostentatious as our own, swathed in Nazi flags and insignia. A thoroughly vulgar vehicle, I thought. I guessed it to belong to some swaggering local dignitary.

We began to move again but then a high-ranking officer in a brown SA uniform emerged from the other side of the car and flagged us down.

We had no option. We slowed to a stop this time. We exchanged the ritual salute, borrowed, I believe, from the film *Quo Vadis*, supposedly how Romans greeted a friend. Once again, Hollywood had added a vulgar gloss to politics.

Noting my uniform and its rank, the SA man was subservient, apologetic. "Forgive me, Herr Standartenführer. This is, I regret, an emergency."

From out of the closed car now emerged an awkward, rather gangling figure in a typical comic-opera Nazi uniform favoured by the higher ranks. To his credit, he seemed uncomfortable in it, pushing unfamiliar frogging about as he walked over to us, offering a jerky salute, which we returned. He was genuinely grateful. "Oh, God be thanked! You see, Captain Kirch! My instincts never let me down. You suggested no suitable car could come along this road and get us to Bek on time—and *voilà*! This angel suddenly materialises." His eyebrows appeared to be alive. His eyes, too, were very busy and he had an intense, crooked smile on his puffy, square face. If it had not been for his uniform, I might have taken him for a typical customer of the Bar Jenny in Berlin. He beamed at me. Raving mad but relatively benign.

"I am Deputy Führer Hess," he told me. "You will be well remembered for this, colonel."

I recalled that Rudolf Hess was one of Hitler's oldest henchmen. In accordance with the papers I carried, I let him know that I was Colonel Ulric von Minct and that I was at his service. It would be a privilege to offer him my car.

"An angel, an angel," he repeated as he climbed into the car and sat beside me. "It is the von Mincts, colonel, who will save Germany." He hardly noticed the case containing the sword. He was too concerned with shouting urgent orders to his driver. "The flasks! The flasks! It would be a disaster if I did not have them!"

The SA man reached into the trunk of the car and carefully took out a large wicker basket which he transferred to our car. Hess was greatly relieved. "I am a vegan," he explained. "I have to travel everywhere with my own food. Alf—I mean, our Führer—" He glanced up at me, like a small boy caught in some forbidden act. Clearly he had been admonished before for making reference to the Nazi leader by his old nickname. "The Führer is a vegetarian—but not strict enough, I fear, for me. He runs a very lax kitchen, from my point of view. So I have taken to carrying my own food when I travel."

The deputy Führer saluted his driver. "Wait with the car," he instructed. "We'll send help from the first town we reach. Or from Bek, if we find nothing else." He sat back in the car beside me, a signal for Oona to put the Mercedes into gear and continue the journey. He was a mass of tics and peculiar movements of his hands. "Von Minct, you say? You must be related to our great Paul von Minct, who has achieved so much for the Reich."

"His cousin," I said. I found it very hard to be afraid of this man.

Hess insisted on shaking my hand.

"A great honour, sir," I said.

"Oh"—he removed his elaborate cap—"I'm one of the old fighters, you know. Still one of the lads." He was reassuring me. Sentimentally he continued, "I was with Hitler in Munich, In Stadelheim and everywhere—he and I are brothers. I am the only one he truly trusts and confides in. It was always so. I am his spiritual adviser, in many ways. If it were not for me, Colonel von Minct, I doubt if any of you would have heard of the Grail story—or understand what it could do for us!"

Confidingly he leaned towards me. "Hitler, they say, knows the heart of Germany. But I know her soul. That is what I have studied."

As the huge Mercedes bowled along familiar country roads, I continued to speak with the man whom many believed the most powerful man in Germany after the great dictator himself. If Hitler were killed today, Hess would assume the leadership.

For the most part his conversation was as banal as that of most Nazis, but laced through with a mélange of supernatural beliefs and dietary ideas which marked him for a common lunatic. Because he understood me to have an affinity for the Grail and all the mysticism surrounding it, he was more forthcoming— about how he had read the Bek legends, how he had read books saying the Grail was the lost Holy Relic of the Teutonic Order. How the Bek sword was the lost sword of Roland, Champion of the Holy Roman Emperor, Charlemagne the Frank. The Franks and the Goths founded modern Europe, he said. The Norsemen were stern lawmakers, with no respect for the Old World's superstitions. Wherever their influence was felt, people became robust, masculine, vital, productive. Latin Christianity weakened them.

The destiny of the German nation, he told me, was to lift its brothers back to glory—to rid the world of all that wretchedly bad stock and replace it with a race of superbeings—super-healthy, super-intelligent, super-strong, super-educated—the kind of breed which would populate the world with the best mankind could be, rather than the worst.

The more I listened to Hess, the more sceptical I became, the more convinced that he was a low-level lunatic with dull dreams and a psychological inability to consider any "truth" but that which he invented for himself.

However, as the man was so fundamentally amiable and clearly trusted me so completely, I had an opportunity to see what he knew of my father. Had he ever met old Count von Bek? I asked. The one who went mad and was burned alive. Killed himself, didn't he?

"Killed himself? Perhaps." Hess shuddered. "A terrible crime, suicide. Betrays us all. On a level with abortion, in my view. All life should be respected."

I had discovered quickly the trick of steering him gently back to the subject. "Count von Bek?"

"He lost the Grail, you see. He was entrusted with it. Father to child—son or daughter—down the centuries. 'Do you the Devil's work!' is their ancient motto. They were at the Crusades. The oldest blood in Germany—but tainted by decadence, madness, Latin marriages . . .

"Legend had it that the von Beks always protected the Grail, until such a time when Satan was reconciled with God. All stupid Christian nonsense, I know, and a corruption of our old, muscular Nordic myths. Those myths made us successful conquerors. It has always been our destiny to conquer. To bring order to the whole world. The myth still retains its power." His eyes were focused on me now, burning into me. "The power of myth is the power of life and death, as we know—for we have restored the power of the Nordic myth. And again we are successful conquerors. We shall challenge that other Nordic race, our natural allies, the British, until they turn with us against the evil East and defeat the tyranny of communism. Together, we shall bring civilisation to the whole planet!"

A typical sample of his droning, pseudo-philosophical nonsense. It explained why the Nazi chiefs in their lunacy placed such value on the Grail and the Sword. These things represented a *mystical* authority. Only with them in harness with their political power were they confident they had secured their victories. Triumph over the admired British Empire would be a kind of epiphany. An armistice achieved, together they would restore the purity of blood and myth to its proper place in the order of things.

"We only have to complete the destruction of their air force and they will call for a truce."

"I am impressed by your logic, sir."

"Logic has nothing to do with it, colonel. Logic and the so-called Enlightenment are Judeo-Christian inventions, deeply suspect by all right-thinking Aryans. Those Nazis who cling to their pro-Christian beliefs are working for the Judaic-Bolshevik cultural conspiracy. The British understand this as well as we do. The best kind of Americans are also on our side . . ."

I think that in all my adventures I have only shown real courage and self-discipline once: when I restrained myself from throwing the glamorous deputy Führer out of my car.

"How," I asked, "did old von Bek lose possession of the Grail?"

"As you no doubt know, he was an amateur scientist. One of those prehistoric gentleman scholars. He knew of the family's trust, to guard the Grail until we, its true inheritors, should come to claim it. But he was curious. He wanted to examine the Grail's properties. Which meant that first he had to master the laws of magic. Of necromancy. His studies drove him mad, but he continued with his examination of the Grail, and in doing so, he summoned a certain renegade Captain of Hell . . ."

"Klosterheim?"

"Just so. Who in turn brought the help of another renegade. One of the company of Law. The immortal, extremely unstable Miggea. Duchess of the Higher Worlds." Hess grinned. He was in the know. He swelled, full of his own secrets. He twitched with supernatural intelligence. "Alf—our Führer—told me to find Gaynor, who was already an adept, and offer to blend our strength with his. Gaynor agreed and, rather later than he'd promised, brought the object of power back to Bek. With it we shall control history—the war against Britain is already won."

In spite of my direct experience of realities he had only heard of, I still found him hard to follow, exhausting in the way mad people often are. Therefore I was deeply relieved when the car began its final drive towards the gates of Bek. Because the deputy Führer was with us, our papers were never inspected. All I had to hope was that Gaynor did not recognise me. My hair was hidden under my military cap and I wore the dark glasses, which were an unofficial part of the uniform, to disguise my albinism.

Chatting easily with Hess, I lifted the encased sword from the car. "For the ceremony," I told him. Hess was by far my best cover and I was determined to stick with him as long as I could. As I moved through my old home, however, it was difficult to restrain myself from exclaiming at what had been done to it.

I would rather Gaynor had destroyed it as he threatened. The house had been thoroughly violated. The place had been redecorated like a Fairbanks film set—all Nazi pomp and circumstance: gold-braided flags, Teutonic tapestries, Nordic plaques and heavy mirrors, freshly made stained glass in the old Gothic windows, one of which showed an idealised portrait of Hitler as a noble knight errant and Göring as some sort of male Valkyrie. A *Rheinejungen*, perhaps? Swastikas everywhere. It was as if Walt Disney, who so admired fascist discipline and had his own ideas for the ideal state, had been hired as Bek's interior designer. The Hitler gang's passion for the garish trappings of the operetta stage was demonstrated throughout. In so many ways Hitler was a typical Austrian.

I, of course, said none of this to Hess, who seemed rather impressed by the house, enjoying his reflected glory as every SS officer stopped to click his heels and give him the Nazi salute. I luckily stood in Hess's reflected glory and Oona in mine, and so we passed as if charmed through our enemy's defences while the deputy Führer spoke warmly of King Arthur, Parsifal, Charlemagne and all the other Teutonic heroes of legend who had borne magic swords.

By the time we reached the armoury, deep within the castle's oldest keep, I was beginning to wish Hess would return to his earlier topic of Nordic veganism. All because of the repressed fear of my own imminent discovery and destruction!

The deputy Führer asked me to hold his canisters of food while he took a large key from his jacket pocket. "The Führer gave me the honour of holding his key," he said. "It is a privilege to be the first to enter and to greet him when he arrives!"

He inserted the key in the lock and turned it with some difficulty. I thought it wise of Hitler to have his friend go ahead of him like that. After all, the Führer could never be sure it was not an elaborate plot to end his life.

Thus, as members of Rudolf Hess's entourage, we passed into the high-ceilinged armoury which had been spared redecoration and was lit by a high, circular window. A sunbeam pierced the dust and fell directly upon a kind of altar, square granite carved with the Celtic sun cross, which had recently been placed there.

Involuntarily, I moved towards this new object. How on earth had they carried such a weight of granite through our narrow corridors? I reached out to touch it. But Hess held me back. Clearly he thought I was eager for other reasons. "Not yet," he said.

As his eyes became used to the dim light, he looked around him in sudden puzzlement. "What's this—what are you men doing here before I ever crossed the threshold? Do you not realise who I am and why I should be here first?"

The shadowy group seemed unimpressed.

"This is blasphemy," said Hess. "Infamy. This is no place for ordinary soldiers. The magic is subtle. It requires subtle minds. Subtle hands."

Klosterheim, automatic in hand, came grinning into the sunlight. "I assure you, sir, we are nothing if not subtle. I will explain as soon as possible. But now, if you don't mind, Deputy Führer, I will continue to save your life—"

"Save my—?"

Klosterheim pointed his pistol at me. "This time my bullets *will* work," he said. "Good afternoon, Count Ulric. I had an idea you would be joining us here. You see! You're fulfilling your destiny whether you wish to or not."

Hess remained outraged. "You are making many mistakes, major. The

Führer himself is involved with this project and will be arriving shortly. What will he think of a subordinate pointing a gun at his deputy and one of his top officers?"

"He will know what Prince Gaynor will tell him," said Klosterheim. He was careless of Hess's words. He hardly heard them. "Believe me, Deputy Führer Hess, we are acting entirely in the interests of the Third Reich. Ever since he was denounced as a traitor and his property confiscated, we have been expecting this madman to make an attempt on the Führer's life—"

"This is nonsense!" I began. "You know it is a lie!"

"But is the rest a lie, count?" His voice grew softer, more intimate. "Do you think we expected you to give up pursuit? Wasn't it obvious that you would make some attempt to reach this place? All we had to do was wait for you to bring us the Black Sword. Which I note you have kindly done."

Hess was inclined to trust to rank. This was my only hope of buying time. As he looked to me for confirmation I shouted in my best Nazi-bark: "Captain Klosterheim, you are overstepping the mark. While we applaud your vigilance in protecting the Führer, we can assure you there is nothing in this room which offers him any danger."

"On the contrary," agreed Hess uncertainly. His eyes, never steady at the best of times, flickered from me to Klosterheim. He was impressed by Klosterheim's handpicked storm troopers. "But perhaps, given the circumstances, we should all step outside this room and settle any confusion?"

"Very well," said Klosterheim. "If you will lead the way, Count von Bek . . ." And he gestured with his Walther.

"Von Bek?" Hess was startled. He looked hard at me and began to think.

I had no more time. I pulled the protective fabric away from my sword. Ravenbrand was all that could save me now.

Klosterheim's gun cracked. Two distinct shots.

He had the sense to know when to stop me.

The sword was only half out of the case as I felt sharp pains in my left side and began to stumble backwards under the impact of the bullets. I struggled to stay on my feet. I wanted to vomit but could not. I fell heavily against the mysterious granite altar and slipped to the flagstones. I tried to get back to my feet. My dark glasses fell off. My cap was kicked away from my head revealing my white hair. I looked up. Klosterheim was standing with his legs straddled over my body, the smoking PPK 9mm still in his right hand. I do not think I have ever seen such an expression of gloating satisfaction on a human face.

"God in Heaven!" I could hear Hess gasping. He peered down at me, his eyes widening. "Impossible! It is the Bek monster! The bloodless creature they were said to keep in their tower. Is it dead?"

"He's not dead. Not yet, your excellency." Klosterheim stepped back. "We'll save him for later. We have an experiment to perform. A demonstration the Führer has requested."

"The Führer," began Hess, "surely would have told me if . . ."

The pointed toe of a boot kicked me efficiently in the side of my head and I lost consciousness.

Dimly, as was constant with me now, I had been sensing what was happening to my alter ego. Suddenly my nostrils were filled with a pungent, reptilian stink and looking up I stared into the familiar eyes of a huge dragon. All the wisdom of the world flickered in those eyes.

I spoke to the dragon in a low, affectionate voice that had no real words to it, that was more music than language, and the dragon responded in the same tones. A thrumming purr came out of its monstrous throat and from its nostrils a few wisps of steam. I knew the creature's name and it remembered me. I had been a child and had changed a great deal. But the dragon remembered me, even though my body was covered in cuts and I was helplessly bound. I smiled. I began to speak a name. Then the pain in my side swept through me like a swift tide and I gasped, going down again into blackness that engulfed me like a blessing.

Had Prince Lobkowitz set this trap for me? Was he now in league with Klosterheim, Gaynor and the Nazi hyena-pack?

And did Elric's fate, in his world, mirror my own? Was he, too, dying in the ruins of his old home?

I was aware of pain, rough hands, but could not bring myself out of sleep. I woke up to the smell of oily smoke. I opened my eyes, thinking at first that the armoury was on fire. But the old flambeaux brackets had been utilised and a flaming brand guttered in every holder, casting huge shifting shadows.

I felt the tight cloth of a gag in my mouth, my hands were bound in front of me and my feet were free. I was relieved that most of my Nazi uniform had been stripped off me. I wore only a shirt and trousers. My feet were bare. I had been prepared for some kind of special treatment. I moved and agony flooded through me. I felt the wadding of a crude dressing on my wounds. My captors were not famous for administering pain relief to their victims.

At that moment they were not interested in me and I was able to watch what was happening. I saw Hitler, a rather short man in a heavy leather military coat, standing next to the plump, frowning Göring. Nearby, SS commander Himmler, with the prissy severity of a depraved tax inspector, was talking to Klosterheim. The two men had a similar quality about them I couldn't immediately identify. Members of Hitler's crack SS guard stood at key points in the hall, their machine guns at the ready. They looked like robots from *Metropolis*.

Gaynor was nowhere to be seen. Hess was talking intensely to a rather bored-looking SS general whose attention was everywhere but on him. Oona was not here. It could mean that she had become alerted to the danger in time. Were her weapons still in the car? Could she at least get the Grail out of Hitler's clutches?

I knew suddenly that I was dying. I had no hope of recovering unless Oona could save me. Even unbound I could not reach my sword, which now lay on the altar like some kind of trophy. While the Nazis were careful not to touch it, they peered at it as if it were a dangerous dormant snake, which might rear up to strike at any moment.

I guessed the sword to be my only hope of life—and that a slim one. I was not Elric of Melniboné, after all, but a mere human being caught up in natural and supernatural events far beyond his understanding. And about to die.

From the dampness of the heavy dressing against my side I could tell that I was losing a great deal of blood. I could not tell if any vital organs were damaged, but it scarcely mattered. The Nazis were not about to send for a doctor. I could not imagine the nature of the "experiment" Klosterheim had in mind for me.

The group had the air of men waiting for something. Hitler, who seemed almost as twitchy as Hess, gave the impression of an impatient street trader, forever on the lookout for trouble. He spoke in that affected German one associates with the Austrian lower middle class and even though he was the most powerful man in the world at that moment, there was a sense of weakness about him. I wondered if this were the banality of evil which my friend Father Cornelius, the Jesuit priest, used to talk about before he went to Africa.

I could hear very little of what was said and most of it sounded like nonsense. Hitler was laughing and slapping his leg with his gloves. The only thing I heard him say clearly was "The British will soon be begging for mercy. And we shall be generous, gentlemen. We will let them keep their institutions. They are ideal for our purposes. But first we must destroy London, eh?"

I was surprised that this was the object of their meeting. I had thought it to do with the "objects of power" Gaynor had brought with him from the Grey Fees.

The door opened and Gaynor stood there. He was dressed all in black, with a great black cloak over his armoured body. He had the look of a knight from one of those interminable historical films the Nazis loved to watch. A copper swastika was emblazoned on his breastplate and another on his helmet. He looked like a demonic Siegfried. His hands were clasped around the hilt of the great ivory runesword. He stepped aside with a dramatic gesture as two of his men bundled in a struggling woman and her unstrung bow.

My heart sank. Our last hope gone. They had Oona.

She was no longer dressed in the Nazi uniform but wore some kind of heavy, oat-coloured dress that engulfed her from head to toe. It, too, had a vaguely medieval appearance. Its collar and cuffs were decorated with red-and-black swastikas. Her wonderful white hair was contained by a filet of silver and her eyes blazed like dark garnets from the pale beauty of her face. She was helpless, bound hand and foot. Her face was expressionless, her mouth set. When she saw me a look of horror came into her furious eyes. Her mouth opened in a silent scream. Then closed more firmly than ever. Only her eyes moved.

I wanted to comfort her, but there was no comfort.

It was clear we were meant to die.

After greeting the others, Gaynor announced with some triumph: "Thus the game I planned reaches its conclusion. Both of these treacherous creatures have been brought to book. Both are guilty of numerous crimes against the Reich. Their fate will be a noble one, however. Nobler than they deserve. The Grail and the Black Sword are now back in our keeping. And we have the sacrifice we need to begin the final sorcery." With a flicker of mockery in his smile, he glanced at Oona. His disgusting appetite was about to be satisfied. "And strike our bargain with the Higher Worlds."

He intended to kill us both—and in pursuit of the Nazis' obscene, half-crazed supernatural nonsense.

The firelight reflected in the eager faces of Hitler and his comrades as they admired the struggling girl. Hitler turned to Göring and made some leering remark to which his lackey responded with a fat chuckle. Only Hess seemed ill at ease. I had the feeling he preferred fanciful daydreams to the actuality of what was evidently to be a bloody ritual.

Goebbels and Himmler, on either side of their Führer, both had tight, chilling smiles on their faces. Himmler's little round eyeglasses positively glinted with hellish glee.

With the sword in one hand, Gaynor reached down and grasped Oona by her moon-coloured hair. He dragged her towards the altar. "The chemical and the spiritual marriage of opposites," he announced, like a showman taking the stage. "My Führer, gentlemen, I promised you I would return with the Grail and the Swords. Here is the white sword of Charlemagne—and there, unwittingly returned to its proper place by this wretched half corpse"—he indicated me—"is the black sword of Hildebrand, Theodoric's henchman. The sword called Son Slayer, with which he killed Hadubrand, his eldest child. The sword of good"— he lifted the ivory sword and pointed towards the altar—"and the sword of evil. Brought together, they will baptise the Grail with blood. Good and evil will mingle and become one. The blood will bring the Grail to life again and bestow its power upon us. Death will be banished. Our great bargain with Lord Arioch will be struck. We shall be immortal amongst immortals. All this King Clovis the Goth predicted upon his deathbed as he gave the Grail into the keeping of his steward, Dietrich von Bern, who in turn entrusted it to his brother-in-law Ermanerik, my ancestor. When the Grail is washed at last with innocent blood, virgin blood, the Nordic peoples will be united in a common bond and come together as one folk, to take their rightful place as rulers of the world."

Insane nonsense, a farrago of myths and folktales typical of the Nazi rationalisers and with scarcely any historical basis. But Hitler and his gang were entranced by the story. Their existence, after all, depended on myths and folktales. Their political platform might have been written by the Brothers Grimm. It was quite possible Gaynor had made up much of this ritual to impress them, for he had told me that Hitler was merely his means to a greater goal. If so, his strategy was proving effective. He was using their power to summon Arioch. Even the most gullible Nazis would not be able to absorb the actuality. Little comfort to me. Whether they were delusory or not, these ideas would not help me accept my coming fate—or avert Oona's bloody death!

Göring, grossly fat, uttered a nervous rumble of laughter. "We shall not rule the world, Colonel von Minct, until we defeat the Royal Air Force. We have the numbers. We have the ordnance. What we need now is the luck. A little magic would help."

"The luck has held. Because it is not mere luck, but the workings of destiny." This was Hitler muttering. "But there is no harm in ensuring our victory."

"It's always a help," said Göring dryly, "to have a god or two on your side. By this time next week, I assure you, colonel, we'll be dining with the king at Buckingham Palace, with or without your supernatural aid."

Hitler seemed buoyed by his Reichsmarschall's confidence. "We shall be the first modern government to reinstitute the scientific use of the ancient laws of nature," he said. "What some insist on denigrating as 'magic.' It is our destiny to restore these marginalised disciplines and skills to the mainstream of German life."

"Exactly, my Führer!" Hess beamed, as if at an outstanding student. "The old science. The true science. The pre-Christian Teutonic science, untainted by any hint of southern decadence. A science which depends upon our beliefs and which can be manipulated by the power of the human will alone!"

All this I heard in the distance as my life began to ebb away from me.

"Nothing will convince me, Colonel von Minct," said Hitler with sudden coldness, as if taking charge of the situation, "until you demonstrate the power of the Grail. I need to know that you really have the Grail. If it is the actual Grail it will possess the power of which all legends speak."

"Of course, my Führer. The virgin blood shall bring the cup to life. Von Bek is dying even now. In a short while he will be thoroughly dead. With the Grail, I will restore him to life. So that you may kill him again at your pleasure."

Hitler waved this last away. A distasteful necessity. "We must know if it has the power to restore the dead to life. When this man is dead, we shall expose him to the Grail's influence. If it is the real thing, he will return to life. Immortal, perhaps. If its power can then be channelled to help our air fleet defeat the British, so much the better. But I will only believe that if its most famous property is displayed. And you have yet to produce the Grail, colonel."

Gaynor laid the white sword beside the black sword, end to end, upon the stone altar.

"And the cup?" asked Göring, borrowing authority from his master.

"The Grail takes many forms," Gaynor told him. "It is not always a cup. Sometimes it is a staff."

Reichsmarschall Göring, in pale Luftwaffe blue and many trimmings, brandished his own elaborate mace of office. His was encrusted with precious stones and looked as if it had been made, with his uniform, by a theatrical costumier. "Like this one?"

"Very similar, your excellency."

For a few moments I lost consciousness. Bit by bit my spirit was leaving my body. I made every effort I could to hang on to life, in the hope I might find a way to help Oona. I knew I had only minutes left. I tried to speak, to demand that Gaynor spare Oona, to say that this ritual of virginal sacrifice was savage, bestial—but I would be talking to savage, bestial men, who embraced the monstrous cause. Death called to me. She seemed my only possible escape from all this horror. I never realised until then how easily one can come to long for death.

"You have still to produce the Grail, Colonel von Minct." Göring spoke precisely, mockingly. Plainly he thought this whole thing a nonsense. Yet neither he nor any other member of the hierarchy dare express scepticism to Hitler, who clearly wanted to believe. Hitler needed the confirmation of his own destiny. He had already presented himself as the new Frederick the Great, the new Barbarossa, the new Charlemagne, but his entire career had been based on threats, lies and manipulation. He no longer had any idea of his own reality, his own effect. But should these ancient objects of Teutonic power respond to him, it would prove that he was indeed the true mystical and practical saviour of Germany. Something he did not always believe himself. All his actions were now determined by this need for affirmation.

Suddenly, as if he realised I was looking at him, Hitler turned his head. His eyes met mine for an instant. Staring, hypnotic eyes. Hideously weak. I had seen them in more than one obsessed lunatic. He dropped his gaze as if he were ashamed. In that moment I understood him to be a creature thoroughly out of its depth, fascinated by its own luck, its own rise from obscurity, its successful dalliance with oblivion.

I knew he could destroy the world.

Through a haze of death I saw them throw Oona onto the altar. Gaynor raised a sword in either hand.

The swords began to descend. She struggled, trying to fling herself off the granite block.

I remember thinking, as I lost consciousness again: Where is the cup?

My mental turmoil was not made better by the knowledge that this scene, or a variant of it, was being played out on every plane of existence. A billion versions of myself, a billion versions of Oona, all dying horribly in violence at the same moment.

Dying so that a madman could destroy the multiverse.

Hidden Virtues

I had not expected to return to consciousness. Dimly I was aware of other forces struggling within me, of some commotion at the altar. For a moment I had the delusion I stood in the doorway of the armoury, the Black Sword in my hand. And I called Gaynor's name. A challenge.

"Gaynor! You would slay my daughter! So no doubt you understand how much you have angered me."

I forced my head up. Gradually I opened my eyes.

Ravenbrand was howling. She was giving off her weird black radiance. Red runes formed agitated geometries within her blade. She hovered over Oona and *refused* to carry out Gaynor's actions. The runeblade shook and writhed in his hand, trying to wrench itself free. Stormbringer lusted to kill, but Raven-brand could not kill certain people. The idea of harming Oona was repulsive. Its semi-sentient constitution did not permit it to harm an innocent. In this it differed from Elric's Stormbringer, which more closely matched the attitudes of Melnibonéans.

Gaynor snarled. The light from the swords and torches painted the watching faces into Bosch grotesques. Those faces turned to look in astonishment at the man who stood in the ruined doorway—an identical black sword in his right hand, a sprawl of brown-shirted bodies behind him. The black blade ran with crimson. He wore torn armour and his own blood-soaked silks. He had the death-heat in his wolf's eyes. He must have been through several battles single-handed, but Stormbringer was still in one bloody fist and his face betrayed the memory of a million deaths.

"Gaynor!" The voice was my own. "You run like a jackal and hide like a snake. Will you meet me here, in this holy place of power? Or will you scuttle as usual into the shadows?"

Slow footsteps, the weariness of centuries. My doppelgänger entered the armoury. For all his exhaustion he radiated a power, a glamour, which the charismatic creatures of the Nazi élite could not begin to match. Here was a true demigod. Here was what they pretended to be. And he was all they claimed, because he alone had paid a price not one of them could even conceive of paying. Had faced such horror, stood his ground against such terror, that nothing could move him.

Almost nothing.

Only a threat to one whom, with all his complex and contradictory emotions, he had given his love. Love most Melnibonéans would never understand. With heavy, measured steps he made his way to the altar.

Gaynor attempted again to strike down with Ravenbrand at Oona's heart. The sword resisted him even more vigorously.

Gaynor screamed an oath, flung the screeching black sword at me, and seized the ivory blade in both hands. This time he would finish Oona.

The black blade did not reach its target. In fact it scarcely moved at all. It hovered in the air long enough for Oona to lift her bonds, cut through them, and scramble clear of Gaynor while making a grab at his belt. I was astonished at the blade's apparent sentience.

With a great deal of shouting and shuffling, Hitler and his people had already retreated behind their storm-trooper guards. They trained a score of efficient modern machine guns at Elric as he made his way to the altar. He ignored all danger. He was oblivious to the Nazis, as one might be in a dream. There was a hard, savage grin on his handsome, alien features. Once certain that Oona was not in immediate danger, he turned his attention to Gaynor.

The ivory sword hummed and bucked as if it, too, would refuse to kill. I wondered if the swords were sentient or if something else checked them.

Gaynor displayed greater control over the so-called Charlemagne Sword. He stabbed again and again at the hobbled Oona, who had yet to cut her feet free. But the sword simply would not do what he wanted. Wild, mystical language began to pour from his twisted mouth as he summoned the aid of Chaos.

But no aid came.

He had not had time to fulfil his bargains.

Elric darted now, swift as a snake. His black blade firmly blocked the white. "There is no pleasure in killing a coward," he said to Gaynor. "But I will do it as a duty if I must."

An arc of black and red. A crescent of silver. Elric's sword met the ivory blade. The two swords screamed in unison in every kind of anguish.

The Black Sword arced again. There was a dull, flat note as it met Gaynor's weapon. The ivory blade began to crack and flake like rotten wood, disintegrating in Gaynor's hand.

Gaynor cursed and discarded it. The thing had always been something of a forgery, with an unclear provenance. Jumping away from the altar, he sought to grab a weapon from the wall. But the weapons had been there years too long and had virtually rusted together. He screamed at the storm troopers to kill Elric, but the guards could not fire without hitting Gaynor or Klosterheim, who levelled his pistol at Elric. The demonic swordsman murmured a single, smiling word.

Ravenbrand plunged towards Satan's ex-servant. Klosterheim gasped. He understood all too clearly what his fate would be if she reached him. He shrieked in Latin. Few of us could understand him. Certainly not the sword, which barely missed him.

Klosterheim flung himself to the ground and Gaynor did the same. At once the machine guns began their mad cacophony, with bullets and spent shells bouncing everywhere in that huge, stone room.

Elric laughed his familiar wild laugh, dodging their fire as if charmed, then ducking behind the altar to be certain that his daughter had not been hit.

She smiled briefly to reassure him and then raced from her cover to where I lay against the wall. Gaynor's razor-sharp Nazi dagger was in her hand. Quickly she reached out, cutting my bonds.

Suddenly Ravenbrand settled herself in my fist, deflecting bullets as the guards turned their attention on me, still surrounding their precious leaders. Hitler and his gang backed hastily toward the ruined main door.

Power surged through me. I too was laughing. With fearless amusement I advanced on Klosterheim. Elric already engaged Gaynor. Oona had only Gaynor's dagger for a weapon, but she ducked behind the altar as the bullets ricocheted around us. They hit only one of the soldiers, causing a yelp of terror from the ranks of the Nazi élite.

Hitler had relied on his luck. But now the luck was with us.

The Nazis stumbled through the gap Elric had carved in the door. They tried to cover the ragged hole. They began to move heavy furniture into it. They could not know what we would do next. They gained time to make a plan.

I made to follow, but Elric held me back. He pointed.

Gaynor and Klosterheim remained at the far end of the hall.

"We still have the Grail," cried Gaynor. In his black armour, almost a parody of Elric's own, he looked like a massive, leathery bird prancing in rage as the firelight flared and faded and his shadows joined the dance. "And we still have aid coming from the Lords of the Higher Worlds. Be careful, my cousins. They'll not be happy if their ally on this plane is unable to bring them through."

Elric snorted. "You think I fear the disapproval of gods and demigods? I am Elric of Melniboné—and my race is the equal of the gods!"

But it was not the equal of Klosterheim's automatic which barked twice more and caught Elric entirely by surprise. "What's this?" Frowning, he fell backwards.

I leaped forward but Oona's dagger had already caught Klosterheim directly in his heart. He looked about to vomit, bending double and trying to pull the Nazi blade free.

Gaynor pushed his dying ally aside and made for the low oaken door which led to von Asch's abandoned quarters. Klosterheim did not move. He was evidently dead.

I was too weak to catch Gaynor. He was through the door and barring it after him as I reached it. I put my shoulder to it and felt a jolt of pain.

I looked down at my side, expecting to see more blood. Only a ragged scar remained. How much time had actually passed? Or was time disrupted as a result of Gaynor's selfish interference? Was the multiverse already beginning to disintegrate around us?

"Friends," I heard Elric gasp. "Up. We must go up . . ."

Oona tried to make a barrier in front of the ruined main door but the Nazis had done much of the work from their own side! We had no means of escape. By now Gaynor could be far ahead of us, taking the Grail back into the Grey Fees.

I continued pushing at the small door, but without success.

The miscellaneous furniture began to move in the main door. It looked like the Nazis had gathered their courage and were returning.

A crash came from the doorway. Hess stood there, waving his machine-gunners forward. He was the only one of his kind with the guts to confront us. Now we had no chance at all of getting free.

I tried my shoulder against the other door, but I was still too weak. I called for Oona to help. She was supporting Elric. He was leaning on Gaynor's altar. Blood poured from his wounds and stained the dark granite.

Impatiently the Melnibonéan straightened himself and took hold of his sword, telling me to stand aside. "This is becoming my habitual method of open-ing doors," he said. Though full of bravado, his voice was feeble.

He gathered his strength and let the sword carry the blow as he brought it down upon the door, splitting the ancient oak in two. The pieces fell aside to admit us. We scrambled across it and up the stairs in Gaynor's wake. Behind us I heard Hess shouting hysterically to his men.

The tower had not been used for years. As we carried Elric through we dis-covered that many of von Asch's possessions were still where he had left them. Trunks, cupboards, chairs and tables were covered in deep dust. Books and maps were long neglected. He had taken his swords and some clothes, but little else. We could see from marks in the dust which way Gaynor had gone. While Elric lay in a collapsed state against the wall, Oona and I dragged heavy furniture out of the rooms to block the narrow staircase. Oona glanced quickly through the books and papers, found something she wanted and put it in her pocket. Carry-ing Elric, we continued upwards until a short corridor led us out onto a broad quadrangle surrounded by narrow battlements broken by chimneys.

Miraculously, Gaynor was still there. He had expected to find help or easy escape. But there was a sheer drop on all sides.

I flung myself after the dark figure I saw ahead of me. It dodged around a buttress, a chimney breast, but I kept it in sight. Then suddenly Gaynor had turned. He was in horrible pain. His whole body vibrated and shook with a wild silvery light. He was growing in size. But as he grew, he dissipated. Like ripples in a pool, each one a slightly larger representation of its predecessor, Gaynor grew bigger and bigger, pulsing and expanding like a great chord of music, high into the sky, into the fabric of the multiverse. He fragmented and became whole at the same time!

I stumbled on, still trying to lay hands on him. I reached him, tried to hold him. Something electric tingled in my fingers, I was blinded for a moment, and then Gaynor was gone. Silence.

"We have lost both Gaynors," I said. I shook with violent anger mixed with fear.

Elric gasped and shook his head. "All of them, for the moment. He has fled in a thousand directions, playing his most dangerous card. Fragmenting into a multitude of versions, each one a slightly larger scale. He dissipates his essence throughout the multiverse, so that we cannot follow. He is at his most unstable. His most dangerous. Perhaps his most powerful. He exists everywhere and no-where. The risk is that he can be everyone and no-one. He spreads his essence thinly. But one thing we do know of him—he has failed to keep his bargain with Arioch. He was attempting to bring the Duke of Hell into this realm.

"If Gaynor hasn't driven himself completely insane, he will do one of two things. He will seek to escape the Duke of Hell, which would be foolish and probably impossible. Or he will go to seek a compromise with him. Which means he must find a place of convergence. Bek denied him, he needs another place of convergence through which he can admit his patron. There cannot be many others in this world."

"Morn," said Oona. "It will be on Morn." She held up the paper she had taken.

"A place of convergence?" I asked. "What is that?"

"Where many possibilities come together," she said. "Where the moonbeam roads meet. I know this realm well. He will go to the Stones of Morn and at-tempt to gather all his many selves back into a single whole."

That was all she could tell me before there came a hammering from within the tower.

"How can we possibly follow him?" I asked.

"I have brought friends," murmured Elric. "Gaynor sought to use them for his own ends. But he lacks our blood. It is how I followed him from Melniboné. Swords call to swords. Wings to wings."

Hess and his men were breaking down the door.

I looked over the battlements. The drop would kill us. There was nowhere left to go. We had no choice but to take a stand. Elric stumbled back towards the tower dragging his sword with both hands. As the door came down he swung the sword. It took the three leading storm troopers by surprise. They went down at once and the blade shrieked its glee. Elric's breath hissed as he absorbed the blade's strength. The stolen energy was quickly restoring him.

Reluctantly I joined him and together we took another five or six men before they retreated into the tower and began shooting at us from a safer distance. The narrow passage made it impossible for them to see us or hit us and their ammunition was wasted.

Elric told us to keep the storm troopers diverted. He limped to the edge of the battlements and looked up into a night sky which boiled with dark cloud stained by an orange moon. He lifted the sword. It began to blaze again with black fire. Elric, in his ruined armour and torn silks, burned with the same flame as he lifted his skull-white face to the turbulent heavens and began the singing of a rune so ancient its words were the voice of the elements, the wind and the earth.

A few more shots from the tower. A cautious storm trooper emerged. I killed him.

Dark shapes roamed the sky now. Sinuous shapes slithered their way amongst the clouds.

Elric had drawn strength from his victims. He stood silhouetted against the battlements, sword in hand, screaming at the sky.

And the sky screamed back at him.

Like sudden thunder, there was a bang, and the sky began to bubble and crack. Forms emerged from the distance. Monstrous flying creatures. Reptiles with long, curling tails and necks, slender snouts and wide, leathery wings. I recognised them from my nightmares. The dragons of Melniboné, brought to my own realm by Elric's powerful sorcery. I knew Gaynor had hoped to recruit these dragons to his cause. I knew he had almost defeated Elric in the ruins of Imrryr. I knew he had found the hidden caves and sought to wake Elric's dragon kin. He had been successful. But he had not understood that the dragons would refuse to serve him. *Blood for blood; brother for brother.* They served only the royal blood of Melniboné. And that blood, by a trick of history, Oona and I shared with her father.

Two huge beasts circled the tower in the orange moonlight. Young Phoorn dragons, still with the black and white rings around their snouts and tails, still with feathery tips to their wings, they had not grown to the size of their elders, whose lifespans were almost infinite, as dragons spent most of their time asleep.

Elric was weakened by his incantation, but his spirits were rising. "I prepared for this. But I had also expected to have the Grail with me when I summoned my brothers." Melnibonéans claimed direct kinship with the Phoorn dragons. In another age they had shared the same names, the same quarters, the same power. In ancient history, it was said dragons had ruled Melniboné as kings. Whatever the truth, Elric and his kind could drink dragon venom, which killed most other creatures. The venom was so powerful that it ignited in the air as soon as it spewed from the dragons' mouths. I knew all this, because Elric knew it.

I knew the language of the dragons. We greeted them affectionately as they landed their huge bodies delicately on the tower. They were steaming and shaking with the turbulence of their journey through the multiverse. They opened their huge red mouths, gasping in the thin air of this world. Their vast eyes turned to regard us. Expectant, benign, their monstrous claws gripped the stone battlements as they balanced there. The patterns of their scales, subtle and rich purples and scarlets, golds and dark greens, glistened in the moonlight. They were very similar in appearance, one distinguished by a blaze of white above its nose, the other with a blaze of black. Their great white teeth clashed when they closed their mouths, and on the edges of their lips, their venom constantly boiled. These were the beasts of the Siegfried legend, but far more intelligent and considerably more numerous. The Melnibonéans had made many studies of dragons, detailing all the various kinds, from the snub-snouted Erkanian, nicknamed the batwing, to these long-nosed hibernating Phoorn, whose relationship with us was oddly telepathic.

Holding his side, Elric approached the nearest dragon, speaking to her softly. Both dragons were already saddled with the pulsing Phoorn *skeffla'a*, a kind of membrane which bonded with the dragon above its shoulder blades, giving it the ability to travel between the realms. The *skeffla'a* was one of the strangest productions of Melnibonéan alchemical husbandry and one of the oldest.

Their names were simple, like most names given to them by men—

Blacksnout and Whitesnout. Their names for themselves were long, complicated and utterly unpronounceable, detailing ancestry and where they had journeyed.

Elric turned to me. "The dragons will take us to Gaynor. You know how to ride?"

I knew. As I now knew most things connected with my doppelgänger.

"He's still in this world. Or at least certain aspects of him are. He could have exhausted himself and no longer have the power to travel the moonbeam roads. Whatever the reasons, the dragons can take us to him."

"To Morn," said Oona. "It must be Morn. Does he still have the Grail?"

"It's not something we'll know until we catch up with him . . ." Elric's voice trailed away as he was overcome with pain. Yet he seemed slightly stronger than a few minutes earlier. I asked him how badly he had been shot and he looked at me in surprise. "Klosterheim shot to kill. And I am not dead."

"I should also have died from Klosterheim's gun," I told him. "The wounds were very evident. I lost an enormous amount of blood. But the wound has now almost vanished!"

"The Grail," said Elric. "We've been exposed to the Grail and haven't known it. So it is either on Gaynor's person or hidden somewhere back there."

Hess's face emerged from the doorway. He ordered his men to stop shooting. His face bore an expression of sincerity, of urgency.

"I must talk to you," he said. "I must know what all this means. What kind of heroes are you? The heroes of Alfheim? Have we conjured our ancient legendary Teutonic world back in all its might and glory? Thor? Odin? Are you—?"

The dragons had impressed him.

"I regret, your excellency," I said, "that these are dragons of oriental origin. They are Levantine dragons. From the wrong side of the Mediterranean."

His eyes widened. "Impossible."

Oona helped Elric adjust his *skeffla'a* on Blacksnout's back. She climbed up behind him, signalling to me to take the other dragon, Whitesnout.

"Let me come with you!" Hess was pleadingly eager. "The Grail—I am not your enemy."

"Farewell, your excellency!" Elric sheathed Stormbringer and wrapped his hands around the dragon's reins. He seemed to regain his strength with every passing moment.

I climbed into the dragon saddle with all the familiarity of one born to the royal line. I was full of a wild, unhuman glee. Alien. Faery. Though I would have scoffed at such an idea a short while earlier, now I accepted everything. There is no greater joy than riding through the night on the back of a dragon.

The massive wings began to beat. Hess was driven back, as if by a hurricane. I saw him mouthing something, pleading with me. I almost felt sympathetic to him. Of all the Nazis, he seemed the least disgusting. Then I saw Göring and the storm troopers burst out onto the roof. The air was once again alive with popping bullets. They were no danger to us. We could have destroyed the tower and all within it by releasing a few drops of venom, but it did not occur to us. We were convinced Gaynor had the Grail and if we could catch him in time it would soon be ours.

The exhilaration of the flight was extraordinary! Elric led the way through the air on Blacksnout's back, while Whitesnout followed. I had no need to control my dragon, though I knew intuitively how to do so.

Every anxiety was left behind me on the ground as the mighty wings beat against the clouds, bearing us higher and higher, farther and farther west. Where? To Ireland? Surely not to England?

England was my country's enemy. What if I were captured, still in the vestiges of my SS uniform? It would be impossible to convince them of my true reasons for being there!

I had no choice. Blacksnout, with Elric and Oona, flew with long, slow movements of her wings, gliding above the clouds ahead of me, sometimes casting a faint shadow. She flew steadily and Whitesnout, her junior by a year or two, let her lead. As the light grew stronger, the markings of the dragon's wings were clearer. They were like gigantic butterflies, with distinct patterns of red, black, orange and glowing viridian, far different from the green and yellow reptiles of picture books. The Phoorn dragons were creatures of extraordinary grace. And beauty with a sense about them that they were wiser than men.

Whenever the clouds parted, I could see the patterned fields and nestling towns of rural Germany. They had known little of direct strife for more than a century and were secure in Hitler's assurances that no foreign bombers would be allowed to enter German airspace.

I wondered if Hitler would be able to keep his promises. My guess was that he would begin relying on magic as political and military means failed him. He seemed like a man riding a tiger, terrified of where it was taking him yet unable to jump clear because of the momentum at which he was moving.

Or a man riding a dragon? Did I think Hitler helplessly caught up in events because I myself was carried along by monumental realities?

Such speculation soon left my head as I relished the beauty of the skies. The smell of clear air. I was so enraptured that I hardly heard the first droning behind me. I looked back and down. I saw a carpet of aeroplanes, so thick, so close together, that they seemed at first to be one huge bird. The droning was the steady sound of their engines. They were moving a little faster than we were, but in exactly the same direction.

I could not see how any country, especially depleted, weary Britain, could stand against such a vast aerial armada. Nothing like it had been assembled in the world's history. The only equivalent sea force had been the Spanish fleet, massed to attack England during Elizabeth's reign. England had been saved that time by a trick of the weather. She could expect no such good fortune now.

I had seen whole civilisations destroyed since this adventure had begun. I knew that the impossible was all too possible, that peoples and architecture could disappear from the face of the Earth as if they had never existed.

Was I, by some ghastly coincidence, about to see the last of England, the fall of the British Empire?

What I had so far seen was a squadron of Junkers 87s—the famous Stuka dive-bomber, which the Luftwaffe had traditionally used in their first attacks on other countries. But as we flew on, obscured by the cloud separating us from the air fleets below, I saw waves of Messerschmitt fighters, squadrons of Junkers and Heinkels, relentlessly moving towards an already battered Britain that could not possibly produce the numbers or quality of aircraft to combat such an invasion.

Was this why Gaynor was leading us to the west? So that we might witness the beginning of the end? The final battle whose winning would ensure the rule of the Lords of the Higher Worlds on Earth? And would those same lords remain at peace? Or would they immediately begin to fall upon one another?

Were we on our way to Ragnarok?

The planes passed. A strange silence filled the sky.

As if the whole world were waiting.

And waiting.

In the distance we began to hear the steady, mechanical thunder of guns and bombs, the shriek of fighters and tracer bullets. Away to our east, we saw oily smoke rising from erupting orange flame, saw flares and exploding shells. Blacksnout banked in a long graceful turn into the morning sun and soon the sound of warfare was behind us. England could not last the day. The war against Europe was as good as won. Where would Hitler turn his attentions next? Russia?

I mourned England's passing with mixed feelings. Her arrogance, her casual power, her easy contempt for all other races and nations, had all been there to the end. These qualities were what had led her to underestimate Germany. But also her courage, her tenacity, her lazy good nature, her inventiveness, her coolness under fire, all these had been invested in her great warships, those fighting islands in miniature, each its own small nation. Those men-o'-war had ruled the world and defeated Napoleon on sea, while together we had defeated him on land. A bloody, piratical nation she might be, ready to boast of her own coarseness and brutality. But her heroes had earned their power through their own determination, by risking their own lives and fortunes. And not a few of those great men had been great poets or historians. If she were decadent now, it was because she no longer possessed such men of integrity and breadth of vision.

This was her day of reckoning. The day to which all great imperial nations come eventually—Byzantium and Carthage, Jerusalem and Rome. Unable to conceive of their mortality, they know the double bitterness of defeat and slavery. Hitler had reintroduced slavery throughout his empire. The British, who had led the world in abolishing that dreadful practice, would again know the humiliation and deep misery of forced labour. Even as she set her national vices aside and called upon her virtues, the Last Post was sounding for her freedom and her glory. She would go to her defeat proving that virtue is stronger than vice, that courage is more prevalent than cowardice and that the two can exist together at a moment to which we can point years later as examples of the best, rather than the worst, that we can be. And show how virtue made us stronger and safer than any cynicism ever could. Why was that a lesson we had to learn over and over again?

Such philosophical meanderings while experiencing the physical exhilaration of riding on a dragon! What a typical thing for me to be doing! But I could not help grieving for that great country which so many Germans thought of as their natural partner, the best that they themselves could be.

Water now. Calm, blue sparkling water. Green hills. Yellow beaches. More water. Lazy sunlight, as if the world had never been anything but paradise. Little towns seemed to have grown from the earth itself. Rivers, woods, valleys. The distinctive domestic beauty of the English shires. What would become of all this once Germany crushed British air power and "Germanified" the world into a comic-opera version of its heritage? The bleak, black cities they all loathed, of course, were defending this tranquillity, this ideal, against the tyranny which, in the name of preserving it, would destroy their way of life for ever.

So powerful were my feelings that I wished I was back facing the dangers of Mu-Ooria. That would have been easier. Had Gaynor really destroyed that gentle race and left only a few survivors?

Over the sea again, gentle in a southerly breeze, to a tiny green spot looking scarcely more than a hillock, jutting out of the water and lapped by white-topped waves. The leading dragon banked again and circled the island, which was about half a mile across. I saw a Tudor house, a ruined abbey, a white peninsula, like a rat's tail, which served as a natural quay. No people were gathering to see us; nothing suggested the place had been occupied for a long time. The centre of the island was topped by a grassy hill which bore a ragged granite crown of stones, marking it as the site of an ancient place of ritual. At one time, long ago, those stones had stood straight and formed a combined observatory, church and place of contemplative study.

And so we came to the Isle of Morn, to Marag's Mount, "whence all the pure virtue of the English race came so long ago," as their epic explorer poet Wheldrake put it. One of the great holy places of the West with a history even more ancient than that of Glastonbury or Tintagel. As the dragons landed gracefully upon Morn's pure white sandy beach, and the sea beat like a warning drum upon the rocks, I knew why Gaynor was here.

Morn was one of the great places of power which even the Nazis acknowledged, though its founders were Celts, not Saxons. The Isle of Morn, where all the old races of the world sent their scholars to exchange ideas and discuss the nature of existence, the differences and similarities of religions, in that Silver Age before the Teuton explosion. Before the violence and the conquest began.

To Morn had come bishops, rabbis and Moslem scholars, Buddhists, Hindus, Gnostics, philosophers and scientists, all to share their knowledge. At the abbey below the hill they had met regularly. An international university, a monument to good will. Then the Norsemen had come in their dragon-ships and it was over.

I climbed down from my dragon, scratching her neck under her scales, and thanking her for her courtesy. I removed the *skeffla'a*, folded it and tucked it inside my shirt. Oona stumbled towards me, still finding her land legs in the soft, white sand. She pointed to the headland. There, at anchor, sat a German U-boat with two sentries standing guard on her low, water-washed decks.

A coincidence? The scouts for the invasion fleet? Or had Gaynor arranged for it to be here, to use it to escape, if need be? But why? He had not known we could follow him. It seemed an elaborate precaution to take on the mere chance of being found here.

Whatever the reason, the Nazi U-boat offered no immediate danger. I doubted they would have believed the reality anyway. Dragons rarely come ashore on small islands in the middle of the Irish Sea.

A word from Elric, and the great beasts were airborne again, arrowing to the upper regions of the air where they would wait out of sight.

Pausing only for a few moments, we struck inland through the cobbled streets of the deserted village, past the great Hall where Morn's independent Duke had ruled until 1918 and which was now boarded up, past a surviving farm or two which had no doubt been evacuated at the outbreak of this war, and up the winding lane which led to the top of the grassy hill and the ring of stones.

So far nothing was unusual about the place. Squabbling gulls cruised the waves and hovered in the air. Blackbirds sang in windswept trees, sparrows hunted in the overgrown hedgerows, and in the distance the surf drummed reassuring rhythms.

With some effort we climbed to the crest of the island where the granite standing stones leaned like old men, one against the other. Their circle was still complete.

We were approaching the stones when I noticed a strange milky light flickering faintly from within. I hesitated. I had no stomach for further supernatural encounters. But Oona urged us on.

"I knew he would have to come here if we defeated him at Bek," she said. "He hopes to contact Arioch. But I think I'll have a surprise for him."

Oona led the way into the centre of the stones. Beyond, the sea was very calm. Perfect weather for an invasion, I thought. I looked for the U-boat, but it wasn't visible from this point.

The translucent light washed around our feet and legs like surf. "Draw your swords, gentlemen," she said. "I will need their energy."

We obeyed her. This beautiful young girl and the confidence she radiated fascinated us. She held up her bowstaff and then dipped it into the opalescent substance, drawing it up like paint and describing extraordinary geometric patterns in the air, linking one stone to another until they were criss-crossed with a cat's cradle of pearly, sparkling force.

At the same time Oona spoke. She murmured and sang, making spells. There was a sense of urgency about her movements and her voice.

Lights began to zigzag wildly until I was thoroughly confused and blinded. She took Ravenbrand from me and described a large oval with it. The oval undulated and formed a tunnel in the light. I saw a figure walking along the tunnel of light towards us.

Fromental!

The Frenchman strolled into the circle of stones as if looking for a good place for a picnic. To confirm this intention, he held in his hand a covered basket. He was completely unsurprised to see us and greeted us with a cheerful wave. Stepping into the stone circle, a crimson light surrounded him, wrapping around him like a bloody coat. It flared and was gone. The milky web also disappeared. A stink of something old and hot remained. I recognised the smell but did not know why.

"Am I in time?" he asked Oona.

"I hope so," she said. "Did you bring her?"

Fromental lifted the basket. "Here she is, Lady Oona. Shall I take her out?"

"Not yet. We have to be sure he is coming. He will get here somehow. As will Arioch. Gaynor expects to meet Arioch at the Stones of Morn. They have been here before."

"My Lord Arioch is with us now," said Elric quietly.

Elric's whole manner changed. He sensed his master's presence in the circle. He spoke rapidly, urgently.

"My Lord Arioch. Forgive us for this intrusion. Give us your good will, I beg, for the sake of our ancient covenants. I am Elric of Melniboné and our blood is bound to the same destiny."

A voice, sweet as childhood, spoke from the air. "You are my mortal off-spring. You represent my interests in other realms, but not in this one. Why are you here, Elric?"

"I seek revenge upon an enemy, my lord. One who serves you. Who offered you this portal."

"One of my servants cannot be your enemy."

"One who serves two masters is nobody's friend," Elric replied.

The voice, whose warmth embraced and comforted like an old, loving relative, chuckled.

"Ah, bravest of my slaves, sweetest of my succulent children. Now I remember why I love thee."

My throat filled with bile. Being in the invisible creature's presence was almost physically unbearable. Even Oona seemed unwell. But Elric was if anything more relaxed than usual, even tranquil. "I am destined to serve thee, great Duke of Hell. The old pact is between my blood and thine. The one who dubs himself 'Knight of the Balance' has already betrayed one Lord of the Higher World, and I know he would betray another."

"I cannot be betrayed. It is impossible. I trust nothing. I trust no-one. I imprisoned Miggea for him. And this was to be my payment. This is a rich, de-licious realm. There is much in it to relieve my boredom. Gaynor swore loyalty to me. He would not dare try my patience further."

"Gaynor's loyalty is to Law before Chaos." I heard myself speak. My voice was a kind of echo in my own skull and sounded like Elric's. "And I assure you, Duke Arioch, I owe you no loyalty. It is not in my interest to allow you to enter my realm. Your forces already destroy too much. But I can offer you the means of claiming your payment from Gaynor."

Arioch was amused. I glimpsed the outline of a golden face, the most beau-tiful face in the multiverse, and I loved it. "Those are not my forces, little mortal. They are the forces of the Lady Miggea. They are the forces of Law who make war against your world."

"Gaynor wishes you to oppose them?"

"I have no interest in his wishes, only his actions. He merely offered me an opportunity. It is in my nature to oppose Law."

"Then our interests are the same," I agreed. "But we cannot strike the same bargain with you that Gaynor struck."

"Gaynor promises me an entry into your realm. By means of his magic and his wisdom. You will not do the same for me?"

"No, master." Elric shrugged almost casually. "We do not have the means. The great object of power is lost to us."

"Gaynor will bring it here."

"Perhaps," said Elric. He spoke with respect but also with the firmness of one who regarded himself the equal of gods. "Master, you have no rights in this realm."

"I have rights in all realms, little slave. Nonetheless, I grow tired of this game. I appear to be playing against my own self-interest. As soon as Gaynor brings the key, I and my armies will pass through to bring unbridled Chaos to a bored little world. Miggea's forces are without the guidance of a vital mind. We shall soon defeat them. Your fears are unnecessary."

"And if Gaynor does not bring the key, your excellency?" said Oona, gazing levelly up at the golden head.

"Then Gaynor is mine. Mine to eat. Mine to regurgitate whenever I choose. Mine to drink. Mine to piss. Mine to tickle. Mine to kiss. Mine to shit and mine to fart. Mine to take his heart. Mine to clothe with iron shoes. Mine to dance. Mine to bruise. Mine to use." The achingly beautiful lips smacked like a troll's in a fairy tale. I began to wonder if it were only Miggea of Law who grew senile amongst the Lords of the Higher Worlds. Could the whole race of gods have grown too old to have any clear idea of their desires or interests? Was the multiverse in the hands of such creatures? Was our own condition reflected in theirs?

Fromental, meanwhile, followed none of this. We spoke a language completely alien to him. He looked from Oona to me, eyebrows raised, asking a silent question.

Elric saw something and pointed. Without a thought, he folded both hands around Stormbringer's hilt.

Gaynor, still in his armour but looking somewhat the worse for wear, appeared on the white beach. Had the U-boat brought him to Morn? He clearly could not see anything within the stone circle and thus believed himself to be alone. He was swordless, apparently with no weapons. And he had no cup with him either.

We took a certain pleasure in watching Gaynor advance.

He paused before entering the circle. He peered in. We remained invisible to him. Ochre light filled the spaces between the stones.

"Master? Lord Arioch?"

Arioch's voice was a gentle invitation. "Enter."

Gaynor stepped through.

And found all his enemies awaiting him.

He turned in startled fury. He tried to step back out of the circle, but he was trapped.

"Have you brought me the key, little mortal?" Arioch spoke again with a delicacy suggesting he tasted each syllable before he released it into the air.

"I could not, sire." His attention was more on us than on the Lord of the Higher Worlds. "The thing has a mind of its own . . ."

"But it is your duty to control it."

"It cannot be controlled, my lord. It has a will, I swear, if not intelligence."

"But I told you all that, little mortal. And you assured me you had the means of gaining control. That is why I helped you. That is why I imprisoned Lady Miggea for you."

Elric laughed as Gaynor's confidence ebbed. "I came for more help," said our enemy almost pathetically. "A little more. But why? How . . . ? These are your enemies, my lord. They who would oppose you."

"Oh, I think they have shown me rather more respect, Prince Gaynor, than I have received from you. You seem to think it possible to lie to a Lord of the Higher Worlds. You seem to think I'm some bottle-imp to give you as many wishes as you desire. I am no such thing! I am a Duke of Hell! I have ambitions which go far beyond your imaginings. And my patience is ended. How shall I punish you, little prince?"

"I can bring you through, my lord, I swear. I just have to return to Bek. Mighty forces even now rise to dominate this realm. Hour by hour they gain more territory, more power. Only you, through me, can defeat them, my lord."

"I have no interest in saving this realm," said Arioch in regal astonishment.

"I just wished to play with it for a while. Now my only pleasure, little Gaynor, will be to play with *you*."

Oona turned to Fromental and snatched the basket from his hands. She reached into it and lifted out its contents.

It appeared to be a miniature model. An intricate ivory cage made of thousands of tiny bones from which a tiny voice raged.

Miggea, still trapped, was furious.

"How did you do that?" I asked Oona in astonishment.

"It is not difficult. Scale is the only thing that varies from realm to realm. Each realm, as I explained to you, is on a slightly different scale, which is how we are able to navigate between them and why we are not immediately aware of their existence.

"I arranged for Lieutenant Fromental to bring her here. Miggea is very powerful, but quite thoroughly imprisoned. Given her own volition she would soon adjust her scale to the realm in which she finds herself. I do not have the power to release her. Only the one who imprisoned her can do that."

"You have brought another of these creatures to my world?" This seemed the height of irresponsibility to me. "To war against the one already here? To turn the whole planet into a battlefield?"

"You will see," said Oona. "But you must all leave the circle now. First, give me your sword."

Against all sense I handed her Ravenbrand. Then Elric, Fromental and I stepped outside the Stones of Morn.

The little we could see became a shadow play. The dark, lounging presence of Duke Arioch, the swift, elegant figure of Oona placing the cage of bone on the ground. Gaynor transfixed. Oona then touched the cage with the point of my sword. I heard Arioch's voice, faintly booming. "Well, my lady, it seems it is no longer in my interest to hold you captive."

A noise like splitting flint.

A terrible *crack*.

Something began to boil and writhe and grow within the circle. Something which cackled and squealed with idiot laughter and pushed against whatever force the stone circle held. Miggea, having escaped the cage, now sought to escape the circle.

The stones shook. They might have been dancing. Then they were still, straight, waiting. They looked to me as they must have looked when the first Druids newly erected them. Tall, white granite, flashing in the light from the sun.

Suddenly a figure of unstable fire stood before us, caught in the circle, writhing uncontrollably, screaming silently out at us. Gaynor's face was burning. His whole body was in flames. Burning with a million conflicts generated in his ungenerous heart. And there he was again, standing beside himself, still flaming, still screaming. He was begging us for something. Could it have been forgiveness? Or merely release? Another dancing, burning figure, and another, until they made a full circle within the circle.

From above, the shadowy golden face of Duke Arioch smiled and whistled as if watching a puppet show, and the senile, drooling, cackling creature that had once been one of Law's greatest aristocrats poked at Gaynor's twisting body, which changed shape and size, became many versions of itself, then one, then fragmented again. I heard his screams. They were like nothing else I had ever heard in all my life.

Arioch and Miggea tugged at him, breaking off pieces of his many identities in their struggle. They played with him as cats might play with a cricket. There was little animosity between them. All their hatred was directed at Gaynor, stupid Gaynor, who had thought he could play one of them off against the other.

He begged them to stop.

I was close to begging for the same thing! A thousand Gaynors filled the circle. A thousand different kinds of pain.

Oona regarded this with quiet satisfaction, in much the same way she might look upon a piece of domestic handiwork and congratulate herself.

"He cannot bring himself back to his archetype," she said. "It is the only way we survive. A sense of identity is all we have. At this moment all Gaynor's many identities are in conflict. He is being disseminated throughout the multiverse. The convergence Gaynor sought to use for his own selfish ends has proved to be his undoing."

"Too many!" Arioch swore. "You promised me the power of Law. I already possess the power of Chaos. Where, fractured Gaynor, is the Grail?"

The replies were various, multitudinous, horrifying. "She has it!" was the only coherent phrase we heard.

Then Gaynor was gone.

Miggea was gone.

Arioch's voice was a satisfied, luscious whisper. "The Grail is still there. At my point of entry, where he promised to bring me through."

Monstrous lips smacked.

And then Arioch, too, disappeared.

Between them, he and Miggea tore Gaynor into a million psychic shreds.

A rustling, like an autumn wind, and sorcery was gone from that realm. The old stones pushed their way up through ordinary grass. A bright sun shone in the sky. The surf washing the white beach was the loudest sound we had ever heard. I turned to Fromental. "You struck this bargain with Oona when you met her at Miggea's prison?"

"We did not know exactly what we would do with Miggea, but it was useful to have her in portable form." Fromental winked. "Now I must return to my friends. Tanelorn is saved, but they will want to know the rest of this story. I am sure we'll meet again, my friend."

"And the Off-Moo? Do you know their fate?"

"They have another city, that is all I know. On the far shore of the lake. They went there. Few were killed."

With the air of a man who had urgent business, he shook hands with me and walked back to the shore. A skiff with two seamen waited for him, offering him a salute as he got into the boat. I had made the wrong presumptions about the U-boat. Fromental had sent it ahead of him. He waved to us again and was then rowed quickly over to the U-boat. Perhaps I would never know how he managed to send a captured goddess to us by submarine!

As I watched the conning tower disappear below the waves, my attention returned to the depressing realities of my own realm. Where a conquering air fleet was ensuring that Adolf Hitler would soon control the world.

I reminded Elric that my work was unfinished. If the Grail was still at Bek, perhaps I could find a way of using it against the Nazis. At the very least it should ultimately be returned to Mu-Ooria.

The dreamthief's daughter smiled at me, as if at an innocent. "What if the Grail always belonged at Bek?" she said. "What if it was lost and the Off-Moo were merely its temporary guardians? What if it decided to return home?"

I scarcely took this in as something else dawned on me. I looked urgently to Elric. "Klosterheim!" I cried. "Both of us survived his bullets because we were in the presence of the Grail and did not know it! The Grail works against dissipation. Gaynor could not have performed his magic with it on his person. The Grail's still there. But that means everyone who was in its presence survived. Which means Klosterheim could even now be in possession of the Grail."

Elric paused. I sensed that he was reluctant to stay in this dream. He wanted to rejoin Moonglum and continue his adventurings in the world he understood best. At last he said, "Klosterheim, too, has earned my vengeance. We'll go back to Bek." He paused, laying a long-fingered hand on my shoulder. For a moment he was a brother.

When we returned to the beach the dragons were already waiting for us, as if they knew we needed them. They were rattling their quills and skipping with impatience from one huge foot to the other. The sun flashed off their butterfly colours, dazzling all around. They were young Phoorn, capable of flying halfway around the world without tiring. They yearned to be aloft again.

We unrolled our *skeffla'an* and saddled our dragons. Climbing onto their broad backs, we settled ourselves in the natural indentations which could, on a Phoorn, take up to three riders.

With a murmur from Elric, still the great Dragon Master, bright reptilian wings cracked and moved the heavy air, cracked again and took us into the afternoon sky with the steady beat of rowers across a lake. They increased speed with each mighty flap, tails lashing and curling to steer us through the rushing currents of the air. With necks stretched out and great eyes blazing, they scanned the cloud ahead. Ancient firedrakes.

We skimmed the sea, then swept gracefully upwards until we were flying east over the gentle wooded hills and dales again, back towards Germany.

This time Elric took a slightly different course, going farther south than I might have expected, perhaps to witness the devastation of the proud hub of Empire in defeat. He, too, understood the peculiar ambivalences of owing allegiance to a dying empire.

But now there was some extra purpose to Elric's flight as he led us down through the clouds and into the late-afternoon light—to where an aerial dogfight was in progress. Two Spitfires wheeled and climbed as their guns blazed at an overwhelming pack of Stukas. The German planes had been deliberately fitted with screaming sirens to make them sound more deadly. The air filled with their dreadful klaxons, but the Spitfires, with extraordinary lightness and manoeuvrability, gave back their best.

Elric was shouting as he urged his dragon down. I heard his voice faintly on the wind as I followed him. After the incredible exhilaration of our dive, Blacksnout turned her long head, narrowed her great yellow eyes, and snorted.

She snorted acid fire.

Fire struck first one Stuka and then another. Plane after plane went down in an instant as the dragon swept the squadron with her terrible breath. I saw looks of astonishment on the thankful faces of the Spitfire pilots as they banked upwards and flew as fast as they could into the cloud.

The few surviving Stukas turned to seek the relative safety of the high skies, but Elric ignored them. We flew on.

Ten minutes later we came upon a great sea of Junkers bombers. It struck me that their crews were my own countrymen. Some of them could be cousins or distant relatives. Ordinary, decent German boys caught up in the nonsense of militarism and the Nazi dream. Was it right to kill such people, in any cause? Were there no other alternatives?

Whitesnout followed her sister down the hidden air trails. Their tails cracked like gigantic whips, venom frothed and seethed in their mouths and nostrils. Our dragons fell upon their prey with all the playful joy of young tigers finding themselves in a herd of gazelle.

Guns fired at us, but not a single shot struck. The dragons' steely scales deflected anything that hit them. For the gunners it was impossible—they must have thought they were dreaming.

Down we went and all I saw were Nazi hooked crosses, a symbol which stood for every infamy, every dishonour, every cynical cruelty the world had ever known. It was those crosses I attacked. I did not care about the crews who flew under such banners. Who were not ashamed to fly under such banners.

Down I dived. Whitesnout's venom seared from her mouth, blown by red-hot air generated in one of her many stomachs. The flaming poison struck bomber after bomber, all still with their loads. They blew into fragments before our eyes.

Some of the planes tried to peel away. Some dropped their bombs at random. But again the dragons circled. Again the planes were destroyed. The few that remained turned tail and raced back towards Germany. What story would they tell when they returned? What story would they dare tell? They had failed, however they explained it.

And thus we gave birth to a famous legend. A legend which took credit for the victory of the RAF over the Luftwaffe. The legend which many believed turned the course of the war and caused Hitler to lose all judgement and perhaps what was left of his sanity. A legend which proved as powerful, in the end, as the Nazi myth unleashed on the peoples of Europe. Ours was the legend of the Dragons of Wessex, which came to the aid of the English in their hour of need. A legend which elevated British morale as thoroughly as it crushed German. Even the story of the Angel of Mons from the First World War was not as potent in its time as the legend of the Dragons of Wessex. King Arthur, Guinevere and Sir Lancelot, it was said, all reappeared. Flying on the fabulous beasts of ancient days, they came to serve their nation in its hour of need. The story would eventually be suppressed, as Hess was to discover. The legend was so powerful that propaganda resources of both nations were devoted to promoting or denying it.

By the time we flew home to Germany, we had destroyed several squadrons of bombers and innumerable fighters. The Battle of Britain had turned significantly. From that moment on, Hitler acted with increased insanity as his predictions lost credibility. From that moment on, his famous luck wholly deserted him.

As the tireless dragon bore me back to Bek, I mourned. I endured the anguish of my own conscience. Though the cause had been right, I had still made war on my own people. I understood all the reasons why I should have done it, but I would never, for the rest of my life, be fully reconciled to this burden of guilt. If I survived and peace was restored, I knew I would meet some mothers whom I would not be able to look in the eye.

The joy of victory, the thrill of the flight, was tempered by a strange melancholy which has remained with me ever since.

By the time we reached Bek, the place was evidently deserted. There wasn't a guard in sight. Hitler and his people had left in disgust and everyone else had made haste to disassociate themselves with the place. There was nothing left to guard.

The place was oddly still as we landed on the battlements and cautiously made our way down into the old armoury.

Scenes of mayhem were everywhere. Blood was everywhere. But no corpses. And no cup.

Where was the Grail? All the evidence indicated it was never removed from Bek. But did Klosterheim somehow take it?

Oona gestured to me to wait for her as she slipped away into the deserted castle.

I felt Elric's hand on my shoulder again, an affectionate brotherly gesture.

"We must find Klosterheim." I turned and started to make my way back up the stairs.

"No!" Elric was emphatic.

"What? It's my duty to follow him," I said.

"I'll follow Klosterheim," said Elric. "If I'm successful you'll never see him again. I'll return to Melniboné. These young dragons have done good work and must be rewarded."

"And Oona? Your daughter?"

"The dreamthief's daughter stays here." With a cold crack of his cloak he turned his back on me and strode for the steps leading from the chamber. I wanted to ask him to return. I had much to thank him for. But, of course, I had served him also. We had been of mutual help. I had saved him from eternal slumber and he had turned the tide of war. The Luftwaffe was crushed. By the courage of a few and with the help of a powerful legend.

Britain would gather strength. America would help her. Eventually the fascists would be ousted from power and democracy restored.

But before that moment came, the blood of millions would be spilled. It was hard to see who would win anything from that terrible conflict.

I looked helplessly around at our old armoury. So much violence had taken place here. How would it ever feel like home to me again?

How much I'd lost since Gaynor's first visit to Bek! When he tried to get the Raven Sword from me in order to kill my doppelgänger's daughter! I had certainly lost a kind of innocence. I had also lost friends, servants. And a certain amount of self-respect.

What had I gained? Knowledge of other worlds? Wisdom? Guilt? A chance to turn the tide of history, to stop the spread of Nazi tyranny? Many yearned to be able to do that. Circumstances of blood and time had put me in a position to change the course of the war in favour of my country's enemy.

The guilt grew more intense as Allied bombing increased. Cologne. Dresden. Munich. All the beautiful old cities of our golden past gone into rubble and bitter memory. Just as we had blown the memory and pride of other nations to smithereens and defiled their dead. And all for what?

What if this pain, this pain of all the world, could be stopped? By the influence of one object? By the thing they called the Runestaff, the Grail, Finn's Cauldron—the object that created a field of serenity and balance all around it. Sustaining its own survival and the survival of the multiverse.

Where was it, this panacea for the grief of nations?

Where was it, but in our own hearts?

Our imaginings?

Our dreams?

Had all I experienced in Mu-Ooria been a complex but unreal nightmare into which the dreamthief's daughter lured me? An illusion of magic, of the Grail, of unending life? Once I was in no doubt of the Grail's properties or of its power for good. But now I wondered if the thing actually *was* a power for good? Or was it self-sustaining and not interested in questions of human morality?

Was Gaynor right? Did the Grail demand the blood of innocents to be effective? Was that the final irony? No life without death?

Oona came through the ruined doorway, a shaft of sunlight behind her. She had found her arrows where she had hidden them.

She looked at me and realised that Elric was gone.

She ran for the old staircase.

"Father!"

She disappeared up the steps before I could reach the door. I called after her, but she ignored me or did not hear.

I went up the stairs rapidly, but something made me slow when I reached the top of the tower and the narrow corridor which led to the roof. I moved reluctantly and looked out at the battlements where Elric held his daughter in a tender embrace.

Behind him the dragons muttered and stamped, anxious to be aloft again. But Elric was slow to leave. When he lifted his face those troubled eyes were weeping.

I watched him place a gentle kiss on his daughter's forehead. Then he strode over to the impatient Blacksnout and stood scratching the great beast under her scales. With a quick, graceful movement, he climbed into his saddle and called in his musical voice, called to his dragon sisters.

With a massive crash of wings the two great reptiles mounted the evening air. I watched their dark shapes circling against the great red disc of the setting sun.

They banked with slow grace into a dark shadow and were suddenly gone.

Oona turned, dry-eyed, her voice unnaturally low. "I can see him anytime I choose," she said. She held something in her hand. A small talisman.

"In his dreams?" I asked.

She stared at me for a moment.

Then I followed her inside.

EPILOGUE

The rest of the story is a matter of public record. Neither Oona nor myself, of course, remained in Germany. Indeed, we were certain of arrest. And, if arrested, we had a clear idea of our likely fate. So Prince Lobkowitz helped us get to Sweden and from there to London. Having helped in the destruction of my own country's air fleet and begun the process of Hitler's defeat, I continued the war against the Nazis. I joined the BBC as a broadcaster for a while and worked as an interpreter with a Red Cross psychiatric unit when the Allies started moving into Germany and Austria. Even I, with my experience of Nazi brutality, could scarcely bear the scenes which every new day brought.

I saw little more of Lobkowitz, who was busy with the War Crimes people, and nothing of Bastable. Oona went to Washington when the United States entered the war and joined a special operations unit.

I saw Bek once more before the Russians took it over. The Red Army had billeted its officers there. Even they remarked on the sense of peace the old place had. I was bound to agree. Though its recent history had scarcely been tranquil, tranquillity is what that house radiated for a mile or more around it in the old Bek estates. I heard that the local authorities eventually turned Bek into a rest home for mental patients, and I was pleased.

When at last the Wall came down and I reclaimed my home, I allowed it to continue in its most recent function, asking only that I have a few rooms in the old part of the house, along with the armoury and the tower. Here I study quietly in the sure knowledge that somewhere I will discover a clue to the Grail's current incarnation. That it lies at Bek, there is no doubt. Here all wounds seem eventually to heal. This is all we saved from the Nazis.

In May 1941 it became clear that the Luftwaffe was no longer capable of conquering Britain. Disturbed that Hitler was attacking the Soviet Union without first securing the alliance of her "natural brothers in arms," Rudolf Hess flew single-handed to Scotland. He parachuted out of his Messerschmitt and landed safely. He spent a few hours at Castle Auchy, the traditional home of the Clan McBegg, which had a bad reputation in those parts. He then set off to find the Marquess of Clydesdale, whom he wrongly believed to be a Nazi sympathiser. What Hess told the marquess and those sent to arrest him was that he had the secret of the Wessex Dragons who rose from their secret caverns under England's most beautiful downs to serve her in her hour of need. He claimed that he knew how to contact King Arthur, Sir Lancelot and Queen Guinevere, and that he also knew the whereabouts of the Holy Grail. He proposed that the Grail was the catalyst to reunite the Nordic peoples against the common Bolshevik/Asian threat. He asked several times to speak to Churchill, but published documents show that MI5 was of the firm opinion that Hess had completely lost his mind. All reports confirm this view. Churchill steadfastly refused to see him.

Hess was sentenced at Nuremberg as a war criminal and became the only surviving prisoner in Spandau prison. He allegedly hanged himself in his prison cell in Spandau in 1987. He was ninety-one. All that time he had been refused permission to publish and had given almost no interviews, though he insisted he had information of crucial intelligence to the authorities. There is a theory that he was murdered by the British Secret Service, who feared what he would tell the public when he was released.

Hess was to play no further part in my story. This would not be true of Elric, however. He is still in my soul. Still shares my mind. At night, when I do dream, I dream Elric's life as if it were my own. I have a sense that I live not only Elric's destiny, but the destiny of hundreds like us. I am never truly free of him. His story continues, and I continue to be a part of it, as does Oona, the dreamthief's daughter, who became my wife. We chose to have no natural children but adopted three girls and two boys. We intend to let our blood die out.

How the Grail was found and what happened to us is a story which, like that of Rudolf Hess, remains to be told.

Meanwhile, we are at rest here for the moment. Glad to enjoy some respite in the great struggle—that game in which we all have important parts to play. The never-ending game of life and death.

THE
SKRAYLING
TREE

THE ALBINO
IN AMERICA

For Jewell Hodges and them Gibsons
with great respect

Thanks, too, as always to Linda Steele for her
good taste and patience

THE SKRAYLING TREE

CONTENTS

PROLOGUE

Nine by nine and three by three,
We shall seek the Skraeling Tree.

—Wheldrake,
A Border Tragedy

The following statement was pinned to a later part of this manuscript. The editor thought it better placed here, since it purports to be at least a partial explanation of the motives of our mysterious dream-travellers. Only the first part of this book is written in a different, rather idiosyncratic hand. The remaining parts of the story are mostly in the handwriting of Count Ulric von Bek. The note in his hand demanding that the manuscript not be published until after his death is authentic.

More than one school of magistic philosophy insists that our world is the creation of human yearning. By the power of our desires alone, we may bring into being whole universes, entire cosmologies, and supernatural pantheons. Many believe we dream ourselves into existence and then dream our own gods and demons, heroes and villains. Each dream, if powerful enough, can produce still another version of reality in the constantly growing organism that is the multiverse. They believe that just as we dream creatively, we also dream destructively. Some of us have the skills and courage to come and go in the dreams of others, even create our own dreams within the host dream. This was the accepted wisdom in Melniboné, where I was born.

In Melniboné we were trained to enter dreams in which we lived whole and very long lives, gaining the experience such realities brought. I had lived over two thousand years before I reached the age of twenty-five. It was a form of longevity I would wish upon only a handful of enemies. We pay a price for a certain kind of wisdom which brings the power to manipulate the elements.

If you were lucky, as I was, you did not remember much of these dreams. You drove them from your mind with ruthless deliberation. But the experience of them remained in your blood, was never lost. It could be called upon in the creation of strong sorcery. Our nature dictates that we forget most of what we dream, but some of the adventures I experienced with my distant relative Count Ulric von Bek enabled me to record a certain history which intertwined with his. What you read now, I shall likely forget soon.

These dreams form a kind of apocrypha to my main myth. In one life I was unaware of my destiny, resisting it, hating it. In another I worked to fulfil that destiny, all too aware of my fate. But only in this dream am I wholly conscious of my destiny. And when I have left the dream, it will fade, becoming little more than a half-remembered whisper, a fleeting image. Only the power will stay with me, come what may.

—Elric Sadric's son,
last emperor of Melniboné

Should you ask me, whence these stories?
Whence these legends and traditions,
With the odours of the forest,
With the dew and damp of meadows,
With the curling smoke of wigwams,
With the rushing of great rivers,
With their frequent repetitions
And their wild reverberations,
As of thunder in the mountains?
I should answer, I should tell you,
"From the forests and the prairies,
From the great lakes of the Northland,
From the land of the Ojibways
From the land of the Dacotahs,
From the mountains, moors, and fen-lands
Where the heron, the Shuh-shuh-gah,
Feeds among the reeds and rushes.
I repeat them as I heard them
From the lips of Nawadaha,
The musician, the sweet singer."

—Longfellow,
The Song of Hiawatha

THE FIRST BRANCH

OONA'S STORY

Nine Black Giants guard the Skraelings' Tree,
Three to the South and to the East are Three,
Three more the Westward side will shield,
But the North to a White Serpent she will yield;
For he is the dragon who deeply sleeps
Yet wakes upon the hour to weep,
And when he weeps fierce tears of fire,
They form a fateful funeral pyre
And only a singer with lute or lyre,
Shall turn the tide of his dark desire.

—Wheldrake,
The Skraeling Tree

I

The House on the Island

Hearing I ask from the Holy Races,
From Heimdall's sons, both high and low;
Thou wilt know, Valfather, how well I relate
Old tales I remember of men long ago.

I remember yet the giants of yore,
Who gave me bread in the days gone by;
Nine worlds I knew, the nine in the tree
With mighty roots beneath the mould.

—The Poetic Edda,
The Wise Woman's Prophecy

I am Oona, the shape-taker, Grafin von Bek, daughter of Oone the Dreamthief and Elric, Sorcerer Emperor of Melniboné. When my husband was kidnapped by Kakatanawa warriors, in pursuit of him I descended into the maelstrom and discovered an impossible America. This is that story.

With the Second World War over at last and peace of sorts returned to Europe, I closed our family cottage on the edge of the Grey Fees, and settled in Kensington, West London, with my husband Ulric, Count Bek. Although I am an expert archer and trained mistress of illusory arts, I had no wish to follow my mother's calling. For a year or two in the late 1940s I lacked a focus for my skills until I found a vocation in my husband's sphere. The unity of shared terror and grief following the Nazi defeat gave us all the strength we needed to rebuild, to rediscover our idealism and try to ensure that we would never again slide into aggressive bigotry and authoritarianism.

Knowing that every action taken in one realm of the multiverse is echoed in the others, we devoted ourselves confidently to the UN and the implementation of the Universal Declaration of Human Rights which H.G. Wells had drafted, in direct reference to Paine and the US Founding Fathers, just before the War. The USA's own Eleanor Roosevelt had helped the momentum. Our hope was that we could spread the values of liberal humanism and popular government across a world yearning for peace. Needless to say, our task was not proving an easy one. As the Greeks and Iroquois, who fathered those ideas, discovered, there is always more immediate profit to be gained from crisis than from tranquillity.

By September 1951, Ulric and I had both been working too hard, and because I travelled so much in my job, we had chosen to educate our children at boarding school in England. Michael Hall in rural Sussex was a wonderful school, run on the Steiner Waldorf system, but I still felt a certain guilt about being absent so often. In previous months Ulric had been sleeping badly, his dreams troubled by what he sometimes called "the intervention," when Elric's soul, permanently bonded to his, experienced some appalling stress. For this reason, among others, we were enjoying a long break at the Frank Lloyd Wright-designed summer house of Nova Scotian friends currently working in Trinidad. They were employed by the West Indies Independence Commission. When they returned to Cap Breton we would then leave their airy home to visit some of Ulric's relatives in New England before taking the *Queen Elizabeth* back to Southampton.

We had the loveliest weather. There was already a strong hint of autumn in the coastal breezes and a distinct chill to the water we shared with the seals, who had established a small colony on one of the many wooded islands of the Sound. These islands were permanently fascinating. The comings and goings of the wildlife provided just the right relaxation after a busy year. While Ulric and I enjoyed our work, it involved a great deal of diplomacy, and sometimes our faces ached from smiling! Now we could laze, read, frown if we felt like it and stop to enjoy some of nature's most exquisite scenery.

We were thoroughly relaxed by the second Saturday after we arrived.

Brought by the local taxi from Englishtown, we had become wonderfully isolated, with no car and no public transport. I must admit I was so used to activity that after a few days I was a trifle bored, but I refused to become busy. I continued to take a keen interest in the local wildlife and history.

That Saturday we were sitting on the widow's walk of our roof, looking out over Cabot Creek and its many small, wooded islands. One of these, little more than a rock, was submerged at high tide. There, it was said, the local Kakatanawa Indians had staked enemies to drown.

Our binoculars were Russian and of excellent quality, bought on our final visit to Ulric's ancestral estate in the days before the Berlin Wall went up. That afternoon I was able to spot clear details of the individual seals. They were always either there or about to appear, and I had fallen in love with their joyous souls. But, as I watched the tide wash over Drowning Rock, the water suddenly became agitated and erratic. I felt some vague alarm.

The swirl of the sea had a new quality I couldn't identify. There was even a different note to a light wind from the west. I mentioned it to Ulric. Half asleep, enjoying his brandy and soda, he smiled. It was the action of Auld Strom, the avenging hag, he said. Hadn't I read the guide? The Old Woman was the local English name for the unpredictable bore, a twisting, vicious current which ran between the dozens of little islands in the Sound and could sometimes turn into a dangerous whirlpool. The French called her Le Chaudron Noir, the black cauldron. Small whaling ships had been dragged down in the nineteenth century, and only a year or two before three vacationing schoolgirls in a canoe had disappeared into the maelstrom. Neither they nor their canoe had ever been recovered.

A harder gust of wind brushed against my left cheek. The surrounding trees whispered and bustled like excited nuns. Then they were still again.

"It's probably unwise to take a dip tomorrow." Ulric cast thoughtful eyes over the water. He sometimes seemed, like so many survivors of those times, profoundly sad. His high-boned, tapering face was as thrillingly handsome as when I had first seen it, all those years ago in the grounds of his house during the early Nazi years. Knowing I had planned some activity for the next day he smiled at me. "Though sailing won't be a problem, if we go the other way. We'd have to be right out there, almost at the horizon, to be in real danger. See?" He pointed, and I focused on the distant water which was dark, veined like living marble and swirling rapidly. "The Old Woman is definitely back in full fury!" He put his arm around my shoulders. As always I was amused and comforted by this gesture.

I had already studied the Kakatanawa legend. Le Chaudron was for them the spirit of all the old women who had ever been murdered by their enemies. Most Kakatanawa had been driven from their original New York homeland by the Haudenosaunee, a people famous for their arrogance, puritanism and efficient organisation, whose women not only determined which wars would be fought and who would lead them, but which prisoners would live and who would be tortured and eaten. So Auld Strom was a righteously angry creature, especially hard on females. The Kakatanawa called the conquering Haudenos-aunee "Erekoseh," their word for rattlesnake, and avoided the warriors as con-scientiously as they did their namesakes, for the Erekoseh, or Iroquois as the French rendered their name, had been the Normans of North America, masters of a superb new idea, an effective social engine, as pious and self-demanding in spirit as they were savage in war. Like the vital Romans and Normans, they respected the law above their own immediate interests. Normans employed so-phisticated feudalism as their engine; the Iroquois, a shade more egalitarian, employed the notion of mutuality and common law but were just as ruthless in establishing it. I felt very close to the past that day as I romantically scanned the shore, fancying I glimpsed one of those legendary warriors, with his shaven head, scalp lock, warpaint and breechclout, but of course there was no-one.

I was about to put the glasses away when I caught a movement and a spot of colour on one of the near islands among the thick clusters of birch, oak and pine which found unlikely purchase in what soil there was. A little mist clung to the afternoon water, and for a moment my vision was obscured. Expecting to glimpse a deer or perhaps a fisherman, I brought the island into focus and was very surprised. In my lens was an oak-timbered wattle-and-daub manor house similar to those I had seen in Iceland, the design dating back to the elev-enth century. Surely this house had to be the nostalgic folly of some very early settler? There were legends of Viking exploration here, but the many-windowed house was not quite that ancient! Wisteria and ivy showed how many years the two-storeyed house had stood with its black beams rooted among old trees and thick moss, yet the place had a well-kept but abandoned look, as if its owner rarely lived there. I asked Ulric his opinion. He frowned as he raised the binoculars. "I don't think it's in the guide." He adjusted the lens. "My God! You're right. An old manor! Great heavens!"

We were both intrigued. "I wonder if it was ever an inn or hotel?" Ulric, like me, was now more alert. His lean, muscular body sprang from its chair. I loved him in this mood, when he consciously jolted himself out of his natural reserve. "It's not too late yet for a quick preliminary exploration!" he said. "And it's close enough to be safe. Want to look at it? It'll only take an hour to go there and back in the canoe."

Exploring an old house was just enough adventure for my mood. I wanted to go now, while Ulric was in the same state of mind. Thus, we were soon paddling out from the little jetty, finding it surprisingly easy going against the fast-running tide. We both knew canoes and worked well in unison, driving rapidly towards the mysterious island. Of course, for the children's sake, we would take no risks if the pull of Le Chaudron became stronger.

Though it was very difficult to see from the shore through the thick trees, I was surprised we had not noticed the house earlier. Our friends had said nothing about an old building. In those days the heritage industry was in its infancy, so it was possible the local guides had failed to mention it, especially if the house was still privately owned. However, I did wonder if we might be trespassing.

To be safe we had to avoid the pull of the maelstrom at all costs, so we paddled to the west before we headed directly for the island, where the gentle tug actually aided our progress. Typically rocky, the island offered no obvious place to land. We were both still capable of getting under the earthy tree roots and hauling ourselves and canoe up bodily, but it seemed an unnecessary exercise, especially when we rounded the island and found a perfect sloping slab of rock rising out of the sea like a slipway. Beside it was a few feet of shingle.

We beached easily enough on the weedy strip of pebbles, then tramped up the slab. At last we saw the white sides and stained black oak beams of the house through the autumn greenery. The manor was equally well kept at the back, but we still saw no evidence of occupation. Something about the place reminded me of Bek when I had first seen it, neatly maintained but organic.

This place had no whiff of preservation about it. This was a warm, living building whose moss and ivy threatened the walls themselves. The windows were not glass but woven willow lattice. It could have been there for centuries. The only strange thing was that the wild wood went almost up to its walls. There was no sign of surrounding cultivation—no hedges, fences, lawns, herb gardens, no topiary or flower beds. The tangled old bracken stopped less than an inch from the walls and windows and made it hard going as our tweeds caught on brambles and dense shrubbery. For all its substance, the house gave the impression of not quite belonging here. That, coupled with the age of the architecture, began to alert me that we might be dealing with some supernatural agency. I put this to my husband, whose aquiline features were unusually troubled.

As if realising the impression he gave, Ulric's handsome mouth curved in a broad, dismissive smile. Just as I took the magical as my norm, he took the natural as his. He could not imagine what I meant. In spite of all his experience he retained his scepticism of the supernatural. Admittedly, I was inclined to come up with explanations considered bizarre by most of our friends, so I dropped the subject.

As we advanced through the sweet, rooty mould and leafy undergrowth I had no sense that the place was sinister. Nonetheless, I tended to go a little more cautiously than Ulric. He pushed on until he had brought us to the green-painted back door under a slate porch. As he raised his fist to knock I noticed a movement in the open upper window. I was sure I glimpsed a human figure.

When I pointed to the window, we saw nothing.

"Probably a bird flying over," said Ulric. Getting no response from the house, we made our way around the walls until we reached the big double doors at the front. They were oak and heavy with iron. Ulric grinned at me. "Since we are, after all, neighbours"—he took a piece of ivory pasteboard from his waistcoat—"the least we can do is leave our card." He pulled the old-fashioned bell-cord. A perfectly normal bell sounded within. We waited, but there was no answer. Ulric scribbled a note, stuck the card into the bell-pull, and we stepped back. Then, behind the looser weaving of the downstairs window, a face appeared, staring into mine. The shock staggered me. For a moment I thought I looked into my own reflection! Was there glass behind the lattice?

But it was not me. It was a youth. A youth who mouthed urgently through the gaps in the weaving and gestured as if for help, flapping his arms against the window. I could only think of a trapped bird beating its wings against a cage.

I am no dreamthief. I can't equate the craft with my own conscience, though I judge none who fairly practise it. Consequently I have never had the doubtful pleasure of encountering myself in another's dream. This had some of that reported frisson. The youth glared not at me but at my husband, who gasped as one bright ruby eye met another. At that moment, I could tell, blood spoke to blood.

Then it was as if a hand had gripped my hair and pulled it. Another hand slapped against my face. From nowhere the wind had begun to blow, cold and hard. Beginning as a deep soughing, its note now rose to an aggressive howl.

I thought the young albino said something in German. He was gesticulating to emphasise his words. But the wind kept taking them away. I could make out only one repeated sound. "Werner" was it? A name? The youth looked as if he had stepped from the European Dark Ages. His unstirring white hair fell in long braids. He wore a simple deerskin jacket, and his face was smeared with what might have been white clay. His eyes were desperate.

The wind yelped and danced around us, bending the trees, turning the ferns into angry goblins. Ulric instinctively put his arm around me, and we began to back towards the shore. His hand felt cold. He was genuinely frightened.

The wind appeared to be pursuing us. Everywhere the foliage bent and twisted, this way and that. It was as if we were somehow in the middle of a tornado. Branches opened and closed; leaves were torn into ragged clouds. But our attention remained on the face at the window.

"What is it?" I asked. "Do you recognise the boy?"

"I don't know." He spoke oddly, distantly. "I don't know. I thought my brother—but he's too young, and besides . . ."

All his brothers had died in the First War. Like me, he had noticed a strong family resemblance. I felt him shake. Then he took charge of his emotions. Although he had extraordinary self-control, he was terrified of something, perhaps even of himself. A cloud passed across the sinking sun.

"What is he saying, Ulric?"

"'Foorna'? I don't know the word." He gasped out a few more sentences, a nonsensical rationale about the fading light playing tricks, and pulled me rather roughly into the bracken and back through the woods until we arrived at the shore where we had drawn up our canoe. The wild wind was bringing in clouds from all directions, funnelling towards us in a black mass. I felt a spot of rain on my face. The wind whipped the turning tide already beginning to cover the tiny beach. We were lucky to have returned early. Ulric almost hurled me into the canoe as we pushed off and took up our paddles, forcing the canoe into the darkness. But Auld Strom had grown stronger and kept forcing us back towards the shore. The wind seemed sentient, deliberately making our work harder, seeming to blow first from one side then another. It was unnatural. Instinctively, I hated it.

What irresponsible idiots we had been! I could think of nothing but my children. The salt water splashed cold on my skin. My paddle struck weed, and there was a sudden stink. I looked over my shoulder. The woods seemed unaffected by the wind but were full of ghostly movement, shadows elongated by the setting sun and hazy air pursuing us like giants advancing through the trees. Were they hunting the young man who was even now running down the long slab of rock and into the water, his braided milky hair bouncing on his shoulders as he tried to reach us?

With a grunt and a heavy splash Ulric gouged his paddle into the water and broke the defences of that erratic tide. The canoe moved forward at last. The wind lashed our faces and bodies like a cowman's whip, goading us back, but we persevered. Soaked by the spray we gained some distance. Yet still the youth waded towards us, his eyes fixed on Ulric, his hands grasping, as if he feared the pursuing shadows and sought our help. The waves grew wilder by the moment.

"*Father!*" The birdlike cry blended with the shrieking wind until both resonated to the same note.

"No!" Ulric cried almost in agony as we at last broke the current's grip on us and found deeper water. There was a high sound now, keening around us, and I didn't know if it was the wind, the sea or human pursuers.

I wished I knew what the youth wanted, but Ulric's only thought was to get us to safety. In spite of the wind, the mist was thicker than it had been! The young albino was soon lost in it. We heard a few garbled words, watched white shadows gathering on the shore as the setting sun vanished, and then all was grey. There was a heavy smell of ozone. The keening fell away until the water lapping against the canoe was the loudest sound. I heard Ulric's breath rasp as he drove the paddle into the water like an automaton, and I did what I could to help him. Events on the island had occurred too rapidly. I couldn't absorb them. What had we seen? Who was that albino boy who looked so much like me? He could not be my missing twin. He was younger than I. Why was my husband so frightened? For me or for himself?

The cold, ruthless wind continued to pursue us. I felt like taking my paddle and battering it back. Then the fog rose like a wall against the wind which roared and beat impotently upon this new impediment.

Though I felt safer, I lost my bearings in that sudden fog, but Ulric had a much better sense of the compass. With the wind down, we were soon back at our old mooring. The tide was almost full, so it was easy to step from the canoe to the house's little jetty. With some difficulty we climbed the wooden staircase to the first deck. I felt appallingly tired. I could not believe I was so exhausted from such relatively brief activity, but my husband's fear had impressed me.

"They can't follow us," I said. "They had no boats."

In the bright modern kitchen I began to feel a little better. I whipped up some hot chocolate, mixing the ingredients with obsessive care as I tried to take in what had just happened. Outside, in the darkness, there was nothing to be seen. Ulric still seemed dazed. He went around checking locks and windows, peering through closed curtains into the night, listening to the sound of the lapping tide. I asked him what he knew, and he said, "Nothing. I'm just nervous."

I forced him to sit down and drink his chocolate. "Of what?" I asked.

His sensitive, handsome face was troubled, uncertain. He hesitated, almost as if he were going to cry. I found myself taking him by the hand, sitting next to him, urging him to drink. There were tears in his eyes.

"What are you afraid of, Ulric?"

He attempted to shrug. "Of losing you. Of it all starting again, I suppose. I've had dreams recently. They seemed silly at the time. But that scene on the island felt as if it had happened before. And there's something about this wind that's come up. I don't like it, Oona. I keep remembering Elric, those nightmarish adventures. I fear for you, fear that something will separate us."

"It would have to be something pretty monumental!" I laughed.

"I sometimes think that life with you has been an exquisite dream, my broken mind compensating for the pain of Nazi tortures. I fear I'll wake up and find myself back in Sachsenburg. Since I met you I know how hard it is to tell the difference between the dream and the reality. Do you understand that, Oona?"

"Of course. But I know you're not dreaming. After all, I have some of the dreamthief's skills. If anyone could reassure you, it must surely be me."

He nodded, calming himself, giving my hand a grateful squeeze. He was flooded with adrenaline, I realised. What on earth had we witnessed?

Ulric couldn't tell me. He had not been alarmed until he saw what appeared to be his younger self at the window. Then he had sensed time writhing and slipping and dissipating and escaping from the few slender controls we had over it. "And to lose control of time—to let Chaos back into the world—means that I lose you, perhaps the children, everything I have here with you that I value."

I reminded him that I was still very much with him, and in the morning we could stroll the few miles down to Englishtown, call Michael Hall and speak to our beloved children, who were happily going about their schooling. "We can make sure they're well. If you still feel uneasy, we can leave for Rochester and stay with your cousin." Dick von Bek worked for the Eastman Company. We had his permanent invitation.

Again he made an effort to control his fear and was soon almost his old self.

I remarked on the distorted shadows we had seen, like elongated mist giants. Yet the youth's outline had remained perfectly clear at all times, as if only he were in full focus! "The effects of fog, like those of the desert, are often surprising."

"I'm not sure it was the fog . . ." He took another deep breath.

That distortion of perspective was one of the things that had disturbed him, he told me. It brought back all the worlds of dreams, of magic. He remembered the threat, which we must still fear, from his cousin Gaynor.

"But Gaynor's essence was dissipated," I said. "He was broken into a million different fragments, a million distant incarnations."

"No," said Ulric, "I do not think that is true any longer. The Gaynor we fought was somehow not the only Gaynor. My sense is that Gaynor is restored. He has altered his strategy. He no longer works directly. It is almost as if he is lurking in our distant past. It isn't a pleasant feeling. I dream constantly that he's sneaking up on us from behind." His weak laughter was uncharacteristically nervous.

"I have no such sense," I said, "and I am supposed to be the psychic. I promise you I would know if he were anywhere nearby."

"That's part of what I understand in the dream," said Ulric. "He no longer works directly, but through a medium. From some other place."

There was nothing more I could say to reassure him. I, too, knew that the Eternal Predator could hardly be conquered but must forever be held in check by those of us who recognised his disguises and methods. Still I had no smell of Gaynor here. The wind had grown stronger and louder as we talked and now banged around the house tugging at shutters and shrieking down chimneys.

At last I was able to get Ulric to bed and eventually to sleep. Exhausted, I, too, slept in spite of the wailing wind. In the night I was vaguely aware of the wind coming up again and Ulric rising, but I thought he was closing a window.

I awoke close to dawn. The wind was still soughing outside, but I had heard something else. Ulric was not in bed. I assumed that he was still obsessed and would be upstairs, waiting for the light, ready to train his glasses on that old house. But the next sound I heard was louder, more violent, and I was up before I knew it, running downstairs in my pyjamas.

The big room was only recently empty.

There had been a struggle. The French doors to the deck were wide open, the stained glass cracked, and Ulric was nowhere to be seen. I dashed out onto the deck. I could see dim shapes down at the water's edge. The ghostly marble bodies were obviously Indians. Perhaps they had covered their bodies with chalk. I knew of such practices among the Lakota ancestor cults but had never witnessed anything of the kind in this region. Their origin, however, was not the most pressing question in my mind as I saw them bundling Ulric into a large birchbark canoe. I could not believe that in the second half of the twentieth century my husband was being kidnapped by Indians!

Calling for them to stop, I ran down to the grey water, but they were already pushing off, the spray causing odd distortions in the air. One of them had taken our canoe. His back rippled as he moved powerful arms. His body gleamed with oil, and the single lock of hair decorated with feathers flowed like a gash down his back. He wore unusual warpaint. Could this be one of those old "mourning wars" on which the Indians embarked when too many of their warriors had been killed? But why steal a sedentary white man?

The mist was still thick, distorting their shapes as they disappeared. Once I glimpsed Ulric's eyes, wide with fear for me. They were paddling rapidly directly towards Auld Strom. The wind came up again, whipping the water and swirling the mist into bizarre images. Then they were gone. And the wind went with them, as if in pursuit.

My instincts took over my mind. In the sudden silence I began to quest automatically out and into the water, seeking the sisterly intelligence I could already sense in the depths far from the shore. She became alert as I found her and readily accepted my request to approach. She was interested in me, if not sympathetic. Water flowed into my entire consciousness, became my world as I continued to bargain, borrow, petition, offer all at the same time, and in the space of seconds. Grudgingly, I was allowed to take the shape of the stately old monarch who lay still and wise in the deep water below the tug of the current, receiving obeisance from every one of her tribe within a thousand miles.

The children of the legendary piscine first elemental *Spammer Gain*, the Lost Fishlings of folklore are a community of generous souls to whom altruism is natural, and this lady was one such. Her huge gills moved lazily as she considered my appeal.

It is not my duty to die, I heard her say, *but to remain alive.*

And one lives through action, I said. *Is one alive who does nothing but exist?*

You are impertinent. Come, your youth shall combine with my wisdom and my body. We shall seek this creature you love.

I had been accepted by Fwulette the Salmon Wife. And she knew the danger I meant to face.

Such ancient souls have survived the birth and death of planets. Courage is natural to them. She let me swim with extraordinary speed in pursuit of the canoes. As I had guessed, they were not heading back to the island but directly towards the whirlpool. While I could feel the current tugging me inwards, I was too experienced to fear it. I had gills. This was my element. I had followed thousands of currents for millions of years and knew that only if you fought them could they harm you.

I was soon ahead of the canoes, swimming strongly towards the surface with the intention of capsizing the larger one and rescuing Ulric. I was as long as their vessel and did not anticipate any hindrance as I prepared to leap upwards under them. To my dismay, my straining back met massive and unexpected resistance. The thing was far heavier than it had seemed. I was winded. Already, as I tried to recover from the self-inflicted blow, the canoe's prow began to dip as she was taken down by the pull of the maelstrom. The whole scale appeared to have altered, but I had no choice. I followed the canoe as it was sucked deep into the centre of the vortex. My supple body withstood all the stresses and pressures I expected, but the canoe, which should have been breaking up, remained in one piece. The occupants, though gripping hard to the sides, were not flung out. I got one clear view of them. They had the fine, regular features of local forest Indians but were dead white, not albino. Their hair was black against oiled, shaven skulls, hanging in a single thick strand. Their black eyes glared into the heart of the maelstrom, and I realised they were deliberately following it to the core. I had to go with them.

Deeper and deeper we went into the wild rush of white and green while all around me great boulders and pillars of rock rose up, their scale shifting back and forth in the unstable water. This was no ordinary natural phenomenon. I knew at once that I had effectively left one world and entered another. It was becoming impossible to orientate myself as the rocks changed size and shape before my eyes, but I did everything in my power to continue my pursuit. Then suddenly the thing was before me, the size of the *Titanic,* and I had been struck a blow directly to the head. I felt myself grow limp. I thrashed my tail to keep my bearings. Then another current was pushing me up towards the surface, even as I fought to dive deeper.

Unable to sustain the descent, I let the current take me back towards shore, exhausted. Fwulette knew we had failed. She seemed sad for me.

"Go with good luck, little sister," she said.

The Salmon Wife returned to her realm, her head slightly sore and, for reasons best known to herself, her humour thoroughly restored.

Fwulette thanked, I called for my own body and returned to the house as fast as I could. We had no telephone, of course. The nearest was miles away. I had no other means of pursuing my husband's abductors, not a single hope of ever seeing him again. I was not the only one whose life had changed totally in the last few hours, but this understanding made my loss no easier. I felt horribly ill as I began looking for my clothes.

Then I saw something I had not noticed in my haste to rescue my husband. Ulric's kidnappers had lost something in the struggle. Presumably I had not seen it earlier because it had fallen down the slats in the stairs and now stood upright against a wall: a large round thing, with the dimensions of a small trampoline, made from decorated deerhide stretched on wicker and attached to its frame with thongs. It was too big for a shield, though the handles at the back suggested that purpose. I had seen the Indians carrying similar shields but in closer proportions to their bodies. I wondered if it was what was called a dreamcatcher, but it lacked any familiar images. It might even be a holy object or a kind of flag.

Made of white buckskin with eight turquoise stripes radiating from a central hub, at the boss was what appeared to be a thunderbird framed by a tree. The entire thing was painted in vivid blues and reds. Ornamented with scarlet beads around the rim, with more coloured beads and porcupine quills throughout the design, it was of superb craftsmanship and had the feel of a treasured possession. Yet its purpose was mysterious.

I left it leaning against the wall while I went upstairs to bathe and get some clothes. When I returned to the main part of the house, the sun was everywhere. I could hardly believe I had not been dreaming. But there was the huge deerskin disc, the cracked glass, and other signs of the fight. Ulric must have heard them come in and delivered himself straight into their hands. There was no note. I had not expected one. This was not an attempt to get ransom.

I was now ready to walk to the filling station. I could do it in under an hour. But I was also reluctant to leave, fearing that if I did so I would miss some important sign or even Ulric's return. It was possible that he could have escaped from his captors after all and been dragged up to the surface as I had been. But I knew this was really a forlorn hope. As I prepared to go, I heard a sound like a car approaching, and then came a knock at the front door. Hoping in spite of all realism, I ran to open it.

The gaunt figure who raised his bowler hat to me was dressed in a neat black overcoat, with black polished shoes, and a copy of the local newspaper under his arm. His hard black eyes shifted in the depths of their sockets. His thin, peculiar smile chilled the surrounding air. "Forgive me for coming so early, countess. I have a message for your husband. Could I, do you think, see him for a moment?"

"Captain Klosterheim!" I was shocked. How had he known where to find me?

He bowed a modest head. "Merely *Herr* Klosterheim, these days, dear lady. I have returned to my civilian calling. I am with the church again, though in a lay capacity. It has taken some time to locate you. My business with your husband is urgent and in his interest, I think."

"You know nothing of the men who were here in the night?"

"I do not understand you, my lady."

I loathed the idea of being further involved with this villainous ex-Nazi who had allied himself with Ulric's cousin Gaynor. Was he the supernatural medium Ulric had sensed? I doubted it. His psychic presence was powerful, and I would have detected it before now. On the other hand he might be the only means I had of discovering where they had taken Ulric, so I drew on my professional courtesy and invited him in.

Entering the big main room he immediately went towards the huge artefact the Indians had left behind. "The Kakatanawa were here?"

"Last night. What do you know?"

Scarcely thinking, I took a double-barrelled Purdy's from the cabinet and dropped in two shells. Then I levelled the gun at Klosterheim. He looked around at me in surprise.

"Oh, madam, I mean you no ill!" He clearly believed I was going to blow him apart on the spot.

"You recognise that thing?"

"It's a Kakatanawa medicine shield," he said. "Some of them think it helps protect them when they go into the spirit lands."

"The spirit lands? That's where they have gone?"

"Gone, madam? No, indeed. They mean here. These are their spirit lands. They hold us in considerable awe."

I motioned with the gun for him to sit in one of the deep leather armchairs. He seemed to spill across it. In certain lights he became almost two-dimensional, a black-and-white shadow against the dark hide. "Then where have they gone?"

He looked at the chair as if he had not known such comfort were possible. "Back to their own world, I would guess."

"Why have they taken him?"

"I am not sure. I knew you were in some kind of danger, and I hoped we could exchange information."

"Why should I help you, Herr Klosterheim? Or you help us? You are our enemy. You were Gaynor's creature. I understood you to be dead."

"Only a little, my lady. It is my fate. I have my loyalties, too."

"To whom?"

"To my master."

"Your master was torn apart by the Lords of the Higher Worlds on Morn. I watched it happen."

"Gaynor von Minct was not my master, lady. We were allies, but he was not my superior. That was mere convenience to explain our presence together." He might even have been a little offended by my presumption. "My master is the essence. Gaynor is merely the vapour. My master is the Prince of Darkness, Lord Lucifer."

I would have laughed if I were not in such bizarre circumstances. "So do you come here from Hell? Is that where my husband is to be found—the Underworld?"

"I do come from Hell, my lady, though not directly, and if your husband were already there, I would not be here."

"I am only interested in my husband's whereabouts, sir."

He shrugged and pointed at the Kakatanawa artefact. "That would no doubt help, but they would probably kill you, too."

"They mean to kill my husband?"

"Quite possibly. I was, however, referring to myself. The Kakatanawa have no liking for me or for Gaynor, but Gaynor's interests are no longer mine. Our paths parted. I went forward. He went back. Now I am something of a watcher on the sidelines." His cadaverous features showed a certain humour.

"I am certain you are not here through the promptings of a Christian heart, Herr Klosterheim."

"No, madam. I came to propose an alliance. Have you heard of a hero called Ayanawatta? Longfellow wrote about him. In English 'Hiawatha'? His name was used for a local poem, I believe."

I had, of course, read Longfellow's rather unfashionable but hypnotic work.

However, I was scarcely in the mood to discuss creaking classics of American liter-ature. I think I might have gestured with the gun. Klosterheim put up a bony hand.

"I assure you I am in no way being facetious. I see I must put it another way." He hesitated. I knew the dilemma of all prescient creatures, or all those who have been into a future and seen the consequence of some action. Even to speak of the future was to create another "brane," another branch of the great multiversal tree. And that creation in turn could confuse any plans one might have made for oneself to negotiate the worlds. So we were inclined to speak somewhat cryptically of what we knew. Most of our omens were as obscure as the *Guardian* crossword.

"Do you know where Gaynor is?"

"I believe I do, in relation to our present circumstances and his own." He spoke with habitual care.

"Where would that be?"

"He could be where your husband is." An awkward, significant pause.

"So those were Gaynor's men?"

"Far from it, my lady. At least, I assume so." He again fell silent. "I came to propose an alliance. It would be even more valuable to you, I suspect. I can guarantee nothing, of course . . ."

"You expect me to believe one who, by his own confession, serves the Mas-ter of Lies?"

"Madam, we have interests in common. You seek your husband and I, as always, seek the Grail."

"We do not own the Holy Grail, Herr Klosterheim. We no longer even own the house it is supposed to reside in. Haven't you noticed that the East is now under Stalin's benign protection? Perhaps that ex-priest has the magic cup?"

"I doubt it, madam. I do believe your husband and the Grail have a peculiar relationship and that if I find him I shall find what I seek. Is that not worth a truce between us?"

"Perhaps. Tell me how I may follow my husband and his abductors."

Klosterheim was reluctant to give away information. He brooded for a moment, then gestured towards the round frame. "That medicine shield should get you there. You can tell by its size it has no business being here. If you were to give it the opportunity to return to where it came from, it might take you with it."

"Why do you tell me that? Why do you not use the shield yourself?"

"Madam, I do not have your skills and talents." His voice was dry, almost mocking. "I am a mere mortal. Not even a demon, madam. Just a creature of the Devil, you know. An indentured soul. I go where I am bid."

"I seem to remember that you had turned against Satan. I gather you found him a disappointment?"

Klosterheim's face clouded. He rose from the chair. "My spiritual life is my own." He stared thoughtfully into the barrels of my shotgun and shrugged. "You have the power to go where I need to go."

"You require a guide? When I have no idea where they have taken Ulric? Less idea than you, apparently."

"I lack your grace." He spoke quietly, though his jaw tightened as if in anger. "Countess, it was your husband's help I sought." Something struggled in him. "But I think it is time for reconciliation."

"With Lucifer?"

"Possibly. I opposed my master as my master opposed his. I scarcely understand this mania for solipsism or how it came about. Once half our lives were spent contemplating God and the nature of evil. Now Satan's domain throughout the multiverse shrinks steadily." He did not sound optimistic.

I thought him completely mad with his weird, twisted pieties. I had made it my business to read old family histories long before I decided to marry Ulric. Half the von Beks, it seemed, had had dealings with the supernatural and denied it or were disbelieved. A manuscript had only recently been found which claimed to be some sort of ancestral record, written in an idiosyncratic hand in old German; but the East German authorities, unfortunately, had claimed it as a state archive, and we had not yet been able to read it. There was a suggestion that its contents were too dangerous to publish. We did know, however, that it had something to do with the Holy Grail and the Devil.

Again he gestured towards the medicine shield. "That will take you to your husband, if he still lives. I don't require a guide. I require a key. I do not travel so easily between the worlds as you. Few do. I have given you all the information

I can to help you find Count Ulric. He does not possess what I want, but what I want is in his power to grant me. I hoped he would have the key."

I was losing interest in the conversation. I had decided to see what the Kakatanawa medicine shield could do for me. Perhaps I should have been more cautious, but I was desperate to follow Ulric, ready to believe almost anything in order to find him.

"Key?" I asked impatiently.

"There is another way to reach the world to which he's been taken. A door of some kind. Perhaps on the Isle of Morn."

"How did you think Ulric could help you?"

"I hoped the door through to that world is on Morn and the key to that door would be in your husband's keeping." He seemed deeply disappointed, as if this was the culmination of a long quest which had proven to be useless.

"I can assure you we have no mysterious keys."

"You have the sword," he said, without much hope. "You have the Black Sword."

"As far as I know," I told him, "that, too, is in the hands of the East German authorities."

He looked up in some dismay. "It's in the East?"

"Unless the Russians now have it."

He frowned. "Then I have bothered you unnecessarily."

"In which case . . ." I gestured with the shotgun.

He nodded agreeably and began walking towards the front door. "I'm obliged to you, madam. I wish you well."

I was still in an appalling daze as I watched him open the door and leave. I followed him and saw that he had come in a taxi. It was the same driver who had brought us from Englishtown. I had a sudden thought, asked him to wait, and went inside. I wrote a hasty note to the children, came out, and asked him to post it for me. As Klosterheim got into his cab, the driver waved cheerfully. He had no sense of the supernatural tensions in the air, nor of the heartbreaking tensions within me, the impossible decision I had to make.

After watching them drive off, I returned to the house and picked up the medicine shield. I had no interest in Klosterheim's ambitions or any conflict he was engaged in. All I cared about was the information he had given me. I was prepared to risk all to let the shield take me to my husband.

Almost in a trance, I carried the thing through a blustering wind that tugged and buffeted at it, down to the jetty. Then I stripped off my outer clothes, threw the shield into the water and gasped as I flung myself after it. Feeling it move under me, I climbed onto it, using it like a raft. The wind wailed and bit at my flesh, but now the shield had a life of its own. It felt as if muscles began to form in the skin as it moved rapidly across the water out towards the island we had visited. I expected it to follow its owner into the maelstrom.

Had the medicine shield come completely alive? Did it have intelligence? Or did it intend to fling me against the rocks? For now it seemed to protect me as the cold water heaved and the cold wind blew.

My fingers dug deep into the edges. Even my toes tried to grip parts of the frame as it bucked and kicked under me.

Then I felt it lift suddenly and move rapidly out to sea, as if it hoped to escape what threatened us. My fingers were in agony, but I would have clung on dead or alive. My will had moulded me to that huge woven frame.

All at once it was diving. I had no time to catch my breath, and I no longer had gills. It was going to drown me!

I saw the high jagged pillars of rock coming up towards me, saw massive dark shapes moving in the swirling water. I cursed myself for an irresponsible fool as my lungs began to fail. I felt my grip on the shield weakening, my senses dimming, as I was dragged inexorably downward.

2

On the Shores of Gitche Gumee

Nine by nine and seven by seven,
We shall seek the roots of heaven.

—Wheldrake,

A Border Tragedy

Suddenly I had burst back out of the water into blinding light. I could see nothing and could hear only the wild keening of a wind. Something icy had me in its grasp. Frozen air wrapped itself around me and effortlessly ripped my hands from the shield. My willpower was useless in the face of such a force. I did all I could to get my grip back, but the wind was relentless. If I had not known it before, I certainly understood it now. This was a sentient wind, a powerful elemental, which clearly directed its wrath specifically at me. I could sense its hatred, its personality. I could almost see a face glaring into mine. I could not imagine how I had offended it or why it should pursue me, but pursue me it did.

There was absolutely no resisting that force. It snatched the shield away and threw me in the other direction. I believe it intended to kill me. I felt myself strike water, and then I had lost consciousness.

I had not expected to awake at all. When I did, I felt a surprising sense of well-being, of safety. I was lying on springy turf, tightly wrapped in some sort of blanket. I could smell the sweet grass and heather. I was warm. I was relaxed. Yet I remained calmly aware of the danger I had escaped and of the urgency of my mission. In contrast to my earlier experience, I now felt completely in control of my body, even though I could barely move a finger! Had I reached the realm where my husband had been taken? Was Ulric near? Was that why I felt safe?

I could see the grey, unstable sky. It was either dawn or twilight. I could not turn my head enough to see a horizon. I moved my eyes. Above me a man's face looked down at me with an expression of stern amusement.

He was a complete stranger, but instinctively I knew I had no reason to fear him. I had found my imagined warrior. The smooth-shaven face was well proportioned, even handsome, and decorated with elaborate tattoos etched across his forehead, cheeks, chin and scalp. His head was mostly shaven, the only piece of hair worn in a long, gleaming black lock interwoven with three bright eagle feathers, but his healthy copper skin told me that he was not one of those who had captured my husband. He wore earrings, and his nose and lower lip were pierced with small sapphires. On his temples, cheeks and chin was a deep scarlet smear of paint. Running down either side of his chest were long, white scars. Between these scars a design had been pricked into his skin. On his well-muscled upper arms were intricately worked bracelets of raw gold, and around his throat he wore a wide band of mother-of-pearl which seemed to be a kind of armour. His tattoos were in vivid reds, greens, blues and yellows and reminded me of those I had once seen displayed by powerful shamans in the South Seas. A nobleman of some sort, confident of his own ability to protect the wealth he displayed with such careless challenge.

He regarded me with equal frankness, his dark eyes full of ironic humour. "Sometimes an angler prays for a catch and gets more than he bargains for." He spoke a language I understood but could not identify. This was a common experience for moonbeam walkers.

"You *caught* me?"

"Apparently. I am rather proud of myself. It was less exhausting than I had expected. I enjoyed the dancing. With the appropriate incantations and trance, I laid out the robe with the head facing the moon and the tail facing the water. I did as I had learned. I invoked the spirits of the wind. I called to the water to give up her treasure. Sure enough there was an agitation in the air. A strong wind blew. Being in a trance, I heard it from a distance. When I at last opened my eyes I found you thus and wrapped you in the robe for your health, your modesty and because the incantation demanded it." He spoke with a sardonic, friendly, slightly self-mocking air.

"I was naked?" Now I recognised the special sensation of soft animal skin against my own. Whatever one's notions about taking a fellow creature's life, that touch is irresistible. While I'd accepted my adopted culture's ways, I had no special concern about being seen undressed. I had far more urgent questions. "But what of the medicine shield?"

He frowned. "The Kakatanawa war-shield? That was yours?"

"What happened to it? I was caught up in a violent wind which seemed to have intelligence. It deliberately separated me from the shield."

The warrior was apologetic. "I believe—you'll recall I was in a trance—I believe that is what I saw spinning away in that direction. A wind demon, perhaps?" He pointed to a thickly wooded hillside some distance away around the lake. "So it was a medicine shield and has been stolen by a demon. Or escaped you both and gone home to its owner?"

"Without me," I said bitterly. I was beginning to realise that this man had, through his magic, somehow saved my life. But had he or the elemental diverted me from following Ulric? "That shield was all that linked me with my husband. He could be anywhere in the multiverse."

"You are of the Kakatanawa? Forgive me; I knew they had adopted one of you in their number, but not two." He was obviously puzzled, but some sort of understanding was dawning, also.

"I am not a Kakatanawa." I was no longer quite so thoroughly in control of my emotions. A note of desperation must have come into my voice. "But I seek the shield's owner."

He responded like a gentleman. He seemed to understand the supernatural conditions involved and lowered his head in thought.

"Where is its owner? Do you know?" I began to struggle in the soft robe. With a word of apology, that elegant woodsman knelt down and untied rawhide knots.

"No doubt with the other Kakatanawa," he said. "But that is where I am going, so it's reassuring for me. I do not know how they will receive me. It is my destiny to carry my wisdom to them. The fates begin the weaving long before we understand the design. We will go together as our mutual fate demands. We will be stronger together. We will achieve our different goals and thus bring all to resolution."

I didn't understand him. I stood up, wrapping myself in the robe. It was wonderfully supple, the skin of a white buffalo, decorated with various religious symbols. I looked around me. It was just after dawn, and the sun was making the wide, still water shine like a mirror. "If you told me your name, your calling and your purpose with me, I would be at less of a disadvantage."

He smiled apologetically and began busying himself with his camp. Behind him was the rising sun, now clearing the furthest peaks of a massive mountain range, its orange light pouring across forest and meadow, touching the small, undecorated lodge erected on the grassy lakeside. From the wigwam came a wisp of grey smoke. It was a hunter's economical kit. The lodge's coverings could be used as robes against the cold, and the poles could function as a travois to carry everything else. A hunting dog could also be used to pull the travois, but I saw no evidence of dogs. The shadows were dissipating, and the light was already growing less vivid as the sun climbed into a clearing sky.

My host seemed in very high spirits. He was a charming man. Nothing about him was threatening, though he radiated a powerful personality and physical strength. I wondered if his tattoos and piercings marked him as a shaman or sachem. He was clearly accustomed to authority.

I was obviously no longer on the Nova Scotian coast, but the surrounding world did not look very different from the landscapes I had just left. Indeed, it was vaguely familiar. Perhaps it was Lake Superior?

Pulled up on the grassy bank of our natural meadow was a large, exquisitely fashioned canoe of glittering silver birchbark, its copper-wound edges finished in wooden inlays painted with spiritual symbols. There was no sign of another human being in the whole of creation. It was like the dawn of the world, a truly virgin America. The season was still early autumn with a hint of winter in the freshening breeze. The breeze did not overly alarm me. I asked him which lake this was.

"I was born not far from here. It is commonly called Gitche Gumee," he said. "You know the Longfellow poem?"

"I understood Longfellow mangled half a dozen languages in the process and got all the names wrong." I spoke, as one sometimes does, in a kind of cultural apology, but I was also remembering something Klosterheim had said. I was fairly certain this man was not just a modern romantic adopting a favourite role in the wilderness. I doubted, if I looked further, I would find a station wagon nearby!

This man was wholly authentic. He smiled at my remark. "Oh, there's nothing wrong with what Longfellow included. The rituals remain in spite of the flourishes. Nobody ever asked the women their story, so their rituals remain secret, undistorted. There are many roads to the spirit's resolution with the flesh. It is with what old Longfellow excluded and what he added that I have my quarrel. But it is my destiny to bring light to my own story. And that is the destiny which I dreamed in that journey. I must restore the myth and address the great Matter of America." He seemed embarrassed by his own seriousness and smiled again. "As if I'd hand over the spiritual leadership of the Nations to a bunch of half-educated Catholic missionaries! There is no trinity without White Buffalo Woman. So it is a triptych missing a panel. That ludicrous stuff Longfellow put in at the end was a sop to drawing-room punctilio and worse than the sentimental ending Dickens tacked on to *Bleak House*. Or was it *Great Expectations?*"

"I've never been able to get into Dickens," I said.

"Well," he replied, "I don't have much opportunity myself." He frowned slightly and looked up at me. "I don't want to take credit for more than is right. While it is my destiny to unite the Nations, I might fail where an alter ego might have succeeded. One wrong step, and I change everything. You know how difficult it is." He fell into frowning thought.

"You had better introduce yourself, sir," I said, half anticipating his answer.

He apologised. "I am Ayanawatta, whom Longfellow preferred to call 'Hiawatha.' My mother was a Mohawk and my father was a Huron. I discovered my story in the poem when I made my dream-journey into the future. Here. I have something for you . . ." He threw me a long doeskin shirt which was easily slipped on and fitted me very well. Was he used to travelling with such things? He laughed aloud and explained that the last man who tried to kill him had been about my size.

He began expertly to dismantle the wigwam. To close down his fire he simply put a lid on the pot he carried it in and secured it with a bit of rawhide. The lodge's contents were folded in the hides and rolled into a tight bundle. The firepot was tied on top. I saw now that the poles were made of long, flint-tipped spears. He laid these along the bottom of the canoe and put the bundle in the middle. He had broken the entire encampment with little evident expenditure of energy.

"You seem very familiar with English literature," I said.

"I owe it a great deal. As I said, through Longfellow's poem I discovered my destiny. I had reached the time of my first true dream-quest. I dreamed a dream in which I saw four feathers. I decided that this meant I must seek four eagles in the places of the four winds. First I went into the wilderness and took the north path called The Eagle, for I thought that was the meaning of the dream. It took me into a land of mountains. It was not a true path. But in leaving that path, I found myself in Boston at the right time. I was looking to see if I had a myth. And if I had a myth I had to find out how to follow it and make it true. Well, you can work out that irony for yourself. I entered a time in the future long after I had died. I learned strange skills. I learned to read in the language of these new people, whose appearance at first astonished me. There were many amiable souls in those parts more than willing to help me, though the self-righteous voices of the bourgeoisie were often raised against my appearance. However, learning to read that way was part of my first real spirit journey. For once I had opened my spirit to the future, I received not just a vision of the founding of the Haudenosaunee, the People of the Same Roof, but I saw what was to follow them, unless I trod a certain path. In order to find the future I desire, I must maintain the immediate future as exactly as possible."

"You weren't offended by Longfellow's acquisition of various native mythologies?"

"Longfellow was genial, lively, kind. And hideously hairy. As a Mohawk I inherited a distaste for male body hair. The Romans were the same, apparently. Yet, for all that, the poet's good nature cut through any prejudice I felt about his appearance. He had an eccentric, springy gait and bounced when he walked. I remember thinking him a bit overdressed for the time of year, but he probably considered me underdressed. I hadn't acquired these." He fingered his tattoos with modest pride.

"I was originally interested in the transcendentalists. Emerson planned to introduce me to Thoreau, but Longfellow dropped into Parker House that day as well. It was by chance that we had occasion to talk. He was not entirely sure that I was real. He was so absorbed in his poem I think he suspected at first he had imagined me! When Emerson introduced us, he probably considered me some sort of noble savage." Ayanawatta laughed softly. "Thoreau, I suspect, found me a little coarse. But Longfellow was good-natured almost to a fault. It was a fated meeting and played an important part in his own journey. I understood his poem to be a prophecy of how I would make my mark in the world. The four feathers I had mistaken for eagle feathers in my dream were, of course, four quill pens. Four writers! I had made the wrong interpretation but taken the right action. That was where the luck really came in. I was a bit callow. It was the first time I had visited the astral realm in physical form. Sadly, that phase of the journey is over. I don't know when I'll see a book again."

Ayanawatta began to roll up his sleeping mat with the habitual neatness and speed of the outdoorsman. "Well, you know we use wampum in these parts, to remind us of our wisdom and our words." He indicated the intricately worked belt which supported his deerskin leggings. "And this stuff is as open to subtle and imaginative interpretation as the Bible, Joyce or the American Constitution. Sometimes our councils are like a gathering of French postmodernists!"

"Can you take me to my husband?" I was beginning to realise that Ayanawatta was one of those men who took pleasure in the abstract and whose monologues could run for hours if not interrupted.

"Is he with the Kakatanawa?"

"I believe so."

"Then I can lead you to them." His voice softened. "I have had no dream to the contrary, at least. Possibly your husband could be or will become the friend of my friend Dawandada, who is also called White Crow." He paused with an expression of apology. "I talk too much and speculate too wildly. One gets used to talking to oneself. I have not had a chance for ordinary human conversation with a reasonably well-educated entity for the last four years. And you, well—you are a blessing. The best dance I ever danced, I must say. I had expected some laconic demigoddess to complete our trio. I wasn't even sure you were going to be human. The dream told me what to do, not what to expect. There is an ill wind rising against us, and I do not know why. I have had confusing dreams."

"Do you always act according to your dreams?" I was intrigued. This was, after all, my own area of expertise.

"Only after due consideration. And if the appropriate dance and song bring the harmony of joined worlds. I was always of a spiritual disposition." He began carefully cleaning one of his beautifully fashioned hardwood paddles, curved in such a way that they were also war-axes. His bow and quiver of arrows were already secured in the canoe. He paused. "White Buffalo Woman, I am on a long spiritual journey which began many years ago in the forests of my adopted home in what you know as upper New York. I am bound to link my destiny with others to achieve a great deed, and I am bound not to speak of that part of my destiny. Yet when that deed is done I will at last possess the wisdom and the power I need to speak to the councils of the Nations and begin the final part of my destiny."

"What of the Kakatanawa? Do they join your councils?"

"They are not our brothers. They have their own councils." He had the air of a man trying to hide his dismay at extraordinary political naïveté.

"Why do you call me White Buffalo Woman? And why would I go with you when I seek my husband?"

"Because of the myth. It has to be enacted. It is still not made reality. I think our two stories are now the same. They must be. Otherwise there would be dissonances. Your name was one of several offered in the prophecy. Would you prefer me to call you something else?"

"If I have a choice, you can call me the Countess of Bek," I said. In the language we were using this name came out longer than the one he had employed.

He smiled, accepting this as irony. "I trust, countess, you will accompany me, if only because together we are most likely to find your husband. Can you use a canoe? We can be across the Shining Water and at the mouth of the Roaring River in a day." Again, he seemed to speak with a certain sardonic humour.

For the second time in twenty-four hours, I found myself afloat. Ayanawatta's canoe was a superb instrument of movement, with an almost sentient quality to its responses. It sometimes seemed hardly to touch the water. As we paddled I asked him how far it was to the Kakatanawa village.

"I would not call it a village exactly. Their longhouse lies some distance to the north and west."

"Why have they abducted my husband? Is there no police authority in their territory?"

"I know little about the Kakatanawa. Their customs are not our customs."

"Who are this mysterious tribe? Demons? Cannibals?"

He laughed with some embarrassment as his paddle rose and fell in the crystal water. It was impossible not to admire his extraordinarily well-modelled body. "I could be maligning them. You know how folktales exaggerate sometimes. They have no reputation for abducting mortals. Their intentions could easily be benign. I do not say that to reassure you, only to let you know that they have no history of meaning us harm."

I thought I might be assuming too much. "We are still in America?"

"I have another name for the continent. But if you lived after Longfellow, then your time is far in my future."

Such shifts of time were not unusual in the dreamworlds. "Then this is roughly 1550 in the Christian calendar."

He shook his head, and the breeze rippled in the eagle feathers. I realised I had never seen such brilliant colours before. Light sparkled and danced in them. Were the feathers themselves invested with magic?

He paused in his paddling. The canoe continued to skim across the bright water. The smell of pines and rich, damp undergrowth drifted from the distant bank. "Actually it's AD 1135, by that calendar. The Norman liberation of Britain began sixty-nine years ago. I think the settlers worked it out on the date of an eclipse. Well, they just picked a later eclipse. They were trying to prove we took the idea of a democratic federation from them."

He laughed and shook his head. "And before them was Leif Ericsson. When I was a boy I came across a Norseman whose colony had been established about a hundred years earlier. You could call him the Last of the Vikings. He was a poor, primitive creature, and most of his tribe had been hunted to death by the Algonquin. To be honest I'd mistaken him for some sort of scrawny bear at first.

"They called this place Wineland. He was bitter as his father and grandfather were bitter. The Ericssons had tricked his ancestors with stories of grapes and endless fields of wheat. What they actually got, of course, was foul weather, hard shrift and an angry native population which thoroughly outnumbered them. They called us 'the screamers' or 'skraelings.' I heard a few captive Norse women and children were adopted by some Cayugas who had survived an epidemic. But that was the last of them."

Though he was inclined to ramble on, he was full of interesting tales and explanations, making up for his years of silence. Now that I knew we sought the Kakatanawa, I devoted myself to finding Ulric as soon as possible. There was a remote possibility that we would arrive before he did, such was the nature of time. But somehow Ayanawatta's endless words had comforted me, and I no longer felt Ulric to be in danger of immediate harm; nor was I so convinced that Prince Gaynor was behind the kidnapping. The mystery, of course, remained, but at least I had an ally with some knowledge of this world.

I reflected on my peculiar luck, which again had brought me into another's dream. I had been attacked by that wind, I was certain. An aerial demon. An elemental. Ayanawatta was supremely confident. No doubt, since this was his final spirit journey and he was back in his familiar realm, he had defeated many obstacles. I had some idea of what the man had already endured. Yet he bore the burden of that experience lightly enough.

A current in the lake took our canoe gently towards the farther shore. Resting, Ayanawatta slid a slender bone flute from his pack. To my surprise he played a subtle, sophisticated melody, high and haunting, which was soon echoed by the surrounding hills and mountains until it seemed a whole orchestra took up the tune. Crowds of herons suddenly rose from the reeds as if to perform their aerial ballet in direct response to the music.

Pausing, Ayanawatta took the opportunity to address the birds with a relatively short laudatory speech. I was to become used to his rather egalitarian attitude towards animals, his way of speaking to them directly, as if they understood every nuance of his every sentence. Perhaps they did. In spite of my fears, I was delighted by this extraordinary experience. I was filled with a feeling of vibrant well-being. In spite of Ayanawatta's company, it had been ages since I knew such a sense of solitude, and I began to relish it, my confidence growing as I was infected by his joyous respect for the world.

By evening we had reached the reedy mouth of a river on the far side of a lake. After we drew the canoe ashore, Ayanawatta pulled some leggings and a robe from the pack. Gratefully I put the leggings on and wrapped myself in the blanket. The air was becoming chilly as the sun poured scarlet light over the mountain peaks and the shadowy reeds. The sachem carefully restarted his fire and cooked us a very tasty porridge, apologising that he should have caught some fish but had been too busy recounting that disappointing meeting with Hawthorne. He promised fish in the morning.

Soon he was telling me about the corrupt spiritual orthodoxy of the Mayan peoples he had visited on an earlier stage of this journey. Their obscure heresies were a matter of some dismay to this extraordinary mixture of intellectual monk, warrior and storyteller. It all turned on certain Mayan priests' refusal to accept pluralism, I gathered. Any fears I had for Ulric were lulled away as I fell into a deep and dreamless sleep.

In the morning, as good as his word, the Mohawk nobleman had speared us two fat trout which, spiced from his store of herbs, made a tasty breakfast. He told me a little more of his dream-quests, of the stages of physical and supernatural testing he had endured to have reached this level of power. I was reminded of the philosophy of the Japanese samurai, who at their best were as capable of composing a haiku as of holding their own in a duel. Ayanawatta's dandified appearance in the wild suggested he cultivated more than taste. He was warning potential enemies of the power they faced. I had travelled alone and understood the dangers, the need to show a cool, careless exterior at all times or be killed and robbed in a trice. As it was, I envied Ayanawatta his bow and arrows, if not his twin war clubs.

After we had finished eating, I expected us to get on the move. Instead Ayanawatta sat down cross-legged and took out a beautiful redstone carved pipe bowl, which he packed with herbs from his pouch. Ceremoniously he put a hollow reed into a hole in the bottom of the bowl. Taking a dried grass taper from the fire he lit the pipe carefully and drew the smoke deeply into his lungs, then puffed smoke to the Earth's quarters, by way of thanks for the world's benevolence. An expression of contentment passed over his face as he handed me the pipe. I could only follow his example with some dread. I hated smoking. But the herbs of the pipe were sweet and gentle to the throat. I guessed they were a mixture containing some tobacco and a little hemp, also dried spearmint and willow bark. I was no smoker, but this beneficent mixture was a secret lost to Ulric's world. A peace pipe indeed. I was at once mentally sharpened and physically relaxed. This world remained intensely alive for me.

In a short while Ayanawatta stood up with stately dignity. He was clearly in a semi-trance. Slowly he began to sing, a rhythmic song that sounded like the wind, the whisper of distant water, the movement of distant thunder. As he sang he began a graceful dance, stamping hard on the ground while performing a complicated figure. Each nuance of movement had meaning. Although I had not been prepared for this display, I found it deeply moving. I knew that he was weaving his being into the fabric of the worlds. These rituals opened pathways for him. Unlike me, he had no natural gift for travel between the realms.

This particular ritual was, however, over swiftly. He made a somewhat shy apology and said that since we were travelling together, he hoped I would forgive him if he performed similar rituals from time to time. It was as important to his religion as my need to pray quietly to myself five times a day.

I had no objection. I knew of some cultures where people devoted their entire lives to learning ways of entering other worlds and usually died before they could accomplish anything. What I had been doing naturally since I was a young child had been inherited from my parents. Such movement was virtually impossible for most people and very difficult for everyone else. We moonbeam travellers have little in common but our talents. We learn the disciplines and responsibilities of such travel at the musram.

Even with my poor sense of direction it did not take me long to realise, as we set off downriver, that the current was not flowing from north to south and that judging by the position of the sun we were probably heading east. Ayanawatta agreed. "The road to Kakatanawa is a complicated one," he said, "and you're wise to approach with the appropriate charms and spells. That, at least, is clear from the prophecy. It isn't possible to go there directly, just as some moonbeam paths are more circuitous than others. And, as yet, I haven't worked out where to expect to find either the giants or the dragon. I intend to dream on the subject as soon as possible." He did not explain further.

With me settled in the front of the canoe, we were now paddling downstream at some speed, with huge stands of pines rising on both sides and the water beginning to dash at the rocks of the banks. The air was misty with white spray, and above us great grey clouds were beginning to build, threatening rain.

Before it finally started to rain, the river had turned a bend and widened and had become lazy, peaceful, almost a lake, with the tall mountains massed in the distance, the forest making swathes of red, gold, brown and green as the leaves turned. All this was reflected in the depths of the river. Heavy drops soon fell into the gentle waters and added to the sense of sudden peace as the narrow torrent was left behind. Our paddling became more vigorous, just to keep us moving at any reasonable speed.

While I understood that my journey could not take place with any special urgency, I remained nonetheless anxious to continue. I imagined a dozen different deaths for the man I loved as we actually headed away from the Kakatanawa territory. Yet I was a dreamthief's daughter. I understood certain disciplines. The direct path was almost never the best. I kept charge of my feelings most of the time, but it had never been harder.

Ayanawatta being unusually laconic, I remarked over my shoulder how much more peaceful the river had become. He nodded a little abstractedly. I realised that as he paddled he was listening carefully, his head cocked slightly to one side. What did he expect? Was he listening for danger? There could be no alligators in these cold waters.

I began to ask him, but he silenced me with a gesture. The wind was rising, and he was straining to hear above it. He leaned to his right a little, expectantly. Then, not hearing what he thought, he leaned forward to where I was now positioned and murmured, "I have powerful enemies who are now your enemies. But we have the medicine to defeat them all if we are courageous."

I shuddered with a sudden chill. It occurred to me to remind him that I was not here to help him in his spirit journey but to find my kidnapped husband. Before my mother vanished, presumably absorbed at last into a dream she had planned to steal, she would have been a more useful ally to him than I. Now, of course, it was unlikely she even knew her own name.

All too well, I understood the Game of Time. Mother had taught me most of what I knew, and the mukhamirim masters of Marrakech had taught me the rest. But it was sometimes difficult to remind myself. Time is a field with its own dimensions and varying properties. To think in terms of linear time is to be time's slave. Half of what one learns as a moonbeam walker involves understanding time for what it is, as far as we understand it at all. Our knowledge gives us freedom. It allows us some control of time. I do not know why, however, there are more women on the moonbeam roads than men, and most of the legendary figures of the roads are women. Women are said to be more able to accommodate Chaos and work with it. There are honourable exceptions, of course. Even the most intelligent man is inclined on occasion to hack a path through an obstacle. But he is also, in the main, somewhat better with a stone lance when it comes to dealing with large serpents.

This last thought came as I watched, virtually mesmerised, while a long, gleaming neck rose and rose and rose from the river until it blotted out the light. Vast sheets of water ran off its body and threatened to capsize the canoe as, with a shout to me to steady us, Ayanawatta took one of the spears from beneath his feet and threw it expertly into flesh I had assumed to be hugely dense. But the spear went deep into the creature, as if into a kind of heaving, wet sawdust, and the water bubbled with the thing's hissing breath. It groaned. I had not expected such a noise from it. The voice was almost human, baffled. It thrashed violently until the spear was flung free, and then it disappeared upstream, still groaning from time to time as its head broke the water, trailing a kind of thin, yellow ichor like smoke.

"I haven't seen anything close to that since I was in the Lower Devonian," I said. I was still shaking. The word *devour* had gained a fresh resonance for me. "Did it mean to attack us?"

"It probably hoped to eat us, but those are known along this river as the Cowardly Serpents. It takes little to drive them off as you saw, although if they capsize your canoe, you are in some danger, of course."

Much as I was trained not to think in linearities I was aware that in this realm gigantic water-serpents had long since become extinct. I put this to Ayanawatta as he paddled to where his spear floated, shaft up, in the reedy, eddying water. A strong smell of firs and the noise of feeding birds came from the bank, and I drank in the simplicity of it to steady myself. I knew the supernatural better than that which my husband insisted on calling "natural," but I felt resentful that I was being forced to take extra risks as I sought to save him. I said as much to Ayanawatta.

The Mohawk prince reassured me. He was simply obeying the demands of his dream-quest. This meant that my own dream-quest was in accordance with his, which meant that as long as we continued in the current pattern and made no serious mistakes our quests would be successful. We should both get what we desired.

The wind was still blustering and slapping at our clothes. I drew my blanket closer. Ayanawatta hardly noticed the drop in temperature. As for the "prehistoric" nature of our dangers, he regretted that some sort of crisis had occurred. Such anomalies were becoming increasingly common. He believed that the source of our own troubles was also causing the disruptions. The great prairies offered natural grazing and ample prey for predators. They were, he admitted, generally moving south these days, and the altering climate took increasing numbers of those that remained.

I said that I had noticed it growing colder.

Still apparently oblivious of the chill, Ayanawatta sighed. "Once," he said, "this was all unspoiled. Those serpents would never have come this far downriver. It means you lose all the river game, and before you know it the whole natural order is turned upside down. The consequences are disastrous. It becomes impossible to lead any kind of settled life. Do you see any villages on the banks these days? Of course not! It used to be wonderful here. Girls would wave at you. People would invite you in to hear your stories . . ."

Grumbling thus, he paddled mechanically for a while. The encounter with the river serpent had not so much frightened as irritated him. Even I had not been terrified of the beast. But Ayanawatta's sense of order and protocol was upset, and he was becoming concerned, he said, about the wind.

Again he surprised me. He had a habit of noticing everything while appearing to be entirely concerned with his own words. For such people, words were sometimes a kind of barrier, the eye of a storm, from which part of them could observe the world without the world ever guessing.

The wind was the king of the prairie, Ayanawatta continued. The most important force. He suspected that we had somehow engaged its anger.

He paused in his paddling and took out his flute. He blew a few experimental notes, then began a high, slow tune which made use of the echoes from the distant mountains and turned them back and forth so that once again it seemed the whole of the natural world was singing with him.

The wind dropped suddenly. And as it dropped, Ayanawatta's flute died away.

The extraordinary scenery seemed to go on for ever, changing as the light changed, until it was close to twilight. The river ahead had begun to rumble and hiss. Ayanawatta said we would have to bypass the rapids tomorrow. Meanwhile we would make camp before sunset, and this time, he promised, he would catch whatever fish the serpent had left us.

In the morning when I awoke, Ayanawatta was gone. The only movement was the lazy smoke from his fire, the only sound the distant lapping of water and the melancholy wail of a river bird. I felt the ground shiver under me. Was this the sound of the rapids he had spoken about?

I rose quickly, hardly able to believe I was not experiencing an earthquake. I heard the chirping of frogs and insects, steady, high. I smelled the smoke and the rich, earthy pines, the acrid oaks and sweet ash. I heard a bird flap and dive, and then I heard a disturbance in the water. I looked up and saw a hawk carrying a bird in its talons. I found myself wondering about the magical meaning of what I had seen.

The earth shuddered again, and wood snapped within the forest. I looked for Ayanawatta's bow and arrows, but they were gone. I found one of his lances, still in the bottom of the boat, and armed myself with it. As I turned, however, it became immediately obvious that a stone lance, even a magic one, might not be much use against this newcomer. Out of the thick woods, scattering branches and leaves in all directions, a fantastic apparition loomed over me.

While I was familiar with the Asian use of domestic elephants, I had never seen a man seated on the back of a black woolly mammoth with tusks at least nine feet long curving out over an area of at least twenty feet!

The rider approaching me was clearly a warrior of the region, but with subtle differences of dress, black face-paint, shaven head, scalp lock worn long, a lance and a war-shield held in his left hand, his right hand gripping the decorated reins of his huge mount. It was impossible to judge the rider's size, but it was clear the mammoth was not young. The old tusks were splintered and bound but could still very easily kill almost anything which attacked their owner.

My heart thumped with sickening speed. I looked for some advantage. At the last moment the mammoth's trunk rose in a gesture of peace. At the same time the painted warrior raised his palm to reassure me.

The mammoth swung her weight forward and began to lower herself onto her knees as the newcomer slid blithely down her back and landed on the turf.

His tone was at odds with his ferocious black mask. "The prophecy told me I would meet my friend Ayanawatta here but only hinted at his companion. I am sorry if I alarmed you. Please forgive the death paint. I've been in a fairly intense dispute."

This thoroughly decorated man had a similar grace of manner to Ayanawatta, but something about his movements was familiar to me. His posture, however, was more brooding. His paint was a black, glowing mask in which two dark rubies burned. I held on to the spear and took a step back. I began to feel sicker still as I recognised him.

Silently, fascinated, I waited for him to approach.

3

A Prince of the Prairie

Do not ask me how I came here,
Do not ask my name or nation,
Do not ask my destination,
For I am Dawandada, the Far Sighted,
Dawandada, Seer and Singer,
Who bore the lance, the Justice Bringer,
Who brought the law out of the East,
Sworn to seek but never speak.

—W.S. Harte,
The Maker of Laws

He was, of course, the same youth I had seen at the house. His face was so thickly painted I knew him only by his white hands and red eyes. He did not appear to recognise me at all and seemed a little disappointed. "Do you know where Ayanawatta is?"

I guessed he'd failed to find fish in the river and had gone hunting in the woods, since his bow and a lance were missing.

"Well, we have some big game to hunt now," the newcomer said. "I've found him at last. I would have reached him sooner if I had understood my pygmy dream better." This was offered as apology. He returned to his mount and led the great woolly black pachyderm down to the water to drink. I admired the saddle blanket and the beaded bridle. Attached to the intricately carved wooden saddle was a long, painted quiver from which the sharp metal tongues of several lances jutted. Beaver and otter fur covered the saddle and parts of his bridle. The mammoth herself was, as I had thought, not in her prime. There were grizzled marks around her mouth and trunk, and her ivory was stained and cracked, but she moved with surprising speed, turning her vast, tusked head once to look into my eyes, perhaps to convince herself that I was friendly. Reassured, she dipped her trunk delicately into the cold water, her hairy tail swinging back and forth, twitching with pleasure.

As his mount quenched her mighty thirst, the young man knelt beside the water and began rubbing the black paint from his face, hair and arms. When he stood up he was once again the youth I had seen at the house. His wet hair was still streaked with mud or whatever he had put in it, but it was as white as my own. He seemed about ten years younger than me. His face had none of the terror and pleading I had seen such a short time before. He was ebullient, clearly pleased with himself.

I chose to keep my own counsel. Before I offered too much, I would wait until I had a better idea of what all this meant. I would instead give him a hint.

"I am Oona, Elric's daughter," I said. This apparently was nothing to him, but he sensed I expected him to recognise me.

"That's a fairly common name," he said. "Have we met before?"

"I thought we had."

He frowned politely and then shook his head. "I should have remembered you. Here, I have never seen a woman of my own colouring and size." He was unsurprised.

"Were you expecting to see me?"

"You are White Buffalo Woman?"

"I believe so."

"Then I was expecting to see you. We play out our parts within the prophecy, eh?" He winked. "If we do not, the pathways tangle and strangle themselves. We should lose all we've gained. If you had not been here, at the time I foretold, then I should have been concerned. But it disturbs me that the third of our trio is missing."

I knew enough of travellers' etiquette not to ask him any more than he told me. Many supernatural travellers, using whatever means they choose, must work for years to reach a certain road, a particular destination. With a single wrong step or misplaced word, their destination is gone again! To know the future too well is to change it.

"What name will you give for yourself?" I asked.

"My spirit name is White Crow," said the youth, "and I am a student with the Kakatanawa, sent, as my family always sends its children, to learn from them. My quest joins with yours at this point. I have already completed my first three tasks. This will be my fourth and last great task. You will help me here as I will help you later. Everything becomes clear at the right time. We all work to save the Balance." He had undone the straps holding the surprisingly light saddle and supported it as it slid towards him, dumping it heavily to the ground, the spears rattling. "We walk the path of the Balance." He spoke almost offhandedly, filling a big skin of water and washing down the black mammoth's legs and belly. "And this old girl is called Bes. The word means 'queen' in her language. She, too, serves the Balance well." With a grunt and a great heave, Bes moved deeper into the water, then lifted her long, supple trunk and sprayed her own back, luxuriating in the absence of her saddle.

"The Cosmic Balance?"

"The Balance of the world," he said, clearly unfamiliar with my phrase. "Has Ayanawatta told you nothing? He grows more discreet." The young man grinned and pushed back his wet hair. "The Lord of Winds has gone mad and threatens to destroy our longhouse and all that it protects." He took bunches of grass and began to clean the long, curving tusks as his animal wallowed deeper into the stream, gazing at him with fierce affection. "My task was to seek the lost treasures of the Kakatanawa and bring them to our longhouse so that our home tree will not die. It is my duty and my privilege, for me to serve thus."

"And what are these treasures?" I asked.

"Together they comprise the Soul of the World. Once they are restored, they will be strong enough to withstand the Lord of the Winds. The power of all these elementals increases. They do not merely threaten our lives but our way of thinking. A generation ago we all understood the meaning and value of our ways. Now even the great Lords of the Higher Worlds forget."

I was already familiar with those insane Lords and Ladies of Law who had lost all sense of their original function. They had gone mad in defence of their own power, their own orthodoxy. Lords of the Wind normally served neither Law nor Chaos, but like all elementals had no special loyalties, except to blood and tradition. White Crow agreed.

"There's a madness in Chaos," he said, "just as there can be in Law. These forces take many forms and many names across the multiverse. To call them Good or Evil is never to know them, never to control them, for there are times when Chaos does good and Law does evil and vice versa. The tiniest action of any kind can have extreme and monumental consequences. Out of the greatest acts of evil can spring the greatest powers for good. Equally, from acts of great goodness, pure evil can spring. That is the first thing any adept learns. Only then can their education truly begin." He spoke almost like a schoolboy who had only recently learned these truths.

Clearly there was a connection with the events Ulric and I had experienced earlier, but it was a subtle one. This battle for the Balance never ended. For it to end would probably be a contradiction in terms. Upon the Balance depended the central paradox of all existence. Without life there is no death. Without death there is no life. Without Law, no Chaos. Without Chaos, no Law. And the balance was maintained by the tensions between the two forces. Without those tensions, without the Balance, we should know only a moment's consciousness as we faced oblivion. Time would die. We would live that unimaginably terrible final moment for eternity. Those were the stakes in the Game of Time. Law or Chaos. Life or Death. Good and evil were secondary qualities, often reflecting the vast variety of values by which conscious creatures conduct their affairs across the multiverse. Yet a system which accepted so many differing values, such a wealth of altering realities, could not exist without morality, and it was the learning of those ethics and values which concerned an apprentice mukhamir. Until it was possible to look beyond any system to the individual, the would-be adept remained blind to the supernatural and generally at its mercy.

I was also beginning to realise very rapidly that these events were all connected with the ongoing struggle we wanted to think finished when the war against Hitler was won.

"Do you journey back to your people?" I asked.

"I must not return empty-handed," he told me, and changed the subject, pointing and laughing with joy at a flight of geese settling in the shadowy shallows of the river. "Did you know you are being observed?" he asked almost absently as he admired the geese, graceful now in the water.

A whoop from the trees, and Ayanawatta, holding a couple of birds aloft in one hand and his bow in the other, called his pleasure. His friend could join us for breakfast.

The two men embraced. Again I was impressed by their magnetism. I congratulated myself that I was blessed with the best allies a woman could hope for. As long as their interests and mine were the same, I could do no better than go with them in what they were confident was their preordained destiny.

I waited impatiently in the hope that White Crow would again raise the subject of our being watched. Eventually, when the two had finished their manly exchanges, he pointed across the river to the north. "I myself have known you were on the river since I took the short cut, yonder." He pointed back to where the river had meandered on its way to this spot. "They have made camp, so it is clear they follow you and no doubt wait to ambush you. It is their usual way with our people. A Pukawatchi war party. Seventeen of them. My enemies. They were chasing me, but I thought they had given up."

Ayanawatta shrugged. "We'll have a look at them later. They will not attack until they are certain of overwhelming us."

White Crow expertly plucked and cleaned the birds while I drew up the fire. Ayanawatta washed himself thoroughly in the river, singing a song which I understood to be one of thanks for the game he had shot. He also sang a snatch or two of what was evidently a war-song. I could almost hear the drums beginning their distinctive warnings. I noticed that he kept a sideways eye on the northern horizon. Evidently the Pukawatchi were an enemy tribe.

I asked White Crow, as subtly I could, if he had ever been to an island house with two storeys and had a vision there. I was trying to discover if he remembered me or Ulric. He regretted, he said, that he was completely ignorant of the events I described. Had they happened recently? He had been in the south for some while.

I told him that the events still felt very recent to me. Since there was no way of pursuing the subject, I determined to waste no more time on it. I hoped more would come clear as we travelled.

I had begun to enjoy Ayanawatta's songs and rituals. They were among the only constants in this strange world which seemed to hover at the edges of its own history. I became increasingly tolerant of his somewhat noisy habits, because I knew that in the forest he could be as quiet as a cat. As he was a naturally sociable and loquacious man, his celebratory mood was understandable.

My new friends added their share of herbs and berries to the slowly cooked meat, basting with a touch of wild honey, until it had all the subtle flavours of the best French kitchen. Like me, they knew that the secret of living in the wild was not to rough it, but to refine one's pleasures and find pleasure in the few discomforts. Ironically, if one wished to live such a life, one had to be able to kill. Ayanawatta and White Crow regarded the dealing of death as an art and a responsibility. A respected animal you killed quickly without pain. A respected enemy might suffer an altogether different fate.

I was glad to be back in the forest, even if my errand was a desperate one. A properly relaxed body needs warmth but no special softness to rest well, and cold river water is exquisite for drinking and washing, while the flavours and scents of the woods present an incredible sensory vocabulary. Already my own senses and body were adapting to a way of life I had learned to prefer as a girl, before I had become what dreamthieves call a mukhamir, before going the way of the Great Game or making my vows of marriage and motherhood.

The multiverse depended upon chance and malleable realities. Those who explored it developed a means of manipulating those realities. They were natural gamblers, and many, in other lives, played games of skill and chance for their daily bread. I was a player in the Eternal Struggle fought between Law and Chaos and, as a "Knight of the Balance," was dedicated to maintaining the two forces in harmony.

All this I had explained as best I could to my now missing husband, whose love for me was unquestioning but whose ability to grasp the complexity and simplicity of the multiverse was limited. Because I loved him, I had chosen to accept his realities and took great pleasure from them. I added my strength to his and to that of an invisible army of individuals like us who worked throughout the multiverse to achieve the harmony which only the profoundly mad did not yearn for.

There was no doubt I felt once more in my natural element. Though fraught with anxiety for Ulric's well-being and my own ability to save him, at least for a time I knew a kind of freedom I had never dared hope to enjoy again.

Soon we were once more on the move, but this time Ayanawatta and I joined White Crow upon Bes the mammoth, with the canoe safely strapped across her broad back. There was more than enough room on her saddle, which was so full of tiny cupboards and niches that I began to realise this was almost a travelling house. As he rode, White Crow busied himself with rearranging his goods, reordering and storing. I, on the other hand, was lazily relishing the novelty of the ride. Bes's hair was like the knotted coat of a hardy hill-sheep, thick and black. Should you fall from her saddle, it would be easy to cling to her snarled coat, which gave off an acrid, wild smell, a little like the smell of the boars who had lived around the cottage of my youth.

White Crow dismounted, preferring, he said, to stretch his legs. He had been riding for too long. He and Ayanawatta did their best not to exclude me from their conversations, but they were forced to speak cryptically and do all they could, in their own eyes, not to disturb the destiny God had chosen for them. Their magical methods were not unlike different engineering systems designed to achieve the same end and had strict internal logic in order to work at all.

While White Crow ran to spy on whoever was following us, we continued to rest on the back of the rolling monster. Ayanawatta told me that the Kakatanawa prince had been adopted into the tribe but was playing out a traditional apprenticeship. His people and theirs had long practised this custom. It was mutually advantageous. Because he was not of their blood, White Crow could do things which they could not and visit worlds forbidden or untraversable by them.

As we moved through those lush grasslands growing on the edge of the forest, Ayanawatta spoke at length of how he wanted to serve the needs of all people, since even the stupidest human creature sought harmony yet so rarely achieved it. His quick brain, however, soon understood that he might be tiring me, and he stopped abruptly, asking if I would like to hear his flute.

Of course, I told him, but first perhaps he would listen to me sing a song of my own. I suggested we enjoy the tranquil river and the forest's whispering music, let the sounds and smells engulf us, carry us on our fateful dream-quest, and like the gentle river's rushing, draw us to the distant mountains and beyond them to that longhouse, lost among the icy wastelands where the Kakatanawa ruled. And I sang a song known as the Song of the Undying, to which he responded, echoing my melody, letting me know his quest was noble, not for self, or tribe or nation, but for the very race of Man. In his dreams the tree of all creation was threatened by a venomous dragon, waiting in angry torment, his tears destroying every root. Too sick to move, the dying dragon had lost his *skeffla'a* and thus lost his power to rise and fly.

He said the Kakatanawa protected some central mystery. He had only hints of what that mystery was and most of that from myth and song. He knew that they had sent their most valued warriors out to seek what they had lost and what they needed. Where they had failed, White Crow had succeeded.

Continuing in grim reflection, he told me how his story was already written, how important to his own quest it was that he return to Kakatanawa, seek their longhouse and their people, bring back the objects they called holy, perform the ritual of restoration, restore reality to the dream. In that final restoration he would at last unite the Nations, at last be worthy of his name. His dream-name was Onatona. In his language that meant Peacemaker. The power of his dream, his vision of the future, informed everything he did. It was his duty to follow the story and resolve each thread with his own deeds. I was in some awe of him. I felt as if I had been allowed to witness the beginning of a powerful epic, one which would resonate around the world.

I agreed his task was mighty. "Unlike you I have no dream-story to live. If I have I'm unconscious of it. All I know is that I seek a husband and father I would like to return to his home and his children. I, too, work to unite the nations. I long to bring peace and stable justice to a world roaring and ranting and shouting as if to drown all sense. I'll help you willingly in your quest, but I expect you in turn to help me. Like you, I have a destiny."

I told Ayanawatta how in my training as a mukhamir my mother had taught me all my secrets, how some of these secrets must be kept to myself, even from my own husband and children. But I did not need to remind him. "I am in no doubt of the power or destiny of White Buffalo Woman. I am glad you elected to act her story. You complete the circle of magic which will arm us against the greater enemies and monsters we are yet to face."

The line of thick forest moved back from the river, making our way easier. Ahead lay rolling meadows stretching into infinity. Gentle, grassy drumlins gave this landscape a deceptively peaceful air, like an English shire extended for ever.

I had enjoyed far more bizarre experiences, but nothing quite like holding a conversation about the socio-economics of dream-visions on the rolling back of a gigantic pachyderm with a mythological hero who had enjoyed the privilege of seeing his own future epic and was now bound to live it.

"There are bargains one strikes," said Ayanawatta with a certain self-mockery, "whose terms only become clear later. It taught me why so few adepts venture into their own futures. There's a certain psychological problem, to say the least."

I began to take more than a casual interest in our conversation, which showed how close to my training Ayanawatta's was. Like the dreamthieves, I had a rather reckless attitude towards my own future and spawned fresh versions without a thought. A more puritanical moonbeam walker took such responsibilities seriously. We were disapproved of by many. They said too many of our futures died and came to nothing. We argued that to control too much was to control nothing. In our own community Law and Chaos both remained well represented.

A sharp, rapid cawing came from our right, where the forest was still dense and deep. Someone had disturbed a bird. We saw White Crow running out of the trees. I was again struck by his likeness to my father, my husband and myself. Every movement was familiar. I realised that I took almost a mother's pleasure in him. It was difficult to believe we were not in some way related.

White Crow's moccasins and leggings were thick with mud. He was carrying his longest spear with a shaft some five feet long and a dull metal blade at least three feet long. In the same hand was a straight stick. He had been running hard. Bes stopped the moment she saw him, her trunk affectionately curling around his waist and shoulders.

He grinned up at me as he rose into the air and patted his beast's forehead. "Here's your bow, my lady Buffalo!" He threw the staff to me and I caught it, admiring it. It was a strong piece of yew wood, ready-made for a new weapon. I was delighted and thanked him. He drew a slender cord from his side-bag and handed that up. I felt complete. I had a new bow. I had left my old bow, whose properties were not entirely natural, in my mother's cottage when I closed it up, thinking I would have no further need of it in twentieth-century Britain.

"They are following us, without doubt," said White Crow, slipping down to the ground, his face just below my feet. He spoke softly. "About half a mile behind us. They hide easily in the long grasses."

"Are you certain they mean us harm?" Ayanawatta asked him.

White Crow was certain. "I know that they are armed and painted for war. Save for me, they have no other enemies in these parts. They are a thousand miles at least from their own hunting grounds. What magic helped them leave their normal boundaries? The little devils will probably try for us tonight. I don't believe they realise we know they are there, so they'll be expecting to surprise us. They fear Bes's tusks and feet more than they fear your arrows, Ayanawatta."

Ayanawatta wanted to maintain our speed. It was easier at this stage to continue overland, because the river curved back on itself at least twice.

We had left the forest behind us and rode towards the distant range. The great pachyderm had no trouble at all carrying her extra passengers, and I was surprised at our pace. Another day or two and we should be in the foothills of the mountains. White Crow knew where the pass was. He had already made this journey from the other direction, he said.

I could now make out the mountains in better detail. They were the high peaks of a range which was probably the Rockies. Their lower flanks were thick with pine, oak, ash, willow, birch and elm, while a touch of snow tipped some of the tallest. They climbed in red-gold majesty to dominate the rise and fall of the prairie. The clouds behind them glowed like beaten copper. These were spirit mountains. They possessed old, slow souls. They offered a promise of organic harmony, of permanence.

With Ayanawatta and White Crow I accepted the reality of the mountains' ancient life. In spite of my constant, underlying anxiety, I was glad to be back with people who understood themselves and their surroundings to be wholly alive, who measured their self-esteem in relation to the natural world as well as the lore they had acquired. Like me, they understood themselves to be a part of the sentient fabric, equal to all other beings, all of whom have a story to play out. Every beggar is a baron somewhere in the multiverse and vice versa.

We are all avatars in the eternal tale, the everlasting struggle between classical Law and romantic Chaos. The ideal multiverse arises from the harmony which comes when all avatars are playing the same role in the same way and achieving the same effect. We are like strings in a complex instrument. If some strings are out of tune, the melody can still be heard but is not harmonious. One's own harmony depends on being attuned to the other natural harmonies in the world. Every soul in the multiverse plays its part in sustaining the Balance which maintains existence. The action of every individual affects the whole.

These two men took all this for granted. There's a certain relaxing pleasure in not having to explain yourself in any way. I realised what a sacrifice I had made for the love of Ulric and his world, but I did not regret it. I merely relished these mountains and woods for what they were, getting the best, as always, from a miserable situation. Only the persistent wind disturbed me, forever tugging at me, as if to remind me what forces stood between me and my husband.

I took the first watch. For all my growing alertness as I strung my bow that night in camp, I heard only the usual sounds of small animals hunting. When White Crow relieved me, I had nothing to report. He murmured that he had heard seven warriors moving some twenty feet from our camp, and I became alarmed. I was not used to doubting my senses. He said perhaps they were only getting the lie of the land.

Before I went to sleep I asked him why people would come so far to try to kill us. "They are after the treasures," he said. He had recently outwitted the Pukawatchi, and they were angry. But all he was doing was taking back what they had stolen.

He said we must be alert for snakes. The Pukawatchi were expert snake-handlers and were known to use copperheads and rattlesnakes as weapons. This did not enhance my sense of security. Although not phobic, I have a strong distaste for snakes of any size.

It was not until Ayanawatta's time of watch that I was awakened by thin shouts in the grey, dirty dawn. Our pasture was heavy with dew, making the ground spongey and hard to walk on. There was no sign of our erstwhile enemies, and I began to believe they lacked stomach for their work.

Then I saw the huge copperhead writhing near the fire, moving slowly towards us. I snatched an arrow from Ayanawatta's quiver, nocked and shot in a single fluid, habitual action. One's body rarely forgets as much as one's mind. My arrow pinned the copperhead to the ground. Its tongue scented in and out between those long, deadly fangs, and I felt less conscience in killing it than I had in eating the birds.

They decided to attack at dawn in the north wind's chill, shrieking high-pitched, hideous war cries and swinging stone clubs almost as big as themselves. They fell back well before they reached us. These tactics were designed to put us on our feet and make us more vulnerable to their next strategy, but White Crow had journeyed among these people and anticipated most of their tricks.

When their arrows came pouring into the camp, we were ready for them. Instantly a fine mesh net was thrown up over us all, including Bes. The net caught the arrows and bounced most of them to the ground.

Two more snakes were hurled into our midst. I dispatched one with the same arrow I had used on his fellow. Ayanawatta killed the other with one of his twin war clubs.

White Crow was no longer interested in our attackers. He was roaring his approval of my archery. I had the eye and arm of any man, he said. He was making an observation, not offering a compliment.

The snakes were abnormally large, especially for this climate, and it was easy to see how the Pukawatchi alarmed their enemies. It quickly became clear, however, why they were not in themselves very terrifying.

Not one of them was over three-and-a-half feet high! The Pukawatchi were perfect pygmies.

I had not realised from the conversations I had overheard that the tallest Pukawatchi could scarcely reach my chest. They were conventionally formed little people. Their scrawny bodies were heavily muscled. They showed a tenacity of attack which made you admire them. I assumed they had evolved in similar circumstances to the African bushmen. Unlike Ayanawatta, they were a square-headed, beetle-browed people, clearly from a different part of the world altogether, yet they dressed in deerskin, with breechclouts, fur caps, decorated shirts and moccasins. But for their features and diminutive size, they might have been any tribe east of the Mississippi.

The trick with the net gave us a certain advantage over the pygmies.

It did not much surprise me that the man leading them was not dressed like a Pukawatchi. He hung back in the grass, pointing this way and that with his sword, directing the attack. He wore a long black cloak, a tall black hat with black plumes, and his weapon was a slender sabre. He looked more like a funeral horse than a man, but there was no mistaking that gloomy skull of a face.

I had seen him recently.

Klosterheim, of course. How long had it taken him to get here? I knew it could not have been an easy path. He seemed older and even more haggard than before. His clothes looked threadbare.

Their attack having failed, the Pukawatchi withdrew around their leader. Either the party had reduced itself since White Crow last saw it, or part of it was elsewhere planning to attack from another angle.

As one of the warriors ran up to him to receive orders I realised with a shock that, like the Pukawatchi who attacked us with such vigour, Klosterheim was scarcely any taller than a ten-year-old boy! He seemed to have paid a radical price for his obsession with the Grail. A moment later he hailed us, his voice unusually high, and suggested a truce.

At that exact moment Bes decided to utter her outrage. Her huge tusks lifted. She raised her head and pawed at the quivering ground. A noise struck our ears like the last trump, and a horrible stench filled the air. Klosterheim's speech was completely drowned. He could not control his fury. Equally, we could not control our amusement. Despite the gravity of our situation, the three of us found ourselves weeping with laughter.

The mammoth's answer to Klosterheim had been to utter a massive fart.

4

Strange Dimensions

Have they told of the Pukawachee,
Fairy people of the forest?
Have they heard of Hiawatha,
Fate's favoured son, the peaceful one?

—*Hiawatha's Song*
(Schoolcraft's tr.)

Klosterheim thought we were merely mocking him for the failure of his attack. Laying down his sword, he signalled for the Pukawatchi to stay where they were while he approached us. His expression was one of gloomy distaste as he reached a small hillock a few yards from where we stood. Here, perhaps unconsciously seeking to be at eye level with us, he paused. He removed his black hat and wiped the inside band. "Whatever sorcerer has blown you up to such gigantic proportions, madam, I trust the spell is easily reversed."

I was able to remain grave now. "I thank you for your solicitousness, Herr Klosterheim. How long is it since we last met?"

He scowled. "You know that, madam, as well as I do." He expelled an irritated sigh, as if I offered just one more frustration for him to contend with in this world. "You'll recall that it was some four years ago, at that angular house of yours near Englishtown."

I said nothing. As anticipated, Klosterheim's route to this realm had been hard. I had a sense of his extraordinary age. How many centuries had he spent crossing from one realm to another in this bleak pursuit? His experiences had changed neither his demeanour nor, presumably, his ambition. I was still not sure exactly what he sought here, but my curiosity was high. Moreover, he was the only link I had to my husband, so I was relieved that we occupied the same realm, if on different scales.

For all his tiny stature, Klosterheim remained entirely solipsistic. His rigid confidence in his own perceptions and understanding was unshaken. He did not doubt himself for a second. He was irritated that I chose not to remember how four years had passed or acknowledge that I had decided to become a giant in the meantime!

I remembered Ulric saying, in the context of Nazi anti-Semitism, that he believed Klosterheim had served the Lutheran Church in some capacity until expelled. The German was clearly of that puritanical disposition uncomfortable with our complicated world's realities. It was a tribute to his great need that he had pursued this goal for centuries. Such minds seek to simplify an existence they cannot understand. All they can do is reduce it to what they believe are fundamentals. Their narrow reasoning demonstrates a complete absence of spiritual imagination. Klosterheim was the apotheosis of Law turned inward and gone sour. Was he aggressively determined to destroy Chaos at its roots and thus achieve absolute control, which is death? Chaos, unchecked, would stimulate all possibility until perception became nullified and intellect died. That was why some of us temperamentally disposed to serve Chaos sometimes worked for Law and vice versa.

Klosterheim knew all this but did not care. His own parochial obsession was with his master, the Satan he had served, rejected and longed to serve again.

White Crow stepped forward, scowling ritualistically. "How do you now lead my enemies? What do you promise these Little People that they follow you out of their ordained hunting grounds to their deaths?"

"They seek only what has been stolen from them." Klosterheim uttered the words with hollow irony.

White Crow folded his arms theatrically. His body language was as formal and controlled as any diplomat's speech. "They stole and murdered to gather the treasures. The lance was never their property. They merely fashioned it. You have persuaded them of honour which they have not earned. The lance blade was made by the Nihrain. The Pukawatchi performed a task. They did not create the blade. You bring nothing but disaster to the Pukawatchi. We serve the Balance, and the lance belongs to the Balance."

"The lance was made by their ancestors and is rightfully theirs. Give them back their Black Lance. You are White Crow the trickster. They simply reclaimed their property. You are White Crow the truth-twister, who deceived them into giving up that property."

"It is not their treasure. I merely argued with that mad shaman of theirs on his own terms. It was my logic won me the blade, not my lies. The Pukawatchi are too intelligent for their own good. They can never resist a philosophical argument, and that is all I offered them in the end. But I won the treasures through clever thought, not cunning. Besides, I no longer have them all. I gave them away."

"I am not here to be a passive audience for your decadent psychological notions," said Klosterheim, only half understanding what had been said to him. "Trickery it was and nothing else."

"Which, as I recall, was the rationale you were using in Germany during the 1930s when we first met?" I pointed out.

"I tell you again, madam, that I never subscribed to that philistine paganism." Even at his reduced height he achieved a kind of dignity. "But one must ally oneself with the strongest power. Hitler was then the strongest power. A mistake. I admit it. I have always been inclined to underestimate women like yourself." He offered this last remark with some venom. Then he considered his response and looked up at me almost in apology. His personality seemed to be breaking up before my eyes. How difficult had it been for him to follow me here, and how stable was his dream self?

One of the Pukawatchi, smeared with brightly painted medicine symbols all over his body, presumably as protection against us, a strutting bantam of a fellow who clearly thought much of himself, came to stand behind Klosterheim, displaying offence and outrage. Upon his head was the skin of a large snake, the head still on it, the jaws open and threatening. Swaying from side to side to his own rhythms, he stretched his arms forward, making the signs of the horned deceiver. I could not tell if he described himself or his enemies. He sang a short song and stopped abruptly. Then he spoke:

"I am Ipkeptemi, the son of Ipkeptemi. You claim much, but your medicine curdles, your spirits wither, and your tongues turn black in your mouths. Give us what is ours, and we will return to our own lands."

"If you continue this war with us," said Ayanawatta reasonably, "you will all die."

The little medicine man made spitting sounds to show his contempt for these threats. He turned his back on us, daring us to strike.

Then he whirled to face us again, shaking his fingers at us. It was clear he feared the power of our medicine. While his was little more than a primitive memory of the reality, he might well have a natural talent. I did not underestimate him or any power he might have stumbled upon. I watched him warily as he continued.

"The Kakatanawa are banished from our land as we are from theirs, yet they came and took the lance our people made. You say we have no business here, but neither have you. You should be living under the gloomy skies of your own deep realm. Give us what is ours, then go back to the Land of the Black Panther."

Again White Crow drew himself into an oratorical stance. "You know nothing, but I know your name, small medicine. You are called Ipkeptemi the Two Tongues. You are Ukwidji, the Lie-Maker. You speak truth and you speak lies with the same breath. You know it is our destiny to make and guard the Silver Path. We must go where the Balance and the tree manifest themselves. You know that is true. Your treasures are gone. Your time is past." White Crow threw his arms wide in a placatory sign of respect. "Your destiny is complete, and ours is not yet accomplished."

The Two Tongues scowled deeply at this and lowered his head as if considering a reply.

From behind me, an arrow flew past my ear. I ducked down. Another arrow fell short of Klosterheim, who, with eyes narrowing, began to stumble back to where his men awaited his orders. I saw him pick up his sword and begin directing the attack on us again. I whirled, my bowstring pulled, and took another sturdy little warrior in the shoulder. I had a habit of wounding rather than killing, although it was not always appropriate! What was strange, however, was how the arrow made a sound as if it had struck wood. The head was barely in the wound. The pygmy pulled it free and ran off. This strange density of physique was common to them all.

The Two Tongues had created a diversion, of course. I had been fascinated by his performance. So fascinated that I had not heard the other Pukawatchi creeping up from the river line. Ayanawatta turned in a single movement to hurl a lance into our nearest attacker. Bes swung her immense bulk around to face the newcomers and stood blaring her rage as a Pukawatchi arrow bounced off her chest. She seemed more upset by the archer's bad manners than by any pain he might have inflicted. He was in her trunk in seconds and flying across the prairie to land, a broken puppet, at Klosterheim's feet.

Grumbling, Ayanawatta stooped to pick up his twin war clubs from the bundle at his feet. Their wide, flat edges ended in serrations, like the teeth of a beast. He spun them around his head, making them sing their own wild warsong as he waded towards the pygmies, slaughtering with a kind of joy I had only seen once before in my father when he had faced Gaynor's men. This battle-rage was cultivated by many adepts who argued that if one had to kill to defend oneself, then the killing had better be done with due consideration, ceremony and efficiency.

White Crow had taken out one of his lances. He did not throw it, but used it like a halberd, keeping his opponents at a distance and then stabbing once, quickly. I had thought at first it was corroded or rusted like so much of the found metal these people used, but now I recognised it for what it was.

The metal was black through and through. As the youth wielded his lance with expert skill, it began to murmur and scream. Red inscriptions flickered angrily at its heart. I was oddly cheered. Surely where that blade sang, Ulric must be near!

I had found the black blade, though I had not sought it. I could see Klosterheim grinning in anticipated triumph. For him, the blade was not nearly as important as the cup his people called the *Gradel*. Klosterheim wanted the thing for his own ambitions. If he took it back to Satan, he was certain he would be restored in his master's eyes. The central irony was that Satan himself sought reconciliation with God. It was as if our danger were so great that the time had come for the two to bury their differences.

Yet it was impossible for Klosterheim to work for the common good. The gaining of the Grail must be by his achievement, I knew, or he would see no respect in his master's eyes. This complicated and contradictory relationship with the Prince of the Morning was, to be frank, somewhat beyond my powers of perception.

White Crow had not seen all the Pukawatchi. A third war party had swept up from a bend in the river. There must have been another forty of the pygmies, all armed with bows. They had walked across the river bottom, like beavers, and had emerged immediately behind us. Our only advantage was that the bows were not especially powerful, and the pygmies were not expert shots.

While we covered him, White Crow repacked Bes's saddle, adjusting straps and other harness until he was satisfied that all was secure. The canoe would now act to guard our backs.

I kept the new party at a distance with my bow. Their own arrows could be shot back, but not with any great power as they were too short. Ayanawatta's arrows, however, were perfect. Slender and long, they were a joy to use. They were so accurate that they might have been charmed. But there were not enough. Fewer and fewer were being shot back by the Pukawatchi. Slowly they were closing the circle.

White Crow adjusted the copper mesh protecting Bes's front and head. She kneeled for us.

White Crow shouted for us to get onto the mammoth, and we scrambled into that massive saddle. We pushed the maddened pygmies back with our bowstaves. Ayanawatta was the last to come up, his twin war clubs cracking skulls and bones so rapidly that it sounded like the popping of a hot fire made with damp wood. He worked with astonishing skill and delicacy, knowing exactly which part of each club would land where. Those dense skulls were hard to crack, but he fought to kill. Each single blow economically took a life. When Bes moved away from the tumbled corpses towards the pygmy archers, they scattered back.

The remains of Klosterheim's band continued to stalk in our wake, but they, too, had few arrows left. They followed like coyotes tracking a cougar, as if they hoped we would lead them to fresh meat.

Their numbers were now badly reduced. They must have been debating the wisdom of continuing with this war party. Klosterheim had not delivered what he had promised them. The Two Tongues probably had some self-interest in leaguing himself with my husband's old enemy. If he had expected Klosterheim to know how to defeat us, he had been disappointed.

I was surprised when they began to drop back. They were soon far behind us. No doubt they were discussing fresh strategies. Klosterheim would, for his part, insist on the pursuit. I understood him well enough to know that.

The woodlands were sparser now, breaking into isolated thickets as the undulating grasslands opened up before us. Huge mountains dominated the distant landscape. The pygmies were among the grasses and wild corn. The smoke we saw behind us showed that at least some of them had made camp. White Crow remained suspicious. He said it was an old trick of theirs to leave one man making smoke while the rest continued in pursuit. After studying it for a while though, he decided most of the Pukawatchi were there preparing food. He could tell by the quality of the smoke that they had made a good kill. This would be the message any stragglers would see, and it would bring them into the camp.

Ayanawatta said the Pukawatchi were a civilised people and would feel shame if they ate their meat raw. The fire told of a beast serving the whole party. While this was not a deliberate message, the Pukawatchi would know how friend and enemy alike would read it. They had called off hunting us, at least for the moment.

"And a big deer will fill a lot of little stomachs!" Ayanawatta laughed.

I asked him if there were many people of Pukawatchi height, and he seemed surprised at my question. "In their own lands, all is to their stature. Even their monsters are smaller!"

"That is what made it both easy and hard for me," chimed in White Crow. "I was easy to see but hard to kill!"

The Pukawatchi were cliff dwellers from the south-west living in sophisticated cave-towns. Most of their civic life was conducted inside. When he had visited Ipkeptemi the Wise, their greatest medicine chief, White Crow had experienced some difficulty crawling through the city's smaller tunnels.

"And did you steal their treasures?" I asked. I had, of course, a specific interest in the black blade.

"I am charged to bring important medicine back to the Kakatanawa. Only I can handle the metal, since they lost their previous White Crow."

"Who was their previous White Crow man?" I asked almost hesitantly. I could not help fearing this road of enquiry would take me somewhere I did not want to go.

His answer was not the one I had anticipated. "My father," he said.

"And his name?" I asked.

White Crow looked at me in some surprise. "That is still his own," he said.

I had offended some protocol and fell silent by way of apology. In this strange world where dream-logic must be followed or consign you for ever to limbo I swam again in familiar supernatural waters, ready for all experience. Old disciplines returned. I was prepared to make the most of what I could. Even the most dedicated adventurers accepted how form and ritual were essential to this life. A game of cards depends upon chance, but can only be played if strict rules are followed.

We played the ball game that evening after we had made early camp. It was a form of backgammon but required more memory and skill. Such games were cultivated by Ayanawatta's people, he said. Those who played them well had special status and a name. They were called *wabenosee* or, more humorously, *sheshebuwak*, which meant "ducks" and was also the nickname for the balls used in their game.

"Presumably we are at the mercy of fate, like the rattling balls," I said. "Do we control anything? Do we not merely maintain the status quo as best we can?"

Ayanawatta was not sure. "I envy you your skills, Countess Oona. I still yearn to walk the white path between the realms, but until now my dream-journeys, dangerous and enlightening as they have been, have been accomplished by other means."

He did not know if I was any more or less at the mercy of fate than himself. He longed to make just one such walk, he said, before his spirit passed into its next state.

I laughed and made an easy promise. "If I ever can, I'll take you," I said. "Every sentient creature should look once upon the constantly weaving and separating moonbeam roads." The women of my kind, of course, constantly crossed and recrossed them. And in our actions, in the stories we played out, we wove the weft and woof of the multiverse, the fabric of time and space. From the original matter, acted upon by our dreams and desires, by our stories, came the substance and structure of the whole.

"Divine simplicity," I said. With it came the full understanding of one's value as an individual, the understanding that every action taken in the common cause is an action taken for oneself and vice versa. "The moonbeam roads are at once the subtlest and easiest of routes. Sometimes I feel almost guilty at the ease with which I move between the realms." All other adepts hoped to achieve the ability, natural to dreamthieves and free dream-travellers, of walking between the worlds. Our unconscious skills made us powerful, and they made us dangerous but also highly endangered, especially when the likes of Gaynor chose to challenge the very core of belief upon which all our other realities depended.

"The path is not always easy and not always straight," I told him. "Sometimes it takes the whole of one's life to walk quite a short distance. Sometimes all you do is return to where you began."

"Circumstances determine action? Context defines?" Grinning, White Crow made several quick movements with his fingers. Balls rattled and danced like planets for a moment and then were still. He had won the game. "Is that what you learned at your *musram?*" And he darted me a quick, sardonic look, to show me that he could use more than one vocabulary if he wished. Most of us know several symbolic languages, which affords us few problems with the logic and sound of spoken language. We are equally alert to the language of street and forest. We are often scarcely aware which language we use, and it never takes us long to learn a new one. These skills are primitive compared to our monstrous talent for manipulating the natural world, which makes shape-taking almost second nature. Quietly, however, White Crow was reminding me that he, too, was an adept.

"To wander the paths between the worlds at will," he said, "is not the destiny of a Kakatanawa White Crow man."

Ayanawatta lit a pipe. White Crow refused it, making an excuse. "We need have no great fear of the Pukawatchi now, but it would be wise to keep guard. I go forward to seek an old friend and hope to be with you in the morning. If I am not, continue as we are going, towards the mountains. You will find me."

And then, swiftly, he disappeared into the night.

We smoked and talked for a little longer. Ayanawatta had had dealings with the pygmies. They had skills and knowledge denied to most and were fair traders, if hard bargainers. When I told him that Klosterheim had been the same size as me when I last saw him, Ayanawatta smiled and nodded as if this were familiar enough. "I told you," he said, "we are living in that kind of time."

Did he know why Klosterheim was now the size of a Pukawatchi? He shook his head. White Crow might know. The dwarves and the giants were leaving their ordained realms. But he and others like him had begun the process, by exploring into those realms. He, after all, had broken the rules, as had White Crow, long before the Pukawatchi began to move north. The dwarves had always lived at peace with those from the other two realms, each with its own hunting grounds. All he knew now was that the closer to the sacred oak one came, the closer the realms conjoined.

I had been taught that the multiverse had no centre, just as an animal or a tree had no centre. Yet if the multiverse had a soul, that was what Ayanawatta seemed to be describing. If the multiplicity of everything was symbolised in a living metaphor, there was no reason the multiverse should not possess a soul. I went to unroll my buffalo robe and wrap myself against the cold.

Ayanawatta was enjoying his pipe more than usual. He lay on his side, staring up at a three-quarter moon over which thin, white clouds floated on a steady breeze from the south. He wore his soft buckskin shirt against the cold. It was of very fine workmanship, decorated with semi-precious beads and dyed porcupine quills, like the leggings and the fur-trimmed cap he also pulled on against the night's chill. Again I had the impression of a well-to-do Victorian gentleman adventurer making the best of the wilderness.

He had already removed and stored his eagle feathers in a hollow tube he carried for the purpose, but he still wore his long earrings and studs. His elaborate tattoos did nothing but enhance his refined, sensitive features. He took a deep pull from the pipe before handing me the bowl into which I placed my own reed to draw up the smoke. "What if that tree-soul which the Kakatanawa guard were the sum of all our souls?"

I agreed that this was a philosophical possibility.

"What if the sum of all our souls was the price we paid should that tree die?" he continued significantly.

I drew the mixture into my lungs. I tasted mint, rosemary, willow, sage. I inhaled a herb garden and forest combined! Unlike tobacco, this spread lightness and well-being through my whole body. "Is that what we are fighting for?" I asked, handing him back the bowl.

He sighed. "I think it is. When Law goes mad and Chaos is the Balance's only defence, some believe we are already conquered."

"You do not agree?"

"Of course not. I have made my spirit-quest into my future. I understand how I must play my part in restoring the Balance. I studied for four years and in four realms. I learned how to dream of my own future and summon for myself both flesh and form. I have read my own story in the books of the horse-people. I have heard my story called a false one. But if I give it life, I will redeem it. I will respect the people it sought to celebrate. I will bring respect to both the singer and the song."

He took another long, delicious pull on the pipe. He was gravely determined. "I know what I must do to fulfil my spiritual destiny. I must live my story as it is written. Our rituals are the rituals of order. I am working to give credible power back to Law and to fight those forces which would disrupt the Balance for ever. Like you, I serve neither Law nor Chaos. I am, in the eyes of a mukhamir, a Knight of the Balance." He let the smoke from his lungs pour out to join that of our small fire, curling gracefully towards the moon. "I have that lust for harmony, unity and justice which consumes so many of us."

The firelight caught his gold and copper, reflected in his glowing skin, drew contrasting shadows. I was, in spite of myself, enormously attracted to him, but I did not fear the attraction. Both of us had been well schooled in self-control.

"It is sometimes hard to know," I said, "where to place one's loyalty . . ."

He experienced no such ambiguities. He had taken his dream-journey. "My story is already written. I have read it, after all. Now I must follow it. That is the price you pay for such a vision. I know what I must do to make sure the story comes true in every possible realm of the multiverse. Thus I'll achieve that ultimate harmony we all desire more than life or death!"

Feeling overwhelmed by my own thoughts, I again took the first watch, listening with an attention which had once been habitual. But I was certain Klosterheim and his pygmies were not out there.

I was ready for sleep when I woke Ayanawatta to take his watch. He settled himself comfortably against Bes's gently rising and falling chest and filled another pipe. For all his appearance of indolence, I knew that every sense was alert. He had the air of all true outdoors folk, of being as securely comfortable in that vast wilderness under the moon and stars as another might be in the luxury of an urban living room.

The last thing I saw before I went to sleep was that broad, reassuring face, its tattoos telling the tale of his life journey, staring contentedly at the sky, confident of his ability to live up to everything his dream demanded of him.

In the morning Bes was restless. We washed and ate rapidly and were soon mounted again. We let the mammoth take her own course, since she evidently had a better idea than we where to find her master.

The only weapon White Crow had taken was his black-bladed lance.

I feared for him. "He might have been overwhelmed by the pygmies."

Ayanawatta was unworried. "With those senses of his, he can hear anything coming. But there is always the chance he's met with an accident. If so, he is not far from here. Bes can find him if we cannot."

By noon we had yet to see a sign of White Crow. Bes kept moving steadily towards the mountains, following the gentle curves of the landscape. Sometimes we could see for miles across the rolling drumlins. At other times we travelled through shallow valleys. Occasionally Bes paused, lifting her wide, curving tusks against the sky, her relatively small ears moving to follow a sound. Satisfied, she would then move on.

It was close to evening before Bes slowly brought her massive body to a halt and began to scent at the air with her trunk. Made long and dark by the sun, our shadows followed us like gigantic ghosts.

Once more Bes's ears waved back and forth. She seemed to hear something she had been hoping for and strained towards the source of the sound. We, of course, let her have her head. She began to move gradually to the east, to our right, slowly picking up speed until she was striding across the prairie at what amounted to a canter.

In the distance now I heard a strange mixture of noises. Something between the honking of geese and the hissing of snakes, mixed with a gurgling rumble which sounded like the first eruptions of a volcano.

All of a sudden White Crow appeared before us, waving his lance in triumph, grinning and shouting.

"I've found him again! Quickly, let's not lose him." He began running beside the mammoth, keeping easy pace with her.

I heard the noise again, but louder. I caught a sweet, familiar smell as we crested a broad, sweeping hill. Setting behind the mountains, the sun turned the whole scene blood-red. And there we saw White Crow's intended prey.

The size of a three-storey building, its brilliant feathered ruff was flaming with a thousand hues in that deepening light. I had never seen so much colour on one animal. Dazzling peacock feathers blazed purple, scarlet and gold, emerald and ruby and sapphire. Such beautiful plumage was the finery of a creature whose nightmare features should have disappeared from the Earth countless millions of years before. Its brown-black beak looked as if it had been carved from a gigantic block of mahogany. Above the beak two terrible brilliant yellow eyes glared, each the size of a dressing mirror. The mouth snapped and clacked, streaming with pale green saliva. As we watched, the thing lifted a yelping prairie fox in its right front claw and stuffed it into its maw, gagging as it swallowed.

The creature had a hungry, half-crazed look to it. It stretched its long neck down to the ground and sniffed, as if hoping to find food it had overlooked. It then stood upright on massive back feet which had a somewhat birdlike appearance, though its forepaws more closely resembled lizard claws.

Any one of the reptile's neck feathers, erect now as he sensed our presence, was the height of a tall man and layered in rich reds, yellows, purples and greens. Ulric would have called it a dinosaur, but to me it was a cross between a huge bird and a giant lizard, its feathered tail train being by far its longest part. Clearly it was a link with the dinosaur ancestors of our modern birds.

As we watched, the tail slashed back and forth like a scythe, cutting and trampling great swathes in the wild corn. I sniffed and realised it was the sweet scent I had smelled earlier. Suddenly awash with totally inappropriate emotions, I longed for the cornfields of the farm where I grew up during the period of my mother's attempted retirement.

"I think," said White Crow regretfully, climbing up into the saddle to sit with us, "I am going to have to kill him."

5

Feathers and Scales

Do you live the tale,
Or does the tale live you?

—Wheldrake,
The Teller or the Tale

"Why kill him?" I asked. "He is offering us no harm."

"He is an invader here," said White Crow. "But that is the business of those who hunt this land. He has moved north with the warming. That is not why he will die." He added almost as an aside, "Many years ago, he ate my father."

The shock which came with this news was horrible. The first time I saw this youth, he had called Ulric "Father."

There was nothing to do or say. My reaction was entirely subjective. For all their resemblance it was obvious there was no close connection between Ulric and White Crow.

"But that is not why we hunt him," Ayanawatta reminded him gently. "We hunt him for what your father carried when he was eaten."

"What was that?" I asked before I thought better of it.

But White Crow answered with apparent easiness, staring at the thing which rattled its huge ruff in frustration and screamed its hunger. "Oh, some medicine he had with him when the *kenabik* took him."

His tone was so inappropriate that I glanced hard at his face. It was a mask.

The feathered dinosaur had our scent, but the blustering breeze was varying and dropping. He kept losing it, turning this way and that and grunting to himself, drooling. He hardly knew what he was smelling. He seemed an inexpert hunter. His nostrils were heavy with ill health. His breathing was a rasp.

The last of the sun now poured over the mountains and drenched the plain with deep light. Big clouds came in behind us with a stronger wind, bringing more rain. Eventually the creature began to lumber away from us, then turned and came back for a few paces. He was still not sure what he scented. He might have been short-sighted, like rhinos. Clearly past his prime, he was scarcely able to fend for himself.

When I mentioned this to Ayanawatta he nodded. "This is not their place," he said. "The *kenabik* do not breed. His tribe have all died. Something as beautiful replaces them, we hope."

He spoke distractedly as he studied the beaked dragon, who was still casting bewildered yellow eyes back and forth. "And of a more appropriate size," he added with a slight smile.

White Crow pulled in our mount. Bes stood still as a rock while her master studied the *kenabik*. The beaked dragon's feathers were layered, pale blue on green, on gold, on silver, on scarlet. There were subtle shades of brown-yellow and dark red, of glittering emerald and sapphire. When that black maw opened it revealed a crimson tongue, broken molars, cracked incisors. There seemed something wrong with that mouth, but I was not sure what.

Then the sun disappeared. It was suddenly pitch-black. From somewhere in that darkness, the *kenabik* began to keen.

That keening was one of the most mournful sounds I had ever heard. The note was absolutely desolate as the monster cried for itself and for its lost kind.

I looked at White Crow again.

His face was still totally immobile, but I saw the silver trail of tears running to his lips. It was hard to know whether he wept for the pain of this creature, the thought of having to destroy it or the loss of his father.

Again, that awful, agonised call. But it grew fainter as the thing moved off.

"We will kill it in the morning," White Crow said. He seemed glad to put off the unsavoury moment for a little longer.

How three humans armed with bows and spears were to set about killing the *kenabik* had not yet been explained to me! Neither was it to happen as White Crow had said.

The monster determined our agenda.

I was awake when the *kenabik* became famished enough to attack. I heard it running towards us over the low hills. It went through the camp in one terrible, violent moment, even as I tried to wake my friends.

Ayanawatta found his bow and arrows while White Crow hefted his spears. "They never hunt at night." White Crow sounded offended.

Bes had stumbled to her feet, still bleary with sleep, her trunk questing about for White Crow. She could not see him, and the feathered dinosaur was coming in rapidly on her left.

Bes was ready. In time to take the *kenabik*'s second attack, she swung her huge tusks in the direction of the noise. The beast came thudding into the camp screaming its own terror at our fire and grabbing about for something, anything, to eat.

Bes stepped forward. A sweep of her great head, and a long, deep gouge appeared along the beast's left side. He shrieked as those ivory sabres began to sweep back the other way.

The old mammoth staggered and was momentarily knocked off balance, but she held her ground, the *kenabik*'s blood streaming from her massive tusk. Her eyes narrowed, her trunk curling, she displayed her pleasure at her own achievement. She was almost skittish as she turned to trumpet after her fleeing foe.

"Why would it behave so uncharacteristically?" I was panting, trying to gather up my few possessions while the others retrieved the rest of our scattered goods.

"It is mad," said White Crow sadly. "It has nothing to eat."

"There must be plenty of prey on the prairie?"

"Oh, yes," he said. "There is. And as you saw, every so often he devours some. What we probably will not see is the *kenabik* disgorging most of what he eats. Unfortunately he was not born a meat eater. What he misses is the rich foliage and lush grass of his native south. The transition from herbivore to carnivore is impossible. The meat he eats is killing him. What vegetation grows here is too sparse and too hard for him to harvest. Even if we did not kill him, he would be dead soon, and it would be a bad, ignoble death. His shame would be great. It would weight his spirit and keep him bound to this realm. He would have long to brood on the ignobility he has brought to himself and his tribe. We can offer him better. We can offer him the respect of our arms. You could say it was his own fault for leaving his grazing grounds, but predators were moving up behind his kind, picking them off as they weakened. He was chased from his homeland. I wish to try to kill him mercifully."

"You show much forgiveness for the beast that ate your father."

"I understand that it was an accident. The *kenabik* probably didn't even know he was eating him. There was no malice involved. My father took a risk and failed." Two red stones shone in White Crow's rigid face.

I turned away.

Ayanawatta had recovered his bow and quiver while White Crow collected all the fire he could find back into the pot. The little lean-to we had put up against the rainy breeze was totally trampled, so again Bes gave us her massive bulk for shelter. The two of us slept warily as White Crow elected to keep watch until dawn.

I woke once to see his profile set against the grey strip of light on the horizon, and it seemed to me he had not moved. When I woke again, his face and head were set exactly as I had seen them hours earlier. He resembled one of those extraordinary, infinitely beautiful marbles of the Moldavian Captives Michelangelo had carved for the French pope. Infinitely sad, infinitely aware of the cold truth of their coming fate.

Once again I felt an urgent wish to take him in my arms and comfort him. An unexpected desire to bring warmth to a lonely, uncomplaining soul.

He turned at that moment, and his puzzled gaze met mine. Then, with a small sigh, he gave his attention back to the distant mountains. He recognised what was in my eyes. He had seen it before. He had a cause. A dream to live out. His destiny was the only comfort he allowed himself.

When we woke it was drizzling hard. White Crow had pulled a robe over his shoulders as he struggled to settle the great saddle on his mammoth's back. Ayanawatta moved to help him. Everything smelled of rain. The whole sky was dark grey. It was impossible to see more than twenty yards ahead. The mountains, of course, had vanished.

I wrapped myself tightly against the cold and wet. The mammoth rose to her feet, groaning and muttering at the winter wind stiffening her joints. We had not tried to make a fresh fire the night before, and our firepot was low, so we ate cold jerky as we rode.

We followed the *kenabik*'s bloodstained trail. Bes had injured him enough at least to slow him down.

We were warier than usual, because we knew the *kenabik* might be waiting in cover to attack. The steady rain finally stopped. The wind dropped.

The world was strangely silent. What sounds there were became amplified and isolated as the going became harder through the soaking grasslands. Occasionally the sky cleared and thin sunbeams banded the distant tundra. The mountains, however, remained hidden. We heard the splash of frogs and small animals in the nearby water. We smelled the strong, acrid aroma of rotting grass from an old nest, and then once again came the sudden hissing wind bringing rain. We heard the steady sound of Bes's feet as she carried us stolidly on after our prey.

We reached a kind of wallow, a muddy bayou filled with weed. It was clear the monster had rested, attempting to eat some of the weed. We also found the half-digested remains of various smaller mammals and reptiles. White Crow had been right. This creature was too specialised to survive here. Also the wound was clearly more serious than we had originally guessed. There were signs that he had made a crude attempt to stanch a flow of blood with some of the grass. How intelligent was this creature?

I asked Ayanawatta his opinion. He was not sure. He had learned, he said, not to measure intelligence by his own standards. He preferred to assume that every creature was as conscious as himself but in different ways. It was as well, he said, to give every creature the respect you would give yourself.

I could not entirely accept this view. I told him that I could not believe, however conscious they might be, that animals possess a moral sensibility. And the most unstable of rocks are poor conversationalists.

Almost immediately, I found myself smiling, amused by my own presumption. Not long before, I had been accusing my husband of being insufficiently imaginative.

Ayanawatta was silent for a moment, raising his eyebrows. "I may be mistaken," he said, "but I seem to recall an adventure I once had among the rock giants. They are, indeed, extremely laconic."

The sideways glance he threw in my direction was humorous.

White Crow slipped suddenly down Bes's flank without stopping her progress and began to pad beside her, studying the muddy creek. It reminded me of what Ulric must have seen in the trenches at the end of the First War. The *kenabik* had clearly been in agony, rolling over and over in an effort to stop the pain.

Our hunt took on a peculiar gravity. It had something of the air of a funeral procession.

The rain came down harder until we could scarcely see for the sweeping sheets of water. As we descended a long hill, we confronted a stand of tough, green grass that reached almost to Bes's shoulder. She found it difficult to walk on through. White Crow told her to turn and move back to a better place. Slowly she crushed her way out of the confining growth and made for the high ground again.

Then through the pounding rain we heard the *kenabik*. No longer did it squawk and scream and moan as it had done. No longer did its voice have the fading note of pain and self-pity. The sound had the fullness of a baritone, rhythmic and slow, the noise of a bull-roarer, booming from that massive diaphragm.

White Crow took a slender spear from the long quiver. The edges were tipped with silver, the shaft bound with ivory and copper. With this, he again dismounted and was quickly lost in the rain and deep grass.

Bes came to a stop, turning her head as if she feared for him.

"What is the *kenabik* doing now?" I asked Ayanawatta.

"I am not sure," said the warrior, frowning, "but I think he is singing his death song."

The beast's voice grew deeper still, and something connected with me. I could feel his bewildered mind reaching into mine, questing for something. Not me. Not me. There was a mutual repulsion. Curiosity. An almost grateful quality as the monster tasted tentatively at my identity.

All the time that song went on. Somehow I believed he was telling the story of his people, of their glory, of their virtue and their destruction. A psychologist would consider this transference, would argue that the beast could not feel such complicated emotions and ideas. Yet, as Ayanawatta said, who are we to measure the value or quality of another's perceptions?

I could not bring myself to bond with the *kenabik*'s brain. It was too unlike anything I understood. It dreamed of tall fields of cane and thick, nourishing ferns, and its song began to reflect this dream more and more. A harmony grew between the strange view of Paradise and the thrumming voice. Whatever it is in sentient creatures that needs to communicate, that is what I heard. It was a confused, frightened mixture of half-understood images and feelings. Who else could the dying creature reach out to? Another voice entered the song, taking the melody until it was impossible to tell which was which.

In response to this, the monster abruptly shifted its attention elsewhere. I was, I must admit, deeply relieved. While it could not be the first time I had attended a dying spirit, this strange, anachronistic being found little comfort from me.

The clouds parted for a moment or two, and the rain passed. We saw that we stood in waist-high grass. Some distance off, with his back to us, was White Crow. From his stance and the position of his head I understood the *kenabik* to be somewhere below him. Then, out of the misty foliage, I saw a beaked head rise. Huge yellow eyes sought the source of the other song. The eyes were filled with baffled gratitude. As it died, the monster received grace.

The clouds rolled in again. I saw White Crow lift his silver-tipped spear.

Both songs ended.

We waited for a long time. The rain lashed down, and the wind blew the grass into glistening waves. We had become used to these blustering elemental attacks. At last Ayanawatta and I made a decision. We dismounted, telling Bes to remain where she was unless she needed to escape danger, and pressed on through the fleshy stalks surrounding us, our moccasins sinking into the thick, glutinous mud. Ayanawatta paused, cautioning me to silence, and he listened. Slowly I became aware of soft footfalls.

White Crow came crashing out of the grass. Over his shoulder he carried his lance and two huge feathers, gorgeous against that grey light. He was covered from head to foot in blood.

"I had to go inside it," he said. "To find the medicine of my father."

We followed him to where Bes waited. The mammoth was visibly pleased at his return. He took the two gigantic brilliant feathers and stuck them into the wool near her head. Her hair was so thick that they did not fall, but White Crow assured her he would attach them more securely later. Bes looked oddly proud of her new finery. White Crow was acknowledging her victory. Then he went back to the creek and washed the blood off his body, and again he sang. He sang of Bes and her hero-spirit. She would find her ancestors in the eternal dance and celebrate her deeds for ever. He sang of the great heart of his finished enemy. And it felt to me as if that monster's spirit were at peace leaving the world to join its brothers in some eternal grazing grounds.

White Crow spent the rest of that day and part of the night washing himself and his clothing. When he came back to the camp he seemed grateful for the fire we had made. He sat down, took a pipe, and smoked for a while without speaking. Then he reached to where he had placed his pouch on top of his freshly washed clothes and slid his hand inside. His fist closed on something, and he withdrew it, opening the palm to show us what he had retrieved.

The firelight threw wild shadows. It was hard for me to see.

"I had no choice but to go into his guts," said White Crow. "It was difficult. It took some time. The *kenabik* had three bellies, all of them diseased. I had hoped to find more. But this was what there was. Perhaps it is all we need."

The fire flared, lighting the night, and I saw the tiny object clearly. Turquoise, ivory, scarlet. Round. It was horribly familiar . . .

I recognised it.

I had an immediate physical reaction. My head swam. I gasped. My mind refused what my eyes saw!

I looked at an exact miniature of the huge medicine shield on which I had made my way into this world. I had no real doubt that it was the same. Every detail was identical, save for the size.

"It was my father's," said White Crow, "when he was White Crow man. I am truly White Crow man now." This statement was made flatly. His voice was bleak. He closed his fingers tightly around the talisman before putting it away in his bag.

I looked at Ayanawatta, as if for confirmation that I was right in recognising the tiny medicine shield, but he had never properly seen it as I had. He had merely glimpsed it in his summoning dream. Every detail was the same, I was sure. Yet how had it become so tiny? Was it some process in the animal's belly? Some supernatural element I had not perceived?

Was Klosterheim a dwarf? Or was I the giant? What had gone wrong with the scale of things? The workings of Chaos? Or had Law, in its crazed wisdom, wished this condition upon the world? "What is that you hold?" I asked at last. White Crow frowned. "It is my father's medicine shield," he said.

"But the size . . ."

"My father was not a large man," said White Crow.

6

The Snows of Yesteryear

Northward to the northern waters,
Northward to the farthest shore . . .

—W.S. Harte,
The Maker of Laws

And so, having reached that particular stage in the dream-quest of my two companions, we continued our journey north. All obstacles seemed to be behind us. The weather, though cooler, was bright and clear. I felt instinctively confident that Ulric still lived and that we should soon be reunited. Only the constant, thrusting, whispering, insistent wind reminded me that I still had mysterious antagonists, those who would stop me seeing my husband again.

Game became increasingly plentiful, and I was able to feed us on antelope, hare, grouse and geese. Now there was wild alfalfa, maize and potato. Both my companions carried bags of dried herbs which they used for cooking and smoking. I was by far the best shot, and the men were content to let me hunt. We became used to eating very well, usually around sunset, while Bes, the mammoth, grazed happily on the rich grasses and shrubs. We enjoyed exquisite light saturating gorgeous scenery, the tall peaks of the horizon, the varied greens and yellows of the prairie. The evening sky was deep yellow, flooded with scarlet and ochre.

We ate heartily, as if to keep our strength against the coming winter.

The wind grew steadily fresher and more invigorating. For a while it was almost playful. There was a sharpness to the air which brought clearer details and keener scents. Beavers worked in the creeks. Prairie dogs were hunted by huge, cruising eagles. We startled a kangaroo rat in a swathe of wild roses whose petals sailed through the twilight as he leaped to avoid us. Families of badgers came squinting into the last of the sun. The occasional possum would play dead when we scared him inspecting our camp at night. Most of the animals were not unusually nervous of us. They had no reason to be. Ayanawatta, lacking a human listener, was perfectly happy to address an audience of thoughtful toads.

More than once we saw herds of bison grazing their way south, but they were not food for us. We had no time to preserve the meat or cure the hide. Buffalo tastes delicious when one has eaten little else, but the tough, gamey meat is not to everyone's favour. Neither were we tempted by the coats of the splendid bulls who guarded their cows and calves. We shared a notion that to kill a buffalo only for its hide was offensive. My companions had been trained as children to kill swiftly and without cruelty and practised all the disciplines of a halal slaughterman. They could not imagine a civilised human being behaving in any other manner. There are few willing vegans on the prairie.

I fell in love with the great, placid bison. I found myself drawn to them. I would leave my weapons behind and stroll among them, touching them and talking to them. They were not in any way afraid of me, though sometimes they seemed a little irritated. I learned not to put my hands on the young. There was a wonderful sense of security at the centre of the herd. Increasingly I understood the deep pleasures of herd life. Our strength was in the herd, in the alertness of the males, in the wisdom of the cows. And we were eternal.

Eventually our ways parted. The huge mass of buffalo—a great, restless sea of black, brown and white—made its way towards the blue horizon. From a hill, I watched it moving slowly across the prairie under the rising sun. Briefly I had an urge to follow it. Then I ran to rejoin my companions.

The mountains, which had seemed so easily reached, were separated from us by scrub, woodland, rivers and swamps, but even these were more easily negotiated than before. Where there was water and shelter, we saw stands of old trees, the remains of a great forest. The ground became firmer as the air grew colder. For her age Bes the mammoth had extraordinary stamina. White Crow said she had not long since walked for five days and nights, pausing only three times to drink.

While White Crow shared my enjoyment of solitude, of listening to the subtle music of the prairie, Ayanawatta remained as talkative as ever. I must admit my own mind was rather narrowly focused.

The wind returned forcefully and erratically. This world had increasing inconsistencies. Klosterheim had become a dwarf. The medicine shield was now small enough to fit on the palm of a hand. Size in this realm was alarmingly unstable. Was this the work of Chaos? Was this changing but persistent wind actually sentient? Dread rose inside me and threatened to consume me. It was some time before I could regain complete control of myself.

Ayanawatta drew his robe around him. "The weather grows chillier with the passing of the hours. This wind never ceases." We wrapped ourselves in the great folds of his wigwam hides and at night built a larger fire. The canoe now acted as a canopy over the saddle, held there by four staves, and protected us against rain. At night two of us could sleep under it and give the other the benefit of the fire.

I remained mystified by the size of the medicine shield and where it had been found. White Crow now wore it around his neck on a beautiful beaded thong. He said nothing else about his father. Etiquette did not allow me to ask. I could only hope coming events would illuminate me.

I was bound to discover more. This careful living of the details of a dreamed future or a granted vision was characteristic of Ayanawatta's people. I understood loyalty to a visionary destiny. I understood the gruelling discipline of his chosen way. Every step was a figure in a formal dance. A masque which must be performed perfectly. By dancing the exact step, the achieved ambition was reached. It was not quite creativity. It was an act of reproduction or interpretation, a strengthening. Following this discipline took the most extraordinary qualities of character. Virtues which I did not possess. Crude folk renderings of this discipline had been discussed during my training in Marrakech, where we had also looked at the Egyptian and Mayan Books of the Dead.

That strict path had no appeal for me. The musram teaches that time is a field and that space could be a property of time, one of many dimensions. By subtle repetition we weave our common threads and give longevity to our particular story. I suppose it was my training to find new patterns. In this sense we represented a balance of the opposite forces of Law and Chaos. Certainly the animism and cosmology of White Crow and Ayanawatta were far more in harmony with the eternal realities than Klosterheim's grim disciplines. If their Law was modified by my Chaos, equally my Chaos was modified and strengthened by their Law.

Klosterheim, in rejecting Chaos completely, rejected any prospect of ever achieving his own particular dream of reconciliation and harmony. In some ways I found the ex-priest a more interesting and complex figure than our defeated enemy Gaynor. Ulric's cousin had been that rare thing, an adept entirely without loyalty to anything but himself. Such creatures achieved their power through means which by definition denied them the harmony of the Balance. Gaynor, or those avatars who played his role throughout the multiverse, tended to come to a sticky end not because they were overwhelmed by the forces of virtue, but because their own flawed characters ultimately betrayed them. Had he, as my husband suggested, drawn all his scattered bodies back into a single self?

I had been unprepared for this adventure. It was occasionally difficult to believe that it was happening at all. At any moment I might take control of my own dream and return to normality.

I found myself missing the advice of my old mentor, Prince Lobkowitz. A tower of strength, a fixed point in my emotional ocean, he understood more of the structure of the multiverse than anyone. He had helped me harness a little of the genetic talent which enabled me to roam the moonbeam roads at will.

Some called the myriad worlds of the multiverse the Shadow Realm or the Dream Worlds. Some understood them to be real. Others believed them an illusion, a symbol, a mere version of something too intense for our ordinary senses. Many believed them to be a little of both. Some suggested we were the vermin of the multiverse, living in the cracks and crannies of divine reality and mistaking a crumb of cheese for a banquet. Many cosmologies recognised only a small group of realms. Whatever the ultimate truth, some of us were able to wander between such worlds more or less at will, as I did, while others endured extraordinary training to be able to take a simple step between one version of their reality and another. The interconnection of human dreams formed its own nexus of reality, its own realm, where travellers wandered or searched for some specific goal. It was in this vast realm of realms, worlds of the soul's dread and the heart's desire, that the dreamthieves earned their dangerous living.

Each slight variance of one realm from another is marked by a change in scale so great that one is undetectable to another. For those of us who walk the moonbeam ways every step takes us through a further scale. Or perhaps we travel beyond scale, as over a rippling pond? Many say this could mean that the matter of our beings is forever forming and re-forming. Instantly re-created by an act of will? Dreaming dust? That said, the reality is almost impossible to describe in mere words. Some achieve their travel through what they call sorcery, others through dreams or some form of creativity. Whatever it is called, it involves a monstrous act of will.

One learns temperance with one's travels. One also learns to live and invite experience. Each twist of a moonbeam branch on the great, eternal tree takes one to fresh knowledge and self-revelation. It is a fascinating and endless life. However, for the likes of myself, who will not steal others' dreams as my mother did, it can become unsatisfying. What Ulric had given me back was a moral focus and a sense of purpose. I had learned to tackle the problems of one small sphere rather than engage in the great, eternal conflict between Chaos and Law.

I no longer felt a particular longing for the moonbeam roads. Sometimes I did yearn for the silver-and-scarlet light warping and sliding in the air around my cottage, that particular music which came when certain spheres intersected and produced their glorious harmonies. But chiefly I hoped my old life, with my husband and my children, would soon be restored.

The days grew shorter and still colder, but they brought some sort of promise. We must soon enter Kakatanawa lands. There, I knew, I would find Ulric. But how would I rescue him or bargain for his release?

The first sign that again we were being followed came during a flurry of sleet, when sheets of grey misery stretched across the plains and hid even the foothills. The curtain parted for a few seconds and revealed a hillock covered in spikey prairie grass and clover, glinting in the thin light. It was just behind us and to our right. Looking over my shoulder at it as we rode along, I thought I saw a figure standing there, its grey robes rising in the wind, its grey face the very personification of winter death.

Klosterheim!

The man was relentless.

Had he returned to his normal size? I had not seen him long enough to be able to tell. I continued to peer back over my shoulder as Bes strode stoically on through the icy rain but did not see Klosterheim again.

No doubt he had his pygmies with him and his ally, the Two Tongues. I warned the others of what I had seen. We agreed it would be wise to mount a guard again when we camped.

We rested Bes regularly. White Crow said normally she would have been put to pasture years before. Then he had talked about this dream, this destined scenario, with her. She had wanted to go, he said. "She believes this journey is good for her and prepares her for the afterlife."

We were lucky. That evening the rain disappeared and left us with a watery sunset brightening a stand of heavy, old oaks. Of the groves we had passed, these were the thickest and most ancient we had seen. The boles and branches were so dense they offered excellent cover. The smell of the ancient glade was intoxicating!

"Good," said Ayanawatta, striding around in what was virtually a cave of woven branches into which a single shaft of sunlight fell upon a slender sapling at the centre. "This is the place to make our medicine. It is a world within the world, with a roof and four corners and the tree at the centre. It will amplify our medicine and make it work as it has to do."

Although he talked more around the subject, he added no further information. We built a small fire in our pot, as you might in someone's home. It felt somehow wrong to disturb the floor of this ancient grove. Many branches were thicker than most trunks. They could be thousands of years old. Perhaps an earlier culture had left a few stands of uncleared woodland? Maybe some natural disaster had destroyed all but a patch or two of these timeless trees?

Ayanawatta burned a little of our food as an offering to the grove for its security. There is a special consciousness which trees have. They respond well to respect. I had the distinct sense that night that I slept in a holy retreat, in a temple.

Strangely for me I dreamed. The tree under which I slept became my multiverse in which I wandered. I dreamed of relatives. I dreamed of the world where my name was Ilian of Garathorm. She was a powerful warrior, an avatar of the Eternal Champion, a soul-cousin to my father. Her world was nothing but ancient trees. To the north-west were the great redwoods, to the north-east the giant oaks and birches. In the south were mangroves and more exotic trees. All were united in one vast world of tangled roots and branches. The entire planet was an organic nest of growing flora, with massive, fleshy blossoms. Magnolias and rhododendrons, vast chrysanthemums and roses bloomed to make a world in which Ilian coexisted with all manner of huge insects and birds. She rode the branches of her world as I strode the moonbeams of mine.

In my dream Ilian was troubled. She saw the end of her world. The death of everything. The withering of her home tree and therefore her own end. She called to her ancestors and the spirits of her world. She summoned them together to aid her in her final fight. She spoke to creatures she knew as silverskins, and as she woke she recalled the story of Peau d'Argent, of Le Corneille Blanc, the silver man, the Prince of Faery, whom the Kakatanawa called White Crow.

Upon waking, my dream fled away from me. I held what I could of it, for there was now a nagging idea somewhere in the back of my mind, something which linked White Crow to someone or something else, some faint memory, perhaps of childhood. I became increasingly certain that we were related.

I looked at the sleeping face of the albino youth. He was completely at rest, yet I knew he could come alert in seconds. I hardly liked to breathe for fear he would mistake any sound I made for an alarm. What had I been dreaming which concerned him? What were these tiny patches of memory he had left me with? I moved a little closer to the fire. My steaming breath was pale on the air. I drew my buffalo robe closer around me and was soon warm.

At last I slept again. In the morning I saw that it had snowed. The thickness of the oaks had protected us. We now inhabited a many-chambered palace of icy greens and golds. We looked out over a prairie purified by the first snowfall of winter. Sitting near our merry little fire and contemplating that immensity of snow, White Crow pulled rather cheerfully on his pipe and, as soon as he knew we were awake, took up a small drum and began to sing a song.

In a lifetime of moving between the realms I had heard few voices as beautiful as White Crow's. The song wove among the branches and glittering icicles. Its echoes turned into harmonies until the entire grove sang with him. Together they sang of ancient ways, of bitter truths and golden imaginings. They sang an elegy for all that had ever been lost. They sang of the morning and of the hours of the day, of the months and the passing of the seasons. As they sang I could barely stop myself from weeping with the beauty of it. Ayanawatta stood straight, with his arms folded, listening with absolute intensity. He wore only his tattoos, his paint, his jewellery and a breechclout of fine beaded vellum. His copper skin glowed in the wonderful light, his chest swelling, his muscles clenching, as he gave his whole being to the music.

Wearing her hero feathers, Bes, too, stirred to this song as if with a sense of security. Yet as well as comfort, the song had power. It had purpose.

Through the surrounding lens of ice, I saw something moving on the horizon. Gradually I made out more detail. It trotted quite rapidly towards us and stopped abruptly about ten yards from where Ayanawatta and White Crow still sang.

Again, I was unsure of the scale, but the beast they had summoned seemed huge. Regarding us with solemn, curious eyes as a fresh curtain of snow began to fall stood a massive white bison, a living totem, the manifestation of a Kakatanawa goddess. Her red-rimmed eyes glaring with proud authority, she stared deeply into mine. I recognised a confirmation. She pawed the snow, her breath steaming.

Bes lifted her trunk and uttered a great bellow which shook the forest and set ice cracking and falling. The white buffalo tossed her head as if in alarm, turned and was gone, trotting rapidly into the deep snow.

Ayanawatta was delighted. He, too, had seen the buffalo. He was full of excitement. Everything, he said, was unfolding as it should. Bes had warned the buffalo of our danger, and she had responded. Powerful medicine protected the land of the Kakatanawa, which in turn protected their city, which in turn protected the eternal tree. Once we crossed the mountains, we would enter the great valley of the Kakatanawa. Then we would almost certainly be safe, ready to begin the last crucial stage of our journey.

I had no reason to doubt him. I kept my own counsel, congratulating him on the beauty, rather than the power, of his voice. I knew, of course, that I was in the presence of skilled summoners. My father was one who could call upon bargains his family had made with the Lords of the Higher Worlds, with powerful elementals. He could invoke spirits of air, earth, fire and water as easily as another might plough a furrow. I could not be sure who had summoned the white buffalo, or whether she had heard both men singing and come to inspect us. If she was as strict with us as she was with her own herd, and indeed with herself, she would soon give us an order. I wondered why I should feel such sisterly feelings towards the animal. Was it simply because Ayanawatta had given me the Indian name of White Buffalo Woman?

The drum continued its steady beating. White Crow rose gracefully to his feet. Swaying from side to side he began to dance. It was only then that I realised what Ayanawatta had meant.

White Crow was opening the gateway for us. We were attempting to pass between the realms. The land of the Kakatanawa lay not in the looming mountains, but in the world beyond them, where this strange tribe guarded their treasures and their secrets in mysterious ways.

As he danced I soon became aware of another presence, something drawn not by his Summoning, but by the *smell* of his magic. And then at last I confirmed the identity of my particular enemy. An elemental but also a powerful Lord of the Higher Worlds, Shoashooan, the Turning Wind, who was native to this realm and therefore more dangerous.

I heard rumbling. A distant storm gathered and moved in our direction. Purples, crimsons and dark greens flooded the sky. They drew themselves across the horizon like a veil, but almost immediately they began to join again, shrieking and threatening and forming into that familiar leering, shifty, destructive fellow: Shoashooan, the Demon Wind, the Son Stealer, the Lord of the Tornadoes, the undisputed ruler of the prairie, before whom all spirits and creatures of the plains were powerless. Lord Shoashooan in all his writhing, twisting, shouting forms, his bestial features glaring out of his swirling body.

Standing on the right side of the Bringer of Ruins stood the Two Tongues, his body burning as his own lifestuff was fed to the summoned spirit. Ipkeptemi would not last long. On the other side of the furious spirit, his ragged buffalo cape flapping and cracking in the blustering force from his new ally, was the ghastly, half-frozen figure of Klosterheim.

He might have been dead, turned to ice where he stood.

His lips were drawn back from his teeth.

For a moment I thought he was smiling.

Then I realised he was profoundly terrified.

7

The White Path

Tread the path that shines like silver,
To the city made of gold,
Where the world-snake slowly dies.
Where a lance moans like a woman,
And the pipe denies all lies.

—W.S. Harte,
Onowega's Death Song

Klosterheim's face was the last human thing I saw before the whirling Elemental Lord screeched and rose into the air. His limbs and organs proliferated so rapidly that he now had a hundred hands, a thousand legs, all writhing and spinning. And every limb held a shivering, slicing blade. The terrible, beastly face glowering and raging, he roared and railed as if something were pulling him back where he had come from.

Still the Two Tongues burned, and still his lifestuff fed the Chaos Lord, giving him the substance he needed to remain in this realm. Yet it was an inexpert summons and therefore perhaps only a partial manifestation. The shaman burned for nothing.

Something *was* driving Lord Shoashooan back.

White Crow was singing. His voice covered two octaves easily and rose and fell almost like the movement of the oceans. His song was taken up by the mountains. Notes rippled from peak to peak, achieving their own strange, extended melody. Raising his arms from where he stood beside that great black pachyderm, he flung back his head and sang again. His handsome, ivory face shone with ecstasy. The red hawk feathers in his white hair were garish against his delicate colouring, emphasising the gemlike redness of his eyes. Behind him, in its quiver, the Black Lance began to vibrate to the same notes. It joined in the song.

Lord Shoashooan growled and feinted and turned and keened, came closer and retreated. Then, with an angry howl, he vanished, taking the two men with him.

"Those fools," said White Crow. "They have neither the skills nor the powers to control such an entity. My grandfather banished him. No human can destroy him once he has established himself in our world. We can only hope he failed to find true substance and could not make a full manifestation." He looked around, frowning. "Though here, it would be easy enough."

I asked about the two men. He shook his head. He was sure they had not gone willingly.

"They summoned a monster, and it devoured them," said Ayanawatta. "Perhaps that is the end of it. If Lord Shoashooan had been able to secure his manifestation, he would be free to feast however and wherever he chose. We can only hope that two amateur sorcerers were enough for him. Lord Shoashooan is infamous for his lethal whimsicalities, his horrible jokes, his relish for flesh."

Glancing to my left I saw the strain on White Crow's face. Here was proof that Lord Shoashooan's disappearance had not been voluntary. I was impressed. Few had the strength and skill to oppose a Lord of the Higher Worlds. Had White Crow's magic driven the creature back to his own plane, taking with him as trophies those who hoped to evoke his aid?

A light wind danced around us.

White Crow lifted his head and began to sing and drum again, and again Ayanawatta joined with him in the music. I found that wordlessly I, too, was singing in harmony with my comrades. Through our song we sought to find our accord again, to set ourselves back on our path, to be true to our stories.

White Crow's small hand-drum began to pound more rapidly, like the noise of a sudden downpour. Faster and faster he moved his stick back and forth, back and forth, around and around, down the side, against the bottom, back up the side to finish in a pulsating rhythm which would strengthen our medicine. Slowly the beats grew further apart.

The wind began to flutter and die away. The sun came out again in a single silver band slanting through billowing clouds and cut a wide swathe across the prairie.

White Crow continued to beat his drum. Very slowly he beat it. And his new song was deep and deliberate.

The shining path of cold sunlight fell until it lay before us, stretching out from our strange ice temple and disappearing towards those wild, high mountains. This silvery trail surely led to a pass through the mountains. A pass which would take us to the land of the Kakatanawa. A pass which began to reveal itself like a long crack in the granite of the mountains.

The clouds boiled in, and the sun was lost again.

But that gleaming, single, silvery beam remained. A magic path through the mountains.

White Crow stopped drumming. Then he stopped singing. The light of day dimmed beneath the heavy snow clouds. But the silver road remained.

White Crow was clearly satisfied. This was his work. Ayanawatta congratulated him enthusiastically, and while it was not good manners to show emotional response to such praise, White Crow was quietly pleased with himself.

He had sung and drummed a pathway into the next realm. He and Ayanawatta had woven it from the gossamer stuff of the Grey Fees, creating the harmonies and resonances necessary to walk safely perhaps only a short distance between two worlds.

Ironically I reflected on their envy of my skills. I could walk at will across the moonbeam roads, while they had immense difficulty. But I was not a creator as they were. I could not fashion the roads themselves. The only danger now was that Shoashooan would follow us through the gateway we had made.

With light steps we restored the saddle to Bes's back and adjusted our canoe canopy. White Crow then urged his old friend to move on.

I watched her set those massive feet on the pathway we could now see through the snow. She was confident and cheerful as she carried us forward. When I looked back, I saw that the road had not faded behind us as we progressed over it. Did that mean Klosterheim or one of his allies could now easily follow us?

Bes trod the crystal trail with an air of optimistic familiarity. Indeed there was something jaunty about the mighty mammoth as she carried us along, her own brilliant feathers now held securely in a sort of topknot. I wondered if there were any other mammoths to whom she could tell her stories, or would she be remembered only in our own tales?

The prairie lay under thick snow. There was nothing supernatural about it. You could taste the sharp snowflakes, see the hawks and eagles turning in the currents high overhead. In a sudden flurry a small herd of antelope sprang from cover nearby and fled over the snow, leaving a dark trail behind them. There were tracks of hares and raccoons.

We had plenty of provisions, and there was no need to leave the tentlike interior of the makeshift howdah. While the mammoth plodded through deep snow, for us this journey was sheer luxury.

Once in the distance we saw a bear walking ahead of us along the trail, but he soon blundered off into the brush near a creek, and we lost sight of him. For some time Ayanawatta and White Crow discussed the possibility that this was a sign. They eventually decided that the bear had no special symbolic meaning. For several hours Ayanawatta expounded on the nature of bear-spirits and bear-dreams while White Crow nodded agreeably, occasionally confirming an anecdote, always preferring to be the audience.

Slowly the mountains grew larger and larger until we were looking up at their tree-covered lower slopes. The silver trail led through the foothills and into the pass. The two men became quietly excited. Neither had been sure the magic would work, and even now they were unsure of the consequences. Would there be a price to pay? I was in awe of their power, and so were they!

The snow started to fall steadily. Bes seemed to enjoy it. Perhaps her great woolly coat was designed for such weather. Snow soon banked itself on both sides of us, as the trail grew rockier. We entered the deep, dark fissure which would lead us to the land of the Kakatanawa. Here little snow had settled, and it was still possible to see the trail ahead.

I had not expected further attack, certainly not from above. But in an instant the air was thick with ravens. The huge, black birds swarmed around us, cawing and clacking at us as if we invaded their territory. I could not bring myself to shoot at them, and neither could my companions. White Crow said the black ravens were his cousins. They all served the same queen.

The noise of the attack was distracting, however, and disturbing to Bes. After some twenty minutes of enduring this, White Crow stood up in the saddle and let out a tremendous cackle of angry song which silenced the ravens.

Seconds later the big birds had settled on outcrops of rock. They sat waiting, heads to one side, black eyes shining, listening as White Crow continued his irritable address. It was clear how he had come by his name and no doubt his totem. He spoke their language fluently, with nuances which even these rowdy aggressors could appreciate. I was amused that he spoke so little in human language and could be so eloquent in the tongue of a bird. When I asked him about it, he said that the language of dragons was not dissimilar, and both came easily to him.

Whatever he said to the ravens, he did not drive them away. But at least it stopped the noise. Now they sat along both sides of our path, occasionally croaking out a complaint or chittering among themselves. Then with a snap and shuffle of their wings, the ravens took to the air, flooding upwards in a long, ragged line towards the distant sky, cawing back at us after they had gained a certain distance. Birds usually felt benign towards humans, but these were clearly the exception.

As we continued down the great cleft in the rock, surprisingly I began to feel a claustrophobia I had never known on the moonbeam roads. The day became so overcast and the cliffs so steep that we could not easily see the sky. The pathway shone no brighter, and we might not have known it was there, save for the banked snowdrifts.

Night fell, and still we followed the glistening path until we came to a place where the trail widened. Here we camped, listening to the strange sounds in the cliffs, where unfamiliar animals scuttled and foraged. Bes was eager to continue. She had not wanted to rest, but we thought it best to catch our breath while we could.

In the morning I awoke to discover that we had again been camping in an ancient holy place. Our shelter was the neglected entrance to a huge stone temple whose roof had long since fallen in. Its walls were carved with dozens of regular pictograms in an obscure language. The elements had worn them to an even more mysterious smoothness. Two vast non-human figures on either side of the pass were obviously male and female. The natural rock overhead had been carved into an arch to represent their hands touching, symbolising the Unity of Life.

Ayanawatta asked if we might pause while he studied these massive pillars. He smiled as he ran his hands over the figures. He seemed to be reading the glyphs, for his lips were moving. Then I thought that he might be praying.

He rejoined us in a good mood and climbed up to find some of his herbs and smoking mixture in his stowed bundle. These he held in one hand while he dismounted again from Bes and ran quickly to both pillars, sprinkling a little of the mixture at the base of each statue.

He sighed his contentment. "They say these two are the first male and the first female, turned to stone by the Four Great Manitoos. It was their punishment for telling the Stone Giants the secret path to the tree which the Kakatanawa now guard. We call them the Grandsires. They gave birth to our world's four tribes. They are monuments to our past and our future."

He frowned at the carvings as we rode past them. He seemed surprised they were so inanimate. "When I was last here, they had more life. They were happier."

He looked up into the dark crags and sighed. "There is great trouble now, I think. There's no certainty we shall save anything from the struggle."

After we passed under the arch, the quality of light subtly changed. Even the echoes were of a different nature. If we were not already in the land of the Kakatanawa, we were beginning to enter their jurisdiction. I thought I saw shadows above us, heard the skip of a stone, a muffled exclamation. But perhaps it was only the clatter of our own progress.

I wondered if the tree the Kakatanawa said they guarded was really a tree or perhaps merely a symbol, a contradictory core lying at the heart of their beliefs.

For long periods in that dark crevasse, I thought we were never going to be free of a universe of rock. The sheer sides threatened to narrow so much as to become impassable, yet somehow we squeezed through even the tightest gap.

The path went relentlessly forward, and relentlessly we followed it until it widened and we saw before us a huge lake of ice which the mountains encircled. Spectacular and vast under the clearing pewter sky, the pale, frozen lake was not, however, what captured our attention.

Ayanawatta let out a high, long whistle, but I could not speak for wonder.

Only White Crow knew the place. He gave a grunt of recognition. Nothing I had heard could have prepared me for my first sight of the Kakatanawa "longhouse."

While it was easy to see how the phrase fitted the conception, the reality was utterly unlikely. Their longhouse was not only the size of a mountain, it appeared to be made of solid gold!

Standing about a mile from the shore, this mighty, glittering pyramid rose at the centre of the frozen lake. The Kakatanawa longhouse dominated even the brooding peaks which completely surrounded it.

Under a paling blue sky reflected in the great plain of ice, Kakatanawa gleamed. An immense ziggurat, as high as a skyscraper, it was an entire city in a single structure. The base was at least a mile wide, and the tiers marched up, step by enormous step, to a crown where what might be a temple blazed.

The city was alive with activity. I could see ranks of people moving back and forth between the levels, the gardens which draped startling greenery over balconies and terraces. I saw transports and dray animals. It was an entire country in a single immense building! While it sat on an island, I guessed that it also extended below the ice. Was there never a time when the ice melted, or were we now so far north that the lake remained forever frozen?

I could not contain myself.

"A city of gold! I never believed such a legend!"

Ayanawatta began to laugh, and White Crow smiled at my astonishment. "All that glisters is not gold," he said ironically. "The plaster contains iron pyrites and copper powder, perhaps a little gold and silver, but not much. The reflective mixture produces a more durable material. And it suits their other purposes to make Kakatanawa shine like gold. I do not know whether the city or the myth came first. There is a legend among the Mayans about this city, but they think it is further south and east. No Kakatanawa can ever reveal the location of his home to strangers."

"Are we not strangers?" I asked.

He began to laugh. "Not exactly," he said.

"The name of the city is the same as that of your tribe?"

"The Kakatanawa are the People of the Circle, the People of the Great Belt, so called because they have travelled the entire circle of the world and returned to their ancestral home. Everywhere they went they left their mark and their memory. They are the only people to do this thing and understand what they have done. Even the Norsemen have not done that. This is Odan-a-Kakatanawa, if you prefer. The Longhouse of the People of the Circle. It is this people's destiny to guard the great belt, the story of the world's heart."

"And is that where I will find my husband?" My own heart had begun to beat rapidly. I controlled my breathing to bring it back to normal. I longed to see Ulric, safe and well and in my arms again.

"You will find him." White Crow for some reason avoided my eye.

There was no doubt in my mind that the Kakatanawa had kidnapped Ulric and brought him here. Now perhaps all I had to do was storm a city-sized pyramid! I hoped that my association with White Crow would make that unnecessary.

I believed I was approaching a people whose motives were mysterious and possibly thoughtless, but who were not malevolent. Of course, my feelings were subjective. I could not help liking the youth, who might have been a son, and there was no doubt I felt a daughter's security in the company of the older sachem, Ayanawatta, so talkative and humorous, so full of idealism and common sense. There was a fitting unity about our trinity. But it was Ulric who remained my chief concern. While certain I would find him here, I still did not know why he had been brought here or, indeed, how White Crow had known where to find the medicine shield.

A sharp wind was beginning to blow from the east, and we sank deeper into our furs. I could smell every kind of sorcery on that wind. I remained confused, uncertain of its source or its purpose.

The faint path of silver continued to cross the ice. It ended at the great golden pillars which supported what could only be the main gate with heavy doors of bronze and copper. The city's architecture was covered in complicated carvings and paintings of the most exquisite workmanship. I remembered the Sinhalese temples of Anuradhapura. Scarcely an inch was undecorated. From this distance it was impossible to make out anything but the largest details. Each tier of the ziggurat's extraordinary structure abounded with doors and windows. The population of a small town must live on each of the lower levels. Other levels were clearly cultivated, so that Kakatanawa was entirely self-supporting. She could resist any siege.

I asked a stupid question. "Will the ice bear Bes's weight?"

White Crow turned his head, smiling. "Bes is home," he said. "Can't you tell?"

It was true that the amiable mammoth looked more alert, excited. Did she still have a family in Kakatanawa? I imagined stables full of these massive, good-natured beasts.

White Crow added, "This ice is thicker than the world. It goes down for ever."

Then, as we continued to move forward, the mountains shook and grumbled. Dark clouds swirled around their peaks. The sky became alive with racing shafts of yellow, dark green and deep blue, all crackling and roaring, rumbling and shrieking. A wild screeching.

I reached for my bow, but I felt sick. I knew very well what that noise heralded.

Lord Shoashooan, the Demon of the Whirlwind, appeared before us.

His dark, conical shape was more stable. The wide top whirled, and the tip twisted into the ice, sending out a blur of chips. I could see his flickering, bestial features, his cruel, excited eyes. It was as if Klosterheim and the Two Tongues had released him from some prison, where he had been frustrated in his work of destruction. We had not driven him away. We had merely made him retreat to reconsider his strategy.

There again on one side of him stood Klosterheim, shivering in his agitated cloak, while all that was left of the Two Tongues lay dying, breath hissing in the corner of his horrible, toothy mouth. Klosterheim had the air of a man who believed his odds of survival small.

White Crow flung up his arm, waving his great black-bladed spear. "Ho! Would a mere breath of air stop me from returning to Kakatanawa with the Black Lance? Do you know what you challenge, Lord Shoashooan?"

Klosterheim spoke through cracked lips over the shriek. "He knows. And he knows how to stop you. Time will freeze, as this lake is frozen. It will allow me to do everything I must do. Your medicine is weak now, White Crow. Soon the Pukawatchi will come and destroy you and take back the things which are their own."

White Crow frowned at this. Was it true? Had he expended all his power in conjuring the Shining Path?

Behind the great Lord of All Winds the golden city sparked and shifted so that sometimes it seemed only a vision, a projection, an illusion. Not a real place at all. Beyond us, nothing moved. Time did indeed seem to have stopped.

White Crow bowed his head. "I am their last White Crow man," he said. "If I do not bring them back the Black Lance, it will not only be the last of the Kakatanawa, it will be the last we shall ever know of the multiverse, save that final, eternal second before oblivion. He has seen that my medicine is now weak. I have no charms or rituals strong enough to defend us against the anger of Shoashooan."

He looked desperately to Ayanawatta, who replied gravely. "You must fly to the Isle of Morn and find help. You know this is what we planned."

White Crow said, "I will use the last of my magic. Bes will stay here with you. I will send you the help you need. But know how dangerous this will be for all of us."

"I understand." Ayanawatta turned to me. "It is for you to help us now, my friend."

Then without another word, White Crow was leaving us. I watched in astonishment as he ran swiftly away. He ran through the foothills and was soon lost from sight. I almost wept at his deserting us. I would never have anticipated it.

Klosterheim cackled. "So the heroes show their real characters. You are not fit enough for these tasks, my friends. You challenge forces far too great."

I took my bow and stepped forward. Perhaps in my right mind I would have shot Klosterheim. I knew a kind of cold anger. I longed to be reunited with my husband, and I was determined not to be stopped. I do not know what instinct informed me, but I forced myself to walk closer and closer to the shrieking madness that was Lord Shoashooan, fitting an arrow to my bow. I could see a face in the centre of the tornado. That same fierce, white-hot anger remained. I knew nothing of fear as I loosed my first arrow into Lord Shoashooan's forehead.

Without thought, I nocked and loosed again. My second arrow took him in the right eye. The third arrow took him in the left eye.

He began to squeal and bellow in outrage. Bizarre limbs clutched at his head. I knew Lord Shoashooan could not be killed so easily. My idea was to try to stay out of his reach and, like a bull terrier, worry at him until he was weak enough to be overcome.

It was no doubt a stupid idea, but I did not have a better one!

I had been too confident. I had only blinded the monster for a few seconds. Before I knew it, he seized me in his icy tendrils and drew me closer and closer to his chuckling maw. I could reach no more arrows. All I had was my bow. I flung the staff into that horrible mouth.

Lord Shoashooan's many eyes glared. He gagged. I had caused some sort of convulsion. He scraped at his mouth and clutched his throat, and suddenly the sentient tornado flung me away.

I saw gleaming white all around me as I fell heavily to the ice. I was dazed and barely conscious. I forced myself to gather my strength.

I knew I had no other choice.

For a moment I refused the inevitable, but it was a pointless rebellion. I knew it as I made it. I could still hear the terrible howling and clawing of Lord Shoashooan as he wrestled with the bowstaff I had flung into his maw.

I, too, had a preordained story in this world. A story which I must follow in spite of myself.

I was reconciled to what was expected of me. I had no other choice, even though I risked a terrible death. In one moment of recovered memory, I knew exactly what had led to this moment. I knew why I was here. I knew what I must now do. I understood it in my bones, in my soul.

I knew what I had to become.

I readied myself for the transformation.

THE SECOND BRANCH

ELRIC'S STORY

I, Elric, called the White, son of Sadric
Am the bearer of the black rune-sword.
Long ran the blood rivers ere the reavers came.
Great was the grieving in the widows' songs.
Souls were stolen by the score
When skraelings sent a thousand to be slain.

—The Third Edda,
Elrik's Saga (tr. Wheldrake)

This was my dream of a thousand years
Each moment liv'd, all joys and every fear.
Through turning time and space gone mad,
I sought my magic and my weird.
For a millennium I trailed what I had lost.
My unholy charge, which e'en my soul had cost.

—Austin,
A Knight of the Balance

8

Conversation in the Devil's Garden

This is my Dream of a Thousand Years. In reality it lasted a single night, but I lived every moment of the dream, risked every kind of death in one last attempt to save myself. I describe it here, through Ulric's agency, because of its relevance to his tale. It was a dream I dreamed as I hung crucified on the yardarm of Jagreen Lern's triumphant flagship, the banner of my own defeat. I had lost my much-needed burden, the demon-blade Stormbringer. I was racking my memory for some means of recovering the sword to save myself and Moonglum and if possible stop the tide of Chaos which threatened the Cosmic Balance and would turn the whole of creation inchoate.

In this dream I was searching for the Nihrainian smith who had forged the original black blade. I had heard of one called Volnir. He lived close to the world's northern edge in what some called Cimmeria but which you know better as North America. If I found him, I should then be able to find Stormbringer. By such means I might save myself, my friend and even my world. I knew the price to be paid for following this dream path.

It would be the second time I had undertaken the Dream of a Thousand Years. To a youth of my genesis it is integral training. It must be done several times. You go alone into the wilderness. You fast. You meditate and seek the path to the world of long dreams. These are the worlds which determine and reveal the future. They offer the secrets of your past. In such worlds one serves more than one rules. Certain knowledge is gained by extended experience as well as study. The Dream of a Thousand Years provides that experience. The memory of those lifetimes fades, leaving the instinctive wisdom, the occasional nightmare.

One does not learn how to rule the Bright Empire of Melniboné without such service. Only in the extreme could I use my skills. I knew the danger involved, but I had no choice. The fate of my world depended upon my regaining, for a few moments, control of the Black Sword.

To attempt this desperate and unlikely magic, I had summoned all my remaining powers of sorcery. I had allowed myself to sink into a familiar trance. Jagreen Lern had already provided me with more than sufficient fasting and physical privations. I sought a supernatural gateway to the dreamworlds, some link to my own youthful past, where our many destinies are already recorded. And it brought me to your world in the year AD 900. I would leave it in the year 2001 upon the death of a relative.

Riding from Vienna, having but recently returned from a conquered Jerusalem, by October I found myself in the rocky Balkan mountains, where a tradition of banditry lived side by side with a tradition of hill farming to break the hearts and backs of most other peasants.

While wolf's-heads might covet my fine black steel helmet and armour, they had the sense not to test the great claymore I carried at my side. She was called Ravenbrand, sister to my own Stormbringer. How I came by Ravenbrand in that place is a tale yet to be told.

Until finding temporary peace with my wife, Zarozinia, I had been a mercenary outlaw in the Young Kingdoms. I had no difficulty making a good living here. Both the blade and I had reputations few were ready to challenge. Already I had served in Byzantium, in Egypt, fought Danes in England and Christians in Cádiz. In Jerusalem through a bizarre sequence of events, coveting a particular horse, I had helped create an order of the Knights Templar, founded by Christians, to ensure that no temporal master should ever claim the Holy Sepulchre. My interest was not in their religions, which are primitive, but in their politics, which are complicated. Their prophets constantly make false claims for themselves and their people.

Because their maps put Jerusalem at the heart of the world, I had hoped to find signs of my smith there, but I was following a fading song. The only smiths I found were shoeing crusader horses or repairing crusader arms. In Vienna I heard at last of a Norseman who had explored the farther reaches of the world's edge and might know where to find the Nihrainian smith.

My journey through the Balkans was rarely eventful. I was soon in the Dalmatian hinterland, where the blood feud was the only real law, and neither Roman, Greek nor Ottoman had much influence. The mountains continued to shelter tribes whose only concession to the Iron Age was to steal whatever they could from those who carried any kind of metal. They used old warped crossbows and spears chiefly and were inaccurate with both. But I had no trouble from them. Only one band of hunters attempted to take my sword from me. Their corpses served to enlighten the others.

I found warm and welcoming lodging at the famous Priory of the Sacred Egg in Dalmatia. Their matronly prioress told me how Gunnar the Norseman had anchored a month since to make minor repairs at the safe harbour of Isprit on the protected western coast. She had heard it from one of his homebound sailors. Gunnar, tired of slim pickings in the civilised ports, was determined to sail north to the colonies Ericsson and his followers had established there. He was obsessed with an idea about a city made entirely of gold. The sailor, a hardened sea-robber, swore never again to sail under a captain as evil as Gunnar. The man spent an unlikely amount of the time with the confessor and then left, saying he thought he would try his luck in the Holy Land.

The Wendish prioress was an educated woman. She said Isprit had known greater glory. The real centre of power had shifted to Venice. The Norseman had made a good choice. Using the local name for the place, the prioress told me the old imperial port was little more than three days' ride on a good horse. Two, the buxom Wend offered with a hearty laugh, if I wished to risk trespassing in Satan's backyard. She hugged my shoulders in an embrace which might have snapped a less battle-hardened invalid. I relaxed in her uncomplicated warmth.

The sailor had said the Norseman was anxious to leave port as soon as possible. He feared they should be trapped there. The Vikings had already angered the Venetians with a raid on Pag, which was successful, and another on Rab, which was not. Those dreaming old Adriatic ports now relied upon Venice for their prosperity and security and were glad to be off the main crusader routes. The knights and their armies brought little benefit and much destruction. The pope had called the Crusade in 1148. He had infected the whole of Europe and Arabia with his own dementia, which he then proceeded to die of. He had invented the jihad. The Arabs learned his lesson well.

I had no quarrel with any of the warring sects, who all claimed to serve an identical God! Human madness was ever banal. Jerusalem commanded no more of my interest. I had all I needed from the city. I had my horse, some gold and the odd ring on my finger. I found myself dragged briefly into the civic business of the city, but it was of no interest to me now whether or not order had been restored. Jerusalem was the turbulent heart of all their sects and would no doubt remain so.

Meanwhile Venice expanded her influence wherever the Turk's attention was distracted. Venice had most reason to see a nuisance in the Norseman. Her navy had already tried to trap him at Nin, but he had escaped, damaging *The Swan* in the attempt. The Viking would not take the risk of his beloved *Swan* being captured. They said she was the last of her kind, as Gunnar was the last of his. The other Vikings had made themselves kings and indulged in imperial expansion, missionaries of their Prince of Peace.

While the Crusades drew the world's attention, the man I sought was raiding through the winter months, taking the rather impoverished towns of the Adriatic, careful never to attract the wrath of Venice. Until recently neither Byzantines, Turks nor any other of the various local powers had will or men to send ships after a sea-raider. His skills and ferocity were infamous, his vessel so fast and lithe in the water many thought her possessed. *The Swan* was as lucky as she was beautiful. But previously neutral or disputed ports now came under the protection of Venice. Venice was rapidly expanding her trade. The Doge coveted Gunnar's legendary ship.

Gunnar, I was told, was not even a Viking by birth. He was a Rus. Outlawed from Kiev he'd returned to the reiving trade of his forefathers more from necessity than romance. Otherwise he was something of a mystery. Evidently neither Christian, Jew nor Moslem, he had never revealed his face, even to his women. Night and day he wore a reflective steel mask.

"Sounds a devilish wicked creature, eh?" the prioress said. "Not plague or leprosy, so I gather."

This matronly prioress, a woman of the world, had, until her retirement, run a brothel in Athens. She had a strong interest in the doings of the region. It was useful, pleasurable and politic to succumb to her charms, even if she found mine a little more supernatural than she bargained for. Before retiring, however, we were joined by another intelligent person of some experience, who was, by coincidence, lodging there for the night.

This guest had arrived a few hours ahead of me. A cheerful, wide-mouthed red-headed little man, he might have been a relative of my old friend Moonglum. My memory, as always in these dreams, was a little dim regarding any other life. This friar was a soldier-priest, with a mail shirt under his heavy homespun cassock, a useful-looking sword of Eastern pattern in an elaborate sheath and boots of fine quality that had seen better days.

He introduced himself in Greek, still the common tongue of the region. Friar Tristelunne had been a Heironymite hermit until his own natural garrulousness took him back, he said, to society. He now made ends meet as best he could, from marriages, deaths, funerals, letter writing, and selling the occasional small relic. Sadly there was often more work for his sword than his prayer book. The Crusade had been a disappointment to him. It no doubt satisfied the Christian appetites of the city's liberators, he said, but it wasn't man's work. He drew the line at skewering old Jewish women and babies in the name of the Lord of Light.

Friar Tristelunne knew the Norseman. "Some call him Earl Gunnar the Ill-famed, but he has a dozen worse names. A captain so cruel only the most desperate and depraved will sail with him."

A pagan, Gunnar's attempt to join and profit from the Crusade had been thwarted.

"Even the realistic, pious and opportunistic Saint Clair could not excuse the recruitment of an unreformed worshipper of Woden."

Gunnar was famous for his treachery, and there was no guarantee that once he reached the Holy Land he would not discover a better master in Saladin.

The only good reason anyone would have to strike an alliance with Gunnar the Doomed was if they needed a good navigator. "His skills are greater than the Ericssons'. He uses magic lodestones. He takes wild risks and survives them, even if all his comrades do not. Not only has he reached the rim of the world, he has sailed completely around it."

Friar Tristelunne had met Earl Gunnar, he said, when the captain was a mercenary in Byzantine employ. The monk had been fascinated by his mixture of intelligence and rapacity. Indeed, Gunnar had tried to get him involved in a scheme for robbing a wealthy Irish abbey said to be the home of the *gradal sante*. But his methods ultimately disgusted the Byzantines, who outlawed him. He had worked for the Turkish sultan for a while but was once again sailing on his own behalf, getting a new expedition ready. He was busy promising every man who would sail with him that even their fleas' shares would be worth a caliph's ransom.

Friar Tristelunne had considered joining the adventure, but he knew Gunnar to be notoriously treacherous. "The chances of returning alive to the civilised world would be slim indeed." He had a passage on a ship leaving Omis for the Peninsula in a few days' time. He had decided to strike out for Cordova, where he could get plenty of translation work and study to his heart's content at their great library, assuming the caliph was still well disposed towards unbelievers.

The friar, like so many in that region, knew me as Le Peau d'Argent or "the Silverskin," and my sword was called Dentanoir. Many avoided me for my sickly looks, but Friar Tristelunne seemed untroubled. He spoke to me with the easiness of an old, affectionate friend. "If, against the good prioress's advice, you choose the short route to the coast, it might be to your advantage to pause when you meet the Grandparents. They might have something to tell you. They speak briefly but very slowly. There is a trick to hearing them. Each deep note contains the wisdom of a book."

"The Grandparents? Your relatives?"

"They are the relatives of us all," said the red-headed monk. "They knew the world before God created it. They are the oldest and most intelligent stones in this part of the world. You will recognise them when you see them."

While I respected his beliefs and judgement, I did not pay a great deal of attention to his words. I was determined to take the shortest route I could through the mountains and down to the port, so was already prepared to ignore the nun's warning.

I thanked the warrior-monk and would have spent longer talking to him if he had not made an excuse and headed for his bed. He could stay here, he said, for only a short time. He had a dream of his own to follow. And I was already engaged for the evening.

In the morning, the prioress told me he had left before dawn, reminding me to pay attention to old stones. Again she warned me not to cross the Devil's Garden. "It's a place of ancient evil," she said. "Unnatural landscapes, touched by Chaos. Nothing grows there. This is God's sign to us not to go there. It is where the old pagan gods still lurk." She had stirred her own imagination; I could tell from her eyes. "Where Pan and his siblings still mock the message of Christ." She squeezed my hand almost conspiratorially.

I assured her that I was comfortable enough with most excesses of Chaos. I would, however, watch for treachery and cunning aggression along the way. She kissed me heartily on the lips. Pressing a bag of provisions and sustaining herbs into my hands, she wished me God's company in my madness. She also insisted on presenting me with a precious text, something from their holy books, which made some mention of the Valley of Death. With this reassuring parchment tucked into my shirt below my chainmail—which I had donned more as a means of quieting the prioress than of guarding against attack in the Devil's Garden—I kissed her farewell and told her that I was now invulnerable. She answered in Wendish, which I hardly understood. Then in Greek she said, "Fear the Crisis Maker." It was what she had told me last night when she had laid out the cards for us both to read.

The other nuns and novices had gathered on the walls of the priory to see me leave. They had, it seemed, all heard tales of the Silverskin. Had their prioress committed the saintly act of sharing her bed with a leper? I suspected those who believed it believed she must have her place in their Heaven already reserved.

With respectful irony, I saluted them, bowed and then spurred my massive black stallion, Solomon, along a rocky road populated in those days by deer, bears, goats and boar, all of them hunted by local farmers and bandits, who were frequently one and the same. The road would take me through the Devil's Garden and down to the western coast.

The local Slavs were in the main a coarse, rather pale people. They had wiped out most of their best bloodstock through complicated and extended family feuding. When they had that romantic touch of Mongolian blood, Dalmatians achieved a stunning beauty.

Elsewhere powerful cultures had arisen and influenced the world, but these rocks offered solace only to the troubled visionary. Along the coasts were a few pockets of civilisation, but most of that was in decay, exhausted by tributes to a dozen powers.

Isprit itself had been the retirement palace of the Emperor Diocletian, who had famously divided the Roman Empire into three, then left its running to a triumvirate who quarrelled and killed one another, as well as Diocletian's daughter. His confusing stamp on the politics of the region would last for millennia. The hapless ex-emperor, who had hoped to balance power between the various warring factions, was the last real inheritor of Caesar's authority. Now the old empire was sustained chiefly by those who had rallied to Charlemagne after he had been crowned Holy Roman Emperor by the pope. Their translation of their greed for booty into a chivalric ideal created an extraordinary expansion whose conquests, frequently under the banner of religious reform, would not stop until they owned the Earth. Already the Normans had imposed their haughty and efficient feudalism onto much of France and England. They in turn would carry these methods across the world. Opinion in Rome agreed that the unruly Saxons and Angles needed the strong hand of the Dukes of Normandy to form them into a nation which might one day balance the power of the Holy Roman Emperor.

At the abbey, in exchange for their hospitality, I had retailed the gossip of the day. Of course, I had only so much curiosity about their world, and most of that related to my search. But much small talk is picked up in the taverns, which a wanderer like myself, largely shunned by all, is frequently forced to use. I had little interest in the details of these peoples' history. It was raw and unsophisticated compared to that of mine, and I was still Melnibonéan enough to feel a superiority to mortals of most persuasions.

Through my senses Count Ulric had the opportunity to witness the genesis of his clan into a nation, and in his dreams he experienced my dreams as if they were his own. He dreamed my dream as I dreamed his. But he did not live my dream as I did, and I suspect he remembers even less. How much he chooses to remember is his own affair.

The late-summer sun was surprisingly hot on my over-armoured head when I became aware of the nature of the landscape changing. The crags were sharper, the cliffs more terraced, and little streams echoed through deep valleys, giving the place an unearthly music. Clearly I had entered the Devil's Garden. The shale became much harder for my horse to negotiate.

The stark landscape was astonishingly beautiful. Little grew here. The smell of the occasional fir invigorated me. The great limestone crags sparkled in the summer sunshine. All the trails were treacherous. Narrow rivers dancing with vivid life poured in falls from level to level among strangely shaped rocks.

The sun cast dense shadows, contrasting extremes of black and white, on the massive glittering cliffs which rose into the sky. Sudden lakes, icy blue beneath the sun, were turned by passing clouds into blinding sheets of reflective steel. Rock pools shone like coral in their delicacy of colour. Groves of dark blue pines and fleshy oaks grew in the few spots of soil. Frequently I heard the rattle of loose rocks as a goat leaped for cover. Crumbling earth on worn stone. Ferns and willowherb growing in crevices. These were the familiar landscapes of a childhood when, as von Bek, I had holidayed here with my family, who kept a villa on the coast. It was also reminiscent of the hinterland of Melniboné, where the Phoorn, our dragon allies, had built their first magnificent city from fire and rock and little else.

As the day grew hotter still, the steady blue sky threw extremes of colour everywhere. I began to feel an unlikely nostalgia. The experience was not entirely pleasant. All I understood was a sense of invasion, as if other intelligences attacked my own. Not merely my dream self intruded, but something older and heavier, something which reminded me again of Mu-Ooria and invoked images, memories of events which perhaps had not yet even occurred in the history of this particular world.

Used to controlling myself in such circumstances, I was still very uneasy. My horse, Solomon, too, was growing nervous, perhaps reflecting my own mood. I wanted to get out of the place as soon as possible. Doggedly, we continued westward, the horse holding with uncanny ease to the path. Loose grey shale skittered and bounced steeply away from us. Sometimes it seemed we clung to the walls of the rock like lizards, staring down at the radically angled slopes, the glittering, weirdly coloured waters far below.

That night I camped in a natural cave, having first made sure it was not the castle of an incumbent bear. It had not seen any kind of human settlement. Nothing in this landscape could sustain human life.

I rose early in the morning, watered, fed and saddled Solomon, set my wargear about me, changed my helmet for a hood, and again was struck by the supernatural quality of the valley. At the far end in the distance was a wide, shimmering lake.

As I urged Solomon forward, I sensed other presences. I knew the smell of them, the weight of them. I had instinctive respect for them even though I was not really conscious of their identity. They were nearby and they were many. That was all I could be sure about. Beings seemingly older than the Off-Moo, who had seen every stage of the Earth's history. They remembered the moment when they had been expelled from the sun's gassy Eden to begin the forming of this planet.

Even the stars of this world's firmament were subtly different from mine. I knew it would be better to learn what the Devil's Garden had to tell me rather than impose my own Melnibonéan speculation on the place. I sensed that this had once been a great battlefield. Here Law and Chaos had warred as they had never warred until now. It was one of the oldest supernaturally inhabited regions in this realm. It was one of the most remote. It was one of the most enduring. I was at last recognising it for what it was. Its denizens were unaffected by the major movements of human history. They were philosophical beings who had witnessed so much more than any others, and they had seen all human ideals brought low by human folly. Yet they were incapable of cynicism. I knew them, just as I knew their young cousins, still hiding goat-footed in the rocks, still sliding in and out of trees and streams, still asking favours of Nature rather than making demands on her, the old godlings whom the Greeks had known, half-mortals who sensed their own extinction. These ancient creatures had such old, slow thought processes they were all but undetectable, yet they were the Earth's memory.

Their name for themselves took several mortal lifetimes to pronounce. Adepts gave them considerable attention. Few consulted them, though more knew how.

Their answers were usually slowly considered, and the one who had asked could be dead before they reached a conclusion. When they slept it was for millions of years. When they awoke it might be for a few seconds. And they never wasted words. I was beginning to understand what Friar Tristelunne had hinted at.

I had passed part of my apprenticeship among such ancients, but I was still uneasy. If Moonglum had been with me, he would have expressed reasonable fear and I should have mocked him for it, but now I was alone. I had survived a hundred great fights with less fear than now.

As I dismounted and led Solomon down to one of the deep valley streams to drink, I looked around me and saw that the sides had widened. I was effectively in a steep, white amphitheatre, scarcely touched by vegetation. A few hardy wild flowers grew here and there, but otherwise the great glade was empty save for the carpet of soft green itself. It had that cultivated atmosphere about its lawns which I had noticed in other places where sheep and goats habitually grazed. Here the limestone crags had split away. Much of the rock stood like tall independent heads or figures. Fancifully I thought I detected expressions. Emotions, life of various kinds, stirred in those huge natural pillars. It was easy to see how the region was rife with tales of ogres.

Old maps referred to the place as Trollheim. Half the legendary giants of Europe were believed to originate here. Remembering the red-headed priest's words, I sought for inscriptions on the stones. I could read Greek, Latin, Arabic easily but had far more trouble with some other languages.

I found no inscriptions. As I ran my hands over the surface of the rock, however, I felt a distinct but very deep vibration, a kind of grumbling, as if I had awakened a sluggish hive. I dropped my hand and stepped back, seeing faces everywhere in the high cliffs, feeling a certain panic. Should these rocks prove sentient and antagonistic, I knew I could not cut myself clear with my sword.

Though my senses were sharper than most mortals', the horse heard the sound before I did. Solomon snorted and whinnied. Then I detected it. A deep, even rumbling, as if from far under ground. It rose rapidly to a heavy hum, and the whole valley swayed to it. All the hillsides shimmered with movement. The stones were dancing. They were singing. Then the note deepened again, and I felt a shock as tremendous vitality flooded up to fill the canyon, as if Mother Earth herself were coming awake.

Solomon, who had been unusually quiet, now voiced a huge snort. I could see that his huge back legs were trembling, and his eyes had begun to dilate badly. My brave beast was actually too terrified to move. His enemy seemed everywhere.

My own emotions were quieter. I still found it difficult to co-ordinate my actions. Then, quite suddenly, the whole vale became suffused with an extraordinary sense of benign good will.

A single enormous throb! The great slow heart of the world had given a beat. The vibrations filled my body with joy and meaning. My hand fell away from my sword, where it had remained from habit. Now with wizard's eyes I saw their faces. I was an actor on a stage. These stones were my audience. Rank upon rank of them, rising up the flanks of the vale, their eyes hidden in deep shadow, their mouths showing a kind of eternal irony that was not judgemental of humanity yet spoke of a wisdom born of their age. As gases they had been conscious. As molten lava they had been wise. As the still-animate crust of the planet they had been moral. And as mountains they were contemplative. That consciousness, old and slow as it was, carried their experience. Their lives had been devoted, down the millions of millennia, to observation and understanding.

Something of great importance to the fate of the multiverse, to their world and my own, had stirred them to speak. Little of their words could be heard by any mortal ear.

They spoke four words, and those words took four days to utter; but that was not our only communication. The mighty heads looked down at me. They studied me and compared me and no doubt recalled all the many others who, seeking their wisdom, had come this way. My horse grew calm and cropped at the grass. I sat and listened to these Grandfathers and Grandmothers, the very spirits of our origin, who in their roaring youth had fled away from the parent sun to form the planets.

Their love of life had slowed, but it had not faded. Their thoughts were as substantially concentrated as their physical forms. Each word translated became several lines in even the most laconic of languages. In comparison old Melnibonéan was baroque and clumsy. Only a trained ear could detect the slight differences of tone. I was forced to recall an old spell and slow down my own perception of time. It was the only way to understand them.

With what they communicated supernaturally, I began to understand a little of what they told me. Why these first stone men and women of the world had chosen to speak to me I did not know. I understood, however, that this was an important part of my dream. I sat, and I immersed myself in a strange, but not unpleasant, communication. In those four days, heedless now of Gunnar's imminent leaving, I listened to the stones.

The first word the Grandparents spoke was:

WHERE THE WINDS MEET
A WOMAN'S HORNS DEFY
THE DESTROYER OF DESTINY
AND MAKE HER YOUR BEST ALLY

I had an image of a white beast, a lake, a glittering building, the whole lying in another natural amphitheatre. I knew this must be my destination, where I would discover the meaning of my dream.

The second word the Grandparents spoke was:

THE BLADE PIVOTS THE BALANCE
THE BOWL SUSTAINS IT
THE DRAGON IS YOUR FRIEND

I had the impression of a sword blade without a hilt, its tip immersed in some kind of basin while in the shadows a great, yellow eye opened to regard me.

The third word the Grandparents spoke was:

ROOT AND BRANCH THE TREE SUSTAINS
BALANCE AND ALL LIFE MAINTAINS

I saw an enormous tree, a spreading oak whose branches seemed to shelter the world. Its roots went deep into the core of the Earth. Its branches covered another image, which was the same thing in a different form. I knew it was the Cosmic Balance.

And the fourth word the Grandparents spoke was:

GO MAKE TRUE

For a fleeting moment I received a glorious image: a great green oak tree against a sky of burnished silver. Then that special vibrancy faded, leaving only the natural grandeur of the stark cliffs and the soft grass below. The Grandparents were silent. Already they returned to sleep. With a sense of added burden rather than revelation I paid them my respects. I assured them I would think upon their words. I admitted to myself that they made little sense. Had the rocks reached a state of senility?

Suddenly I was struck by the stupidity of my excursion. I had crossed the Devil's Garden to save time. I had then lost a day rather than gained one. The Norseman might already be leaving Isprit. From the slowest of mortals, I became one of the fastest. I needed my stallion to do his best.

Solomon had carried me all the way from Acre. I had acquired him from a Lombardian knight who, like so many of my crusader comrades, had joined the expedition entirely for the land it promised. Finding the promised land a little barren, he had joined the Templars, turned to disappointed drinking and gambling and from there to the inevitable duel. I had let him pick it. I had long coveted his horse. Being of a weakly disposition, I also needed a soul or two for my sustenance and preferred my food ripe.

The religious posturings of these brutes were as corruptly self-deceiving as anything I had witnessed. Religions so at odds with mankind's nature and its place in the natural order only produce a kind of madness, where the victims are constantly attempting to force reality to confirm their fantasies. The ultimate result must be the ultimate destruction of the realm itself. In their histories, wherever the banner of pious Law was raised, Chaos quickly followed.

Though their people were said to have visited Cimmeria, there was still every possibility that the Norseman would not be able to help me. I would soon know.

I had been to Isprit before, but from the sea. The mountains became greener and more forested and the ride to the port pleasant, if hurried. I arrived above the city just before sunset. The Adriatic stretched, tranquil pewter, beneath a golden sun. Protected by a huge promontory, the port had been chosen by Diocletian for its views and air. Parts of walls and columns along the harbour were clearly from Roman times. But where imperial sails had blossomed on bulky triremes, the ships were now traders, fishing craft. There was only one reefed sail on a tall, slender mast, her crow's nest decorated with vivid dragons curling around the tip, where a black flag flew. The sail was recognisable to anyone but an inlander. It was the typical scarlet-and-azure stripes on a white field of the old Norseman. Gunnar was still in port.

From this height the town looked unplanned and ramshackle, a sprawl of huts and badly thatched houses standing among the marble ruins of a vast Roman compound. As you drew closer, the real wonder of the place made itself evident, as did the rather pungent smell of the dust heaps and sewage dumps inland of the harbour. None of this was noticeable, however, when you looked out over a dark blue sea turning to a pool of blood in the dying sunlight. I rode down the old trade trail from the mountains into that extraordinary port.

Several hundred years before, the emperor had built himself a palace here overlooking his private moorings and the Adriatic. An extensive complex of buildings, its entire purpose was to comfort the abdicated emperor and help him forget the troubles of the world, many of which were his own creation. The walls were high. There were cloisters and fountains; pleasant walks and groves; benches and tables of basalt, marble and agate; temples and chapels. The baths were exquisitely luxurious. When I had last been here the decay was less extensive.

When Rome's power faded, the barbarians' power over Isprit had grown. Byzantium lacked the resources to claim much in the way of sovereignty, so the port had filled with free fishermen, scrap-metal shippers, slavers, timbermen, traders, pirates, furriers and all the other honest and outlaw callings known to men. It was not an important port, strategically, but it was a lively one. The ostentatious palace was now the core of an entire community. They occupied its rooms and galleries, used its gardens for growing food, its halls for trading and meeting, its baths—those still in working order—for supplies of running water. Even to me this infestation of brawling, squabbling, embracing, praying, shrieking, giggling uninhibited human life had a certain charm.

The fountains had long since dried up. Some had been turned into the hubs of dwellings, their fanciful masonry in contrast to the simplicity of the people. Pigs, sheep and goats were kept in pens on the outskirts, so the stench increased as you approached but lessened as you reached the streets.

I rode through shacks and shanties of driftwood and stones which looked like the débris of a dozen sea-raids in which everything of wealth had been taken. Yet there was probably more life here now than when the emperor came. In those imperial ruins the fallen mighty had given way to the vital mob. This was one of the lessons I had tried to teach my countrymen. Their final lesson came when I demonstrated their weaknesses and the strength of the new, human folk who challenged them.

I had led those human reavers. I had destroyed the Dreamers' City. It was no wonder that I preferred this dream. Here I was merely a leprous wizard with a talent for warfare. There I was the prince who had betrayed his own people and left them scattered, homeless, dying from their world's memory. My actions had allowed Jagreen Lern, who always sought to emulate Melnibonéan power, to raise the Lords of the Higher Worlds, to threaten the Cosmic Balance in the name of the Gods of Entropy.

The forces of Law and Chaos were not themselves good or evil. It was by their actions that I judged such Higher Lords. Some were more trustworthy than others. My own patron Lord of Chaos, Duke Arioch, was a consistent if ferocious being, but he had little power in this world.

The only lighting in the warren of cobbled streets and apartments came from the taverns and dwellings themselves. Behind the oiled vellum of windows, the candles and lamps gave the twilit town a sepia look. I searched for a sea-men's hostelry Friar Tristelunne had told me of. The smell of ozone was strong in my nostrils, as was the smell of fish. I was hungry for some fresh octopi, which Melnibonéans had always eaten with great respect. The creatures possess intelligences greater than most mortals. Certainly their flavour is considered subtler.

My own Melnibonéan appetites and impulses were forever at odds with the ideas I had inherited from my human companions. Cymoril, while she was alive, never knew that cannibalism disgusted me. She had taken her place at the ritual tables without a thought. I derived very little pleasure in the arts of torture cultivated by Melnibonéans for thousands of years. For us there were formal methods of dying as well as of killing.

As a youth I began to doubt the wisdom of these pursuits. Cruelty was scarcely a trade, much less an art. My fears for Melniboné had been practical. I had lived and travelled in the lands of the Young Kingdoms. I understood how soon they must overwhelm us. Had that been the reason that I had joined the ranks of my enemies? I dismissed this guilt. I had no time for it now.

I found the tumbledown, straw-roofed shingle building with a dim fish-oil lamp illuminating a sign that read in old Cyrillic *Odysseus's,* which was either the name of the owner or of the hero with whom he wished to be associated. The tavern had declined a little since the Golden Age.

Not trusting the Dalmatians, I dismounted from Solomon to lead him into the tavern. It stank of stale wine and sour cheese. The straw on the floors had not been replaced in months. There was a dead dog in one corner. The dog offered the advantage of attracting most of the flies and covering up the worst of the smells. The majority of the other customers were collected at a bench playing backgammon. A couple of men who sat talking quietly in the corner farthest from the dog attracted me. They had the filthy fair hair of the typical Danish pirate, arranged in two greasy plaits which had enjoyed as much of their meat gravy as they had. But they seemed in good humour and spoke enough kitchen Greek to make themselves understood. Clearly they were not disliked, for the landlord's girl was relaxed with them and told a joke which had them all laughing until they saw me a little more clearly.

"Nice horse," said the taller, his eyes narrowing a little, though he tried to disguise his expression. I was familiar with the response. He had recognised me as the Silverskin. He was wondering if he was going to find out what it was like to contract leprosy. Or have his immortal soul turned to roughage.

"I'm looking for a boy to keep an eye on him," I said. "He might even be for sale." I held up a silver Constantine. Shadow rats appeared from everywhere. I selected one and told him the Constantine was his as long as the horse was safe and well groomed. If he knew of a likely customer he would get a commission. Then I stared into the unhappy faces of the Vikings and told them I was looking for a man named Gunnar the Luckless. The men understood this subtle snub. "He's called Earl Gunnar the Wald, and he has a liking for good manners," said the younger, clearly wishing he had not been put in this position. They were Leif the Shorter and Leif the Larger.

As the boy took away my horse to the ostler's, I turned to one of the serving women and ordered a skin of their best yellow wine. I, too, I said, appreciated good manners and would feel snubbed if they did not join me. The group with the backgammon board, hearing us speaking Norse, displayed only a passing interest in me, having identified me as an outlander. I heard one of them refer to me as Auberoni and was amused. I was no king of the fairies. The men were Venetian fishermen who had settled here recently and clearly had never heard of Le Peau d'Argent or his sword, which was still known in Venice as Il Corvo Noir after its legendary maker, who had not actually forged the sword but had made the fanciful hilt. A large body of opinion believed the sword had taken its first soul from Corvo.

I dusted off the crusader's surcoat I still wore and joined the wary lads, Leif and Leif, who typically had hands as carefully groomed as their hair was greasy. I supposed if they ate mostly with their fingers, there was a point to keeping them clean. Needing neither to shave nor, in the conventional sense, pass faeces, few Melnibonéans were familiar with beards or urinals. Many human habits remain deeply mysterious to us.

The Vikings probably thought me some effete Byzantine affecting Oriental manners. They had enough respect for my reputation, however, and showed me perfect courtesy. Renowned for their love of poetry and music and fine workmanship, Vikings enjoyed cultured living and hospitality. These two sea-robbers, though they served under one of the most evil captains known, were well informed and told me they had discussed deserting Gunnar for crusading or working as mercenaries in Byzantium. But they had no real choice. Their fate was to sail with Gunnar until the Valkyries came to carry them to Valhalla. They found a boy to run to Gunnar.

By the time we finished the skin, there came a stirring and a chorus of greetings. Earl Gunnar had arrived.

He hated to show his face. They said his wounds were so hideous he could not bear to look on his own features. I was surprised at the baroque workmanship of his mask, fashioned like a gryphon's head with an open, threatening mouth, but where the gullet would be was a face of silvered steel. Of Eastern origin, the helmet's crest had been cleverly crafted in silver and pewter: gryphon ascendant. But it was my own face I saw when I first looked at him. He was coming towards me, striding with dangerous inelegance.

Gunnar the Doomed was a bear. He was twice my width and slightly taller. I could imagine this terrifying figure on the bridge of his ship. He wore fine-woven plaids and linens and, like all his kind, his hands were girlishly tended. Hanging down over his shoulders his hair showed a little grey. With his well-trimmed, flowing locks, his rich clothing and knee-high doeskin boots, he could have been a Danish noble of the previous century. There was a generally archaic air about the man. It had been a hundred years since the last Vikings had gone on raiding expeditions.

The Norse sailors most reminded me of my old friend, the bluff, direct and solidly realistic Smiorgan Baldhead of the Purple Towns. As an individual Gunnar struck me as Smiorgan's opposite. There was something unwholesome about him. He affected the rough manners of a nobleman too long in the company of brutes. Yet he was a real diplomat. He knew enough not to threaten me. Instead he preferred to charm me. He ordered another skin of Bulgar wine and had it brought to the table where I still sat with his men. I could, of course, read nothing from the face, completely covered by the mirrored steel of the helmet. There were dark cavities in the mask. Through two of these he stared at me. Through another he fed himself tiny scraps of some kind of meat he carried in his hand. Otherwise he had the familiar manner of those who do not know me. He kept a little distance between us on the chance that I was actually a leper. Courteously I refused his wine. I had drunk my fill, I said. "I have some business with you, Earl Gunnar."

Gunnar shrugged. "I'm not a merchant, and my ship is not for hire."

"You are an adventurer, like myself, and your ship is your own. I'm not here to hire you, Earl Gunnar. A man like yourself does not strike me as one who would sing to another's tune no matter how sweet the melody."

"You've come overland, have you? Where from? Constantinople? Did you ride through the Devil's Garden?"

I told him that I had. He nodded. He sat back in his chair, that more-than-enigmatic mask regarding me with some interest. "So you saw all those massive heads. You'd think they were alive, eh? I saw something like them when I sailed with the Rose on her twin-hulled ship *The Either/Or*. We passed an island which marked the boundaries of that people's empire. Huge eyes staring from these stone faces. An island of giants. We did not go closer."

Gunnar had a certain witch-sight. No ordinary mortal would have seen those stones for what they were. I held my own counsel and let Gunnar continue.

"So you know me by my reputation, as I know thee, Sir Silverskin. And it pleases you to flatter my pride. Yet you know I do indeed work for hire on occasions. So, while I appreciate your courtesy, I'd be as happy to get down to business, if we have any, as not. I sail on the morning tide, and my crew is already aboard, save for these two, whom I came to find." He paused. Taking a reed from within his jerkin he placed one end in his wine-cup and the other in the aperture in his mask. He sipped delicately. "My destination's already determined."

"I understand that also." I dropped my voice. "North and west to the World's Rim?"

He was too canny a captain to respond immediately. "You know more than I do, Sir Silverskin. We are merely setting sail for Las Cascadas to find fresh crewmen. Winter approaches, and at this time we normally go down to Zanzibar, where we take an interest in the slave trade. It's a poor business, but there are few other ways for an independent captain to make a living in these over-settled times."

I opened my palm and showed him what was there. "Give me a berth on your ship, Earl Gunnar, and I'll tell you more about this."

It was not in his nature to hesitate.

"The berth is yours," he said. "We sail on the first tide."

9

Peau d'Argent

Darkling dragon, reiver's pride,
Rides high upon the turquoise tide.
His weird-drenched wave
Shall bear him to a rich retreat.
Darkling dragon, reiver's pride,
Lord of the Last, destined to die.
In Woden's waves he'll find no grave
His death's pre-written on his own black blade.

—Longfellow,
Lord of the Lost

A little before dawn I was down at the harbour looking over the long, slender ship lying against the dock. Solomon had been sold for a fair price to a Greek merchant who had some fancy to show himself off as a knight. I threw in the surcoat for good measure. At least he could pretend to fellow Christians to have been a crusader. Solomon would be making his way home to Lombardy shortly after we sailed. If he was lucky, the merchant would not be on the stallion's broad and cunning back.

Narrow, seemingly delicate, yet full of sinewy power even at anchor, *The Swan* pulled eagerly at her traces, haughty and confident as her namesake. I heard Gunnar had bought her from the impoverished Greenlanders who had made her but lacked the skills to sail her.

I admired the lines of the ship. Her fine, beaky figurehead might deliberately have been a cross between a swan and a wyvern. She had the swan's calm stateliness, but also an air of menace, which had something to do with the rake of her deck, the set of her mast.

In the old Viking manner there were shields strapped to the rail above the board which ran between the rowing benches and the shut-beds where men could store their goods and get sleep when utterly worn out. I knew that many Vikings preferred to sleep at their oars and had developed ways of hanging over the great, golden sweeps to find the total rest of the thoroughly exhausted. But half the shield spaces were empty. I suspected they were not filled by born Norsemen.

I waited patiently near the gangplank as the sea-raiders arrived. They represented most nations, from Iceland to Mongolia. "By Ishtar," murmured a Persian, seeing me, "Gunnar's more desperate for men than we knew." Some of the races I did not recognise at all, but there were tall, thin East Africans, a couple of burly Moors, three Mongols and a mixture of Greeks, Albanians and Arabs. All of them had the grim look of men who knew violence more thoroughly than peace. Settling in to the ship, some of them took places by shields they had clearly acquired from the dead. The two Ashanti had brought their own long shields. Others had no shields at all. There was a miscellaneous mixture of weaponry. If ever a crew was born to sail a ship into the realms of Chaos, it was *The Swan*'s.

Out on the far horizon something moved. I glanced up. Melnibonéans were also a seafaring people, and I had their way of scanning the ocean out of the corner of my eye. One of the Mongols ran up the mast like a rat to yell out his urgent fear.

"Venetian war galleys. Making good speed."

Gunnar came brawling down to the dock, half a dozen whores and hounds forming a living train behind him, shouting orders which were followed like thoughts by his obedient men. He took a moment to turn his faceless head to me and yell "We sail for Las Cascadas. We'll be safe there. Come aboard. If we can't strike a bargain, I'll set you off on the island." He swung his heavily cloaked body up over his rail and headed for the stern.

Las Cascadas was a notorious rock in the western Mediterranean with a single port. It was still some days' sail away, and we had the Venetians, possibly the Turks, perhaps the Byzantines, the Italians and the Caliphates to deal with, all of whom claimed authority over these seas. Gibr al Tairat itself was not so thoroughly untakable, but Las Cascadas's harbour was so well protected no enemy fleet could hope to enter. Any attempt to attack by land was thwarted by the steep, volcanic cliffs which rose sheer from the water. As a result the place had become a refuge for every corsair on the Red Coast and beyond and had its own queen, the infamous pirate known across the seafaring world as the Barbary Rose, whom Gunnar boasted of sailing with. Her strangely named twin-prowed ship was unmistakeable and had been built apparently by shipwrights the Rose had brought with her from the South Sea Empire, which few European navigators even believed existed. Only the two tattooed giants, who still served the she-captain, knew the secret of making such vessels.

The black-and-gold sails of Venice were slightly larger on the horizon now. The tide was beginning to run our way, and I squeezed into a space between the mast and the deckhouse, marvelling at the efficiency of these seamen. With a single woollen sail, they could get a ship into battle order in moments.

The oars bit the water as Gunnar roared the beat. We leaped out of the harbour, oblivious of everything but escape. Dhows and wherries scattered as we shot through the outer walls and into open sea, oars and sail combining to bring the ship about as Gunnar himself stood at the steering sweep, making adjustments with the touch of his hand, the balance was so beautiful. The unshipped oars moved in amazing uniform, like a neatly choreographed dance, and *The Swan* darted like a live thing under our feet, thrusting out into the deep water long before the Venetians saw us. We were already running for the Mediterranean, and unless they had laid a real trap for us there, we might even leave them behind completely. Once we were seen to reach the safety of Las Cascadas, any other pursuers would give up. Earl Gunnar had always made a point of staying on good terms with the Caliphates.

Two-masted, slave-rowed, heavy in the water and clumsy fore and aft, built more for endurance and protection than attack, the Venetian ships needed good weather and great luck even to keep pace with us. We quickly saluted farewell as our glorious pursuers fell below the horizon. Then we ran down the Illyrian coast and, with oars at full speed, sail bellying with a powerful south-wester, rounded the Italian peninsula with a strong wind for Sicilia and the Tyrrhenian Sea, where we ran into a small flotilla of black-sailed ships expectantly lying in wait for us. Two brigantines and a brig.

Gunnar stood on his own bridge holding his sides and jeering with laughter as we sped by the lumbering vessels. "Three!" he shouted. "Three ships! Only three to catch *The Swan!* Your wealth makes you stupid!" He then turned to me. "They insult us, eh, Sir Silverskin?"

It was clear he felt a bond with me which I did not share.

I was exhilarated by the ship's performance. Gunnar, however, continued to act as if being overtaken by the Venetians were imminent. Like me he had learned not to relax too soon.

Later that night he finally gave the order to slow oars. His men slept instantly over their sweeps. Almost at her own volition *The Swan* continued to glide through the water. Gunnar planned to hug the Numidian shore all the way to the Maghreb. In the west, only a few miles of sea separated the coast from Las Cascadas.

Gunnar joined me in the prow, where I had found a little solitude and was looking up at the great splash of the Milky Way, staring at stars which were at once familiar and unfamiliar. I had wrapped myself in my deep indigo oilskin cloak. Golden autumn touched the ocean. I remembered the story told to Melnibonéan children of the dead souls who walk the star-roads of the Milky Way, which we called the Land of the Dead. I was, for some reason, thinking of my father, the disappointed widower who blamed me for my mother's death.

Gunnar made no apology for interrupting me. He was in good spirits. "Those fat merchant bastards are still wallowing their way around Otranto!"

He clapped me on the back, almost as if feeling for a weakness. "So are you going to tell me how you think you know my plans? Or am I going to throw you overboard and put you out of my mind?"

"That would be ill-advised," I said. "But also impossible. You know I am effectively immortal and invulnerable."

"I won't know that until I put it to the test," he said. "But I do not believe you are any less mortal than myself."

"Indeed?" I saw no point in quarrelling with him. He recognised the token I showed him. The ring which seemed fresh-minted.

"Aye, Elric Sadricsson, I know you from King Ethelred's time, when he paid you with that ring for your aid against the Danes. But the ring's far more ancient, eh. I thought the Templars had it now."

"Ethelred ruled a century and a half ago," I said. "Do I seem so old? I am, as you know, not a well man."

"I think you are much older than that, Sir Templar," Gunnar said. "I think you are ageless." There was a sinister note to his voice, a mocking quality which irritated me. "But not invulnerable."

"I think you mistake me for Luerabas, the Wandering Albanian, whom Jesus cursed from the tomb."

"I know for a fact that story's nonsense. Prince Elric of Melniboné, your story is far from being finished. And far from judgement."

He was trying to disturb me. I did not show him he had succeeded. "You know much for a mortal," I said.

"Oh, far too much for a *mortal*. It is my doom, Prince Elric, to remember everything of my past, my present and my future. I know, for instance, that I shall die in the full knowledge of the hopelessness and folly of existence. So dying will be a relief for me. And if I take a universe with me, so much the better. Oblivion is my destiny but also my craving. You, on the other hand, are doomed to remember too little and so die still hoping, still loving life . . ."

"I do not plan to die, but if I do, I doubt if it will be hoping," I said. "The reason I am in this world is because I search for life, even now."

"I search for death. Yet our quest takes us to the same place. We have common interests, Prince Elric, if not desires."

I could not answer him directly. "You have a place, no doubt, in this dream," I said. "You are some sort of dream-traveller. A dreamthief, perhaps?"

"You seem determined to insult me."

I would not rise to this. I was beginning to get the man's measure. He did know a great deal more about me than anyone else in this world. True, when I first entered this realm I served King Ethelred, known as the Unready. I travelled with a woman I called my sister, and we were both betrayed in the end.

But my apparent longevity was only the stuff of dreams, not my own reality. Gunnar was enjoying my supposed bafflement. I had shown him the ring because I had thought it might have meaning for him. It clearly bore more significance for him than I had guessed. I had acquired the thing in Jerusalem, off the same knight from whom I had taken Solomon.

"Come," Gunnar said. "I've something to show you. It will be interesting to know if you recognise it." He led me amidships into the little deckhouse. Inside was a chest which he opened without hesitation, swinging the bronze oil lamp over it so that I could see inside. There was a sword, some armour, some gauntlets, but on top of these was a round shield whose painted design was elegantly finished in blues, whites and reds, the pattern suggesting an eight-rayed sun. Was it of African origin? Had he found it in that famous expedition to the South Seas with the Rose? It was not metal, but hide covering wood, and when Gunnar put it into my hands it was surprisingly light, though about the same size and proportions as a Viking shield. "Do you know this plate?" he asked, using the Norse meaning.

"I had a toy like it once perhaps. Something to do with my childhood? What is it?" I balanced it in my hands. It seemed vibrant, alive. I had a momentary image of a non-human friend, a dragon perhaps. But the workmanship was in no way Melnibonéan. "Some sort of talisman. Were you sold it as a magic shield? That could be the Sign of Chaos as easily as it could be the points of the compass. I think you have placed too high a value on this thing, Earl Gunnar. Was it meant to enchant me? To persuade me to your cause?"

Gunnar frowned. He simply did not believe me. "I envy you your self-control. You know the nature of that ring! Or is it self-deception? Lack of memory?"

"I seem to have little else but memory. Far too much memory. Self-deception? I remember the price I pay for slaying my own betrothed . . ."

"Ah, well," said Gunnar, "at least I am not burdened by such depressing and useless emotions. You and I are each going to die. We both understand the inevitable. It is merely my ambition to achieve that fate for the whole of creation at the same time. For if Fate thinks she jokes with us, I must teach her the consequences of her delusion. Everything in the multiverse will die when I die. I cannot bear the idea of life continuing when I know only oblivion."

I thought he was joking. I laughed. "Kill all of us?" I said. "A hard task."

"Hard," he agreed, "but not impossible." He took the bright "plate" from my hands and placed it back on top of his war hoard. He was disgruntled, as if he had expected more from me. I almost apologised.

"You'll have a great desire for that shield one day," he said. "Perhaps not in this manifestation. But we can hope."

He expected no real response from me. It seemed he sought only to pull me down to his level of misery. My own was of a different order. I had no "memory" of the future, and it was true my memory of the past was often a little dim. My concern was with my own world and an ambitious Theocrat who had summoned forces of Chaos he could not now control. I needed to be free of him. I needed to be able to kill him slowly. I was still Melnibonéan enough to need the satisfaction of a long and subtle revenge. To achieve this end I must find the Nihrainian smith who forged the archetype of the black blade. Why it should be here, in a world given over to brutality and hypocrisy, I did not know.

Having baffled me when he hoped to intrigue me, the faceless captain let an edge creep into his voice. I was reminded of his essential malevolence.

"I have always envied you your ability to forget," he said. "And it irks me not to know how you came by it."

I had never met the man before. His words seemed like the merest nonsense. Eventually I made an excuse, settled myself in the forward part of the boat and was soon asleep.

The next day, with a heavy sea mist at last beginning to burn off, we came in sight of the Tripolitanian coast. Gunnar sent a man up the mast to look for ships and obstacles. Few others would sail in such weather, but most of the ships in the region were coast-luggers, transporting trade goods from one part of the Moorish Confederacy to another. The richest and most cultured power in the region, the Arabs had brought unprecedented enlightenment. The Moors despised the Romans as uncouth and provincial and admired the Greeks as scholars and poets. It was to those oddly opposed forces that this world owed most of its creativity. The Romans were engineers, but the Moors were Chaos's thinkers. Romans had no real notion of balance, only of control. A pattern so at odds with the rhythms and pulses of the natural and supernatural worlds seemed destined to produce disaster.

Las Cascadas, called by the Moors Hara al Wadim, was a haven in a region too full of ships to be safe for us. I prayed that the Venetians or Turks had not taken their place in the meantime and were lying in wait for us. It was highly unlikely. Though nominally under the authority of the Caliphates, the strongest power in the region, Las Cascadas was a law unto herself, with one easily defended harbour. While the Mussulman Fatimids and their rivals continued to quarrel over stewardship of Mecca, as the Byzantines quarrelled over the stewardship of Rome, and so long as the Matter of Jerusalem was the focus of the world's attention, the island remained safe.

The Barbary Rose was prudent. She confined her activities to those waters not claimed by the Caliphates or Empire. First fortified by Carthage, Las Cascadas was considered safe, too, because she was ruled by a woman. I had sailed with that woman in my time. Gunnar told me her twin-hulled ship I greatly admired, *The Either/Or,* was wintering in North Africa, probably in Mirador with an old ally of hers and mine, the Welsh sea-robber and semi-mortal, Ap Kwelch, who had also been hired by King Ethelred. Ap Kwelch was known in English waters for a cunning foe but an awkward ally.

I was relieved I would not have to encounter Kwelch. We had an unresolved argument not best settled at Las Cascadas where all weaponry was collected and put under lock and key at the dock.

Before we ever saw the island, Gunnar ran up his flags, as if they would not recognise *The Swan* for who she was. Perhaps he had a code to let the defenders know he was still captain.

We sighted Las Cascadas at midday, approaching her from the harbour side. At first the island fortress was like a mirage, a series of silver veins twinkling in the sunlight. Then it became clear those veins ran down the sides of cliffs formed by the crater of an enormous volcano. There were no evident signs of a harbour entrance, only the still lagoon within. It seemed to me that this mysterious island could only be occupied from the air or from below, and such supernatural forces were no longer summonable.

I had seen the fate of those forces of nature and supernature, exiled to bleak parts of the world like the Devil's Garden and slowly dying. When all such souls died, it was thought by our folk, the Earth died also. This war had been going on for centuries between Law and Chaos. Soon Arabia might be the only region not conquered by thin-lipped puritans.

Gunnar again took the steering sweep. He wrapped his huge arm around one of the sail ropes, guiding his ship as if it were a skiff. Beyond the rocks which guarded the harbour, I saw a great cluster of houses, churches, mosques, synagogues, public buildings, markets and all the dense richness of a thriving, almost vertical city. It was built up the sides of the harbour. The rivers and waterfalls which gave Las Cascadas its name sparkled and gushed between buildings and rocks. The whole island glinted like a raw silver ingot. Pastel-coloured houses were dense with greenery and late-summer flowers. From their roofs and balconies, their gardens and vineyards, people raised up to look at us as we came about before the sea-gates of Las Cascadas. Two enormous doors of brass and steel could be drawn over a narrow gap between the rocks, just wide enough for a single ship to come or go. I was reminded vividly of Melniboné, though this place lacked the soaring towers of the Dreamers' City.

I heard shouted greetings. Figures moved about the stonework which housed the doors, levers turned, slaves hauled huge chains and the sea-gate opened.

Gunnar grunted and touched his steering sweep a little to port, then a little to starboard. Delicately he guided us through the narrow gaps, swift and smooth as an eel. The gates groaned closed again behind us. We rowed in slowly beneath the gaze of Las Cascadas's citizens. Everyone here lived off the proceeds of piracy. They were all devoted subjects of the pirate queen. The beautiful Barbary Rose had diplomatic skills which made her the equal of Cleopatra.

A great variety of ships already stood at anchor in the harbour. I recognised a Chinese junk, several large dhows, a round-hulled Egyptian ship, and the more sophisticated fighting galleys, most of modified Greek pattern, which were the favourite vessels of corsair captains. I had a feeling I might meet old friends here, but not recent acquaintances. Then, as I hauled my gear to the dock, I heard a name being called. "Peau d'Argent, is it you?" I turned.

Laughing, the little red-headed Friar Tristelunne came bustling along a quayside already crowded with the riff-raff of Las Cascadas turning out in hope of casual employment. But whatever booty Gunnar brought to Las Cascadas to pay for his security, it was not cargo. For a while Tristelunne disappeared in the crowd, then bobbed up again nearby, still smiling. "So you took my advice," he said. "You spoke to the old ladies and gentlemen?"

"They spoke to me," I said. "I thought you headed for Cordova."

"I was about to disembark. Then I heard Christians and Jews were again out of favour with the caliph. He believes there has been a fresh conspiracy with the empire. He's considering expelling all Franks. Indeed, he is wondering if expelling might not be too good for them. I thought it wise to wait out the winter here, administering to what faithful I can find. I'll see how the weather feels in spring. My alternative, at present, is the Lionheart's England, and quite honestly, it's no place for a gentleman. The forests are full of outlaws, the monasteries full of Benedictines and worse. Their divinely appointed king remains a prisoner in Austria, as I understand it, because his people have no particular interest in paying his ransom. John is an intellectual and therefore not trusted by anyone, especially the Church." Gossiping continually, Tristelunne guided me up steep, cobbled streets to the inn, which he insisted was the best on the island.

Behind me Gunnar roared a question. I told him I would see him at the inn.

I sensed his unease with my independence. He was used to control. It was second nature to him. He was baffled, I suspected, rather than angry.

Amused by all this, Friar Tristelunne led me into the inn's sunny garden. He sat me down at a bench and went inside, returning with two large shants of ale. I did my best with this hearty stuff, but yellow wine was the only drink that suited my perhaps over-refined palate. The fighting friar was not upset by this. He fetched me a cup of good wine and finished the ale himself. "You got advice, I hope, from the Grandparents?"

"They seemed more in a prophetic mood," I said. "Some mysterious visions."

"Follow them," he said firmly. "They'll bring you the thing you desire. You know already, in your heart, what the thing you desire will bring you." And he sighed.

"I have no interest in foreknowledge," I said. "My fate is my fate. That I understand. And understanding it releases me to drift wherever the tides of fate take me, for I trust in my own fortune, good or bad."

"A true gambler," he said. "A veritable mukhamir!"

"I'd heard all that before," I told him. "I belong to no society nor guild. I practise no formal arts, save when necessary, and I believe in nothing but myself, my sword and my unchangeable destiny."

"Yet you struggle against it."

"I am an optimist."

"We have that in common." He spoke without irony. He sat back against a post and stared around him at the flowers which flooded the entire courtyard.

These blossoms vied with the bright colours worn by the customers, none of whom paid us much attention. I knew the people of Las Cascadas thought it ill-mannered to show excessive attention to strangers.

On my first visit to Las Cascadas I had had status. The Rose and I were lovers then. On my second visit I had been a captive and something of her dupe. My ultimate turning of the tables had not made her any less aggrieved. But it was unlikely she had left any instructions about my fate, since she would hardly expect me to visit her stronghold again.

The friar confirmed that she was away until spring. She had sailed south again, he said. She always returned with exotic spices and jewels, and the occasional string of exquisite slaves. Ap Kwelch had gone with her. "That twin-prowed ship can sail faster and further than anything afloat," said Tristelunne. "She can sail to China and back in a single season. While we winter against the Atlantic, she's enjoying the sunshine and spoils of the Indies!"

"I thought Gunnar had taken *The Swan* there?"

"They both went in *The Swan*. She returned in *The Either/Or* after some dispute between them." He stopped suddenly and looked up. I knew Gunnar had come into the courtyard. The friar began to laugh, as if at his own joke. "And then the other dog said, 'No I only came in to get my claws trimmed.'"

Gunnar's hand fell on my shoulder. "We still have business to discuss," he said. "You, Sir Priest, have no business with me, I understand."

Pulling his worn cassock about him Friar Tristelunne got up. "I will never be desperate enough, sir, to seek the devil's employment."

"Then I was right," said Gunnar. "Is there no service in here?" He went inside. The friar seemed completely amused. He shrugged, winked at me, told me that our paths were bound to cross again and slipped out of the gate as Gunnar came back holding a boy by his ear. "All the girls are elsewhere, is it?"

"It is, sir," said the boy, dropped back to the paving of the yard. "I'm all that is left."

Gunnar cursed the urgency of his own men's drives and bellowed at the boy to bring ale. I told the lad to bring one more shant, tossed him a coin and got up. Gunnar's glittering mask looked at me in evident astonishment.

"You have the advantage of me, sir, and I cannot judge you for that," I said, "but it's clear you've no experience of partnership. I do not wish to hire your ship. I think you have some misunderstanding about me. You already told me that you know my blood and position. While I expect little from these kulaks and other rabble, I expect far more from one who claims to know my rank."

A sardonic bow. "Well, I apologise if that suits you. A breath of air and all is settled between us."

"Actions impress me more than words." I made to leave. I was, of course, playing a game, but I was playing it by following my own natural inclinations.

Gunnar, too, knew what was going on. He began to laugh. "Very well, Sir Silverskin. Let's talk as equals. It's true I'm used to bullying my way through this world, but you see the kind of company I'm forced to keep these days. I, too, was a Prince of the Balance. Now you find me a wretched corsair, clutching at legends for booty when once I crushed famous cities."

I sat down again. "While I am certain you have no intention of telling me your whole story, I suggest you let me know when you intend to sail for Vinland. Only the god-touched would venture into those seas in winter."

"Or the damned. Sir Silverskin, the course I propose to sail is directly through the realms of Hel. The entrance is on the other side of Greenland. Through the Underworld, through the moving rocks and the sucking whirlpools, through the monstrous darkness, to a land of eternal summer where riches are for the taking. The land is lush, growing wild what we cultivate with the sweat of our brows. And for wealth, there is legendary gold. A great ziggurat made entirely of gold and mysteriously abandoned by her people. So since we venture into the super-natural world, I suspect it makes little difference whether the season be summer or winter. We sail to Nifelheim itself."

"You sail to the north and the west," I told him. "I have useful experience and something you value."

He sucked thoughtfully through one of his straws. "And what would you gain from this voyage?"

"I seek a certain famous immortal smith. A Norseman maybe."

The noise from within the helm might have been laughter. "Is his name Volund? For Volund and his brothers guard that city called Illa Paglia della Oro by the Venetians. It stands in the centre of a lake at the place where the edge of the world meets Polaris. That is where I am bound."

Gunnar was not telling me the whole truth. He wanted me to think a city of gold his goal. I guessed he sought something else at the World's Rim. Something he could destroy.

For the moment, however, I was content. *The Swan* was going where I wished to go. Whether the realm of Hel was supernatural or natural scarcely mattered if we sailed the North Sea in December or January. "You trust your boat completely," I observed.

"I have to," he said. "Our fates are intertwined now. The ship will survive as long as I survive. I have magic, as I promised, and not the mere alchemical nonsense you hear in Nürnberg. I follow a vision."

"I suspect I do, also," I said.

IO

The Mouth of Hel

Norn-curs'd Norsemen, nature-driven to explore Earth's End,
Followed their weird to Fimbulwinter's icey land.
Longswords lay unblooded in lifeless hands
When warriors went the way of Gaynor, call'd the Damn'd.

—Longfellow,
Lord of the Lost

When we left port a few days later, the seas were still calm. Gunnar hoped to make headway through a good autumn. We might even reach Greenland before the ice settled in.

I asked him if, beyond Nifelheim, he did not expect to find empires and soldiers as powerful as any in this sphere. He looked at me as if I were mad. "I've heard the story from a dozen sources. It's virgin land, free for the taking. The only defenders are wretched savages whose ancestors built the city before they offended the gods. It's all written down."

I was amused. "So that makes it true?"

We were in his tiny deckhouse. Stooping, he opened a small chest and took out a parchment. "If not, we'll make it true!" The parchment was written in Latin, but there was runic scattered through the text. I glanced over it. The account of some Irish monk who had been the secretary of a Danish king, it told the story, in bare details, of a certain Eric the White. He had gone with five ships to Vinland and there established a colony, building a fortified town against those whom they called variously *skredlinj, skraelings* or *skrayling.* This was the Viking name for the local people. As far as I could tell it meant "whiner" or "moaner," and the Vikings considered them wretches and outlaws.

On this evidence Gunnar was prepared to sail through Nifelheim. I had heard similar stories from every Norseman I had known. Moorish philosophers proposed that the world was the shape of an elongated egg with the barbarian, godless races somehow clinging to the underside in perpetual darkness. In all such matters, as one is taught to do in the Dream of a Thousand Years, I remained silent. This was a dream I could not afford to have truncated. This was the last possible dream I could occupy before Jagreen Lern destroyed our fleet and then destroyed Moonglum and myself.

"So we will have only a land full of savages to conquer," I said sardonically. "And, say, thirty of us?"

"Exactly," said Gunnar. "With your sword and mine, it will take us a couple of months at most."

"Your sword?"

"You have Ravenbrand"—the faceless man tapped the swaddled blade at his side—"and I have Angurvadel."

He pulled away some of the covering to reveal a red-gold hilt hammered with the most intricate designs. "You'll take my word that the blade has runes embedded in it which flame red in war and that if it be drawn it must be blooded . . ."

I was, of course, curious. Did Gunnar carry a faux-glaive? Or did his sword have genuine magic? Was Angurvadel just another cursed sword of which the Norse folktales abounded? I had heard the name, of course, but it was an archetype I sought. Even if it were not false, Angurvadel was only one of the Black Sword's many brothers.

As Gunnar had hoped, the sailing was fair into the Atlantic. We stopped to take in provisions at a British settlement far from the protection of Norman law. There were only a few villagers left alive after Gunnar's men had finished their slaughter. These were forced to help kill their own animals and haul their own grain to our ship before they were in turn disposed of. Gunnar had an old-fashioned efficiency and attention to detail in his work. Like mine, his own sword was not drawn during this time.

We sailed on, knowing it would be some while before anyone considered pursuing us. Gunnar had a lodestone compass and various other Moorish instruments, which was probably what his men considered his magic. This made it far easier to risk quicker routes. As it happens, the sea was extraordinarily calm and the pale blue skies almost cloudless. Gunnar's men ascribed the weather to a damned man's luck. Gunnar himself had the air of a man thoroughly satisfied with his own good judgement.

During the few hours we had, I talked to some of the crew. They were friendly enough in a generally uncouth manner. Few of these reavers had much in the way of imagination, which was perhaps why they were prepared to follow Gunnar's standard.

One of the Ashanti, whom we called Asolingas, was by now wrapped in thick wool. He spoke good Moorish and told me how he and ten others had been captured after a battle and taken down the coast to be sold. Bought to row a Syrian trader, they had overwhelmed the rest of the ship within an hour of being at sea and, with the few other slaves who had joined them, managed to get themselves to Las Cascadas where, he said, they had been cheated out of the boat. The others had all been killed in later raiding expeditions.

Asolingas said he was homesick for Africa. Since his soul had already died and returned there, he supposed it would not be long before he followed it. He knew he would be killed sometime after we made our final landfall.

"Then why do you go?" I asked.

"Because I believe that my soul awaits me on the other side," he said.

A sigh came from starboard as the wind rose. I heard a gull. It would not be long before we made landfall.

In Greenland the colonists were so poor that the best we could get for ourselves was their water, a little sour beer and a weary goat that seemed glad to be slaughtered. Greenland settlements were notoriously impoverished, the settlers inbred and insular, forever at odds with the native tribes over their small resources. I said to Gunnar how I hoped that the entrance into Nifelheim was close. We had provisions for two weeks at most. He reassured me. "Where we're going, there won't be time for eating and drinking."

When we put out from Greenland, heading west, the weather was already growling. A sea which had been slightly more than choppy began sending massive waves against the bleak beaches. We had considerable trouble getting into open water. We left behind perhaps the last European colony, struggling no more in that harsh world. Gunnar often joked that he was God's kindest angel. "Do you know what they call this blade in Lombardy? Saint Michael's Justice." He began telling me a story which rambled off into nothing. He seemed to absorb himself psychically in the mountainous waves. There was a massive, slow repetition to the sea, even as it howled and thrashed and tossed us a hundred feet into the air, even as the wind and rain whistled in the rigging, and we dived another hundred feet into a white-tipped, swirling valley of water.

I grew used to the larger rhythm to which the ship moved. I sensed the security and strength which lay beneath all that unruly ocean. Now I knew what Gunnar and his men knew, why the ship was thought to be a magic one. She slipped through all that weather like a barracuda, virtually oblivious and scarcely touched by it. She was so beautifully constructed that she never held water between waves and almost always rose up as another wave came down. The exhilaration of sailing on such an astonishingly well-made vessel, trusting her more than one trusted oneself, was something I had never experienced before. The nearest experience I knew was flying on a Phoorn dragon. I began to understand Gunnar's reckless confidence. As I stood wrapped in my blue sea-cloak and stared into the face of the gale, I looked at the ship's figurehead in a new light. Was this some memory of flight?

Gunnar began swinging his way along the running ropes, a great bellow of glee issuing from within his faceless helm. Clearly he was almost drunk on the experience. His head flung back, his laughter did not stop. At length he turned to me and gripped my arm. "By God, Prince Elric, we are going to be heroes, you and I."

Any pleasure I had felt up to that moment immediately dissipated. I could think of nothing worse than being remembered for my association with Gunnar the Doomed.

The Viking moved his head, like a scenting beast. "She is there," he said. "I know she is there. And you and I will find her. But only one of us will keep her. Whoever it is shall be the final martyr."

His hand fell on my back. Then he returned to the stern and his tiller.

I was, for a moment, reminded of my mother's death, of my father's hatred. I recalled my cousin's bloody end, weeping as the soul was sucked from her. Who was "she"? Who did he mean?

The waves crashed down again, and up we rose on the next, constantly moving ahead of the turbulence so that sometimes it really did seem we flew over the water. The ship's half-reefed sail would catch the wind and act like a wing, allowing Gunnar to touch the tiller this way and that rapidly, and swing her with the water. I have never seen a captain before or since who could handle his ship with his fingertips, who could issue a command and have it instantly followed in any weather. Gunnar boasted that however many he lost on land, he almost never lost a man at sea.

Foam drenched the decks, settled on the shoulders and thighs of the oarsmen. Foam flecked the troubled air. Black, red, brown and yellow backs bent and straightened like so many identical cogs, water and sweat pouring over them. Above, the sky was torn with wet, ragged clouds, boiling and black. I shivered in my cloak. I longed to be able to call Mishashaaa or any of the other elementals, to calm this storm by magic means. But I was already using my magic to inhabit this dream! The power of Ravenbrand was potent only in battle. To attempt anything else might result in uncontrollable consequences.

All day and all night we plunged on through the wild Atlantic waters. We used oars, tiller and sails to answer every change of the wind and, with the help of Gunnar's Moorish lodestone, now ran like an arrow due north until Gunnar called me into his deckhouse and showed me the instrument. "There's sorcery here," he insisted. "Some bastard's bewitched the thing!"

The stone was spinning in its glass, completely erratic.

"There's no other explanation," Gunnar said. "The place has a protector. Some Lord of the Higher Worlds . . ."

A howl came from the deck, and we both burst out of the deerskin deckhouse to see Leif the Larger, his face a frozen mask, staring at a vast head erupting from the wild water, glaring with apparent malevolence at our vulnerable little ship. It was human, and it filled the horizon. Gunnar grasped the Norseman by the shoulder and slapped him viciously. "Fool! It's a score of miles away. It's stone! It's on the shore!" But at the same time Gunnar was lifting his head to look upward . . . and then upward again. There was no question that what we saw was a gigantic face, the eyes staring sightlessly down from under the cloud which covered its forehead. We were too small for it to see. We were specks of dust in comparison. What Gunnar had noted was true. The thing did not seem to be alive. Presumably, therefore, we had nothing to fear from it. It was not a sentient human or god, rather an extraordinarily detailed sculpture in textured and delicately coloured granite.

Leif the Larger drew in a breath and mumbled something into his golden beard. Then he went to the side and threw up. The ship was still tossing about in the ocean, was still on top of the waves. She continued the course we had set before our lodestone was enchanted. A course which took us directly towards that gigantic head.

When I pointed this out to Gunnar he shrugged. "Perhaps it's your giant who lives at the North Pole? We must trust the fates," he said. "You must have faith, Elric, to tread your path, to follow your myth."

And then, in an instant, the head opened its vast, black mouth and the sea poured down into it, taking us relentlessly towards a horizon which was dark, glistening and thoroughly organic.

Gunnar roared his frustration and his despair. He made every effort to turn the ship. His men back-rowed heroically. But we were being drawn down into that fleshy pit.

Gunnar shook his fist against the fates. He seemed more affronted than terrified. "Damn you!" Then he began laughing. "Can't you see what's happening to us, Elric? We're being *swallowed*!"

It was true. We might have been the contents of a cup of water with which some monstrous ogre refreshed himself. I found that I, too, was laughing. The situation seemed irredeemably comical to me. And yet there was every chance I was about to perish. If I did so, I would perish in both realities.

All at once we were totally engulfed. The boat banged and buffeted, as if against the banks of a river. From somewhere amidships rose the sound of a deep, chanting song, its melody older than the world. Asolingas, the Ashanti, clearly believed his own particular moment had come.

Then he, too, fell silent.

I gasped and coughed at the foulness of the air. It was as if a street cur had breathed in my face. A whole series of fables I had heard about men being swallowed by gigantic fish came to mind. I could not recall a story about a ship being swallowed by a giant. Or was it a giant? Had we simply let ourselves see a configuration of rocks and made it into a face? Or was this some ancient sea-monster, large enough to swallow ships and drink seas?

The stink grew worse, but since it was the only air to breathe, we breathed it. With every breath, I filled my lungs with the dust of death.

And then we were in Nifelheim.

Leif the Shorter, from somewhere in the middle of the ship, cried out in frustration. "I should not be here. I have done nothing wrong. I killed my share. Is it my fault that I should be punished simply because I did not die in battle?"

I wrapped my sea-cloak more closely about me. It had become profoundly cold. The icy air was hard against my skin, threatening to strip it off. Breathing became painful. I felt I inhaled a thousand shards of glass.

There was no wind—just cold, pitch-darkness, utter silence. I heard the sound of our oars dipping and rising, dipping and rising with almost unnatural regularity. A brand flared suddenly. I saw Gunnar's glittering mask, illuminated by the rush torch. I caught a faint impression of the rowers as he came back up the central board. "Where are we, Prince Elric? Do you know? Is this Nifelheim?"

"It might as well be," I said. The deck then slanted again, and we ran downwards for a short while before righting ourselves.

As soon as we were back into still water, the oars began to dip and rise, dip and rise. All around us was the sound of running water, like glaciers melting—a thousand rivers running from both sides of the narrow watercourse on which we now rowed.

Gunnar was jubilant. "Hel's rivers!"

The rest of us did not respond to his joy. We became aware of deep, despairing groans which were not quite human, of bubbling noises which might have been the last moments of drowning children. There was clashing and sibilant shushing, which could have been the sound of whispering voices. We concentrated on the dip and rise, dip and rise of our oars. This familiar slap was our only hold on logic as our senses screamed to escape.

Leif the Shorter's rasp came again. He was raving. "Elivagar, the Leipter and the Slid," he shouted. "Can you all hear them? They are the rivers of Nifelheim. The river of glaciers, the river of oaths, the river of naked swords. Can't you hear them? We are abandoned in the Underworld. That is the sound of Hvergelmir, the great cauldron, boiling eternally, dragging ships whole into her maw." He began to mumble something about wishing he had been braver and more reckless in his youth and how he hoped this death counted as a violent one. How he had never been a religious man but had done his best to follow the rules. Again he wailed that it was scarcely his fault he had not been killed in battle. Leif the Larger economically silenced his cousin. Yet even Leif the Shorter's wailings had not interrupted the steady rise and fall of our oars. Every man aboard clung to this effortful repetition, hoping it would somehow redeem him in the eyes of Fate and allow him entry into Paradise.

Now imploring voices called out to us. We heard the sound of hands on the sides of the ship, attempts to grasp our oars. Yet still the men rowed on at the same pace, Gunnar's voice rising over all the other sounds as he called out the rhythm. His voice was aggressive and bold and commanded absolute obedience.

Down dipped the oars and up again they rose. Gunnar cursed the darkness and defied the Queen of the Dead. "Know this, Lady Hel, that I am already dead. I live neither in Nifelheim nor in Valhalla. I die again and again, for I am Gunnar the Doomed. I have already been to the brink of oblivion and know my fate. You cannot frighten me, Hel, for I have more to fear than thee! When I die, life and death die with me!" His defiant laughter echoed through those bleak halls. And if, somewhere, there was a pale goddess whose knife was called Greed and whose dish was named Hunger, she heard that laughter and would think Ragnarok had come, that the Horn of Fate had blown and summoned the end of the world. It would not occur to her that a mere man voiced that laughter. Courage of Gunnar's order was rewarded in Valhalla, not Nifelheim.

Gunnar's defiance further heartened his men. We heard no more of Leif the Shorter's discovery of religion.

The sound of clashing metal grew louder, as if in response to Gunnar. The human voices became more coherent. They formed words, but in a language none of us knew. From out of that chilled darkness there emerged other, less easily identified sounds, including a gasping, bubbling, sucking noise like an old woman's death rattle. Yet still *The Swan* rowed on, straight and steady, to Gunnar's beating fist and rhythmic song.

Then he stopped singing.

A great silence fell again, save for the steady thrust of the oars. We felt a tug at the ship as if a great hand had seized it from below and was lifting it upward. A howling voice. A whirlwind. Yet we were being dragged into rather than out of the water.

I gasped as salt filled my mouth. I clung to whatever rigging I could find in the darkness while behind me Gunnar's laughter roared. He began to sing again as it seemed that he steered us directly into the drowning current. The ship creaked and complained as I had never heard before. She tilted violently, and at last the rhythm of her oars no longer matched the rhythm of Gunnar's song.

There was a tearing sound. I was convinced we were breaking up. Then came a great thrumming chord, as if the strings of an instrument had been struck. The chord consumed me, set every nerve singing to its tune and lifted me, as it lifted the entire ship, until we were driving upwards as rapidly as we had gone down. A white, blinding light dominated the horizon. My lungs filled entirely with water. I knew that I had failed in my quest, that in a few moments my only grasp on life was what was left to me as I hung in Jagreen Lern's rigging.

The ship began to yaw and spin in the water until I lost what little sense of direction I had. Suddenly the light faded to a pale grey. The noise became a steady shout, and again I heard Gunnar's laughter as he bawled to his men to return to their oars. "Row, lads. Hel's not far behind!"

And row they did, with the same extraordinary precision, their muscles bulging to bursting from the effort of it, while Gunnar lifted his gleaming helm towards heaven and pointed. Here was proof that we had left the supernatural world.

The bright light faded. Above us was a grey, darkening sky. Behind us some kind of maelstrom danced and sucked, but we had escaped it and were even now rowing steadily away from it.

Ahead of us lay a high, wooded coastline with a number of small islands standing off it. The cloud cover was heavy, but from the nature of the light sunset was not far off.

The sounds of the maelstrom fell away. I wondered at the extraordinary sorcery it had taken to achieve such a strange transition. Gunnar presented the coast to me with a proprietorial hand.

"Behold," he said with sardonic triumph, "the lost continent of Vinland!" He leaned forward, drinking it in. "The Greeks called it Atlantis and the Romans called it Thule. All races have their own name for it. Many have died seeking it. Few ever made the pacts I made to get here . . ."

A mist was rising. The coast vanished into it, as if the gods had grown tired of Gunnar's posturings. As we slowed oars and came in on a long, cold surf, we began to make out the darkening outlines of a fir-crowded coast edged by dark rock and small, unwelcoming beaches. Gunnar steered us between rocky, fir-clad islands as if he knew where he wanted to go. By the nature of the waves we had entered a bay and must be nearing a mooring of some sort, but there were still many small islands to negotiate.

I began to smell the land. It was rich with pine and ferny undergrowth, verdant with life. Gunnar's sense of that had been right, at least.

Asolingas saw the house first. He pointed and yelled to get Gunnar's attention.

Gunnar cursed loudly. "I'll swear to you, Elric—and I paid heavily in gold and souls for this information—I was told Vinland held nothing but savages."

"Who says they are not?" After all these years I was still confused by the fine distinctions.

"That manor could have been built in Norway last week! These aren't like the wretches we dealt with in Greenland." Gunnar was furious. "Leif's damned colonies were supposed to have perished! And now we're sailing into a port that probably has a dozen Viking ships in it and knows exactly what we're here for!"

He gave the order to back water and up oars. We drifted close in to the island and the house. The lower windows were already lit against the twilight and cast a mottled pattern on the surrounding shrubs. These windows were typically of lightly woven branches which admitted light and afforded privacy during the day but could be covered against the night. I wondered if the place was some sort of inn. There was thin smoke rising from its chimneys. It looked a good solid place, of big oak beams and white daub, such as any rich peasant might build from Normandy to Norway. If it was a little taller, perhaps a little more circular in shape than average, that was probably explained by local materials and conditions.

The manor's existence, of course, suggested exactly what Gunnar feared—that the Ericsson colonies had not only survived but prospered and produced an independent culture as typically Scandinavian as Iceland's. A house of these proportions and materials meant something else to Gunnar. It meant there were stone fortifications and sophisticated defences. It meant fierce men who were conditioned to fighting the native skraylings and had a code of honour which demanded they die in battle. It meant that one ship, even ours, could not take the harbour, let alone the continent.

I was not, of course, disappointed. I had no quarrel with this folk and no eye on their possessions. Gunnar, however, had been promised a kingdom only to discover that apparently it already had a king.

As we passed the house we looked in vain for the city which we now expected to see. The shoreline was virgin woodland or harsh, pebble beach, with occasional slabs of rock rising up directly from the water. When night at last fell it was very clear there was no thriving harbour nearby. Gunnar was careful. He did not relax his guard. There were a dozen headlands which could be hiding a fair-sized fortified town. His position as a leader was threatened. He had promised an abandoned city of gold, not a city of stone crammed with warriors. The politics of our ship were beginning to shift radically.

The only light gleaming through all that watery, pine-drenched darkness was from the house on the island. At least we were not immediately threatened. If challenged, Gunnar would greet the Vikings as a brother, I knew. He would bide his time, search for their weaknesses, while he praised and flattered and told exotic stories.

Gunnar sighed with relief. He gave the order to row towards the island. I found myself hoping that the inhabitants were capable of defending themselves. Just as we began to look for an anchoring place, the lights in the house went out.

I looked up at the stars. They were far more familiar in their configuration than those I had most recently left behind. Had I somehow returned to the world of Melniboné? Instinctively I felt that my dreams and my realities had never been closer.

II

Klosterheim

Famous in fierce foam the reivers raged,
Swords bared against their barren fortune.

—Longfellow,
Lord of the Lost

Apart from the lamp which had burned in the front windows, there was no evidence that the house was occupied at all. Our men were by now totally exhausted. Gunnar knew this and told them to stop rowing. The Persian was sent forward with the plumb line. The water seemed shallow enough, but when we dropped anchor it would not hold. We were touching rock. The big millstone we used was slipping. Eventually we were able to get some sort of purchase in what was probably organic tangle. The ship drifted about before settling slowly with her dragon bird prow staring imperiously inward at the mysterious continent. Had Gunnar really thought it could be taken by thirty men commanded by a faceless madman?

I had no need of sleep the way the others had. I told them I would take first watch. I spent it in the little buckskin shelter we had made in the prow, which gave me a view of the water ahead. I heard what I thought were seals and checked the ship for swimmers. By the time my watch was up the night had been uneventful.

When I awoke just after dawn I heard birdsong, smelled wood-smoke and forest and was filled with a sense of quite inappropriate well-being. From within the house, some sort of animal croaked, and I heard a human voice that was faintly familiar to me.

We drew anchor and rowed slowly around the island looking for a better landing place. Eventually we found a slab of rock jutting directly into the sea. A lightly clad man could stand on the rock and wade up easily to get a rope positioned for the rest of us. We would drown in our war-gear if we slipped.

At length, having left a small guard, we stood on the bank of the island. Out to sea, gulls and gannets fished on grey, white-flecked water. They flew low against a sky of windswept iron, with tall firs and mixed woodlands rising inland as far as we could see. Nowhere, save from the house, was there any smoke.

With a habitual curse, Gunnar began to march forward through the undergrowth leading his men. We were approaching the back of the house. There was no sign we had been detected until, as we came close, a bird inside began to screech in the most urgent and agitated manner. Then there was silence.

Gunnar stopped.

The Viking led us in a wide circle until we could see the front of the house with its solid oaken door, heavy iron hinges and locks, the bars at the windows in front of the lattice. A well-maintained and defendable manor house.

Again the bird made a noise.

Were they hoping we would go away?

Were they expecting us to attack?

Gunnar next told half the party to stay with me at the front while he circled the house. He was looking for something in particular now, I could tell. He murmured under his breath and counted something off on his fingers. He had recognised the place and feared it.

Certainly his manner changed radically. He yelled for us to get back, to get down to the ship immediately.

His men were used to obeying him. Their own superstition did the rest. Within seconds they were all stumbling back through the undergrowth, catching their hasty feet and cursing, using their swords to hack their way clear, thoroughly infected by their master's panic.

And panic it was! Gunnar was clearly terrified.

I would have followed had not the door opened and a rather gaunt, black-clad individual whom I did not recall greeted me with cold familiarity.

"Good morning, Prince Elric. Perhaps you'd take a little breakfast with me?"

He spoke High Melnibonéan, though he was a human. His face was almost fleshless, a cadaverous skull. His eyes were set so deep in their sockets it seemed a vacuum regarded you. His thin, pale lips forced a partial smile as he saw my surprise.

"I think my former master, Lord Gunnar, knows the nature of this place, but do not fear, my lord. It cannot do you harm. You do not recall me? I understand. You lead so many and such varied lives. You meet people far more remarkable than myself. You don't remember Johannes Klosterheim? I have been waiting here for Earl Gunnar to arrive for some fifty years. We were once partners in sorcery. My own satanic powers are used elsewhere. But here I am."

"This house was brought here by sorcery?" I asked.

"No, sir. The house was built by my own and others' honest sweat. Only the stone posts were already in place. We erected the beams, the walls and floors. Each corner of the house is stone, as are many of the interior supports. We found the circle already here when I arrived."

"We? You and your pet?"

"I must apologise for the bird, sir. My only protection against the savages. But I was not referring to him. No, sir, I am lucky enough to be chief of a small tribe of native skraylings. Travellers like myself. We found this land already settled. It was the settlers helped me build my house."

"We saw no other lights, sir. Where would those settlers be?"

"Sadly, sir, they are all dead. Of old age. We fell out, I fear, myself and the Norsemen. My tribe triumphed. Apart from the women and children adopted to make up our numbers, the rest are now enjoying the rewards of Valhalla." He uttered a barking caw. "All mongrels now, eh, sir?"

"So settlers built this place for you?"

"They did most of the necessary work, yes. It's essentially circular, like their own houses. The island itself was a holy place locally. The natives were frightened of it when we arrived. I knew it would be a long while before you got here, so I needed somewhere comfortable to wait. But my tribesmen will not live here. A few remain with me but make their own camp in the mountains over on the other side of that ridge." He pointed inland at a distant, pine-covered terrace. "They bring me my food and my fuel. I am, these days, a kind of household god.

Not very important, but worth placating. They've waited years, I suspect, for a more suitable Easterner. Gunnar could well be what they want, if he does not kill them before they have a chance to talk. You had better take me to him. I place myself under your protection, Prince Elric."

Without locking the house, Johannes Klosterheim closed his front door, left his jabbering bird inside and followed me. Some Vikings had already reached the gang-rope. *The Swan* rocked and bobbed under the weight as they pulled on the rope, hauling themselves through the water and up the side.

"Earl Gunnar," I called. "The master of the house is with me. He says he means us no harm. He can explain these paradoxes."

Gunnar was still half-panicked, raving. "Paradoxes? What paradoxes? There are no paradoxes here, merely dark danger. I will not risk my men's lives against it."

His men paused. They were not as impressed or terrified as he was. Gunnar gathered himself. He spoke with a slightly forced authority. He could not afford to show any further failures of judgement, or he would not last long.

"The master of the house is captured?"

"He comes as a friend. He says he awaits us. He is glad we have arrived."

Gunnar wanted no more of this in public. He grunted and shrugged. "He can come aboard with us, if he likes. We need fresh water, and there's none I can see here."

Smiling faintly to himself Klosterheim held his own counsel. He bowed. "I am much obliged, Earl Gunnar."

Gunnar pushed back through his men to take a better look at the newcomer. "Do you know this realm?"

Klosterheim changed his language to Greek. "As well as anyone," he said. "I would imagine you are hoping for a guide."

Gunnar snorted. "As if I'd trust you!"

"I know why you fear this place, Gunnar the Doomed, and I know you have reason to fear it." Klosterheim spoke in a low, cold voice. "But I have no particular cause to fear it, and neither has any other man here, save you."

"You know my dream?" said Gunnar.

"I can guess what it must be, for I know what happened at that place. But you have nothing to fear in the house now."

"Aye," said Gunnar. "Call me a cautious old man, but I see no reason to trust my fortunes to you or that place."

"You had best trust me, Gunnar the Doomed, since we have goals in common."

"How can you know so much living at the World's Rim? Do vessels come and go every week from here to the Middle Sea?"

"Not as many as there used to be," said Klosterheim. "The Phoenician trade at its height was thriving on other shores than these. I have been to a country far from here where the folk speak Breton and are Christians. Slowly the land will change them. They will become as the others here. Men change not as they would, but as nature demands. The Norse and Roman trade was minimal. The Phoenicians and their Celtic allies fled here after the fall of Carthage. This continent has always absorbed its settlers. And made them its own."

Gunnar had lost interest. "So you say there's no big Norse settlement here? No major defences? No fleet?"

"Just myself and the Pukawatchi now," said Klosterheim, almost humorously. "Patiently expecting your coming. I know what you carry with you here. How came you so swiftly to Vinland?" He spoke knowingly.

Gunnar saw the last of his men into the ship, then came back to talk further. "You mean that war plate?" he asked. "That skrayling shield?"

"It was more than luck brought you here before the winter snows," said Klosterheim. "It was more than one thing allowed you to take a short cut through Hell!" He spoke with unusual force. "You need me, Earl Gunnar the Doomed, just as you do Prince Elric, if you are ever to see the Golden City and look upon the wonder of the Skrayling Tree."

"Do you know what I seek?" Gunnar demanded.

"Might it have something to do with the ring worn by our pale friend?"

"That's enough," said Gunnar.

He lapsed into uncharacteristic, brooding silence.

"And why am I here?" I asked. I held up the ring.

"You are not here, as you well know," said Johannes Klosterheim with narrowed eyes. "You are in peril in some other realm. Only desperation brings your dream self here."

"And you know what I seek?"

"I know what you would do. I cannot see how it can be done whether you serve Law or Chaos." He interrupted himself, looking to Gunnar. "Come back with me to the house. Leave your men to guard the ship. You can sleep, and we can talk further. I need your strength as you need my wisdom."

But Gunnar shook his head again. "Instinct tells me to avoid that house at all costs. It is associated with my doom. If you have warriors and would join forces, we'll improve our security. So I'll agree provisionally to an alliance. Until I see the mettle of your men. Should you reveal to me tomorrow that your tribe's no more visible than the average elf or dwarf, you'll have waited fifty years just to lose your head. Do you too claim to be a demi-mortal like our leprous friend here? The world is filling up with us. The best of these die bloodily at forty or so. Few live to sixty, let alone two hundred."

"I was born out of my time," Klosterheim offered by way of explanation. "I am an adventurer, like yourself, who seeks a certain revenge and recompense. I cannot die until Time herself dies. A young dreamthief's apprentice has tried to steal something from me and has paid a price for it. Now I travel as you do, with the help of sorcery. Why Time should accommodate us so thoroughly, I cannot tell, but we might learn one day."

"You're of a scientific disposition?" I asked.

"I have been acquainted with natural scientists and students of the Khemir and the Gibra for many years. All grope for wisdom as greedily as their lords and kings grope for power. To protect their wisdom from abuse by the temporal forces of this world, various brotherhoods have been formed down the centuries. The most recent is the Brotherhood of the Holy Sepulchre. All understand that the sum of human wisdom, the secret of human peace, resides in a certain magical object. It can take the form of a cup, a staff or a stone. It is known by the Franks as the Grey Dale, which is a name they give to a ceremonial bowl used to greet and feast visitors. Some say it is a bowl of blood. Some say the heads of enemies swim in that bowl and speak of secret, unnatural things. Or it is a staff, such as Holy Roman Emperors carry to symbolise that they rule justly and with balance under the law. The Gauls and Moors are convinced it is a stone, and not a small one. Yet all agree the Grey Dale could take any of these forms and still be what it is, for sight of it is hidden from all but the most heroic and virtuous."

Again Gunnar was laughing. "Then that is why I am the Doomed. I am doomed to seek the cup but never see it, for I cannot claim to be a virtuous man.

Yet only that cup could avert my fate. Since I'll never see it, I intend to ensure that no others shall ever set eyes on it . . ."

"Then let us hope," Klosterheim interrupted dryly, "that we are able to help you avert your fate."

"And you, Master Klosterheim," I said. "Do you, too, seek this staff, stone or cup?"

"To be honest," said Johannes Klosterheim with thin, terrifying piety, "I seek only one thing, and that is the cure for the World's Pain. I have one ambition. To bring harmony back to the world. I seek to serve my master, the Prince—"

"—of Peace?" Gunnar was feeling confident again now, and as usual this came out in a form of aggression. "I mistook you for a soldier or a merchant, sir, not a priest."

"My master inspires in me the greatest devotion."

"Aye. That devotion evaporates when you are forced to eat your own private parts," said Gunnar with a reminiscent chuckle.

He had regained whatever he had momentarily lost in his terror to get away from the house. Such weaknesses in one who was usually as courageous as he was ruthless! It made me curious. No doubt this curiosity was shared by his men, who trusted him only while his judgement remained impeccable. He knew, as well as anyone, that if he began to falter, there were thirty souls ready to challenge him for the captaincy of *The Swan*.

He had fired them with dreams of kingdoms. Now Klosterheim promised to take them to the Golden City. But Gunnar had by now seen the sense of that. He was no longer disputing our need for the skullface and others.

"And I must admit," added Klosterheim, "to have had some real trouble from the one who calls himself White Crow. One of your people, Prince Elric?"

"It is not a familiar name in Melniboné," I said. These humans believed anyone who was "fey" to be of Faery or some other imagined supernatural elfland.

I looked across at the shore with its great, wooded hills, its deep, ancient forest rolling like green waves back into the interior. Was this truly Atlantis, and did the continent surround the World's Pole? If so, would I find what I sought at the centre, as I predicted?

"Tomorrow," Klosterheim continued, "we shall meet with my tribe, and together we shall find the Shining Path to the Golden City. Now we have allies, and all the prophecies combine to say the same thing. White Crow will give us no more trouble now. He'll soon vanish from this realm for ever. That which he stole shall be mine. This is what the oracle says."

"Aye, well," grumbled the faceless earl, "I have a habit of mistrusting oracles as well as gods."

Again Klosterheim offered us the hospitality of his home, and again Gunnar declined it. He repeated that Klosterheim should accept a place in the ship. Klosterheim hesitated before refusing. He had matters he must settle before joining us in the morning. He stated that his hall was our hall, and he had good venison and a full vegetable cellar if we cared to join him. My own appetite not being hearty and it being politic to keep my alliance with Gunnar in place, I refused. Accepting this with a baffled shrug, Klosterheim turned and made his way through the tangled undergrowth. There were no well-trodden paths to his house. From within came the agitated cackling of a bird.

It was now noon. The sun blazed through the gold and green of the late-autumn trees from a sky the colour of rust and tarnished silver. I followed Klosterheim with my eyes as far as I could, but he was soon hidden in the brushy shadows.

Who was the young skrayling? A local leader, no doubt. Clearly Klosterheim hated the man. Yet what had he meant? White Crow was of my people? Was this land occupied by descendants of Melnibonéans?

The place being no longer occupied by Norse settlements, Gunnar was reassured. Once we were back aboard he gave the order to row towards the shore. He saw a good, low-rising beach with easy anchorage. We could easily wade from the boat to the shingle now. Soon Gunnar had men cutting down branches and setting up camp while the ship was secured and the guard determined.

At supper he asked me what I thought of Klosterheim. Was he a magician? I shook my head. Klosterheim was not himself a sorcerer but was employing sorcery. I did not know where he got this power or if he had other powers. "He's waited as long as he has and built that house for himself knowing he might have to wait for us even longer. Such patience must be respected. His need for an alliance might be of mutual benefit. He won't, of course, keep any bargain he might make with us."

Gunnar chuckled at this. The sound echoed in his helm and ended suddenly.

"We'll keep no bargain we make with him. Who wins has the quickest wits and anticipates the others' moves best. This is the kind of game I like to play, Elric. With life and death to win as the only stake." Having escaped the terrors of that house, he was in unnaturally good spirits. I suspected an element of hysteria under his repeated reassurances that the future looked better than ever. With a larger fighting force, our chances of taking the City of Gold were immeasurably improved.

His ambitions were beyond me. I was prepared to bide my time and see what transpired. I, too, had my own ambitions and goals and did not intend to let either these or some mysterious dreamthief's apprentice stand in my way.

Next morning we roasted and ate a doe Asolingas and his friend killed. A little canoe rounded the island and slid rapidly towards us. The black-clad Klosterheim paddled it. I went down to the beach to greet him. Not a natural oarsman, he was out of breath. He let me help him beach the craft, gasping that the Pukawatchi were now assembled and awaiting us above the ridge, where they had built a peace camp. He pointed. Smoke puffed into the dawn sky.

The Pukawatchi, he explained, were not from these forests. Originally they had come with him from the south in search of their sacred treasures stolen by White Crow the trickster. The tribe had linked its destiny with his. Now they felt ready to ally with us and attack their ancient enemies.

We dragged *The Swan* ashore and disguised her deep in the forest. We removed all our war-gear, which included the great blue, red and white shield Gunnar had shown me that first night. As I had no shield, he loaned me that one. But there was a strict condition. Before we left the deckhouse, Gunnar flung me a cover. He helped me tie it over the outside of the shield. We would need that shield later, he said, and he did not want the Pukawatchi to see it. If I showed it, under any circumstances, it could be the end of us. I suspect Gunnar also thought the shield stolen. If it were discovered, he would rather I be thought the thief. It made no difference to me. Even with its cover, the thing was light, useful if attacked by spears and arrows, and practical if I needed something to throw at a horse to bring it down. Not that Klosterheim had said anything about horses when I asked him how long we had to go. He described everything in terms of marches. As one who hated to walk, who had ridden the wild dragons of Melniboné, I was not used to marching. Nor did I enjoy the prospect.

Following what appeared to be deer trails, we lumbered through the forest in our war-shirts and our iron helmets like so many ancient reptiles. I was impressed by the Viking hardiness. They had scarcely rested before they were again on the move, their legs doing the same kind of work their arms had done earlier. Gunnar knew the Norseman's secret of the loping march, which they had learned from the Romans.

We went uphill and down, through the heavy, loose soil, the root-tangled undergrowth of an endless green-gold forest. Hawks circled above us. Unfamiliar birds called from the trees. Our rhythmic tramping was relieved by what we saw. Rivers dammed by beaver, curious raccoons, the nests of squirrels and crows, the spoor of deer, bear and geese.

Then Klosterheim slowed us, lifting both hands in reassurance. We came out of the trees into a deep autumn meadow beside a narrow, silver stream where some forty lodges had been erected, their cooking smoke moving lazily in the air. The people reminded me very much of the Lapps I had encountered in the service of the Swedish king. They had much the same features, being rather short, stocky and square. They had dogs with them and all the other signs of an established camp. Yet something was slightly awry about the scene. They had posted no guards and so were surprised when we came into their village, Klosterheim leading the way.

There was an immediate cacophony when they saw me. It was something I was used to, but these people seemed to have some special animosity towards me. I remembered Klosterheim's reference. I could see he was trying to reassure them that I was neither their enemy nor one of their enemy's tribe.

He said something else I did not hear which cheered them. They began to sing, to raise their spears and bows in greeting. All were fairly short, though one or two of them were almost as tall as Klosterheim. They had certainly not gone soft during their wait. Displaying the physiques of men who lived by hunting, they wore jerkins and leggings of buckskin, softened and tightly sewn and decorated with all kinds of pictograms. The shoulders and sleeves of the jackets, the back and bottom edges of the leggings, were sewn with fringes of buckskin, handsome costumes on a somewhat unlovely people. The clothing all looked as if it had been cut down to fit. I asked Klosterheim how his tribe had learned to make such fine cold-weather garments.

The gaunt man smiled. "They discovered in the usual way. These lodges and most of these tools and weapons are what were left after the Pukawatchi came upon the original owners. The Pukawatchi have a policy of taking no long-term prisoners unless they need to replace their own dead. In this case the attack thoroughly surprised the tribe, whom my people wiped out to a child. So there are no more Minkipipsee, as I believe the indigenous folk termed themselves. You have no cause to feel insecure. Nobody cares to avenge them, even for the sport of it."

We entered the camp proper, a large public area encircled by the lodges. The tribe sent up a great wail of greeting. They seemed to be waiting for something or someone, and meanwhile they were painting for the war trail, Klosterheim told me. Something about their square, stern faces reminded me of Dalmatia. Daubed with white, scarlet and blue clay on their bodies, they smeared yellow clay on their hands and foreheads. Some wore eagle feathers. The men's weapons were elaborate, carved lances tipped with bone, obsidian and found metal. Both men and women raised their voices in this strange ululation, which sounded to my unpractised ear more like a funeral lament. We responded as best we could and were made welcome.

These woods were not lacking in game. There were patches of vegetables where the Pukawatchi had made gardens. Again our party ate well. The men relaxed. They asked the skraylings if perhaps they could spare a little beer or wine, as they did not know what to make of the proffered pipes. They had the sense, however, to note that none of our hosts was drinking anything but water and a rather unpleasant tea made from spearmint and yarrow. Eventually, after trying the pipe, they resorted to explaining in some detail how beer was brewed.

With due ceremony we were introduced to the rather sour-faced individual whom Klosterheim called Young Two Tongues or Ipkaptam. With a scar across his cheek and lip, as if from a sword cut, his was a handsome, ungiving face. He had become the sachem, or speaker, of these people on his father's death. "Not because heredity demanded it," said Klosterheim in Greek, "but because he was known to have medicine sight and be lucky."

The local language was largely impossible for the Vikings to understand. The Pukawatchi thus tended to focus their attention on Gunnar and myself. We must have seemed demigods or, more likely, demons to them. They had a name for us which was impossible to translate.

But there was plenty to eat. The women and girls brought us dish after dish to enjoy, and soon a convivial atmosphere developed.

Klosterheim quelled the uncertainties of the still-grim Ipkaptam, who had added more paint to his face. When Klosterheim suggested we retire to the talking lodge to discuss our expedition, Ipkaptam shook his head and pointed first at my sword and then at my face, uttered the word "Kakatanawa" more than once and was adamant that I not be allowed into their councils. Klosterheim reasoned with him, but Ipkaptam stood up and walked away, throwing down an elaborate bag, which had been attached to his belt. I took this to mean he did not intend to share his wisdom with us.

Kakatanawa! The same word, spat as an oath and directed at me. Klosterheim spoke to him, brutally, urgently, no doubt encouraging some sort of common sense, for gradually Young Two Tongues glowered and listened. Then he glowered and nodded. Then he glowered and came back, fingering his scars. He picked up his bag and pointed to a large tepee set aside from the others near a stand of trees and a tumble of rocks. He spoke seriously and at some length, gesticulating, pointing, emphatic.

He grumbled something again and called to some women standing nearby. He gave orders to a group of warriors. Then he signalled that we should follow him as, still sour-faced, he walked grudgingly towards the big lodge.

"The talking lodge," said Klosterheim, and with a crooked grimace, "their town hall."

Gunnar and I followed Klosterheim and his friend towards the talking lodge. I gathered we were to prepare our assault on the City of Gold. Our weapons were left in the safe-keeping of our men. Their own war-tools were so superior, they had little to fear from any "skraylings."

Nonetheless I entered the shaman's lodge with a rather uneasy sense of privilege.

12

The Vision in the Lodge

Ask me not my name or nation,
Ask me not my past or station,
But stay and listen to my story
Listen to my mystic calling
How I saw my path unrolling,
How I dreamed my dream of patience,
Dreamed how all might work together
Make their laws and peace together
Make their lodges one great cover,
And a mighty people fashion
Who will walk and seek with passion
Seek the justice of the mountains
Seek the wisdom of the forests
Seek the vision of the deserts
Then bring all this learning home.

Then we light the redstone peace pipe,
Pass the pipe that makes the peace talk,
Lets us speak of valorous virtue.
Pass the red bowled, smoking spirit
Declaim our noble deeds and dreams.
Let speakers see themselves in others,
Let listeners listen to their brothers,
Listen to sisters and their mothers,
To the dwellers in the forest
And the spirits of the sky.

Our tales are strong and live forever
Tales of luck and skill and cunning
When the White Hare she came running,
When the cackling Crow was flying,
When the Great Black Bear was charging,
When in War we faced our foes.
Speak to all, for all are brothers,
Speak of deeds and dreams of valour,
Breathe the smoke that soothes the soul.

—W.S. Harte,
The Hobowakan

It was already very hot inside the large lodge, and it took a while for my some-what weak eyes to clear. Slowly I made out a central charcoal fire around which were arranged rich piles of animal hides. On the far side of the fire was a larger heap of furs. Those had a white skin thrown over them. I guessed this to be Ipkaptam's seat. Willow branches had been woven around it to make a kind of throne. I did not recognise several of the pelts used. Some must come from indigenous beasts. The air was thick with various herbal scents. A smouldering fire in which several round rocks were heated gave off heavy smoke, sluggishly rising to the top of the tepee. A strong smell of curing hides, of animal fat and what might have been wet fur permeated the room. I was also reminded of the smell of worked iron.

I asked Klosterheim the purpose of this discomfort. He assured me that I would find the experience engrossing and illuminating. Gunnar complained that if he had known it was going to be this sort of thing he would have hacked co-operation out of the bastards. Recognising his tone, Ipkaptam smiled secretly. For a moment his knowing eyes met mine.

Once inside, the flaps of the lodge were tied tight, and the heat began to rise considerably. Knowing my tendency to lose my senses in such temperatures, I did my best to keep control, but I was already feeling a little dizzy.

Klosterheim was on my left, Gunnar on my right and the Pukawatchi shaman directly ahead of me. We made a very strange gathering in that buffalohide wigwam. The lodgepoles were strung with all kinds of dried vermin and evil-smelling herbs. While I had known far worse ways of seeking wisdom in the dreamworlds, I have known better-scented ones. Yet I was struck by a strong sense of familiarity. My brain would not or could not recall where I had experienced a similar conference. Decorated as he now was with a white feather crown, turquoise and malachite necklaces and copper armbands, together with his medicine bag and its contents, Ipkaptam looked even more striking. He reminded me vaguely of the old Grandparents, the gods who had talked to me in the Devil's Garden. I tried desperately to remember what they had told me. Would it be of use here?

The shaman produced a big, shallow drum. He beat on it with long, slow, regular strokes. From deep within his chest, a song grew. The song was not for us to hear but for the spirits who would help him in performing this séance. Half its words and cadences were outside the range of even my own rather sensitive ears.

Klosterheim leaned forward over the fire to splash water on the heated stones. They hissed and steamed, and Ipkaptam's chanting grew louder. I struggled to keep my breathing deep and regular. The scar on his face, which I had seen as an irregular wound, now took on shape. Another face lurked beneath the first, something baleful and insectlike. I tried to remember what I knew. I felt nauseated and dizzy. Were the Pukawatchi human? Or did their race merely take on human characteristics? According to Klosterheim such ambiguous creatures were quite common here.

As I came close to losing consciousness, I was alerted by Klosterheim's changing voice. He sounded like a monk. He was chanting in Greek, telling the tale of the Pukawatchi and their treasures. He threw fuel on the fire, blowing until the stones were red-hot and then splashing on more water. The fire danced up again, casting shadows, increasing the heat until it was impossible to think clearly. All my energies were largely devoted to remaining conscious.

The beating drum, the rhythmic chanting, the strange words, all began to take me over. I was losing control of my own will. It was not pleasant to feel that somewhere I had experienced all this before, yet I was also somewhat heartened by the thought. I hoped a higher purpose was being served by my discomfort.

During my youthful training I had been absorbed into many such rituals. I, therefore, made no particular effort to hold on to individual identity but let myself be drawn into the dark security of the heat and the shadows, the chanting and the drumming. I say security because it is like a kind of death. All worldly and material cares begin to disappear. One is confronted with one's own cruelties and appetites, experienced as a victim might experience them. There is remorse and self-forgiveness, an incisive glance into the reality of one's own soul, as if we stand in judgement on ourselves. This creates a peculiar psychic spiral in which one is redeemed or reborn into a kind of purity of being, a state which enables one to be open to the visions or revelations which are almost always the result of such formalities.

Apologising to us that he no longer possessed the tribe's traditional redstone pipe bowl, Ipkaptam produced a large ceremonial pipe and lit it with a taper from the fire. He turned to the four points of the compass, beginning in the east, chanting something I could not understand, puffing the smoke as he did so. He held the pipe aloft. Again he chanted and puffed. Then he passed the pipe to Klosterheim, who knew what to do with it.

Now Ipkaptam began to speak of the tribe's great past. In rolling tones he described the Great Spirit's creation of his people deep below the ground. The very first people had been made of stone, and they were slow and sleepy. They had in turn made men to run their errands for them, and then made giants to protect them against rebellion. The men ran away from the giants to another land, which was the land of the Pukawatchi.

The smaller Pukawatchi were too weak to fight so many; thus they fled under ground. The giants had not pursued the men. The tall men had not pursued the Pukawatchi, and soon they were at one with men and giants.

All had been equal, and all had gifts the others could use. Warmed in the womb of Mother Earth herself, they had no need of fire. Food was plentiful. They were at peace. Every year the great Eternal Pipe, the redstone smoking bowl of the Pukawatchi, which they had won in war against the green people, was produced and presented to the Spirit. The pipe was smoked by every tribe and every people in creation. It was always full of the finest herbs and aromatic bark, and it never needed to be lit. Even the bear people and the badger people and the eagle people and all the other peoples of the plains and forests and mountains were invited to the great pow-wow, to confirm their bond. All lived in mutual harmony and respect. Only in the world of spirits was there conflict, and their wars did not touch on the lands of the Pukawatchi, nor of the tall men, nor of the giants.

I realised I was no longer hearing Klosterheim's Greek but Ipkaptam's own language in his own voice. Ipkaptam easily made the mental links necessary for me to understand their language. At last the words had found their way directly to my mind.

With the words came pictures and narratives, crowding one upon the other. All were sufficiently familiar. I absorbed and understood them quickly. I was learning the whole history of a people, its rise and fall and rise again. I was hearing its own legends. Would I learn about a lost sword with a habit of escaping or killing those who possessed it?

More water was poured on the stones. The pipe was passed again and again. As I learned to inhale its strange smoke, my sense of reality grew even dimmer.

Ipkaptam's insectoid features seemed those of a great ant and his crown of feathers antennae. I refused to lose either my life or my sanity. I pretended his disguise was all that was visible to me. I remembered the teachings of a people I had lived among briefly, who spoke of a god they called the Original Insect. He was supposed to be the first created being. A locust. The story was told how the locust could not eat, so the spirits made it a forest where it might graze. But the locust was so hungry he ate the whole forest, and now he cannot do anything else. Unless stopped, he will attempt to eat the whole world and then eat himself.

I found nothing sinister in the tale the shaman told of his people's history. Perhaps there *was* nothing sinister in the tale itself, only in the teller. What Two Tongues had learned might not have been from his fathers. Nonetheless, I listened.

The steam and the smoke continued to make me very faint. My heart sank when the great red sandstone peace pipe was passed again. Once more it was offered to the spirits of the four winds. Klosterheim took a small, mean puff and passed it to me. I inhaled the fragrant barks and leaves and came suddenly alive. It was as if the smoke curled through every vein and bone in my body, inhabiting all of me and filling me with a sense of well-being, leaving none of the effects of my usual desperate drug-supported state. Those drugs fed off my spirit as I fed off their energy. These were natural plants, dried but not cured. I felt as if I inhaled all nature's benefits in one long pull on the pipe. I was hugely invigorated.

Ipkaptam took back the pipe with reverence. Again he offered it to the sky, then to the earth, then to the four winds, and only then replaced it on the stone before him. His widening lizard eyes glowed huge in the firelight.

"Many times," he said, "the spirits tried to involve us in their wars. We would fight neither for one side nor the other. These were not our wars. We did not even have the means to fight them. We did not have the will to kill our fellows." He seemed to grow in stature as he spoke with reminiscent pride. "Once all peoples, giants and men, came peacefully to trade with the Pukawatchi in their underground realm. We traded the metal we chipped from the rocks. With this metal the whole world tipped its arrows and lances and made fine ornaments." Iron was more highly prized than gold, said Ipkaptam, for with iron a man might win himself gold, but with gold he was always vulnerable to the man with iron. Metal was even more highly prized than agate and quartz for the edge it would take.

Men were cunning, had fire, but they did not know where to look for the metals and stones. Their tools and ornaments, their weapons, were made of flint and bone, so they traded furs and cooked meat for the Pukawatchi iron. Giants had sorcerous powers and ancient wisdom, for they were the folk of the rock. They had the secret of fire, and they knew how to burn metal and twist it into shapes. All had to come to the Pukawatchi for their metal, and the most prized of all the metals was the sentient iron mined at the heart of the world.

The Pukawatchi were small and clever. They could find the crevices where the metals and the precious stones lay and prise them out. They had the patience to mine them and the patience to work them. They made hammers and other tools strong enough to flatten the iron, the copper, the gold. Striking them over and over again, they made beautiful objects and impressive weapons.

They lived in their great, dark realm for untold aeons until massive upheavals occurred below the ground and all around them people went to war. The Pukawatchi were forced to the surface. Terrified of the sun, they became night dwellers, hiding from all other peoples and keeping their own counsel. Sometimes they were forced to steal food from villages they found. At other times the villages left food for them, and they in turn repaired pots and the like.

So the Pukawatchi wandered until they came to a place far from the lands of other men. Here they built their first great city. Now they were no longer brothers with their fellows. Now all were at war. Yet the Pukawatchi brought their skills with them when they fled, and they still had knowledge of the earth and what was to be found there. After a while they built a great city deep into the rock face of the land they had reached. The city was fashioned like the dark tunnels and chambers they had known below the ground. Now it was above the ground, but inside it was as it had always been. And the people were safe and the people prospered, living in their cool, dark cities. At last, against all sane instinct, against the very will of the spirits, they began to work with fire.

Soon the giants heard that the Pukawatchi had survived and could be traded with. The Pukawatchi learned the secret of fire and began to deal again with everyone except the spirits, who remained mindlessly at war. The war spread to men. The Pukawatchi made weapons for all peoples and grew rich as a result. The men were exhausted by war. The Pukawatchi cities had prospered and pro-liferated until the whole of the south and west became their empire.

The Pukawatchi grew rich with all things men valued. They had extended their rule further and further across the surface—the Realm of Light, as they called it. They conquered other tribes and made them subject to the Pukawatchi, and in the conquering they won great treasures, among them the famous Four Treasures of the Pukawatchi.

Each treasure had been won by a different hero, then lost in a series of complicated epics, then won again. All these stories were told to us in such a way that we absorbed them as we sat smoking and sweating in the lodge, our ordinary human senses completely lost to us.

The Four Treasures of the Pukawatchi were the Shield of Flight, the Lance of Invulnerability, the Perpetual Peace Pipe which never required filling, and the Flute of Reason, which, if the right three notes were played upon it, could restore a mortally wounded creature to life.

These treasures they kept in their city, deep within the complex of caves, in chambers they had hewn and elaborately decorated from the living rock. Pukawat-chi cities could be defended easily against attack by abandoning the lower levels and defending the upper. No other tribe had ever defeated the Pukawatchi, who had gloried in their treasures, celebrating them each year with the stories of how they came to be won by the heroes of the tribe in deeds of extraordinary warfare.

Ipkaptam began to draw in the air. He painted pictures there for us to see. He showed us the perpetually filled redstone pipe, which had belonged to the green people who lived along the lakes in stilt huts and who refused to pay the Pukawatchi a tribute of fish. So the Pukawatchi hero Nagtani went against the green people and destroyed their villages and took their pipe as a trophy. The green people were driven from the land.

Next the Kakatanawa, far in the north, asked the Pukawatchi to fashion a great lance of magical iron which the Kakatanawa had cut from the mother metal. This was the first great treasure of the Pukawatchi, for they had made it themselves. The Kakatanawa sent the magic metal to be made into a lance, but they refused to pay the higher price the Pukawatchi asked. The blade was more valuable, so the Pukawatchi kept it.

He showed us a vision of the lance, its shaft carved and decorated, its black blade running with scarlet letters. I was shocked. It was my sword, but turned into a spear! Then he showed us the Flute of Reason, and it seemed to me that Klosterheim responded with surprised recognition. I, too, experienced a flash of memory. And then Two Tongues showed us the Shield of Flight, the shield which allowed its owner to travel through the air. It was identical to the one I carried. I knew that the stolen artefact was only a few hundred yards from us at most, in the safe-keeping of Asolingas.

Ipkaptam continued. "All these were our treasures and our history. Then White Crow came, and he was smiling. White Crow came, and he told us he was our friend. White Crow promised to teach us all his secrets and because he did not seem a Kakatanawa and therefore not our enemy, we accepted him. His medicine was brought to us, and he was our good luck. Because he was not of our people, he could not take a wife among us, but he had many friends in the great men of our tribe, and their daughters admired him. Our people welcomed him, for he said he came only to learn our wisdom. We understood that he followed his dream-journey, and we wished him well.

"And White Crow went away. We said: It is true. White Crow desires nothing from us. He is a good man. He is a noble man. He is a man who follows his way. He runs his own path. And we said that some great man was lucky indeed to have such a son.

"Then the next year and the year after that, White Crow returned. And still he was a model guest. He helped with the hunting, and he lived among us. What was difficult for us to do was easy for him. His strength and his height and his cleverness were such that we were glad of his company.

"Then the fourth spring White Crow came again and was welcome among us and shared our food and lived in our city and told tales of all the places he had visited. But this time he asked to see our sacred treasures, the Black Lance of Manawata, the only spear which can kill spirits; the Shield of the Alkonka, the only defence against the spirits; the Cherooki Pipe, the great redstone pipe which brings peace wherever it is smoked, even with the spirits. And the Flute of Ayanawatta, which, if the right notes are blown on it, will confer on the owner the power to change his ordained spirit path, even from death to life. It will heal the sick and bring harmony where there is strife.

"And White Crow tricked us and stole our treasures and took them away with him. An evil spirit seized him. He journeyed to the great wilderness, where there are no trees. There, at the foot of the mountains, White Crow called a great gathering of the Winds. He planned to make the Winds his friends. So he called to the South Wind. And the South Wind came. He called to the West Wind. And the West Wind came to his calling. And to each spirit of the wind he gave a gift to take back to their people. Even before we knew he had stolen them, he had given the Perpetual Pipe to the People of the South; the Shield of Flight he gave to the People of the West. He himself took the Flute of Reason to the People of the East. And each of them gave him a gift in return.

"Now he has set violent events in motion. There are prophecies, omens, portents. It is the end or the beginning for the Pukawatchi. So much is confused. But there is hope that we can recover our treasures. To the Kakatanawa themselves in the north, White Crow planned to carry the Black Lance. They are his most powerful friends, and his folk have always been allies of their folk, since the beginning of things. His people also made their great obscene pact with the Phoorn and so began the rule of ten thousand years. But if White Crow fails to take the Black Lance back to the Kakatanawa, then all our destinies can be changed. Thus we do everything we can to stop him and his allies. Already they stand on the final part of the path to the city of the Kakatanawa . . ."

"Where," Klosterheim told us, in more normal tones, "our magic defeats them. White Crow is prisoner, but his brother and sister carry the lance. We must stop them! They are held captive on the Shining Path by a great ally of mine, who makes it impossible for them to continue on the last part of the Shining Path. Time does not pass there. They are unaware of it, but they have remained under that spell for half a century, allowing us to grow strong again. They have tried all their sorcery against my ally, but he is too powerful for them. Only White Crow escaped, but I was too clever for him. Yet even my pact with Lord Shoashooan is finite, and that busy elemental will soon grow hungry. He must have his promised reward. So we must reach Kakatanawa as soon as possible. Alone we might not defeat White Crow and his talented friends, but together we will make their end inevitable."

"What of your other lost treasures?" I said. "How will you get those back?"

"It will be easier once we have the Black Lance," said Klosterheim. He added softly to me in Greek, "The treasures of the Pukawatchi are as nothing to the prize to be found in the city of the Kakatanawa."

"I am only interested in one damned treasure," said Gunnar, to Ipkaptam's disapproval. "And that's a jewelled cup I've been seeking for some centuries. Failing that, I have some business with Death."

I had sudden insight. "You call it the Holy Grail! The Templars were obsessed with it. Supposed to contain some god's blood or head? The Welsh also have a magic bowl. My erstwhile comrade Ap Kwelch told me he once discovered it. There are too many of these magic objects loose in a world so ambivalent towards sorcery! Your learned priests say it's a myth, a will-o'-the-wisp?"

"I know that it is not, sir," said Klosterheim disapprovingly. "There are many legends but only one Grail. And that is what I expect to find in Kakatanawa."

Again the shaman was singing. He sang to apologise for our behaviour to whatever spirits he had summoned. As we became quiet he spoke of his own destiny, the dream he had dreamed in his youth: to revenge his grandfather, who had died in the summoning of Lord Shoashooan. In that dream he had sought his people's treasures and he had led his people home.

"That is my destiny," he said. "To redeem my father's house. To reclaim our treasures and our honour. For too long we have followed a false dream."

13

The Trail of Honour

I am the God Thor,
I am the War God,
I am the Thunderer!
Here in my Northland,
My fastness and fortress,
Reign I forever!

Here amid icebergs
Rule I the nations.
This is my hammer,
Mjolner the mighty.
Giants and sorcerers
Cannot withstand it!

—Longfellow,
The Saga of King Olaf

Behold, this pipe. Verily a man!
Within it I have placed my being.
Place within it your own being, also,
Then free shall you be from all that brings death.

—Osage Pipe Chant
(La Flesche's tr.)

Gunnar the Doomed was in good spirits as we stumbled from the heat of the lodge out into the cold slap of a northern autumn evening. "By Odin," he said, "we are lucky men this day!" But I hardly heard him. I was still stupefied by the smoke and the heat of the lodge. I felt I was on the verge of understanding some great truth.

I looked up and almost reeled at the sight which met us. It took me a moment to realise that the Pukawatchi were decorated for battle. They looked like a hive of human-sized insects. They buzzed faintly. In all my travels I had never seen a people quite like this.

A sudden wilder buzzing—an ululation went up from the gathered warriors. Layers of different-coloured paint in this light gave their faces the same quality I had noticed in that of their sachem, Ipkaptam the Two Tongues, as we sat in the lodge. Their eery, insectlike quality was given further substance by a translucent black sheen which spread over the surface of the other colours. They had the dark iridescence of a beetle's wing. Some wore insectlike headdresses. The black overlay was symbolic. It meant they were prepared to fight to the death. The red-rimmed eyes announced they would show no mercy. Ipkaptam told me with some pride that they had named their path the Trail of Honour and would return with the nation's treasures or die nobly in the attempt.

Again something nagged at the million memories which shadowed those of my immediate incarnation. Who did these people remind me of? Was there a Melnibonéan folktale I had read? About machines become fish who became insects who became human? Who had followed a Trail of Honour to establish a city in the south? I was unsure of all I could recall. With somewhat sentimental notions of intelligence, sensibility and virtue, the story did not feel like a Melnibonéan tale. Perhaps I had heard it in the Young Kingdoms or in another dream of baroque life and rococo death spent in a realm far less familiar to me than this?

In my youth I performed the five journeys and dreamed the Dream of Twenty Years, then the Dream of Fifty Years and then the Dream of a Hundred Years. Each of those dreams I had to dream at least three times. I had dreamed some several more times than that. But this was only the second time I had dreamed the Dream of a Thousand Years, and this was no longer the quest of an education but the hope of saving my own life, and that of most of surviving humanity, from unchecked Chaos.

Perhaps this moment was what one trained for? It seemed I was born and reborn for crisis. It was what the nun had told me at the Priory of the Sacred Egg in the Dalmatian highlands. She had read my fortune that night in the light of a tallow candle while we sat naked in the bed. Fetching the cards had been her response, as passion was satisfied, to her first real sight of my physique, of its scars and marks. She asked in some seriousness if she had shared herself with a demon. I told her that I had been a mercenary for some time. "Then perhaps you yourself have slept with a demon," she joked.

Fear the Crisis Maker, she had warned, by which I had decided she meant that I should fear myself. What was worse in a fully sentient universe than one who refused thought, who feared it, who was sickened by it? Who inevitably chose violence and the way of the sword, though he yearned for peace and tranquillity?

Fear the child, she had said. Again, the child was myself—jealous, greedy, demanding, selfish. Why should her God choose such a man for his service?

I had asked the matronly prioress this question, and she had laughed at me. All soldiers she met seemed to be soul-searching in one way or another. She supposed it was inevitable. "In some eras," she said, "the sword and the intellect must be as one. Those are our Silver Ages. That is how we create those periods we call Golden Ages, when the sword can be forgotten. But until the sword is fully forgotten, no longer part of the cycle, and men no longer speak in its language of gods and heroes and battles, every Golden Age will inevitably be followed by an age of Iron and Blood." She had spoken of the Prince of Peace as if he might actually exist. I asked her about this. "He is my soul's salvation," she had said. I told her without irony that I envied her. But it was hard for me to understand the kind of man who was prepared to die on the chance that it might save others. In my experience, such sacrifices were rarely worth making. She had laughed aloud at this.

Her kind of Christianity, of course, was almost the apotheosis of what we Melnibonéans see as weakness. Yet I had also seen ideas growing from the common soil which, when examined, actually had the hope of becoming reality. It was not for me to denigrate their softness and their tolerance. My father frequently argued that where you exalted the weak above the strong, thus you turned your nation from predator into prey. However much the thinking of the Young Kingdoms influenced me, it had never occurred to me to choose to become a victim!

A Melnibonéan of my caste is expected to put himself through at least most of the tortures he will in the course of a long life bestow on others. This produces a taste, an intimacy, a conspiracy of cruelty which can give a culture its own special piquancy but in the end brings it to collapse. Imagination rather than inventive sensation will always be a nation's ultimate salvation. I had tried to convince my own people of this. And now the Pukawatchi faced a similar dilemma.

Indeed, as I came to know them, I discovered I had more in common with the Pukawatchi than with some of the crew of *The Swan*.

Preparations made, routes discussed, plans laid, we helped the Pukawatchi strike camp. Our somewhat ragged army slowly made ready for its long trek north. More pipes were smoked. More talks talked. The Vikings and the skraylings, as they still called their new allies, developed a reasonable camaraderie— good enough for the expedition, at least. Morally they shared much. The Pukawatchi understood the need to make a good death, just as the Vikings did. The warriors prayed for the right circumstances and the courage to display their virtues while they died.

These ideas were far closer to those of my immediate ancestors. Among the rest of what I still considered the Young Kingdoms, there had been developing a tradition which was as mysterious and as attractive to me as my own was familiar and repellent. It was that culture, not my own, I fought to save. It was those people whose fate would be decided by my success or failure in this long dream. I had no love for the millennia-old culture which had borne me. I rejected it more than once in preference to the simpler ways of the human mercenary. There was a certain comfort in taking this path. It demanded little thought from me.

There was some urgency to my situation, of course, as I hung in Jagreen Lern's rigging waiting to die. But there are no significant correspondences between the passage of time in one realm and another. I had elected, after all, to dream of a thousand years, and now the full thousand must be endured even if my object were achieved sooner. It is why I am able to tell you this story in this way. What I achieved in this dream would reflect through all the other worlds of the multiverse, including my own. How I conducted myself in this dream was of deep importance. A certain path had to be followed. When the trail was left it had to be left knowingly.

The path had already taken on a certain relentless momentum. From being a group of raiders or explorers, we were now an army on the march. Egyptians and Norsemen tramped side by side with the same extraordinary stamina they showed at the oars. Asolingas and the Bomendando jogged ahead with the Pukawatchi scouts.

Ipkaptam, Gunnar, Klosterheim and I marched at the centre of the main group. The Pukawatchi went to war in finger-bone armour, with lances, bows and shields. They had jackets of bone and helmets fashioned from huge mammoth tusks decorated with eagle feathers and beads. The bone armour was decorated with turquoise and other semi-precious stones and was lighter than the chainmail most of our crew favoured. Some warriors wore the carapaces of huge turtles and helmets made from massive conch shells. Braids were protected by beads and otter fur.

Just as I had noted the size of some of the huge pelts within the wigwam, I wondered at the size of the sea-life which supplied the Pukawatchi with so much. Klosterheim said somewhat dismissively that sizes were unstable in these parts, something to do with the conjunction of various scales. We were too close to "the tree," he said.

None of this made much sense to me. But as long as our journey took us forward to where I hoped to find the original of the Black Sword, I scarcely cared what rationales he presented.

We were now an army of about a hundred and fifty experienced warriors. Some of the women and youths and old people were also armed. At the far end of this mixed force of pirates and Pukawatchi came the unarmed women, the infirm, children and animals who would follow us until we began to fight. From what I had seen thus far, I expected the city to be a primitive affair, probably a stockade of some kind surrounding a dozen or so longhouses.

The Pukawatchi had no real beasts of burden, unless you counted their coyote dogs that pulled the travois on which they carried their folded lodges. Women and children did most of the work. The warriors rarely did anything except, like the rest of us, march at a steady, dogged pace. Those women who had what they called "men's medicine" dressed and armed themselves like the men and marched with the men, just as one or two of the men with "women's medicine" walked with the group at the back. Klosterheim told me such practices were common among many of the peoples of this vast land. But not all tribes shared values and ideas.

Ipkaptam, joining in, spoke of certain tribes who were beneath contempt, who ate insects or who tortured animals, but even those peoples they had exterminated he spoke well of, as people of honour. We Melnibonéans had never experienced noble feelings for people we sent to oblivion. Melnibonéans never questioned their own ruthless law, which they imposed on all they conquered. Other cultures were not of interest to us. If the people refused to accept our scheme of things, we simply slaughtered them. But we had become too soft, my father complained, looking always at me, and allowed the Young Kingdoms to grow arrogant. There had been a time when the world never dared question Melniboné. What we defined as the truth *was* the truth! But because it suited us to have fat cattle at our disposal, we allowed the people of the Young Kingdoms to proliferate and gain power.

Not so, the Pukawatchi! They believed in the law of the blood feud, so gave their enemies no chance to retaliate. Every member of the rival tribe had to be eliminated or the babies taken to substitute for any Pukawatchi killed. Once they had been so few they had stolen infants from stronger tribes. Now they needed no foreign babies.

Yesterday the Pukawatchi had been despised, said Ipkaptam, both for their stature and their intelligence. Today all took them seriously. Their story would survive. And when the Kakatanawa were conquered, the Pukawatchi would dominate all worlds. They had grown strong, he said, until they were the strongest of all.

They were certainly sturdy. When walking and water were the only two means of travelling long distances, the calves and the arms became capable of enormous endurance and power. Their means of transport ensured them success in battle.

The Pukawatchi would have preferred the greater speed of water, but we were moving north and upstream of a small river which was too narrow to take any kind of craft. Klosterheim said there was a mooring rendezvous about two days ahead of us where we would acquire canoes so that the war party could make better progress. He seemed to have a greater sense of urgency than the rest of us. Of course, it was his magic, his energy, which was holding our rivals at bay. He suggested that soon the army should move on at a trot to the rendezvous, leaving the armed women and children with a small guard of warriors. I elected to command this guard. The idea of trotting did not appeal to me.

For the time being, we all continued at our regular pace.

Again I was impressed by the size to which everything in the region grew. Plants were far larger than anything I had seen before. I should have liked to have stopped and examined more. The terrain we were crossing was wooded and mountainous, and we travelled through a series of valleys, still following the winding course of the river, as we drove deeper and deeper into country nobody was familiar with. It had been deserted of people, Ipkaptam told me, since a great disaster had struck here. He believed that the whole country around the Kakatanawa land was dead, like this. As you got closer, even the game began to disappear. But he had only heard this.

Before the beginnings of this war, no Pukawatchi had ever been allowed to cross the human lands, let alone visit the land of the Kakatanawa. They had come east in his grandfather's time. Equally, the Kakatanawa were forbidden to leave their own land. Until recently they, too, had kept to their pact. But others, such as the Phoorn, had done their work for them. Some of these Phoorn adopted human form and bore a resemblance to me, though my physique was different. Others were monstrous reptiles. Now that he knew me, said the sachem, he realised I was more like a Pukawatchi, yet it was still difficult, he said, to trust me. His instinct was to kill me. He could not be sure this was my natural form.

The Pukawatchi had never been this far north, and Ipkaptam worried that he did wrong. But wrongdoing had become the order of the day. Once the people of the south, north, west and east had respected one another's laws and hunting grounds. They had a saying: The West Wind does not fight the East Wind. But since White Crow had come to the world, Chaos threatened on all sides. In their fighting the Lords of the Air produced the hawk-winds which destroyed whole peoples and created demons who ruled in their place. These demons were called Sho-ah Sho-an and could only be defeated by the lost Pukawatchi treasures.

Ipkaptam also admitted that he was nervous of being sucked off the back of the world. At some point you must tumble into the bottomless void, fall for ever, eternally living the sharp, despairing moment when you realise your death is inevitable. Far better to die the warrior's death. The clean death, as some called it. To Pukawatchi and Viking alike a noble death remained more important than longevity. Those who died bravely and with their death songs on their lips could live the simple, joyous warrior's life for eternity.

My own responses to these notions were rather more complex. I shared their idea that it was better to make a noble death than lead an ignoble life. There was not one among us, save Klosterheim, who did not think that. The Ashanti, the Mongols, the Norsemen knew the indignities and humiliations of old age and preferred to avoid them, just as a promise of inevitable defeat made them anxious to take as many of their enemies with them as they could.

The Pukawatchi, so provincially self-important and so certain of their imperial rights, had a shared sense of afterlife which favoured those who had died bloody deaths and sent as many others as possible to equally bloody deaths. The fate of women and children in these cosmologies was vague, but I suspect the women had their own more favourable versions which they told among themselves. For all their domestic power, they were more frequently the unwilling victims of the warrior code. Certain warriors prided themselves on their skill at dispatching women and children as painlessly as possible.

As we began to speak the same language I learned more about the skraylings, as Gunnar still insisted on calling them. The supernatural understanding of these natives was sophisticated, though their powers of sorcery were limited and usually restricted to needs of planting and hunting. Only the great line of shamans, of whom Ipkaptam was the latest, understood and explored the world of the spirits. This was where he drew his power.

Ipkaptam's was not an especially popular family. They had often abused their privileges. But the Pukawatchi believed in the family's famous luck. When that luck failed, I suspected, Ipkaptam would no longer be revered, tolerated or perhaps even alive.

Gunnar walked by himself much of the way. Few sought him out. The Pukawatchi suspected him to be some kind of minor demon. They displayed an instinctive dislike of me as well. Some were still convinced I was a renegade Kakatanawa.

Our alliance could break down at any moment. Gunnar and Klosterheim had common goals, but there would come a day when they would be at odds. Equally, no doubt, Gunnar was scheming how he would dispatch me when I had served my turn. Like my late cousin Yyrkoon, Gunnar spent a great deal of time planning how to gain the upper hand. Those of us who did not think competitively were always surprised by those who did. For my own part I responded with appropriate cunning or ferocity to whatever situation I found myself in. When one has had the training of a Melnibonéan adept, one rarely needs to anticipate another's actions. Or so I thought. Such thinking might well have led to our extinction as a people.

Yet Gunnar's weakness was also typical, as he believed me to be scheming as hard as he was. This might have been true of Klosterheim and Ipkaptam, but it was certainly not true of me. I was still prepared to believe that I could easily be following a chimera. The black blade's maker was my only interest.

The Vikings remained fairly cheerful. They had seen enough to know that there might be a city somewhere which could be looted, even if it was not made of gold. They knew the superiority of their iron weapons and had a fair idea of the way back to the sea and their ship. They probably believed a longer sailing would avoid the more terrifying aspects of the journey here. So most of them saw this as a standard inland expedition from which they might emerge with wealth and knowledge. They knew the value of the Pukawatchi furs and quickly understood how the Pukawatchi valued iron. The only iron the Pukawatchi worked was moon metal or ingots chipped from the rock. Somehow they had lost their legendary power to mine and smelt metal. As a result, a small iron dagger would buy a lot of valuable furs.

In my company, at least, the Vikings also had the sense that they carried secret power. I was surprised that my shield, the Pukawatchi stolen Shield of Flight tight under its cover, had not been sensed by their shaman, seemingly so sensitive to the supernatural. It remained to be seen whether it would give the gift of flight to anyone who carried it or whether spells and chants were involved to invoke the spirits associated with the shield.

Experience shows most magic objects depend far more upon the gullibility of the purchaser than on any blessing by the spirits. The shield could have no particular properties at all, except those of superstition and antiquity. How

Gunnar found it in Europe, he refused to explain, but I had the impression he had come by it in trade some while ago, perhaps from one of the People of the West to whom, Ipkaptam said, it had been given. But here the People of the West would live far away from the sea, unless we were on a large island. If we were on an island, then it was possible the People of the West had somehow sailed around the rim of the world, as Gunnar would have it, from the China Seas, as he himself had done with the Rose. Or was this a treasure Gunnar had brought back from the expedition they made, when he had returned in *The Swan* while the Barbary Rose captained her own twin-prowed ship, *The Either/Or*?

There was some dispute among us as to whether we should make the quick march at all or keep to our present pace, so that we remained together. Klosterheim spoke of the gathering winter. It was becoming noticeably colder by the day. We were marching north. Normally, both Pukawatchi and Vikings reserved raiding expeditions for the spring. Winter made movement almost impossible. Ice would form on the rivers soon, and they would not be able to use the canoes.

So we called a further conference. Eventually it was decided that the two Ashanti, Asolingas and the Bomendando, who were our fastest runners, together with a Pukawatchi called Nagatche, would go ahead for a few miles to get the lie of the land. Then we could make a better-informed decision.

The three runners set off as the evening sky grew black overhead. An east wind began to blow steadily, biting through layers of clothing. I felt the lash of sleet against my cheeks.

Night fell. Ipkaptam, Klosterheim, Earl Gunnar and I again conferred around an uncertain fire in a small temporary lodge. Ipkaptam believed that the season was coming unusually early. He would have expected another month before the snows arrived. Again he spoke anxiously about offending the winds. It would be best to reach the water as soon as possible. With snow, our journey to Kakatanawa would be far more difficult. With ice it might be impossible, and we would have to wait until the next year. He turned to Klosterheim for suggestions. Were there any other magical allies he could summon? Was there some way to placate the wind so that it blew the snow away from them? What if he were to offer the Snow Wind his most valuable possessions? His children's lives?

Klosterheim pointed out in Greek that most of his powers were already being used to sustain his supernatural ally Lord Shoashooan threatening our enemies. He had only been able to summon the demon in the first place because of the strange nature of this realm's semi-sentient winds, which Ipkaptam had already remarked on. It was even possible that Lord Shoashooan was drawing the bad weather to them. But if White Crow was allowed to take the Black Lance back to Kakatanawa, then the Pukawatchi would never defeat their ancient enemies, never redeem their honour. As for summoning powerful spirits, that was now entirely beyond him. With all his experience of the supernatural, he had never been able to control two such forces. Gunnar mumbled something about having made too many bargains already and said he was thinking on the problem. I—whose powers were virtually non-existent here, but needed fewer drugs and sorcery to survive—was equally helpless.

"Then we must do our best with our natural brains," said Klosterheim with some humour.

The next morning one of the Ashanti returned. The Bomendando was glad of the camp. He stood by the fire shivering, his lanky body wrapped in a buffalo robe. He was uneasy and seemed frightened. He said he had left the other two guarding their find while he came to tell us what it was. They also would return if it became too dangerous. They had remained in case they should catch a glimpse of what they guessed was occupying the hills.

I had never seen such a disturbed look on the Bomendando's face. Clearly, he thought he might not be believed.

"Come on, man," demanded Gunnar, reaching a threatening hand toward him. "What have you seen out there?"

"It's a footprint," said the Bomendando. "A footprint."

"So there are other men here. How many?"

"This was not a man's footprint." The Bomendando shivered. "It was fresh, and we found others, fainter, when we looked. It is the footprint of a giant. We are in the realm of the giants, Earl Gunnar. This was not part of our agreement. You told us nothing of giants, nothing of the Stone Men. You spoke only of a poorly defended city. You said how the giants had been driven from this land by men and halflings. You said giants were forbidden to go outside their city. Why did you not tell us of these other giants? These roaming giants?"

"Giants!" Gunnar was contemptuous. "A trick of the eye. The track had spread, that was all. I've heard tales of giants all my life and have yet to see one."

But the Bomendando shook his head. He held out his spear. With his hand he measured off another half-length again. "It was that wide and more than twice as long. A giant."

Ipkaptam became agitated. "They are not supposed to leave their city. They cannot leave it. They are forbidden. The giants have always guarded what they are sworn to guard. If they left, the world would end. It must have been a human you saw."

The Ashanti was adamant, tired of talk. "There is a giant out there, in those hills," he said. "And where there is one giant, there are often others."

There came a shout from the margins of the camp. Warriors ran towards us, pointing over their shoulders.

In the slanting sleet I saw a figure emerging. He was indeed very tall and broad. My head would scarcely have reached his chest, but he was a third the size of any giants I had previously encountered.

He was dressed in a heavy black coat, covered by a fur-lined cloak. On his head was an oddly shaped hat, its brim turned up at three corners, sporting a couple of plumes. His white hair was tied back with a loose, black bow.

I heard Klosterheim curse behind me.

"Is that our giant?" I asked.

Ipkaptam was shaking his head. "That's no giant," he said. "That's a human."

The newcomer took off his hat by way of a peace sign. "Good evening, gentlemen," he said, "my name is Lobkowitz. I was travelling in these parts and seem to have lost my way. Is there any chance, do you think, that I could warm my bones a little at your fire?"

He loomed over us, almost as tall as our tepees. I felt like a ten-year-old boy in the presence of a very burly man.

Klosterheim came forward and bowed. "Good evening, Prince Lobkowitz," he said. "I had not expected to see you here."

"It's a turning multiverse, my dear captain." The broad-faced, genial nobleman peered hard at Klosterheim. He frowned in apparent surprise. "Forgive me if I seem rude," he said, "but is it my impression, sir, or have you shrunk a foot or two since last we met?"

14

The Gentleman at Large

But the mischievous Puk-Wudjies,
They the envious Little People,
They the fairies and the pygmies,
Plotted and conspired against him.
"If this hateful Kwasind," said they,
"If this great, outrageous fellow
Goes on thus a little longer,
Tearing everything he touches,
Rending everything to pieces,
Filling all the world with wonder,
What becomes of the Puk-Wudjies?
Who will care for the Puk-Wudjies,
He will tread us down like mushrooms,
Drive us all into the water,
Give our bodies to be eaten,
By the wicked Nee-ba-naw-baigs,
By the Spirits of the Water!"

—Longfellow,
The Song of Hiawatha

Klosterheim and Lobkowitz had been acquainted in Christendom. They were not friends. Klosterheim was deeply suspicious of every word the newcomer uttered. Lobkowitz, while more affable, seemed equally wary of Klosterheim.

Gunnar said something about two peoples forever at odds. He believed the races must be natural enemies.

As Prince Lobkowitz stood with his back to our fire, Gunnar asked him what brought him to the region.

"Very little, sir. My business was with another party, but you know how it is, this close to a node on the great tree of time. Although it makes travel between the worlds a little easier, it also makes it confusing. Variances of scale, which would be so vast as to be unnoticed elsewhere, are not so great here. The closer to where worlds connect, the less we are, as it were, divided. We do our best, sir; but the Balance must be served, and the Balance determines everything in the end, eh?" The huge fellow had a rather quiet manner. It seemed odd to find delicacy in one of his size.

His apparent diffidence put a swagger into Gunnar the Doomed. He was the only one of us to be amused. "My men described your footprint. To hear them talk you were at least ten feet tall, though I must admit you're the biggest human being I've ever met. You're even bigger than Angris the Frank, and he is still a legend. Are they all your size where you come from?"

"Pretty much," said Prince Lobkowitz. Gunnar did not miss the sardonic tone. His faceless helm turned to regard the huge man with some curiosity. I, too, felt I was missing what might have been a joke.

The sleet continued to fall. It was not settling as snow. Ipkaptam decided it was too warm for bad snow, that what we had was no more than an autumn squall. In a couple of days it might even seem like summer again. He had experienced the phenomenon many times.

Now that we thought Lobkowitz was our giant, Ipkaptam was far more at ease. It was decided we would indeed send the main warriors ahead at a rapid trot while I would bring up the rear. Prince Lobkowitz, who knew the terrain no better than I did, elected to stay behind with us. "At least until it becomes possible to rejoin my party!"

While the prince went off to relieve himself, I was warned secretly by Gunnar to keep an eye on Lobkowitz and to kill him if he acted at all suspiciously. Klosterheim was especially uneasy. He said that the man was not necessarily malign but that his presence suggested there were other, possibly dangerous, elements involved in this adventure.

I asked him to be more specific. What did he know about Lobkowitz? Had the newcomer followed us here? Was he in league with the Kakatanawa?

"He has no more right to enter the Kakatanawa stronghold than I," said Klosterheim. "But he has friends who also seek what I seek and what Gunnar seeks. I believe he shares a mutual interest. It will do no harm to make an ally of him now. It's best he's kept in the rear, at least until we know what we are facing. He might be a spy, for instance, sent to learn our secrets. If not, we could use someone of his size."

Gunnar was unhappy. "There are too many unknown elements in this. My idea was to come here, take what I needed, and leave. I had not expected Klosterheim, the Pukawatchi—nor giants . . ."

"That man is not a giant," insisted Ipkaptam. "He is human. You would know if he was a giant."

With a scowl, Klosterheim agreed. "This is a strange area of the multiverse," he confirmed. "It is, as Lobkowitz says, a node. Where the branch joins the tree, eh? Usually we are too far away from a node to experience this phenomenon, but here I would guess it is common."

I accepted this oddness was familiar to them and trusted their judgement. Only Gunnar continued to be ill at ease. He kept muttering about superstition and repeating what was clearly a simplification if not a lie—that he was here for one reason only, and he had promised his fighters the loot of the City of Gold.

Ipkaptam signalled for Gunnar, Klosterheim and the others to follow and set off at a lope. The main war party fell in behind him, and all were soon lost in the mists of the deep valleys. I was glad to keep a slower pace. It gave me a chance to speak to the gigantic man, to ask him how he had found himself here. He said he was travelling with a friend and they had become separated. The next thing he knew, he said, he spotted our camp. His friend was clearly nowhere in the area.

"And is this friend similar in size to you?" I asked.

Prince Lobkowitz sighed. "These are not my natural surroundings, Prince Elric, any more than they are yours."

I agreed with some feeling that they were not mine. If I discovered I was on a wild-goose chase, then Gunnar should pay with interest for all my wasted hours. While I had once sought the seclusion and isolation of the countryside, nowadays I again preferred the alleys, the noisy streets and crowded public places of urban life. Nonetheless, events had curious resonances, I said. It made me think that perhaps this adventure had parallels with a life I could not quite remember.

As Ipkaptam predicted, the snow held off and the sleet continued to fall. The Pukawatchi boys and women were not loquacious. Lobkowitz and I were thrown together as a result. He was oddly close-mouthed on some subjects, and when I accused him, half joking, of talking like an oracle, he laughed loudly. "I think that's because I am talking like an oracle," he said.

He explained that this age was not his own. He was something of an interloper. But this realm, or one like it, was similar to his own past. As he was sure I understood, he did not dare inadvertently reveal anything of the future, yet he was constantly tempted to use his knowledge.

It was the reason, he said, for prophecies and omens to be so obscure. A directly related account of coming events automatically changed those events. Knowledge of them meant that some could act to avoid what they disliked. This not only made prophecy dangerous, it added to the multiplicity of the worlds. A few ill-judged words could create branch after branch of additional alternatives. It served no general purpose, he said. Few such branches survived for long.

I remembered the Stone Giants and their meaningless prophecies, but I said nothing to Lobkowitz, even though we were together, tending to walk behind the main party, following tracks the Pukawatchi and Vikings had made.

Then as we began to approach the foothills of the mountains, the sleet changed to snow. By the following morning it had settled and the sky had cleared. It was a blue day. Snow lay before us all the way to the mountains, and tracks were rare. Where a buffalo had passed, you could see immediately. Also hare and birds had used the land ahead, but of the Pukawatchi trail there was nothing.

Prince Lobkowitz seemed both amused by and sympathetic to this turn of events. He suggested that with his extra height he could go on ahead and see if he could find the Pukawatchi camp. Not entirely trusting him I said that we could travel together. That way I could stand on his shoulders, perhaps, and get a longer view. Thus we could make the best use of each other's relative size.

This seemed to amuse him even further. I said I thought my suggestion perfectly reasonable. He was recalling another event, he said, which had nothing to do with me directly, and he apologised.

He agreed; so we increased our pace. When the going became difficult for me, I was able to ride his mighty shoulder or otherwise make use of his unusual size and strength. It was the strangest riding I have ever done and was something of a change for me, though again I was troubled by vague memories of distant incarnations. Yet as far as I know I have always been Elric of Melniboné, for all that various seers and sorcerers insist otherwise. Some people relish the numinous the way others value the practical. I have had enough experience of the numinous to place great value on what is familiar and substantial.

When Lobkowitz raised the subject, I told him what I knew for certain. While I hung in some distant realm facing the death of everything I loved, I also dreamed the Dream of a Thousand Years, which had brought me here. He would probably think I was mad.

He did not. He said that he was familiar with such phenomena. Many he knew took them for granted. He had travelled widely, and there was little that was especially novel to him.

As it happened, we did not go far before the snow began to melt, revealing enough of a trail for our trackers to follow again. But a certain valuable camaraderie had developed between Prince Lobkowitz and myself. I had the impression he, too, had more in common with me than with the others, even Klosterheim. I asked him about that gaunt-faced individual.

"He is an eternal," Lobkowitz said, "but he is not reincarnated, simply reborn over and over again at the point of his death. This is a gift he received from his master. It is a terrible gift. His master is called in these realms 'Lucifer.' As I understand it, this Lord of the Lower Worlds has charged Klosterheim with finding the Holy Grail. This was the pivot, the regulator of the Great Balance itself. But Klosterheim also seeks some sort of alliance with the Grail's traditional guardian."

I asked who that was. He said that I was distantly related to the family who would become its guardians. The Grail had disappeared more than once, however, and when that happened, it must be sought wherever the path leads. The stolen artefact had a habit of disguising itself even from its protectors. He had never been directly involved in this Grail quest, he said—not, at any rate, as far as he could recall—but the quest continued through a multiplicity of pasts, presents and futures. He envied me, he said, my lack of memory. He was the second to make that remark. I told him with some feeling that if my condition was what he called a lack of memory, I was more than glad to have nothing else to remember. He made an apology of sorts.

Soon we reached the rendezvous with the rest of our party. They had little to report. The original owners of the canoes had fled, leaving most of their camp intact, so we spent a good night. In the morning we began to load the canoes when the blizzard hit us. It howled through the camp for hours, heaping up snow in huge banks. A wild east wind. By the time we were able to go out again, we found three feet of snow and ice already forming on the river. Up ahead the snow was bound to be thicker. We would either have to winter here or go on by foot. Ipkaptam said we could load the canoes and use them as sleds. That would keep the tribe together, as it would be foolish to leave the women and children. And so we set off, first carrying the canoes and then, as it became possible to drag them, pulling them behind us until we had reached the mountains proper. The sharp crags rose darkly above us, threatening the evening sky.

"They're evil-looking peaks," said Gunnar the Doomed, bending to pick up a handful of snow and rub it with relish into his neck. "But at least the weather's improving." I had forgotten how much Norsemen love snow. They yearn for it the way Moors yearn for rain.

Klosterheim pointed out the pass through the mountains. A dark gash ran between peaks glinting like black ice, probably basalt. Already the mountain-sides were heavy with snow, and more snow weighed down the pines and firs of the flanks. There was no moving water. Game was rarely seen. Occasionally I glimpsed a winter hare running across the snow, leaving black tracks in a white flurry. Hawks hung high in the sky, seeing no prey below. I do not think I had ever seen such a winter wasteland. In its own grandeur, its uncompromising bleakness, it was impressive. But unless some magical paradise lay within those mountains, protected from the weather, we were none of us likely to survive. All common sense told us to turn back while we could and spend the winter in more agreeable conditions.

Klosterheim and Gunnar were for going on. Ipkaptam pointed out that it would be stupid to continue. We would lose all our men and be no closer to what we sought. Prince Lobkowitz also advised prudence. I, who had the better part of a thousand years still to dream, said that I had no special thoughts, one way or another, but if Vikings could not survive a little cold weather, I would be surprised.

This spurred a general growling and posturing and, of course, we were on our way, leaving the weaker members of our band to keep camp if they could. If they could not, they were advised to rejoin the others and wait until we returned.

I do not know what happened to those Pukawatchi. It was the last I ever saw of them, the boys and the girls with their bows and lances, the women and old people giving us the sign of good journeying. Yet even as we left them behind, they still had something of the look of insects. I would never understand it.

I voiced my disquiet to Lobkowitz. He took me seriously. He said he believed they were in some kind of transition, and this was what gave them their insectlike appearance. Further generations might develop different characteristics. It would be interesting to see what they became. My guess was that most of these would soon be meat for the coyotes and bears. For all my aversion to their appearance, I felt a twinge of sympathy for them.

Ipkaptam's own wives and daughters were among those we left behind. He said that he had now given everything he valued most to the spirits, to use or treat as they wished. The spirits could be generous, but they always required payment.

My own instinctive belief, of course, was that the situation had driven him mad. All he could do now was go forward until he died or was killed. Or did Klosterheim have a special use for him?

I had a sense that the journey itself would require more sacrifice. Both Gunnar and Klosterheim swore that Kakatanawa was on the far side of the range. Once it was reached, the city was theirs for the taking. Klosterheim asked Prince Lobkowitz directly, "Do you want a share of the loot? You'd be useful to us because of your size. And we'd give you a full warrior's portion."

Lobkowitz said he would think over the proposition. Meanwhile he would march with us in the hope of catching a glimpse of his missing friend.

I asked him about the friend, whom I had gathered was of his size. Had they travelled here together?

Yes, he said. The situation demanded it. He added mysteriously that this was not what he had chosen. He had become disorientated. He would not forgive himself if he had to leave without his friend. He hoped they would find some sign of him in the mountains.

At last our mixed force of well-wrapped Pukawatchi and Vikings reached the opening of the pass. The sides, high and narrow, had the effect of keeping the worst of the weather out, and little snow had fallen here. We were even able to find easily melted water, but there was still no game. We relied on dried meat and grains to sustain ourselves. But then, one afternoon, as we set about making camp, a Pukawatchi scout came running down the canyon towards us. He was trembling with news, the horror still on his face.

An avalanche had come down on them. Many Pukawatchi and two Vikings who had lagged behind were buried. It was unlikely they would survive.

Even as the man told his story, there came a rumbling sound from above. The earth quaked and trembled, and a huge rush of snow began to course down the flanks of the canyon. In the aurora of this second avalanche I could have sworn that I saw a great, shadowy figure step from one mountain flank to another. The avalanche had been directed at us, and it seemed, indeed, to have been started by a giant. Then I saw that Prince Lobkowitz had begun to run in the opposite direction to everyone else.

Without thinking, I followed him.

I was running upwards through deep snow. In order to keep up I stepped in his tracks where I could. I heard him calling a name, but the whipping wind took it away. Then the clouds opened, and blue sky filled the horizon and broke over me like a wave. Suddenly everything was in stark contrast to the white of the snow, the deep blue of the sky and the red globe of the falling sun sending golden shadows everywhere. The avalanche was behind us, and I heard nothing of my companions, though every so often the voice of Lobkowitz came back to me as he stumbled on through the snow, sometimes falling, sometimes sliding, in pursuit of the giant.

It was almost sunset by the time I caught up with him. He had stopped on a ridge and was looking down, presumably into a valley, when I joined him.

I saw that the mountains surrounded a vast lake. The ice was turning a pale pink in the light. From the shore a glinting silvery road ran to the centre of the lake, to what might have been an island in summertime, and there stood one of the most magnificent buildings I had ever seen. It rivalled the slender towers of Melniboné, the strange pinnacles of the Off-Moo. It rivalled all the other wonders I have ever seen.

A single mighty ziggurat rose tier upon tier into the evening sky, blazing like gold against the setting sun. With walls and walkways and steps, busy with the daily life of any great city. With men, women and children clearly visible as they continued their habitual lives. They were apparently unaware that a black whirlwind shivered and shrieked at the beginning of the silver road to the city. Perhaps it protected the city.

There was a sudden crack, a flap of white wings, and suddenly a large winter crow sat on Lobkowitz's shoulder. He smiled slightly in acknowledgement, but he did not speak.

I turned to ask Prince Lobkowitz a question. His huge hand reached to point out the warrior armed with a bow, who sat upon the back of a black mammoth seemingly frozen in mid-stride. Was this the enemy Klosterheim kept in check? He was too far away for me to see in any detail. The threatening whirlwind, however, was an old acquaintance, the demon spirit Lord Shoashooan.

Then from behind them I caught another movement and saw something emerging out of the snow. A magnificent white buffalo with huge, curving horns and glaring, red-rimmed blue eyes, which I could see even from here, shook snow from her flanks and trotted past the mammoth and its riders. I could see how big the buffalo was in relation to the mammoth. Her hump almost reached the mammoth's shoulder.

The white buffalo's speed increased to a gallop. Head down, the creature thundered full tilt at the roaring black tornado. From behind me Prince Lobkowitz began to laugh in spontaneous admiration. It was impossible not to applaud the sheer audacity of an animal with the courage to challenge a tornado, the undisputed tyrant of the prairie.

"She is magnificent," he said proudly. "She is everything I ever hoped she would become! How proud you must be, Prince Elric!"

THE THIRD BRANCH

ULRIC'S STORY

Thraw weet croon tak' the hero path.
Thraw ta give and thraw ta reave.
Thraw ta live and thraw ta laugh.
Thraw ta dee and thraw ta grieve.

> —*Thraw Croon/Three*
> *Crows*, trad.
> (Wheldrake's version)

Three for the staff, the cup and the ring,
Six for the swords which the lance shall bring;
Nine for the bier, the shield, the talisman,
Twelve for the flute, the horn, the pale man,
Nine by nine and three by three,
You shall seek the Skraeling Tree.
Three by seven and seven by three,
Who will find the Skraeling Tree?

> —Wheldrake,
> *The Skraeling Tree*

15

The Chasm of Nihrain

Let me tell you how I tarried,
Tarried in the starry yonder,
Tarried where the skies are silver,
Tarried in the tracks of time.

—W.S. Harte,
Winnebago's Vision

My struggle with the pale giants was brief. They were armed with spears and round shields, obsidian clubs and long flint knives, but they did not threaten me with their weapons. Indeed, they were careful not to harm me. They used their full strength only to pin my arms and collapse my legs. I did not give up readily and grabbed at their weapons, getting my hands first on a tomahawk, then on a war-shield. I was lucky not to be cut, for I had difficulty gripping them.

My attackers were very powerful. Though I am almost as fit as I was twenty years ago, I was no match for them. When I resisted them, my limbs seemed to sink into theirs. They were certainly not insubstantial, but their substance was of a different quality, protecting them and giving them added strength. Whatever their peculiar power, they soon bundled me into my own canoe and struck off towards the Old Woman as my beautiful wife, wide-eyed with fear, ran down to the jetty in pursuit. A wild wind was beginning to rise. It blew her fine, silvery hair about her face. I tried to call out to her, to reassure her, but it snatched away my words. Somehow I was not afraid of these creatures. I did not think they meant me harm. But she could not hear me. I prayed she would not risk her own life in an effort to rescue me.

You can imagine the array of emotions I was experiencing. Every fear I had dismissed a few hours earlier threatened to become reality. I was being drawn from a dream of happiness and achievement back to some parallel existence of despair and threatened failure. But I sensed this was not a desperate fantasy of escape created by my tortured brain and body in a Nazi concentration camp. In spite of all my terrors and anxieties, it was Oona I feared for most. I knew her well. I knew what her instincts would tell her to do. I could only hope that common sense would prevail.

With extraordinary speed this bizarre raiding party neared the Old Woman, whose voice lifted in a strange, pensive wail. And from somewhere another wind rose and shrieked as if in frustrated anger. At one point it seemed that it extended fingers of ice, gripping my head and pulling me clear of my captors. It was not trying to rescue me. I was certain that it meant me ill.

I was relieved to escape it when suddenly the canoe dipped downwards, and we were beneath the surface. Everywhere was swirling water. I was not breathing, yet I was not drowning. Great eddies of emerald green and white-veined blue rose like smoke from below. I felt something bump the bottom of the canoe. On impulse I sought the source of the collision, but it was already too late.

Like an arrow, the canoe drove down through the agitated currents, down towards a flickering ruby light, tipped with orange and yellow. I thought at first we had begun to ascend and I was looking at the sun, but the flames were too unstable. Down here, deep at the core of the maelstrom, a great fire burned. What could this mean? We were heading for the very core of the Earth! Where else could fire burn in water? Could these gigantic Indians be messengers of the Off-Moo, that strange subterranean people whom Gaynor had driven from their old cities? Were these their new, less hospitable territories? The flames licked through the water, and I was sure we would be consumed. Then the canoe twisted slightly in the current, and immediately we were above an unfathomable abyss lit by dark blue-and-scarlet volcanic fires.

All sound fell behind us.

A great column of white flame stabbed upwards erratically from the depths and dissipated into roiling smoke. We drifted in neither air nor water, descending slowly through the foaming fumes into the chasm itself.

My captors had not uttered a word. Now I struggled in the strips of leather which bound me and demanded they tell me what they were doing and why. Could my words be heard? I was not sure. While they acknowledged me with some gravity, they did not reply.

The blackness of the chasm grew more intense in contrast to the vivid tongues of fire, which licked out every few seconds and illuminated my immediate surroundings before vanishing. Everywhere brooded a sense of massive stillness behind which was frenetic activity. I felt as if something had been bottled up in this chasm, and I could not guess if it was a physical or some crude supernatural force.

The glinting obsidian of the vast sides was veined with brilliant streams of fire. The mouths of caves, many of them clearly man-made, often glowed scarlet, like the open maws of hungry animals. Sounds were loud, then quickly muffled and echoing. My nostrils filled with the stink of sulphur. I choked on the thick air, almost drowning in it. The canoe continued to sink between the mighty black walls. I could see no surface, no bottom. Only the red-and-indigo flames gave us light, and what that light revealed was alien, ancient, unwholesome. I am not given to fanciful imaginings, especially at such times, but I felt as if I was descending into the bowels of Hell!

After a very long time the canoe began to rock gently under me, and I realised with a shock that we were floating on a great, slow-moving river. For a moment I wondered if it was the source of the river which both fed and lit the world of the Off-Moo. But this was almost the opposite of phosphorescent. This river seemed to *absorb* the light. I could now see that we drifted on water dark as blood which reflected the flashes of flame from above. By the weird, intermittent light my captors paddled into the entrance of a wide old harbour, its bizarre architecture built on a huge scale.

Every piece of stone was fluid and organic, but seemingly frozen at the moment of its greatest vitality. The sculptors had found the natural lines of the rock and turned these forms into exquisite but chilling imagery. Great eyes glared from agonised heads. Hands twisted into their own petrified flesh, as if trying to escape some frightful terror or seeking to tear their own organs from their bodies. I had half an idea that the statues had once been living beings, but the thought was too terrible. I forced the idea from my mind. Desperately my eyes darted everywhere, hoping to see some living creature among all this inanimate horror, while at the same time fearing what I might be forced to confront. What kind of life chose to inhabit such a hellish landscape? In spite of my situation, I began to speculate on the kind of minds which had found this place good and built their city here.

I was soon rewarded. My abductors carried me bodily to the slippery quay-side whose cobbles were made dangerous by disuse. There was a musty smell of age in that rank air. A smell of resisted death. But death nonetheless. This place had passed its time and refused to die. It spoke of an age and an intelligence which had lived long before the rise of my own kind. Might it even be the natural enemy of my kind? Or perhaps just of myself? A wild proliferation of half-memories swam just below my consciousness but refused to come to the surface.

I fought confusion. I knew I must keep my head as clear as possible. Nothing here offered me immediate harm. That strange seventh sense I had developed since my encounters with Elric of Melniboné drew upon almost infinite memory. To say that I knew the peculiar feeling of repeating an experience, which the French call déjà vu, would give some idea of what I felt if multiplied many times over. I had somehow lived these moments many, many times before. It was impossible to rid myself of a sense of significance as I was carried away from the quayside. I looked towards an avenue which ran between the statues. I had heard a sound.

From out of the ranks of twisted sculpture there stepped a group of tall, graceful shadows. I at first mistook them for Off-Moo, since the steamy atmo-sphere gave them that same etiolated appearance. Like my captors, they were very tall. My eyes hardly reached the level of their chests. Unlike the Off-Moo, however, these people had refined, handsome human features and superb phy-siques, reminding me of the Masai and other East African peoples. Their bodies were half-naked, their exposed flesh glinting ebony, its depth emphasised by their silky yellow robes, not unlike those of Buddhist priests. These men, however, were armed. They carried heavy quartz-tipped spears and oblong shields. Their heads were as closely shaved as my captors', but bore no decoration. They were warriors, perhaps? They moved towards the pale giants with gestures of con-gratulation. Clearly they were compatriots. The newcomers stood and looked gravely down on me. Gently I was helped to my feet. I am a tall man and not used to being overlooked. It was a strangely irritating feeling. My instinct was to take a step or two back, but they were in the process of removing my bonds.

As I was freed, an even taller and more heavily muscled man stepped through the ranks. He carried a tangible charisma, an air of complete authority, and it was evident that the other handsome warriors deferred to him. There was nothing sinister about their leader. He had an air of peculiar gentleness as he reached forward and took my hand in his. The raven-black palm and fingers were massive, engulfing mine. The gesture was evidently one of pleasure. He again congratulated his friends in that wordless way I somehow understood. His strange eyes shone with triumph, and he turned to his companions as if to display me as proof of some argument. These people were not mutes; they simply did not need sound to communicate. He was clearly pleased to see me. I felt like a boy in his presence, and I knew immediately that he was not my enemy. I trusted him, if a little warily. These were, after all, the people who had presumably built this dark city.

I was at a disadvantage. They all seemed to have some idea of my identity, but I still knew nothing of theirs.

"I am the Lord Sepiriz," the black giant told me, almost apologetically. "My brothers and I are called the Nihrain, and this is our city. Welcome. You might not forgive us this uncivilised way of bringing you here, but I hope you will let me explain so that you will at least understand why we need you and why we had to claim you when the opportunity presented itself to us. It was not you the Kakatanawa sought, but a lost friend. Their friend was freed, but they brought you here with them in the hope you will elect to serve our cause."

"It only disturbs me further to think you had not planned to kidnap me," I said. "What possible purpose could you have in such reckless action?" I told him that my first concern was for my wife. Had he no idea what trauma my abduction had created?

The black giant lowered his eyes in shame. "It is our business sometimes to cause pain," he said. "For we are the servants of Fate, and Fate is not always kind. She has a way of presenting her opportunities abruptly. It is up to us to take advantage of them. Her service sometimes brings us disquiet as well as pride."

"Fate?" I all but laughed in his face. "You serve an abstraction?"

This seemed to amuse and please him. "You will have little trouble under-standing what I must tell you. You are by instinct a servant of Law rather than Chaos. Yet you are married to Chaos, eh?"

"Apparently." I understood him to mean my strange relationship with Elric of Melniboné, with whom I had had a conscious but inexplicable connection since he had come to my aid in the concentration camp all those many years before. "But have you any conception of my family's anxiety?"

"Some," said Sepiriz gravely. "And all I can promise you is that if you follow your destiny, you will almost certainly see them again. If you refuse, they are lost to you—and to one another—for ever."

Now my pent-up fears burst out in anger. I walked towards the giant, glar-ing up into his troubled eyes. "I demand that you return me to my wife at once. By what right do you bring me here? I have already done my duty in the fight against Gaynor. Leave me in peace. Take me home."

"That, I fear, is now impossible. This was ordained."

"Ordained? What on earth are you talking about? I am a Christian, sir, and believe in free will—not some sort of predestined fate! Explain yourself!" I was deeply frustrated, feeling like a midget surrounded by all these extraordinary, gigantic men.

A fleeting smile crossed Sepiriz's lips, as if he sympathised. "Believe me in this then—I possess knowledge of your future. That is, I possess knowledge of what your best future can be. But unless you work with me to help this future come about, not only will your wife and children perish in terrible circumstances, you, too, will be consigned to oblivion, erased from your world's memory."

As we spoke Sepiriz began to move with his men back into the shadows. I had little choice but to move with them. From one shadow to another, each deeper. We entered a great building whose roof was carved with only the most exquisite human faces all looking down on us with expressions of great tran-quillity and good will. These faces were caught by the dancing flames of brands stuck into brackets on walls inscribed with hieroglyphs and symbols, all of which were meaningless to me. Couches of carved obsidian; dark, leathery draperies; constantly moving light and shadow. Sepiriz's own face resembled the ones look-ing down from the roof. For an instant I thought, *This man is all those people.* But I did not know how such an idea had come into my head.

While the giants arranged themselves on the couches and conversed quietly, Lord Sepiriz took me aside into a small antechamber. He spoke softly and reasonably and succeeded in calming my temper somewhat. But I was still outraged. He seemed determined to convince me that he had no choice in the matter.

"I told you that we serve Fate. What we actually serve is the Cosmic Balance. The Balance is maintained by natural forces, by the sum of human dreams and actions. It is the regulator of the multiverse, and without it all creation would become inchoate, a limbo. Should Law or Chaos gain supremacy and tip the scales too far, we face death—the end of consciousness. While linear time is a paradox, it is a necessary one for our survival. I can tell you that unless you play out this story—that is, 'fulfil your destiny'—you will begin an entirely new brane of the multiverse, a branch which can only ultimately wither and die, for not all the branches of the multiverse grow strong and proliferate, just as some wood always dies on the tree. But in this case it is the tree itself which is threatened. The very roots of the multiverse are being poisoned."

"An enemy more powerful than Gaynor and his allies? I had not thought it possible." I was a little mocking, I suppose. "And a tree which can only be an abstraction!"

"Perhaps an abstraction to begin with," said Sepiriz softly, "but mortals have a habit of imagining something before they make it real. I can tell you that we are threatened by a visionary intelligence both reckless and deaf to reason. It dismisses as nonsense the wisdom of the multiverse's guardians. It mocks Law as thoroughly as it mocks Chaos, though it acts in the name of both. These warring forces are now insane. Only certain mortals, such as yourself, have any hope of overcoming them and halting the multiverse in its relentless rush towards oblivion."

"I thought I had put supernatural melodrama behind me. I weary of this, I can tell you. And where are your own loyalties, sir? With Law or Chaos?"

"Only with the Balance. We serve whichever side needs us more. On some planes Chaos dominates; on others Law is in the ascendancy. We work to keep the Balance as even as possible. That is all we do. And we do anything necessary to ensure that the Balance thrives, for without it we are neither human nor beast, but whispering gases, insensate and soulless."

"How is it that I feel we have met before?" I asked the black giant. I stared at my surroundings, the strangely decorated ceiling, the resting figures of my captors.

"We have a close association, Count Ulric, in another life. I am acquainted with your ancestor."

"I have many ancestors, Lord Sepiriz."

"Indeed you have, Count Ulric. But I refer to your alter ego. You recall, I hope, Elric of Melniboné . . ."

"I want no more to do with that poor, tortured creature."

"You have no choice, I fear. There is only one path you can follow, as I explained. If you follow any other, it will take you and yours to certain oblivion."

My emotions were in turmoil. How did I know that this strange giant was not deceiving me? Yet, of course, I could not risk destroying my beloved family. All I could do was keep my own peace, wait and learn. If I discovered Sepiriz was lying to me, I vowed to take vengeance on him come what may. These were not typical thoughts for me. I wondered at the depths of my rage.

"What do you want me to do?" I asked at last.

"I want you to carry a sword to a certain city."

"And what must I do there?"

"You will know what to do when you get to the city."

I recalled the bleak chasm beyond these walls. "And how will I get there?"

"By horseback. Soon, I shall take you to the stables to meet your steed. Our horses are famous. They have unusual qualities."

I was hardly listening to him. "What is your interest in this?"

"Believe me, Count Ulric, our self-interest is also the common interest. We have given up much to serve the Balance. We have chosen a moral principle over our own comfort. You may wonder, as we sometimes do, if that choice was mere hubris, but it scarcely matters now. We live to serve the Balance, and we serve the Balance to live. Our existence is dependent upon it, as, of course, ultimately is everyone's. Believe me, my friend; what we do, we do because we have no other choice. And while you have choice, there is only one which will enable you and yours to live and thrive. We tend the tree that is the multiverse, we guard the sword that is at the heart of the tree, and we serve the Cosmic Balance, which pivots upon that tree."

"You are telling me the universe is a tree?"

"No. I am offering a useful way of formalising the multiverse. And in formalising something, you control it to a degree. The multiverse is organic. It is made up of circulating atoms but does not itself circulate in prefigured order. It is our chosen work to tend that tree, to ensure that the roots and branches are healthy. If something threatens them, we must take whatever drastic steps are necessary for their rescue."

"Including kidnapping law-abiding citizens while they are on holiday!"

Sepiriz permitted himself another quiet smile. "If necessary," he said.

"You are barking mad, sir!"

"Very likely," replied the black giant. "It is madness, I think, to choose to serve a moral principle over one's own immediate interests, eh?"

"I rather think it is, sir." Again, I had no way of challenging Sepiriz.

I turned to the pale giants Sepiriz had called "Kakatanawa." I could not think of them in relation to the normal-sized native population. These warriors rested in the attitudes of tired men who had worked well. One or two of them were already stretched out on the stone benches and were close to sleep. I felt physically as if I had been pummelled all over, but my mind was alert. If nothing else, adrenaline and anger were keeping me awake.

"Come," said Sepiriz. "I will show you your weapon and your steed." Clearly I had no real choice. Controlling my fury I strode after him as he led the way deeper into that strange, hewn city.

I asked where the rest of the inhabitants were. He shook his head. "Either dead or in limbo," he said. "I am still hoping to find them. This war has been going on for a long time."

I mentioned my past encounters with the Off-Moo, whose own way of life had been savagely disrupted by the coming of Gaynor and Klosterheim to their world. Lord Sepiriz nodded with a certain sympathy and seemed merely to add that to a list that was already larger than any sentient creature could absorb. Somehow, without his saying a word, I had the impression of battles being fought across a multitude of cosmic planes. And in all those conflicts, Sepiriz and his people had involved themselves. A race which lived to serve the Balance? It did not seem strange.

"What is your relationship with the men who seized me?" I asked him. "Are they your servants?"

"We are allies in the same cause." Sepiriz let out a massive sigh. "Just as you are, Count Ulric."

"It is not a cause I volunteered for."

Sepiriz turned, and again I thought he seemed strangely amused. "Few of us volunteered, Sir Champion. The war is endless. The best we can hope for are periods of tranquillity."

We reached a great slab of rock decorated with elaborate scenes carved in miniature from top to bottom. The whole formed a half-familiar shape which hinted at something in my memory.

Lord Sepiriz turned, opened his arms and began to chant. The sound found an echo somewhere, like a string resonating to its perfect pitch.

The great slab quivered. The scenes on it writhed and for a second were alive. I saw great battles being fought. I saw bucolic harvesters. I saw horror and joy. Then the song was over and the slab was motionless—

Except that it had moved closer to us, revealing a dark aperture behind. A door! Sepiriz had evidently opened it with the power of his voice alone! Again this struck a distant chord in me, but I could attach no specific memory, only the same sense of déjà vu. No doubt that peculiar duality I had with my half-human alter ego, Elric of Melniboné, caused these sensations. It was no comfort to know that I searched for the memory of another man, a man with whom I had shared a mind and a soul and from whom I knew now I would never be entirely free.

Taking a flickering brand from the bracket on the wall, the black giant signalled me to follow him.

Crimson light splashed over the stones, revealing a multitude of realistic carvings. The entire history of the multiverse might be depicted here. I asked Sepiriz if this was the work of his ancestors, and he inclined his head. "There was a time," he said, "when we had more leisure."

From being uncomfortably warm, the air now turned very cold. I shivered in spite of myself. I half expected to find this was a tomb full of preserved corpses. The figures looming over me, however, were of the same carved obsidian as the others I had seen. We seemed to spend hours beneath them until we came to an archway only just high enough to permit Lord Sepiriz to pass under it. Here he raised the brand in the air, making the faces writhe and change their expressions from serenity to twisted mockery. I could not rid myself of the idea that they were watching me. I remembered how the Off-Moo were capable of suspending their life functions so successfully that they effectively became stone. Was this quality shared with Lord Sepiriz and his people?

But my attention was quickly drawn from the carved faces to the far wall and what appeared to be a background of rippling copper. Framed against it was a familiar object. It was our old family sword, which I thought in the hands of the communists.

It hung against the living copper which reflected the erratic light of the torch. That black iron, so full of an alien vitality, was caught as if by a magnet. Within the blade I was sure I detected moving runes. Then I thought they might have been mere reflected light from the brand. I shuddered again, this time not from cold but from memory. Ravenbrand was a family heirloom, but I knew little of its history, save that it was somehow the same sword as Elric's Stormbringer. In my own realm of the multiverse the blade had supernatural qualities, but in its own realm I knew it was infinitely more powerful.

Some deep strain within me yearned to hold that blade the moment I saw it. I remembered the wild bloodletting, the exhilarating horror of battle, the joy of testing your mettle against all the terrors of natural and supernatural worlds. I could almost taste the pleasure. I reached for the hilt before I had formed a single, conscious thought to do so. Then I reminded myself of my manners, if nothing else, and withdrew my hand.

Lord Sepiriz looked down on me with that same half-humorous expression, and this time there was a distinct sorrow in his voice when he spoke. "You will take it. It is your destiny to carry Stormbringer."

"My destiny! You confuse me with Elric. Why does he not claim this sword?"

"He believes he seeks it."

"And will he find it?"

"When you find him . . ."

I was sure that he was deliberately mystifying me. "I never entertained ambitions to act as your courier . . ."

"Of course not. That is why I have your horse ready. Nihrainian horses are famous. Come, leave the sword for the moment, and we will hurry to the stables. If we are in luck, someone is waiting there to meet you."

16

Fate's Fool

If you tell me what my name is,
Should you tell me what my station,
I will speak of the Pukwatchis,
I will lead you to their nation.
I will show you what to steal.

—W.S. Harte,
The Starry Trail

Though I grew familiar with this city's grotesque and fantastic sights, I was unprepared for the Nihrainian stables. Little of that intricately hewn city lay outside the great caverns into which it was carved. We made our way through miles of impossibly complicated corridors and tunnels, every inch of which was etched with the same disturbing scenes.

The muggy air tasted heavily of sulphur, and I had difficulty breathing. Lord Sepiriz did not slacken his steady gait and was hard to pace. Gradually the roofs grew higher and the galleries wider. I had the impression we were entering the core of the original city. What we had passed through up to now was a kind of suburb. Here the carvings seemed older. There was greater decay in the rock, some of which seemed almost rotten. Everywhere volcanic fires flared through windows and doorways and fissures in the ground, illuminating what seemed to me an astonishing desolation. Here was not the tranquillity of the Off-Moo chambers, but the stink of death so violent that its ancient memory permeated this living rock. I could almost hear the screams and shouts of those who had died terrible deaths, almost see their reflections trapped in the obsidian and basalt of the walls, writhing in perpetual torment. Once again I wondered if I was in Hell.

Lord Sepiriz touched his brand to another. This in turn lit the next until in a flash of light I saw we stood at the entrance of a huge amphitheatre, like a massive Spanish bullring with tiers of empty stone benches stretching up into a darkness, heavy and threatening. Yellow flames lit the scene from without while from within came an unstable scarlet glow. I felt I stood on the threshold of some strange necropolis. Our very life seemed an insult to the place, as if we intruded on every kind of agony. Even Lord Sepiriz seemed borne down by the sadness and horror. We could have been in the killing fields of the universe.

"What happened here?" I asked.

"Ah." The black giant lowered his head. He was lost for words, so I did not press the question.

My foot stirred dark dust. It eddied like water. I imagined the blood which had been spilled in this arena, yet could not easily imagine how it had happened. There was no sense it had ever been used for gladiatorial fights or displays of wild beasts.

"What was this place?" I spoke with some hesitation, perhaps not wishing to hear the answer.

"At the end, it was a kind of court," said Lord Sepiriz. He drew in a deep, melancholy breath, like the soughing of a distant wind. "A court where all the judges were mad and all the accused were innocent . . ." He began to walk across the arena, towards an archway. "A place of judgement which sentenced both court and defendants to a terrible death. This is why there are only ten of us now. Our fate was as preordained as yours as soon as we forged the swords."

"You made them? You mined the metal here . . . ?

"We took the original metal from a master blade. War raged as always between Law and Chaos. We thought to make a powerful agent against one of them. The swords were forged to fight against whichever power threatened to tilt the Balance. Law against Chaos or Chaos against Law. We drew on all our many powers to make them, and when they were finished we knew we had found the means to save worlds and perhaps destroy them at the same time. A mysterious power entered one of the blades. While they were otherwise identical and could feed great vitality to those who wielded them, Stormbringer was subtly different. Those who made that particular blade and summoned the magic required to enliven it knew they had created something that was oddly, independently evil. Somehow, though Mournblade, the sister sword, had little such power, those who handled Stormbringer developed a craving for killing. Honest blacksmiths became mass murderers. Women killed their own children with the blade. Ultimately it was decided to put both the handlers and Stormbringer on trial . . ."

"Here?"

Sepiriz lowered his head in assent. "Here, in the stables. This is where the horses were exercised and exhibited. We loved our beautiful horses. But it seemed the only suitable place. Originally this ring was used for equestrian displays. Our Nihrainian horses are very unusual in that while they exist on this plane, they simultaneously exist on another. This gives them some useful qualities. And some entertaining ones." Sepiriz smiled as a happy memory intruded on the sadness.

Then, pulling himself together, he straightened his shoulders and clapped his enormous hands.

The sound was like a shot in the huge, silent arena. It brought an almost instant reaction.

From within came a whinny, a snort. Something pounded the hard surface. Another great whinny, and out of the archway, mane flaring as if in the wind, sprang a horse of supernatural proportions. A monstrous black stallion, big enough to carry Sepiriz. He reared, flailing bright jet hoofs and glaring from raging ochre eyes. The beast's mane and tail became a wild mass of black fire. He was muscular, nervous. This gigantic beast expressed impatience rather than anger. But at a word from Sepiriz, the horse cocked his ears forward and immediately settled. I had never seen a creature respond so swiftly to human command.

Although there was no doubting the animal's physical presence, I quickly noticed that for all his activity, he scarcely stirred the dust of the arena floor and left no hoofprints of any kind.

Noting my curiosity, Sepiriz laid a hand gently on my shoulder. "The horse, as I told you, exists on two planes at once. The ground he gallops on is unseen by us."

He led me up to the horse, who nuzzled at him, seeking a familiar treat. The beast already wore a saddle and bridle and seemed equipped for war as well as travel.

I reached a hand towards the mighty head and rubbed the animal's velvet nose. I noted the bright, white teeth and red tongue, the hot, sweet breath.

"What is his name?" I asked.

"He has no name in your terms." Sepiriz did not elaborate. He looked towards the walls, searching for something he had expected to find there. "But he will carry you through all danger and serve you to the death. Once you are in his saddle, he will respond as any horse, but you will find him, I think, unusually intelligent and capable."

"He knows where I am to go?"

"He is not prescient!"

"No?" For a moment the ground beneath my feet shifted like liquid, then as quickly resettled. Again Sepiriz refused to answer my unspoken question. He was still searching. His eyes scanned the long, empty stone benches stretching into the gloom. I noticed that the darkness seemed to have absorbed some of the upper tiers. Smoke or mist swirled and gave carved figures expressions of gloating glee, then of wild, innocent joy.

Sepiriz noted this at the same time I did. I was certain I saw a flash of alarm in his eyes. Then he smiled with pleasure and turned as another horse emerged from the archway into the stadium. This horse had a rider. A familiar rider. A man I had met more than once. Our families had been related for centuries. His was a branch which had supported Mozart and been famous for its taste and intelligence.

This rider had first introduced himself to me in the 1930s as a representative of an anti-Nazi group. His handsome, heavy features were enhanced now by an eighteenth-century wig, a tricorn hat and military greatcoat. He looked like one of the famous portraits of Frederick the Great. Of course it was my old acquaintance, the Austrian prince Lobkowitz. His clothing was bulky, completely unsuitable for this volcanic cavern. His face was already beaded with sweat, and he dabbed at himself with a vast handkerchief of patterned Persian silk.

"Good morning, sir." His voice a little hoarse, he reined in and lifted his hat, for all the world as if we met on a country bridle path near Bek. "I'm mightily glad to see you. We have a destiny to pursue. Sentient life depends upon it. Have you brought the sword?"

Lobkowitz dismounted as Lord Sepiriz came towards him, towering over the Austrian, who was not a short man. Sepiriz kneeled to embrace him. "We were unsure you could perform so complicated a figure. We had other means ready, but they were even more fragile. You must have succeeded thus far, or you would not have joined us."

Prince Lobkowitz put his hand on Lord Sepiriz's arm and came to shake my hand. He was in high spirits. Indeed, I found his attitude a little unseemly, considering my circumstances, if not his. His warm charm, however, was impossible to resist.

"My dear Count von Bek. You cannot know the odds against your being here and our meeting like this. Luck, if not the gods, seems on our side. The dice are tossed by a fierce wind, but now at least there is a little hope."

"What is the task? What do you seek to accomplish?"

Lobkowitz looked at Lord Sepiriz in surprise. He seemed to expect the black giant to have told me more. "Why, sir, we seek to save the life and soul of your dear wife, my protégée, Oona, the dreamthief's daughter."

I was horrified. "My wife is in danger? What is happening back there? Is someone attacking the house?"

"In relation to our position in the scheme of things, she is no longer at your house in Canada. She is further inland, deep in the Rockies, and facing an enemy who draws his strength from every part of the multiverse. Unless we reach her at exactly the right moment, where our story intersects with hers, she will perish."

I could not control the pain I experienced at this news. "How did she come to be where she is? Could you not have helped her?"

Prince Lobkowitz indicated his costume. "I was until lately, sir, in the service of Catherine the Great. Where, I might add, I met your unsavoury ancestor Manfred."

For one of such habitual grace, he seemed in poor temper. I apologised. I was a simple man. I had no means of understanding this topsy-turvy tumble of different worlds. It was more than I could normally do to try to imagine the space between the Earth and the moon. Yet my veins beat with anxious blood at the thought of my beloved wife in danger, and I feared for my children, for everything that had meaning to me. I wanted to turn on this pair and blame them for my circumstances, but it was impossible. Another intelligence lurked within my own.

Gradually his presence was growing stronger. Elric of Melniboné, who believed in the reality of only one world, understood perhaps instinctively the complexity of the multiverse. His experience, if not his intellect, told him how one branch sometimes intersected with another and sometimes did not, how branches grew quickly, took on bizarre shapes, and died as suddenly as they appeared.

Elric understood this science as his own sorcerous wisdom, captured over years of education in the long dreams which gave the Melnibonéan capital its nickname of the Dreamers' City. For Elric's people extended their lives through drug- and sorcery-induced dreams which assumed their own reality, sometimes for thousands of years. By this means, too, did their dragon kin, to whom they were related by blood, sleep and dream and manifest themselves, no doubt, in others' dreams. It was dangerous for anyone but the full adept to attempt such an existence. And dangerous, I knew, to try to change a narrative which gave some kind of uneasy order to our lives. At best we could create a whole new universe or series of universes. At worst we could destroy those which now existed and by some mistake or unlucky turn of the cards consign ourselves and everything we knew to irreversible oblivion.

My twentieth-century European sensibilities were repelled by such ideas, yet Elric's soul was forever blended with my own. And Elric's memory was filled with experiences I would normally dismiss as the fantasies of a tormented madman.

Thus I accepted and refused to accept at the same time. It was a wonder I had the co-ordination to mount the huge horse. He was at least as large as the famous old warhorses of past legends. I looked for Sepiriz, to ask him a question, but he had gone. The saddle and stirrups were modified for a man of my size, yet the saddle still felt huge, giving me an unfamiliar sense of security.

There was no doubt my horse was pleased to have a rider. He moved impatiently, ready to gallop. At Lobkowitz's suggestion I cantered the stallion around the arena. The Nihrainian steed trod the ground with evident familiarity, tossing his great black mane and snorting with pleasure. I noted the strong, acrid smell he exuded when he moved. It was the smell I normally associated with a wild predator.

Lobkowitz followed me, saying little but clearly noting my handling of the animal. He congratulated me on my horsemanship, which made me laugh. My father and brothers had all despaired of me as the worst rider in the family!

As we rode, I begged him to tell me more about Oona and her whereabouts. He asked that I respect any reticence on his part. Knowledge of a future could change it, and it was our task not to change the future but to ensure that, in one realm at least, it be a future I desired for my loved ones and myself. I must trust him. With some reluctance, I bowed to his judgement. I had no reason, I said, not to trust him, but my head ached with many questions and uncertainties.

Sepiriz returned bearing a scabbarded sword. Was it the sword I knew as Ravenbrand, which Elric called Stormbringer? Or was it the sister sword, Mournblade? Sepiriz did not tell me. "Each sword is of equal power. The power of the other avatars weakens in proportion to their distance from the source. It is as well it happened this way," he said. "The Kakatanawa have already gone home. The circle tightens. Here."

As I reached to accept the sword, I thought its metal voiced a faint moan, but it could have been my imagination. There was, however, a distinct, familiar vibrancy to the hilt as it settled into my right hand. Automatically I hooked the scabbard to the heavy saddle.

"So," I said, "I am prepared to follow a road for which I have no maps, in a quest whose purpose is mysterious, with a companion who seems scarcely more familiar with the territory than I am. You place much faith in me, Sepiriz. I would remind you that I remain suspicious of your motives and your part in my wife's endangerment."

Sepiriz accepted this, but clearly he did not intend to illuminate me further. "Only if you are successful in this adventure will you ever know more of the truth concerning the swords," the black seer told me. "But if you do, indeed, succeed in fulfilling your destiny, of serving Fate's purpose, then I promise, what you hear shall hearten you."

And with that Lobkowitz yelled for us to be off. We must be free of Nihrain before the new eruption, when all here will be destroyed, and Sepiriz and his brothers will ride out into the world to fulfil another part of their complex destiny.

I could do nothing but follow him. The prince bent over his horse's neck and rode with impossible speed out of the huge amphitheatre and down corridors of liquid scarlet veined with black and white and tunnels of turquoise, milky opal and rubies. All carved in the same relief. Faces begged and twisted in agony. Their eyes yearned for any kind of mercy. Vast scenes stretched for miles, every figure minutely detailed, all exquisitely individual. Landscapes of the most appalling beauty, of elaborate horror and hideous symmetry, rose and fell around me as I rode. All were given movement by my own speed. Were they designed to be seen thus? A creative style best appreciated from the back of a galloping warhorse?

I began to believe that I inhabited a fantastic dream, a nightmare from which I must inevitably wake. Then I remembered all I had learned from Oona and realised that I might never wake, might never see her or my children again. This infuriated me, firing me with a righteous anger against Fate or whatever less abstract force Sepiriz and his kind served.

I put all that emotion into my riding, into following the expert Lobkowitz through tunnels, chambers, corridors of dazzling diamonds and sapphires and carnelians, down long slopes and up flights of steps, our horses' hoofs never quite touching the ground of the paths we traced. I gasped and braced myself to fall the first time the horse galloped across the air separating one part of the mountain from another. By the second experience I had learned to trust its sure-footed pace over an invisible landscape.

We galloped through oceans of lava, through foaming rivers of dust, over blue-veined pools of marble, sometimes blinded by a fiery light, sometimes plunging through pitch-darkness. The great black horses never tired. When we passed through caverns of ice, their breath erupted like smoke from their nostrils, but they were otherwise undisturbed by any natural obstacle. Now I understood what a valuable animal Sepiriz had loaned me.

In spite of my anxieties, I began to know an old, familiar elation. The sword at my side was already wrapping me in her bloody gyres, sending me a taste of what I would experience if I unsheathed her. I dared not draw the thing from her scabbard, for I knew what she would make of me, what pleasures I would taste and what mental torments I would experience.

I was filled with a dreadful mixture of fear and desire. Knowing my wife was even now in danger, I longed to feel the hilt in my hand again and taste the most terrible drug of all, the very lifestuff of my foes. What some called their souls. As the spirit of Elric combined with that of the sword, together they threatened to overwhelm the part of me who was Ulric von Bek. Already far too much of me longed to charge into battle on this magnificent horse, to hack and pierce, to slice and skewer, to lift my arm and let death come wherever it fell.

All this horrified Ulric von Bek, that exemplar of liberal humanism. Yet perhaps here was a time when a rational, modern man was not best suited to deal with the realities around him. I should give myself up wholly to Elric.

Should I do that, I thought, I would in some way be abandoning my wife and children. I had to hang on to the humanistic person I was, even though increasingly Elric lurked just below the surface, threatening to take me over and make me a willing tool of his killing frenzy.

How I yearned never to have known this creature, nor ever to have had to rely on his help. Yet, I thought, if I had not involved myself with Elric and his fate, I should not now be married to his daughter, Oona, whom we both loved in our own ways. At least in this we were united. What was more, the last emperor of Melniboné had saved me from torture and degrading death in the Nazi concentration camp.

This final thought helped me sustain a balance within myself as the Nihrainian steed carried me higher and higher out of the depths, up into the roaring chasm and then down black shale, rivulets of red lava, a rain of pale ash. The Nihrainian horses continued to follow their own peculiar route parallel to this reality. The stink of sweat and sulphur remained in my nostrils. The neck of the great beast steamed, bulging with straining muscles as it continued down the flanks of the black mountain and out into a world which turned by degrees from night to dawn and from lifeless ash to rolling meadowlands with copses of oak and elm.

I was tiring. The horse's pace slowed to a steady canter as if to enjoy the cool, autumnal air, the scents of sweetly fading summer. The leaves of the trees turned gold and brilliant yellow and russet in the low, comforting light. Lobkowitz, still ahead of me, his greatcoat and tricorn hat covered with light grey ash, turned in his saddle to wave. He seemed jubilant. I guessed we had crossed another barrier. Our luck was holding.

At last we rested beside a pond on which a few white ducks squabbled. There were no signs of human beings, although the whole area had a pleasant, cultivated look. I mentioned this to Lobkowitz. He said he thought that we were in a part of the multiverse which for some reason had ceased to be inhabited by human beings. Sometimes entire futures vanished, leaving the most unexpected traces. He guessed that this land had once been settled by prosperous peasants. Some action in the multiverse had affected their existence. Their natural world had survived as they left it. Everything they had made had vanished. Every little pact they believed they had with mortality brushed aside.

He gave a small, sad shrug.

Lobkowitz said that he had witnessed the phenomenon too often not to be convinced that he was right. "You might note, Count Ulric, a certain barrenness to those gently rising and falling hills, those old stones and trees. They are a dream without its dreamers." He rose from where he had been washing his face and hands in the pond. He shivered, drying his palms under his arms as he waited for me to drink and wash. "I am afraid of places like this. They are a kind of vacuum. You never know what horrors will choose to fill it. An untrustworthy dream at best."

I followed his reasoning, but did not have his experience. I could only listen and try to understand. I knew I did not have a temperament for the supernatural, and I thus would never be thoroughly comfortable in its presence. Not all my family had a natural affinity with infinite possibility. Some of us preferred to cultivate our own small gardens. I wondered with sudden amusement if I might be the horror who chose to fill this particular vacuum. I could see Oona and our children cultivating a farm, a pleasant house . . .

And then I understood what Lobkowitz feared. There were many traps of many kinds in the multiverse. The harshest climate could hide the greatest beauty, the most attractive shireland could disguise hidden poisons. With this realisation, I was glad to remount the big, tireless stallion and follow Lobkowitz through endless meadows until starless, moonless night fell, and I heard the sound of water far below me.

I hardly dared look down. When finally I did, I saw little, but it seemed the big Nihrainian horse was galloping across a lake. We slept in our saddles. By morning we rode over the high, tough grass of a broad steppe. In the distance we saw grazing animals which, as we drew closer, I recognised as North American bison.

With some considerable relief I realised that we were probably upon the same continent as my imperilled wife. Then the bison vanished.

"Is she nearby?" I asked Prince Lobkowitz when we next stopped on a rise overlooking a broad, winding river. All wildlife seemed to have disappeared. The only sound we heard was the remorseless keening of the west wind. We dismounted and ate some rather stale sandwiches Lobkowitz had carried in his knapsack from Moscow.

His reply was not encouraging. "We must hope so," he said. "But we have several dangers to overcome before we can be certain. Many of these worlds are dying—already as good as dead . . ."

"You take much in your stride, sir," I said.

"'Some polish is gained with one's ruin,'" he said. He quoted Thomas Hardy, but the reference to our circumstances was obscure to me. He threw the remains of his sandwich onto the ground and watched it. It did not move. I was puzzled. Why were we studying a piece of discarded food?

"I see nothing," I told him.

"Exactly," he said. "There is nothing to see, my friend. Everything around it is unaffected. Nothing comes to investigate. This place looks very tranquil, but it is lifelessness. Eh?" He kicked at the stale bread. "Dead."

Lobkowitz stamped back to his horse and mounted.

At that moment I do not believe I had ever seen a more heavily burdened individual.

Thereafter I treated my companion with a different respect.

17

Against the Flow of Time

Moons and stars saw many passings
Many long suns rose and fell
Many were the women dancing
Many were the warriors singing
Many were the deep drums calling
Calling to the Gods of War!

—W.S. Harte,
The Shining Trail

The rolling hills of that ersatz Sylvania behind us, we found ourselves in a grey terrain of shale and old granite. The world had changed again. Ahead was a succession of bleak, shallow valleys with steep, eroded flanks. High in the cloudy skies carrion eaters circled. At least they were a sign of life or, if not, the promise of death. The floors of the silvery limestone valleys were rent with dark fissures, long cracks which ran sometimes for miles. A leaden, sluggish river wound across the depressing landscape. In the distance were low, wide mountains which from time to time gouted out red flames and black smoke. This was not unlike the dead world Miggea of Law had created.

I asked Lobkowitz if anything had caused the withering of these worlds we crossed, and he smiled wryly. "Only the usual righteous wars," he said. "When all sides in the conflict claimed to represent Law! This is characteristically a land which has died of discipline. But that is Chaos's greatest trick, of course.

It is how she weakens and confuses her rivals. Law will characteristically push forward in a predictable line and must always have a clear goal. Chaos knows how to circle and come from unexpected angles, take advantage of the moment, often avoiding direct confrontation altogether. It is why she is so attractive to the likes of us.

"You do not want the rule of Law?"

"We could not exist without Chaos. Temperamentally I serve Law. Intellectually, and as a player in the Game of Time, I serve Chaos. It is my soul that serves the Balance."

"And why is that, sir?"

"Because, sir, the Balance serves humanity best."

We were cantering through the shallow dust of a valley. A few hawthorn trees had managed to grow in the hollows, but mostly the scenery was bare rock. Slowing to a walk, Lobkowitz turned in his saddle and offered me a white clay pipe and a tobacco pouch. I declined. As he filled his own bowl, tamping it with his thumb, he sat back in the big wooden saddle and gestured towards the horizon. "We have kept our co-ordinates, I do believe. At this rate it will not be long before we reach our destination."

"Our destination?"

Almost apologetically Prince Lobkowitz said, "It is safe to tell you now. We travel, with a little luck, to the city of the Kakatanawa."

"Why could we not have gone back with the Kakatanawa when they returned home?"

"Because their path is not our path. If my judgement is accurate, when we find them, they will have long since been back at their positions. Those warriors are the immortal guardians of the Balance."

"Why are we all from different periods of history, Prince Lobkowitz?"

"Not history exactly, my friend, for history is just another comforting tale we tell so that we do not go mad. We are from different parts of the *multiverse*. We are from the multitude of twigs which make up this particular branch—each twig a possible world, yet not growing in time and space as we perceive, but growing in the Field of Time, through many dimensions. In the Time Field all events occur simultaneously. Space is only a dimension of time.

"These branches we call spheres or realms—and these realms are finely separated, usually by scale, so that the nearest scale to them is either too large or too small for them to see, though perhaps the physical differences between the worlds are scarcely noticeable."

Prince Lobkowitz gave me a sideways look to check if I was following his argument. "Yet there are occasions when the winds of limbo breathe through the multiverse, tossing the branches to and fro, tangling some, bringing down others. Those of us who play the Game of Time or otherwise engage with the multiverse attempt to maintain stability by ensuring that when such winds blow, the branches remain strong and healthy and do not crash together or proliferate into a billion different and ultimately dying twigs.

"Nor can we let the branches grow so thick and heavy that the whole bough breaks and dies. So we maintain a balance between the joyous proliferation of Chaos and the disciplined singularities of Law. The multiverse is a tree, the Balance lies within the tree, the tree lies within the house, and the house stands on an island in a lake . . ." He seemed to shake himself from a trance, in which he had been chanting a mantra. He came smartly awake and looked at me with half a smile, as if caught in some private act.

It was all he would tell me. Since I could now anticipate further answers to my questions as it became possible for him to offer them, I grew more optimistic. Was he relaxing because we were getting closer and closer to where Oona was in some mysterious danger? If Lobkowitz was so optimistic, there was every chance we would be there to rescue her.

On we galloped as if we rode on the soft turf of an abandoned shire, although the limestone now was melting and turning to a sickly, sluggish lava beneath the Nihrainian horses' hoofs. The stink of the stuff filled my nostrils and threatened to clog my lungs, yet not once did I feel afraid as we crossed a sea of uneasy pewter and reached a shore of glittering ebony far too smooth to accept any mortal steed's hoof. The Nihrainian stallions took the slippery surface with familiar ease. Ducking as large trees came towards us, we found ourselves in a sweet-smelling pine forest through which late-afternoon sunlight fell, casting deep shadows and calling the sap from the wood. Lobkowitz let his horse stop to crop at invisible grass and turned his face upwards to admire what he saw. The sun caught his ruddy features. In the heightened contrast he resembled a perfect statue of himself. Great shafts of sunlight broke through the silhouettes of the trees and created an incredible mixture of forms. For a moment, following Lobkowitz's gaze, I thought I looked into the perfect features of a young girl. Then a breeze disturbed the branches, and the vision was gone.

Lobkowitz turned to me, his smile broadening. "This is one of those realms all too ready to mould itself to our desires and take the form we demand. It is particularly dangerous, and we had best be out of it soon."

We cantered again, across sparsely covered hills and through valleys of sheltered woodlands, and entered a broad plain, with a greying sky hovering over us and a cold breeze tugging at our horses' manes. Lobkowitz had become grave, turning his head this way and that as if expecting an enemy.

The clouds streamed in towards us, thick and black, and lowered the horizon. In the far distance I could make out the peaks of a tall mountain range. I prayed they were the Northern Rockies. Certainly this great, flat plain could be part of the American prairie.

It began to rain. Fat drops fell on my bare head. I was still wearing the clothes Sepiriz had first given me and had no hat. I lifted a gloved hand to hold off the worst of it. Lobkowitz, of course, was now dressed perfectly for the weather and seemed amused by my discomfort. He reached into one of his saddlebags and tugged out a heavy, old dark blue sea-cloak. I accepted it.

I was soon even gladder for the cloak as the wind came whipping in from the north-east and hit us like a giant fist. Doggedly the Nihrainian stallions maintained their pace. As their great muscles strained harder, there was a hint of tiredness now. The endless veldt stretched all around us. Still no obvious signs of beaver, birds or deer. Once, as the wind howled fiercely and caused even my stallion to reduce his speed to a dogged plod, there came a gap in the clouds. Red sunlight brightened the scene for a moment and revealed a herd of deer running for their life before the wind. The first I had seen. They were clearly trying to escape the region. I had the distinct feeling we were not heading in the sensible direction. I remarked on the wind during a lull. Lobkowitz looked concerned as he confirmed my guess that we were heading into a tornado. Knowing little of such things in Europe, I could not recognise one. All I understood was that it was wise to find shelter.

Lobkowitz agreed that, as a general rule, it was usually wise to seek cover.

"But not this time. He would find us, and we would be more vulnerable. We must continue."

"Who would find us?"

"Lord Shoashooan, Lord of Winds. He commands a dangerous alliance."

Then, as if to silence my friend, the wind again became a shouting bully. The rain was a giant's fingers drumming on my back as we cantered on, crossing marshes, rivers and grassland with equal ease. The only thing powerful enough to slow us was that cruel, relentless wind. It seemed to carry hobgoblins with it, tugging at my body and teasing my horse. I could almost hear its hard, cackling laughter.

Lobkowitz rode in close now, stirrup to stirrup, so that we should not lose each other in the weather. Every so often he tried to speak over the wind, but it was impossible. I was sleeping intermittently in my saddle when the horses slowed to a walk. My body ached, yet they were almost tireless. This seemed to be the nearest they came to resting.

Mile by mile the prairie became low hills, rolling towards the mountains, slowly transferring into the range that rose tall and ragged into the soughing sky. The wind seemed to give up once we reached the foothills. Suddenly the clouds parted just as the sun was sinking, and the mountains were a vivid glow of ochre, russet, sienna and deep purple shot through with bands of darker yellows and crimsons. All mountain ranges have their characteristic beauty. I had seen such magnificent colour only in the Rockies.

"Now we must be *more* than careful." Prince Lobkowitz dismounted on the slope and was leading his horse up towards a wide cave-mouth above. "We'll shelter here tonight and ensure our sleep. We shall need to be alert. Perhaps take watches."

"At least that damned wind has dropped."

"Aye," said Lobkowitz, "but he remains our main enemy here. He is cunning, often seeming to depart, then licking around at you from a fresh point on the compass. He loves to kill. The more he can devour at a sitting the more content he is."

"My dear Lobkowitz, 'he' is an insentient force of nature. 'He' no more plans and schemes than do those rocks over there."

Lobkowitz looked with some mild alarm towards the rocks. Then he shook his head. "They are benign," he said. "They follow the Balance."

I was becoming convinced that my cousin was a little eccentric. While he could lead me to Oona, however, and back to the safety of our home and children, I would continue to humour him. As it was, I could not always tell what he saw or how. I was reminded of visionaries like Blake, who inhabited a world quite as real as that of those who mocked him. Certainly I judged people like Blake with a different and greater respect once I understood that his world had been as vividly real to him as this world was to me. I was still a sufficiently modern gentleman, however, not to relish the social circumstances of meeting and speaking with an angel.

Lobkowitz built a little fire deep inside the cave. The smoke was drawn to a narrow crack at the back which doubtless led into some larger system.

Like all experienced travellers, he was economical with what he carried and yet seemed to want for nothing. With ease he prepared a kind of savoury pancake from various dried powders he carried in a small cabinet which fitted, with a little forcing, into one of the big gun-pockets in his coat.

I asked him why he was so anxious about the wind. True, it was bitter cold, but it had not, after all, turned into a tornado and blown us away. I took my first bite of the food. It was excellent.

"It is because Lord Shoashooan dissipates his power in various strategies. Had he drawn upon his power and concentrated it, we should doubtless be dead by now. But his main strength is elsewhere."

"Who is this entity who commands the wind?"

"He once had a pact with your family, for mutual defence, but that was on another plane altogether. Lord Shoashooan is an elemental who serves neither Law nor Chaos. At this time, he seems to have chosen to ally himself with our enemies, which means inevitably we shall soon be challenging him. Meanwhile the White Buffalo struggles against him on our behalf, which is why he is so weak. Yet for all the White Buffalo is his most powerful enemy, Lord Shoashooan will not be held for much longer. His allies grow strong, both in numbers and in the range of powers they command. Lord Shoashooan tastes his new freedom."

He spoke with such knowing familiarity of this high lord that I wondered for a moment if I should suspect him of being in the creature's service. Meanwhile, it would be wise to take care what I asked him. I then decided he was speaking of a person, or a totem, and asked no more questions.

I was becoming used to this kind of patience. We were situationalists, of sorts, he said, responding to whatever opportunities were presented to us by fate and making the most of them. That was why, as Pushkin knew, the gambler's instinct was so important.

I had become distracted. The thought that we were only a short distance from Oona made my sleep intermittent. I kept waking and wanting to get back in the saddle, to reach her as soon as possible, but Lobkowitz had already pointed out how ordinary time meant little in this business. It was more a matter of choosing to act when the right co-ordinates presented themselves. He remarked again that Pushkin would have made a good member of the Guild of Time, though he was something of an amateur. The best gamblers, like himself, were careful professionals who earned their livings by winning.

I remarked that I could not see Prince Lobkowitz as a card sharp. He laughed. I would be surprised, he said, at his reputation in the coffee houses of London, where every kind of game was played. Putting away his cleaned utensils he suggested that I get as much sleep as possible and prepare myself for whatever the coming days would bring.

I was up soon after dawn. I stepped from the cave into the cold autumn morning. The mist had lifted, and I looked out into stunning natural beauty whose wonderful shapes and colours were all touched by the rising sun. I felt like opening my arms to the east and chanting one of those songs with which Indians were said to greet the return of the sun.

Lobkowitz arose soon after me. With his shirtsleeves rolled up to the elbow, he cooked a piece of bacon and some beans. The fresh dawn air made me hungry, and the smell was delicious. He apologised for what he called his "cowboy breakfast," but I found it excellent and would have eaten another portion had there been one. I asked him if he knew how much longer it would be before we saw Oona. He could not say. First he had some scouting to do.

Only then did I notice that the horses were gone. Our saddlebags and weapons lay just inside the cavern. It was as if a thoughtful thief had led them away in the night.

Lobkowitz reassured me. "They have returned to Nihrain, where they will be needed for another adventure involving your ancestor and alter ego Elric of Melniboné. We cannot ride horses into the territory we now explore. No horses exist there."

"Are you telling me we are in pre-Columbian America?"

"Something like that." He put a friendly hand on my shoulder. "You are an exemplary companion for a man like myself, Count Ulric. I know that you are impatient for more information, but understand how I can only reveal it to you a little at a time, lest we change our future and further weaken the branch. Believe me in this: my affection for your wife is, in its own way, as great as yours. And what is more, her survival depends upon our success quite as much as our survival depends on hers. Many branches are being woven together to make a stronger one, Count Ulric. But the weaving involves considerable skill and good fortune."

"It is taking me a little while," I told him, "to think of myself as a strand."

"Ah, well," he said with the suggestion of a wink, "imagine instead that you are lending the weight of your soul to the souls of a small company who together might save the Cosmic Balance and rescue the multiverse from complete oblivion. Does that make you feel more important?"

I said that it did and, laughing, we picked up our kit and with a spring in our steps set off along the high mountain trail, admiring the peaks and forests which lay below us and revelling in all the wildlife that now inhabited them. Such scenery eased my soul. I was strengthened by it more, I suspected, than I was strengthened by the sword.

Lobkowitz walked with the aid of a crooked staff. I wore the big blade balanced on my back. It was so beautifully forged that it felt far lighter than it actually was. I must admit I had always thought a Luger or a Walther a more reliable weapon in a pinch, but also I had once seen what happens when someone attempts to fire such a weapon in a realm where it should not exist.

We were comfortable while we walked, but when we stopped we felt the chill in the wind. Before the end of that first day, a little light snow had touched my face. We were steadily moving towards winter.

The season seemed to be coming upon us rather swiftly, I said.

"Yes," said Lobkowitz. "We are walking against what you would usually conceptualise as the flow of time. We could be said to be walking backwards to Christmas."

I was about to respond to this whimsicality when a pale face some seven feet high blocked the narrow mountain path ahead. A giant peered at us from eye level. When I peered back at the face, I realised it was a realistic carving. What mighty force had placed a great stone head directly in our way, blocking the path? The thing stared at me with a smile which made the Mona Lisa's seem broad, and I found myself charmed by it. Indeed I admired its beauty, running my hand over the smooth granite from which it had been sculpted. "What is it?" I asked Lobkowitz. "And why is it blocking our path?"

"It is a creature called an Onono. A tribe of them used to live in these parts. What you cannot see are the useful legs and arms hidden within what looks like a singularly thick neck. They are extinct in this realm, everywhere but in Africa, where they are a distinct species of their own. You should be pleased this one has petrified. They are formidable and savage enemies. And cannibals to boot." With his crooked staff Lobkowitz levered the thing towards the edge. It began to rock almost at once and then suddenly flew over and down. I watched it tumble into the gorge far below. I expected it to land in the river, but instead, with a snapping crash it went into a stand of dark trees. I found myself hoping it had managed a reasonably soft landing. The way ahead, though a little chipped and eroded, was now clear.

Lobkowitz moved cautiously forward and was wise to do so, for as the path widened and turned we confronted not a stone guardian, but several living versions of the creature we had just sent over the edge. Long, spindly, spiderlike arms and legs were extended from within the shoulder area. Their huge heads, filed teeth and great, round eyes were like something out of Brueghel.

Parleying with the Ononos was not a possibility. Six or seven of them crowded across the pathway. We had to fight them or retreat. I guessed that retreat would sooner or later involve us in fighting them anyway. Lobkowitz unsheathed the monstrous cutlass under his coat, and with a guilty sense of relief I drew Ravenbrand from her scabbard. Immediately the black blade howled with a mixture of joyous delight and horrible bloodlust. I was dragged towards my foes, Lobkowitz in my wake, as we ran to do battle with these grotesque failures of evolution.

Spindly fingers gripped my legs as I swung my sword full into the face of the first Onono, splitting it like a pumpkin and covering his companions and myself in a gruesome mixture of blood and brains. The things had massive but relatively delicate craniums. Two more of the monsters fell to Ravenbrand, who now shrieked with a disgusting and undisguised love for blood and souls. I heard my voice shouting Elric's Melnibonéan war-cry "Blood and souls! Blood and souls for my Lord Arioch!" Part of me shuddered, fearing that to invoke that name might be the worst thing I could do in this world.

Yet it was Elric of Melniboné who dominated now. Wading into the hideous Ononos, I drew their crude lifestuff into my own. Their coarse blood pulsed through me, giving me a foul, virtually invulnerable energy.

Soon they were all dead. Their twitching hands and feet lay strewn everywhere on the path. Some had sailed down towards the trees. Other parts had landed on the mountainside. The remaining two creatures—who looked like young females—were bounding away on their knuckles and would offer us no further trouble.

I licked my lips and wiped my blade clean on coarse black Onono hair. Nearby Prince Lobkowitz was examining those corpses still more or less in one piece. "These were the last of Chaos in this realm, at least until now. I wonder if they will welcome their cousins." He sighed. He seemed to feel sympathy for our defeated attackers.

"We are all Fate's fools," he said. "Life is not an escape plan. It is an inevitable road. The changes we can make in our stories are not great."

"You are a pessimist?"

"Sometimes the smallest of changes can become significant," said Lobkowitz. "I assure you, Count Ulric, that I am anything but a pessimist. Do not I and my kind challenge the very condition of the multiverse?"

"Which is?"

"Some believe the only power which makes existence in any way choate is the imagination of man."

"We created ourselves?"

"There are stranger paradoxes in the multiverse. Without paradox there is no life."

"You do not believe in God, sir?"

Lobkowitz turned to regard me. He had a strange, pleasant expression on his face. "A question I rarely hear. I believe that if God exists he has given us the power of creativity and has left us with it. If we did not exist, it would be necessary for him to create us. While he neither judges nor plans, he has given us the

Balance—or, if you prefer, the *idea* of the Balance. It is the Balance I serve, and in that, perhaps, I am serving God."

I became embarrassed, of course. I had no wish to pry into another man's religious beliefs. But, raised as I was in the Lutheran persuasion, there were certain questions which naturally occurred to me. His was a religion of triumphant moderation, it seemed, whose purpose was clear and whose rules were easily absorbed. The Balance offered creativity and justice, a combination of all human qualities in harmony.

A harmony not mirrored in the busy wind which again began to lick at what little flesh we had exposed. It lashed us with rain and sleet. It blinded us and chilled us to our bones, but we continued to follow the mountain trail. Winding around great cliffs and across narrow ridges, on both sides were drops of a thousand feet or more. The wind seemed to attack us when we were most vulnerable.

In certain parts of the mountains' flanks, high overhead, some snow had begun to settle. I became alarmed. If we had heavy snow, we were finished, I knew. Doing his best to reassure me, Lobkowitz failed to convince himself. He shrugged. "We must hope," he said. "'Hope ahead and horror behind, tell of the creatures I have in mind.'" He seemed to be quoting from the English again. Only when he made such quotations did I realise that our everyday speech was German.

From somewhere in the distance came the faint, cawing voice of a bird. Lobkowitz became instantly alert.

We rounded a great slab of granite and looked out over a descending cascade of mountain peaks towards a frozen lake. I must have gasped. I remember my own breath in the air. I heard my own heart beating. Was this Oona's prison?

Far out in the lake I could see an island. On the island had been raised some sort of gigantic stepped metal pyramid which dazzled with reflected light.

Leading from shore to island, a pathway, straight and wide, shone like a long strip of silver laid across the ice. What sort of thing was this? A monument? But it seemed too large.

The wind then slashed stinging sleet into my eyes. When they cleared, a rolling mist was covering the lake and the surrounding mountains.

Lobkowitz's face was shining. "Did you see it, Count Ulric? Did you see the great fortress? The City of the Tree!"

"I saw a ziggurat. Of solid gold. What is it? Mayan?"

"This far north?" He laughed. "No, only the Pukawatchi have ventured up here, as far as I know. What you saw was the great communal longhouse of the Kakatanawa, the model for a dozen cultures. Count Ulric, give thanks to your God. Intratemporally we have followed a dozen crooked paths all at the same time. The odds on accomplishing that were small. By chance and experience, we have found resolution. We have found the roads to bring us to the right place. Now we must hope they have brought us to the right time."

Lobkowitz looked up with a broad smile as out of the air a large bird dropped and settled on his extended forearm. It was an albino crow. I looked at it with considerable curiosity.

The crow was clearly its own master. It walked up Lobkowitz's arm, sat on his shoulder and turned a beady eye on me.

Lobkowitz's manner revealed that he had held little hope of our success. I laughed at him. I told him I was not pleased with my fate. He admitted that overall he believed we had been dealt a pretty poor hand in this game. "But we made the best use of the cards and that's the secret, eh? That's the difference, dear count!"

Fondling the proud bird affectionately and murmuring to it, he obviously greeted a pet he had thought lost. I suspect, too, that he was half-mad with disbelief at his own successful quest. Even now I could tell he was torn between greeting the bird and craning for another glimpse of the golden pyramid city. I understood his feelings. I, too, was torn between fascination with this new addition to our party and peering through the swirling clouds for another view of the fortress, but the clouds now made it impossible to see more than a few feet ahead.

It was dark before we decided to stop in a small, natural meadow. We drew the big cloak over a little shelter in the form of tough bushes rooted into the mountainside and were thankfully able to light a small fire. It was the most comfortable we had been for some time. Even Lobkowitz's pet crow, roosting in the upper parts of a bush, seemed content. I, of course, immediately wanted Lobkowitz to tell me whatever new details it was possible for him to reveal. Anything which would not affect the course of our time-paths.

There was very little, he apologised. He did not think we had much further to go. He frowned at his bird, as if he hoped it would provide him with advice, but the creature was apparently asleep on its perch.

Lobkowitz was awkwardly cautious, perhaps fearing that we were now so close to our goal that he dare not risk losing it. A pull or two on one of his numerous clay pipes, however, calmed his spirits, and he looked out with some pleasure at the dark red and deeper blue of the twilight mountains, at the clearing sky and the hard stars glittering there. "I once wandered worlds which were almost entirely the reflection of my own moods," he said. "A kind of Heathcliffian ecstasy, you might say."

He seemed emboldened and continued on more freely. "Our business is with the fundamentals of life itself," he told me. "You already know of the Grey Fees, the 'grey wire' which is the basic stuff of the multiverse and which responds, often in unexpected forms, to the human will. This is the nourishment of the multiverse, which in turn is also nourished by our thoughts and dreams. One kind of life sustains another. Mutuality is the first rule of existence, and mutability is the second."

"I have not the brains, I fear, to grasp everything you tell me." I was polite, interested. "My attention is elsewhere. Essentially I need to know if we are close to rescuing Oona."

"With considerable luck, more courage and any other advantages we can find, I would say that by tomorrow we shall stand on the Shining Path which crosses to the island of Kakatanawa. Three more have come together. *Three by three and three by three, we shall seek the Skrayling Tree,* ha, ha. This is strong sorcery, Cousin Ulric. All threes and nines. That means that every three must come together and every nine must come together to link and form a force powerful enough to restore the Balance. There is much to overcome before you will see the interior of the Golden City."

Our fire sustained us through the night, and in the morning ours was the only patch of green in a landscape covered by a light snow. We packed our gear with care and secured everything thoroughly, for we knew the dangers of slipping on that uneven trail.

The wind came back before noon and blustered at us from every angle, as if trying to uproot us from our uneasy balance on the mountain face and hurl us into valleys now entirely obscured by thick, pale cloud. We kept our gloved fingers tight in the cracks of the rock face and took no chances, advancing step by careful step.

At last we were climbing down, moving into a long valley which opened onto the lakeside. In contrast to the frozen water, the valley was green, untouched by the snow on the upper flanks. It felt distinctly warmer as we reached the shelter of pleasant autumn trees.

Lobkowitz's face was now a stark mask as he kept his eye upon the gap in the hills through which we could sense the glittering golden pyramid.

Soon enough the clouds parted again, and the sun shone full down on an unimaginably vast fortress. As we neared it I began to realise what an extraordinary creation it was. I had seen the Mayan ziggurats and the pyramids of Egypt, but this massive building was scores of storeys tall. Faint streamers of blue smoke rose from it, obviously from the fires of those living in it. An entire, great city encompassed in a single building and constructed in the middle of the pre-Columbian American wilderness! How many brilliant civilisations had risen and fallen leaving virtually no records behind them? Was our own doomed to the same end? Was this some natural process of the multiverse?

These thoughts went through my head as I lay staring at the multitude of stars in the void above me that night. Sleep was almost impossible, but I finally nodded off before dawn.

When I awoke, Prince Lobkowitz was gone. He had taken his cutlass with him. Only his saddlebags were left behind. There was a note pinned to one of the bags:

MY APOLOGIES. I HAVE TO GO BACK TO COMPLETE SOME UNFINISHED WORK. WAIT FOR ME A DAY THEN CARRY ON TOWARDS THE SHINING PATH. LET NOTHING DIVERT YOU.
—LOBKOWITZ

I guessed that the albino crow had gone with him, until for an instant I spied it circling above me before disappearing down into a canyon. Perhaps it followed Lobkowitz?

With little to do but nurse my fears, I waited all that day and another night for Lobkowitz. He did not return. Superstitiously I guessed we had celebrated too early.

I mourned for him as I took up his belongings and my own. I wondered where the bird had gone. Had it followed him to his fate or taken another path? Then I began the long climb down towards the frozen lake and the silvery trail which led across it.

I prayed that I would at last find Oona in the great, golden pyramid the Kakatanawa called their longhouse.

18

The Hawk Wind

Then he told the deed he'd done,
Told of all that endless slaughter,
Red beneath the setting sun.

—W.S. Harte,
The War Trail

The trail down to the lakeside was surprisingly easy at first. Then, as usual, the wind came up, and I had to fight it to stay on my feet. It attacked me from every point of the compass. Now I, too, had the strangest feeling that not only was it intelligent, but it actually hated me and wanted to harm me. This made me all the more determined to get down to the valley floor. Gales forced their way through layers of my clothing, sliced me across the throat and drove icy needles into my eyes. My hand felt lacerated from trying to protect my face.

Several times, on a difficult part of the mountain trail, the gusts sprang from nowhere to grab me and more than once almost succeeded in flinging me down into the distant gorge. Sometimes they struck like a fist into the small of my back and other times attacked my legs. I began to think of this wind as a devil, a malignant personality, it seemed so determined to kill me. In one terrible moment I set off an avalanche I barely escaped, but I pressed on with due care, keeping a handhold on every available crack and clump of grass as the full-force gale tore and thrashed at me. Somehow I eventually reached the valley.

I stood at last on the flat, staring up a long, narrow gorge towards the lake.

I could see a few dots on the shore, and I hoped one of them might be Lobkowitz awaiting me. I could not believe he had betrayed or abandoned me. He had seemed so elated the night before, anticipating our sighting of the causeway and the golden ziggurat of Kakatanawa.

The ziggurat became more impressive as I approached.

From this distance I could see signs of habitation. It was evidently a huge and complex city to rival any of the great cities of Europe, yet arranged as a single vast building! From various parts of the ziggurat, which was verdant with gardens, hanging vines, even small trees, I saw the blue smoke of small fires rising into a clearing sky. Everywhere was busy movement. The place was thoroughly self-contained and virtually inviolable. It could have withstood a thousand sieges.

A huge wall ran around the whole base. It was extremely high and capable of withstanding most kinds of attack. The tiny specks were people amid large, animal-dragged passenger vehicles and commercial carts. The general sense was of busy activity, casual order, and unvanquishable might. If such a city had ever existed in my world's history, then it survived only as a legend. How could something so magnificent and so enormous be completely forgotten?

In contrast to the order of the city, the activity on the shore was confused. I saw a few figures coming and going. Some sort of dispute seemed to be taking place. I tried to see who was arguing with whom.

Foolishly I had let my attention focus on the distance rather than on my immediate surroundings. The gorge had narrowed. The trail dipped down into a shallow, green meadow blanketed with a light coating of snow. Enclosed by high rocks, the depression might have once been a pond or old riverbed. I was so busy craning my neck to see the group on the shore that I was taken entirely by surprise.

I slipped, losing both my bundle and Lobkowitz's. My feet slid from under me, and I fell headlong.

When I came to rest I found myself surrounded by a large band of Indians. They were silent, menacing. They emerged from among the rocks, glaring in full warpaint. Though they had the appearance of Apache or Navajo, their clothing was that of woods Indians, like the Iroquois. They were clearly intent on butchering me. But there was something wrong.

As they drew closer, spears and bows at the ready, I began to realise how small they were.

I tried to tell them I came in peace. I tried to remember the Indian signs I had learned in the Boy Scouts in Germany. But these fellows were not concerned with peace. The tiny men screamed unintelligible insults and orders at me. There was no doubting their belligerence but I hesitated before defending myself. Not one of them reached much above my knee. I had been flung into some children's fairyland, some elfin kingdom!

My first impulse was laughter. I began to make some remark about Gulliver, but the spear that narrowly missed my head was unequivocal. I continued to try to avoid bloodshed.

"I am not your enemy!" I shouted. "I come in peace!"

More miniature arrows zipped past me like bees. They were not deliberately trying to miss me. I was amazed at their bad marksmanship, as I was not, after all, a small target. They were clearly terrified. After one last attempt to persuade them to see reason, I acted without thinking, without any hesitation, and with a growing frisson of relished destruction.

Reaching over my shoulder I sensuously slid the shivering, groaning rune-blade from her hard scabbard and felt the black silk mould to my hand, the black steel leap to life as she scented blood and souls. Scarlet runes veined her ebony blade, pulsing and flickering within the steel as she sang her terrible, relentless song. And it seemed I heard names in the humming metal, heard great oaths of revenge being taken. All this bonded me even closer to the weapon. My human self remained horrified, distant. Whatever else inhabited me anticipated a delicious feast. As well as drawing on the experiences of Elric of Melniboné I also became, in some hideous way, *the sword itself.*

I gasped with the joy of it even before the gleaming metal took her first little souls. Strong little souls. They were helpless against me, yet despite their fear they would not run. Not at first. Tough, hardy bodies pressed around my legs, and I had to force a certain delicacy upon the blade in order to slice away their embracing limbs. They behaved like men who had reached their limit and now did not care if they died. As I pressed forward against them, cutting them down like vermin, they fell back around something they were clearly protecting.

I was curious, even as I continued to kill. My sword possessed my will. She would not cease her feasting. She would not stop drinking until she had drunk every shred of every soul and drawn them shrieking into my eager veins. Half of me was disgusted with my actions, but that half did not control my blood-lust nor my sword-arm. I stabbed and slashed and chopped with slow, steady strokes, like a man stropping a razor.

They were now entirely fearless, these little men, as if reconciled to their violent deaths. Perhaps even welcoming them. They came at me with tomahawks and knives and spears and arrows. They even used a kind of sling to fling live snakes at me. I let them strike if they chose. There is no venom known which can kill a Melnibonéan noble. We are weaned on venom.

The snakes and arrows were brushed aside by the sword I knew as Raven-brand. Her speed was a bloody blur. Flint clubs and short, stone swords grazed me but did not cut me. Every pygmy who died wailed in sudden understanding as he gave me fresh life. I laughed aloud in my killing. I let the stolen energy fill me with godlike invulnerability. I lusted to murder and celebrated every stolen soul! Small they might be, but the pygmies were near-immortals and thus rich with supernatural lifestuff. After the crude souls of the Ononos, this fairy blood was a delight. It poured into me until I felt my physical form would contain it no longer, that it would all burst out of me.

I fought on, carrying the attack. I laughed at their agony and their fear. Even those who tried to surrender, I killed. I sighed with the sweetness of their slaughter. The majority, however, battled on with enormous courage, preferring to die bravely, because they knew death was their only future.

Up and down, my sword-arm rose and fell as, driven by my old berserk blood-craze, I pursued groups of the warriors and continued to slaughter even when most of them had finally lost heart for a fight. At last there was only one band left. With their buffalo-hide shields and quartz-tipped spears, they had formed a ring around a pair of large boulders and clearly intended, like their fallen comrades, to defend their position to the death.

I slipped the blade of my sword between the legs of the nearest warrior and dragged the razor-sharp blade upward to cut him neatly in two. He squealed and wriggled like a tortured cat. Most, however, I simply beheaded. It was hard, precise, mechanical work. The creatures were considerably denser than they looked.

At last all that was left of the pygmies was what they had defended. He lay in a small clearing formed by the boulders. A wizened old man spread over the primitive stretcher like a stain. Everywhere around him were piled the corpses of his warriors. Not one was remotely alive. Small, headless corpses, like so many slaughtered chickens. Spattered with the blood of his people, the man must have been over a hundred years old. His skin was thin as tissue paper, and his fingers were like picked bones. He was an animated corpse, an unwrapped mummy, a husk of a creature, yellowed and fading into nothingness with none to mourn him. But his eyes burned with life, and his lips moved, whispering violently and with considerable pain in a patois I could barely understand. A much corrupted Old French dialect? I had learned that it was often a mistake in the multiverse to try to identify a language too closely.

"Would you loot the last of our honour, Prince Silverskin?" He glared angrily at me and tried to lift a hand weakly shaking a bloody rattle decorated with small animal skulls. All he had left was his mockery. "Your folk have taken everything else from us. You leave us nothing but our shame, and we deserve to die." He was neither strong nor unreconciled to death. There was no need for me to finish him. I had always had a distaste for killing the helpless, which had made me something of a laughing stock as a boy in Melniboné. The old man was already as good as dead, his raspy breath coming with increasing difficulty and slowness. In spite of his afflictions he was able to whisper at me from the rough stretcher on which he lay. "I am Ipkaptam, the Two Tongues."

He was a grey man. The life had been sucked out of him, but not by the sword I now resheathed.

"Are all my people dead?" he asked me.

"All those whom you sent against me," I said. "Why should you wish to have me killed?"

"You are our enemy, Pale Crow, and you know it. You have no soul. You keep it in the body of a bird. You use our own iron against us. You would steal our best-kept treacheries and learn too much about our masters' whims. Does it matter where we are or what we face now? All human aspiration is brought low by human greed and human folly. Now we are tainted by the human curse, and so we fade from this sphere. Is our epic to tell of our self-deception, of our certainty in our own superiority? It is the end of the Pukawatchi. There are only two important realities in this world: starvation and sudden death . . ."

This speech exhausted him. I motioned him gently to silence. But he said: "You are the man the boy became?"

I could not follow this. I thought he was raving. Then he said clearly, "There are only old people, women and children to weep for the Pukawatchi. Our ancient tribe reconciles itself to the end. We are no more. One day even our name will be forgotten."

My impulse, now that the blood frenzy had passed, was to comfort him, but I did not know how to do so.

I knelt among the raw, red meat I had made of his men and took his withered hand in my gauntleted one. "I meant you no harm and would have gone on my way if you had not attacked me."

"I know," said the old man, "but we also knew that our death time had come. It was written that the black blade would destroy us if we let it go. We have failed in all our ventures. Our oaths lie dry and unfulfilled in dying mouths. It is time for us to die. All our treasures are gone. All our boasts are empty. All our honour has been taken from us. We have nothing to return with save our shame. So we died with honour, trying to take back our black blade. Is it your son, then, who stole it?"

The old man's gaunt features were parchment on bone. His eyes sparked and then faded before I could try to answer.

"Or are you another self altogether?" The shaman rose from his stretcher and reached out, trying to touch me. A soft song whispered on his lips, and I knew that he spoke not to me but to the spirits he believed in. He looked into a world becoming far more real to him than the one he was leaving.

He died upright in an attitude of pride and did not fall back until I laid him down and closed his eyes. His people had died, as they wished, in battle and with honour against an old foe. Their remains looked frail, like children's corpses, and I knew a pang of conscience. Yet these people had been trying hard to kill me. They would be stripping my still-warm body even now, had they won.

In the end I made no attempt to bury them, but rather left them to be cleaned by the carrion-eating birds congregating overhead, drawn in by the stink of a blood-drenched wind.

Soon I could clearly make out what lay before me, but I was no less mystified. I saw a tall black elephant carrying a huge open howdah with what appeared to be a birchbark canoe used as a canopy. Astride the beast was a handsome Indian whose style of costume and decoration resembled the Kakatanawas and was typical of the Indians who had once inhabited the North American woods. A Mohican, perhaps? I guessed him to be some sort of chief. His concentration was not upon the arriving buzzards but on what lay immediately in his field of vision. The scene was made worse by its absolute silence.

A black, horrible and completely *silent* tornado, thin and vicious at the base, lowering, thick and menacing above, was almost a perfectly reversed pyramid. This edifice of frozen, filthy air blocked the way from shore to island and, with the city as its background, formed a terrifying harmony. The silver trail ended suddenly, as if the tornado had somehow eaten it up. The path across the ice to the city ended as well. I felt I neared the very centre of the world. But compared to this, my journey had been easy until now.

All the forces who opposed the Balance were gathering to defend against its saviours. We faced not the opposing philosophies of Law and Chaos, but the Spirit of Limbo—the mindless yet profound creature which yearns for death, which aches for death, but not merely for itself. It demands that all creation shall know oblivion, for all creation is the only equal to that monstrous ego. If other persuasions fail, self-murder and the murder of as many others as possible become the only logical option. I knew from Nazi Germany that from small, mean dreams such egos grow until their nightmares become the condition of us all.

Against all my usual scepticism I was now in no doubt that this barely frozen force was a supernatural tornado. There was also no doubt it intended to block the way of those who confronted it. I knew I looked upon a magical event of some magnitude. From where I had paused, taking what cover I could, I could feel its vibrant evil. A whole world of evil concentrated into this unmoving whirlwind. Were I still a believer, I would have thought myself in the presence of Satan incarnate. I marvelled at the courage of the single warrior facing it.

All around me now was that awful, oppressive stillness. Progress forward was nearly impossible. I felt as if I waded through heavy water rather than air.

The great beast was a mammoth, and like the Indian it was frozen in motion.

Then I saw a woman's figure in the shadow of the giant pachyderm. An arrow fitted to her bow, she faced the tornado. Over her slender shoulders was a beautiful white robe, thrown back to allow her the shot.

Time was standing still here. Even my own actions grew more sluggish by the moment.

I forced my way forward, hoping that my eyes were not merely trying to console me that the figure I saw was who I thought it was.

A little nearer and I was certain. It was Oona! I tried to move in her direction when suddenly I was overwhelmed by a mighty, deafening noise. It was like the note of a horn, echoing through every dimension of the multiverse. Echoing on and on for ever.

The tornado shrieked and sniggered and raged. It had come fully alive now! I saw fiendish faces within it and limbs of sorts.

My hair and clothes were whipped backward. I felt my body sucked at, clutched at, investigated. The wind became even more aggressive. The whole scene was alive now.

Through all this wild bluster came the sweet, clear note of a flute. My wife was nocking her arrow to her bow. I feared to call out and distract her. What did she hope to do? Did she think she could kill a whirlwind—and a supernatural whirlwind at that—with an arrow? Why was Oona walking so calmly towards her death? Did she not sense the thing's power? Was she in a fresh trance? Dreaming within a dream?

And who, or what, had sounded the horn I heard?

Again, instinct took charge of my will, and without a second thought I ran towards the causeway, shouting to Oona to stop, to wait. But she did not hear me above the terrible shriek of the tornado. She walked slowly, with an odd, unnatural gait. Was she entranced?

The tall Indian seemed to know me. He tried to stay me with his hand. "Only she can make the Silver Path across the ice. Wherever she passes, that will give us our way. But she goes against the Winds of the World. They are Winds gone mad. She goes against Lord Shoashooan."

I yelled something back at him, but that, too, was snatched from my mouth by the railing currents.

A sudden cut of cold wind slashed across my face, momentarily blinding me. When I could see again, Oona was gone. Behind me I sensed a presence.

The Indian was climbing back onto the mammoth. Behind him, marching down the beach, came a group of warriors who appeared to have stepped off the set of *Götterdämmerung*. Save for the fact that not all were Scandinavians, I confronted as unwholesome-looking a bunch of hardened Vikings as I had ever seen. Immediately I reached for my sword.

The leader stepped forward out of the press. He wore a silvered mirror helm. I had seen it before. I knew him. And something in me, however terrified, knew the satisfaction of confirmed instinct. My instincts had been right. Gaynor the Damned was abroad again.

If I had not recognised him by his helm I would have known him by that low, sardonic laughter.

"Well, well, cousin. I see our friend heard the sound of my horn. He seems to have inconvenienced you a little." He held up the curling bull's horn, covered in ornate copper and bronze, which hung at his belt. "That was the second blast. The third will bring the end of everything."

And then he drew his own blade. It was black. It howled.

I was desperate. I had to help my wife. Yet if I did so now, I would be attacked from behind by Gaynor and his brutish crew.

Then it was as if Ravenbrand had seized my soul, conscience and common sense, and I found that I'd drawn it again without thought.

I began to advance towards the armoured Vikings.

I heard the thin, sweet sound of a bone flute. It echoed like a symphony around the peaks. Gaynor cursed and turned, flinging his hatred towards the Indian, who sat cross-legged upon the neck of the mammoth, his eyes closed, his lips pursed, playing his instrument.

Something was happening to Gaynor's sword. It twisted and shivered in his hand. He screamed at it. He took it in *both* hands and tried to control it, but he could not. Was I right? Did the flute actually control the sword?

Then my own sword almost dragged me towards the causeway and my wife. Behind me I heard the shouts of Gaynor and his men. I prayed they were diverted by the Indian. I had to help my wife, my dearest love, my only sanity.

"Oona!"

My voice was turned to nothing by mocking breezes. Every time I tried to call out, the wind stole my every sound. All I could feel and hear were the vibrations in the sword which had somehow found a common harmony with the whirlwind. Did I carry a traitor weapon? Did this sword bear some loyalty to the howling black tornado in whose depths I now made out a glaring, gleeful face, delighting in what it would do to the lone woman still walking towards it, arrow nocked to bowstring, stance resolute, as if she were about to take a shot at a stag?

Black fog jetted out of the tornado. Long tendrils swam to surround and engulf Oona, who stepped in and out of the tangle like a girl playing hopscotch, her arrow still aimed.

And then she loosed the arrow.

The gigantic, inverted pyramid of air and dust began to shout. Something very much like laughter issued from it, a sound which turned my stomach. I ran all the faster until I was standing on the causeway which now moved like mercury under my feet. It took me several moments to regain my balance and discover that I did not need to sink into it. With an effort of will I could walk along it. With even more effort, I could run.

And run I did as Oona let fly a second arrow and a third, all in a space of seconds. Each arrow formed the points of a "V" in the thing's face. It raged and foamed, seeking to shake the arrows loose. Its eyes were full of a knowing intelligence, yet one which had lost all control of itself. Lord Shoashooan was still grinning, still laughing, and again his tendrils were curling, tightening, drawing my wife into the depths of his body.

The flute's note rose for a third time.

Oona was violently ejected from the body of the tornado. Clearly the arrows had worked some mysterious magic in conjunction with the flute. She was flung back to the Shining Path and lay, a tiny heap of bones, covered by that bright, white buffalo robe, on the shifting quicksilver.

I yelled to her as I ran past with no time to see if she still lived, so determined was I to take revenge and stop the creature from attacking her again.

I was swallowed by an ear-piercing shriek, inhaling foul air and confronting an even fouler face which leered at me from the depths of the wind. It licked dark blue lips and opened a yellow maw and extended its tongue to receive me.

Instead, the green-brown tongue was cut in two by my Ravenbrand, which yelped its glee like a hound in chase. Another movement of the blade and the tongue was quartered. Intelligence again bloomed in those hideous eyes as it realised it was not dealing with an ordinary mortal but with a demigod, for with that sword bonded to my flesh I knew that I was nothing less. A mortal able to wield the powers of gods and to destroy gods.

Nothing less.

I began to laugh at those widening eyes. I grinned in imitation of its bloody mouth as it swallowed its parts back into its core and re-formed them. And while it used its own energy to restore itself, I struck again, this time at one of the glaring eyes, cutting a slender thread of blood across the pupil. The monster moaned and cursed in painful anger. Oona's arrows had weakened him.

I struck at the smoky tendrils as if they were flesh, and the sword cut through them. But Lord Shoashooan was constantly forming and re-forming himself, constantly spinning himself into new guises within his inverted cone as if he tried to find the best way of destroying me.

But he could not destroy me. I fed off the stolen souls of scores of the recently dead. Fresh souls and, moreover, no demon duke to share them with. I knew that familiar, horrible ecstasy. Once tasted it was always feared, never forgotten, always desired. The vital stuff of all those I had killed filled my human body and turned it into something at once unnatural and supernatural, the conduit of the sword's dark energy. Oona was a forgotten rival. Now I belonged to the sword.

Deep into the being's vitals the sword plunged. Only Ravenbrand knew where to stab, for only she was completely on the same plane as the demon lord whose powers I had once sought to harness myself. Now I had no such fine ambition. I was fighting for my life and soul.

The black energy pouring into me sharpened my senses. I was hideously alive. I was completely alert. I parried every tentacle's attempt to seize me. I laughed wildly. I drove again and again at the head while all around me the thing's whirlwind body shrieked and screamed and thrashed, threatening to destroy the mountains.

Whatever part of me was myself and whatever was Elric of Melniboné, I clung to those identities, and it seemed a thousand other identities were drawn to them. Drawn by the power of the Black Sword. Could good come out of evil, as evil often came from good? This was no paradox, but a fact of the human condition. I struck two-handed at something which might have been the thing's jugular and was rewarded. The tornado suddenly collapsed into a wide, filthy cloud, and I was covered with what I supposed was its inner core, its blood. A green sticky mess which hampered my every move, for all my extraordinary strength, and seemed to be hardening on my flesh.

I had struck the thing a crucial blow, but now I was helpless, whirling around and around and suddenly flung, as my wife had been flung, out onto the Silver Path. I landed winded, but I still clung to the sword and was able to stumble to my feet just in time to see a monstrous white buffalo charging down on me.

My instinct and my sword's natural bloodlust worked together. I brought the great black battle-blade up like a skewer and gored the massive bison in the chest. A second blow and the buffalo went down. A third and her blood was gouting onto the ice.

I turned in triumph, expecting to receive the congratulations of those I had saved.

The face that met mine was that of a second newcomer. It was as bone-white as my own with eyes just as crimson. He could easily have been my son, for I guessed him to be no older than sixteen. There was an expression of disbelieving horror on his face. What was wrong? He was the boy I had seen on the island, of course. Who was he? Neither my son, nor my brother. Yet that grim face had a distinct likeness to the rest of the family.

"So," I said, "the enemy is vanquished, gentlemen. Is there more work to do?" I was met with silence. "Have you no stomach for the adventure?" I was still strutting with egocentric euphoria which came with so much bloodletting.

Then I realised that these men were looking at me with considerable gravity, as if I had committed some error of taste or perhaps even a crime.

Ayanawatta stepped forward. He reached out and wrenched the sword from my hand, flinging it to the path. Then he turned me around and showed me what lay behind me. "She was to lead us across the ice. Only White Buffalo Woman can walk the Shining Path. Now she is dead."

It was Oona. Her white buffalo robe was stained with blood. She had three sword wounds. The wounds were exactly where I had struck the white buffalo.

Slowly the horror of what I had done infused me. I picked up the sword and flung it far out across the ice.

In my battle madness, as she had come to save me, I had killed my own wife!

19

The Shining Path

Golden was the city ere Rome were mud,
Philosophies she dream'd ere Greece was form'd,
Senses she explor'd before the rise of Man;
Long was her glory before decline began.

—Austin,

Ancient, In Ancient Days
Atlantis Dream'd

Disbelievingly I stumbled towards the frail corpse. Had I really killed my wife? I prayed that this was the illusion and not the bizarre beast I had cut down with my sword.

The wind had fled in defeat and left behind it a deep, triumphant silence. I heard my own footfalls on the silvery path, smelled the sweet salt of fresh blood as I knelt and reached towards the warm, familiar face.

Then I was knocked sprawling. The albino youth I had first seen on the island stooped and swiftly wrapped my wife in the buffalo robe. Without hesitation he began to run towards the great pyramid city. As he ran, the Silver Path extended before him and remained behind him where he passed. I raised myself to follow him, but I was exhausted. I had no sword. All my stolen energy was draining from me.

I stumbled and fell on the unstable causeway. My hands sank into mercury. I tried to crawl. My cry filled worlds with sorrow.

Then Lobkowitz was there, and with the Indian stood over me and helped me to my feet.

"He seeks to save her," said Lobkowitz. "There is a chance. See? Even in death she has the power to make the path."

"Why did you let me—?" I stopped myself. I had never been one to blame others for my own follies, but this was worse than anything I could possibly have imagined. There were terrible resonances within me as Elric's memories confronted mine and came together in common guilt. Only now did I remember who I really was. How had Elric managed to take me over so thoroughly? I looked about me, expecting him to appear as he had first appeared to me in the concentration camp. But our relationship was by now far more profound.

Lobkowitz signed to the Indian. "Ayanawatta, sir. If you would take his other arm . . ."

Ayanawatta responded immediately, and I was hauled bodily up as the two men mounted the massive pachyderm who waited impatiently for us.

Now I could see the reasons for their urgency.

The Vikings were returning. Already they were running towards the pathway, which would be as useful to them as it would be to us. They had reassembled around their leader, who, in his mirror helm, still looked for all the world like my defeated enemy, Gaynor the Damned. I heard their voices echoing across the ice. Were they gaining on us?

I struggled to find my sword, but the two men gripped me tightly, and I was too weary to fight them.

"Do not fear Gunnar and company," said Prince Lobkowitz. "We will reach the safety of the city before they catch up with us."

"Once we are through the gates, he cannot harm us," the other man agreed.

I was relieved to see that at least the youth was safe. His pace dropped to a walk as he passed beneath the gateway and disappeared within. I looked back again. Gunnar—or Gaynor—was still pursuing us. There was something odd about the perspective. They seemed either too far away or too small in relation to the gigantic mammoth. Perhaps all this was an illusion or another dream? Should I trust my own eyes? Could I trust any of my senses? I felt as if I had swelled enormously in size and lost substance at the same time. My skin felt like a balloon about to burst. My head was fuzzy with a kind of fever. All perspective around me seemed to be warping and shifting. The mammoth became smaller, then larger. I felt sick. My eyes ached, and I could hold my head up no longer.

As the pair dragged me towards the city I lost my senses entirely. By the time I recovered we were behind the tall walls of the Kakatanawa city, and an unexpected security filled me. The youth with my wife's corpse was nowhere to be seen. Indeed, to my astonishment, the great courtyard around the gigantic city was completely deserted. And yet I had noted complex activity earlier as I approached the ziggurat. It seemed that everything had become an inchoate illusion, like a dream without rational meaning. How could such a vast city now give the impression of being empty?

Even the mammoth appeared surprised, lifting her huge trunk, her tusks actually making whistling noises in the air as she raised her head, and trumpeting out a greeting which received no response, save from the echoes among the empty tiers and the distant peaks.

Where were the Kakatanawa, the giant Indians who had brought me to the Chasm of Nihrain and ultimately to this world? I tried to free myself from the friendly hands still holding me. I needed to find someone who would give me the answers. I think I was babbling. At some point thereafter I fell into a deep sleep. But it was not a comforting sleep. My dreams were as disturbed as my life had become, and as mysterious.

In those dreams I saw a thousand incarnations of Oona, of the woman I loved, and in those same dreams I killed her a thousand times in a thousand different ways. I knew a thousand different kinds of remorse, of unbearable grief. But out of all this spiritual agony I seemed to find a tiny thread of hope. I saw it as a thin, grey wire which led from tragedy towards joyous resolution, where all fear was driven away, all terror quietened, all gentle dreams made real. And I wondered if Kakatanawa were just another name for Tanelorn, if here I might rest and have my love and my life restored.

"This is not Tanelorn." I awoke refreshed. The black giant Sepiriz was staring down at me. He held a goblet in his hand which he offered me. Yellow wine. I drank and felt better still. But then memory came back, and I sprang off the dais on which I had been lying. I looked around for my sword. Apart from the platform on which I had slept, the room was entirely empty. I ran into the next room, out of a door, into a corridor. All empty No furniture. No occupants.

"Is this Kakatanawa?"

"It is the city of that people, yes."

"Have they fled? I saw them . . ."

"You saw what travellers have seen for centuries now. You saw a memory of the city as she was in her prime. Now she dies, and her people are reduced to those few you have already met."

"And where are they?"

"Returned to their positions."

"My wife?"

"She is not dead."

"Alive? Where?"

Sepiriz tried to comfort me. He offered me more of the wine. "I told you that she was not dead. I did not say she was alive. The tree alone no longer has that power. The bowl alone no longer has that power. The disc itself alone has no power. The staff alone no longer has the power. The blade alone no longer has that power. The stone alone no longer has that power. The pivot is gone. Only if the Balance is restored can she live. Meanwhile, there is some hope. *Three by three, the unity.*"

"Let me see her!"

"No. It is too soon. There is more to do. And unless you play your prescribed role, you will never see her."

I could only trust him, though his assurances had hidden aspects to them. He had promised me I would see Oona again, but he had not told me she might take a different form.

"Do you understand, Count Ulric, that the Lady Oona saved your life?" asked Sepiriz gently. "While you fought Lord Shoashooan most bravely and weakened him considerably, it was the dreamthief's daughter who dealt him the final, dissipating blow, which sent his elements back to the world's twelve corners."

"She shot those arrows, I remember . . ."

"And then, after you precipitously attacked the demon duke, thinking you saved her, she aided you again. She at last took the shape of the White Buffalo whose destiny was to make our final road across the ice. She had the greatest tradition of resisting Lord Shoashooan. Do you understand? She became the White

Buffalo. The Buffalo is the trail-maker. She can lead the way to new realms. In this realm, she is the only force the wind elementals fear, for she carries the spirit of all the spirits."

"There are more elementals?"

"They combined in Lord Shoashooan, who was ever a powerful lord with many alliances among the air elementals. But now he has taken them in thrall. Although the twelve spirits of the wind are conquered by his powers, they can still re-form. All the winds serve him in this realm. It is why he succeeds so well. He commands those elementals who were once the friends of your people."

"Friends no longer?"

"Not while that mad archetype enslaves them. You must know that the elementals serve neither Law nor Chaos, that they have only loyalty to themselves and their friends. Only inadvertently do they serve the Balance. And now, against their will, they serve Lord Shoashooan."

"What is his power over them?"

"He it was who stole the Chaos Shield which should have brought your wife to this place. Lord Shoashooan waylaid her and took the shield. That was all he needed to focus his strength and conquer the winds. Had it not been for Ayanawatta's medicine, she would not have been with us at all! His magic flute has been our greatest friend in this."

"Lord Sepiriz, I undertook to serve your cause because you promised me the return of my wife. You did not tell me I would kill her."

"I was not sure that you would, this time."

"This time?"

"My dear Count Ulric." Prince Lobkowitz had entered the room. "You seem much recovered and ready to continue with this business!"

"Only if I am told more. Do I understand you rightly, Lord Sepiriz? You knew that I would kill my wife?"

The black giant's expression betrayed him, but I saw the sadness that was there also. Any blame I felt towards him dissipated. I sighed. I tried to remember some words I had heard. Was it from Lobkowitz, long ago? We are all echoes of some larger reality, yet every action we take ultimately decides the nature of truth itself.

"Nothing we do is unique. Nothing we do is without meaning or consequence." Lobkowitz's soft, cultured Austrian accent cut into Sepiriz's silence. The black giant seemed relieved, even grateful. He could not answer my challenge and feared to answer my question.

The ensuing silence was broken by a loud noise from outside. I walked past the dais on which I had been sleeping. I was almost naked, but the room was pleasantly warm. I went to the window. There was a courtyard outside, but we were many storeys above it. Old vines, thicker than my legs, climbed up the worn, glittering stonework. Autumn flowers, huge dahlias, vast hydrangeas, roses the span of my shoulders, grew among them, and it was only now I understood how ancient the place must truly be. Now it was a better home to nature than to man. Large, spreading trees grew in the courtyard, and tall, wild grass. Some distance below on another terrace I made out an entire orchard. Elsewhere were fields gone to seed, cattle pens, storehouses. There had been no-one here for centuries. I remembered the tales told of the Turks capturing Byzantium. They had believed they brought down an empire, but instead found a shell, with sheep grazing among the ruins of collapsed palaces. Was this the American Byzantium?

In the courtyard the great black mammoth, Bes, was being washed down by the youth, White Crow, and his older companion, Ayanawatta. The two men seemed good friends, and both were in the peak of physical fitness, though White Crow could not have been more than seventeen. His features, of course, were those of an albino. But it was not my family he resembled. It was someone else. Someone I knew well. My urge was to call to him, to ask after Oona, but Sepiriz had already assured me she was no longer dead. I forced myself to accept his leadership. He did not simply know the future—he understood all the futures which might proliferate if any of us strayed too far from the narrative which, like a complicated spell involving dozens of people in dozens of different actions, must be strictly adhered to if we wished to achieve our desire. A game of life or death whose rules you had to guess.

Looking up, the youth saw me. He became grave. He made a sign which I took to be one of comradeship and reassurance. The lad had charm, as had the aristocratic warrior at his side. Ayanawatta now offered me a faint, respectful bow.

Who were these aristocrats of the prairie? I had seen nothing like them in any of the wonderful historic documents I had studied about the early history of northern America. I did, however, recognise them as men of substance. Warriors and superbly fit, they were expensively dressed. The quality of workmanship in their beaded clothing, weaponry and ornaments was exquisite. Both men were clearly prominent among their own people. Their oiled and shaven heads; their scalp locks their only body hair, hanging just so at an angle to the glittering eagle feathers; the complicated tattoos and piercings of the older man; the workmanship of their buckskins and beading—all indicated unostentatious power. I wondered if, like the Kakatanawa, they too were the last of their tribes.

Again I was struck by the sense that, from within, the city seemed totally deserted. I looked back at tier upon tier fading into the clouds which hid the city's upper galleries.

Turning I could see beyond the great walls to the lake of ice and the ragged peaks of the mountains beyond. The whole world seemed abandoned of life. What had Sepiriz said about the inhabitants of this city? It must have housed millions of them.

I asked Lobkowitz about this phenomenon. He seemed unwilling to answer, exchanging looks with Lord Sepiriz, who shrugged. "I do not think it unsafe, any longer," he said. "Here we have no control of events at all. Whatever we say, the consequences will not change. It is only our actions which will bring change now, and I fear . . ." He dropped his great chin to his chest and closed his brooding eyes.

I turned from the window. "Where are the Kakatanawa, the people of this city?"

"You have met the only survivors. Do you know the other name for this city—the Kakatanawa name? I see you do not. It is Ikenipwanawa, which roughly means the Mountain of the Tree. Do you know of it? Just the tree itself, perhaps? So many mythologies speak of it."

"I do not know of it, sir. It is mainly my wife who concerns me now. You suggest she might live. Can time be reversed?"

"Oh, easily, but it would do you no good. The action has already taken place. And will take place again. Your memory cannot be changed so readily!"

"What *has* changed within these walls?" I asked him.

"Nothing. At least, not in many hundreds of years. Perhaps thousands. What you saw from the ice was an illusion of an inhabited city. It is one which has been maintained by those who guard the source of life itself. The reflective walls of the city serve more than one purpose."

"Has no-one ever come here and discovered the truth?"

"How could they? Until recently the lake was constantly boiling with viscous rock, the very lifestuff of the planet. Nothing could cross it, and nothing cared to. But since then cold Law has worked its grim sorcery and made the lake as you see it now. This is what Klosterheim and his friends have been doing. In response the pathway was conjured by Ayanawatta and White Buffalo, but of course it is now being used by our enemies. We make the paths, but we cannot control who uses them after us. It will not be long, no doubt, before they realise the trick and find a way of entering the city. So we must do all we have to as quickly as possible."

"I understood that time, as we know it, does not exist." I was becoming angry, beginning to think they tricked me. "Therefore there is no urgency."

Prince Lobkowitz allowed himself a small smile. "Some illusions are more powerful than others," he said. He seemed about to leave it at that, then added, "This is the last place in the multiverse you can find this fortress physically. Everywhere else it has transformed itself."

"Transformed? This was a fortress?"

"Transformed by what it contains. By what it must guard. At one stage in the multiversal story, this was a great and noble city, self-contained and yet able to help all who came to it seeking justice. Not unlike the city you call Tanelorn, it brought order and tranquillity to all who dwelled here.

"The human story is what changes so drastically. Passion and greed determine the course of nations, not their ideals. But without change we would die. So simple human emotions, those which have brought down a thousand other empires and destroyed a thousand Golden Ages, worked to bring about the destruction of this stability. It is a story of love and jealousy, but it will be familiar enough to you.

"This fortress—this great metropolis—was built to guard a symbol. First, a symbol was chiefly all that it was. Then, through human faith and creativity, the symbol took on more and more reality. Ultimately the symbol and the thing itself were one. They became the same, and this gave them strength. But it also gave them dangerous vulnerability. For once the symbol took physical shape, human action became far more involved in its destiny. Now symbol and reality are the same. We face the consequences of that marriage. Of what, in essence, we ourselves created."

"Are you speaking of a symbolic tree?" I asked. I could only think of old German tree worship, still recalled in our decorated Yule pines. "Or of the multiverse itself?"

He seemed relieved. "You understand the paradox? The multiverse and the tree are one, and each is encompassed by the other. That is the terrible dilemma of our human lives. We are capable of destroying the raw material of our own existence. Our imaginations can create actuality, and they can destroy it. But they are equally capable of creating illusion. The worst illusion, of course, is self-deception. From that fundamental illusion, all others spring. This is the great flaw which forever holds us back from redemption. It was what brought an end to the Golden Age this place represented."

"Do you say we can never be redeemed?"

Lobkowitz brought his hand to my shoulder. "That is the fate of the Champion of Humanity. It is the fate of us all. Time and space are in perpetual flux. We work to achieve resolution in the multiverse, but we can never know true resolution ourselves. It is the burden we carry. The burden of our kind."

"And this dilemma is repeated throughout countless versions of the same lives, the same stories, the same struggles?"

"Repetition is the confirmation of life. It is what we love in music and in many forms of art and science. Repetition is how we survive. It is, after all, how we reproduce. But when something has been repeated so many times that it has lost all resonance, then something must be done to change the story. New sap must be forced into old wood, eh? That is what we try to do now. But first we must bring all elements together. Do you understand what we are hoping to achieve, Count Ulric?"

I had to admit that I was baffled. Such philosophies were beyond my simple soul to fathom. But I said, "I think so." All I really knew was that if I played out my role in this, I would be reunited with Oona. And nothing else much mattered to me.

"Come," said Sepiriz, almost taking pity on me. "We will eat now."

We walked outside to a wide path curving around the city.

"What is the exact nature of this place?" I asked. "Some centre of the multiverse?"

Lobkowitz saw how mystified I was. "The multiverse has no centre any more than a tree has a centre, but this is where the natural and the supernatural meet, where branches of the multiverse twine together. These intersections produce unpredictable consequences and threaten everything. Size loses logic. That is why it is so important to retain the original sequences of events. To make a path and to stick to it. To choose the right numbers, as it were. It is how we have learned to order Chaos and navigate the Time Field. Have you not noticed that many people out there are of different dimensions? That is a sure sign how badly the Balance is under attack." Lobkowitz paused to look up. Tier after tier, the vast building disappeared into wisps of white cloud.

"The Kakatanawa built this city over the centuries from the original mountain," Lobkowitz told me as we continued past deserted homes, shops, stables. "They were a great, civilising people. They lived by the rule of Law. All who sought their protection were accepted on condition that they accepted the Law. All lived for one thing—for the tree which was their charge. They devoted themselves to it. Their entire nation lived to serve and nurture the tree, to protect it and to ensure that it continued to grow. They were a famous and respected people, renowned across the multiverse for their wisdom and reason. The great kings and chiefs of other nations sent their sons to be educated in the ways of the Kakatanawa. Even from other realms they came to learn from the wisdom of the People of the Tree. White Crow, of course, follows his family's long tradition . . ."

I said that I understood Kakatanawa to mean "People of the Circle." Why did he say "tree"?

He smiled. "The tree is in the circle. Time is the circle, and the tree is the multiverse. The circle is the sphere in which all exists. Space is but a dimension of this sphere."

"Space is a dimension of time?"

"Exactly." Lobkowitz beamed. "It explains so much when you realise that."

I was saved from any further contemplation of this bewildering notion by a sharp wailing sound. With sinking heart, I rushed to the nearest balcony. I saw dark clouds drawing in on the jagged horizon, gathering around one of the tallest peaks and writhing and twisting as if in an agonised effort to assume some living form. The clouds were making one huge figure, drawn by all the winds now in thrall to Lord Shoashooan. A long streamer of cloud sped from the central mass, across the ice, over the walls of the great fortress city, and lashed at our flesh like a whip, then retreated before we could respond.

Even Sepiriz bore a thin welt across his neck where the cloud had caught him. I imagined I saw a flash of fear in his eyes, but when I looked again he was smiling. "Your old friends march against us," Lobkowitz said. "That is the first taste of their power. From this moment on, we shall never know peace. And if Gaynor the Damned is successful, we shall know agony for eternity."

I raised an eyebrow at this. Lobkowitz was serious. "Once the Balance is destroyed, time as we know it is also destroyed. And that means we are frozen, conscious but inanimate, at the very moment before oblivion, living that death for ever."

I must admit I had begun to close my ears to Lobkowitz's existential litany. A future without Oona was bleak enough to contemplate.

Food forgotten, we watched the blue-black bruise of cloud forming and re-forming around the peaks of the mountains. A shout from another part of the gallery and we could see over the great gateway to the city, to the half-faded path which Ayanawatta had created with his flute. It now spread like dissipating mercury across the ice with men moving through it, leaping from patch to patch. The figures were tiny. They were not Kakatanawa. I thought at first they were Inuit, bulky in their furs, but then I realised that the leader had no face. Instead the light reflected from a mirrored helmet which was all too familiar to me. Another man strode beside him, one whose gait I recognised, and on the other side of him a smaller man, also familiar. But they were too far away for me to see their faces. They were without doubt his warriors.

The same Vikings who had tried to stop us reaching the fortress.

"Time is radiant," said Lobkowitz, anticipating my question. "Gaynor the Damned is now Gunnar the Doomed. Merely a fraction of movement sideways through the multiverse. He has gathered himself together, but he dare not live now without that helmet—for all his faces exist at once. Otherwise he is here in your twelfth century, as indeed is this city and much else . . ."

I turned to look at him. "Does Gunnar still seek the Grail?"

Lobkowitz shrugged. "It is Klosterheim who longs for the Grail. In his warped way he seeks reconciliation. Gunnar seeks death the way others seek treasure. But not merely *his* death. He seeks the death of everything. For only by achieving that will he justify his own self-murder."

"He is my first cousin, yet you seem to know him better than I do." I was fighting off a creeping sense of dread. "Did you know him in Buda-pesht or Mirenburg?"

"He is an eternal, as you are an eternal. As you have alter egos, fellow avatars of the same archetype, so he takes many names and several guises. But the relative you know as Gaynor von Minct will always be the criminal Knight of the Balance, who challenged its power and failed. And who challenges it again and again."

"Lucifer?"

"Oh, all peoples have their particular versions of that fellow, you know."

"And does he always fail in his challenges?"

"I wish that were so," said Lobkowitz. "Sometimes, I must say, he understands his folly and seeks to correct his actions. But there is no such hope here, my dear count. Come, we must confer. Lord Shoashooan gathers strength again." He paused to glance out of another opening in the great wall winding up the ziggurat. "Gaynor and his friends bring considerable sorcery to this realm."

"How shall we resist them?" I looked around at the little party, the black giant, Prince Lobkowitz, the sachem Ayanawatta and White Crow. "How can we possibly fight so many? We are outnumbered and virtually unarmed. Lord Shoashooan gathers strength while we have nothing to fight him with. Where's my sword?"

Sepiriz looked to Lobkowitz, who looked to Ayanawatta and White Crow. Both men said nothing. Sepiriz shrugged. "The sword was left on the ice. We cannot get the third until . . ."

"Third?" I said.

Ayanawatta pointed behind him. "White Crow left his own blade down there with Bes. His shield is there, too. But again, we lack the necessary third object of power. There is no hope now, I think, of waking the Phoorn guardian. He dies. And with him the tree. And with the tree, the Balance . . ." He sighed hopelessly.

The silence of the city was suddenly cut by a squealing shriek, like metal cutting metal, and something took shape above the ice directly behind where Gaynor and his men were moving cautiously along the dissipating trail.

I was sure we could defeat the warriors alone, but I dreaded whatever it was I saw forming behind them.

It shrieked again.

The sound was full of greedy, anticipatory mockery. Lord Shoashooan, of course, had returned. No doubt, too, Gaynor had helped him increase his strength.

White Crow turned away from the scene. He was deeply troubled. "I sought my father on the island, in my crow form. I thought he would help us. That he would be the third. But Klosterheim was waiting for me and captured me. At first I thought that you were him, my father. If you had not been near . . . The Kakatanawa came to rescue me after Klosterheim went away. They released me and found you. My father is, after all, elsewhere. He followed his dream and was swallowed by a monster. I thought he had returned to the Dragon Throne, but if he did, he has come back for some reason. This must not be." He lowered his voice, troubled. "If that man is who I am sure it is, I must not fight him. I cannot fight my own father."

I frowned. "Elric is your father?"

He laughed. "Of course not. How could that be? Sadric is my father."

Ayanawatta touched his friend's arm. "Sadric is dead. You said so. Swallowed by the *kenabik*."

White Crow was genuinely puzzled. "I said he was swallowed. Not that he was killed."

20

The Pathfinder

Pour the beer and light the feasting fires,
Bring you in the tall Yule trees,
Without, let Father Frost and Brother Death reside
Let Mother Famine fly to farther fields,
Raise high the trees and high the ale-cup lift,
Let good will rule and to ill will all folk give short shrift.

Old Moorsdale Song

Lord Shoashoon did not merely take shape above the fading causeway. He drew strength from the surrounding mountains. Storm clouds boiled in from north, south and west, masses of dark grey and black shot through with points of white, tumbling swiftly towards us.

Shale and rocks began to fly towards his spinning form, and from within that bizarre body his grotesque face laughed and raved in its greedy rage, utterly deranged. He was now more powerful than when either Oona or I had fought him. His size increased by the moment. Pieces of ice flew up from the lake to join the whirlwind's heavy débris. And when I looked deep into it, I saw the twisting bodies of men and beasts, heard their cries mingled with the vicious shriek of the cruel Warlord of Winds.

Realising suddenly what he faced, White Crow frowned, murmured something to himself, then turned and began to run back down the long, curving roadway between the tiers. Sepiriz and Ayanawatta both cried out to him, but he ignored them. He flung some cryptic remark over his shoulder and then disappeared from sight. Was he deserting us? Where was Oona? Did he go to her? Was she safe? And who did he think his father was? Gaynor? How did White Crow hope to avoid conflict?

Questions were impossible. Even Sepiriz seemed flustered by the speed with which Lord Shoashooan was manifesting himself. The maddened Lord of Winds was already ten times more powerful than when he had sought to block our way across the ice.

Prince Lobkowitz was grim as he hurried up the ramps. Higher and higher we climbed, and the tornado rose to match our height. The causeways grew tighter and narrower as we neared the top of the city, and the wind licked and tasted us, playing with us, to let us know there was no escaping its horrible intelligence, its vast destructive power.

As we neared the top, heavy pieces of earth and stone flew against the walls of Kakatanawa, chipping at surfaces, slashing into foliage. A large rock narrowly missed me, and Sepiriz shook twice as he was hit. Part of an outer wall fell. Through the gap I saw the tiny figures of the Vikings on the ice moving in closer, but we were momentarily safe from any immediate confrontation with them. We had no way to resist the invader even if we could engage him. Lord Sepiriz carried no sword. Save for Ayanawatta's bow and Prince Lobkowitz's cutlass, we had no weapons.

We had reached a broad-based tower with dark red walls and a deep blue ceiling and floor; a central spiral staircase led like a cord of silver up to a platform and what was clearly an experimental laboratory. An alchemical study, perhaps? Certainly Prince Lobkowitz had expected to find it there. He began at once to climb the stairs.

"Let's have a better look at our enemies," he murmured.

We followed him up. Here was an assortment of large, chunky machinery, mostly constructed of stone, like an old mill with huge granite cogwheels and smaller ones of beaten gold and platinum. Apparently this people, too, had no notion of smelting iron. The strange, bulky cogs and levers worked a series of lenses and mirrors. There was something familiar about all this.

Of course. My father had experimented with a smaller version at Bek before the First War. I realised we were looking at a rare form of camera obscura, which, by means of mirrors, could show scenes of the surface around the city. It was not entirely mechanical in nature. There were other forces involved in its construction, more common to Melniboné than Munich. Indeed, when Lord Sepiriz joined the stocky prince, he easily made parts move by a murmured command and a gesture. Gradually the two men brought the scene outside the gates into view.

I had been right. Gaynor the Damned led them. Near him was his turncoat lieutenant Klosterheim. The third man also wore a helmet, which obscured most of his face, but his eyes were shockingly familiar. He had an edgy, wolfish air, as did all the Vikings, but his was of a different quality. There was something fundamentally self-contained about the figure, and I feared him more than the others.

The Vikings did not look as if they had slept or eaten well for some time. Their journey here had clearly not been an easy one. I had rarely seen a hungrier bunch of cut-throats. They watched the Wind Demon with considerable wariness and did not look happy to be of Gaynor's party now. They were almost as nervous of the huge whirlwind as we were! Only the stranger in the black helmet seemed to be in a different mood. His eyes in shadow, his pale lips half-hidden by the upwardly thrusting chin-guard, the man was smiling. Like his eyes, his smile was one I recognised and feared.

Still larger rocks smashed into the walls, leaving deep gashes. Sepiriz was furious, muttering about the age of the place and what it had meant for so many millennia.

I think he had believed us safe, at least temporarily, in the remote fortress city, but these events were proving far more dangerous and whimsical than he had expected. He realised he may have underestimated the danger. The developing situation appeared to have defeated his imagination.

A gritty wind howled into the tall camera and whistled around the complicated confection of copper wires and polished mirrors, the worn granite cogwheels and brass pivots, the pools of mercury. There was a busy humming, a rattling and buzzing as the wind touched the delicate, half-supernatural instruments. Polished glass flashed and blinded me. Thin tubes rattled and hissed and scraped together.

Lord Shoashooan's voice whispered through the tall rooms, finding strange, ugly echoes. "Mortals and immortals both, you face your end without dignity or grace. Accept the fact that the Balance is finished. Its central staff has been lost, its scales discarded. Soon the tree itself will die. The regulator of the multiverse has failed you. Law triumphs. The steady calm of complete stability awaits you. Time is abolished, and you can anticipate, as do I, a new order."

"The order you promise is the stasis of death," Lord Sepiriz replied contemptuously. "You it is, Lord Shoashooan, who dishonours your own name. You it is who lacks both dignity and grace. You are a busy noise surrounding a vacuum. To destroy is your only effect. Otherwise you are less than a bird's dying breath."

A groan of anger. The walls rattled and cracked as the whirlwind's strength increased still more. Outside another great crash as masonry loosened and tumbled.

Lord Sepiriz's hands played over the strange instruments. His shoulders were hunched with the urgency of his actions. His eyes flashed from one point to another as if he sought a weakness somewhere.

He was reading signals within the mirrors, frowning over swirling glasses and tubes.

The chamber shook. It was like a heavy earthquake. My companions looked at one another. Clearly they had never anticipated such a force. Though outwardly artificial, this city had once been a wild mountain. Within she was *still* a living mountain. And Lord Shoashooan had the power to challenge this mountain, to threaten its destruction!

Outside, the entire landscape was filled with the wildly whirling débris. Below, at the apex, stood Gaynor and his men, looking up at the once invulnerable gates of the city as the wind remorselessly battered them to destruction. I could already see the gates beginning to bulge and split. Their iron bands and hinges, which hitherto could withstand any attack, now warped and twisted under the pressure.

We were deafened by the roaring sound, and our hair and clothing lashed violently in every direction. Lord Sepiriz shouted at me. He signalled. I could not understand what he wanted.

The mercury pool that was a mirror swirled again, and I saw a man's face in astonishing detail. It was the stranger who had come with Gaynor and Klosterheim. He stared upwards, presumably at his supernatural ally. His eyes, like mine, were crimson. They contained profound and complex experience. I wondered how any human soul could bear the burden of knowledge revealed in those eyes. Only Elric of Melniboné was sorcerer and warrior powerful enough to consider taking that burden. I doubted if there had ever been a human character equally strong.

The pool's surface flickered to show, full-length, a black-armoured, blackhelmed warrior. He had a huge round war-board on his arm, canvas covering its blazon. With some surprise I saw that he carried a black sword identical to my own. Then, for the first time, the truth began to dawn on me. It was so enormous it had eluded me. Three of us? Three swords? Three shields? But who carried the shields?

Sepiriz pulled me away from the mirror pool. "It is drawing you in. You'll drown in that if you're not careful. Many others have."

"Drown?" I laughed. "Drown in a reflection of myself?"

Ayanawatta came to join me. "So you understand." He radiated a certain calmness. He represented common sense in all this insanity. "You would not be the first to do that." His smile was quiet, comradely. "Some might say that was your friend Gunnar's fate!"

The more I knew this tall red man, the more I liked and respected him. He was a natural leader. He was unassuming, egalitarian, but acted decisively and with due caution. All the great leaders, like Alexander, could sit at backgammon with common soldiers and still have them believe him a living god.

I wanted to ask Ayanawatta where the rest of his people were. His tribal style was familiar to me, but I was not sufficiently knowledgeable to identify it. This was no time to satisfy such curiosity. Events were moving too swiftly. We had all been thrown together by our different circumstances. I had no idea how Gaynor and company had reached Kakatanawa or why they were here.

The shrieking air was painful. My ears felt as if needles were being inserted and twisted in them. I covered them as best I could and noted that my companions were equally affected. Lord Sepiriz found some wax and handed it out to us. Stuffing the slick, malleable material into my ears relieved the worst of the howling. I could hear Prince Lobkowitz when he approached me. Cupping his hand around my ear, he spoke into it.

"We cannot fight Lord Shoashooan or his allies. We lack the necessary tools to destroy him, so all we can do now is retreat. We must abandon the outer city and seek the deeper reality within. We must fall back to the Skrayling Oak."

That was all he was able to say before the screeching wind grew even louder and fingers of ice wormed their way into my clothing and found the flesh beneath. I knew piercing agony and swore aloud at the fierceness of it just as White Crow reappeared in the doorway. There was something behind him. Something dark and looming. I longed to draw my sword, to run to his assistance, and then I realised it was a beast with him, his trusty pachyderm, Bes. Fearing for her safety, he had returned for her. Her saddle was on her back, and her burdens were covered by a great white buffalo robe edged with blue and scarlet, which made it seem as if she had a dromedary hump. Whether she would be better off with us or without us was an open question at that moment.

Bes moved as rapidly as the rest of us as we dashed through the camera obscura and through various other chambers, all of which were clothed in different raw metals, many of them precious. Our feet slipped and slid on the floors of these tunnels. Our reflections were distorted by the curving, polished walls. Twice my own face appeared, enlarged and transformed into something leering and hideous. The others scrambled to get away from the place. I found myself laughing in my grief-madness. How close these people had been to changing the eternal verities! What had destroyed them?

At last we were all crammed into a crystal room scarcely large enough to take the curling tusks of the great mammoth, let alone the rest of us. My hand was on the huge, curved ivory surface of one tusk as she turned her mild, unfrightened eye to regard me. A wall had fallen away behind her, revealing that we were above an unstable lake of rising and falling crystals.

Sepiriz muttered and growled, motioning with his staff over the crystals. They hissed in reply. Sluggishly they formed a rough shape and then fell back into the same amorphous mass. Again Sepiriz spoke to the crystals. This time they swirled rapidly and formed a cone with a black centre.

Then we fell!

I shouted out, trying to resist the descent as the entire top of the city was enveloped in a sulphuric cloud. The crystals opened like a mouth threatening to swallow me. I stared in awe into a world of intense green foliage. Every shade of green, so vivid it almost blinded me.

The rest of the world roared into a void and disappeared.

We stood in the swaying top branches of a huge tree. The ground was so far away that I could see nothing below. Only endless leaves. Foliage stretched out and downwards from the canopy. I peered through giant limbs, heavy twigs and myriad leaves, into the complexity of all that grew from a single, vast trunk. For what might have been miles I could see massive branches, themselves supporting other branches which supported still more branches. I was dazed with wonder. The city had contained a mountain that in turn contained this measureless oak!

With a sign, Sepiriz jumped into the foliage. I saw him sink slowly, as if through water; and then I followed, and we were all descending little by little through womb-rich air, salty and thick with life. Everywhere the branches of that great tree stretched into infinity. The trunk of the tree was so large we could not see the whole of one side. It was like a wall stretching on for ever. The thickest limbs were equally difficult to accept for what they were.

I was overwhelmed by the scale of it all and wondered if I would ever find my wife again. Impotent fury bubbled in me. Yet I remembered the admonition I had heard more than once since my adventures began so long ago in Nazi Germany: *Every one of us who fights in the battle, fights as an equal. Every action we take has meaning and effect.* My moment was bound to come. This hope sustained me as we drifted like motes of living dust down through the lattice of intersecting realities, of dreams and possibilities. We sank down into the multiverse itself and let it embrace us.

Countless shades of green were dappled by a hidden sun. Sometimes a shaft of golden or silvern light blinded me or illuminated a mysterious, twisting corridor of foliage. Leaves that were not quite leaves, yet which proliferated and reached enormous distances. Branches that were not quite branches became curling, silver roads on which women and men walked, oblivious of the intricacy around them. And these branches turned back and put out further branches, which in turn formed a matrix within a matrix, a billion realities, each one a version of my own.

Oona! I struggled in the hope of glimpsing my wife.

Down we sank in Sepiriz's supernatural wake, down through what was at once concrete reality and abstract conception, passing through countless permutations, each one telling the same human story of conflict without and within:

the perpetual conflict, the perpetual quest for balance, the perpetual cycle of life, struggle, resolution and death which made us one with the rest of creation. What put us at odds with creation was, ironically, the very intelligence and imagination which was itself creative. Man and multiverse were one, united in paradox, in love and anger, life, death and transfiguration.

Oona!

Through golden clouds of delicate tracery, through russet, viridian and luminous lavender, through great swathes of crimson and silver, we fell. Looking up I saw only the wide branches of a tree stretching to where the roof of the pyramid would be. It became obvious the area enclosed by the Kakatanawa city was far greater than the city itself. The city could have rested on the topmost branches of the multiversal tree. If it guarded the crown of the tree, who or what guarded the trunk and roots below?

Where was my wife? Was I being led towards her or away from her?

Oona!

Slowly I fell, unable to decrease or otherwise control my descent. Save for my concerns over my wife, I had no real sense of fear. I was not sure if I had died or if I was still alive. The question was unimportant. What seemed solid as we dropped towards it became less dense as we passed through it. And in turn the tenuous grew solid.

I could not imagine the variations in scale involved. Outside the pyramid, I was a speck of dust in the quasi-infinite multiverse. Within, I was the size of galaxies.

I passed through the substance of the tree as through water, for here mass and scale were the means by which the multiverse ordered its constantly proliferating realities, enabling them to coexist. Perhaps it was *our* mass that changed as we fell and not the tree's. I realised that I felt no ordinary physical sensations, merely occasional electrical pulses from within my body that altered in intensity and rhythm with every breath I took. I had the feeling I was not breathing air at all but sweet ichor, what some might call ectoplasm. It flowed like oil, in and out of my lungs, and if it had any effect on me at all it was only to sharpen my vision.

Where was Oona? I had the peculiar impression that I was not only "seeing" with my eyes, but with all my other senses, including the ordinary ones of touch, smell and hearing. Unfamiliar, dormant senses now wakened in response to some recognisable supra-reality, this vision of a living multiverse.

Perhaps a man of more intellectual bent might have understood all this better, but I was helplessly in awe. In my exhilaration I felt I was in the presence of God.

I fell through a field of blue, perhaps a sudden patch of sky, and as I did so my soul filled with a rare sense of peace. I shared a contented tranquillity with all the other human souls who occupied this place. I had passed briefly through heaven.

Once more I floated among green-gold branches and could see my companions above and below me. I tried to call out to Lobkowitz, who was nearest, to ask where Oona was, but my voice made only broad, deep rolling sounds, not recognisable words.

These tones took on shape and a life of their own, curling off into the depths of blossoming scarlet. I tried to move towards the colour field, but a gigantic hand seized me and set me back on course. I heard only what seemed to be the words "Catch up cave," and looking back I saw that the hand was Lobkowitz's though he seemed of ordinary size and some distance off. The hand and arm retreated, and I accepted this as a tacit warning that I should not try to stop my descent or change my course. The peculiarities of scale and mass which seemed so odd to me were clearly the natural conditions of this place. But what exactly was the place? The multiverse? If so, it was contained in a single mountain on a single planet of a universe. How could that be?

My emotions seemed to be dissipating. My whole being was evaporating, joining the ectoplasmic atmosphere through which I floated. Terror, anxiety, concern for my loved ones, became abstract. I lost myself to this sense of infinity. I did not expect to stop my fall nor ever know an ending to my adventure. I was mesmerised by the experience. We were all in the embrace of the Tree of Life itself!

I remembered the Celtic notion of the Mother Sea to which the wandering spirit always returned. Its presence became increasingly tangible. Was this what dying felt like? Were my loved ones already dead? Would I join them?

Unconcerned now, I was content to drift down and down through the verdant lattice and not care if I ever reached a bottom. Yet increasingly I began to notice areas I could only describe as desolate. Branches had withered and broken as vitality had been drained from them by Law or by Chaos or by the ordinary, inevitable processes of decay. And slowly it began to dawn upon me that perhaps the entire tree was truly dying.

But if the multiverse were no more than an idea, and this was only then its visualisation, how could it possibly be saved by the actions of a few men and women? Were our rituals so powerful that they could change the fundamentals of reality?

Below me now I saw an endless flow of pale green-and-yellow dunes racing and rippling, as if blown by a cosmic wind, crossed by curving rivers of chalky white and jade, dotted with pools which bubbled and gasped. I smelled rich salt. I smelled a million amniotic oceans. Around me a dark cloud gushed rapidly upwards and spread away, forming its own tree shape. Another followed it, dark grey, white, boiling foam. Another. Until there was a forest of gaseous trees. A hissing forest that rose before me and then collapsed into shivering star clusters. More green-gold branches. More peace. Eternal tranquillity . . .

The whispering gases arose again, the darkling turbulence, and a shrill voice yelling into a gorge of bubbling blood. I was losing my own substance. I could feel everything that was myself on the very brink of total dissipation. At any moment I would join the writhing chaos all around me. Whatever identity I had left slipped towards total destruction. Intellectually I felt some urgency, but my body did not respond.

Only when I remembered Oona did any sense of volition return.

Looking about me and down I saw three huge human figures standing on a surface of glittering, rainbow rock. To my horror, I recognised them. How had they arrived here before us? How much more powerful had they become?

Three giants. Klosterheim and Gaynor the Damned I identified at once. The third was the black-armoured man I had seen with them earlier. But now I recognised him completely. It was indeed Elric of Melniboné. The canvas cover had been removed from his shield, which displayed the eight-arrowed Sign of Chaos. A black runeblade trembled on his hip. There was no doubting his identity. But what of his loyalty?

The three had obviously come here by supernatural means. Now standing to my left on a great limb they were completely unaware of me and were arguing fiercely among themselves. I was apparently too small for them to see just as they were almost too huge for me to contemplate. I looked up at Lobkowitz above me. He was staring at the three figures with open dismay.

A gust of wind raced past us unexpectedly, and we were swept away from the gigantic figures, losing them among the branches.

I saw Sepiriz leaping and rolling towards me in an extraordinary sequence of movements. Thus he negotiated this strange version of space. He spoke, but his words were meaningless to me. Lobkowitz then said something. I saw White Crow and Bes, with the white-skinned youth clinging to the beast's thick fur. Where was Oona? Imitating Lord Sepiriz's strange tumbling method of locomotion, Ayanawatta trailed him as they came rolling towards me.

Is Oona with you?

Their voices were enormous, booming, on the verge of being incoherent. Their bodies were huge. Bigger even than Gaynor and company. But the hands that reached towards me were only as large as my own. Each hanging on to one of my arms, Sepiriz and the Mohican sachem were concentrating on guiding me slowly through our descent.

I stood on spongey material that reminded me, stupidly, of my childhood, when we had played on our feather beds. I saw myself in a field of multicoloured flowers. There were millions of varieties and colours, but the petals were all small and tight and gave the picture the quality of a pointillist painting. I half expected to see that my companions were also made up of tiny dots. They did, indeed, have a slightly amorphous quality.

The vivid colours; strong, amniotic scents; the warm, womblike air—all emphasised the total silence around us. When I spoke I communicated with my companions, but not in any familiar way, and it made me economical with words.

A fern as big as the world opened its fronds to embrace me. A million shades of green turned slowly to black as they disappeared into the distance. Endless slender saplings, silver and pale gold, appeared so substantial I expected at any moment to see a woodsman padding through them.

White Crow and the mammoth were nowhere to be seen. Where *was* Oona? I longed for a glimpse of my wife. I wept with guilt at my own hasty folly. I hoped with impotent optimism.

Ayanawatta, Lobkowitz and Sepiriz surrounded me and moved with me, guiding me in long, wading steps. Their outlines were now sharper, and everything had a more tangible quality. Were they taking me at last to Oona? The sweetness of the wild flowers began to dominate the saltier tastes of the sea. Ahead of us was another blinding mass of varied green. With wonder I looked upon the Skrayling Oak, the object of so many dream-quests.

I was distracted from this vision by a sense of more than one self nearby. It was hard enough for me to cope with the presence of Prince Elric, whose experience was supernaturally mingled with my own and manifested itself always in my dreams if not continually in my conscious mind. It felt as if these other intelligences, these alter egos, were also Elric. Mentally I was in a hall of repeating mirrors, where the same image is reversed and reflected again and again to infinity. I was one of millions, and the millions were also one.

I was intratemporally infinite and contained by the infinite. Yet that infinity was also my own brain, which contained all others. The mind of man alone was free to wander the infinity of the multiverse. One contains the other and one is contained in the other . . . Not only were these paradoxes of particular comfort to me, they felt natural. For all my fear of the place, I now knew a resounding resurgence of hope. I was returning home. I would soon be reunited with Oona. In this long moment, at least, I knew she was safe, hidden between life and death.

Only if the tree itself died would she die. But whether it was certain she would live again, I could not tell.

The green, gold and silver lattice of the mighty tree filled the horizon. Framed against it I saw three groups of three men. Each of the men had his head bowed, and each had his hands wrapped around a tall, slender spear. At their belts were polished war clubs. They wore their hair in single scalp locks decorated with eagle feathers, and their bodies were tattooed and painted in a way I had seen before. All were pale and distinctly similar, in both physique and face, yet every one was different. I knew who they were. They were the last of the Kakatanawa, the guardians of the prophecy, of the tree. Perhaps they now stood funeral watch for the tree itself. There was something sombre about the scene when there should have been joy.

"The tree is sick, you see." Sepiriz's deep voice sounded in my ear. "The roots are being poisoned by the very creature enjoined to protect them. That which regulates the Balance was stolen by Gaynor, then found by another . . ."

"What creature is it that guards the roots?"

"Gunnar's Vikings would probably tell you it was the Worm Ouroboros, the great world snake who eats his own tail—the dragon who both defends and gnaws the roots. Most of your world's mythologies contain some version. But Elric would know him as a blood relative. You have heard of the Phoorn?"

Already there were too many echoes. I might have replied that Elric would no doubt recognise the name, but I was not Elric! I refused to be Elric! The Phoorn name, in my present state, had no more significance to me than any other. Yet I did know what he meant. I was simply denying the memories which came unsummoned from my alter ego. Images crept insistently into my consciousness. My being was suffused with a deliciously terrifying sensation. My blood recognised the word even as my brain refused it.

"Why have you brought us to this place, Lord Sepiriz? And why are those three here? Why so gigantic? I thought we had escaped them. I thought we came here for our security. I also thought we came to find my wife! Now you confront me with my worst enemies!"

The ground rose and fell beneath my feet like a breathing beast.

"Elric is not your enemy. He is yourself."

"Then perhaps he is indeed my worst enemy, Lord Sepiriz."

I could see them now, wading towards us in all their martial weight, swords drawn and ready to spill blood. Again I was all too aware that we were virtually unarmed.

Something vibrated forcefully against my feet. I looked down, half expecting the ground to be thoroughly alive. Wild flowers swept like a tide around my legs. There was activity in the depths below. I imagined infinite roots spreading out to mirror the boughs above. I imagined caverns through which even now the dark reversals of ourselves prowled, seeking bones to break and spirits to suck. Was this the route the giants had taken to arrive here now? Had Shoashooan been unable to gain access to this oddly holy place?

Then far away and below I heard a wild, angry howling. I understood Lord Shoashooan had not been left behind.

There was more movement over near the tree's wide trunk. The multiverse was shaken by a long, mournful groan. I breathed in a familiar scent. I could resist the memory no longer.

"I know the Phoorn," I said.

21

The Skrayling Tree

Seeking the worm at the heart of the world,
Wild warriors carried carnage with their swords
To Golddune, the glittering gate of Alfheim.
Bold were these bears in their byrnies of brass,
White-maned horses bore them in their boats,
To wild Western shores and rich reiving,
Where three kings ruled in Hel's harsh realm.
Bravely they defied Death's cold Queen,
So came in conquest to the Skrayling Tree.

—The Third Edda,
Elrik the White (tr. Wheldrake)

I was surrounded by the finest flowing copper spreading like a woman's auburn hair, lock after lock, wave after wave into a crowd of people hiding among tall grasses, waiting to join with me. Did they protect my wife? I sought only Oona. I prayed Oona had lived long enough for me to save her. As I came closer to the riders, I saw they were not people. They were instead intricately shaped and coloured scales, dimpled by millions of points of light, flashing with a thousand colours, each one of extraordinary beauty. I was aware that I saw only a shadow of an older glory. And where another might have known wonder, I knew sympathy.

I looked on the body of a sickly Phoorn, blood-kin to my ancestors. Some said we were born of the same womb before history began.

The Phoorn were what the people of the Young Kingdoms called dragons. But these were not dragons. These were Phoorn, who flew between the realms, who had no avatars, but made the whole multiverse their flying grounds. The Phoorn had conquered entire universes and witnessed the deaths of galaxies. Blood-kin to the princes of Melniboné—who drank their venom and formed bonds of flesh and souls with them, creating even more terrible progeny, half-human, half-Phoorn—they had loyalties only to their own kind and the fundamental lifestuff of the multiverse.

My blood moved in harmony with this monster's, and I knew at once that it was ill, perhaps dying, its soul suffused with sadness. I understood our kinship. This Phoorn was a brother to my forefathers. The poor creature had known past anguish, but now he was near complete exhaustion. From a half-open mouth his poison dripped into the roots of the tree he was sworn to protect. He was too weak to drag his head clear. Massive quicksilver tears fell from his milky, half-blind eyes.

His condition was obvious. His *skeffla'a* was gone. The membrane which drew sustenance from the multiverse itself and allowed the Phoorn to travel wherever they chose was also the creature's means of feeding. They might take thousands of years in their passing, but ultimately, without a *skeffla'a*, the Phoorn were mortal. There were few of them left now. They were too curious and reckless to survive in large numbers. And this one was the greatest of the Phoorn, chosen to guard the Soul of Creation. It was rare enough for these elders to grow weak, almost unheard-of for one to sicken.

"What supernatural force is capable of stealing a *skeffla'a* from the great world snake?" said Sepiriz from somewhere nearby. "Who would dare? He guards the roots of the multiversal tree and ensures the security of the Cosmic Balance."

"He sickens," I said. "And as he sickens his venom increases its effect . . ."

"Poisoning the roots as the Balance tips too far. Virtue turned to vice. This is a symbol of all our conflicts throughout the multiverse." Lobkowitz joined us. Wild flowers ran around our legs like water, but their nauseating stench was scarcely bearable.

"A symbol only?" I asked.

"There is no such thing as a symbol only," said Sepiriz. "Everything that exists has a multitude of meanings and functions. A symbol in one universe is a living reality in another. Yet one will function as the other. They are at their most powerful when the symbol and that which it symbolises are combined." Lord Sepiriz shared a glance with Prince Lobkowitz.

Out of nowhere came the high, lovely sound of the flute. I knew Ayanawatta had begun to play.

The Kakatanawa were aroused. They lifted their great heads and stared around them. Their eagle feathers trembled in their flowing scalp locks. They shifted their grip on their war clubs and lances and made their shields more comfortable on their arms. They readied themselves carefully for battle.

Was this to be the final fight? I wondered.

The sound of the flute faded, drowned by a harsher blare. I sought the source.

There above us was Elric of Melniboné, blowing on the heavily ornamented bull's horn Gaynor had brought with them. Elric's black helm glowed with a disturbing radiance as he flung back his swirling cloak and lifted his head, making a long, sharp note which cut through the quasi-air; caused great, dark green clouds to blossom and spread; shook the ground beneath my feet and made it crack. Through the cracks oozed grey snapping paste which licked at my feet with evident relish.

I jumped away from the stuff. Was it some monster's tentacle reaching up from the depths? I heard it grumbling away down below.

Defended by the Kakatanawa, I approached the Phoorn. In relation to this ancient creature I was about the size of a crow compared to Bes, the mammoth. I walked through a forest of tall stalks which might have been oversized grass or saplings of the original tree, and eventually I stood looking up at those huge, fading eyes, feeling a frisson of filial empathy.

What ails thee, Uncle? I asked.

Thin vapour sobbed from the beast's nostrils. His long, beautiful head lay along the base of the tree. Venom bubbled on his lips with every laboured breath and soaked into the roots below. His mind found mine.

I am dying too slowly, Nephew. They have stolen my skeffla'a and divided it into three parts, scattered through the multiverse. It cannot be recovered. By this means they stop me from finding the strength I need. I know the tree is being poisoned by my dying. You must kill me. That is your fate.

Some cruel intelligence had devised the death of this Phoorn. An intelligence which understood the agony of guilt the Phoorn must feel at betraying his own destiny. An intelligence which appreciated the irony of making the tree's defender its killer and of making the Phoorn's own kin his destroyer.

I have no weapon, Uncle. Wait. I will find one.

I looked over my shoulder to question Lord Sepiriz. He was gone.

Instead, Gaynor the Damned stood behind me, some distance away. His armoured body glistened with brilliant, mirrored silver. On his right hand was Johannes Klosterheim in his puritan black. On his left hand was Elric of Melniboné in all his traditional war-gear. Gaynor's dark sword hung naked in his mailed hand, and Elric was drawing another black blade which quivered and sang, hungered for blood.

They stepped forward as one, and the effect was startling. As they moved closer towards me, their size decreased until by the time we were face to face, we were all of the same proportions.

I peered past them. Something lurked behind them, but I could not determine what it was.

"So good of you to grant the dragon mercy, Cousin Ulric." Gaynor's voice was quiet within his helm. He seemed amused. "He will die in his own time. And you have killed your wife, too, I note. Your quest has scarcely been a success. What, in all the worlds, makes you believe that you will not continue to repeat these tragedies down the ages? You cannot escape destiny, cousin. You were ordained to fight for ever, as I am ordained to carry the instant of my death with me for eternity. So I have brought us both a blessing. Or at very least a conclusion. You were never fated to know peace with a woman, Champion. At least not for long. Now you have no destiny at all, save death. For I am here to cut the roots of the multiversal tree, to send the Cosmic Balance irredeemably to destruction and take the whole of creation with me to my punishment!"

He spoke softly and with certainty.

I had no reason to listen to him. I refused to let my annoyance with his crazy mockery show in my voice. I was greedy for my lost sword, which I had flung out over the ice. What could I do against such odds?

"So," I said, "the void has a voice. But the void is still a void. You seek to fill up your soulless being with empty fury. The less you are able to fill it, the more furious you become. You are a sad wretch, cousin, stamping about in all your armour and braggadocio."

Gaynor ignored this. Klosterheim allowed himself a slight glint of amusement. From his bone-white face Elric's crimson eyes stared steadily into mine.

All I thought when I looked at him was *Traitor.* I hated him for the company he kept. How was it that he had been on my side against Gaynor on the Isle of Morn and now stood shoulder to shoulder with the corrupter of universes?

Klosterheim looked worn. He had drained himself with his conjuring and spell-casting. I was reminded of the dying pygmy I had encountered on the way to Kakatanawa. Klosterheim, like me, had no natural penchant for sorcery. "You are unarmed, Count Ulric. You have no power at all against us. This evil thing that you call 'uncle' will be witness to the final moments of the Balance as it fades into non-existence. The tree falls. The very roots are poisoned and can be attacked with steel at last. The multiverse returns to insensate Chaos. God and Satan die and in death are reconciled. And I shall be reconciled."

These supernatural events, like a constant, ongoing nightmare, had clearly affected his sanity rather more than mine. But I had something to focus on. Something more important than life or death, waking or dreaming. I had to find my wife. I needed to know that I had not destroyed her.

Where was White Crow? What had he done with Oona? Through the dark, gorgeous mist roiling at Gaynor's back, shadows stirred and drew closer.

The Kakatanawa.

Where is my wife? I asked. *Where is Oona?* But they were silent, moving to enclose the three threatening me.

Gaynor seemed unworried. As the Kakatanawa advanced, they reduced in scale, so that by the time they confronted Gaynor and his henchmen, they were equal in size. They remained, however, impressive warriors, handsome in their beautifully designed tattoos which rippled over their bodies and limbs from head to waist, a record of their experience and their wisdom.

"This is blasphemy," intoned one. "You must go." His voice was resonant, very soft, and carried enormous authority.

Gaynor remained unconcerned. He gestured to Elric, who again took up the big horn. Elric placed the instrument to his lips and drew a deep breath.

Even before he began to blow, the noise below my feet increased. Out of the subterranean caverns, an ally was rising, the echoes of his voice whispering and whining through the caverns and crags of the underworld. I imagined all those ethereal inhabitants, the Off-Moo and their kin, seeking shelter from that destructive malice. I feared for friends I had last seen in those endless caves lying between the multiverse and the Grey Fees. Did they perish below as we were to perish above?

But there was also something happening above us. A distant shrieking, almost human. It consumed everything with its sinister aggression.

The growing noise alerted the Kakatanawa. All simultaneously looked skyward in surprise and alarm. Only Gaynor and his friends seemed careless of the commotion.

There came a thrashing and slashing from far above. A metallic chuckling. A muttering, rising voice became a distant howl. Louder and louder it grew, crashing through the branches of the great Skrayling Tree, sending jagged shards of light in all directions. It seemed that entire universes might spin to land and be crushed underfoot. I felt a sickness, a realisation of the magnitude of Death accompanying Lord Shoashooan's descent towards us.

It could be nothing else but the Lord of Winds. Summoned by that traitor Elric! What possible promise could Gaynor have made to him?

My cousin intended to destroy the multiverse and destroy himself at the same time.

And Lord Shoashooan was stronger than ever, hurtling at us from above and below!

Gaynor stepped forward, his sword held in his two mailed hands, and swept the dark blade down towards the tree's already dying roots.

NO! I moved without thought and leaped forward. Unarmed I tried to wrestle the pulsing sword from his fists.

Klosterheim advanced with his own blade drawn. But Elric had turned and leaped towards the dragon, using his pulsing sword to climb the glinting peacock scales, a tiny figure on the dragon's side. I heard his crooning song join with that of his sword, and I knew the Phoorn heard it, too. What did Elric want? The creature was too weak to move its head, let alone help him.

Then it came to me that Elric intended to kill it. That was to be his task. To kill his own brother as I had killed my own wife. Was all our ancient family to die in one terrible, unnatural bloodletting?

I hardly knew what to do. I had no sword. I could not stop them all. The Kakatanawa had held their positions. I realised that they were guarding something. Not the tree any longer, but the same shadowy shape I had glimpsed before.

Lord Shoashooan howled downwards while beneath our feet the other wind was beginning to test at the ground. I was convinced it must soon erupt under us.

Elric reached a point close to the dragon's back. He had his sword in hand, his shield on his arm, the horn at his belt. His cloak swirled around the ivory whiteness of his skin. His crimson eyes flashed wolfishly, triumphantly. I saw him raise the sword.

I forgot Gaynor, who pointlessly continued to hack with compulsive energy at the tree's roots. I left Klosterheim stumbling in my wake. Over that heaving, spongey ground, with one tornado advancing from above and another apparently from below, I ran back towards the dragon. White Crow appeared at my side. He did not pause but reached out towards me. He tore the talisman from his neck and placed it around my own. Why had he given me the miniature of Elric's great shield? How could a trinket possibly protect me?

I will bring her now. It is time . . .

He shouted something else, but I did not hear him. I began to climb in Elric's wake. Even against his own wishes, I had to save the Phoorn, for only he could ever save us. I had no clear idea of what to do next, but since Elric had gone mad and was trying to kill his brother, I had to try to stop him.

Another sound trumpeted over the noise of the winds. Looking back I saw Bes. Her body was covered in dark copper mesh which swayed as she trotted. As she came nearer, I realised her size was almost the equal to the Phoorn. Her great, linen-covered platform swayed on her back, its flaps wild in the wind. Riding on the neck of the beast, spear in his hand, was White Crow in all his paint and finery, his pale scalp lock lying along his left shoulder. His face was prepared for war. Behind him came the buffalo-hide-draped platform resembling a circular bier laid out with a body which clutched a sword to its chest. I knew this had to be Oona.

I was torn. Was I to continue on and try to stop Elric, or should I turn back to tend to my wife? This all seemed part of my torment. I wondered how much of it Gaynor had planned.

The unstable ground began to heave like quicksand. Bes had difficulty keeping her footing. White Crow signalled for me to go on. I looked up. Elric was putting the horn to his lips.

And then, from somewhere, sweetly cutting through the raging howl of the wind, I heard the crystalline sound of Ayanawatta's bone flute.

As Elric blew another blast on the horn, the notes immediately blended with the music of the flute. Rather than cancelling each other out, they resonated and swelled into a grand harmonic. Urgently I continued to climb up the clattering dazzle of the Phoorn's scales.

The tornado was still tearing its way downwards, and from below, the ground around the tree's roots was beginning to spit and bubble.

I lost sight of Elric above me but noticed the Phoorn's breathing had changed. Did he understand that Elric was trying to kill him, as he had begged me to do?

Lord Shoashooan crashed in upon us. His grinning, whirling heads flashed rending teeth. His wild, swinging arms ended in long claws. His feet had scythes for nails. And everywhere he danced he brought destruction.

I was certain that once Lord Shoashooan joined with his twin elemental, even now dancing just below the surface as Shoashooan danced above it, everything would begin to collapse in a final appalling cataclysm!

From behind me the nine Kakatanawa advanced upon Lord Shoashooan. Ayanawatta's flute rose above the din, sounding delicate and sombre now.

Lord Shoashooan blustered and swung wildly about him, but his belligerence had no force. The sound of the flute had some effect on him. Perhaps it calmed that berserk rage?

I thought I glimpsed the outline of White Crow and Bes moving below. They, too, were bound to be destroyed.

Then all at once the nine Kakatanawa surrounded the base of the tornado. Their hair and clothing streaming out from their bodies in that hideous turbulence, they held their ground. Linking arms and shields and with lances thrust outwards, war clubs at their sides, they formed a circle around the whirling base—a ring strong enough to contain Lord Shoashooan as soon as he touched the exposed roots of the tree at which Gaynor maniacally continued to hack while Klosterheim looked on impassively.

I saw Ayanawatta walk into the circle formed by the Kakatanawa, still playing his flute. It was clear from the buffeting that he would not hold Lord Shoashooan for long, but it was incredible that he could hold him at all. I pushed on, climbing those yielding, pulsing scales, while above me, I was sure, Elric prepared to deal his brother a death blow.

I willed myself to find more energy. We must all be weakening before the force of this stupendous supernatural threat. I reminded myself that we almost certainly witnessed the end of everything. If I did not discover further resolve within me, I should reach the moment of my death knowing that I had not done enough.

This spurred me to complete my climb. I danced along the Phoorn's back while above me the branches of the great multiversal tree stretched out for ever, damaged but not yet destroyed. I saw Elric. His sword had indeed made a cut in the Phoorn's vulnerable spine, where it met the head. Yellow blood oozed from the long incision.

I climbed on, determined to stop him. But before I could reach him he took his shield and pressed it down onto the bloody patch he had made in the beast's hide. The shield fitted the patch exactly. Blood soaked it through instantly as it was absorbed into the Phoorn's flesh. What was Elric doing? He stretched out his hand to me now. It was as if he had expected me, even welcomed me.

I made my way forward as the Phoorn's back rippled and stirred under my feet. *What is it? What do you do?*

Give me what White Crow gave you! Quickly. I have deceived Gaynor until now. He still controls Lord Shoashooan but is distracted. This is our moment. Give me the talisman, von Bek!

Without hesitation I ripped it from my neck and threw it to him. He caught it in his gloved fist and, kneeling, placed it at the centre of the wound he had made. A plume of bright red fire shot up like a beacon, higher and higher until it disappeared among the branches of the Skrayling Oak. Then, burning brilliant white it sank slowly back, spreading out as it turned to pale blue and covered the Phoorn's wound. The Phoorn let out a long, deep sigh which blended with the sound of the flute.

Sensing what was happening, Lord Shoashooan yelled and feinted at the Kakatanawa warriors. But they held their ground. They stabbed at him with their spears. They swung their war clubs against his whirling sides, struggling to control the spin of their weapons as the winds flung them back.

White Crow was immediately below. He had brought Bes to a stop. The patient mammoth paused, kneeling in the midst of all this wild confusion.

Ayanawatta drew another extended breath and continued to play. Above me on the Phoorn's shoulders, Elric raised the horn to his lips again.

At this blast Gaynor ceased his ferocious hacking and glanced up, his mirrored helm catching the green-gold light of the dying tree.

Guided by the horn and the flute in unison, the great round bier began to rise into the air, the white hide falling away beneath it to reveal my own wife, Oona, seemingly dead, lying upon yet another version of the Kakatanawa war-shield. This one was twice the size of the shield Elric had put between the Phoorn's shoulders. Seeing it at last Gaynor let out a frustrated shout and looked around him for his men. There was only Klosterheim. Gaynor beckoned to him. Rather reluctantly the ex-priest came forward to join him, crying out in a peculiar sing-song as the Kakatanawa attempted to tighten their circle about the raging Lord of Winds.

Higher rose Oona, lifted on Ayanawatta's and Elric's music. I saw that she lay in the position of old knightly tomb figures, her legs crossed at the ankles, a long black sword clasped between her breasts and a red sandstone bowl on her chest from which rose a willowy plume of smoke.

White Crow dropped down from Bes's neck and ran towards the Phoorn. He slung his lance over his back and began to climb up the breathing scales as Oona's floating platform, buoyed by the notes of the flute, drifted high over the Phoorn's back, paused and then began to descend as Elric and White Crow called out in unison. They were chanting a spell. They guided Oona's flight with their sorcery, bringing the great round shield, the third part of the missing *skeffla'a*, down towards the faintly glowing blue wound. The shield completed the membrane which all dragons must have if they are to fly between the worlds, and which is in so many unknown ways their sustenance.

They had re-created the stolen *skeffla'a* and brought it back to the dying Phoorn! Was it this which sustained my wife between life and death?

At last the great disc covered the dragon's back, and Elric gently lifted Oona from it as I joined him. She seemed unusually at peace in his arms. But was it the peace of death?

I touched her. She was warm. Upon her chest the faintly smoking bowl, one of the great treasures of the Kakatanawa, their Grail, rose and fell with her slow, even breathing.

Instantly now the Phoorn drew in a full breath. It took all our efforts to cling to those swelling quasi-metallic scales and move towards one another.

The wind still shrieked and raged, but the Kakatanawa ring held. The warriors all called out the same strange, high-pitched ululations, their actions and voices completely in unison. The spears ran in and out of the spinning darkness, containing the howling thing but scarcely harming it.

The scales of the Phoorn steadily changed colour. They deepened and ran with dozens of different shades, taking on a fire that had not been there before. White Crow clambered towards me. He pointed to Oona, lying half held in the blue-grey membrane where Elric had placed her, still unmoving, as if she lay in a womb. Elric was beside her on his knees. He took the large ring from his finger and reached through the membrane to place it on Oona's forehead. I tried to call out to him but failed. Surely he could not mean her ill. He was her father. Even a Melnibonéan would not be so ruthless as to kill his own child.

I felt a light hand on my shoulder. White Crow had reached me. Clearly exhausted, his eyes gleamed with hope. "You must take up the sword," he said. "Oona has brought it to you." And he pointed to where the black blade still lay, clutched in her hands, but outside the peculiar organic stuff of the Phoorn *skeffla'a*.

"*Take it!*" he commanded.

Crimson eyes locked onto mine as Elric looked up at me. He raised the sword in his fist and all but hurled it at me. "We have no grace!"

"Fear not." White Crow gasped. "He is of our blood and of our party. We three shall do what has to be done."

At that moment it occurred to me again that Elric could be White Crow's father, which meant that the young Indian was Oona's twin. The evident discrepancy in their ages added a further mystery to the conundrum.

Would it ever be explained? None of us was dead yet, but Gaynor, Klosterheim and Lord Shoashooan appeared to have the greater power!

The Lord of Winds still screamed and raged in the Kakatanawa circle. It seemed the disciplined warriors could not hold much longer. Already there were weaknesses showing as the giants used every ounce of mental and physical energy to contain him.

But I was reluctant to accept the sword. Perhaps I feared I would use it to kill Oona again? I shuddered. A coldness filled me. I was consumed by guilty memory.

"Take it!" Elric shouted again. He rose to his feet, his eyes still fixed on his daughter. "Come. We must do this now. Lobkowitz and Sepiriz say it is the only way." He thrust the sword towards me again.

How had Lobkowitz communicated with Elric? Had they been in league all along? Lobkowitz had explained nothing to me, and I might never understand now.

I accepted the sword. I knew I could not deny the inevitable. There was time only for action now.

As my hand closed on the silk-bound hilt I felt a sudden shock of energy. I looked down on my wife. Her face was tranquil. On her breast the red sandstone bowl glowed and smoked. On her forehead the deep blue stone swirled with a life of its own. Somehow I knew it was the bowl that sustained her life.

Elric's face was shadowy. He moved closer to stand with his body pressed against mine. White Crow came nearer from the other side until both men were almost crushing me. I could not resist. The blade demanded it. All three blades were in our hands now. All three were touching. All three were beginning to sigh and murmur, their black fire mingling, their runes leaping back and forth from one to the other. They conferred.

Oona opened her eyes, looked at us calmly and smiled. She sat up, the silvery web of membrane falling away to merge with the Phoorn *skeffla'a*. She took the red sandstone bowl and blew gently into it. White smoke poured upwards and surrounded us. I breathed it in. It was sweet and delicate, the stuff of heaven. With every breath we took in unison, White Crow, Elric and I moved closer together. The swords merged until there was only one massive blade, and I knew, as I grew in both size and strength, wisdom and psychic power, that the swords were reunited with their archetype as we were reunited with ours. Three in one.

"Now!" It was Sepiriz. He, too, was as enormous as the single creature I had become. "Now you must climb. Now you must restore the tree and return the Balance."

I could see Lord Shoashooan whirling wildly below me. The Kakatanawa could no longer hold him. I heard Lobkowitz's voice. "*Go!* We will do all we can here. But if you do not go, nothing will be worth it. Gaynor will win."

Once again Elric's familiar personality was absorbing my own. I had no sense of White Crow's individuality. For me it was exactly as it had been before when only Elric and I had combined. But now I felt even more powerful. The Black Sword had become a monstrous and beautiful object, far more ornate and intricate in design than anything I had ever wielded in battle. Her voice was melodic, yet still as cold as justice, and her metal blazed with life. I had no doubt that I held the *first* sword, from which all others had come. I looked up at the flaking bark, the decaying pulp that now blotched the base of the Skrayling Oak. Gaynor's work had been well done.

I flung my arm forward towards the oak, and the sword did the rest, carrying me deep towards the core of the trunk. The closer I came, the larger I grew, until the tree, though tall, was of more familiar size.

I scabbarded the sword and climbed. I knew what this ascent meant. I knew what I had to do. Elric's blood and soul informed my own as mine informed his. While Lobkowitz had given me only hints, he had told Elric everything he needed to know. Since the time they first saw White Buffalo Woman and Kakatanawa city, Elric had schemed against Gaynor while pretending to serve his cause. And now, too, I knew who White Crow was.

On my belt was Elric's horn, and I moved with the agility of White Crow. The outer bark of the supernatural tree was very thick and layered, forming deep fissures and overhangs which afforded me handholds on my route upwards.

I heard a sound below and looked down. Far away the Kakatanawa were being pressed back by the power of the Lord of Winds. Lord Shoashooan had widened their circle until it must surely break. I knew in my bones that unless the Phoorn had more time to heal and recover he would still perish. Oona was doing her best for the great beast, but if Lord Shoashooan were to break free now, the Phoorn would not yet be strong enough to destroy him.

I thought I glimpsed Ayanawatta, Sepiriz and Lobkowitz on the edge of my vision, but then I could not look away any longer. I needed all my faculties to climb the constantly changing organic fissures in the tree.

Noise from the tornado crashed and wailed. Every part of the tree began to shake. I had to exert even more effort to cling to the weird bark. Often pieces crumbled away in my hands. I feared I would soon weaken and lose my grip completely.

An inch at a time I climbed. The air grew thinner and colder and the sounds of the Lord of Winds more shrill. Then something grabbed at my body. It felt as if a giant skeletal hand seized me about the waist. The cold went deep into my guts, and I knew Lord Shoashooan was free.

I fought to keep my grip on the tree. Being held so, I could not climb any further. It was all I could do to hang on.

The Lord of Winds' voice trumpeted a vainglorious note now. Once I thought I glimpsed the Kakatanawa below as they were flung backwards, their ring broken. Lord Shoashooan attacked me and the Phoorn with all his strength.

I heard the pure whistle of Ayanawatta's flute cutting through the roar and bluster. Again I was gripped by the tendrils of wind as Lord Shoashooan tried to prise me loose. Without the strength of my avatars, I should surely have been lost.

But the sound of the flute came clearer and sweeter through all that cacophony and joined with another sound coming from far below, equally high but by no means sweet. This sound writhed around the tree's roots. The sound was the other Lord of Winds. If the lords succeeded in joining, there would be no overwhelming their combined strength.

With that thought came the energy to force myself up the trunk. At last I stood in the swaying upper branches looking out across a world at night, at the frozen lake, at the rubble to which the great city had been reduced. At my will the sword sprang into my hand. I held the blade high above my head as power flooded into it. I offered myself as a conduit for this huge, supernatural force.

Then I reversed the sword and aimed it at the topmost tip of the tree, plunging it down, down into the soul of all-time, the heart of all-space, down into the centre of the Skrayling Tree.

Immediately the sword left my hand and remained in the tree, its point driving deep through the inner wood to the soul of the Skrayling Oak. As it moved down the tree, it did not split but rather expanded the trunk until sword and tree had merged, and a great, black blade lay at the core of the ancient oak.

Then I lurched backwards, grabbing frantically at boughs to stop myself falling towards the faraway ice and the inevitable death of all my avatars. If I fell, we might never know if our sacrifice had been worth anything. Even now I heard the wind rising, higher and higher, ever more vicious. I was losing my grip on the bough. I was surely about to fall, and I had given up my weapon.

A shadow passed fleetingly through the whirlwind's dusty crown. It was Oona, and she was riding the Phoorn.

The great white-gold spread of a Phoorn rising on his wide peacock wings into the air above a storm was a breathtaking sight! On my reptilian relative's broad back, merged with his gleaming iridescent *skeffla'a* but clearly visible, was my wife Oona, vibrantly alive, her head thrown forward in the sheer pleasure of the flight, a bowstaff clutched in her right hand and the redstone smoking bowl balanced in her left.

When I fell, the Phoorn fell beside me, almost playfully. His soft breath slowed my descent, and he slid underneath me. I landed gently, painlessly, in his *skeffla'a*. I lay prone just behind my wife. I could see the tree outlined in a golden glare. Within the spreading oak was the deep black of the sword blade, the guard stretching out across the branches, the pommel pulsing like a star. The black blade had completely merged with the oak and become part of the tree's life-force.

I was held within the membrane, only able to watch as Oona put down her bow, took the redstone pipe bowl and spread her hands in a magical gesture that produced two bowls, one on each palm. I saw her reach out and put a smoking redstone bowl at each end of the Black Sword's guard. They hung suspended there as she lifted both hands to her head and took something from it. She then placed this object on the sword hilt between the bowls. The ritual was done, and I looked upon the Cosmic Balance.

Oona began to laugh with joy as Shoashooan redoubled his attack. The storm raged on and shot up cold tendrils wrapping around us, still trying to draw us back. Yet she turned towards me, laughed again, and embraced me.

The Balance still swung erratically. It could destroy itself if its movement back and forth became too violent. Nothing seemed to have even the promise of stability as yet.

Below us, seemingly even more powerful, the great plume of the tornado fanned out, gathering stronger and stronger substance. The limbs of the tree began to thrash uncontrollably again as Lord Shoashooan unleashed a desperate anger.

Once more I heard the clear note of the flute. Oona heard it, too. The Phoorn began to bank through the dirty light, sweeping through the edges of the whirlwind, down through the green-gold haze of the tree, down past the slender black shaft which glowed at the centre of the trunk. Down towards the greedy Lord of Winds.

I had done everything I could do. I prepared myself for the death Lord Shoashooan undoubtedly planned for us. If I could have thrown myself into his centre and saved Oona I would have done so, but the membrane prevented any dramatic movement.

This was how my ancestors had travelled with the Phoorn, protected by the *skeffla'a* which allowed the monsters to sweep like butterflies so delicately between the realms of reality. Few Melnibonéans had made such flights, though my father Sadric was said to have voyaged longest and furthest of any of us, after my mother had died giving birth to me.

It was only now that the realisation came. My shame was coupled with a sudden rush of relief. The Kakatanawa Grail had done its holy work! The wounds I had inflicted upon Oona were thoroughly healed.

With decreasing energy, the Phoorn fought valiantly against the sucking wind drawing us to it. His massive wings beat upon the ether as he strained to escape. Oona became increasingly alarmed. Filling the entire world before us was the spreading bulk of the Skrayling Oak framing the pulsing black sword. Its crosspieces formed the Cosmic Balance, which again began to sway wildly. The conflict was by no means decided.

Looming behind us was the ever-growing presence of Lord Shoashooan. The Kakatanawa warriors were nowhere to be seen. Lord Sepiriz, Ayanawatta and Prince Lobkowitz had disappeared. Neither was there any sign of Gaynor or Klosterheim.

Then I heard the flute's refrain. Ayanawatta's clear, pure tones cut through all the raging turmoil.

The Phoorn lurched this way and that in the force of the tornado. The air grew colder and colder. We were slowly freezing into immobility. I became drowsy with the cold.

Again the flute piped.

The Phoorn's wings could no longer beat against the thinning ether. His breath began to stream like gaseous ivory from his nostrils. Slowly we were losing height, being pulled deeper and deeper into the heart of the whirlwind.

The voice of the Phoorn sounded again in my mind. *We have no strength to escape him* . . .

I prayed that I could die with Oona in my arms. I pushed with all my strength against the clinging membrane, too weak now to reach her. She was holding tight to the scales as the freezing wind sought to dislodge her from the Phoorn.

I was now convinced that Sepiriz, Lobkowitz and the Kakatanawa had all perished. Somehow Ayanawatta continued to play his flute, but I guessed he could not survive for long.

I love you. Father—Ulric—I love you both.

Oona's voice. I saw her turn, seeking me, yearning towards me with her eyes. She could not loose her grip, or she would be torn from the back of the Phoorn. Again I strained against the membrane. It flickered with scarlet and turquoise and a soft pewter brilliance. It did not resist me, but neither did it allow me to break free.

Oona!

From below something roared and spat at us. The whole of the surface erupted, fragmenting into millions of spores which spun away past us into the infinite cosmos. Scarlet and black streamed up at us, as if the whole world exploded. Searing hot air was a sudden wall against the cold. Silence fell.

I heard a distant rumbling. A roaring. I knew what this meant. What shot upwards towards us was magma. Rock as swift and lively as a roaring river and far more deadly. We were directly above an erupting volcano. We would burn to death before the whirlwind destroyed us!

But Oona was pointing excitedly up towards the distant balance, clearly visible now on the staff that had replaced the Black Sword. I knew then that this was the original iron which Sepiriz and his people had stolen to make Stormbringer. This was the metal the Kakatanawa had told the Pukawatchi to fashion. She was what whole nations had died to possess. Her magic was the magic of the Cosmic Balance itself. Her power was strong enough to challenge that balance. Those who mastered her, mastered Fate. Those who did not master her, were mastered by her.

What Oona showed me was not significant at first, but then I realised why she was elated. The bowls that formed the twin weights of the balance were gradually finding equilibrium.

The boiling air struck hard against Lord Shoashooan's cold turbulence. I saw his face, closer this time, as his teeth snapped at us and his flailing claws grasped and held the Phoorn. The beast beat his wonderful wings helplessly and would surely perish.

But the hot air was consuming Lord Shoashooan. He was collapsing in it. Slowly his grip loosened, and he began to wail. I felt my head would burst with the volume. What I had taken for another aspect of Lord Shoashooan's strength had been his opposite, conjured from the benign underworld whose denizens had helped us in the past. A counterforce as powerful as the Lord of Winds, which could only be rising from the core of the Grey Fees.

Shoashooan had weakened himself in his pursuit of us. At last we felt his grip relax, and we were free. And he in turn was now pursued. One great Lord of Winds gave chase to another! We watched the turquoise-and-crimson air, foamy masses of creamy smoke roiling in its wake, as it enclosed and absorbed its filthy opposite. It purified the Lord of Winds with its grace alone and brought at last, against Lord Shoashooan's will, a kind of uneasy harmony. With the tornado still grumbling from within, the flute's simple tune faded into one single note of resolution.

We stood looking up at the Skrayling Tree, looking up at the great black staff of the Balance, at the cups which must surely be the Grail, which had restored Oona to life. At the central pivot of the Balance Oona had placed the blue jewel of Jerusalem, my ring. The same Templar ring which Elric had carried from Jerusalem. The ring which resembled our small, ordinary planet, seen from space. The ring which had helped us restore the Balance.

The Kakatanawa resumed their watch, again immobile. The great Phoorn settled near the roots of the tree, and my wife and I dismounted and embraced at last. Almost at once the huge beast curled himself about the base of the tree. He returned peacefully to his stewardship. The roots were already restoring themselves.

At the moment of our embrace, we stood beneath a sharp, blue sky, with a sweet wind blowing surrounded by ruins. The tree grew larger and larger as the Balance grew stronger, until it filled the entire firmament, and the roots were green and fresh again, winding out from the ruined Kakatanawa city, out through the deep, deep ice—

Where the surviving avatars of Gaynor, Klosterheim and their men still moved with weary determination towards us.

The Vikings' eyes stared sightlessly. Their lips moved wordlessly. They held their weapons tightly, the only reality the Vikings could be certain of. It was clear they longed for the release of a slaughtering. They no longer cared how they died.

It was still not over. I looked around for a sword but found nothing. Instead I saw the prone bodies of Elric and White Crow. I saw Prince Lobkowitz, Lord Sepiriz and Ayanawatta, all unarmed, standing together around Bes, the mammoth. The great Phoorn seemed to have immersed himself in the trunk of the tree.

We did not have a weapon among us, and Gaynor and his men were still armed to the teeth. They understood their advantage, because their pace quickened. Like hungry dogs scenting blood, they hurried towards us. Elric and White Crow slowly revived only to become aware of their threatened destruction.

Had I survived so much to see my wife cut down before my eyes? I dug around among the rubble for a sword. There was nothing. Lord Shoashooan had reduced the entire great city to dust.

They were almost on our island. I urged Oona to flee, but she held her ground. Ayanawatta had come to stand with us. His handsome, tattooed features were calm, resolute. He slipped his bone flute from his bag in one fluid movement and placed it to his lips. We watched Gaynor and his men advance across the ice.

As Ayanawatta played, no note issued from the flute itself, but I began to hear a strange, subterranean sound. Groaning, creaking and cracking. A distant rushing. And another eruption of warm air at our feet. Things burst upwards through the shattering ice. They glistened with fresh life.

Gaynor saw them, too. He yelled to his men, instantly understanding the danger, and began to dash towards us, sword drawn. But the fresh, green roots of the Skrayling Oak spread everywhere, smashing up through the ice, overturning great blocks and collapsing back into what was rapidly becoming water once more.

Desperate now, Gaynor persevered. He laboured to the edge of the ice, our island shore only a few paces away.

And there he stopped.

Bes the mammoth stood facing him. She shook her tusks, menacing him, all the while her mild eyes regarding him with a terrifying calm.

He turned. Hesitated.

Further up the shore Klosterheim and several of his men leaped to our island as the last of the ice around them melted. Sheets of clear, pale water appeared beneath the winter sky. A great fissure had torn apart the remaining ice sheets and was widening rapidly as Gaynor, trapped between two dangers, still hesitated, not knowing how to avoid defeat. Bes stomped relentlessly towards him, and he was forced back onto the ice. He began to run, slipping and sliding, towards a nearby spur of rock jutting out from the beach.

He almost reached the rock, but his armour and his sword became too heavy for him. He sank as quickly as the ice vanished. He stood up to his waist in black water, raging to survive, roaring out his anger and frustration even as he slipped suddenly beneath the waves and was gone.

Gone. A warm, gentle breeze blew from the south.

I could not believe that angry immortal had simply disappeared. I knew by now that he would never die. Not, at least, until I, too, died.

Oona tugged at my arm. "We must go home now," she said. "Prince Lobkowitz will take us."

Klosterheim and the other survivors looked listlessly at the spot of water where their leader had vanished. Then, turning towards us, the leading Viking shrugged and sheathed his sword. "We have no fight with you. Take our word on it. Let us make our way back to our ship, and we will return to where we belong."

Elric had affection for some of these men. He accepted their offer. "You can sail *The Swan* back to Las Cascadas. And take that disappointed wretch with you." Smiling he indicated a gloomy Klosterheim. "You can tell them what you witnessed here."

One of the tall black warriors laughed aloud. "To spend the rest of our days as reviled madmen? I have seen others cursed with such reminiscences. They die friendless. You'll not come with us, Duke Elric? To captain us?"

Elric shook his head. "I will help you get back to the mainland. Then I have a mind to go with Ayanawatta when he returns to take the Law to his people and fulfil the rest of his destiny. We are old friends, you see. I have some eight hundred years until my dream is ended, and only then shall I know if I had power enough to summon Stormbringer to me in that other world. My curiosity takes me further into this land." He lifted a gloved hand in farewell.

Sepiriz shrugged and spread his hands in gentle acquiescence. "I will find you," he said, "when I need you."

White Crow came close to look directly into Elric's face. "My future does not seem to hold much joy," he said.

"Some," said Elric, staring back. He sighed and looked up at the snow-capped mountains, the silver sky, the few birds which flew in the warm, clean air. "But most of that is in slaughter." He turned away from White Crow as if he could no longer bear to look at him. At that I finally understood that White Crow was neither son nor brother nor nephew nor twin. White Crow was completing his own long dream-journey, part of his apprenticeship, his training as an adept, his preparation for his destiny, to become Sorcerer Emperor of Melniboné. White Crow was Elric himself, in his youth! Each had been moved in his own way by what he saw in the face of the other. Without another word, White Crow returned to stand with Bes. He would be the last Melnibonéan of noble blood to be sent to Kakatanawa for his training. Their city gone, the giants had only one duty, to guard the tree for ever.

"It is done at last," said White Crow. "Fate is served. The multiverse will survive. The treasures of the tree have been restored, and the great oak blooms again. I look upon the end of all our histories, I think." He clambered up into the big wooden saddle and goaded Bes towards the lapping water.

None of us tried to stop him as White Crow guided the noble old mammoth into the waves and began to descend until Bes had submerged completely. He turned in the saddle once and raised his bow above his head before he, too, disappeared back into his particular dream, as we all began to return slowly to our own.

"Come," said Lobkowitz. "You'll want to see your children."

EPILOGUE

And so another episode in the eternal struggle for the Balance was completed and resolution achieved. How human endeavour has the power to create and make real its most significant symbols I do not know, but I do know that a logical creator might build such a self-sustaining system. In spite of my adventures, my belief in a supreme spirit remains.

Ayanawatta believed strongly in his dream, somehow reinforced rather than contradicted by the Longfellow account, and went on to found the Iroquois Confederacy, a model for the federal system of the United States. Ulric and I worked first for the UN and later for Womankind Worldwide, whose work becomes increasingly important.

Passing without incident from one realm to another, Ulric, Prince Lobkowitz and I returned, travelling chiefly by rail, from Lake Huron to the Nova Scotian coast.

As dreamers, we both experience dreams and we create them. The experience brings us wisdom, which is why such dreams are coveted by dreamthieves. But they place equal value on creative dreams. These can be more volatile and hard to negotiate, let alone control. In the so-called Ghost Worlds, where everything is malleable, one learns to value the power of supernatural logic.

Ulric and I were to know only one more unusual adventure together, but there is no question that our relationship had altered. Our love, our understanding of the value of our public work, was deeper, yet there was an uneasy, rarely mentioned memory. Ulric had, indeed, killed me as I tried to help him in my assumed shape of White Buffalo. And he did almost destroy the Skrayling Tree as a result. These thoughts continue to burden him.

He has other dreams. We do not live in a linear multiverse. We do not tell a simple history with a beginning, middle and end. We weave instead a tapestry.

We depend upon repetition but not upon imitation, which is mere corruption, confirming nothing. Each strand must be new, though the pattern might be familiar.

Gunnar's expedition to America left little to show for itself, unless the destruction of Kakatanawa was an achievement. But a few legends were made and others confirmed. As for Gaynor, we would meet him again in a final adventure.

The strange mathematics of the multiverse, which orders the weft and woof of the great tapestries, is the means by which we order Chaos. But the strict formality of the design demands an adherence to ritual similarly found, for instance, in the Egyptian Book of the Dead. Every word uttered, every step on the destined path must be exact, or that destiny will change. The choreography for such actions is the special skill of Prince Lobkowitz and Lord Sepiriz.

As for Elric of Melniboné, he lived out his dream of a thousand years. How that dream ended and its effect on the von Bek family is the last story still to be told.

Oona, Countess of Bek,
Sporting Club Square,
London, S.W.

THE WHITE WOLF'S SON

THE ALBINO
UNDER GROUND

In memory of
Jerico Radoc:
a generous spirit
who died too young

and for Alan Wall
and all the regulars down
at MWM, with thanks

THE WHITE WOLF'S SON

CONTENTS

CONTENTS

PROLOGUE

And then did Sir Elrik spye Sir Yagrin and say to him "Fast thou, villain. Where goest thou this Daye?" Whereupon Sir Yagrin saith: "On my Honour, I shall answer ye with arms." Whereupon one charged the other. Ten speares did they brake until Sir Elrik had killed Sir Yagrin and lay close to his deathe bedd with none in all that Woode to help him.

—The Romance of Prince Elrik
tr. from the Portuguese.
Anon., London *ca.* 1525

The albino hung captive in the rigging of the great battle-barge, spreadeagled on the mainmast, barely able to open his red, glaring eyes. He was mumbling to himself, calling out a name, as if he felt that name would save him. Although dreaming, he was at the same time half-awake. He could see below him the foredeck of the ship, with its massive catapult whose cup slaves were already filling with flaming pitch. There, too, the White Wolf's captor strutted in his seething rosy armour. Upon his head was the glowing scarlet helmet bearing the Merman Crest of Pan Tang, the island of the theocrats who had long envied Melniboné her power. High-shouldered, black-bearded, full of raging triumph, Jagreen Lern threw up his face and laughed at his enemy. He was delighting in his power, in the movement of his galley through the water, its huge bulk pushed by the oars manned by five hundred slaves. He turned to his followers, men made utterly mad by all they had witnessed, by their own demonic bloodlust, by their own cruel killing.

"Let fly!" he roared. And another shot was discharged, arcing over the water and dropping into the boiling sea just short of the fleet which had assembled to defend what was left of the world from his conquest.

"We'll get their measure with the next one," declared the Theocrat, turning again to look up at Elric. He spat on the deck. There was a terrible, crooked grin on his face. He was full of his victories, swollen like a leech on blood.

"See! The whiteface is nothing without that black sword of his. Is this the hero you feared? Is this all Law could summon against us—a renegade weakling?"

Jagreen Lern strutted beneath the mainmast, jeering up at the man whose crucifixion he had ordered.

"Watch, Elric. Watch! Soon you shall see all your allies destroyed. All that you love turned to heaving Chaos. Lord Arioch refuses you help. Lord Balan refuses you help. Soon Law and all its feeble creations shall be banished from our world, and I shall rule in the name of the great Lords of Entropy, with the power to make what I like of inchoate matter and destroy it again and again at a whim. Can you hear me, White Wolf? Or are you already dead? Wake him, someone! I would have him know what he loses. He must learn his lesson well before he dies. He must know that by betraying his patron Chaos Lords he has betrayed himself and all he loves."

Some part of the albino heard his enemy. But Elric of Melniboné was desperately sending his mind out into the unseen worlds around him, the myriad worlds of the multiverse, where he believed he might find the one thing which could help him. He had deliberately fallen into a slumber known by his sorcerer ancestors as the Dream of a Thousand Years, by which he had earlier learned his wizard's craft. He was now too weak to do anything else but send his failing spirit out into the astral worlds beyond his own. By this means he sought his sword, Stormbringer, calling its name as he slept, knowing that if he died on this, his last desperate dream-quest, he would die here, also.

He dreamed of vast upheavals and forces as powerful as those which now captured him. He dreamed of strange lands and stranger creatures. He dreamed of heroes like himself, heroes with a destiny similar to his own. He dreamed of brutal warriors, of wonderful supernatural beings, of beautiful women, of exotic, secret places where the destiny of worlds was created. In this dream he crossed whole continents, negotiated vast oceans, fought men and monsters, gods and demons. And he dreamed of a boy who, obscurely, he felt might be his son, though he had no son in this world. He dreamed, too, of a little girl, who played unconsciously and happily around her house, knowing nothing of the enormous forces of Law and Chaos, of Good and Evil, which clashed in worlds but a shadowed step removed from her own . . .

The albino groaned. The bearded Theocrat pushed back his pulsing scarlet helm, looked up at Elric and laughed again.

"He lives, right enough. Wake him, someone, so that I might relish his agony all the better."

A crewman obeyed. Knife in belt, he began his ascent of the rigging. "I'll tickle his toes with my dagger, master. That'll bring him round."

"Oh, draw a little of his thin, deficient blood. Maybe I'll drink a cup of it to celebrate his final agonies." Jagreen Lern, master of all the once-human creatures who now gibbered and slavered and anticipated their final triumph over Law, reached out his red-gauntleted hand, as if to receive a goblet from one of his minions. "A libation to the Lords of Chaos!"

Elric muttered and stirred in his bonds, high above the ship's main deck. A word formed on his lips.

"Stormbringer!" he gasped. "Stormbringer, aid me now!"

But Stormbringer, that unholy black sword which had preserved his life so many times before, did not materialise.

Stormbringer was *elsewhere*, imprisoned by powerful sorcery, manipulated by men and supernatural monsters whose ambitions were even darker, even more dangerous than those of the creatures of Chaos who sought to rule Elric's world.

Stormbringer was being used in a Summoning powerful enough to challenge the combined might of Law and Chaos and to bring about the end of everything, of the multiverse itself.

Again the albino whispered his sword's name. But there was no reply.

"*Stormbringer* . . ."

Nothing but the silence of the cold, unpopulated ether. The silence of death.

And into that silence came laughter, cruel laughter full of the cold joy of slaughter.

"Open his eyes for him, you scum! Watch, Elric! Watch all that you love perish!"

The laughter blended with the crashing noise of the sea, the terrible sounds of the war-catapults, the groaning of the slaves, the creaking of the oars.

The pale lips parted, perhaps for the last time, barely able to utter the word again:

"Stormbringer!"

PART ONE

A MUCH SOUGHT-AFTER YOUNG LADY

Lord Elrik sate in his own red bludde
His vanquishéd foe beside him;
Saith he, "Thou kepst my Treasure near
In Castle Lorn do ye reside in."

"Take all, take all" cried his noble foe,
"Take all that I have defended
My soul's now Carrion for the bold black Crowe
But my Conscience hast thou mended."

IV

Heal'd and alone, Lord Elrik rode,
Till Castle Lorn lay behind him
"No Gold shall I need in Manor Bonné,
Where I'll finde my fair, forlorne one."

—Lord Elrik and Sythoril,
ca. 1340
Coll. Wheldrake,
Ballads and Lays of the
Britons, 1856

I

Then Elric sped out of Tanelorn, seeking Mirenburg, where the next step of his destiny must be taken. And he knew that the doom of ten thousand years lay upon him; and that of himself he'd made bloody sacrifice, having found the Stealer of Souls.

Now his true dream began to resume; now his destiny marched to remorseless resolution.

—*The Chronicle of the Black Sword*
(Wheldrake's tr.)

y name is Oonagh, granddaughter of the Countess Oona von Bek. This is my story of Elric, the White Wolf, and Onric, the White Wolf's son, of a talking beast in the World Below, of the Guild of Temporal Adventurers, the Knights of the Balance and those who serve the world; of the wonders and terrors I experienced as the forces of Law and Chaos sought the power of the Black Sword, found the source of Hell and the San Grael. All this happened several years ago, when I was still a child. It is only now that I feel able to tell my story.

As usual, I was spending my summer holidays at the old family house in Ingleton, West Yorkshire. My father had been born there before his natural parents were killed in Africa, and he had inherited it when still a small boy. It was kept in trust by my grandparents until he was twenty-one.

Tower House was an old place. The main part dated back to the seventeenth century. There was a big late Victorian addition, built from local granite, put on when the building was turned into a girls' boarding school in the 1890s. By the 1950s it had been split into several dwellings and sold to separate owners. My grandparents had helped my father turn the house back to its former glory. This meant that any guests generally had an entire wing to themselves. There was even a flat over the old stables, now a garage, where the permanent housekeepers, Mr and Mrs Hawthornthwaite, lived.

My grandparents, Count and Countess von Bek, had come to love the place and now remained there almost permanently, only going down to London for the theatre season or to visit doctors and dentists. They were a hearty old couple. My grandfather was at least ninety, and my grandmother, though she did not seem it, must have been close to seventy. Everyone remarked on how youthful she looked. I was not the only family member to notice how, beneath her make-up, her face was actually younger, softer. "Good skins run in the family," said my mother. She never seemed to notice the oddness of that remark. Even Granny's slower movements and apparent absent-mindedness seemed designed to deceive you into thinking she was older. Of course, she *should* have looked older, given that she had married my granddad in the 1940s, after the Second World War. But at that time in my life I didn't really think much about it. Perhaps she aged herself to save my grandfather's pride? No-one else in the family mentioned it, so I didn't think a lot about it, either.

We had been going up to Yorkshire for the summer holidays ever since I was tiny. My mum and dad had spent the summers there long before I was born. I knew every inch of Storrs Common, the brook, the old caves all around the area, the abandoned mine workings down past Beesley's farm on the path to the famous waterfalls. The falls themselves roared through a deep gorge in thick woods. The farms on the other side of the dale tried to charge tourists for walking in that beauty spot. This kept them fairly free of all but the most dedicated visitors! In Victorian times, trains had run special excursions to the Ingleton Falls, but now there was no station, let alone a railway.

All that was left of Ingleton's former glory were the reproductions of old photographs showing ladies in bustles and big hats posing beside one of the main falls. School parties came occasionally, little crocodiles of captive kids with packed lunches in their haversacks, trudging moodily along the high paths above the river. But most of the time it was still fairly remote country. I saw the occasional big red English squirrel in the oaks and hazels, and I had seen my first crayfish by the stepping stones through that part of the river we called "the shallows." You could sometimes catch trout if you fished patiently, but the water was too fast-running to attract most anglers. During high summer and autumn there were few visitors. People were no longer allowed to park on the common across from our house, mainly because of the erosion so many walkers had created. Instead they had to park in the village, and for many the paved road up to the common was too steep.

We were used to that road. It was only half a mile, a bit less if you went the back way. Although a trip to the village took you about an hour, you could still get down to buy fish and chips, the occasional sweets and comics, or have a look in the souvenir shop. If it took more than an hour, it was because someone wanted to chat. We were on good terms with almost everyone there. It had taken my mum and dad a few years to be accepted, especially by our neighbouring hill farmers, but now even they remembered my name most of the time.

The place nearest to us was another half an hour up the hill. Without running water, the big old farmhouse was accessible by a rough cart track which even four-wheel-drive Jeeps found hard to handle. Having no significant land attached to it, the house tended to change hands quite often. We rarely saw much of the occupants, who were almost always natural recluses. The place was known as Starr Bottom, and when we were small, my older brother and sister had sworn it was haunted. Shaggy free-range sheep still grazed up to the foundations of its rather neglected drystone walls.

Tower House had no gas, but it had electricity, central heating, fireplaces and a huge coke-fired stove in the big granite-flagged kitchen which had once served the whole school. It was built on the side of Ingleborough, one of the famous Three Peaks, and had a view over twenty miles of rolling hills and dales to the Atlantic at Morecambe Bay. On a clear day you could see even further from the central tower: a beautiful, rugged landscape, whose limestone glittered in the sunshine and whose hawthorns bowed close to the crags, telling of our high winds and winter snows. Our scenery was made famous in old TV series like *All Creatures Great and Small*, and preserved in its original beauty by the National Trust and the farmers who loved it.

We were a short distance from the Lake District and in easy driving distance of Leeds, so the house was convenient for almost any kind of activity. Sometimes we would drive into Leeds for the fun of it, visit one of Dad's old friends and spend an afternoon in those wonderful covered markets, the

Arcades, all dark green Victorian iron girders and sparkling glass. I loved our trips to Leeds.

Only one episode spoils the memory of my early childhood in Yorkshire. I would wake in my bed with a full moon streaming into the window, showing me all the things of my daytime life: toy-boxes, modelling table, audio stuff, books, various projects I had half started, but they had all taken on a mysterious and even sinister quality. As I sank back into sleep, I remember screaming a loud, terrible scream which did not wake me, but which I learned later woke the rest of the house. I don't remember much else. I always woke up very frightened.

I remember one dream which was especially terrifying and which remained in my memory (whereas the others tended to fade): *I was out on the common and had somehow wandered into a deep cave. I was lost but knew home was fairly close. I just had to find it. Below me, in semi-darkness, was some sort of city with pale, slender towers like spikes of rock. And these strange creatures were coming towards me, pointing. They were not particularly unfriendly, these figures in high, conical hats, almost like elongated Ku Klux Klansmen. I couldn't make out their faces, yet I was sure they weren't fully human. I heard a shout and looked back. There was a man following me. I was more frightened of him than of the creatures approaching me. His face, too, was in shadow, beneath the broad brim of a black hat. He had a wide white collar worn over a black jerkin. A Puritan. Trying to escape them all, I darted aside and was suddenly in a deep, peaceful greenwood. For a moment I felt safe. Then I saw a man with bone-white skin and red eyes standing on a large bough over the path I was on. He was dressed in a long turban, vividly coloured cloak and sashes swirling around him, his large black sword held high as he reached towards me across the tree-tops. "How . . .?" he said. He was mouthing a question I couldn't hear. He could only help me if I answered him. He reminded me of my granddad, but was much younger. I knew he was trying to save me, but something was stopping him. "How . . .? Grunewald? Mittelmarch?" Those are the only words I remembered.*

Then I was running from him, too, running down towards where the men in conical hats waited for me, running straight into the tall body of yet another bizarre creature who looked down at me with kindly brown eyes. I think he was a friend of my grandfather's. A huge red fox, dressed elaborately in late-eighteenth-century finery, who smiled his pleasure at seeing me, displaying sharp, white teeth.

"*Well, I suppose I'm in good hands,*" I said, trying to show I was grateful for his friendship.

"*Paws,*" he said, with the literal logic of a dream, "*actually. My dear mademoiselle, we must hurry . . .*"

Then the Puritan was behind him, his skull-like face grinning as he lifted a huge pistol and shot the fox in the back. With a look of surprise and grief, the fox fell.

I began to run again . . .

I was screaming.

The local doctor was called, but he wasn't much help. After trying me on a few different prescriptions, he eventually admitted he was baffled. I then had a psychiatrist for a few sessions until I started to get better on my own as the dreams, or feelings, never recurred. I could still remember the people of that dream, but Mr Handforth, the local vicar and a bit of a family friend, was the most help. He took me seriously and said I seemed to have quite a lot of "guardian angels" looking out for my safety. In his deep, cultured accents he spoke of my troubled spirit. He thought I had been a soul under attack.

"And should we worry that she believes herself under attack?" I remember my father asking him.

"Mr Beck, she *was* under attack," the vicar insisted. "I'm convinced of it. There is no saying those forces will never be back. But meanwhile . . ." He spread his hands and sighed.

"Strange that of all of us, she should not have been spared," I was puzzled by my grandmother saying one day. I had no idea what she meant, and didn't really let it bother me much. Then, as my dreams stopped coming, I forgot all about it, though I did like the idea of the giant fox. He was like something out of *Alice in Wonderland*!

My grandparents' family estate had been in Germany, but my grandfather had given the whole place over to the nation years ago to use as a rest home for aged people suffering from dementia. Granddad was a tall, rather gaunt man, strikingly handsome as my granny was beautiful. She was stockier, though equally striking. Remarkably, they were both pure albinos with rare red eyes, just like the man I had seen in those dreams. The two of them were clearly deeply in love. As he grew frail, she grew ever more solicitous of his health. Though my parents clearly loved the count and countess, they sometimes thought them a little old-fashioned with their decided opinions about modern pop culture! My mum and dad liked rock-and-roll, but Countess von Bek, for instance, had decided opinions about modern pop music! The only light music she was willing to accept was played by the 1930s big bands.

My grandparents' own circle of friends occasionally visited Ingleton. An odd, often bohemian collection of old people, they sometimes seemed a little remote from us but evidently took pleasure in seeing children about and almost always brought us gifts. They would disappear off to my grandparents' wing of the house or go for long walks, talking about obscure and mysterious things. We were never particularly curious about them. Some, we gathered, had been anti-Nazis in Germany and had known our parents during the Second World War.

We spent most of the year in London, so we knew how to look after ourselves, but we enjoyed immense freedom in Yorkshire. We were allowed to range across the fells at will as long as we took our mobile phones. We weren't idiots. We avoided going down into the various cave systems which ran under large parts of the hillside. These systems were the haunt of cavers, desperate to discover new and connecting routes, just as the high, shining terraces were favourite places for climbers, some of whom returned every year and were known to us. Gradually, under their expert if slightly condescending supervision, my brother and sister and I learned technical rock climbing as well as caving. Yorkshire was just the greatest place I knew in the whole world.

My adventure began on one of those slow, wonderful, dreaming, sparkling summer afternoons you get in the dales. The whole landscape takes on a magical quality. It's easy to imagine you're in fairyland. The lazy air is full of insects, the grass full of surprising little plants, such as wild orchids and fritillaria, all different kinds of mosses and the tiny creatures living in them. The hills seem endless and the days infinite. Only an idiot couldn't love it. But that day I had no company.

My dad had driven my grandparents into Lancaster to get the train to London, and my mum had gone with him, taking my brother, Alfy, and sister, Gertie, to shop for new shoes and some art supplies. They had a few other plans, so they would probably not be back until the evening. I had stayed behind because I thought one of my favourite old films was coming on the television. They had left Mrs Hawthornthwaite, a kindly dumpling of a lady, in charge of me. Only after they'd gone did I discover that I had misread the TV Guide; my film, The Thief of Bagdad, had been on the previous week. Now I had nothing to look forward to and was doubly bored.

After lunch Mrs H., probably irritated by my deep sighs, told me it was all right if I wanted to go down to the shallows (our end of the river where it emerged from the woods) to look for fish. It wasn't the most exciting option, but it was better than hanging around watching her load and unload the washing machine, since she wouldn't allow me to help her.

As usual, I took the mobile phone. I had instructions to phone her if I needed her or got into any sort of trouble. "Mr H. can be down there in a minute or two," she assured me as she saw me off. "It doesn't matter how silly or trivial a feeling you get; just phone up. He'll know what to do. And if there's nowt to do, so much the better. He needs to be kept busy."

Mr Hawthornthwaite, an amiable man with a shock of snow-white hair and with startling blue eyes in ruddy features, was up in the tower mending a pipe and could be heard cursing mildly from time to time as metal clanged against metal.

I put one of Mum's old Indian bags over my shoulder. Its tassels hung down almost to the ground, but it was the best thing I had to carry my bits and pieces in, including the phone. On the way to the river I spent some while playing around in a ruined building we called the Castle. It was actually part of an old quarry, with a loading platform and rail tracks still running into it where the First World War graphite trucks used to unload, transferring the stuff to the steam train which ran along a narrow-gauge line to Ingleton Station. The remains of the graphite mill was on the other side of the village. It had blown up in 1917. Some thought it was the work of German saboteurs, but my dad said it was probably due to someone's neglect.

Rural Yorkshire has dozens of similar abandoned workings and buildings. There was still an active gravel quarry up the road from us. Occasionally we could hear them dynamiting. Their explosives were why we were never allowed to go into any local caves. A man and his two children had been trapped in White Scar Cave some years ago, hiding from a bull, and only luck had saved them. The quarrymen were not the only ones to use explosives. Even today you would hear a thump and the house would shake, usually because the least responsible cavers, the hooligans of the caving world, were dynamiting new routes into the systems below!

I had quite a decent game running in the Castle, but by about three o'clock in the afternoon I had begun to wonder about going back for tea or continuing down to the river. Then I heard a sharp crack from the direction of the woods above and assumed that the quarry was blasting, though I hadn't noticed the usual warning siren. When there were no further explosions, I swung my feet from the platform and continued on down the grassy bank from the dirt path to the river. Taking off my shoes on the bank, I waded into the clear water and was soon absorbed in seeking out whatever swam over the pebbles.

I was hoping to find freshwater crayfish, those tiny, almost transparent relatives of the lobster, but the sun on the water was too bright, and all I found were a few minnows. My mobile phone was in a little holder swung across my body, and I thought I heard it start to ring. False alarm. I was on the point of giving up on the fishing trip when suddenly the phone began to make a very peculiar noise, almost as if it was warning me that my battery was low. Although I had recharged it while I was having lunch, I pulled it out and flipped it open, wondering if Mrs Hawthornthwaite was trying to get in touch with me. She sometimes rang at teatime if there was something special, like toasted scones or crumpets, which were best eaten hot.

The phone was completely dead. I pressed the recognition button without success. There were no text messages. So I put the thing away again, thinking, a passing fluke of the hills, and returned my attention to the river until a noise from above me told me that someone was on the path. I got up in a hurry. This was all a bit spooky. There he was, a monster of a man, swinging out of the woods: a tall, bulky figure wrapped in a big leather overcoat, his head shaded by a wide-brimmed felt hat, his eyes hidden by reflecting sunglasses, with a scarf drawn up to his nose, as if it were winter and he were feeling the cold. Perhaps he was worried about inhaling dust from the quarry's latest blast.

I must admit I felt a little more vulnerable than usual as the burly man stopped on the path high above me and lifted a gloved hand in greeting. His accent was thick, deep and vaguely familiar. "Good afternoon, young lady."

He was probably trying to sound friendly, but I gave him a cold nod in response. I hated people calling me "young lady." It seemed condescending. Perhaps a little ostentatiously I sat down and began buckling the straps of my shoes.

But the man did not walk on. "You live around here, do you?" he asked. There was an edge, an undertone to his voice, that I really didn't like.

Again I nodded. I couldn't see anything of his face at all and began to wonder if he was deliberately hiding it. He reminded me of the pictures of the Invisible Man I had seen in the Alan Moore comics my brother collected. He hardly seemed any better tempered than that character. Was that why I was so wary of him?

"Am I on the right path for the village of Ingleton?" he asked.

"You're on the back road," I told him. "Keep going and it'll take you to the middle of the square across from the butcher's. The newsagent will be down on the main road to your right."

He thanked me and began to move on. Then he hesitated. He turned, fingering the lower part of his face, still covered by the scarf. "Has anyone else come this way recently?"

I shook my head.

"I'm looking for a rather thin, pale gentleman. A foreigner. Likes to wear black. He would have arrived a day or so ago. Mr Klosterheim? Might he be staying in these parts?"

"You could ask at the newsagent for the Bridge Hotel," I told him. "They'll put you right for where the Bridge is, on the other side of the viaduct." There were also a couple of guest houses closer, but I didn't feel like offering him too much information. His had been a very odd question for anyone to ask in Ingleton. I wondered where he could have come from. He wore high, thick, flat-soled boots of battered leather, reaching to his knee. His trousers were tucked into the boots. He had no haversack, and he didn't look like any kind of hiker I'd ever seen. The clothes were old-fashioned without being identifiable with any historical period. Instinctively I was glad of the distance between us, and intended to keep it. Slowly I finished fastening my shoes.

He grunted, thought over what I'd said, then began moving. He was soon gone, clumping along the track like a campaigning soldier. The track was used by everyone local and curved downwards into the village. It was the shortest way and roughly paralleled the main paved road which passed our house above.

For us it could often seem just as quick to go down that back road than to take the car and try to find a parking space in the village.

The encounter had unsettled me. I was getting flashes of those old, bad dreams. Nothing specific. Not even a tangible image. It was also possible I had eaten something which disagreed with me. Standing on the riverbank, I tried my phone again. It still wasn't working, although now I got a buzzing, like the sound of distant bees. I decided it was time to go home.

I wasn't used to feeling the shivers on the sunlit commons of Ingleton during a golden summer afternoon.

I scrambled up the grassy bank, reached the path, then ran up through the green hillocks over the common, past Beesley's, until I got to the back gate of our house. Mrs Hawthornthwaite was hanging white linens up to dry on a line stretched beside part of our vegetable garden. She insisted it was the best place for laundry, since the linens especially were refreshed by the growing carrots and brussels sprouts. As a girl she had read the tip in *Woman's Weekly*, and always applied it. Her whites glittered, reflecting the bright sunshine. Starched or un-starched, they blossomed in the breeze like the sails of fairy ships.

The main walled garden was to the front of the house, still landscaped much as it had been in the seventeenth century, with junipers, cedars and poplars sur-rounding what was mostly smooth lawn arranged in terraces. The lawn was not good for much except looking at, since there was such a slope on it. When we wanted to play cricket or some other game, we had a flattened area out of sight behind the row of poplars and willows on the far side of the tiny stream which dropped under ground long before it reached the main river. You could just see down to the back road from there.

I was half-tempted to check if the stranger was still on the path, but he would probably have reached the village by now. Something about him contin-ued to bother me. His heavy, menacing masculinity had made its way into my head.

"You feeling hungry, dear?" Mrs Hawthornthwaite was surprised to see me back. She looked at her watch as if wondering why I would be home so early on such a beautiful sunny day.

"A bit," I said. "Is Mum home yet?" I knew the answer.

"Not yet, dear. They were going to wait for the fresh fish to be landed in

Morecambe, remember? They might have gone to the pictures, but there wasn't much on in Lancaster." She frowned. "Are you all right?"

"Yes, thanks," I said. "It's just that I saw a man on the back road. He scared me a bit."

She grew alert. "He didn't—"

"He didn't do anything except ask me the way to Ingleton and if I knew some foreign visitor," I told her. "Then he went on to Ingleton. I suggested he ask about his friend at the Bridge. It's okay. I just thought I'd come home. For some reason my phone's not working."

She accepted this. Mrs Hawthornthwaite had a way of trusting our instincts, just as we trusted hers.

I went into the big, warm living room which looked out towards More-cambe. It got the western sun from two sets of windows. Through them you could see the roofs of the village below. I took the binoculars from the shelf and focused them on the little bit of the back road that was visible. All I saw was the vicar's wife, coasting her bike down the track. As usual, Mrs Handforth had her big orange cat, Jerico, in the front basket. They both seemed to be enjoying the ride. Nobody else was about. I went up to my own room, planning to plug the phone in and recharge it, but when I got it out it was working perfectly. I wondered if the weather had something to do with the problem. Sunspots? I had only the vaguest idea of what sunspots were.

A bit later I had some bread and jam and a glass of milk in the kitchen. Now I was really bored. Mrs Hawthornthwaite suggested I find a book and go outside again. I didn't have a better idea. I took one of my mum's favourite E. Nesbit books, *The House of Arden*, and went downstairs, out of the front door, through the yard, and crossed the paved road to Storrs Common.

"Watch out for that chap!" she called as I left.

Immediately opposite the house was a levelled spot, originally designed to provide parking space for visitors who planned to climb the mountain. Now, as I said, they had to park in the village. From that flat area the hill continued to rise up towards the distant peak of Ingleborough. We always said living at Tower House developed strong calf muscles if nothing else. You were either straining to go up or bracing to go down. Whenever we found ourselves on flat ground we walked so rapidly nobody else could keep up with us.

On the peak of the mountain were the remains of a Celtic hill fort. The story of the fort was that the last of the Iceni had gone there to make their stand against the Roman invaders. Armed to the teeth behind a heavy wall, they prepared for the attack. But the Romans had taken one look at them and decided to go round on their way to Lancaster and Carlisle. The Celts were nonplussed. After about fifty years of living in the wind and cold of the peak, the remains of the Iceni eventually came straggling down and got jobs on the docks at Lancaster.

I had soon found one of my favourite spots in the common, a dip in the grass where it was impossible to be seen. Here, if it was windy, you could swiftly find yourself in a complete cone of silence. The common was full of such holes, where the ground had fallen in over the cave systems which riddled the entire area. Here and there were deeper, larger holes, where the rock was exposed and which seemed like the entrances of caves but never really led anywhere.

Once below the level of the ground in the inverted cones, you couldn't hear a thing. There was no better sense of isolation, and yet anyone who knew you could easily find you and you could be back at home within a few minutes.

With a sense of pleasurable anticipation, I opened the covers of *The House of Arden*, a companion to another favourite, *Harding's Luck*. It was all about time paradoxes and people meeting themselves. My earlier exertions must have tired me more than I thought, because I fell asleep in the middle of the first chapter. The next thing I remember is rolling over on my back and blinking up into the late-afternoon sun. As I yawned I saw some large, round object drifting across the sky, a thin plume of smoke coming from it, a bit like the vapour trail of a plane.

Waking up rapidly, I recognised the aircraft as a hot-air balloon. A local group of enthusiasts took visitors up over the Dales during the summer, but they rarely came down this low. Nor, I realised, as the shadow of the basket fell across my hiding place, were they usually so big or so colourful. Next thing the balloon filled up my entire field of vision, and I could smell the smoke. The silk of the canopy blazed in the sun. Glittering scarlets, greens and golds dazzled me. From the rigging flew the cross of St Andrew, the blue-and-white Scottish flag. I saw tongues of fire from the brazier in the basket and two very pale faces staring down at me. Then something whooshed past, and I heard a thump, a yell. As

I scrambled up and out onto the common, there came the roaring sound of a powerful engine in high gear.

On turning, the first object I saw was the big antique convertible. Not the Lexus containing my parents, as I had half hoped, but a great, dark green monster with massive mudguards and a huge radiator decorated with an ornamental "B," a single blue-clad occupant, swinging off the road and onto the flat parking space. The driver's dark goggles gave him the appearance of a huge, mad lemur.

At the sound of another yell I looked back to see the balloon still dragging up the common, the silk bouncing and brilliant, the gasbag booming like a drum. The passengers had leaped from the basket. One of them had thrown out a great iron anchor and was trying to dig this into the ground, seeking to stop the balloon's progress over the grass-grown rocks. The other passenger was clinging hard to the wicker, clearly not at all happy about his situation.

This happened so swiftly, I could barely take in what was going on. None of the people seemed to need help from me, and none seemed especially menacing. It occurred to me that I ought to duck down and hide, but the driver of the car had already seen me and was waving a gauntleted hand and calling out.

"Pardon me, miss. Could you tell me if I'm at the right place? My name's Bastable. I'm looking for some friends of ours." Pushing up his goggles, he began to climb from the car, gathering the folds of his cotton dust-coat which covered what appeared to be a light blue military uniform. On his head was a peaked cap of the same colour.

"Good afternoon," was all I could think of to say.

Another voice came from behind me.

"Good afternoon, my dear beautiful young woman."

Somehow I wasn't a bit offended by those rich, flattering tones, offered in the most delicious Scottish brogue I had ever heard. I turned round again. Grinning at me, the balloonist, in full Highland dress, including a brilliant kilt, was testing his anchor line now, having stopped the vessel's drift. His companion was stamping heavily on bits of flaming wood threatening to set the grass alight. Then he reached into the basket and took something out. A black, undecorated oblong box, narrow and long. Clearly an electric guitar case. He was tall and very nifty in what appeared to be European evening dress. I wouldn't have guessed he was a rock musician. When he faced me, I was surprised. I had seen him before. In my dreams! Though considerably younger, he could have been a relative of my albino grandfather or grandmother. He had the same refined, angular features, the same long, graceful body, the same slender fingers, the same white hair and subtly tapering ears, and he had the same scarlet eyes. He greeted me with an inclination of his head, then shouted across to the Scot.

"You promised us a smoother landing, St Odhran."

The man he addressed waved a dismissive hand and removed his befeathered bonnet, revealing a shock of red hair above lively blue eyes. With a broad, charming smile which reflected something of the swagger in his manner, he approached me. Reaching out an elegant hand, he made a deep bow, kissing the tips of my fingers. "You are the young countess, I take it? I am the Chevalier St Odhran, forever at your service."

"I'm not a countess," I told him, still fascinated by his albino friend. I was a bit distracted. "But I'm pleased to meet you. Would one of the people you're looking for happen to have a German-sounding name? If so, there's another gentleman wants to see him down in the village."

"We are all British, I fear," said the driver of the car, also presenting himself in that same charming, old-fashioned way. "Even my friend here"—he indicated the man in evening clothes—"has sufficient residency to claim citizenship." He saluted. "At your service, Colonel Bastable of the GTA, ma'am." His manner was playful and won me over. He reminded me a bit of Sting and Hugh Grant combined. "I must say, we seem to have timed our arrival to the second. That's not always the case. I wonder if you'd mind my asking a question. Would that house be Tower House, the residence of the Count and Countess von Bek?"

"I'm Oo Beck," I said. "The youngest in the whole family."

I was surprised that Mr or Mrs Hawthornthwaite had not yet come out to investigate, but if they were at the back of the house, perhaps watching the cricket, they might not have heard the visitors arrive. I had no instinctive suspicion of the three men and in fact trusted the albino just because I remembered someone like him in my old dreams, so I answered perhaps more freely than was sensible. I agreed that the Count and Countess von Bek did usually live across the road but that they had gone to London. My own parents, their son and daughter-in-law, were due back from Lancaster fairly soon.

"Ah," said the tall albino rather sonorously. "The one thing we had not bargained for!" Putting his long case carefully down, he shook hands with me. His were the strongest, hardest fingers I had ever touched before. "I apologise, Miss von Bek. My manners have become crude." He introduced himself. "I am usually simply known as Monsieur Zodiac."

"That's the name of a conjuror who used to appear at the Palladium," I said. "You look rather like his picture." I had seen the programmes which my grandfather and grandmother had kept. "Are you a relative?"

"I had a small reputation on the halls," he admitted. "But I had not expected to be recognised by someone so young!" His smile was pleasant, melancholy, rather distant. "Your grandfather and I go back sixty years."

I explained the circumstances while the Chevalier St Odhran, employing Colonel Bastable to help him, ran back to press the hot air from his balloon's canopy. "I'm fascinated by all those old theatre things," I told him. "I mean to be an actress one day. Did you perform with the Beatles?"

He regretted that he hadn't known the group. "I was only once on the same bill. In Preston. In the early days. Now, if I might leave this in your care for a few minutes . . ." Setting his guitar case down, he excused himself and went to the assistance of the others.

I watched the three press and fold the silk and pack it into the balloon's basket. They were all tall, athletic men and plainly old friends, exchanging jokes and laughing as they worked. Yet there was a purposefulness to them which gave me a lot of comfort. I could feel myself beaming with inner contentment. Boredom was no longer threatening to spoil my holidays.

2

There seemed nothing for it: I must try to be a good hostess and invite the strangers in for a cup of tea. Mrs Hawthornthwaite entered the big kitchen just as my guests and I reached the hall. She was a bit taken aback, especially when the tall men told her they already knew the von Beks and were here by arrangement.

"I'm surprised," she said a little stiffly. "Usually Mr and Mrs Beck let me know when visitors are expected." My parents, who under German custom could use their titles, preferred not to be known as Count and Countess.

But St Odhran soon charmed Mrs H., establishing his credentials with a reminiscence or two of shared early days with her employers, until the more formal apologies of his companions had her insisting to them that they should stay even when, with perfect manners, they suggested they find a tea shop in the village and return later.

"I should also warn you, Mrs Hawthornthwaite, that up to four other members of our little band also expect to join us here," said Colonel Bastable, offering her a salute of thanks. "It would be pure imposition . . ."

She took this in her stride. I had never seen her so friendly to anyone outside the family as she was to these well-dressed yet somehow battle-scarred men, whom I think we both instinctively understood to be heroes, seasoned in unimaginable wars. "Then I'd better get out the old tea set," she said with some satisfaction. "We've had bigger parties for the Three Peaks race, gentlemen." She wondered if she shouldn't try to contact my mum and dad on their mobile phone. It was sometimes harder to find a signal for Morecambe than it was for London, in spite of what the servers always promised you. I said I'd try as soon as the big men were settled. I got them down in our comfy leather sitting-room chairs, admiring our pictures and our wonderful views. Their orders for tea were hearty and manly, though Colonel Bastable generously said that while he would also find Darjeeling or something like that splendid, it really didn't matter to him if Assam was preferred by the others, so I went off to sort out what I could from our miscellaneous packets of antique teas. All we used at home was Yorkshire Gold. I decided to put that beside the big teapots Mrs Hawthornthwaite was warming. Then I went up to our tower via the "secret" door through the upstairs bathroom, the highest point in the house, and tried to phone.

I didn't put the light on in the tower, because I wanted to enjoy the last of the evening. It was getting on for twilight now, and the mist was like a filmy blue blanket over the village below. Yellow lamps shone here and there from under twisted eaves and above rippling slate roofs touched blood-red by the setting sun. Ingleton had never looked more beautiful and unworldly. In the other direction were the lights of villages all the way to Morecambe Bay: lights of homes, streetlamps, window displays, all burning the same dense yellow against the deepening blue. I could smell the fells as night came creeping up over the limestone shelves and rooks began to call out the evening round-up and turn for home.

I dialled my mum's number. It crackled and rang, crackled and rang. Then I thought someone picked up. In the hope that they could hear me, I told them we had visitors and who they were. Colonel Bastable and company had insisted they would not impose on us and had proposed taking us to supper at the Inglenook or, if we could order in time, the Hill Inn. The Hill Inn offered basic ham suppers, about the best in Yorkshire, and my vote was for the Hill. I always voted for the Hill, and I had a feeling I wouldn't be overruled tonight if all went well. Visitors, especially if from the south, always got the ham tea and the Theakston's Old Peculier. It was a sort of provincial showing off, I suppose. But it was hard to imagine a decent world which didn't have at least one of those two things in it.

Just before I opened the door to go down, I saw two figures on the main road up from the village, where it turned radically under the high limestone wall of the police station. It seemed that Sandy, our policeman, *really* wasn't in. Usually you could see the light in his back room as he watched TV and pretended he was called on a case. I recognised the heavy cloak worn by one of the figures. He was the man I had met earlier. The second man filled me with alarm because he reminded me of my old dream. He wore that same kind of wide-brimmed black hat. I told myself not to be stupid. The two strangers had managed to meet, probably at the Bridge as I had suggested. I moved away from the window in case they looked up and saw me. Seeing their shadows still unmoving, I stared into the night and wondered what they were up to.

I then went back to attend to our guests, not mentioning the strangers outside. I must admit I enjoyed playing hostess and having all those grown men responding with grave respect as I offered Eccles cakes and refilled their teacups with a brew they all agreed was the best they'd had since the various foreign parts they had all come from. I asked them if they had enjoyed their journeys.

Colonel Bastable said they had all most recently travelled from St Odhran's place in the Highlands and before that, in his own immediate case, from Salisbury. They were surprised they had not been expected, since the message to meet had come from the count and countess, my grandparents. Just as they were tucking into a second round of Eccles cakes, home-made by Mrs Hawthornthwaite, there came a knock at the door, and she went to answer it. Soft masculine voices in the hall. Further apologies. Then my original three visitors were standing up to shake hands with the newcomers.

These weren't the men I'd seen outside in the shadows. These were clearly all old friends and did not seem to have met for a while. They were careful to include me in their conversation, though much of it, of course, was lost on me. The newcomers were equally impressive. One had silver hair and seemed roughly the age of my grandfather, though not as frail. He was shorter and stockier than the rest, with a square face and light blue eyes, a manner of solid integrity, though a little self-mocking, with a faint accent I took to be German. Prince Lobkowitz embraced one of my tiny hands in both his massive ones. His kindly eyes were intelligent, and whereas the others had the demeanour of men of action, Prince Lobkowitz appeared to be some sort of professor. The man with him had a more pronounced accent and was clearly French. Lieutenant Fromental was a huge, gentle man with a large head, dark skin and black eyes beneath a shock of curly white hair. Although still insisting he was a legionnaire, he wore jeans, a white shirt and an enormous leather jacket, which he was reluctant to remove. As he accepted a china teacup and saucer in his hands the china seemed to turn into the dolly's tea set I still had upstairs. Prince Lobkowitz looked like a dwarf beside him.

I don't know why these men seemed familiar to me. Even their names rang a bell. While they behaved like my granddad's contemporaries, some were too young, but I was sure some of their names were the same as those I'd heard talked about. And, of course, it was actually my grandfather and grandmother these men had come to see. I got the impression they had once belonged to some sort of think tank at Oxford or Cambridge or maybe Westminster.

"I can't work out why my grandparents would make such an important appointment and then zip off for London," I said. "They're not like that. It's not as if they get a vast number of visitors. They'd have been talking about your turning up for weeks, normally. Yet I know for certain they won't be back for at least another day."

"They could have had a reason for calling us here early," suggested Prince Lobkowitz. "Something might have to be defended."

"You mean from those men I saw outside?" I asked. "When I was in the tower."

"Which men? Are you talking about this German chap?" Colonel Bastable came to kneel beside me as I popped the last bit of Eccles cake into my mouth.

"Well, yes," I agreed, "that man, possibly, with his friend that I saw when I was at the river. They were coming up the main road from the village. Not used to that hill, I bet. They had stopped to get a second wind, I'd guess."

To my surprise, the whole atmosphere changed. Immediately Colonel Bastable was on his feet while someone else doused the lights. Monsieur Zodiac peered cautiously out of the window, from where you could, if you flattened your head against the wall, just see a bit of road. It all seemed a bit melodramatic to me, and I wanted to giggle, yet there was something so serious in their manner that I soon calmed down.

"What is it?" I asked. "Are those the bad guys?"

"Never invite them across your threshold," St Odhran said seriously. "They mean you and your family only ill."

"Granny would certainly know what to do," I said. "But meanwhile I suppose we shall just have to be prepared."

"Prepared it is, my dear," said Colonel Bastable. "Those are beasts of prey out there this evening, and they are hungry for our blood. But even that evil pair would not come wandering into our territory so readily if they meant to start trouble at once. They are just sniffing around us, I suspect."

"Unless they possessed some enormous power which they were convinced could defeat us," said Monsieur Zodiac. He seemed the most on edge of the men. He was constantly checking the watches he wore on both wrists.

"And decided to employ it because they knew our numbers would never be weaker," murmured Lieutenant Fromental.

"You mean this is a trap that pair set for us?" Prince Lobkowitz put his head down, his hands behind his back, and began to pace. "Yet how could they have known the roads?"

"We grow too used to conspiracy, gentlemen." Monsieur Zodiac had recovered himself and leaned against the piano, lighting a cigarette and waving a dismissive hand. "They are here to spy on us. They travel in our wake." He stepped to the French windows and flung them open. The air was warm, and his action had the effect of dispelling any anxieties entertained by his companions. He flicked his ash contemptuously out into the darkness. But he moved, I thought, with wary speed, ready to contain, with instant strategies, any attack on us. I was sure I heard the mumble of conversation beyond the tall garden wall. "They trace the detritus of our passing," added the albino, addressing only the sweet-smelling garden. Then the mumbled voices stopped abruptly, and Monsieur Zodiac laughed under his breath. "If they have the power, they are saving it."

"What power? Saving for what?" I couldn't help asking.

"Power to tip us out of the world's saucer!" As Colonel Bastable glared at him, the Chevalier St Odhran burst into raucous laughter. "Well, colonel, she might as well know these aren't your usual child abductors. And with whatever small powers we have among us, we fight the forces of annihilation itself."

"No child should carry such burdens," murmured Monsieur Zodiac, his voice suddenly soft.

St Odhran agreed. "But we have all known children who have borne such burdens well. True?"

It was pretty clear to me that something had gone wrong. The way they exchanged glances and lowered their voices when they didn't want me to hear was a bit of a clue. When St Odhran began to speak rapidly in French, it was all

I could do to keep up with him, though I could understand the Frenchmen when they replied to him. "They have selected their ground, then," said Lieutenant Fromental. "They must feel pretty confident."

"No doubt. We have more than enough to keep them at bay." Prince Lobkowitz sounded a bit on the grim side. "And there is much they must achieve, even after the ground has been taken and named. They were ahead of us there, I'll grant you."

"Never try to be too subtle with these people," said Monsieur Zodiac. "They are brutes. They should be disposed of like brutes."

Colonel Bastable and some of the others seemed a little embarrassed by this, as if Monsieur Zodiac's ruthless remedies might be theirs, also.

"We shall certainly take every precaution against them." Prince Lobkowitz reopened the French door and looked out into the night, sniffing the night-scented stock and jasmine. "Nothing here now."

His reassurance was enough for them. They relaxed at once. I was envious of any group of people who could trust one another so thoroughly.

Mrs Hawthornthwaite came in. She had evidently been counting sheets and towels and so on. "I'm sure it would be no problem to put you up for a few days, gents. We've had parties of cavers and campers and even a rock-and-roll band staying before now. I'll have to wait and check with Oo's parents when they get back, of course. They shouldn't be long now. All they had to do was pick up some fish in Morecambe. Then they were on their way home. They'd have phoned if they had any other plans."

"Certainly not, dear lady." The Chevalier St Odhran shook his head vigorously. "Ingleton has more than one hostelry, I take it?"

"Lots more," I said.

Mrs Hawthornthwaite gave me a bit of a look. I realised then she really wanted to have the company of these men for more than just the kudos and pleasure of it. She was more anxious than she was letting on.

"Quite a lot," I said stupidly, realising what I'd done.

"Oh, yes, gentlemen," she was forced to say gamely. "Ingleton's a famous resort, or was. Though," she added, "it's possible there won't be room for you all in the same place. And you'd want to stay together, I expect."

"We have my Bentley," Colonel Bastable pointed out. "We can easily go over to Settle or some larger town. However, if you would allow us to telephone to Count and Countess von Bek to let them know we're here . . .?"

I hadn't thought of phoning my granddad and granny at their London flat. They'd probably be there by now. If I'd had my computer working, I would have emailed them hours ago. I showed Colonel Bastable into the hall, where the telephone sat on a table covered in an old green velvet cloth. Beside it were two cut-off tree trunks—log seats. He tried to sit on one and then decided to make his call standing up. I felt a bit of an idiot for not thinking of this sooner. I gave him the London number.

"I'll be glad to pay for the call," he told me as he dialled.

I had become particularly fascinated by Colonel Bastable, who seemed to have stepped out of one of the old movies I loved to watch on the Turner channel. He even looked a bit like Ronald Colman. He certainly talked like him! He had an air of early-twentieth-century dignity about him, a way of speaking and moving which made me think of soldiers ready to die for Empire, of Kipling and "the thin red line"; yet his eyes carried a knowledge, a sadness even, which denied the stereotype, as if all his experience and wisdom, perhaps even his self-knowledge, were exceptional.

St Odhran was the most cheerful of our visitors, and Monsieur Zodiac probably the saddest. Prince Lobkowitz had considerable gravity yet seemed the most ordinary, together with Lieutenant Fromental, who appeared awkwardly embarrassed to be here, as if he felt he should be out defending his fort from Tuareg freedom fighters. For all their differences, however, the men were a glamorous and substantial group, a little reluctant, in spite of my direct questions, to go into details about why they were here. My French was not good enough for me to be a very effective eavesdropper.

When Colonel Bastable finally got through to London, it was only to leave a message on my granddad's incredible old-fashioned answering machine, which he insisted on keeping purely on the strength that it had outlasted something like twenty-six generations of upgrades.

At length, after several more telephone calls and conferences among themselves, our guests had made up their minds. To be on the safe side I phoned the Hill to tell them we'd be coming up for a ham supper.

Thanking us for our hospitality, the visitors declared that Messrs Lobkowitz and Fromental would stay at the Bridge, where there was room. St Odhran would stay at Oakroyd's in the village. Bastable would go on to a small hotel in Settle, some ten miles from Ingleton. I, of course, was disappointed they were not going to stay with us, though St Odhran asked if he could leave his balloon in our unused stables. I asked if they were going to look for those men at the Bridge, and this seemed to re-engage their attention. "No, but we'll keep an eye on them while we're staying there. If you don't mind, Monsieur Zodiac will take your spare bed. We determined one of us would be needed here." He paused. "If your parents agree, of course."

"Of course. Who exactly are those two men, Colonel Bastable?"

"Two wrong 'uns, dear young lady, as I said. So no invitations to come in, eh? And stay away from them when you're outdoors," insisted Bastable, glancing meaningfully at St Odhran.

"Well, we'll be staying at the hotel tonight and will have our chance, no doubt, to get their measure." Prince Lobkowitz exchanged a glance with Lieutenant Fromental. "But you must be ready for any trick here, mademoiselle. The man you met on the road today is sometimes known as Paul von Minct, sometimes as Prince Gaynor. The man he sought and found is Herr Klosterheim. A thoroughly bad egg. Together they defy both God and Satan and plot the end of the created universe, every world in it."

"Why would they do that?" I wondered.

"Because they hate our way of life," said Colonel Bastable without any apparent irony.

After a moment's hesitation, St Odhran and the others nodded.

"Or perhaps just because they hate any form of life," said Prince Lobkowitz.

They began to talk among themselves again, and I missed most of what they said.

Mrs Hawthornthwaite and I were both very upset they weren't all staying. I think she felt a bit abandoned after so much talk of danger, but I quickly realised they had not half abandoned us, as it had first seemed; but rather were repositioning themselves. I had a fair idea that Colonel Bastable wouldn't be driving to Settle and, if he did, that he wouldn't be looking for a good twelve hours' sleep at some local hostelry. We were being protected very thoroughly, almost as if they wove a web around us. They created a shield against those who wished us ill. It was all that boring stuff I'd always heard from my mother. I thought I'd never really absorbed it, but now I was astonished at how quickly I was taking this knowledge for granted. I knew the danger in my bones. I had dreamed of it before. I knew how important it was to build all the defences we were currently building. We were dealing with the threat of supernatural attack. And it wasn't the kind Mrs Hawthornthwaite kept away by remembering which kind of lilac was best put in the bowl on the threshold and if it was better or worse luck to use your left hand to pick up a fallen fork.

I remembered something else from those early nightmares I'd had. I was experiencing the benign form of the power which had assaulted me. I recognised it now only because I had known its opposite. I knew that I couldn't be safer than with Monsieur Zodiac.

Naturally we had orders to contact people at their hotels should anything alarming happen, but I knew we were in perfect hands.

Monsieur Zodiac seemed pleased with my obvious confidence in him. I felt a strange connection between myself and those pain-filled crimson eyes.

Prince Lobkowitz patted my shoulder in a comradely fashion. "We'll go now but will be back in time to meet Mr and Mrs Bek. Will you promise me you won't let the bad 'uns talk you into anything, no matter what crisis they will pretend you have initiated?"

"Of course." Again I was touched by his old-fashioned language and concern.

"And we won't let them cross the threshold of our house, no matter what arguments and sweet inducements they do offer." Mrs Hawthornthwaite indicated her husband, nodding beside her. "We're used to witches and their ways in these parts, gentlemen."

This was news to me, but it was a kind of comfort, too. Mrs Hawthornthwaite didn't mean cackling old ladies in big pointed hats, sailing over your head on their broomsticks. Mrs Hawthornthwaite meant an invasion of pure evil into the dale, an invasion you could almost feel like mist curling up from the bottoms of pits and riverbeds to spread itself through every street, every room of our village. And the only forces left to fight it were the unsuspecting, unimaginative folk the likes of Colonel Bastable represented: the honest, virtuous long-term inhabitants of these valleys.

I felt absolutely safe in Ingleton. I wondered if this was, after all, the best strategy of our enemies, to attack here. Even with the deep caverns in the limestone below booming far away in the underground distance, I always felt safe at Tower House. She had no ghosts I feared.

With Monsieur Zodiac I watched the news. I was growing impatient, wanting Mum and Dad, Alf and Gertie, to come home in the expectation that our visitor would confide more in them. I might not be allowed to stay in the sitting room, but Tower House's acoustics were so good that I'd be bound to hear the important bits of whatever was said, even if I kept out of sight on the landing which led to my room.

But Monsieur Zodiac said little more to my parents when they came in. They seemed to know who he was and were very welcoming. Dad, who was almost as thin and wiry as our guest, picked me up and hugged me as if I'd been rescued from actual danger, and Mum told me I could stay up for supper at the Hill Inn. I felt slightly guilty for having invited everyone. At that point Mum didn't actually know I'd done it. I knew she had planned on cooking haddock. She seemed genuinely grateful, however, for Monsieur Zodiac's presence and was pleased to know that his friends would be coming with us for the meal. I was rather proud of her. She was dignified and gracious, like a queen.

Messrs Lobkowitz and Fromental came up from the Bridge after a while and waited with us for St Odhran and Colonel Bastable. They hadn't seen the two strangers there. Mum and Dad put out snacks and got drinks for all who wanted them. I helped Mum in the kitchen while my brother, Alfy, and my sister, Gertie, tried to persuade Monsieur Zodiac to open his case and show them his guitar. With good humour, he refused, saying he had no amplifier and refusing the offer of Alfy's. "I fear my instrument would be a little too powerful, Mr Bek."

"Alfred," said Mum, looking up from our big Raeburn stove, "come in and help me with the nuts. Gertie and Dad can look after our guests." Alfy came in reluctantly, his big blond head bowed in disappointment, his red cheeks ruddier than usual. I think Mum had made him feel a bit of an idiot. When I tried to be friendly he snatched away and started pouring out nuts, but I knew he wouldn't stay in a bad mood for long. We heard the TV go on again. Both Monsieur Zodiac and Dad seemed to be taking a keen interest in the news.

"He reminds me of the Winter brothers," said Mum. "Do you know who they are?"

"Some old pop stars of yours and Dad's?" I asked.

"I used to love them when I was in college." She pushed back her mop of brown, curly hair.

"Bloody awful R and B." Alf was being mean.

"Don't say 'bloody,' Alfy," she remonstrated mildly. "Have you finished doing those nuts?"

"I love blues," I said. "Were they like Howlin' Wolf?"

"A bit." She grinned at me and winked. We both knew Alfy would regret his snit, as he did within five minutes, when Gert came in. She was as tall as Mum and skinny. I thought she was the most beautiful girl I'd ever known, much better-looking than any of the pop stars or actresses I'd seen. She had Mum's curly hair, but it was red, and she had big hazel eyes, full lips, and a fair skin, like Alf's. She said there had been a series of earthquakes in the Middle East and another one on the American West Coast. "The worst for some time. I think that's what Mr Z. wanted to hear about. He thought we might even feel a few shock waves here. Remember the last time?"

I took some fizzy water in for Monsieur Zodiac. The others were having wine and whisky.

Monsieur Zodiac and my dad were talking about the news. "Would that be why you and your friends have come here?" Dad was asking.

"Well, sir, it has something to do with our expedition, I'll grant you."

"And what of those others at the Bridge? Assuming they are still at the Bridge."

"A wicked pair, sir. They mean your family no good. But with luck we'll see them off in a few days. We await only the arrival of the count and countess. We spoke to them on the telephone, and they are taking the early train home in the morning. They hoped you could pick them up at Lancaster Station."

"Of course. We'd better think in terms of an early night, I suppose."

"We'll be ready to be off to the Hill, I think, as soon as everyone's here. Your daughter did us the courtesy of booking supper."

Until then nobody had known I had already booked the Hill. "How thoughtful . . ." said Dad with a bit of a grin.

I had my fingers crossed everyone would be here in good time for the ham tea I anticipated. In the end there was no problem. All the men returned in time, and Colonel Bastable ferried quite a lot of us up in his Bentley while the others had to go in the old Lexus. It was a happy, busy night at the Hill. My parents didn't know everything about *their* parents' adventures, but they knew enough to understand that all these people turning up was a bit of an honour for us. Monsieur Zodiac wasn't hungry, so I had most of his tea, too!

Soon we were back at the house, and various people were saying goodnight. Monsieur Zodiac stayed with us while the others went their separate ways. Again I had that sense of people posting watch. Again I felt very secure.

I drank my cocoa in front of the fire with the handsome albino. I'd heard the others speak of Monsieur Zodiac a little warily, as if he were very fierce and temperamental, but I found him very easy to get along with. I felt sort of sorry for him, I suppose. He bore his sadness, as Wheldrake says somewhere, like a steel sheath about him, so that not even the blade of his wit could strike and harm.

Before I went up to bed, the albino patted my shoulder and looked down at me through his brooding crimson eyes. He made an attempt to smile. It was kindly meant, and I saw something very much like a parent's love in his expression. I was surprised, but I smiled back.

"Look after yourself, little mademoiselle," he said.

That night I woke up several times with bad dreams. They weren't exactly nightmares, for I was always rescued before anything got close enough to me, but they left me weak and feeling unpleasant, so much so that when Dad got up early, even though the train didn't arrive for a few hours, I got up, too. He wanted to go out for a walk, and I begged him to let me go with him. I think I persuaded him while he was still sleepy; otherwise he might have remembered the warnings of the night before. But I was used to testing my safety by the limits adults set on my freedom, so, because Dad let me go with him on his walk, I thought it was perfectly okay.

It was another beautiful summer morning. As we climbed up the slopes and terraces above the house, we looked back. Tower House, all sparkling granite and glass windows, looked as magical as the limestone, with the hills rolling away behind it across to the distant, glaring sea. The West Yorkshire dales at their best.

We climbed over a stile and were soon in the fields, with a long drystone wall below us in a shallow valley and a small flock of shaggy sheep grazing above. We paused to enjoy the view again.

Dad and I had often gone on this walk. It was one of our favourites. This morning we had to cut it short, because Dad needed to get back and make the long drive to Lancaster along the twisting lanes which crossed the border from Yorkshire to Lancashire. There are still people on that border who fight those Wars of the Roses, at least verbally, and usually in the pub.

We were back safe and sound and ate breakfast before anyone else was up. Only when I had finished did I realise that Monsieur Zodiac must have left while we were on our walk. He clearly planned to come back, said Mum, scruffy as ever in her old dressing gown, because his door was open and his bag and clothes were still in his room, although his long, black instrument case was gone. Mum, who wasn't at her best in the morning, wondered where he could be taking his guitar at this time.

"He couldn't have a gig around here. Not even a rehearsal. Could he, do you think?"

Alfy, still half-asleep, made a weak joke about playing in the sunrise with the hippies in Kirby Lonsdale, at which Gertie expressed her disgust. The smell of coffee filled the room, followed by the acrid smell of burning toast. Alf preferred his breakfast black.

I saw Dad off and went back out onto the common for a minute. I climbed the hill so that I would see the last of his car, waved, and began to ascend again. Which was when the earth shuddered. Then stop. Then shudder again. Then shake.

As I got to the house, the earth tossed me up and threatened to throw me into the wall before I could get through the gate.

I was winded and scared. More explosions from the cavers, was my first thought. They'd gone too far. My second thought was earthquake. I tried to remember how you were supposed to respond in such circumstances. I only knew what we'd been told to do in the hotel, on our trip to Disneyland, about getting under a secure beam and so forth.

I suddenly felt myself slipping, as if the ground had tilted beneath my feet, and I knew I was sliding towards the mouth of what we sometimes called Claffam's Cave—not a real cave at all, but a deep indent in the grass-covered limestone. I could hardly make out the grassy bottom. How had it happened that one moment I was near our quadrangle door and the next I was sliding down towards dark, slippery shale? I managed to get a strong grip on a bit of rock and hung on tight, stopping my descent.

The smell of rock dust clogged my nostrils, and I couldn't get a foothold on anything. I didn't have the breath to scream. Surely someone in the house knew what was happening and was taking the proper action.

The shale continued to clatter and hiss past me, and I was shocked to see the foreign-looking man, Paul von Minct, in the big greatcloak, shaking his dusty head out of the pit below me, his clawlike slate-coloured fingers pushing back the shale as he came upwards, his long, grey face intense in its determination to keep climbing towards me. At last I started screaming. But nothing came out of my throat. This man, already described as my greatest enemy, was between me and my house. I couldn't shout, so I let go of the rock, landed on his face, knocked him over, pushed past him, and was out of the hole and back on the green of the common. I had lost my bearings. Where was the house? I heard his heavy feet running behind me, and ahead of me I saw another cave opening. I jumped in to avoid his seeing me, but I could still hear him nearby.

"Miss Oonagh. Could I have a word with you, perhaps?"

I kept my head down.

He must have known I was close enough to hear him. "You have broken the spell," he snarled. His voice was like the hard bluster of the wind. "You have shredded the net they put around you. Now you are ours!"

Then came the Puritan, Klosterheim, speaking in tones like a keening, shrieking blade on glass, behind his master. Could anyone ever forget that grating voice? Or those black-and-white clothes, straight out of my old nightmares? "You proved your own will, dear child. Your *own* will. You prefer to be with us . . ."

That was both so blatantly false and so nonsensical, I found some energy from laughing at it. I managed to stand, see where I was, spot the house, and start running for it.

To my relief, I saw Monsieur Zodiac beckoning to me from overhead. I had not recognised him before, since he had discarded the formal English evening dress. Now he looked just as I'd seen him in those old dreams, as if he had stepped out of one of those Hindu movies I love, with long turban ends and a flowing costume, scarves and sashes, all of bright, beautiful colours. Why was he dressed so differently?

A growl from behind me.

"Here!"

There came a single deep note from the rock at his feet, and releasing me he reached down to pick up the black sword. "Only this blade remains unchanged."

He gasped and reached towards me, but I was drifting past him while he shouted my name. I knew I was lost from his protection, possibly from all protection. Then I was running on solid ground in the dark, then slipping. All the others had disappeared, and I could see no opening to the cave.

As I turned while falling, the only light before me now was in the green, reflecting eye of a very large cat!

Then this light, too, blinked out.

3

I wasn't scared at that point, because I was confident someone would come and rescue me. I didn't think anyone had planned to trap me in the cave system. Monsieur Zodiac had, I was sure, protected me as best he could from von Minct and Klosterheim. So it was hours before I gave up and began to feel my way downwards to where I was sure I saw a faint light. It could, of course, just be the glaring eyes of the big cat I had seen in the dark, but I had no choice.

I moved carefully, trembling with cold. All I wore was a Tshirt and shorts. I was going steadily downwards, hoping to find cavers there who could get me back to the surface. Then behind me I heard a loud crack, and the ground shook faintly. Bits of stone rattled down, but nothing hit me. I had a sick feeling in my stomach, but I was trying to keep control of myself. If Klosterheim could scare me so readily, then I ought to have all my wits about me. I climbed over a ridge of rock and suddenly was looking down into a deep underground valley and the strangest city I had ever seen. It was like something out of a silent black-and-white sci-fi film. I knew it, of course. I had seen it in those old, terrifying dreams.

Crystal spires, which could almost have been natural formations, rose a thousand feet or more below me. A silvery river ran through the city centre, and strange, elongated beings, scarcely different in appearance from the crystalline spikes, came and went on the slopes. As in those dreams, I felt no fear of them or their city. In fact, I knew a sense of relief and wasn't really surprised by my own lack of surprise. After all, I had known the city and its strange beings all my life.

Then I realised some inhabitants had seen me and were coming towards me.

Just as in those dreams, I started to run away from them, even thought they offered me no harm. Then I saw the outlines of a gigantic fox ahead, standing on his hind legs. My thought was, I can't let him be killed by that Puritan. So I turned and ran back towards the denizens of the city. I was prepared to do almost anything to make sure the bad part of the dream didn't come true.

Two of the weird-looking creatures in pointed hoods were approaching me now. I knew they were harmless. I just *had* to change the dream, make sure the fox wasn't shot. I let them come towards me. They must have been nine or ten feet tall, with hands so elongated they reminded me of bones. The tall, pointed hoods, which could have been some kind of carapace, made them look like priests in an *auto-da-fé* or members of the Ku Klux Klan. Beneath these long, pointed skulls were faces at once alien and amiable, with stone-coloured folds of skin, their features seemingly formed from flowing volcanic rock and suddenly frozen, utterly unhuman and beautiful. Within their strange masklike faces were eyes like ice, which clearly held nothing but good will towards me. When they spoke, it reminded me of the soft music of wind chimes, and though I could not understand their language, I accepted the first being's cold, long-fingered hand when he offered it. He knew I had no business being where I was. I felt confident he would soon get me home. Taking his hand, I noticed an ordinary black cat with a thin body and long ears, which had situated itself at the feet of the two alien beings. It regarded me with its almond-shaped eyes. As my hosts led me back towards their city, the cat followed. Soon several similar cats, tails high, joined us. We made a strange procession as we walked slowly down towards crystal spires.

At that point I was still convinced I would soon be reunited with my parents, or that at least Monsieur Zodiac would be contacting me. Somehow I thought they already knew about this world. I had no possible notion of the adventure on which I was about to embark.

At last we reached the city. The tall, irregular towers had an extraordinary and profound beauty. I felt an emotion similar to one I had known when visiting York Minster and Westminster Abbey, but far more intense. I had sensations of tremendous joy and was so absorbed in the experience, I did not notice the creature standing in the nearest doorway, smiling at me.

"I see the city of the Off-Moo has impressed you, young miss."

I was being addressed by that same large fox, somewhat bigger than the average man and standing a little uncertainly on his hind legs, dressed with exquisite taste in the finery of a late-eighteenth-century fop. With one paw the fox held a tall ornamental pole, with which he kept his balance. The other he extended to me. "How do you do, mademoiselle." His pad was soft and sensitive, with a living warmth to it. "I am Renyard von Grimmelshausen, Lord of the Deep City, hereditary keeper of the secrets of the centre. Oh, and many other things. I am named, I must admit, for one of my favourite authors. Have you read *Simplicissimus*? I've written a few books of my own, too. I will be your guide, young mistress. At your disposal. Not in this city, of course, which is not mine, but the other city, parts of which *are* mine."

"There's someone wants to shoot you," I said, shaking his paw. "You'd better be careful."

"I am used to it," he assured me. "I am always careful. And you are . . .?"

"I am Oonagh Beck. I'm hoping to get back to Ingleton as soon as possible."

Lord Renyard frowned, not understanding everything I said. Then he bowed again. "Enchanted, mademoiselle." He spoke in faintly accented English. "You appear to have won the approval of our friends the Off-Moo."

"Who's that, again?"

"Those gentlemen. They are the builders and inhabitants of yonder city. I think it's safe to say they are allies of mine. They'll not harm you."

"But Klosterheim's around!" I looked, but I could no longer see the skull-faced Puritan.

"Oh, he'll not bother us for a while yet, believe me. He cannot come here. How can I help you?" He was serenely confident. I calmed down.

"Maybe you could point me in the right direction for the village," I suggested. There had to be another exit or entrance or whatever. "Or even take me a bit of the way to Ingleton . . ."

"Ingleton, my dear child?"

"It's where I live."

"Is that where you entered the World Below?"

"It is." My granny had told me bedtime stories about the World Above and the World Below when I was a little girl. I'd forgotten all about them. "So? Any ideas about Ingleton?"

He shook his long head. For the first time I became genuinely worried. "Then how can I find my way home?"

"We'll have to look, I suppose."

"Is it possible to stay lost for a long time?"

"It's always possible." He was regretful. "But I'm sure I can help. I have a good many maps where I live. A very extensive library on all subjects. I was paying a casual visit to my friends the Off-Moo, so we can leave without risking offence. I come here to relax. They see nothing strange in me, whereas most of your kind and mine are suspicious of a fox who not only wears human clothes but is also educated, as I am, in all the Encyclopaedists."

"I don't know much about encyclopaedias, Lord Renyard." I felt a bit silly saying that. Had he read them all?

"I am an intellectual child of Voltaire and Montaigne." He spoke with a slight air of self-mockery. "Of whom, no doubt, you've never heard."

"I've heard of Voltaire, but we don't really do much French history or philosophy yet at school."

"Of course you don't." He opened his muzzle and barked several times. It took me a moment to realise that he was laughing. "How old are you, mademoiselle?"

"I'm twelve."

"Another six years before you go to university."

"About that. My sister goes next year."

He asked after my family, and I told him. I said our family name was really von Bek, and at this he barked again.

"Von Bek? It could be I know your father. Or one of your relatives at least. Is his name Manfred?"

"It's one of his names, but they have so many names. I don't think there's been a Manfred first name. Not for about two hundred years at least."

"That could easily be, of course. I met him in about 1800."

"Over two hundred years ago." Was I dreaming or not? Somehow the logic seemed to be that of a dream. "What's the year here?"

"The Off-Moo don't have calendars as we do. But in Mirenburg, the City in the Autumn Stars, where I rule as a prince, it would be about, I don't know, 1820 perhaps. To tell you the truth, my dear, it could as easily be 1920. If I had any means of measuring, I'd be better able to compute exactly what year it was in comparison. When we arrive there I'll be able to help you more."

"Then I suppose we'd better get off to Mirenburg. My mum and dad will be worrying. We can probably phone from there."

"Perhaps they won't be worrying, child." His voice softened in reassurance. "Time has substantial variations, and only a moment or two might have passed in Ingleton while days and weeks go by out here."

For some reason I was reassured by him, just as I had been in my dreams.

"Or several years," added Lord Renyard. Then, realising he might have disappointed me, he leaned down, offering something like a smile. "But it's generally only a matter of moments. I was just finishing my business here. Would you like to come with me to my home? From there it might be possible to reckon a little more specifically."

"I don't seem to have much choice," I said.

"You could, of course, also stay with the Off-Moo. That gentleman over there is Scholar Ree, their spiritual counsellor. He can be very kind."

"I think I'd better stay with you, Lord Renyard, if it's all the same . . ."

"I shall be glad of the company." The handsome fox again offered me his paw and began to lead me back to the larger group of stonelike beings. "First we'll make our adieux."

With grace Lord Renyard bowed to his hosts, then led me out along a narrow trail of smooth rock. Above us the enormous cave widened. The roof of the cavern seemed miles overhead. Instead of stars, crystals glittered and a silver river ran away into the distance, its luminous waters lighting a landscape of stalagmites and stalactites and what seemed like forests of fronds, all pale, shimmering and ethereal.

Reconciled to my inability to contact my parents at that moment, I felt better when Lord Renyard's soft padded paw grasped my hand and we left the Off-Moo city behind. As we walked, he told me a little of the people inhabiting the land he called Mu-Ooria. They had lived here long before the surface of the earth was occupied by sentient beings, he said. Their world was sometimes known as the Border Land or the Middle March, existing on a plane shared in common by many aspects of the multiverse. I was familiar with the idea of alternative universes, so I grasped what he told me fairly easily, though I had never really expected to experience what old-fashioned writers sometimes called "another dimension," and had until now pretty much taken the ideas as fiction. Most of the children's stories that my brother and sister and I read were the kind which describe another world parallel to ours, and I had never thought the idea strange. That said, I knew it might be difficult to escape from such a universe once you had fallen into one, and I remained concerned for my worried parents, feeling somewhat guilty that the fascinating underground world kept distracting my attention.

The Off-Moo had few natural enemies and were peaceful, Lord Renyard told me. The cats I had seen often visited them and communicated between them and certain humans. "Felines often come and go from that city. They have a special fondness for it. I know not why."

Lord Renyard said he found the intellectual stimulus he craved by visiting the Off-Moo. Most of his colleagues in Mirenburg were positively anti-intellectual, he said. "Many are outrageously superstitious. But if they were not, I should probably not rule them."

"You are Mirenburg's ruler?"

"Not the whole city, dear young lady." As we strolled along he told me that he had enjoyed the company of my great-great-great-umpteenth-grandfather and that of another adventurer, his friend the famous aerial navigator, the Chevalier St Odhran.

"You know the Chevalier St Odhran? I met him yesterday!" I was excited to have a friend in common with him.

"Indeed? Not his descendant?"

"Only if his descendant is also a balloonist."

He described his friend who often visited Mirenburg. It was my St Odhran to the letter. And sometimes, I heard, he came here with two friends who *had* to be Lobkowitz and Fromental. This gave me more hope. If the Scot had been able to fly his balloon to Ingleton, then it suggested there was a way I could easily be reunited with my parents and that the Chevalier St Odhran might also know where to look for me. In that way kids can do, I made up my mind not to worry and to enjoy the experience as much as possible. If a minor earth tremor had opened the world to me, there was a good chance that a similar tremor would get me out.

Lord Renyard had a taste, it emerged, for abstraction. He reminded me a bit of my dad, who was always inclined to wander off the practical point into speculation. I began to lose the thread of the fox's arguments and was glad whenever he paused to point out a spectacular view or describe some flora or fauna of the surrounding world.

I was beginning to get tired and hungry by the time the tottering towers of the City in the Autumn Stars came in sight: a sprawl of tall tenements and chimneys, spires and domes. High overhead I could see pale, bright spots of faded colour, rusty reds and dark yellows, which might indeed have been ancient stars. I wondered if I would find my other protector, Monsieur Zodiac, there in the city.

Lord Renyard told me to be careful where I put my feet. "We shall be at my home soon, but the path can still be treacherous." He pointed to the skyline of Mirenburg. "What you observe," he explained, "is a mirror of the city you will find on the surface. Do not ask me how this phenomenon can be. I lack the intellect to explain it. But in a certain place the upper city and the lower city connect and allow us to move from one into the other. I think you will find that upper city more familiar. I cannot be sure, but it might even exist on the same plane as your own."

"In which case they'd have long-distance telephones," I said. "And I'll be able to get in touch with my parents."

He hesitated, doubtful. "Our Mirenburg—*my* Mirenburg—is not an especially progressive city, though she has lately accepted some modest manufacturing reforms."

As we descended towards the city walls, the silence of the huge caverns was broken by a rapid drumming sound. Looking around him, Lord Renyard drew me back into the shadow of a slab of granite. He put his paw to his muzzle, indicating to me that I shouldn't talk. Far away across the ridge, under the dim light of the "autumn stars," I saw two men on horseback. I couldn't make out their features until they rode quite close. I would have called to them if I hadn't remembered Lord Renyard's instructions. When I saw their faces, I was glad I hadn't. It was the mysterious visitor and the other man from the dreams, the Puritan with the pale, gaunt head. Klosterheim. I suspected they were looking for me.

Soon we had reached the high walls of Mirenburg. It was a cold, rather alarming place. I gripped the fox's paw still tighter as he led me through unguarded gates, explaining where we were. "The larger, outer city we call, these days, the Shallow City. But my people inhabit the core of the place. The quarter known as the Deep City. The Shallow City is ruled by the Sebastocrater, descended from Byzantine knights. But I have little intercourse with them. They are very poorly educated, having forgotten their old wisdom and skills. They never leave the city and certainly never venture under ground, as I do."

We walked through black, unlit streets and eventually came to a wide boulevard. A single globe of light, very dim at this distance, lit this area of the city. The globe was seated on top of a monolith of black marble, block upon gigantic block, ascending to cubes of basalt.

"The palace of the lower city's Sebastocrater," Lord Renyard murmured. "No threat to us."

Many of the other buildings had the look of public offices or apartments of important officials. Only rarely did I see a yellow light in a window. The buildings were high and close together. I was reminded of New York, except that this city was weirdly silent, as if everything slept. The only time I'd been to New York, I'd been astonished at the noise of traffic and police sirens going all night.

Lord Renyard seemed nervous, murmuring that this part of the city was not one he was familiar with. "Mine is the oldest quarter, what most these days call the Thieves' Quarter."

"Thieves?"

"I am not an entirely respectable person," he murmured, as if embarrassed. "Though I strived to educate and civilise myself all my life, those amongst whom I am doomed to dwell still consider me a monster. Many are deeply conservative. Even their religion is of a very old-fashioned kind. Only in that district, where no decent citizen will enter, can I find any kind of rest."

This sounded rather melodramatic to me. Personally I found a talking fox cool. My guess was that he'd be on every TV chat show there was, if he moved to London. I meant to tell him this as soon as we arrived at his house. After all, if I could travel so easily to his world, he could as easily come to mine.

The big buildings began to open out until we reached a wharf district on what was either a lake or a very wide river. The horizon turned a faint pink as the sun began to rise. Black water glittered. Overhead the stars grew dim. Lord Renyard led me down some watersteps, and then, amazingly, he led me up them again as the sun rose behind us and Mirenburg awoke and began to greet the morning. It was the same city we had just left, but utterly transformed!

Cocks crowing, dogs barking, maids calling from window to window, hawkers beginning to cry their wares, bells ringing, the sounds of carts rolling over cobbles, the bustle of people everywhere. It was the people, however, who rather alarmed me, not because they were sinister in any way, because they were not. They were fresh-faced, round-headed for the most part and of a generally cheerful disposition. They were dressed like people out of another century. Spiral streets wound up towards the town centre, where a vast castle tottered. The smells convinced me that I had almost certainly gone back in time.

Now I really was beginning to worry. I blurted out my anxiety. "Lord Renyard, I don't think you're taking me back to my parents. I'm beginning to be concerned about them. I really *do* need to get home."

Lord Renyard paused. Ahead of us were lofty tenements which seemed to sway in a kind of dance. Even the chimney pots hopped and shuddered. "Visitors here sometimes know of ways of going back and forth across the multiverse." He seemed almost sorrowful.

I didn't mean to start crying. Why had it taken so long for the reality to sink in? I had no idea what was happening. I was lost in time as well as space, and however kind Lord Renyard was, he had no easy way of helping me. It was some comfort to be held in his huge paw, to have his stammers and snuffles of sympathy, but it wasn't enough.

I pulled myself together. I was fairly certain Prince Lobkowitz and the others would guess where I was and would find me. I told myself I had every chance of returning home. The fox was greatly relieved when I stopped crying. "It's not too far now, mademoiselle. And as soon as I am in my apartments I promise I will begin the search for those people who can help you."

Again I took his soft paw, and soon we were in the canyons of what he called the Deep City, where tall, dilapidated buildings creaked and swayed around us. Lord Renyard assured me it was in the nature of this part of Mirenburg to behave so and that only rarely did a building actually fall down. "It helps us keep our privacy, however. That and our reputation." His wink included me in a conspiracy whose ramifications I could never hope to understand. To distract myself I changed the subject.

"You said you are a thief, Lord Renyard. What do you steal?"

His big red-furred ears flattened a little, as if with pride. "I am the Prince of the Thieves, as I told you. That is why you are so safe with me. I myself do not steal, but I command as rascally a gang of footpads, pickpockets and tobymen as you've ever had the pleasure of meeting."

"Tobymen?"

"The toby is the highway, my dear. They are highway robbers. Knights of the road, as they're sometimes termed."

"And murderers?"

He was disapproving. "We don't encourage murder."

Among the shadows of the tenements, I began to see shadows lurking. Sometimes I glimpsed a pale, ratlike face, and sometimes I detected a glinting eye in a basement area or heard a scuttling, a shuffling, a sniggering.

Then, outside a tavern whose sign was so weather-stained and peeling I couldn't easily make out its name, Lord Renyard stopped. "Here we are!" I spelled it. "R-A-S-P-A-Z-I-A-N'S."

Raspazian's Tavern was a basement drinking den. The strong smells of alcohol and tobacco roiled up towards us as we descended dirty steps to its door, which was immediately flung open, inviting us to step through.

I heard a sound all around us, as if we had disturbed a colony of rats, but the interior, lit by oil lamps, had an unexpectedly pleasant atmosphere. At the tables groups of men and women dressed in patched and ragged finery, none of it very clean, saluted my friend with their tankards and weapons and called out respectfully.

"Morning, Captain. Who's the chicksa mort?"

"Enough of that, you rogues." Suddenly Lord Renyard adopted a haughty manner. I guessed that was how he kept his followers in order. I was glad to be under his protection at that moment. We stepped through the tavern to a door at the back, and up a flight of steps into a spacious room much cleaner than the one we left.

Judging by the table and chairs, the room was used for dining. On the other side of this was another flight of stairs. Lord Renyard ushered me ahead and up into a comfortable apartment with two bedrooms. It was the quaintest set of rooms I'd ever seen. I had expected a prince of thieves to live in a palace, but these were the simple, comfortable apartments of a gentleman who enjoyed reading. There were bookshelves everywhere. There was even a shelf of small leather-bound volumes next to a spice rack.

The smaller bedroom was for me, he said. There he let me clean up while he sent servants out to find clothes for me. Before long his maid brought me everything I needed, including a mobcap. At least I would look normal when I went out. While I was dressing, I smelled cooking food. At the table Lord Renyard now sat before a pile of various breads, butter and jam, which he offered me while his smiling black-haired maid brought him in a plate of undercooked chicken. Civilised and erudite as he was, the fox remained a fox.

"I have already sent my men abroad, mademoiselle. They seek St Odhran's friends Prince Lobkowitz and Lieutenant Fromental, who have apparently been sighted and have visited here before. If anyone can discover your friends, my people will."

"What do you know about Klosterheim and Gaynor?" I asked.

"Very little. They are here, too, by now, of course. They work with powerful allies these days, I gather. I have come up against Klosterheim in the past. Although I made a friend of your ancestor, I'm not entirely sure the friendship was beneficial."

"How do you mean?" I asked.

"Well, there were repercussions. It is not something I wish to speak about, dear mademoiselle." He would not let himself be drawn out by me, and I couldn't see much point in questioning him further. The important thing at the moment was to get in touch with my grandfather's friends.

We sat in the cosiness of this strange being's apartment while my brain tried to absorb all that had happened to me in the past hours, and as Lord Renyard talked of where and how his men would be looking for my friends, I gradually fell asleep in my chair. I was only dimly aware of him picking me up in his awkward, delicate paws and putting me into a bed so comfortable it must have more than one feather mattress.

I dreamed again. *I was back in the strong embrace of the albino, his silks and samite swirling about him, his great, growling runeblade pulsing in his right hand. "I battle with a friend!" he declared. He began to laugh. "Come!"*

And in a storm of white we lighted on black crystalline rocks, where the great Lord Renyard, splendid in his ruffles and tailored silks, his beribboned dandy cane in his left paw, his quizzing glass to his right eye, bowed with great respect to us both. Then it was as if the albino had blown me like dandelion flax towards Lord Renyard, with his blessing and his strength.

I looked back, and over my shoulder were the distant spires of Mu-Ooria, the black granite and crystalline landscapes of dreams and enduring illusions. I felt Lord Renyard's paw around my shoulder. The albino was nowhere to be seen, but the great fox's delicate perfume was unmistakeable.

Then I was dreaming of Tower House. *My parents were wondering where I'd been, but their pleasure at finding me far outweighed their anxiety. Sometimes I felt I was telling them how protected I felt in the care of Lord Renyard, who sat at the kitchen table, a teacup held between two paws, looking at a brace of unplucked pheasants my mum and dad had given him. His nose was twitching and his teeth were slightly bared, as if he could not wait to begin devouring the succulent birds.*

4

From this dream, I woke up. It was dark. A sliver of light came through my door. I tiptoed to it and opened it a crack. There was no-one in the main room, but I heard voices coming from downstairs. Laughter, oaths, the clatter of crockery and pewter. And over it all the sharp, barking tones of Lord Renyard, speaking a language I had never heard before in my life.

"Two pops and a galloper says she's a pike off."

"Dids't challenge the mish of yon dimber mort!"

Out of sheer curiosity I did my best to hear as much as possible of the queer speech which everyone here used. It sounded a bit like English, a bit like Irish, perhaps, but I was lucky if I understood one word in ten. Nowadays, having read my ancestor's book, in which he offered an account of a visit to Mirenburg around 1800 (cf. *The City in the Autumn Stars*), I know that what I overheard was called "the canting tongue," a language which derived from Gypsy and was used, in one form or another, by thieves and vagabonds in England and other parts of Europe.

When I went back to bed, however, I knew they had been talking about me. I had heard my name mentioned. I had a feeling Lord Renyard's men and women were objecting to my presence, partially because they thought he had kidnapped me. I smiled at this until I realised it was quite possible. How could I have been subtly induced to move further and further from my home, where even now our local friends and acquaintances thought I must still be—unless I had been kidnapped? Could the fox be holding me for ransom and merely pretending to help me?

No, I thought as I returned to the warmth and security of my feather bed. If he had entertained such a plan, Lord Renyard would have betrayed himself. If he had been lying to me, I would have caught something of his intention in his face. Yet it was still possible he could be persuaded to hold me captive or, worse, hand me over to the man who sought me and against whom I had already been warned. I was beginning to realise that I could not trust everything I heard or everyone who told me something. If I was to get back home, I would have to rely increasingly on my own instincts and judgement.

I slept, with brief intervals of wakefulness, until early the next morning, when the light through my little window showed that it was dawn. I looked out onto crooked, cobbled streets, swaying tenements, a bustle of people and animals. Seen in this light, the buildings seemed hardly less organic than the people and beasts. The smell of coffee mingled with the smell of smoke from the city's myriad chimneys. The sky behind those tall buildings grew first rust-red and then yellow and then blue, until the sun was up in all its glory, shining off windows, milk cans, pitchers of pewter, buckets of zinc, and the steel of swords and daggers stuck in the belts of the men swaggering towards the eating houses and grog shops. If I had been on holiday, I would have been fascinated by all this variety and difference, but now I longed to see something familiar, to reassure me that I could soon be on my way home.

Lord Renyard's pretty maid knocked on my door to tell me the table was laid for breakfast. I washed, dressed in my new clothes, and stumbled out to sit down before an array of ham, cheese, dark bread, butter and jam. Not sure of their customs, I helped myself to bread and butter and made myself a ham and cheese sandwich. I was eating this when the maid brought in coffee and hot milk. A moment later Lord Renyard appeared. He looked a little dusty, as if he had been busy during the night. He explained that he'd had to issue orders to his men who were not natural early birds. "But I have a habit of rising at dawn, though I'll often sleep during the day. I put it down to my ancestry. And you, my dear, did you sleep soundly?"

"Yes, thank you, Lord Renyard. But I did get a bit homesick during the night."

"Of course you did. Of course you did." He patted my hand with a soft forepaw. "I expect news of your friends at any moment. My men have been everywhere in the Upper, Lower and Middle City. They have reports of the man Klosterheim, who pursues you, but nothing save rumours about any who pursue *him*. Strangers have all been sparing with their names, it appears." Lord Renyard shared a cup of warm milk with me, wiping his muzzle with his napkin. "For the moment it would be wise for you to remain here until I get some substantial intelligence."

I was bound to agree. "Maybe I could borrow a book or something?" I begged. "Since you don't have TV. I mean, I'd like to take my mind off things or I start worrying about my mum and dad."

Lord Renyard was sympathetic. He brightened, glad of something he could do for me. "I will introduce you to my library, though I fear it is primarily in the French language. Are you fluent?"

"Not really. Maybe you've *something* in English?"

"We'll go there and we shall see," he promised. He took a key from his waistcoat and moved slowly towards a room he had not yet shown me. Almost with reverence, he unlocked the door and opened it, walking to the far wall and drawing back a pair of curtains to allow a dim light to shine upon the orderly shelves of a large and impressive library. I loved the smell of old vellum and paper, the faintly glinting titles. I took some pencils and paper, intending to note down titles that interested me. Unfortunately, when I came to look at them more closely, they were all very old or, as Lord Renyard had warned, mostly in French or German. What weren't in those languages were as often as not in Greek or Latin. I eventually found a translation by Henry Fielding of *Gil Blas*, but frankly it was a bit stuffy. I hadn't by that time become a fan of Smollett and Fielding. The only old books I had read were John Bunyan's *Pilgrim's Progress* and children's versions of *Gulliver* and *Robinson Crusoe*.

After going up and down the ladders for a while I gave up. Thanking the fox politely, I kept the pencils and paper and wrote down what had happened since I'd left home. I didn't know it then, but I was starting what became a journal and the basis of this account. While it didn't take my mind off my problems, it did help me focus on the situation and put it in some perspective.

Lord Renyard prepared to leave after a while, begging me to remain, as he put it, under his protection. I promised, though I longed for a telephone just so I could reassure my parents that I was okay. He told me that he was doing his best to get a message to them somehow. "But I would guess your grandparents' friends are here looking for you. I mentioned the rumours." He picked up his elaborate feathered hat, took a firm grip on his long cane, and bent to pass through the low door, closing it behind him.

While he was gone I heard a lot of activity in the tavern below, and a few words, and these sounded like nonsense. I heard a great deal of high-pitched laughter from the women. They scared me. Again I found myself wondering whether Lord Renyard was on Klosterheim's side or Monsieur Zodiac's.

When the fox came back he was in good humour. He had heard that newcomers were looking for me. It was thought they were in audience with the Sebastocrater, the city's ruler. What they intended to do when they left his palace, Lord Renyard didn't know, but he had men watching the palace, and they would contact my friends (if that was who they were) as soon as they could. Meanwhile someone else wished to see me. She might be able to help.

Who else could know I was here? I was baffled. She?

Lord Renyard bowed, offering me his arm. "Would you mind coming with me, mademoiselle? It is only a short way from here."

My head filled with questions I couldn't voice. I replied lamely. "I'll be glad to," I said, "thanks." Hand on paw, we left the tavern and went out into the pleasant evening air. As we walked, Lord Renyard tried to tell me something of the history of the City in the Autumn Stars, why it was called what it was, who had founded it, who now ruled it and so on. It was a huge city, very well ordered in the main. "The centre alone is reserved for the criminal and bohemian classes and all those associated with us. I am the acknowledged chief of those classes. Nowhere else is wickedness allowed to thrive." He seemed faintly embarrassed. "You should know that I am a monster but never had any choice in my calling."

We went down another alley, emerging into a wide courtyard.

On the far side of the courtyard stood a small, picturesque house with two windows and a door. The roof was thatched, and a white lattice supported a huge mass of pink and white roses, which gave the cottage a resemblance to a human face. I had never seen anything quite like it and wasn't even surprised when the windows opened suddenly to reveal two huge blue eyes. Then the door creaked and the house began to speak.

My instinct was to run. I seemed to be able to take a talking fox in my stride, but not a house which behaved like a human head.

"Good evening, child," said the house in a severe feminine voice.

Lord Renyard's paw steadied me, but my voice was shaking when I replied. "Ggood evening—um—ma'am."

"I heard you were in the city. Did your friend the fox explain who I am?"

"N-no, ma'am, h-he d-didn't."

"You are not dreaming, at least no more than the rest of us dream, there being no such thing as one particular reality. We pass through the multiverse as best we can, using whatever logic we can, understanding what is possible for us to understand. You are surprised that a house can speak. I would be surprised, for instance, by a box which showed me events on the far side of the world as they happened, yet you take such a phenomenon for granted, if I am not mistaken."

"You're not mistaken, ma'am. That's television."

"I have spoken of them with other visitors. But I did not ask my friend Lord Renyard to bring you here to discuss the nature of realities. I wanted to tell you that you are in considerable danger."

"Klosterheim? Is he close?"

"You have been in danger since the day you were born. You carry fated blood, you see. You carry a power. Have you ever heard of the Graal Staff?"

"No—um—Miss . . ."

"You may call me Mrs House. I am famous locally as an oracle and have occupied this spot, off and on, for five or six thousand years, though I think the time is coming due when I must move again." Her windows closed for a moment, as if in thought. "I might have to found my own city . . ."

"Thank you, Mrs House."

"You have not heard of the Blood, yet you are the virgin your enemies believe is destined to carry it. Whether you keep it or not is not yet decided."

"I'm sorry, Mrs House. You'll have to explain a bit more."

"Oracles aren't especially adept at explanations," she said almost apologetically. "We are best at large predictions, especially if we are bound to one place, as I am so frequently bound."

"Why should I be singled out to take charge of some blood?" I asked.

She seemed almost impatient with me. "If you find the Blood, you or someone you decide upon must take it home and keep it safe for ever."

"But I can't find my home. That's the problem!"

"Solving one problem will solve both. The Blood is the blind boy. One will reveal the other."

"Can I find my home first?"

"You will find it eventually, of that I am certain. Unless they put you and the blind boy together. If that happens, you could easily die in terrible circumstances. You must make it your business for them not to catch you."

"Catch me? Who do you mean . . .?"

"Those who know only the secret of the Blood and the Stone but not their function."

My heart was beating so hard that I was short of breath. I think I had begun to cry. "Tell me who wants to hurt me," I begged.

Her expression quickly became sympathetic. Her roses rustled quietly.

"One, as you know, is called Klosterheim," she declared. "He is here already. But the other is more fearsome. The creature with whom Klosterheim habitually travels. Yes, I see him. Once the greatest Knight of the Balance, now a Prince of Chaos. Paul von Minct." Again her window eyes closed as if in pain. "Ah! He has no face! He has too many faces! Beware of him. Seek your uncle in the fires of industry!"

And suddenly her eyes closed, and I was looking at an ordinary little country house again, with a rather shaken fox motioning for us to leave. I took his offered paw.

"Sometimes, my dear," he said as he led me out of the courtyard, "this world of mine defeats all logic. Its terrors make me speculate whether or not I should believe in a deity, for it seems I am consigned to Hades. I am so sorry you were frightened." We were again in the bustle of the city. "I had only her message. She is known to be very accurate. Yet this time she was also mysterious. Do you have a brother here?"

"No," I said. "Nor an uncle. Not even a cousin I know about."

"Are you by any chance adopted?"

"Of course not! I was just a bit of an afterthought, Mum said. Besides, there was the blood test we did before we went to India, which showed we were all related. Why?"

"Just a foolish idea," he apologised. He was still thinking hard. "The fires of industry she sees are no doubt the many factories on the far side of the river. It is possible that your friends also journey there."

"She said something about getting home. Could there be a way home on the other side of the river? Might it be safer for us there?"

"I doubt it, my dear."

In deep thought we returned to Lord Renyard's apartments. It seemed to me we were more confused than before we had left.

I was beginning to get used to the miraculous, but it took a while for what I had just experienced to sink in. Lord Renyard wore an air of faint pride as we headed towards Raspazian's. Mrs House did not send for just anyone, he said. Although she had warned me, she hadn't really told me much that I didn't already know. I was curious, of course, about what she'd called "the Graal Staff," and asked the fox several questions about it on the way back. He had heard of the Holy Grail, he said, and knew of the Black Sword, but he wasn't sure he'd read more than a reference to a staff.

"It could be that it has yet to be found, that you are the one destined to discover it. After all, powerful blood flows in your veins, eh?"

This mystified me even more. When I tried to quiz him about it further, he merely put a paw to his snout in a knowing gesture and winked at me.

To be honest, I was a bit alarmed by Mrs House's predictions, wondering if I hadn't entered some kind of grand loony bin. It had to be a strain, as Lord Renyard had hinted, being so strange. I wondered if I wouldn't be better off in what they called the "Shallow City," where people seemed more normal.

As we approached Raspazian's faded sign, one of the swaggering, befeathered rogues who served the fox came towards us and, leering at me in a disturbing way, bowed to his master.

"Well, Kushy?" said Lord Renyard.

"Ye've a visitor, my lord. We've seen him before, if I'm not mistaken. Pale cove. Looks like death. Has a cold."

"His name?"

"Didn't mean much to me, your worship." Kushy lapsed into the language I'd heard before.

A brief conversation, and we were on our way again, with the fox frowning and looking down at me. Before we reached the tavern, he had further words with Kushy, who was off like a shot, coming back with a sizeable hemp sack.

"What's that for?" I asked.

"For you, my dear. I want you to climb into it."

"I'm not sure that seems like a good idea."

"I don't want this Klosterheim to see you. This way I can get you past him and into my quarters without revealing your presence."

Reluctantly I agreed. The sack didn't smell as bad as I expected it to. In fact it was rather sweet. It must have contained sugar or something similar. Kushy hoisted me onto his shoulders, groaning that I seemed precious heavy for a little girl, and I felt him carrying me into the tavern and setting me down inside the door while a voice I recognised announced itself as Klosterheim.

"I remember you," I heard Lord Renyard say. "You are a friend of Tom Rakehell's—Manfred von Bek."

"The same, sir." Klosterheim's cold tones were also familiar to me. "I trust you are well."

"Well enough, after all the damage you and your party caused here. I hope you found what you sought. Too many died in that pursuit. I was forced to take sanctuary in another city for a while."

"Aha! You have been in Tanelorn!"

"That's my business, Herr Klosterheim. What's yours?"

"I fear I call upon you again for help, sir."

Lying still as a corpse in the sack, I managed to get an eyehole parted but, even so, couldn't see much of either Lord Renyard or Herr Klosterheim. But I knew for certain it was the same man I had been warned against.

"I believe you have taken the young countess, Oonagh von Bek, under your protection," Klosterheim said, cutting to the chase. "The granddaughter of Count Ulric and Oona, the Dreamthief."

I'd never heard Granny described like that, and I strained to listen.

"I was privileged to be of some small service to the child when she became lost in Mu-Ooria. A confusing country for those who do not know it."

"As is the whole world of underground."

"Quite so."

"She journeyed on, I take it."

"You may take it, sir."

"Would you oblige me by telling me where she has gone?"

"I would not, sir." I heard ice in the fox's voice. Plainly he didn't like Klosterheim one bit. Which made me feel a little better since at least he shared this with my grandparents' friends.

"I need to speak to her urgently. She is in considerable danger."

"From whom, sir? From you?"

"I am not her enemy."

"Your allies are not her friends, from what I hear."

"You refer to Paul von Minct, otherwise known as Gaynor the Damned. Why should he and I be allies now?"

"Perhaps I have news that you came to our city in his company."

"Where I learned his true plans. Where, I should tell you, sir, we quarrelled and went our separate ways."

"Yet you both seek the girl?"

"I need to get her to safety."

"Where would that safety be?"

"I refer to the city of Tanelorn."

"Until recent times there was no certainty the city was a place of safety. And I seem to recall that Gaynor had something to do with putting Tanelorn in jeopardy."

"Be that as it may, I had nothing to do with that attack. Neither do I mean the child harm. If you could arrange for me to speak to her . . ."

"I must ask her that question. I promise she shall know all that passed between us."

I smiled at Lord Renyard's foxy joke, which he knew I would appreciate.

"She's a high-strung creature with an overactive imagination," said Herr Klosterheim portentously. "We must do our best to protect her from herself."

"Quite so," said Lord Renyard.

Eventually Herr Klosterheim left, and Lord Renyard opened the sack. "Well, mademoiselle? What do you think of that?"

"I was warned not to believe him, no matter what he said."

"And I'd be inclined to follow that warning," he agreed. "Still, it suggests he or his spies will be looking out for you. We must be careful."

"I agree, Lord Renyard. But how can I hide from him and try to do what Mrs House told me to?"

"She gave you no specific instructions, mademoiselle. She is not a mistress but an oracle!"

I nodded. "But if Prince Lobkowitz can't be found soon, I'll have to do something, don't you think?"

"I understand your frustration, my child." He sighed. "But we should not keep Klosterheim far from our consideration. He has a determined air to him, and I suspect he'll not go far away, even if it's true and he has fallen out with his partner, von Minct. Those two are more than common rogues. They both possess a will towards evil. I sensed it the first time I met him, when he came here with your ancestor."

I wanted to satisfy a question which had been nagging at me. "You speak of the time you met my ancestor, yet he lived two hundred years ago. When did you actually meet him?"

"Perhaps some fifteen or twenty years since. As I said, mademoiselle, time in our city passes at a different pace to the time you experience. I do not know why this is so, though I have heard more than one man attempt to explain it, and I myself once kept an orrery and all manner of astrological instruments until they were stolen from me in one of the wars which occasionally shake our city. It coincides with some cycle of the planes which make up our universes moving at a different rate, much as planets go about the sun according to their own pace. I am not an unlearned being, yet I have been unable to discover any treatise which sets out to explain this phenomenon satisfactorily. Be assured, however, that you are not the first visitor to observe it. It could mean your parents have not even noticed you are missing."

This seemed to cheer him up. It was only then that I realised how my kindly captain of rogues had been as anxious as I about my parents' fears for me. I moved forward and embraced him. His nose twitched; he made a gulping sound deep in his throat, and I thought I saw something like a tear in his big vulpine eye.

The next few days were very frustrating. Lord Renyard's men reported that Messrs Lobkowitz and Fromental had indeed presented themselves at the palace and had even met Klosterheim and von Minct, though the encounter hadn't been friendly. Whenever one of the rogues of the Deep City had tried to contact my friends, they had failed for a variety of reasons. Lord Renyard wanted to hand me into their safe-keeping but thought it unwise to risk a journey across town. We must wait until they come looking for us, he thought.

"They do not know where to search for you. Klosterheim has clearly not shared any of his knowledge with them."

Meanwhile I tried to puzzle out what Mrs House could have meant in her reference to the one with no face, the Graal Staff and so on. I wondered if the strange oracle was in her right mind. Maybe she was a bit senile. As Lord Renyard had hinted, being a monster, being cut off from common experience, was inclined to make you lose your grip on ordinary reality. I was getting very bored at Raspazian's even though I had now made friends with Kushy and some of the other "tobymen" and "divers" and had begun to pick up a bit of their language.

Lord Renyard eventually, reluctantly allowed them to take me out with them as long as I was disguised, usually as a boy. They showed me their secret routes through the city, even taught me a way of crossing bridges underneath the general traffic.

Kushy called me his rum doxy, which was a compliment, meaning I was a pretty girl, and Kushy's lady friend Winnie said she thought I was a sweet lathy of a girl with a fine little knowledge box, who she wished her own daughter might be. Within a week I became a bit of a mascot to those vagabonds and footpads and felt honoured to be liked by them, even though I'm not sure my mum and dad would have approved of my spending so much time in their company. Since I wasn't often allowed to leave Raspazian's, my new friends brought their own children to play with me. To pass the time, I let them teach me their tricks, including how to pick a pocket or shoplift without being spotted!

Lord Renyard was gone more frequently, on mysterious business. I guessed he was looking for my friends. Kushy, Winnie and the other denizens of Raspazian's were careful to look after me, and I knew that although I was in perfect hands, I couldn't bear to stay there for much longer, no matter how slowly time was passing on my own plane of the multiverse.

Then one morning the decision was taken out of all our hands when, without warning, the tavern door burst open and there stood Klosterheim, his pale eyes glaring in his skull-like face topped by a black, wide-brimmed hat. The rest of his clothes were of the same Puritan cut as before, with a wide, white collar and cuffs. A big belt supported a sword and two pistols, which he drew as he entered, flanked by soldiers with drawn swords, wearing the archaic armour of the ancient Greeks but with necklaces of what I first took to be onions around their throats. They were tall, dark men with glistening black beards. Kushy and company regarded them with some nervousness until, with a sweeping bow, Kushy took off his feathered hat and said with that whining, mocking courtesy his kind always adopted to authority:

"Good morrow, gentlemen of the City Watch. Your visit's a rare pleasure. What can we do for you?"

Klosterheim pointed at me. "That girl. She's the one you kidnapped. Kill them all, guards, if they resist. You are safe now, fräulein. I am here to take you home."

I looked from Kushy to the guards. For a moment I was confused. "He's the one wants to kill me," I said.

Then, instinctively, I raced for the back room and slammed the door behind me, bolting it as Lord Renyard had taught me. From the other side came the firing of shots.

I felt fairly certain that Klosterheim, having somehow got the city authorities on his side, would win this round. At any moment they'd come bursting in. With my heart pounding, I opened the window of my bedroom and hopped out onto the tiles of the roof below. I slid down it, grabbed a drainpipe and shinned down into the little paved yard at the back of the tavern. I was hoping to hide somewhere nearby until they were gone. I took the bar out of its lugs, opened the gate and slipped into the alley. By the time I had found a dark doorway in which to hide I heard shouts from the courtyard. Men raced towards me. I had no choice. I crept into the yard behind me and hid among some stacks of crates and barrels. Fortunately their feet pounded past in the alley. Only when it was dark did I risk sneaking out and making my way back to the tavern, just to find the gateway closed again. I would have to risk going out into the street and entering through the front door.

As I slipped into the street leading to the square I saw a glint of armour. The city guards were still there, maybe left behind by Klosterheim. I kept walking, dodging in and out of shadows with no clear idea where I was going. Eventually I came to the unstable black marble that was the river, rows of deserted warehouses, and scuttling rats. I felt comparatively safe by the water if I kept in the dark. Across the river the new town didn't seem so full of soldiers. Sparks and flames gushed up in the black factory smoke. I could smell that smoke from here. A weird hard-boiled-egg smell; it reminded me of Guy Fawkes Night fireworks.

I thought I recognised the nearest bridge, the one Kushy and the others had shown me how to cross. A narrow walkway, used by builders to make repairs, ran underneath. You could get onto it, if you were nimble and small enough, by climbing up some ornamental ironwork and wriggling through a pipe.

Very slowly and carefully I made my way to the base of the bridge. I could hear the rumble of carts, horses' hoofs, marching soldiers. But nobody bothered to look down as I quickly shinned up the ironwork, squeezed through the short section of pipe. I climbed over the protective metal roof and swung down to drop on the walkway on the other side of a locked gate.

Then it was nothing to run softly over the wooden slats until I got to the other side, repeated the operation and found myself beside more rows of warehouses, whose stink, I should add, was not any more attractive than that of the first. I had been right. There were no soldiers on this side at all. They were all concentrating on the far bank.

I kept to side streets. The heat increased as I got closer to the great walled factories. Here Mirenburg made the steel for which, in my own world, she was famous, producing a well-known make of East European car, the Popp. Now she was probably making pikes and swords and cannons and stuff, more suitable for the customers of this age!

And then, as luck would have it, a squadron of mounted soldiers galloped along the thoroughfare ahead of me, just as I reached the middle of a factory wall, with no street I could easily dodge into. They weren't looking for me, I was sure, and were probably on their way to the bridge, but they would recognise me if they saw me. There was a small door in the factory wall, which I fully expected to be locked or jammed; to my astonishment, the handle turned. Without even a squeak of hinges I stepped into the overheated darkness and closed the door behind me. I began to wonder if some goddess had her benevolent eye on me.

The door led into a bleak passage, at the end of which were three more doors. Rather than waiting for the soldiers to go, I let curiosity take me down the passage. Had I been sensible, I would have just hidden for a moment and then gone back into the street. But I walked down the corridor, then opened the middle door a crack. I saw a turnstile and, behind that, people doing various kinds of office work. Apart from their clothes, they could have been in any ordinary office from my own time. Beyond them came the noise and bustle of the factory itself. I saw an occasional bright tongue of flame leaping into the air.

The door to the left was a disused office by the look of it, with a dusty desk and filing cabinets. But there was another interior door beyond it. I had no light once I closed the door behind me, and had to fumble my way across the room until I got to the other side. Again I expected this door to be locked. It was. But as I groped down its face, I felt a big key still in its lock. With difficulty I turned it. Unlike the door in the wall, this one had been badly kept. I twisted the handle, hearing a high-pitched sound. It cut through my eardrums and yet wasn't completely unpleasant. There was a strangely thrilling note to it. Then the noise died away. Something rumbled. Something raced and gushed. Something hissed.

I opened the door wider. It led out onto a gantry overlooking a busy factory. Molten steel splashed like lava from huge buckets hauled on chains by sweating half-naked men, overseen by shouting foremen and other specialist workers, who helped guide the buckets and tip them over a series of moulds. The light was glaring, and the heat was like a wall against my body. Flaming liquid steel gushed and splashed.

Through squinting eyes I saw the blind albino boy. He stood in a pulpit made of metal. His head was raised and set to one side, as if he was listening keenly. At a certain moment he raised his slender white hand in the air. All work stopped. He listened again, his crimson eyes reflecting the red-hot metal around him. Overhead more buckets rumbled and hissed; more molten steel flowed down gullies. It was a very hectic factory, but I couldn't really work out what was being made. The moulds were at most three inches wide and about three feet long. Were they forging rods of some kind?

I managed to wriggle into a space behind rolls of unused chain and get a better look at what was going on below me. As I watched, one of the workers yelped. A tear of boiling steel had fallen on his shoulder. A medic came from the side of the room and put a patch on him. He went back to work. I noticed that several workers had more than one patch. This had to be a dangerous occupation. Why, I wondered, didn't the factory supply them with protective clothing? I had a poor grasp of economics in those days.

The blind boy fascinated me. He was about four years older than me. Like Monsieur Zodiac, he had long, milk-white hair, while his skin had the sheen of bone. Unlike the workers, he had few patches. Even at that distance I could tell he was sweating. His glaring crimson eyes seemed completely sightless. Had the glowing metal blinded him? His hearing, however, was unnaturally sharp. For it was his hearing, I realised, they were employing.

The men paused so that a bucket of boiling metal was near him, and he listened. Then he spoke to them and pointed in the general direction of some of the moulds. The workers finessed the bucket to their moulds and again poured liquid metal. Occasionally some kind of boss came along and spoke to the men. They kept their distance from the boy. They carefully avoided touching him.

I watched for over an hour as the albino paused, listened carefully, almost always rejecting the steel, very occasionally pointing and giving directions. As the steel cooled in the moulds, the lengths were brought to him, and again he would hold them close to his ears, listening intently. Some of them he accepted, but most were rejected. This seemed to be the norm, judging by the way the workers treated the routine. He was listening for some flaw, I was sure.

There wasn't much doubt in my mind that the boy was related to my granny and Monsieur Zodiac. Even the way he held himself was familiar. Was he a prisoner in the factory? I couldn't be certain. There were no guards about.

He worked constantly, listening, directing, listening, rejecting. Eventually I realised they were forging sword blades, which would no doubt be polished, honed and decorated by other hands. But he didn't pass many of them. I could tell he was listening to the music within the steel. The blades spoke to him, and he accepted almost none of them, rejecting most.

Suddenly a klaxon sounded throughout the factory. Work was stopped, and men moved away to open packets of sandwiches and eat. The blind boy was led to a spot only a yard or two below where I was hiding. As the men ate, the boy merely drank from a large cup handed to him by a guard. The guards were not rough to him. In their own way they seemed to like him, but they treated him very much as an alien creature, not one of their own. Now I had my chance. When the space was deserted around him I risked calling to him, barely lifting my voice above a whisper.

"Boy! Blind boy?"

He looked up. He had heard me. He did not reply in a loud voice himself, but murmured.

"Girl? Overhead? Yes, she lies on the walkway above, hidden by chains, and—"

"I've seen how clever you are," I told him. "But I'm not here to admire you."

"Why *are* you here? Did McTalbayne send you to find me?"

"I don't know who that is. I'm lost. This is an accident. I have relatives who look like you. Does the name Beck mean anything?"

He shook his head and finished his drink. The klaxon sounded again. The boss approached him to guide him back to his station.

"You must get me away from here," whispered the boy suddenly. "If you are a friend, you must help set me free. What's your name?"

"Oonagh," I said.

"That's like my mother's name! Do you know Tufnell Hill?" A desperate expression crossed his face. "Those two brought me here, but . . ."

"What's yours? What's your name?"

"They call me Onric here," he said. "My father—"

The guard came too close. He stopped whispering.

"I'll try to free you," I said, "but I'll have to get help. I'm only a little girl."

"You have given me more hope than anyone else," he said, his voice dropping so low that I could scarcely hear it. Then the foreman was beside him and leading him back to his post.

I was confused. How could I be related to this boy I had never seen, who dwelled in a different age, in a different part of the multiverse? I stepped out from behind the chains. Somebody shouted. Had they seen me? I bolted for the next door, entered into the darkness behind it, remembered to turn the key and then tiptoed to the door into the corridor, which was still deserted. Where could I get help for this Onric, I thought ironically, when I couldn't even get help for myself!

I returned to the street. Maybe Lord Renyard would find someone to help me rescue Onric and get us both out of harm's way! Were we really related? Was this who Klosterheim and von Minct were searching for? Were they hoping I would lead them to the boy? Did I, after all, have some sort of affinity with him?

In a daze, I managed to reach the bridge and return the way I'd come. Where was I going to find help? Raspazian's seemed the only likely place. I had to hope the Sebastocrater's guards had left, as there was still a fair amount of activity on the bridge.

I crossed over into the warehouse district, found a street I recognised and began to make my way up it. I heard the marching feet of guardsmen behind me. I was so exhausted, I was almost ready to be captured.

Stepping back into a doorway, I felt sick with fear as a hand covered my mouth and an arm encircled my body and lifted me. I struggled until I heard Kushy's murmur in my ear. "Hush, little mort." When we were back in the alleys he let me go. His face was badly battered, and he had a wound in his left side. He seemed ashamed of himself and kept apologising to me. "His lordship's still not returned. There's talk he's captured."

I was horrified. "What can we do?"

"Get you away from here," he said. "Get you somewhere safe. I've no idea how Klosterheim has the guards on his side. It probably means he's persuaded the Sebastocrater that you've been kidnapped by us."

"Prince Lobkowitz and Lieutenant Fromental were supposed to be at his palace. They wouldn't have let him do it!"

"We don't know what's happened, missy." He was leading me into the tangle of twittens running between the buildings. "We need to find the chief. Meanwhile you can hide out here." He opened a door, and we slipped into a poorly furnished room. There was a cot in the corner, a table and some crudely made chairs. "Get some sleep," he advised. "I'll bring you some food in the morning."

I lay down to rest.

When Kushy still hadn't returned by noon the next day, I became sure he was dead or captured. If they tortured him, they'd learn where I was. The plight of the blind albino boy was still on my mind. I couldn't just leave him. He had asked for help. Taking the blanket from the cot, I left the hovel and made my way out into the creaking, tottering streets. First I must find food. Then I must find the Sebastocrater. At least I would be able to tell him that Klosterheim had tricked him, and maybe I could find and recruit Lord Renyard to help save the boy.

5

Leaving in daylight was a risk, but I really needed to eat. At least I was no longer conspicuous. Dirty and poorly dressed, I slipped out into the streets with no idea how I would find food. The Deep City was crowded with frightened people unused to the presence of the city guards, even though the guards kept their distance according to ancient tradition. With Lord Renyard gone, there was no-one to demand a return to those old agreements. The guards, in their peculiar antique Greek armour, did not look comfortable. Most of them wore strings of garlic around their necks. Apparently they thought it warded off disease. Only Klosterheim carried pistols. They were armed with swords, lances, shields and bows, while the Deep City's denizens had plenty of guns. Any uprising would be hard to control.

Eventually I applied the bad lessons I'd learned from Kushy and his friends. Feeling rather guilty, I easily pinched a loaf and a pie from a distracted baker in the market. Ravenously I ate them in a quiet doorway. I think anyone as hungry as I would have done the same. But I was very glad my mum hadn't been there to see me! I wondered if I should try to find Mrs House again. She had foreseen some sort of future for me, and she had mentioned the boy. Then I reminded myself that the best thing to do was to go into the Shallow City and try to find out what had happened to Lord Renyard or Prince Lobkowitz, so I took one of the spiralling alleys, intermittently hiding and walking slowly, getting closer to the wide basalt boulevards.

By midnight I had reached the black marble avenue which ran roughly from east to west with a huge Greek palace in the middle, at the top of which burned a massive single light, illuminating much of the city around it. From a new perspective I was looking at the Sebastocrater's monolithic home.

I had better sense than to walk out into the open, but I kept that great dark dome, glinting with lacquer, gold and silver, in constant sight. Using trees and buildings for cover, I avoided patrols and got much closer to the palace, which was surrounded by black walls lit at intervals by blazing braziers, their flames flowing and guttering in the night air. Overhead the ancient ochres, yellows, browns and deep greens of the Autumn Stars looked down on me.

I heard a sound behind me and smelled something familiar. I retreated into the shadows. Turning, I saw, to my astonishment, that same black panther I had first encountered beneath Ingleton common. I guessed she meant me no immediate harm, because she narrowed her eyes in what, for a domestic cat, would have been a smile. The panther's whiskers twitched, and a heavy rattling sound came from her throat—something which could have been a purr. Her friendly posturing was somewhat at odds with the beautiful ivory sabre fangs which grew from the top of her mouth. She lay down in front of me. Somehow I knew she wanted me to climb onto her back so that she could help me escape.

"I can't," I whispered. "I have to get to the palace to see if I can find Lord Renyard."

The cat's purr became a noise of enquiry. Then she stood up and waited expectantly for a moment. I shook my head again. Then, since I would not ride, looking back at me from time to time, she began to lead me through the darkness, closer to the palace. Thinking she might know a secret way in, I followed her until we stood in dense shrubbery beside the great obsidian wall. It was apparently unclimbable, however, and I could see no other way in. Again the panther lay down, clearly indicating that she wanted me to jump on her back, and this time I did what she demanded, wrapping my arms around her powerful neck just in time, before she made a terrific spring. Air rushed through my hair, and I felt suddenly exhilarated as her incredible muscles moved under me. We landed on a broad lawn. A short distance away I could just make out a fountain playing near a summer house built like a miniature Greek temple. Not far from the fountain I saw the stiff outlines of about a dozen men, probably guards. The panther loped across the lawn towards the summer house. Another leap and we jumped out of the night, into brilliant day!

It took a moment for my eyes to adjust. Then I saw them. Inside the bright summer house stood not only Lord Renyard but Prince Lobkowitz and Lieutenant Fromental. I think I was only slightly less astonished to see them than they were to see me. I tumbled off the back of the panther and ran to embrace Lord Renyard, who looked delighted and troubled at the same time. I turned to stroke the head of the big black cat, but she had gone. In her place stood a woman who was my grandmother's exact twin, though much younger. She was an ivory-haired, pale-skinned albino with unusually brilliant crimson eyes.

"You're a hard-headed child," she said. She was dressed in a red jerkin and black tight-fitting trousers. There were leather boots on her feet, and on her back was a quiver of arrows. In her left hand was an unstrung bow. "What made you go off like that?"

"Granny?" I stammered in astonishment.

"Well, in a manner of speaking."

"Are you related to Monsieur Zodiac?"

"I am."

"You—the panther—how?"

"We have a special rapport," she said with a slight smile. "I'm sorry about the mystery, but we knew no other way to find you."

"Are you prisoners here?"

"I am not," she said. "But my men were also caught. Klosterheim has convinced this city's prince that they are to be feared and were responsible for holding you prisoner."

"But why should he be interested in me?"

"Because of oracular warnings concerning the Graal Staff. With the best motives in the world, he wants to take on the burden of guarding the Staff. I suppose he doesn't accept that you're worthy of the job."

"I don't even know what the job is. I don't even know what the Staff is. But I certainly don't have it, and neither do I know where it is." I wanted to ask her about the blind boy, Onric, but I couldn't find a way of starting.

"We understand all that, Oonagh, dear." Prince Lobkowitz stepped forward to kneel down and embrace me. "But Gaynor, the other man you saw in Ingleton last night, is convinced you are the key to its possession. I think they might be misguided, but we let ourselves be captured before we could find you and take you home. You're safe here for a while. It won't occur to them to look for you in our prison, I'm sure."

"How did they capture you?"

"Magic," said Lieutenant Fromental simply and unequivocally. "Powerful sorcery which defeats all our knowledge of such things. None of us, save Oona the Dreamthief here, has any such power. We scarcely know how to defend ourselves, let alone attack it. But you can help us."

Although it baffled me, I suspected that Oona the Dreamthief was my grandmother but at an earlier time of her life. "Help *you?*" I said. "I can't even help myself. I still don't really believe in magic. At least, I didn't until I met Mrs House, and even she could be just another kind of life form."

"I quite agree with you, dear young lady." Lieutenant Fromental's big brow clouded. "But rationalism cannot entirely explain things I have witnessed in this world they call the Middle Marches. For instance, look outside." He pointed. It was now daylight outside, and the figures I had seen on the lawn were in fact about a dozen American Indians in colourfully decorated breechclouts, leggings and leather shirts. Their heads were shaven, apart from long scalp locks, and their fierce faces were painted. In their hands were various weapons, including stone tomahawks, lances, bows and shields. They looked as if they had walked off the set of *The Last of the Mohicans*. Yet each one of them was frozen in mid-movement.

"Who are they?" I asked.

"They are my friends," said Oona. "My clansmen. They came with me to look for you, dear. But since we arrived I haven't been able to communicate with them, and they haven't been able to move. Some spell has been put on them. All the men are under the power of the Sebastocrater, the Prince of Mirenburg."

"Am I a prisoner, too?" I asked.

"Probably not—nor the panther. Nor me. That is how we were able to bring you here and explain what has happened. Our friends came to beg the help of the Sebastocrater. All of us were tricked into entering his grounds and this building. But why he should league himself with such villains as Paul von Minct and Herr Klosterheim, we cannot think. As I say, either they have alarmed him with some trumped-up terror or they have promised him something he can't resist."

"What could that be?" I asked.

"The Stone, I suspect," said Prince Lobkowitz. "He showed an uncommon interest in it when we arrived here looking for you. He asked if we knew where it was. We told him truthfully that as far as we knew, it was lost. He said it and its guardian had last been heard of in Mirenburg. We know, of course, that it was recently stolen from your grandparents' London flat. That's why they couldn't meet us, as they had arranged. Do you the Devil's work, eh? Could the Stone have acquired a new keeper? It determines its own situation, as we well know."

I wanted to ask Oona what her relationship was with me. I was sure she was my grandmother. But there were more urgent questions. "Are they feeding you?" I asked.

"So far we have not been offered food," said Lieutenant Fromental. He pointed to a big pair of saddlebags lying on a couch. "But Prince Lobkowitz packed plenty of provisions before we left Ingleton in search of you. You see, only a few hours have passed in this building since we arrived. I suspect, like the city, it exists outside the ordinary laws of time and space. Try a sandwich?"

I wanted to ask about Onric, but Prince Lobkowitz spoke first.

He seemed awkward. "We mustn't alarm"—he looked at me—"mademoiselle."

"It's all right," I said. "I know everything here is odd. Well, more than odd. I'm not scared. Especially now I've found you all. There's this boy—"

"You and I are the only ones who can leave," said Oona. "We are the only two not under the spell."

"This Sebastocrater? What's his game?"

"None, I suspect. He means well, but he's none too bright," said Lord Renyard. "It's my guess that Klosterheim and von Minct have fed him lies and have almost certainly frightened him into doing some stupid things, including invading the Deep City, which is protected by so many ancient spells. It could set off catastrophic consequences here. If Klosterheim and von Minct have convinced him they are helping you against us, that might be the answer to what's happening. Of course, I don't know him well. He and I never socialised, except at ceremonial occasions. He ruled here, and I ruled in the Deep City. Everything was as it should be. In equilibrium."

"Why is that equilibrium disrupted?"

"It began some years ago," said Lord Renyard. "When Manfred von Bek first visited us. He was not the cause of the disruption, merely an early sign of it. Some serious movement of the Cosmic Balance."

Prince Lobkowitz answered. "I have known this city and her rulers for many years. I have enjoyed conversations here and never had cause to suspect the kind of trick which has imprisoned us. My suspicion is that von Minct and Klosterheim have placed the Sebastocrater under some kind of charm or debt and are using him in their own plans."

"To find me?" I asked.

"I think you either have something they want, my dear, or access to something they want."

"The Staff which Mrs House mentioned."

Lord Renyard explained how he took me to see the oracle. Could Onric have been the boy Mrs House was talking about? I gave up trying to introduce this. Nobody was listening to me. Understandably, they were focused on their own immediate problems.

"Then it's as we all guessed," said Oona. "The Grail has disappeared again. What force works to disrupt the Balance over and over in increasingly close episodes?"

"I believe it is our friend's dreaming that creates the problems," said Prince Lobkowitz. "Yet that dream is due to end very soon, and when it does it could mean oblivion for all."

"No." Oona shook her head. "The dream's merely ending will not bring destruction, of course, but what is in place at the moment of its ending will decide between continuing life or complete annihilation. He will die to ensure that equilibrium, but without our help he might die for nothing."

"And the child"—Prince Lobkowitz glanced at me as if apologising for speaking of me in the third person—"she carries the secret?"

"Klosterheim and von Minct evidently believe that. This will be their third attempt, however, to gain control of the Grail. Twice we have frustrated their plans. This time they hold more power than ever. A certain mademoiselle here plays a significant role in their machinations. That is why it is important you get to safety, child."

"All I want to do is get home." My response was heartfelt. "But I did promise a boy I'd try to help him. He works in the factory over the river. He said—"

"I don't want to be gloomy," said Oona, "but we could be moving further away from our world, not closer to it."

Seeing my alarm, she softened. "In terms of the multiverse, which is vast and infinitely varied, we are not too far away," said Oona. "All realities meet in the Middle March. You have no doubt already experienced that."

I nodded. Then I paused. "Did you say you had plenty of food, Lieutenant Fromental, because if you have, I wonder if it would be possible—?"

"Of course, my dear. Of course. Bon appétit!" And he flung open the basket with a grand gesture. I saw now that Mum had packed some of it with my favourite snack foods. I picked out a sausage roll, some salt-and-vinegar crisps, an apple pie and a diet Dr Pepper, consuming them rather greedily. Almost at once I felt like a new girl!

"Now you and I had better get out of here," said Oona. "My warriors lack my particular gifts and were caught in the spell before I understood what was happening. I have to free them. They were loaned to me by one of my oldest friends. I doubt he would be amused by what I have led them into."

I looked at the Indians. "What tribe are they?"

"They're related to the Iroquois," she said. "They call themselves the Kakatanawa, the People of the Circle."

"Who's your friend?"

She smiled widely. "You'd know him as Hiawatha. Do they still teach that poem at school?"

"My granny reads it," I said, giving her what I thought was a penetrating look.

"No doubt," said Oona, with a sudden grin. She was my granny, all right! Every instinct told me she was. I gave up trying to work out the logic of it. That only confused me more. So I stopped.

Again the panther stood regally in front of me. I climbed on her back, and before I could turn and say goodbye to the others, the big cat leaped forward, raced across the lawn and jumped over the wall, into the wide avenue running beside it.

I jumped down and ran into the shadows. Oona, a foot or two behind, joined me.

"What are we going to do next?" I asked.

"Find Klosterheim and von Minct," she said. "It's all we can do, I'm afraid. I'm going to have to use you as bait."

"What do you mean?"

"The only way to lure them out into the open is to have you return to Raspazian's and be seen there. Then we have to hope that Klosterheim or his companion will seek you out. As long as they don't come with the Sebastocrater's guards, we might have a chance."

"But what will happen if they capture me?"

"I'll be there to rescue you. It's all I can promise."

"Okay," I agreed doubtfully, thinking the plan sounded pretty desperate. Still, I couldn't suggest anything better.

"So let's get back to Raspazian's," she said.

The panther had faded into the darkness. Oona seemed to know how to get to the Deep City the quickest way. We were at Raspazian's before dawn. The Sebastocrater's guards were no longer to be seen. Some of the mobsmen had returned and were hanging around outside the tavern, though they had lost much of their old spirit. Kushy appeared from the basement. He had another bloody bruise on his forehead and was hatless. His clothes were even more torn. But his gap-toothed smile widened as he recognised me.

"'Arry 'Awk be praised! You're in one piece! And free! We thought the watch had you, missy. They only left a few hours gone. You'll have to be careful 'cause they could easily come back anytime. It's you they're after and no mistake, missy. You didn't find Lord Renyard, then?"

"I found him. He's the Sebastocrater's prisoner in the grounds of his palace. Unharmed but incapacitated."

"Kept there by sorcery," added Oona.

"That's it, then, ma'am," said Kushy. "Sorcery's the only thing that could keep the master imprisoned. The Shallow City has broken its age-old compact with the Deep City, has it? The capturing of one king by another was always against our rules, so Lord Renyard told me."

"They say the times are desperate, Kushy," I told him.

"They must be, little missy. They must be," he said bitterly.

"And sorcery's what's needed to free him," said Oona. "Who can help us, Herr Kushy?"

He led us down the steps into Raspazian's. Inside, the place was crowded with thieves and their doxies. All were heavily armed. All looked anxious. They gathered around us, wanting our news, horrified to hear that magic was at work.

It was rare enough in Mirenburg. They weren't so much shocked by the evidence of magic as by the use of it. Magic was unsporting, outside the accepted traditions. The Sebastocrater played unfairly. They began to speculate among themselves. Why would he do that? Was he in someone else's power? Were the Lords of Law and Chaos taking an interest?

At last Oona raised her hand. "I can only say that Klosterheim and von Minct are certainly somehow involved. Does anyone here know what power exactly they have over the Sebastocrater's decisions?"

"What do they want?" asked Mrs Nagel, one of the "diver-divas."

"Put simply, they want this young lady."

"What does she have that they seek?"

"I honestly don't know," I insisted. "I'm just—I'm just a little girl . . ." I had never sounded so pathetic to my own ears as I did then. How lame! I thought.

"Why should we protect you?" someone else wanted to know. "Lord Renyard's already captive. Ancient agreements have been broken, and magic's abroad. Why shouldn't we give you up to the Sebastocrater's men?"

I couldn't answer. I tried but gave up. I felt very guilty, and I was beginning to cry. Oona's arm around me was a small comfort.

She spoke coolly. "Keep her safe and you can bargain. Give her up and you've nothing."

This calmed them. Sharp-featured Kushy stepped forward. He had found his plumed hat. His expression was grim and set. He spoke in a low, desperate voice. "We have our honour. We need magic of our own. We've no choice now. We must ask Clement Schnooke to help us."

I didn't like the sound of Herr Schnooke. Neither, it seemed, did anyone else.

Oona started to speak but then was interrupted.

"I find such confidence flattering, gentlemen."

I turned my head towards the door. A round-faced, cheerful little man stood there. His shiny black hair was slicked down against his skull. His coat was a patchwork of red, gold and green. His brass-buckled shoes were dark green. His neck cloth was bright yellow. He looked like a clown, but the hiss of the crowd and the way they drew back from him told me he was disliked and feared by everyone.

Kushy said in a defeated tone, "Mornin', Clement Schnooke. Talk of the devil, eh, sir?"

"I've been telling you for years that your snotty Sebastocrater deserves a spot of sorcery to put him in his place, Kushy. Now that zoological monstrosity you call a master has failed to save you from the Greek's soldiery, you turn at last to Clement Schnooke. Suppose I refuse my services? Have you some other sorcerer who'll make it his business to represent the interests of the Deep City the moment he gives his word on the matter?"

"Lord Renyard forbade you to practise magic on pain of banishment," said one of those furthest from him.

The harlequin whirled to find him, pointing. "Banishment? Just as well I didn't take my leave when it suited me, eh? What is it I can do for you? Now, I mean? Now I'm needed. Lord Renyard forbade—what was it? Where is Lord Renyard, by the way? Ah, you wish me to free your master from some imprisoning spell. So that he'll return here and punish me for using sorcery? Doesn't seem sense to me, fellow citizens. I'll need a suitably generous stipend, I suggest, if I'm to risk releasing your haughty master. Then I'll ask for a free hand to use black sorcery against the city. 'Tis time that the old arts were practised here again, and Clement Schnooke given the justice and rewards he deserves!"

Another actor, I thought, whose success on stage had gone to his head. I felt cold and clammy in his sibilant presence as he preened and pranced defiantly in the faces of those who loathed him. He removed his cap and bowed to me. But he addressed Oona.

"I've heard of you, dreamthief. And I met your mother once. She, too, insulted and demeaned me. You show me no respect. Tell me why I should show you any!"

"I don't want your respect," said Oona evenly. "I want your services. What's your price?"

He cocked his wicked head to one side. "Price? A soul or two, perhaps?" He smiled his horrible smile again and danced before us in triumph, wriggling and writhing, pointing his toes and fingers, so that I half expected him to begin shedding his glittering skin. "But gold's more useful. I need enough gold to take me out of here and see myself where I belong. Where I came from."

"Where's that?" I asked.

His cold, sardonic eyes fell on me. "Where's *that*, little miss?" he hissed. "Where's that?"

I looked him back in the face. I knew evil by its eyes, and I knew the extent of its power by the depths of those eyes. "That's what I asked."

He dropped his gaze and sighed. "I was once a prince in Cincinnati. Not the Cincinnati you may know, but a fabulous city, all slender towers and ziggurats, whose cats can speak in complex tongues, where my success as a sorcerer was acknowledged and appreciated, where the fair sex were sweet and plentiful. All I need for happiness is in Cincinnati."

"Why do you need gold to get there?"

"Gold's what I said I'd seek, and gold's what will preserve my reputation. I can find my way on the moonbeam roads but never find my nation. The maps must be bought fresh every six months. And such maps are expensive."

"What if I put you on your way? The secrets of the silver roads are mine." Oona stepped towards him.

"I would still need gold."

"We'll give you gold," said Kushy. "And if Fräulein Oona can guide you to your home, will you free our master and his friends?"

"I'll do my best with my rusty powers," promised Clement Schnooke. "You all know me and what I'm capable of. For in spite of Lord Renyard's repression, half of you have sought me out for potions and spells over the years, and I've obliged."

"At high prices," declared an old woman.

"Reasonable, sister, given the risks."

"You've killed more than one customer," accused another. "You're hated here and you know it. Frau Fröhlich caught the palsy, and Herr Nipkoch shrieked his life away for days before he died. We know Fröhlich the carpenter failed to pay you to harm his wife. And then his *nose* turned black and his head dropped off."

Clement Schnooke smiled and bowed. "I appreciate your endorsements, my friends. They have brought me customers and added to my small savings."

"Well," said Kushy. "We'd be rid of you, so here's a way we can all be served."

Schnooke sneered and postured. "Give me a day or so and I'll have your master free. It will cost you a century in gold."

"By weight?"

"No, fool! By time! Yes, of course by weight. A hundred kilos."

This caused noisy concern among the denizens of Raspazian's. But after a while his terms were agreed to, and Clement Schnooke departed.

"I must return to the Sebastocrater's prison and warn Lord Renyard what's soon to happen," said Oona. "Kushy and the rest will keep you safe."

Soon she was gone; I was back on my own in Lord Renyard's library. But this time I looked for specific books, for what I guessed was the source of Clement Schnooke's sorcerous craft. I found several books and studied them with an intensity I'd never given to my lessons.

By the following evening Oona was back. She brought me another pork pie, some crisps and a pickled onion. I couldn't help suspecting she had stopped off at the pub as an afterthought, but I've always loved pickled onions and was famished. There weren't too many English pubs in Mirenburg.

"How's Lord Renyard and the others?" I asked.

"No change. And my Kakatanawa are still frozen. Horrible as he is, I'm desperately hoping that this man Schnooke can do something, though Klosterheim and von Minct will probably counter him. What would you think of paying a visit to the Sebastocrater?"

"Wouldn't that be dangerous?"

"Maybe. But with Clement Schnooke attacking from one direction, that might distract our enemies enough for us to find out how they are persuading the prince to behave so uncharacteristically."

"What if we fail?" I asked.

"We have my bow. And the panther." Her grin reassured me. "And while I have no desire to place you in danger, I somehow feel you would be safer in my company than if I left you here."

"I know I'd certainly feel safer," I agreed.

"Then let's wait a while just to see what Clement Schnooke can do."

For the rest of the day I slept and ate or talked to the dreamthief. She answered many of my questions, but she avoided those to do with her family and her relationship to mine. "And if we were related, you'd no doubt be in greater danger from that pair," she said. "All you need to know is that I'm the dreamthief's daughter."

Laughing, she told me to mind my own business, that what were dreams in one world of the multiverse were realities in another.

"What exactly is a dreamthief?" I asked.

"I'm not a dreamthief," she told me.

"Schnooke said you were."

"I'm a dreamthief's *daughter*. I know some of the simpler tricks of the profession, but I didn't want to follow my mother's calling. I took a small inheritance from her, when it seemed she had died. I became a wanderer across the multiverse, walking the moonbeam paths, looking for my ideal world and a companion to share it with."

"And did you ever find them?"

"I certainly did. But I had to give them up again."

"Why was that?"

"Someone we loved was in danger. Something we valued was threatened."

"You won't say any more?"

"Not yet. I promise I'll tell you more when I can be sure it's safe to do so."

"You have enemies of your own, not just Klosterheim and his mate?"

"I think it's fair to say that you and I have common enemies." She wouldn't be drawn any more. "I've been on your trail since Ingleton. It has taken me almost two years to find you."

"Two *years*! But I've only been away a few days at most."

"Time passes at different rates in different dreams," was all she would say.

"When shall we go?"

"Let's give Herr Schnooke what he needs. I don't know how quickly they will be able to pay him or how swiftly he'll perform once paid. He's working on some sort of rain spell and a creature made of water which will set our friends free. Even if he's not entirely successful, his sorcery will create a diversion. Meanwhile we must be on our guard. The Sebastocrater's men could return at any time."

With some anxiety, though fairly convinced that the dreamthief's daughter knew what she was about, I settled down to wait.

6

The Sebastocrater's soldiers came back to Raspazian Square in the early light. Still wearing their garlic necklaces, as if they expected a vampire attack at any moment, they emerged from the surrounding alleys.

They didn't attempt to enter the tavern but remained on the outskirts of the square, looking this way and that, gesturing in alarm towards the mobsmen who approached them. The guards were stern but scarcely belligerent. The old lack of aggression between the Shallow and the Deep Cities, which all had taken for granted, was still there. Even the arrival of Klosterheim and von Minct had failed to drive serious rifts between them. Oona and I were both puzzled by it.

"They seem reluctant to be here," she said. "What does this mean when neither side wishes to be at odds? Yet I am sure, if we went out there now, we'd immediately be clapped in irons and dragged off to prison!"

"What have Klosterheim and von Minct told them?"

"We must try to find out. If we can learn that, we'll know better how to act. This is like playing three-dimensional chess, isn't it?"

At nightfall we slipped out into the back alleys and evaded the guards for a second time, but now, with Oona in the lead, we were soon back at the black marble palace, observing it from the shadows of the shrubbery and wondering how we might most easily gain entrance. Eventually she determined the weakest part of the wall and made a short huffing sound. "I'll send the panther," she said. "You first." And she disappeared into the greenery. A moment later the panther, clearly always nearby at her command, appeared and crouched for me to jump onto her sleek back. Again we leaped the wall into the grounds but this time did not head for the ornamental summer house, where the frozen Kakatanawa still stood guard, but rather loped up a wide, white path towards the palace itself.

The huge overhead lamp, apparently fired by naked electricity, created deeper and deeper shadows the closer we came to it. The blazing light was blocked by heavily and colourfully decorated stoneworks in the classical-oriental traditions of Byzantium. The deeper shadows were illuminated by flickering firebrands, which in turn created another layer of mobile shadows, suggesting to an overtired mind they might be populated by all kinds of guarding monsters. Once I had dismounted, the panther slipped away, and a few moments later I heard Oona whispering from the shrubbery. As she had expected, most of the Sebastocrater's men were now in the Deep City. There remained only a skeleton guard.

Very soon we were inside the palace, dodging from column to column, seeking out its ruler. We heard distant music. A few servants came and went, but they weren't for a second suspicious. Only in the tall central halls, under a dome inset with gold, precious jewels and mosaic scenes, was there much activity.

A concert was in progress. On his throne sat a slender young, golden-haired man, wearing a circlet of silver inset with diamonds and rubies. The musicians consisted of a harpist, a lute player, a flute player and a drummer. The music was stately and, though not to my taste, surprisingly modern in feel. I was distracted by it.

Then suddenly Oona made a decision. With a bound she was at the young Sebastocrater's side, her sword blade resting against his throat. The music stopped abruptly.

Even I was surprised by this turn of events. Oona had said nothing of threatening the monarch's life.

The Sebastocrater's response at seeing me was spectacular. He jumped up, surprising Oona and knocking her backwards. She barely held on to her sword. Then he, too, fell back again. He was clearly panicked by the sight of me and seemed hardly interested in Oona at all until he looked around and found that she had risen, rescabbarded her sword and now held on her drawn bowstring an arrow directed at his heart.

His eyes darted from side to side, seeking his soldiers. He was breathing rapidly. I moved towards him, and he backed away as if in fear.

"Please," he said, "I beg you. I've done you no harm."

"Well, that's a matter of opinion," I said. He was incredibly good-looking in the typical Greek manner, with a long straight nose and bright blue eyes. "I want to know why you've imprisoned my friends and betrayed your ancient compact with the Deep City."

"For all our good," he said. "Your friends are merely in quarantine. As you should be. At least until a cure is found."

"A cure?" repeated Oona and I in unison. "Cure for what?"

"For the disease you bring with you from your world."

"Is this what Klosterheim and von Minct have told you?" Oona asked.

"Doctor Klosterheim explained how the child carries a deadly plague, which has wiped out Frankfurt, Nürnberg and Munich and left other great German cities almost without a population, without enough living people to bury their own dead. All those in proximity to her have almost certainly been infected." The Sebastocrater now had the air of a man who faced his own inevitable end. "It is irresponsible of you to bring her here."

"I'm not sick," I said. "There's nothing wrong with me, and I haven't made any other people sick. I haven't even given my white rat my cold this year!"

"They warned us you would say that. You have no signs of the plague yourself, but you have the power to infect others."

I remembered the stories of Typhoid Mary I'd heard from a radio programme, and briefly wondered if perhaps I actually *was* the carrier of some deadly virus.

"That's nonsense," said Oona briskly. "The child's as healthy as I am. As healthy as Lobkowitz and Fromental, who saw her days ago. As healthy as Lord Renyard, for that matter."

"It would be irresponsible of me not to isolate them as I isolated your friends. This is an ancient city. I cannot have its citizens infected. That is why we had to act swiftly to occupy the Deep City. If we had not, who knows how swiftly the plague would have spread."

"Then why haven't any of my friends at Raspazian's been infected?" I asked. "Not one of them's ill!"

"It takes time to manifest itself."

"This is ridiculous," said Oona. "You have allowed yourselves to be tricked and panicked by a couple of wicked men. They're responsible for untold deaths. They will kill this child if they need to and are given the chance."

The Sebastocrater seemed only half-convinced. He looked back and forth from the bow-woman to me, to his subjects and musicians.

"Doctor Klosterheim assured me . . ."

"*Doctor* Klosterheim!" she snorted. "He is better qualified as a butcher than a doctor!"

"What do you know of this great medical man? He risked his own life to warn us of our danger."

"Danger? From what?"

At that moment two men had entered the hall and stopped in the flickering shadows cast by the flambeaux on the walls. I recognised them immediately. I could see more of von Minct's heavy, handsome Germanic face, its cold blue eyes and thin lips. Dressed in black, he wore a steel breastplate. Beside him was gaunt, gloomy old "Doctor" Klosterheim, his eyes glistening in their deep sockets. He had a head like a fleshless skull, narrow and vicious. I would certainly never have taken them for a couple of heroes.

"From that child." Klosterheim raised one long, bony finger and pointed at me.

"And how can a little girl offer you danger?" said Oona, resetting the arrow on her bowstring.

"She offers the whole world grievous danger." Gaynor von Minct's voice was brutal, coarse.

"I wasn't hurting anyone in Yorkshire." I began to be annoyed. "I hadn't hurt anyone in London. I was perfectly happy at home in Ingleton until you turned up and started laying siege to our house!"

"Trying to avert the danger we foresaw," broke in Klosterheim. "The plague which has wiped out half your country."

I was furious at these lies. "Plague? There was nothing wrong with England when I left."

"You poor girl. After that terrible destruction of Londra, your own grandparents were taken with the plague. Did you not know that?"

A wave of horrified misery hit me. "What?" I looked at Oona.

"That's a foul lie, Prince Gaynor. How low you stoop! And for what gain?" Oona drew her arrow back on the bow as she prepared to shoot him.

The Sebastocrater looked at me with some alarm and raised a kerchief smelling strongly of garlic to his face. Now I understood why the guards were wearing garlic necklaces. They thought garlic was a way of warding off the plague. And vampires, too, of course.

I believed that Oona and my imprisoned friends would have told me if the story were true. "I'm perfectly healthy," I said, "and so are my grandparents."

Oona, for reasons of her own, was grinning widely at the two villains. "They certainly are," she said. "I can guarantee it."

The Sebastocrater frowned. "Who am I to believe? My responsibility is to the people of Mirenburg. Why would Doctor Klosterheim and Prince Gaynor von Minct have come to tell me such a terrible lie?"

"I think they want to kidnap me," I said. "They have already tried it once or twice. That's why I'm so far from home—and so eager to get back there."

"Don't perjure yourself," murmured Klosterheim. "It's not becoming in one so young."

"Agreed," said Oona. "Though it's a habit with you, Herr Klosterheim. You know me and you know my power. You seek what you think this girl possesses. I suspect you have the other half of your recipe already in your power. Fresh caught, eh? But half a spell is worse than none. Either way, the chances are, you'll kill her."

The Sebastocrater's handsome features clouded, and he ran his fingers through his golden curls. He didn't like the thought of being responsible for my death.

"I was already warned about them by my parents," I said. "It's true, your honour. They mean me no good."

"Yet they are so convincing."

"They are clever servants of the Master of Deceit himself," said Oona. "They serve only the Prince of Lies."

"You lie, not I!" cried Klosterheim. But she had struck home.

Oona threw back her head and laughed again. "Ah! Liar! Liar! You no longer *know* what is truth and what is falsehood!"

"What do you demand of me?" asked the Sebastocrater, rather more impressed.

"Release my friends and my warriors, and we shall all leave Mirenburg," promised Oona. "Save for Lord Renyard, who will return to rule the Deep City by tradition, as he has always done."

"And if we should then have an epidemic?"

"You will not. I have told you. Klosterheim and von Minct lie."

"Perhaps you merely wish to rescue your friends. The girl does not show plague. We did not say she did. We know she carries it." Prince Gaynor stepped towards me. "Doctor Klosterheim has explained all this. He was physician to more than one royal court."

"And no doubt poisoned more than one round of royal cocoa," I said, getting a glare of pure hatred from the "doctor" in question. "I've told you. He's a liar."

"Yet *you* could be the liar."

Oona was getting pretty tired of this. She took her bowstring back another inch. "We have no motive. If you give this child up to Klosterheim and von Minct, you almost certainly sentence an innocent to a dreadful death."

I believed her and felt slightly faint. I stared at the two villains. They stared back. They didn't seem to be denying anything. Klosterheim's cold eyes were angry. Von Minct's face was hidden again in the depths of his cloak.

Were we at an impasse?

The Sebastocrater sighed. "It would seem that if I quarantined the child, and you, too, fräulein, until such time as we are certain of the truth, I would be exercising my duty."

"And Klosterheim and von Minct?"

"They, too, shall be quarantined."

Klosterheim hissed his disagreement with this decision, but he was unsure what to do next. They both glared at me. I felt like a steak being eyed by two famished men. I moved a little closer to Oona.

"No," I said, "there's nothing wrong with me, and I should be getting home. My parents will be worrying."

"We'll take you home," growled Gaynor von Minct. Klosterheim drew a large pistol from within his cloak. "I believe this puts you all at a disadvantage," he said.

Von Minct also had a pistol. He cocked it with a heavy click.

Oona did not release her bowstring. She kept her weapon levelled at them as I began slowly to back out of the concert room, out of the palace, with von Minct, Klosterheim and the Sebastocrater glaring at me, not daring to follow.

I moved towards the summer house where, in the moonlit garden, the band of Kakatanawa stood frozen.

I hadn't expected it to be dark again. Time was playing the most peculiar tricks. Once again I was convinced I experienced some kind of waking dream.

Oona wasn't far behind me.

"Someone is already taking liberties with the machinery of the multiverse," she murmured. She looked up to where the Autumn Stars, like blossoming dahlias in dozens of deep, rich colours, poured down their light. A light which had tangible warmth.

Then a wild, cold wind whipped through the streets of the city. I heard a wailing command which I was sure I recognised. Could it be the disgusting Clement Schnooke? He had been paid and was beginning his spell without waiting to co-ordinate with us.

The voice uttered an invocation, I was sure. It summoned up weather elementals. That was about all I knew. My mother hadn't wanted me to know too much of such supernatural details.

Suddenly a great bolt of lightning cracked down. The light on top of the palace went out. Then came on again.

I felt fine mist in my face. The mist turned to rain, and I shivered with cold.

And then a shot rang out in the night. I looked back. This was definitely Schnooke's work. Rain swept in with long scimitar strokes, and the light from the palace cut through the glinting silver. The effect was almost stroboscopic. I saw the Sebastocrater clutching a wounded arm, with a look of pure astonishment on his face, while von Minct placed a pistol at his head and Klosterheim reloaded.

"The advantage is ours, I believe," snarled Prince Gaynor.

At that moment a huge splitting noise echoed through the garden, and golden light burned all around us, blinding me for a second. I heard a roar like a distant waterfall. A swift shadow moved, and the Sebastocrater went down. Instinctively I began to run.

Soon I heard water pounding on water. A great rush of water. Everything was flooding!

The Indians were suddenly coming to life. Behind them the fountain had flooded.

I had to get above the water. With relief, I felt the ground rising gradually beneath my feet. I was labouring up a slope. For the moment at least, there was a good chance I was safe.

But what of my friends? Were they also managing to escape from the drowning city?

PART TWO

DIVERGING HISTORIES

'Twas moonlight when Sir Elrik rode
His mighty steed from Old Nihrain
With anger such a needless load
Upon his heart; a bane upon his brain;
Yet anger like a plague infected every vein.

—Wheldrake,
    The Black Sword's Song

INTERLUDE

UNA PERSSON

Then, with joyous heart, Sir Elrik cried,
Why, this be Tanelorn, *the Citadel of Peace;*
And all the old man did desire and say is true.

—Wheldrake,
The Black Sword's Song

It had been some years since I had received a visit from my old friend Mrs Persson. I had reconciled myself to the idea that I might never see her again. In the past her stories had generally involved Bastable, Cornelius or the denizens of the End of Time. Only once or twice had she told me anything concerning Elric of Melniboné, whose adventures I drew largely from other sources, especially from Mr John D—, that contemporary manifestation of the Eternal Champion, whom I knew best. Mr D—, as I might have mentioned elsewhere, married a distant relative of mine and eventually settled in the North. It wasn't until a later occasion, when my wife and I spent a year or two in the English Lake District, that I had the pleasure of his company once more.

At the time I met Mrs Persson again, however, Linda and I had grown rather settled in our rural Texan life and had developed a pleasure in unexpected visitors, the way you hardly ever do in the city.

One late October evening we sat in rocking chairs on our screened porch, enjoying the warmth and watching the sun set over our property's low hills and wide, shallow streams, when a car approached on the dirt road. The machine threw up a great "dust ghost" which rose into the darkening sky like a pale fairytale giant.

It fell back as the car passed under the tall gateposts on which hung the sign of the Old Circle Squared. My great-uncle had named the ranch when he settled in the Lost Pines area and made his first fortune in timber, his second in cattle, his third in river trade, his fourth in oil and his fifth in real estate. Because of bad advice from accountants, we had made almost no money. Now most of our remaining land is part of the Lost Pines State Park, and for a small tax break we raise a modest herd of longhorns, as much a part of the family as any one of our other domestic animals. We name them all, as they pay their own way like true Texans. The balance of our land, not kept for grazing or in forest, we employ for organic gardening.

Because of the garden we were used to the occasional neighbour dropping by for a bunch of carrots or a pound or two of tomatoes, and so thought nothing of it until the car drew up at our porch steps and a slender, dark-haired woman got out. She had a boyish, startling beauty. She wore a long coat of the kind we call a "duster" in Texas, and her hair was cut in what used to be known as a pageboy. From underneath those Prince Valiant bangs two bright grey eyes smiled at us. I recognised her at once, of course. Mrs Persson strode up the steps of the porch as I rose to open the screen door for her. My wife let out an expression of pleasure. "My dear Una! What brings you to the back of beyond?"

Linda drew up another rocker for Mrs Persson while I went to fix her a drink. Still standing, she received it gratefully. Again I offered her a chair, but she said she'd been driving for some hours and preferred to remain standing for the time being. She was in Austin, she told us, to see a colleague at UT, and while she never knew our phone number, she found our address and decided to drive out to see if we were in.

I assured her that we had become lazy; I was pretty much retired and had absolutely nothing to do. I asked after old friends as well as some of those I regarded as friends from her stories.

She said she saw little of anyone except her cousin and someone whose adventures she knew would interest me. "Elric of Melniboné?" She made the words sound delicious, like exotic food. There might have been a hint of irony, the kind a woman gains from living too long in Paris.

"Really? You've been enjoying more adventures in space and time?"

"Not at all. He has only recently returned to his own era. That is, whatever physical manifestation we take with us between one plane of the multiverse and another. What his people know, I understand, as 'dream-quests.'"

"You are not now embarked upon any such quest, are you?" my wife asked gently.

Una Persson bowed her head a fraction and winked.

"We are all embarked upon dream-quests," she said. "Those of us who are not wholly dead. Wholly dead."

"But your time on the stage, and so on—that wasn't a dream-quest," said Linda. "That was a dream come true."

I laughed.

"I wasn't raised to know the difference," said Una, settling at last into the rocking chair beside Linda. "Dreams and identities are there, like the multiverse, to be negotiated, to be tested and tried and sometimes adopted."

"I think I would prefer not to have that choice," I said.

"I know I would prefer not to have it," she agreed vehemently.

"You didn't enjoy your time on stage?" Linda was implacable. She was a huge fan of musical comedy, and Una had for a while a very successful career both in the West End and on Broadway.

"I think I enjoyed it most of all," she said. "It was a long career, because of my peculiar circumstances. I came in with the great dowager halls, the massive palaces of variety like the Empire, Leicester Square. I went out with revue and the sophisticated topical songs of the 1960s. It was rock-and-roll and satire ruined me, my dear." And she laughed. She had enjoyed it while it was fun, but never seemed to care that it was over. She had done so much more with her life, in political terms, since the mid-1960s. Her main association then, of course, was with Jerry Cornelius and his odd assortment of travelling players, who had been so typical of the situationist theatre which had grown up on the Continent but which had never really caught on in the United States or UK. I had heard that the theatre had been a cover for other kinds of more serious activity, but I was never curious about so-called secret-service stories.

Una had, in fact, a new Elric tale—or at least part of one—to tell us. Most of the facts, she promised, came from Elric himself. Others had been verified beyond doubt by various people she had met on the moonbeam roads in recent months.

I mixed her a fresh drink while Linda went into the house to see about dinner. Then, when Linda had returned, Una began her tale.

7

Elric of Melniboné, Una told us, had embarked involuntarily on what he called the Dream of a Thousand Years. Having arrived in England some years before the Battle of Hastings, in the reign of Ethelred the Unready, he served as a sea-going mercenary against the encroaching Danes until Ethelred, impoverished as a result of his own poor planning, failed to pay him. Therefore the albino took what was his and left for the Middle Sea, where for a while he fell in with a female pirate known as the Barbary Rose, striking merchant ships from the security of her island stronghold of Las Cascadas. Later he went adventuring into the wildern lands of the Moors, beyond the High Atlas into the desert, where, it was said, he came upon a country ruled by intelligent dragons. Little was then heard of him until he turned up as a crusader, becoming the ally of Gunnar the Doomed and sailing with him to America.

Elric, who had used a variety of names, founded a nation. He carved it from the old German and Slavic lands in a place called Wäldenstein, whose capital was the city of Mirenburg. There he and what seemed to be his progeny ruled by virtue of dark magic and a fabulous black sword said to drink souls as readily as it drank blood. Terrible legends surrounded the princes of Mirenburg until the nineteenth century, when the city appeared to have been abandoned by the crimson-eyed albinos who occupied it. At the early part of the twentieth century, though a few stories still existed in Mirenburg concerning a soul-eating demon called Karmesinaugen, the old tales of the vampire prince and his vampire sword continued to circulate. They soon merged with those of Nosferatu and the hero-villains of German cinema. Meanwhile an albino resembling Elric began to entertain with a magic act on the English stage. Monsieur Zodiac, as he was called, was a very popular attraction, and his son, who might have been his twin, later took over the act as well as the name.

Mrs Persson believed that his thousand-year sojourn in our world, where his dream self took on solid flesh, was coming to an end. She wanted to help him return to his world, "where he hangs crucified on a ship's mast," but was afraid he was now too weak to resist the controlling power of his massive runesword, which, she believed, had been stolen and carried across the multiverse. He was desperate to rediscover it and convinced he would die if he awoke from his dream without it.

"Why will he die?" I asked.

"There's a symbiosis between the blade and the man. The blade's the essence of Chaos. It might even have a mind. *His* mind. The blade lends him vitality in return for the souls it feeds upon. Yet the sword could be a holy object associated with the Cosmic Balance itself. We must never forget that the Balance maintains the structure of the multiverse. When it tips one way, Chaos rules across the multiverse. When it tips the other, Law grows dominant. One way lies madness and hideous death; the other, sanity and relentless nothingness. It is the Eternal Champion's fate to ensure that the Balance is maintained. Our fate, I suspect, is to help him in this task."

"Our fate?"

"I'm afraid so. There's also the problem of the Runestaff. Its existence or lack of substance could determine the issue. Many believe the Staff and the Stone are the fundamental components of the Balance itself. Of course, we are also discussing an abstraction." She shrugged. "The symbols of power are not the power themselves. Unless you're a magician, of course."

"I understood the Grail was involved in that equation."

"The Grail takes many forms. One of those could be the Staff. Anyway, the fact is that several people would like to control one or all of these forces represented by those objects, because of the enormous power such possession would give them. This is doubtless why, under great threat, it has again divided itself into its chief components and again gone out of the protection of the family sworn to defend it—the von Beks.

"One of those pursuing the Stone across time and space for his own ends is Gaynor the Damned, a former Knight of the Balance, disgraced and exiled, Elric's most implacable enemy. He goes by many names but is best known in these times as von Minct."

"He's sailed with Elric to America?" asked Linda.

Una nodded. "Gaynor once drew on the power of the Balance, using it for his own benefit. Needless to say, he lost his calling and became an outlaw, the enemy of all who served the Balance. Yet he yearned at the same time to be reconciled with what he had been bred to respect. And if reconciliation's not possible, he'll destroy the Balance and the multiverse with it. This is what fuels his unquenchable hatred. The Balance, of course, is essentially only a symbol of the forces which rule the multiverse. Yet those forces are real enough, created out of the seminal stuff which exists in the place we call the Grey Fees. Forces created by the common will or by an uncommon imagination. That is what we call reality."

"And reality can be destroyed? Is that it? By an act of will?"

Mrs Persson took a sip of her drink, rocking slowly back and forth, her face turned up to the emerging evening stars. "By an act of extraordinary will, channelled by ritual and superhuman desire. We are dealing with a creature who has honed and channelled that will and that desire for millennia."

"What keeps him alive?" I asked.

"Some believe his very hatred sustains him. Neither he nor Elric is immortal, though their longevity is, of course, phenomenal. Elric is not even conscious of his longevity. Both move from one dream-quest to another, though Elric has not often walked the moonbeam roads. It's hard for some of us to understand. How do we count age when so much of your life is spent in dream-quests centuries long, in which you scarcely move in your sleep nor grow older?"

Sitting there in the warm Texas twilight discussing the nature of the infinite multiverse was a little odd, but our pleasure in seeing our old friend was more than enough to make us forget the incongruity. Besides, it had been some while since I had learned of any manifestation of the Eternal Champion, let alone Elric of Melniboné, whose adventures I first heard from Una Persson in the 1950s, when I began recording them.

Apparently Elric, in his guise of Monsieur Zodiac, the stage conjuror, was visited by two men he had met during the 1930s, when he discovered himself at odds with various Nazis, including Gaynor, who had transformed himself into a minor German nobleman, cousin to Ulric von Bek. Elric had founded the family line in his first years in Mirenburg. The extraordinary coming together of von Bek and Elric, whose identities blended into a single physical being, was something neither had experienced and which almost defeated description. These disruptions in the order of time had come about, Mrs Persson had told me, as a result of Gaynor and his ally Klosterheim seeking to use for themselves the power of the Grail and the black sword Ravenbrand, sometimes called Mournblade, the sibling sword to Stormbringer.

Meanwhile, Mrs Persson said, Elric went to Portugal, searching for the Black Sword, which had passed out of his hands sometime in 1974 in the course of an adventure she promised to relate to me on another occasion. Having only a few years left to repossess the blade before his dream-quest ended, Elric eventually found himself and his recovered blade in Cintra, outside Lisbon, where the Chevalier St Odhran in turn discovered him. From there the two men journeyed via St Odhran's Scottish estates to Ingleton in West Yorkshire, to Tower House, not far from my own ancestral home of Moorcock, near Dent. There they met Prince Lobkowitz and his old friend Lieutenant Fromental and Colonel Bastable, all able to negotiate the moonbeam roads, all Knights of the Balance and members of the Guild of Temporal Adventurers, founded in the mid-twentieth century. They had expected to discover the von Beks there. Oona von Bek, a relative of Mrs Persson, was Elric's daughter and had, like Count von Bek, fought at his side against Gaynor the Damned on more than one occasion.

"What was the reason?" I asked her. "Isn't it unusual for so many heroes to gather in one place?"

"Yes, it is unusual," she agreed. "Indeed there's some danger in it. But it appears they learned von Bek's young granddaughter was being sought by Gaynor, and they went there to protect the little girl."

"They succeeded, I hope."

"Not entirely. The child has a mind of her own and disappeared. It was thought at first that Gaynor and Klosterheim had been successful in their intentions. But the real cause of her disappearance was a weakening in the fundamental fabric of time and space, the Grey Fees, the very DNA of the multiverse. She vanished during a minor local earthquake caused by this chaotic movement. Gaynor and Klosterheim were seen in the vicinity, but it's pretty clear they didn't set out to kidnap her. They are opportunists, and they were lunging after her as clumsily as the rest of us. The presence of so many people from alternate spheres of the multiverse seems to have produced a certain amount of cosmic turbulence.

"Lobkowitz and Fromental set off to find the little girl while the others waited to join forces with the von Beks—Ulric and Oona. Ulric remained with his other children while his wife, who had sworn never to revisit the moonbeam roads—by which means travellers cross between the worlds—took up her old calling. Her mother was a dreamthief, but Oona had been content merely to explore the worlds her mother had once entered with the intention of stealing dreams to sell to her clients. It was in one such world that her mother met Elric and conceived their twin children, as I believe you already know."*

"And the male twin?" asked my wife. "What became of him?"

"He disappeared before his sister even remembered him. He was kidnapped."

"By von Minct and Klosterheim?"

"As it happens, probably not. They found him later and bought him from his master."

"So what became of Elric? Did he ever contact the child? Or his own lost son?"

"Why don't I tell you the story from the beginning," she said, "as best I can."

Over the next few days, as our guest in Texas, my old friend told me everything she knew of the events concerning Elric of Melniboné and the last months of his dream-quest, when his body, suffering extreme pain, hung in the rigging of Jagreen Lern's flagship moments before a mighty sea-fight. The naval battle's outcome would be a crucial factor in events which were to change the whole course of his world's history. It would begin actions whose consequences would resonate throughout the multiverse.

How Mrs Persson knew so much concerning the private lives of some of those featured in this narrative, she would not at that time say. In many cases I have been unable to verify what she told me, and have set it down here without checking.

According to Mrs Persson this is what happened: Elric, St Odhran, Fromental and Colonel Bastable, having conferred with the old Count and Countess von Bek, agreed that the countess should set off on her own. They then travelled together to Mirenburg by conventional means, from Heathrow, London, to

---

* See *The Fortress of the Pearl*

Munich, Germany, and from there to Mirenburg, capital of the newly independent principality of Wäldenstein, where Germany, Austria and Bohemia came together.

Though still beautiful, the city had yet to recover entirely from the poverty of her communist past. German had been her official tongue before the Russian conquest, but her people still spoke a Slavic language akin to Polish. Her parliament, however, returned primarily to the German form, so that her seat of government was known as the Reikstagg, and the chief executive of her elected city council was called her majori, or mayor.

The travellers went immediately to the Berghoff and, thanks to letters from Count von Bek, received a swift audience with Mayor Pabli, who put his city's law enforcers at their disposal on the assumption that young Oonagh von Bek would be found there.

Meanwhile Elric, who was most familiar with the city's secrets, set about on his own explorations, glad, he told my friend, to be back in his old haunts. In no time he found his familiar secret back alleys and explored the tunnels only he and a few others knew about, eventually emerging in the underground "looking glass" city which lay alongside their time and space (an area known in German as the Mittelmarch), close to the borders of that exquisitely beautiful land of Mu-Ooria. He found this manifestation of the city largely deserted and in ruins. The Off-Moo told of a terrible internal war where the people of the Deep City, the interior of Thieves' Quarter, had clashed with the forces of the Byzantine Sebastocrater.

Realising he was not in a place where he was likely to find the girl, Elric returned to the Mirenburg of the early twenty-first century to report to his friends, only to find them gone, leaving him a message to let him know they were following other important clues.

Modern Mirenburg, with its decaying industrial section and impoverished working class, was not to Elric's taste, but he had come to love the old city, which still retained much of her beauty and quaintness. He decided, however, to waste no further time and employ what little sorcery was still available to him in a world where the Lords of Law and Chaos exhibited themselves in alien and rather prosaic ways and where the great elementals, his old traditional allies, had either disappeared or died.

Unlike his daughter, Elric had only limited experience of the silver strands of the moonbeam roads, where adepts walked between the worlds, crossing from one level of the multiverse to another, from one alternative Earth to another; but he decided that if he was to find his daughter's grandchild, he would have to explore more than one version of the World Below. Thus he gathered his strength, performed the necessary exercises and rituals, and found himself on the roads between the worlds.

Mrs Persson had described these roads in the past, but much as I longed to see them for myself, I never had the privilege of even so much as a glimpse. To the mortal eye, she said, they appeared like an infinite lattice of silver ribbons, wide enough to take a number of travellers, most of whom walked and all of whom represented an enormous variety of peoples and cultures, some extraordinarily different from our own and some very similar. The travellers reached the roads by several means and interpreted this experience in quite different ways. Most would readily exchange information, and few were antagonists.

Elric had used these roads only in his youthful dream-quests, through which his people gained wisdom and made compacts with supernaturals. He was scarcely aware of them in his waking world, where a great fight was brewing between Law and Chaos, waged for control of the Balance, and echoed in many different forms across the multiverse.

After buying himself a horse, Elric made enquiries of his fellow travellers and soon discovered that young Oonagh was to be found in a particular place and had, in fact, not yet left Mirenburg. So he plunged again into the strange, almost limitless underground domain of the Middle Marches, through the infamous Grey Fees, unformed Chaos reacting unpredictably on the imagination. In his wisdom Elric feared his own mind more than he feared any being, mortal or supernatural. Only his need to ensure the safety of the little girl drove him on, and he hated himself for what he considered his own weakness.

Yet in the familiar deep chasms and jagged peaks of Mu-Ooria, following the glowing silver river towards Mirenburg, he was surprised not to see the outlines so familiar to him in his numerous travels. The lake—actually a great widening of the river—had extended itself. The cries of birds, almost deafening, were baffling to him, for they were not the voices of waterfowl but rather were the anxious voices of birds finding what nesting space they could among the towers, eaves and taller trees of a recently flooded city.

The city's phosphorescent liquid had lost much of its lustre. Elric felt a vague sense of alarm. When, after several hours' ride, he came to a village of shacks and makeshift houses built from the rubble of more magnificent buildings, he recognised the spires and domes and roofs of that ancient, drowned metropolis, where, in cavernous shadows, naked men dived, disappearing into still deeper darkness, into the faintly glowing silver depths, and occasionally reappearing clutching sodden trophies. Sad, ill-fed women tended sputtering fires outside their dwellings. Elric dismounted beside one of them and asked her what this place was called and what the men were doing.

They were surly creatures, ruined by work that was hard and hopeless. They asked him for any spare food he carried. He gave them what he could, a soldier's rations meant to sustain him for several days, and the citizens fell upon it as if it were a feast. They were willing to help him if they could. Their watery city was all that was left of Mirenburg, where they had once lived under the secure rule of the Sebastocrater and his opposite number, Lord Renyard, until terrible misdirected magic, long banished from the city by ancient treaty, caused a great catastrophe, drawing in both the city and its mirror version in the World Above. Now men dived for whatever food had been preserved, be it in sealed jars or barrels, but the supply diminished daily. They had no way of appealing to any higher being, for they were all cursed.

"How did this curse come about?" asked Elric.

"We have told you," said one grey crone, her black eyes catching faint reflected light from the lake. "Sorcery. The ancient compact made with the gods was broken. The Balance tipped. The result is what you see. A great cataclysm which shook the city to the core and brought the waters pouring in and down upon us. We are all that survived. Perhaps it would have been better had we also drowned with the folk of the Outer and Inner, Deep and Shallow Cities. I saw the towers crumble and collapse. I saw all the people engulfed. I saw the river rush into the craters. Within the hour, this was all that was left of a great and ancient metropolis. Her centuries-old agreements destroyed within a few days, chiefly as the result of fear. Of unknown fear. Of fear of the unknown . . ." And she began to cackle to herself happily. "What destruction we bring upon ourselves, master!" She accepted a useless coin, which she hid in her clothes. "What insects we are! No more able to guard against the future than we can against the day. Time remains our lady, and death our lord, eh?"

Elric, used to such views from the moment he could walk and talk, found her boring and ignored her. She spat at him and cursed him, almost affectionately. He smiled to himself, feeling no insult. She found the coin somewhere in her rags and threw it after him. To both of them the encounter had stirred life. In Klosterheim's hell, he thought, this was what passed for affection. He felt safe enough to dismount and show that he offered them no violence.

Then Elric asked after the child he sought. They told him she had almost certainly drowned.

"As she deserved," continued the crone, "if it's the one I think you seek, master. A little blue-eyed diddicoy, she was. All innocence and winsome manners. It was my guess she was the one what brought this here disaster. Before she came, and those who followed her, we had not known any serious change for two hundred years."

I'm told, said Mrs Persson, that Elric returned to the more familiar Mirenburg, desperately hoping he had taken the wrong route and that the child he thought of as his own flesh and blood had survived. Perhaps in this aspect of the multiverse, he insisted to himself, she had survived Mirenburg at the time of the city's drowning. He needed expert help.

Where he would find her, where he should begin looking for her, was a mystery. At least he knew that sorcery, though banned, worked on this plane. Should he stay here or attempt to find a world where magic was even more potent? Did he have enough time?

As before, he was welcomed in Mu-Ooria. What language differences they had, what problems were thus created, they accepted in good faith, no matter how outrageous the other seemed. Elric, however, knew no way of asking a direct question of the Off-Moo, or they might have helped him better. Not that it would have made an improvement to the story.

His oldest acquaintance among this people was Scholar Ree, the most widely travelled of the Off-Moo, and his people's spiritual leader. Ree felt something like affection for the albino. With his delicate, elongated lips fluttering, his deep-set eyes glowing with faint phosphorescence, he embraced Elric. It was the strangest experience, like being hugged by hesitant tissue paper.

That wise old creature agreed to help Elric, and together they consulted books and charts while the albino did all he could to curb his impatience, fearing irrationally that time was wasting, that in the meantime the former Knight of the Balance and Satan's ex-servant might be subjecting the girl to horrors he would rather not imagine.

Why they wanted her, Elric was not be sure. Perhaps she was a pawn in a much larger game. Perhaps she had been abducted in order to distract him and his allies while some other plot was hatched, but none of this affected his determination to find her. His bone-white features were tense, his crimson eyes narrowed in concentration, as he bent over Scholar Ree's documents, seeking a road to Mirenburg which would have him arrive before disaster visited the city, where he might consult his own sorcerous allies, most of whom were denied time by the nature of his existing dream-quest.

In his whispering voice like the rustling of long-dead leaves, Scholar Ree debated in a kind of pidgin High Melnibonéan with the albino. It was difficult for the Mu-Oorian to engage with equal passion in pursuit of an answer to his friend's problem, but he devoted his whole attention to it.

At last the two determined the co-ordinates required for the exercise.

"It will be dangerous for you, Elric, considering your situation," said Scholar Ree. "These worlds have much in common. There is the likelihood of your encountering an avatar of yourself. Moreover, that avatar could be serving Law and you Chaos, and you'll find him your enemy. Such mighty power does not always work for the common good. These are unstable times, old friend. The Balance tips this way and that; a great Conjunction of the Worlds takes place over and over again as if Creation awaits a final, single action. You could come to great physical harm, or worse."

"Worse?"

"You could *cause* great harm. The fate of millions of worlds is being decided, and you and yours could be lost, unnoticed in such a struggle."

"But I must find her, Scholar Ree."

"I understand that. Pray she is not the catalyst for limitless destruction. That's all I mean to imply."

Elric sighed. "Well, I'll rest a little, then make my way to this other Wälden-stein, this other Mirenburg, where this other empire rules! I heard you give it a name . . .?"

"The Empire of Granbretan, like your own, is an island nation which has conquered whole continents. Like yours, it's feral yet overcivilised. Like yours, its supernatural compacts are chiefly with Chaos. And, like yours, it is thoroughly hated, ruling by force and threat of bloody violence."

Elric laughed at this.

"Then I shall feel thoroughly at home," he said.

Very shortly he again took his heavy steed in rein and set off through the Middle March.

A rare rain was falling, silver tears against the black fangs of the rock. He held his face up to receive it. It smelled like all the spices and flowers of the world. Just for a moment it reminded him of a garden where he had walked with a child. They had both remarked on it. An extraordinary concentration of scents. And then it was gone.

Elric was careful to follow Scholar Ree's map to the letter.

As it happened, the albino easily found his way to Wäldenstein in the age of the Dark Empire of Granbretan, a world I myself know something about. Of course, there are a million versions of the same era, most of which vary only by the faintest degree, but evidently the world in which Elric found himself did not vary much from those of which I had already heard. In it the oppressive empire of Granbretan—Britain in our world—had emerged from a Dark Age known as the Tragic Millennium, brought about by conflicts in which terrible, mysterious weapons had been employed. Using a mixture of sorcery and science, Granbretan had conquered Europe and set her sights on the rest of the world. In many aspects of the multiverse she had been opposed by a few heroes, chiefly Dorian Hawkmoon, Duke of Köln, and Count Brass, Lord Guardian of Kamarg. In some they had succeeded in their challenge. In others they had failed.

Elric emerged from the Mittelmarch into a huge cave deep in a mossy forest of old oaks, elms and ash trees. The foliage was so thick, it had almost knitted together to form a canopy, through which the sun managed to cast a green, hazy light, cut occasionally by bright, golden rays through which birds and small mammals moved. The air was filled with a constant fluttering and whistling, an indication of rich life. The colours glowed and gave the canopy itself the appearance of stained glass. Elric found his surroundings restful. He was reminded of the deep Shazaarian woods of his native world. For a moment he almost fancied himself home, until he remembered that the armies of Chaos, guided by his blood enemy Jagreen Lern, had laid that nation waste. Jagreen Lern must soon destroy the lands of the Eastern Continent unless Elric could summon Stormbringer back and defeat the Theocrat.

Mrs Persson thinks so many shadowy concerns filled Elric's mind in those days, when a thousand realities and the memories of so many men crowded his brain, that only one rigorously trained in the arts of Melniboné, who had undertaken so many dream-quests, could remain even remotely sane. I believe that it is less arduous than she thinks, for most readers can keep a multitude of stories in their heads. I grew up reading and watching a score or so of serials a week, at least, and had no trouble separating the threads of my favourite detective tale from a historical yarn, or a story about a trip to Mars and another involving people fighting some evil genius's attempt at world domination. We are complex and robust creatures, we humans, able to give our attention to a thousand concerns.

To Elric the forest offered a welcome tranquillity after the vicissitudes and setbacks of his journey, and he was tempted to take his time, but he could not dawdle while the child remained in danger. At last he found a path, well trodden by horses and vehicles, and followed it until it led him to a tall, moated castle, all steep-pitched towers and crenellations, flying half a dozen unfamiliar standards, its granite walls almost white against the deep blue of the sky and the rich greens of the woods.

Elric went forward with his usual arrogant lack of caution, calling out to the gatekeepers to show that he did not come as a stealthy enemy.

A rattle of armour and a head appeared in a narrow window at ground level.

"Who comes?" The language was Old Slavonic, which Elric knew.

"Elric, Prince of Melniboné, seeking your master's hospitality."

More sounds as guards ran to receive instructions; then, in a few moments, the drawbridge above the moat creaked, chains tightened and a groaning winch let down the wide wooden bridge across to the far bank, revealing an ornate portcullis with just enough room for a mounted man to pass under.

Elric looked down at the dark, unpleasant waters of the moat as he dismounted and crossed. From the bubbles rising to the weedy surface, there were creatures of some size swimming there; he saw dark shapes darting through the reflective gloom.

A man in somewhat bulky, almost medieval garb stood to greet him in the cobbled bailey. Clearly an important personage, he had a rippling scarlet surcoat, chainmail, glinting greaves and a helmet completely covering his face. The helmet was wonderfully moulded in the features of a snarling wolf, every detail perfect, utterly belligerent as if about to charge. Such a helm had been designed to frighten whoever saw it, but the albino scarcely noted it. He only wondered what kind of creature was insecure enough to require such a mask.

He removed his gloves as he advanced towards the fierce wolf and held out his right hand.

"I thank you for your hospitality, sir. I have made a long journey and would trouble you for some minor assistance."

After some hesitation the wolf unbuttoned his right gauntlet and, removing it, extended his own hand to Elric.

"I am Sir Edwold Krier, Knight Lieutenant of the Order of the Wolf. I rule this province on behalf of our great King Huon, whose throne is in distant Granbretan, at the very centre of the world. I fear I am unfamiliar with your rank and station."

"Prince Elric of Melniboné." Elric offered the man a slight bow. "My lands are far from here. Ours is an island nation. We have heard a little of this continent, and I come as an emissary, in peace."

"Then you are welcome, for we of the Empire of Granbretan wish only peace to our neighbours. We fear the aggression of those who envy us our wealth and way of life."

The masked man bowed and signed for Elric to follow some servants into the interior of the castle.

"Granbretan?" Elric pretended to be puzzled. "But that, too, I understand, is an island, some many leagues from here."

"Indeed it is. I miss its sophistication, its pleasures. But I have my duty to do here. Sometimes it is fated that a man serves his nation best in some far-flung corner of a foreign land . . ."

Now they were inside a rather starkly furnished hall, with functional chairs, benches and tables, some wall hangings, a few battle flags, a rather moth-eaten collection of large animal heads, some of which were unfamiliar to Elric. There was a melancholy air about the whole place. Clearly Krier had no family here, but the man was a good host. Wine was called for and brought. Out of politeness, Elric sipped a little, though he had little taste for what these people cultivated in their vineyards.

"I sympathise," said Elric, who missed the complex and varied pleasures he had forsaken when Imrryr had fallen to his own hand. Only as he grew older did he fully appreciate what he had destroyed. "Is there nothing you can do here? Some musicians, perhaps? I take it you are lord of this castle."

"I am governor commander, which they call Raulevici or Seneschal, of this province in the County of Wäldenstein."

"Your nation has conquered Wäldenstein? They attacked you?"

"Europe is full of those who plot against Granbretan. We attacked them before they and their allies attacked us. They are no longer a serious threat to us."

"Very wise," said Elric dryly. "And the threat is now averted, I take it."

"Apart from a few insurgents. Supporters of the old, unjust régime we supplanted. Such terrorists represent only a small fraction of Wäldensteiners, who are essentially a peaceful people with no great interest whether their prince or the protector general rules in Mirenburg."

If Elric expected Edwold Krier to remove his ornate helmet once they were inside, he was wrong. Only local troops went unmasked, it seemed. The wide, Slavic faces of the ordinary guards were visible, but those who commanded them were Granbretanners whose grotesque beast-masks were never removed.

Even when wine was poured for them, Sir Edwold sipped his through a specially shaped mouthpiece. Elric felt as if he were being entertained by some non-human creature. Yet Edwold Krier was pleasant enough, bidding Elric sit and rest while a female slave removed his boots and bathed his feet. He found this surprisingly refreshing.

"You must stay the night, Lord Elric, and tell us something of your lands. We are starved for news here, as you can tell. Have you travelled through many of our towns? What kind of horse is that hairy steed of yours? I have seen nothing like it. And you are so lightly clad and armed!"

"Thieves," said Elric, "in the Bulgar Mountains. I was set upon, my retinue slain, save for those who were able to retreat. It is possible they made it home. My gold and horses stolen, all but the one. My horse Samson has a preference to remain with me. His speed got me clear of the brigands." He shrugged, almost daring his host to disbelieve him. "We wandered a good distance, I think, before I recovered my senses in your forest."

"My condolences. You have travelled many leagues. I am surprised our border patrols did not help you. Even though we do all we can to secure this savage land, insurgents still manage to form bands. Be assured, sir, those who have done this will be hunted down and captured. They must learn that the protection of the banner of Granbretan is real. Tomorrow you will, I hope, show me on the map where you were attacked, and I will send a message. Your property will be recovered, and justice will be delivered."

"I am grateful, sir." Elric was to some degree amused by such pompous boasts. He knew that the Bulgar Mountains were very far from here and almost certainly outside Granbretan's effective jurisdiction.

"Granbretan's laws shall not be broken," continued Edwold Krier. "From ocean to ocean one rule shall apply in the name of our noble King Huon, who lives for ever, as our power lives for ever."

Elric was scarcely able to repress his sardonic tongue at all this vainglory. He had heard such boasts once made by his own people, who had lived to see Melniboné's towers crumble, her people slain or in chains and all her power turned to pain in the space of a single day. He wondered at the hubris of empires and whether their very size made them collapse so swiftly and decisively when they did fall.

The two men passed the time in less boastful discussion, with Elric remarking on the beauty of the woods and the architecture of the castle while Edwold Krier told him of the original Wäldensteiner aristocrats who had lived there until they were unwise enough to rise against the empire. Then dinner was served, and Elric was astonished at the ingenuity of his host, who managed to eat heartily without once removing his helmet.

The hall was lit by tall oil lamps with reflectors of beaten silver to amplify and spread their flames. The light was caught by the bronze and steel of Sir Edwold's wolf mask as, in response to Elric's courteous questions, he explained that it was considered poor manners in Granbretan to remove the helm of one's clan. He had the honour of belonging to what was the most prestigious and noblest, the Order of the Wolf, the same as that of Baron Meliadus, the Order's Grand Marshal, second only to King Huon the Immortal, and the greatest active power in the empire.

Clearly Sir Edwold Krier hero-worshipped the grand marshal, eulogising his valour, his wisdom, his influence, so that Elric pretended to be open-mouthed with admiration while he sat concocting a plan which would involve some modest sorcery and might get him into Wäldenstein's capital undetected. He had to hope that he had not been misled and that his powers would be effective in this world. He then feigned sleep in his chair and was wakened by Sir Edwold's good-natured suggestion that he retire.

"You are a kind host, sir. I must admit that my energy is not as other men's. Were it not for potions prepared for me by my people's apothecaries, I fear I would hardly be able to move abroad."

"I have heard this is a trait amongst people of your colouration," said Sir Edwold. "You have weak eyes, I gather. And are lassitudinous by nature."

Elric smiled and shook his head. "My albinism is different to any you might be familiar with. My eyesight is no worse than any of my other frailties. Few albinos in your lands have red eyes. Generally they are blue or grey. Just as with your people's albinism, mine is inherited, blood which from time to time recurs in my family. But I assure you, neither true albinos nor albinos of my kind are necessarily unhealthy for want of a little pigment."

"Forgive me—I had not meant to—"

"You made a common judgement, sir. I am not offended."

The wolf rose in his seat. "Then I'll let you restore yourself, Lord Elric. Tomorrow you must, if you will, tell me more of your land. I admit I have never before even heard of a red-eyed, ivory-skinned race with tapering ears. I am a poorly educated man, I fear."

He seemed to have missed Elric's point.

"Believe me, sir, I am as ignorant of your world as you are of mine." Elric got up from his chair to follow a servant to his room. The young fellow was broad-faced with fair hair and pale blue eyes, evidently of local stock. His features also had a closed, self-possessed quality Elric noticed at once, and there was a sense of contained anger, which Elric understood. When they reached his room Elric closed the door. "How long have you served your master?" he asked in the Slavic dialect he had learned hundreds of years earlier.

The man was surprised, frowning. "Since the fall of Mirenburg," he said, "my lord."

"Those Granbretanners seem excellent warriors, eh?"

"The Dark Empire conquers all she makes war upon."

"She's a just empire, is she?"

The man looked him in the eye. "They are the law, my lord, so we must assume they are just."

Elric could tell he dealt with a man of great education and not a little irony. He smiled. "They seem insecure braggarts to me. How did they come by their power?"

"By growing rich, my lord. By building great engines of destruction. By controlling the trade and manufacturing of every nation they conquered. They mean to destroy the world, my lord, and rebuild it in the image of Granbretan." Now there was a glimmer of fire in the young eyes. Elric was sure he had rightly judged his man.

"So it would seem. Do they all wear masks?"

"All, my lord. Only their lowlier slaves and servants go naked-faced, as they call it. This is one of the means by which they distinguish the conquered from the conquerors. To them it is an outrage to go about unmasked. Most wives, for instance, have never seen their husbands' faces."

"Does Sir Edwold Krier have many visitors of his own kind?"

"We are a remote province, my lord, and no threat to the empire. I believe Sir Edwold has relatives in his native Vamerin, a town not far from Londra. They maintain a certain influence at Court, I understand, and obtained the stewardship of our little province for him. I gather"—the Wäld dropped his gaze to the carpet—"I gather there was no other employment for him. He has few friends. He relies on clan loyalties and his clan's influence at Court."

"So few know him?"

"I understand that to be the case, my lord." There were questions in the young man's eyes when he next looked up.

"Do you know Mirenburg?"

"I was educated there, before the conquest."

"It's a rich place, I gather. A manufacturing centre. Could you guide me about the city, if I needed it?"

"I think so, my lord. But I don't believe Sir Edwold would permit such a thing. And if I left without his permission, I would be killed."

"Your master will gladly order you to accompany me."

"With respect, I find that unlikely, my lord."

"What's your name?"

"Yaroslaf Stredic, my lord."

"What is your background?"

"I was once cousin to the prince of this place. Now that he is dead, I am its hereditary prince."

"And would you earn a title for yourself again?"

Stredic's face was a mixture of expressions. Elric's smile was thin, questioning.

"Well, Master Stredic, I intend to take you into my confidence. I possess certain powers in what some of your folk call the Dark Arts."

"You're a sorcerer?" Stredic's pale eyes widened.

"I have a few small skills in that direction. I hope to employ some of them tonight."

Now Stredic frowned. For a moment he seemed genuinely afraid. Cautiously he murmured, "I am not sure I entirely believe in magic, my lord."

"I have learned how to call on beings who are invisible to the majority of us, marshal energies which others cannot summon easily. I have gained certain disciplines."

Elric preferred to be counted as a clever conjuror or a charlatan. He was amused by Stredic's mixture of superstition and disbelief, even a hint of disapproval. He took something of a risk by trusting the man but guessed Stredic hated Granbretan enough to co-operate. Swiftly he explained what he intended to do and what the risks were.

Two hours later, when the castle slept, Elric left his room and, led by Yaroslaf Stredic, found Edwold Krier's apartments. Only one armed guard stood on duty outside his door, and the man had no suspicion. His wolf mask turned casually as the two men approached.

MICHAEL MOORCOCK

Elric smiled as he greeted him. "I wonder if you have seen the twin of this object." He held up his hand to display what was in his palm. The wolf mask looked, and its eyes were instantly fixed on the mirror Elric showed him. His limbs slackened, and his eyes grew dreamy. Then, slowly, he sank to the floor.

Stredic was impressed. He kept silent as Elric opened the door and entered the antechamber. It was empty. A lantern burned from a central chain. It gave off light enough for the two men to pass into the bedroom, where Edwold Krier, his face covered by a Granbretanian "night mask" of gauze, slept the sleep of the just.

This time Elric used what he called "low sorcery" to keep Sir Edwold sleeping. Next he removed the man's mask to reveal a small, sharp face, more like a common rodent's than an aggressive wolf's. The flesh was almost repulsively pallid, kept as it had been from normal sunlight. The brown, sightless eyes, which Elric prised open, were vacant, bovine. The fleshy lips were slack, the teeth dull, yellowed. Elric smiled at a small joke Yaroslaf Stredic made regarding the true nature of the wolf.

Then, with a warning to his companion to step away, Elric began his spell.

Stredic looked on in some fear as the albino's head fell back and his long, milk-white hair streamed out from his head in an invisible wind. Alien words poured from his pale lips, and his crimson eyes blazed with impossible fires. His voice rose and fell, creating mountains and valleys of sound. The bedchamber began to stir with shadows half-seen in the flickering light. Stredic felt the movements of chill breezes upon his flesh, so that he was tempted to back out of the room and seek cover. But Elric had reassured him that he would come to no harm, so he watched in fascination as Elric's own face writhed and warped and his red eyes slowly changed to the colour of Edwold Krier's. When he next turned and spoke to the Wäld, it was in the voice and accents of the prone Seneschal.

Then Elric stretched out his hand and touched the sleeping man's arm. Slowly he leached all the colour out of Edwold Krier's flesh and took it for himself. When his skin was identical in colour to the governor's, and the governor's pale as his own, he next went to a specially constructed stand at the head of the bed and removed the great wolf mask, raising it up and settling it down over his own head.

"It fits. I'll need no spell to change its size." His voice was muffled by the helmet. He took it off again and set it back on its stand.

Yaroslaf Stredic noticed how strange Elric's long, handsome skull looked with its brown eyes and darker skin, but he was even more disturbed by what appeared to be Krier's bloodless corpse lying on the bed.

"Now, said Elric, "as soon as we have moved this pale object to my room, set certain checks on his memory and left a few misleading clues, we ride for Mirenburg, you and I!"

Yaroslaf Stredic looked with barely controlled horror at Elric as the Melnibonéan flung up his naked head and howled with laughter.

8

Protector Olin Desleur, Knight Commander of the Order of the Wolverine, Governor of the City of Mirenburg, hero of the Battle of Snodgart, rose from his great bed of furs and silks, naked in all his manly glory, a thin helmet of gold and platinum snarling on his shoulders, giving him the appearance of a waking werewolf. He stretched and yawned. His boy slaves still lay sleeping in the bed. He ignored them as women came forward to bathe him with hot towels. He felt relaxed and sated, having enjoyed a night in which two of his boys had met their deaths pleasuring him. Their bodies had already been removed. Now he let the women bring his day mask, its massive jewelled helm thick with sharp silver teeth in a grinning muzzle of dark platinum, and place it over his head skilfully, on pain of death, as they slipped his night mask from beneath the more substantial one in such a way that his face was not glimpsed even for a moment. He then strolled onto his balcony to breakfast while Mirenburg began to move about her business.

Olin Desleur was reasonably content with what he was inclined to call his exile from the Court of Londra, where ancient King Huon, artificially kept alive in a globe of fluid, schemed further conquest with his favourite, Baron Meliadus of Kroiden, Grand Master of the Wolf, conqueror of Kamarg. While Mirenburg could be boring, and he missed his native fells, there was a certain security in being absent from the intrigues of the Court.

At Court one could die suddenly and in great humiliation merely for taking half a step in the wrong direction or being overheard insulting the wrong person. With all Europe under the imperial flag, the courtiers took to complicated scheming, unwilling, at least yet, to turn their warlike attention to Amarehk or Asiacommunista, whose alien inhabitants were said to be almost as powerful as the Dark Empire and must surely be the next threat to be averted by striking them before the empire itself was struck. But for now no-one considered it politic to begin much further expansion until the empire was at peace or, at least, thoroughly under Huon and Meliadus's heels.

The Protector of Mirenburg found the province relatively easy to govern, for it was used to conquerors and had only known brief intervals of independence when it had not had to accommodate them. A few exemplary executions, one or two public torturings a week, and the population proved considerably more malleable than some of the other provinces which had fallen under his protection in the course of a successful career. Köln, for example. Then there had been Kamarg, which had proved so ungovernable under its rebellious Countess Yisselda, daughter of the empire's great enemy, Count Brass, that there had been nothing for it but to deport the entire population to the Afrikaanish mines and install more agreeable Muskovites (always grateful for a little warmth) in their place. The countess herself had come under the eye of the great Meliadus, who had made her a ward, so it was rumoured, of Flana, with whom he was said to keep an exceptionally perverse liaison. But then it was rumoured that Yisselda of Brass had recently escaped and gone to join her lover with some miscellaneous bunch of raggle-taggle insurgents. Some even believed that her father, though wounded, still lived.

Olin Desleur occasionally missed his wild West Thirding, where he had grown up in the picturesque town of Beury. He was used to hills which shone like copper in the autumn sun, and limestone pavements that formed natural causeways, glinting silver against the summer green. He loved the mingling of snow with the smell of spring at equinox. One day he intended to retire there, to his promised estates, with nothing but a few favourite boys for company.

"And perhaps a little girl or two," he murmured aloud as he looked up from his cheese, "to add variety."

But he would have to earn the privilege first, and that meant keeping the peace in Mirenburg and the province of which it was the capital. A backwater, maybe, but a fairly strategic backwater. They were now producing the majority of the empire's most advanced war machines.

A sound, half-heard, drew his attention away from his morning meal. From where he sat on a high balcony of what had once been the prince's palace, he could see the city's gates opened for the morning traffic. People and vehicles of all kinds came and went through those gates. His was a rich little fiefdom, he thought with some satisfaction. He watched it all, relishing all the marvellous and quaint sights, from the great steam-powered battle-engines of the empire to the peasants' donkeys. But this morning his eyes were attracted to a party just passing through the gates, the early sunshine glancing off their armour and masks.

Meliadus? was his first thought, voiced to no-one. But while the banner was that of the Order of the Wolf, the entourage was far too small. The secondary flags announced the little group as belonging to his provincial governor, Sir Edwold Krier, a man for whom he had little respect but who was far too well connected to be ignored. After all, they were at St Remus's together. Members of the same club, to this day. Immediately he was on his feet, calling for his ceremonial armour, his helm of state.

As he prepared to greet his countryman, a guard in the mask of his Wolverine Order brought him news that two emissaries had arrived that night by ornithopter and had landed in the east field, having flown all the way from Londra. The emissaries carried letters from the capital. Two Germanians, apparently, in the employ of Baron Meliadus. They were to be treated as honoured guests.

The protector gave orders that the emissaries be entertained in the guest hall while he went first to greet Sir Edwold Krier and bid him welcome. Protocol gave more or less equal status to both parties. His fellow countryman had best be dealt with first, however, since it was likely he was here on some business of the province. It was unusual for him to come to the capital on personal business. He assumed, since Meliadus's fellow Wolf had sent no message, there must be some urgency. Or could there be something the matter with the heliograph? The Dark Empire was as proud of her communications systems as she was of her battle vessels. Had some heliographer been drinking at his vanes, or a post or two blown up by terrorists? His captain of engineers would be reporting to him on the matter, no doubt.

Thus, with his own entourage and guards, the Lord Protector of Mirenburg was waiting when the wolf masks came into the courtyard of the great castle, and Sir Edwold Krier's Wäldish servant helped his master from his saddle, taking his banner and following at a respectful distance as he clanked up the steps to give the salute.

"Good morning, Sir Edwold. We are honoured to receive you at the capital. Your business, we take it, is of great importance to the empire."

"Of greatest importance, my lord. You are gracious to receive me thus at such short notice."

"I take it the heliograph is down again for some reason?"

"Sadly, yes, my lord. Three attempts we made to repair it, and even put a new man in. Then the attacks spread to other stations. My warriors are stretched thin, Lord Olin Desleur. But the rest I must discuss with you in private."

"So you shall. Have you breakfasted?"

Sir Edwold said he had eaten at dawn before breaking camp. Once they were together in Lord Olin Desleur's wonderful library, its windows looking out into the gardens of the palace with its ornamental lake and fountains, the spines of the books, dark reds, blues and greens, reflecting the predominant colours of his flowers outside, Olin Desleur's tone turned from one of public courtesy to one of private confidence. He personally shut the door and asked Sir Edwold what was the urgency of such an untimely visit when he, Lord Olin, was needed to entertain visiting dignitaries with letters from Quay Savoy in Londra.

Sir Edwold told him what he knew of the planned uprising.

Olin Desleur turned his back to his books and stared out over the lake. "How did this information come to you, Sir Edwold?"

"I had a visitor a few days ago. An odd fellow, belonging to a race I never encountered before. He was set upon by brigands to the north of us and, while in their power, had heard that a force of men was being raised to attack first our outlying defences and then Mirenburg herself. It seemed to me that it was my duty to tell you of the danger and perhaps go on to Londra by the speediest route to beg Meliadus for more troops."

Lord Olin gave this some thought. First he had to consider the tranquillity of the province and how best to maintain it. If he failed in these duties he would be humiliated, recalled to Londra, dismissed from his Order, even tortured and killed. If, however, he allowed Sir Edwold to take the news to Londra, he would not be able to present his case, and Sir Edwold could depict him in an unfavourable light if he so chose. He was in a quandary.

"What became of your informant?"

"By now, Lord Protector, he has probably died of his wounds. But I had every reason to believe he spoke truth. There have been rumours of a rebellion in the province for some while, as you will of course know."

"Quite so." Lord Olin had not heard a single rumour, but it would not do to reveal this to Sir Edwold.

"Is there an ornithopter ready, my lord? I believe I should go at once to tell the King-Emperor of our need for more troops here."

"Best that I carry the news. They will listen to me more readily."

"But would they not wish to hear the news first hand—?"

"It will carry more authority if I give it."

"If you say so, my lord." The wolf mask bowed in agreement and some disappointment. "I thought perhaps that your responsibilities here . . ."

"You will have to carry that burden, Sir Edwold, while I warn Londra. I'll make you deputy protector in my absence."

"You do me great honour, my lord." There was still a hint of disappointment in Sir Edwold's voice.

"It will be your duty to gather intelligence and send spies abroad, to watch for any danger."

"Of course, Lord Protector."

Now Lord Olin Desleur recalled the two Germanians who awaited an audience in the antechamber. Politely he took his leave of the governor and hurried through the banner-draped galleries to the room where the two men waited. Normally he would have received them in his great hall, but he needed to know as privately as possible if their visit concerned the potential rebellion. He must have as few available ears listening as possible.

He soon looked with barely concealed disgust upon the naked face of one of the emissaries. The other creature at least had had the grace to mask.

The better-mannered of the pair was huge, heavy and broad-shouldered, much like Baron Meliadus in physique. He wore simple travelling clothes, his homespun britches tucked into riding boots of plain leather. His empty scabbard showed that he had left his sword with the guards. His cloak was pushed back over his shoulders. He carried a broad-brimmed "Bremen" hat in his hand, and his face was covered by a plain mesh mask.

The man's companion was slighter in build and had deep-set black eyes in a gaunt, skull-like face which, to be fair, might have been mistaken for a mask.

He was dressed all in black and also carried a broad-brimmed hat. He looked more like the big man's clerk than his squire, thought Lord Olin. They rose and bowed to him as he entered the room, averting his eyes from the bare-faced man and addressing the other.

"Forgive us, Lord Protector. We are Germanians serving the Protector of Munchein and are searching for an individual who offers the empire great harm. We have been commissioned to seek her out and capture her. There is some understanding that she has sought help in Mirenburg and might be found living amongst your workers in the manufacturing district."

"Unlikely," mused Lord Olin, his busy hands behind his back. He felt just a little less confident about the situation. "Those workers are handpicked. Each of them has more than one reason to be loyal to the empire. We depend upon them. The empire's most crucial work is done here in Mirenburg. Our very latest machines are being built and tested here. The fastest ornithopters, the most effective battlecraft. I have made this province the armoury of the empire! We cannot, therefore, afford to let a single sweeper on the factory floor be in any way disloyal."

"Which is why we are here, Lord Olin," intoned the maskless one. "Mirenburg, as you rightly say, is critical to the whole power of the empire. Because of your efficiency and the need to locate a manufacturing zone near the centre of the empire rather than at the edge, this city is now the *most important* to the empire save for *Londra herself.*"

Lord Olin's strut became at once less spontaneous and more emphatic as he crossed towards the window to look up the long drive which led from the ceremonial doors below him on the ground floor. "I think the peace of the empire has come to depend upon us here in Mirenburg," he said proudly. "And be assured, gentlemen, we shall continue to construct machines at the same rapid rate. Already 'Made in Mirenburg' is stamped on the barrels of our latest flame cannon, on the bellies of our mechanical rhinoceri and on the wing levers of our fastest, deadliest ornithopters. We also produce rapid-fire gas projectors and explosives." This, he told himself, was what he had to lose if he failed to keep the King-Emperor's good will. His success here would give him an opportunity to rule an entire nation within the empire, enabling him to build up enough power to secure his family from the most arbitrary of King Huon's decisions. And then, he thought, there was his retirement. If he did especially well, some less fortunate aristocrat would be banished from his Lakeland estates, and those lands renamed as Lord Olin's. Olin of Grasmere, he thought. That would be sweet, especially if he could choose which of his rivals to oust.

"You think we are especially in danger here?" Lord Olin asked. "Because others will soon begin to realise what an important centre of the empire Mirenburg is?"

"That is what is to be feared," agreed the naked one. His companion growled something about "focus of attack" and "strategies of terrorism."

"Well, as it happens, I take to the air this very morning. I go to Londra to speak to the King-Emperor and ask him for more troops. Your report will give substance to my own request."

"You have heard nothing of a child, then?"

"Nothing. What is she? Some sort of oracle?"

"Just a little girl," said the masked one, "but of ancient blood. Could we ask you, my lord, to put soldiers at our disposal while you go to Londra? They will serve the double purpose of allowing us to continue our search for the traitors and discover the whereabouts of the child, as the King-Emperor commissioned us to do. Meanwhile, we have other duties, as these papers will show."

The lord protector unrolled official scrolls and broke the seals off letters of introduction. The two Germanians were Gaynor von Minct and Johannes Klosterheim, loyal servants of the empire. The crucial message from the Quay Savoy, headquarters of his nation's secret service, suggested that some kind of cult had developed, apparently around the defeated Duke of Köln and his Kamargian allies. Those insurgents should have been destroyed when ornithopters dropped powerful bombs on Castle Brass in the final battle, when Meliadus had brought his troops against Hawkmoon. With a certain aid from the sorcerer-scientists of Granbretan, Meliadus had decisively defeated them, claiming all Europe, from Erin to Muskovia, from Scandia to Turkia, as the empire's.

"This child holds a secret which could lead us to these rebels," said the naked one called Klosterheim. "The girl," added the masked Gaynor, "is related to a hero these people believe can defeat the empire."

At this Lord Olin chuckled. While rebellions might occasionally disrupt the empire's tranquillity, the idea of Granbretan knowing defeat was clearly ludicrous. They were the most powerful nation on Earth. Nonetheless he took their warnings seriously. "I will inform my deputy and tell him to give you all possible help in tracing this child," he promised. "I have pressing business which takes me to Londra. The child hides in the factory district, you say?"

"So it's thought, my lord."

"Well, do what you must. But do not slow down production. If you do, it will be you who will take responsibility before the King-Emperor."

"We understand, my lord."

"No disruption. I will emphasise that to my deputy, Sir Edwold Krier. You will report directly to him. I will speak to King Huon about you. He will—"

"This business is secret, my lord. It concerns the Quay Savoy."

"Of course. Nothing public. There is much to be concerned about. In the last nine months we have increased our ornithopter and battle-engine production and trained operators for them. We have modified the Brazilian system, and our steam engines are now considerably more efficient. We have one of our Granbretanian scientists working on a powerful bomb. These factories are the most advanced in the world. We are also developing an aerial battle cruiser—a flying ironclad—together with new guns. These models will be fully steam-powered and considerably more accurate at long range. Mirenburg's factories have become the model for others which will spring up all over the empire as our might spreads. Once our new ships take to the air, no rebel will dare defy us. And the rest of the world shall tremble at the appearance of our fleets in their skies."

"Perhaps the child is part of a plot to sabotage these factories, great lord," suggested the gaunt Klosterheim.

Lord Olin found the naked man's opinion unwelcome and ignored it, addressing the other, Gaynor of Munchein. "I have business to attend to. My deputy will give you the assistance you need."

And with that he swept from the room. There was much to prepare. It would, he decided, be politic not to be in Mirenburg when any rebellion occurred. His garrison would easily put it down, but it would prove his point and show that without his controlling hand, Mirenburg's factories were in danger. Also, Sir Edwold could be blamed for any failures. Meanwhile he would be gathering a stronger force, bound to defeat the rebellion and thus gaining him credit for success.

When he had gone, the two Germanians exchanged looks of triumph. Their story was believed. They had the run of the city as well as the governor's assistance in hunting down the dreamthief's little granddaughter, Oonagh von Bek. It would be, they were sure, but a matter of time before the girl and her elusive kinsman were within their power. Then they could perform the final bloody deed, which must be completed if the power they sought was to come into their hands. The child's life was the key to control of the multiverse. To eternity.

The two old allies, who had given up so much of themselves to avert the fate they so feared, were determined that whatever threatened their souls now should never threaten them again.

9

Elric was amused by Yaroslaf Stredic's astonishment at the success of his plan. Sir Edwold Krier remained entranced in his own castle, his guards sent upon errands into the woods. He could wander where he liked but had been robbed of all his masks and most of his clothes, as well as his memory and his identity. And now Lord Olin had taken Elric's bait. He had left by the latest and swiftest ornithopter, fresh from his own factories, for Londra. He had placed his supposed governor in control of the city. Elric had plenty of time to find his great-granddaughter without interference.

"We'll have every available guard looking for her," said Elric. His helmet off, his witch-colouring remained intact. He bit into a piece of fruit and looked out over the town. To the east was the smoke and sparks of great chimneys, showing the location of the manufacturing district. To the west rose the domes and sloping roofs of covered markets, where traders displayed their wares. To the north were the steeples of places of worship, where the people of Mirenburg were allowed to confer with any strange gods as long as King Huon the Immortal commanded a shrine dedicated to him and the priests praised him in their prayers. King Huon was not one to deny the conquered their comforting abstractions.

The people of Mirenburg were not especially devout, but more people now attended the temples than before the conquest. So many spies were among the priests, priestesses and congregations that it was well known the temples were decidedly not places of secret sedition. The most radical hopeful could not have said that Mirenburg seethed. Indeed, superficially, Mirenburg was a city which, with the deaths and disappearances of its ancient families, had pragmatically accepted its return to provincial status under the empire. Even the kulaks, the landed peasants of the rural communities, seemed to have accepted Londra's rule with a certain philosophical air. Periodically their country was conquered. They judged their conquerors more on the levels of taxes they charged than any other criterion. Granbretan had, in fact, eased taxes a little in the past year. They were still high, of course, and the laws still strict, but a certain security prevailed within those parameters. As is true the world over, the average kulak preferred authoritarian stability to the responsibility of freedom. Even when they had the opportunity to vote, most of those farmers and villagers and tradesmen preferred bellicose displays of strength rather than representation and intelligence in their leaders. Not so the industrial workers, however, who shunned the temples and spoke cryptically among themselves, disguising their outrage and anger as a matter of honour.

Stredic told Elric that to the north lay the wealthier suburbs, whose inhabitants liked to complain about Londra but would only support an uprising if one was thrust upon them. Elric was not particularly interested, however, in rebellion, in spite of what he had told the lord protector. If some action of his helped overturn Mirenburg's conquerors, he would not be distressed, but his only real interest was to rescue Oonagh and leave. If Yaroslaf Stredic chose to use his moment to organise resistance, so much the better. Confusion would help him get her clear. It had cost him much exhausting sorcery to find her, and it would not be long before he began to run out of the much needed serum he had purchased from an apothecary in Brookgate, for a large amount of gold, shortly before embarking upon this expedition.

"We'll initiate an intensive search," he informed his companion. "And we'll help lead it ourselves. The first man to find her will be well rewarded, if not in money, then in whatever else he decides. But we do not have limitless time. Soon the real Sir Edwold must wake from his trance and begin to remember at least a little of who he is, while Lord Olin could return with specific orders from Londra—orders which might not suit our plans."

Yaroslaf Stredic saw the sense of this. He meant to take advantage of every hour his strange new ally had bought him. He was interested in the factories. He knew that the quietly angry slave workers were his most likely recruits. He could also recruit the pilots and many of the auxiliaries to his cause. His planned rebellion would have men to fly the machines and mechanics to maintain them. He coveted the ordnance as much as he wanted to free the workers. It had been these war-engines that had achieved Granbretan's conquests, not the unquestioned ferocity of her commanders, or their lust for land and resources.

The same day that Lord Olin left for Londra, Elric of Melniboné, disguised by the helm stolen from the real Edwold Krier, demanded a marshalling of the city's entire garrison in the sprawling Square of the Salt Traders. In ringing tones he informed the men of their duty.

"A great plot is being hatched beyond the mountains. Some of the intriguers are already here, amongst us. These terrorists and rebels will do all they can to distract us from the nobility of our crusade. They hate us for the very security and freedom we enjoy. They live for strife, while we serve the forces of serenity. They are evil creatures who must be rooted out and destroyed. But we must not kill them. Any suspects must be taken to the dungeons of the Oranesians, the St-Maria-and-St-Maria, and interrogated by my handpicked investigators. They will soon give us the information we seek. Meanwhile, be alert for the child of whom I spoke. She must not be harmed. She must be brought to me at once, no matter what the time or what else is told to you."

"And what of the youth, my lord?" one captain wished to know.

"Youth?"

"The Germanians wish us to seek and capture a youth as well. A young albino. They were clear on the matter. If any harm befalls him, or should he escape, those responsible will be publicly tortured and killed."

"The Germanians?" He had yet to meet these other newcomers. "It seems they exceed their orders, captain. But if an albino youth is found, you must let me know and bring him to me. Under no circumstances is he to be given up to them. They exceed their authority!"

On dismissal the guards broke up into small groups, talking among themselves. Their tone was puzzled, even slightly confused. But they had a feeling in their blood that great events were in preparation and that they would be involved in some historic moment.

Watching this from their apartments in the nearby Martyr's Tower, the two "Germanians," Gaynor von Minct and Klosterheim, glowered in rage. What right had this provincial upstart to countermand their orders when, only an hour before, they had been congratulating themselves on the powerful help they had so easily secured with documents obtained by the expenditure of a few shillings in the forger's art and the aid of certain powerful plotters in Londra? The girl and the youth had been as good as in their hands! Once the children were in the prison of St-Maria-and-St-Maria (the feared Oranesians), it would have been relatively easy to get them out and carry them off to their ultimate destination. Now this fool had thwarted them!

"It seems we chose a poor moment for our little charade," announced Gaynor, pouring a beaker of fresh wine.

And Herr Klosterheim, nodding slowly, permitted himself a small grimace.

The search of the factory district began the next morning. Soldiers of the Wolverine, Dog and Lynx clans went from tenement to tenement rounding up every girl who remotely fitted Oonagh's description, yet she could not be found. Mothers wailed and fathers groaned as their children were ripped from their arms and inspected. Cupboards were smashed open, and anything hidden in them not a girl-child was discarded, ignored. Floorboards were lifted, lofts were combed and basements disrupted. Overseen by their grim leaders, the soldiers were unsubtle in their methods. Of course, the guards did not dare to harm any of the girls. They had been warned how they would die if a drop of Oonagh's blood was spilled. At the end of five days, however, they were unable to bring the deputy protector any news.

Meanwhile the frustrated Germanians conducted their own secret searches and failed to be granted an audience with Sir Edwold, who seemed singularly reluctant to see them. They were beginning to feel suspicious of this deputy commander.

Only when Gaynor, unable to restrain himself, demanded that a soldier hand over some poor, shivering blonde-headed girl to him, did Sir Edwold's captain-of-the-day challenge him and, in exasperation, put both Germanians under guard. Elric, concerned they might recognise him by his own, slowly returning voice, was forced to confront them as they marched arrogantly into the interrogation chamber, surrounded by a detachment of city soldiery and brandishing their documents.

Elric disguised his voice as best he could. He sat well back in his great chair, observing them through the eye slits of his mask, his gloved, beringed hands tapping on the arms as if in impatience.

"What's this? Treachery?" he growled.

Hearing him, Gaynor frowned for a moment, and Elric feared he would be discovered. Then von Minct spoke levelly, a note of interrogation colouring his demands.

"My lord protector, we carry letters from the Quay Savoy, which serves the emperor directly in all matters of homeland and overseas security. In these letters you are requested"—he spoke with growing emphasis—"nay, *commanded*—to give us all aid we request in this matter. The children whom your soldiers seek are the same as those we came to find. They are crucial to our imperial security, yet your men seem positively to be hampering us. I would remind you, sir, that you challenge the emperor himself!"

"*Commanded?*" Elric feigned anger. He was fairly certain that the documents could not be genuine. Why would Huon or his diplomatic police send these two, who had no credentials as far as he knew? "*Commanded?*" He made as if to give orders to his men. He was acting out a dangerous charade, countering a similar attempt by von Minct and Klosterheim, who might also be play-acting.

Klosterheim, always more of a natural diplomat, stepped between them. "I assure you, my lord, that we acknowledge your station and responsibilities. We have no intention—"

"Show me those documents!" Elric saw a glint of surprise in Klosterheim's deep-set eyes. Had the Puritan recognised him? Discovery at this stage would be extremely inconvenient . . .

"They are in our apartments, my lord."

"Very well! Take these men to the St-Maria-and-St-Maria," Elric ordered. "And search their rooms for these documents. Our emperor would be seriously angered if we did not show due caution in this matter. Then bring the documents to me and I will inspect them!"

Gaynor von Minct bellowed a refusal, but Klosterheim quickly calmed him, turning to Elric. "We have no quarrel in this matter, my lord protector. You will see that the documents are genuine. We both seek to protect the security of the empire . . ."

"Let us hope so, Herr Klosterheim." Again Elric noted a flash of suspicion in the Puritan's eyes as he half-recognised the albino's voice. He fell back silently into his chair while the guards marched the men away. He had gained a little time for himself, but he could not be sure how much longer he could maintain this untypical masquerade.

Now Lord Olin neared Londra. He flew in one of the new, faster ornithopters, fashioned in the likeness of a great dragon, its green, red, blue and black metallic wings clashing, powered by compact, sophisticated steam turbines spreading grey smoke in the vehicle's wake. The pilot, of the Order of the Crow, circled the great machine over Kroiden Field, as much to display it as to find a landing space. From there a massive steam tram, running on bright steel rails, took Lord Olin to the capital. Londra, with her brooding basalt buildings fashioned in the likenesses of beasts and grotesque men, was where the fiercely belligerent Baron Meliadus, King Huon's chancellor, awaited him.

From Kroiden it was already possible to see signs of the capital, the dark green fog which swirled in the sky above the glassy towers reflecting the gloomy fires of Londra, where sorcery and science mingled uneasily, drawn from the half-forgotten arts of the Tragic Millennium, when madness and folly had combined to bring the whole Earth close to destruction.

Now Londra's natural philosophers, her alchemists and masters of learning, all wished to restore the lost arts and discover new ones. Night and day her manufactories poured out their unlikely creations, moulded metal and constructions of wood and precious gems, fearsome vehicles, war-engines, suits of armour, flame lances, all fashioned in grotesque, baroque shops reflecting the inspired insanity of her masked aristocrats.

Lord Olin, who was familiar with the capital and the Court, who had never grown fully used to either, realised, with a pang of anger, how he regretted being posted so far from home. Would he ever know the peace of his native hills again? What was it that drove him to develop his addiction to cruelty, which he had never known before coming here to be trained in the realities of Dark Empire administration?

He was already regretting his habit of intrigue, which had brought him here. He had no love for Baron Meliadus, for Lady Flana (King Huon's cousin), for Taragorm, Master of the Palace of Time, or for Taragorm's scheming colleague Baron Bous-Junge of Osfoud, Commander of the Order of the Snake, and Londra's chief scientist. He suspected them of treachery but had no proof. And though he would not breathe this to his own shadow, he was actually disgusted by ancient King Huon, who spoke with a stolen voice, who lived off stolen energy, a wizened homunculus maintaining himself in a sphere of life-giving liquid, his long, insectile tongue serving him as hands, his sole desire to preserve his own life, even if whole continents were sucked of their vitality for the purpose.

Yet here he was again, thought Lord Olin, driven by some survival mechanism as warped as those he despised, behaving like any other fearful courtier and now, as it dawned on him how he was acting, hating himself for it.

As the tall ceremonial tram, all black steel and ornamental chrome as befitted his station, bore him rapidly towards the city, Lord Olin seriously considered turning back. But there was no protocol which allowed it. No-one would know how to obey him. The tram could not stop to be repositioned until it reached the Londra terminal known as Blare-Bragg-Bray Station, where ceremonial guards no doubt waited to receive him. He was arriving in state, in all the honour and ceremony Granbretan could bestow upon her great nobles.

The tram was driven by a man in the elaborate helm of the Order of the Ox, whose members traditionally took the levers of such transports. On either side, on upper and lower decks, on seats of brass and polished oak, sat an honour guard drawn from the Order of the Dog and his own client clan, the Order of the Wolverine. These men had always supplied the ceremonial soldiery protecting the great and the good of Granbretan. Their long-snouted masks gave the assurance of loyalty and resilient steadfastness. Red bronze and copper glittered on their armour—ten warriors, a drummer boy, three standard-bearers carrying the flags of their Orders, the imperial banner of Granbretan and Lord Olin's own quartered standard, showing his House, his Order, his position and his honours.

Seated across from Olin was one of King Huon's own Seneschals, in green iron and the expressionless mask of the Order of the Mantis. To behave eccentrically now, thought Lord Olin, would be to sentence himself to death. He had no choice, if he wished to survive, but to continue into the city, to march through the great palace and the vast doors of King Huon's throne room, and then to stride in full honour through a hall from which hung the flags of five hundred provinces, once sovereign nations, with guards drawn from all but the lowliest aristocratic families lining the long approach. There he must prostrate himself before the great Throne Globe, that huge sphere of amniotic fluids which hung overhead, and wait until it pleased King Huon to receive him.

Sometimes even Baron Meliadus must wait thus for an hour or more before the King-Emperor deigned to reveal himself, a yellowed embryo with a long, flicking tongue with which it operated the controls of its globe.

This morning, however, Lord Olin did not need patience. The globe came to life almost immediately. The mellifluous voice of a god spoke to him.

"Well, my lord viscount, what news of Mirenburg, that productive jewel in our skull of state?"

"I am honoured, great King, to oversee such a massive achievement. I am here to assure you, as always, of my life and loyalty. Before you beats a devoted heart concerned only with your well-being and the well-being of our great nation, which are one and the same. I came because my underlings brought me rumours of something which has the potential to threaten the tranquillity of your realm. I would not bother you, sire, of course, had not you ordered me to report directly to you and not to the noble Baron Meliadus, Your Majesty's greatest and most faithful steward . . ."

"Baron Meliadus is not at Court. He pursues certain errands on my behalf. You can save some of your flummery, Lord Olin."

"Thank you, great King-Emperor."

"You have proven yourself a conscientious servant, Lord Olin, and I have no reason to believe you would waste our time . . . ?"

"I would rather kill myself, great King."

"So you had best make haste and tell me why you need more soldiers, for no doubt that is why you are here."

"A planned rebellion, sire. For all I know, it will not occur. The rebels might lose their resolve; we might arrest their leaders; their numbers might dwindle; the moon might not be in the correct corner of the quadrant; their wives might—"

"Yes, yes, Viscount Olin. We are aware of all the factors involved. But it surprises us that the province should offer defiance. Are we not generous to it, compared to our dealings with Germania or Transylvania, for instance?"

"Very generous, great King. Wäldenstein is a model province, supplying us with many of the raw materials we need, as well as sturdy workers. That is why Mirenburg was chosen to be the site of our most advanced manufactories. Her inhabitants enjoy privileged tax status close to that of our own people here in Londra. In the past five years she has returned splendid harvests, and other revenues have been raised through the sale and trade of her women, who are famously fair and strong, and of her glassware and her china. Her kulaks know rare contentment and would seem the last to offer us trouble. Yet my provincial governor warns me a rebellion is already begun, that a larger uprising against our benign authority could take place at any moment, with armies coming from the East, perhaps from Asiacommunista. Our heliographs have been attacked and destroyed. I have my spies abroad, of course. However, I thought it wise to report this directly to Your Majesty, to beg for more soldiers and war-engines that we might snuff out this rebellion before it can inflame more of our territories. Examples must be made."

The arrogant, glittering eyes stared intently down at Lord Olin. "Examples, yes. Wäldenstein is so placed as to be central to our future defence plans. We would not want our armies tied down there while forces from Asiacommunista attack some weaker flank."

"Your Majesty's knowledge of strategy is, as always, acute."

"This is not the only disruption to our realm at present. Indeed, we begin to suspect a concerted plan. Baron Meliadus investigates this possibility elsewhere. And others of Granbretan's finest turn their complex minds to such a problem. How did your man grow aware of this plot?"

"A visitor, great King-Emperor, who was waylaid in the Bulgar Mountains. The bandits let slip they would soon be helping in some uprising against us."

"We shall consider your request for troops, Lord Olin, but we must remind you that it is your duty to protect our manufactories at all costs. Even the most minor of failures will carry severe penalties."

"I understand, sire. Mirenburg has become a key city in the defence of the empire . . ."

"Indeed she has. You are a born manager, Lord Olin. You must tell your King-Emperor all your news. What have you heard, for instance, of the Silverskin?"

"The name is unfamiliar to me, great King-Emperor."

"Aha. And what, perhaps, of the Runestaff?"

"The Runestaff, my lord. I—I thought our lord protector had care of it."

"The thing's not what we thought it was. We held a gorgeous fake. Few are familiar with the actual artefact. We hallow it, respect it, even pray to it and swear oaths upon it, yet who truly knows its real function or even its preferred shape? Some do not believe it takes the form of a staff at all. Instead, it resembles a beautiful, golden cup or a block of dark green stone, a giant emerald, some say. So, Lord Olin? Any news of it?"

"I have heard nothing at all, my lord."

"You had visitors from Germania, eh?"

"Indeed, sire. Sent by the Quay Savoy. With letters bearing your own seal. But I thought you had given orders for no mention of that to be made here . . ."

"Fool, those were forgeries!" The voice was like a snake's sudden hiss of warning. "We suspect traitors at Court and have been following them. They, too, I'd guess, seek the Runestaff. Did you not have their luggage and clothing secretly searched? Were they not drugged and their bodies inspected? Have you all become such sentimentalists in Mirenburg, my lord, that you pamper these naked savages as if they were a favourite dog?"

"Great King, the scrolls bore the Quay Savoy's unbroken seals of office!"

"Even so, Lord Olin."

"I beseech your forgiveness, my lord." Lord Olin still lay visor-down upon the flagstones. He could not abase himself any further without breaking his own bones, or so it seemed.

"We would suggest, Lord Olin, that when you return to Mirenburg, you be a little more rigorous in your dealings with barbarians and such. You yourself have said how important the city is to our security and tranquillity."

"I will return at once and see to it, sire."

"Not at once, Lord Olin." There was a terrible kind of happiness boiling at the back of King Huon's strangely reptilian eyes. "You can only hope your deputy is more suspicious than you are! I want you to confer with Baron Brun of Dunninstrit, and before that with Baron Bous-Junge of Osfoud. They will ask you specific questions. Granbretan will show her gratitude for your speedy decision in bringing your news directly to us. Let us hope you are first strong enough to pay the price for your lapses of intelligence."

An onlooker would have sworn how at that moment Lord Olin merged with the flagstones. From his great mask helm, there came what might have been a muffled weeping.

As the prehensile tongue flicked out, slowly the Throne Globe dimmed until only those awful eyes were visible. Then all was swirling darkness and silence.

After some moments, when nothing had happened, Lord Olin rose. There was something incongruous in the snarling wolverine head which topped that slumped and defeated body as it got to its feet and walked unsteadily down the long hall towards the distant doors. Through them he was directed to another antechamber and another, conscious of the eye of every courtier upon him. Finally he stood in a chamber fashioned of obsidian warped to resemble human figures and symbolic creatures from Granbretan's most distant past.

A servant in the mask and livery of the Order of the Snake signalled to him. With a deep bow the servant led the way to the newly installed moving pavement, which carried them rapidly through miles of palace and many levels of offices until they reached Baron Bous-Junge's apartments, which had an unsavoury reputation even in Londra. From inside came screams of such a timbre and pitch that even Granbretan's most jaded courtiers, used to the variety of shrieks and groans achieved through uniquely extracted pain, found them exciting.

On shaking legs, with dry mouth and stinging eyes, Lord Olin dared not pause. He must appear to go willingly to whatever fate Lord Huon had decreed, for if he did not, he would suffer a worse punishment. If he took his punishment as was expected, he might yet live to fulfil his ambitions of a peaceful retirement.

The smell coming from the baron's quarters, a mixture of alluring scents and the most disagreeable stinks, was enough to ensure that most men and women gave the place a wide berth. The main concentration of gases emanated from a low, squat doorway through which the servant led him.

Baron Bous-Junge, leaving his bench, his tubes and retorts, greeted Lord Olin warmly. The cobra mask nodded on Bous-Junge's shoulders, and he moved as if the weight of all his ceremony slowed him down.

"My Lord Olin, you honour me. I hear you came to report trouble in your province."

Lord Olin stammered his greetings in return. "A—a—rumour, 'tis all, my lord baron. We shall sssee what develops anon . . . mmmm . . ."

As was traditional in Londra, no mention was made of the punishment, the horrible public humiliation, Lord Olin would soon be suffering.

Baron Bous-Junge took Lord Olin by the arm and steered him through what seemed like miles of benches and equipment, where his specially trained slaves worked, many of them disfigured by chemicals or other forces, some of them probably not even human.

"Let us hope it doesn't have anything to do with this troubling rumour concerning the Runestaff and the men who seek to discover its ancient resting place," murmured Bous-Junge.

But Lord Olin did not want to know anything more than he knew already. He wondered: if he had sent Sir Edwold to Londra, might he have been spared his coming torture? He was suffering complex regrets.

"Many do not believe there is such a thing as the Runestaff," continued Bous-Junge conversationally as they left his laboratories and moved into the rather shabby and neglected luxury of his living apartments. "Even though I search for it, sometimes I myself am inclined to believe it doesn't exist. I have studied all the legends concerning it." Baron Bous-Junge's sinister green mask tipped to one side. Behind it the hard, old eyes seemed amused. "But it is a troubling coincidence that we should hear all those rumours from different sources. The empire stands for Law, for Balance, for the power of justice and equity. Our empire is represented by such symbols as the Runestaff. There is always a certain power invested in these symbols. Could we ourselves have willed the Runestaff into existence, out of sheer need?"

"Indeed, indeed, indeed," babbled Lord Olin, his mind on his future.

"After all, our own religion is a matter of ritual and tradition, little else." An almost inaudible hiss of words, and Lord Olin, already trapped, was quick to sense further snares. "We worship our immortal King-Emperor, Baron Bous-Junge!"

"Of course we do, Lord Olin. Have you ever sworn an oath on the Runestaff?"

Lord Olin, within his armour, was like a terrified rat in a cage. "Oath? No? Yes! No . . . No, of course not—too—too powerful . . ."

"Exactly. If we swear an oath by the Runestaff, that oath is binding. We do not invoke the Runestaff lightly."

Lord Olin racked his poor scrambled brains to remember if he had ever lightly invoked the Runestaff. He could not recall. He began to sweat. The sweat soaked into his underclothes, ran along channels in his moulded helm and breastplate. He had begun to blubber. His snarling wolverine helm was like a greenhouse.

"Exactly," declared Baron Bous-Junge in answer to his own question. "My dear Lord Olin, I suspect there are plans afoot to obtain power over the original Runestaff and by this means affect the histories of our own realm in time as well as space."

Lord Olin was still unable to utter anything resembling intelligent speech. Baron Bous-Junge did not seem to mind. Equably he threw an arm about Lord Olin's shoulders.

"Are you curious about what gives me that suspicion?" The snake mask lifted to glance right and left. "Have you, I wonder, in your readings and travels, in your conversations, even in your dreams, heard of a creature not altogether human, with red eyes and bone-white skin, whom you might know in that part of the world as Count Zodiac?"

"C-c—?"

"Some reference, I understand, to an ancient Middle European outlaw or trickster. Anyway, he might well be the worst problem we face. Some suspect one of these Germanians to be a disguised Zodiac. Lord Taragorm's oracles suggest it. Are you sure you haven't heard of him? He has other names? Crimson Eyes? White Wolf? Silverskin? Some know him as Elric of Melniboné."

10

In his assumed identity Elric of Melniboné experienced a frisson he had not known for some time. It had been many years since he had enjoyed the luxuries of so much power, and this was both attractive and relaxing to him. He had been raised, after all, in such opulence, and for a while, as emperor of his own nation, had taken it for granted.

Yet Oonagh had not been found, and he knew his own role must soon be discovered. Every possible man and woman had been set to the task of seeking the girl out, with no success. They had not so much as seen or heard a breath of her. Although the mysterious albino boy might have travelled on, Elric had been certain Oonagh would be found here. All he and Scholar Ree had been able to divine indicated that she hid in this version of Mirenburg. If he had not been so certain, he would scarcely have concocted so elaborate a plot. As it was, he now had to fear the possibility of his sorcery wearing off even more, and of being exposed to the vindictive masters of the empire.

Even his co-conspirator, Yaroslaf Stredic, was growing nervous. Elric seemed determined to alert the Lords of the Dark Empire to the very rebellion Stredic planned. Why anger the Quay Savoy by locking up the two "Germanians"? He began to suspect that all his divinations had been wrong. Yet why would Klosterheim and von Minct, who most wanted to find her, also be looking here? Their presence seemed to confirm Elric's own understanding.

On the fourth morning of the search, Elric was close to calling it off when there was an incident in the factory quarter. Three ornithopters took off directly from the plant, flapping crazily into the air on metal wings, and from just above the topmost roofs, fired down into the city, aiming directly for the governor's quarters and the garrisons. Soldiers returned their fire before the ornithopters lumbered off into the distance and disappeared. They were commandeered by the very slave workers employed to build them. These men learned everything they knew from studying their masters.

Elric was not pleased with this development. Still posing as deputy protector, he now had to pretend to take measures against the factory district. He sent men in with orders to arrest the heads of the factories. When they went in, the guards were met with sustained fire and were driven back. Their captains came to Elric for further orders. He told them that the rebels had taken over all communications, and sent them off to the internal heliograph posts to destroy them. It was his belief, he said, that the rebellion would burn itself out.

Next morning the rebellion had spread across other parts of the city. Rebels were well armed and well disciplined. Elric ordered more of his soldiers into the forests and hills, seeking the girl. He explained that she held the key to their defence.

Eventually, he knew, the Dark Empire would retaliate. But he aimed to give the citizens all the time he could to take control of the city, believing that if the girl was hiding, she would come into the open once the rebels had won. A messenger was dispatched to the border, to the nearest intact heliograph, to signal that all was well with Mirenburg.

By now the citizens had some fifty ornithopters and a variety of battle-engines of the very latest design. If Londra attacked, they would almost certainly be driven back until more troops and machines were brought to the war zone.

Elric made one last use of his stolen power. He sent his soldiers marching towards Munchein, allegedly to relieve an even more embattled force there.

And he gave orders for the two Germanians to be brought to him.

The first order was obeyed. The second was not. The Germanians had disappeared. Their cell in the St-Maria-and-St-Maria was empty!

Elric understood their power. No doubt they had discovered that Oonagh was not, after all, in this part of the multiverse.

He would have given a great deal, however, to know where they had gone. The few spells he could readily cast gave him no further clues.

It was time to look elsewhere for his great-granddaughter. Every instinct told him that she was now in even greater danger.

Leaving the young Prince Yaroslaf in charge of the rebellion, he discarded his disguise, left his helm and armour behind, and set off into the Deep City to discover a gateway through to the roads between the worlds. He would have to begin his search all over again.

Elric had begun to understand how strong were the other forces in play, supernatural forces more powerful even than the two Germanians, the Dark Empire or even the old empire of Melniboné. He suspected the agency of Law or Chaos, and while he had no certain proof, he was fairly certain that his little great-grandchild and the mysterious boy had in some way been selected to become their means to the ultimate power. Though he knew loyalty to Chaos yet fought for Law, Elric hated both. Too much horror had befallen those he loved as one struggled to gain ascendancy over the other. He trusted none of the Higher Worlds. They cared nothing for the mortals they used in their eternal struggle for ascendancy. And as Elric well knew, few mortals could refuse whatever fate the Lords of the Higher Worlds determined for them. His own struggles, even in the thousand years of his long dream-quest, had rarely succeeded. The illusion of free will was maintained in spite of the evidence. Even our most private thoughts and yearnings, he suspected, were dictated by some preordained scenario in which Law battled Chaos. The best that we could hope for was a brief respite from their eternal war.

Elric could now do nothing else but search for his young kinswoman and attempt to save her from the worst that might befall her. He shook his fist at the gods and rode off to find the moonbeam roads, leaving his young friend to build what looked to be a substantial force against the infamous war leader Shenegar Trott and the other feared military lords of the Dark Empire. Yaroslaf Stredic might not defeat his conquerors, but he would set an example which might spark further revolutions across Europe.

Meanwhile, Dorian Hawkmoon, Duke of Köln, unknown to Elric, Baron Meliadus, Klosterheim or anyone else, returned to his cave two days after he had left to forage for food. The hero of Köln, still good-looking in spite of his grim experience, his blue eyes like honed steel, his blond hair streaked with grey, had news which might be good. In far-off Mirenburg, many miles from the foothills of the Bulgar Mountains, the citizens had at last risen against the Dark Empire.

Hawkmoon's friend, the wiry little mountain man Oladahn, was sceptical that any rebellion could succeed. The weapons of the Dark Empire were far too sophisticated. He scratched his red, hairy body and shook his head. They had attempted to withstand that final great attack upon Castle Brass and been defeated, in spite of their flamingoes, their towers, their flame lances. Only by chance had the defenders found security in the secret marshes surrounding the castle before Meliadus and his forces had ruthlessly destroyed the majority of the flamingoes, the horned horses and any human who had resisted them. They wanted no survivors, had completely destroyed the watchtowers, the old towns, every house and shed, bringing in an entirely new population from the Muskovian steppe, intending to ensure that not even a name would survive their conquest of Kamarg. Neither had Meliadus been greatly disturbed by the probability that a few Kamargian peasants had escaped. They would never be able to rally fighters the way Dorian Hawkmoon of Köln had rallied them. Count Brass's only child, his daughter Yisselda, had been plucked by Meliadus from the fires of Castle Brass and, no longer worthy of being Meliadus's wife, made a slave at Meliadus's court until she had disappeared, killed no doubt in Londra by some rival for another slave's affections. Bowgentle, the poet, was dead, as were all other defenders, or so Meliadus believed.

But he was misled. Una Persson herself had visited the survivors soon after they escaped into the great Slavian Forest, where they had lain low for over a year before they felt safe enough to move on. They found refuge at last among Oladahn's folk, the mountain brigands.

Oladahn could not believe the news. "Meliadus, or whoever represents him there, would have swiftly put down any uprising. They are superior in weapons, if not numbers."

Hawkmoon was not so certain of this. His informant had been a Bulgar who had the news from a Slavian merchant. "Apparently they took over a new kind of flying machine and turned it against the Granbretanners."

"Well," said Oladahn, scratching his hairy red arms, "it would not be the first time we've heard such rumours. If we believed them all . . ." His wide mouth clamped shut.

Hawkmoon said he was inclined to believe this. "It seems that many of those outlawed by the empire are flocking to Mirenburg to strike while they may. At the first sign of imperial gains they will melt away, to strike elsewhere— and disappear again. If they never attack Londra, they at least whittle away at the empire." The Duke of Köln had known defeat three times at the hands of the Dark Empire, yet he would fight Huon's people until the end, even if he never defeated them.

Hawkmoon passed a strong, bronzed hand through grey-blond hair. He was a handsome man. The dull black jewel at the centre of his forehead somehow enhanced his looks. He frowned as he considered what he had heard. All the power of the sorcerous science he had once employed against the Dark Empire was now gone. He had only his sword, his armour and his horse with which to fight Granbretan, while two of the people he most loved in the world, his wife and his father-in-law, slept under the security of that cave's roof, perhaps destined never fully to recover from the horrors they had experienced. He regretted refusing the help of that servant of the Runestaff, the Warrior in Jet and Gold, whose proffered gift might have given them the chance of defeating Meliadus when he brought all his force against Kamarg. But the opportunity had passed, and Hawkmoon had lost too much. Now he wondered if he had the courage to risk any more. His own life was nothing. The lives of those he loved were everything to him.

With a sigh, the Duke of Köln considered his options.

Should he lend his strength to the citizens of Mirenburg and the peasants of Wäldenstein, or should he wait for a more propitious moment? What were the chances of such a moment ever coming?

As he turned to go deeper into the cave system, he heard a movement outside. He picked up his flame lance from where it lay hidden beneath a pile of straw. That and its recharger were almost all he had carried away with him from Castle Brass. He could not possibly have trusted the Warrior in Jet and Gold. The warrior had already betrayed him at the Mad God's court, then returned at a critical moment, pretending to bring them help against Meliadus. Yet should he have rejected that? Could he have misinterpreted the warrior's intentions? Could they have turned the tables against Meliadus, saved hundreds of thousands, perhaps millions, of lives, if he had accepted that help?

Warily he returned to the cave entrance. Had he conjured that strange being back into existence? Riding towards him over the rolling foothills came the unmistakeable figure in armour of glowing black and yellow, his face, as always, covered by his helm. This refusal to display his face was one of the things which had always made Hawkmoon suspicious. It was a Dark Empire trait. Yet here he came again, at another crucial moment. What did he want this time?

Hawkmoon smiled bitterly to himself. All was doubt these days.

The Warrior in Jet and Gold might be an agent of the Dark Empire, though he represented himself as an opponent. Would it even make sense to let the warrior know he was here? He shrugged. Clearly the warrior always knew where to find him. He could therefore have betrayed the survivors of Kamarg many times.

Hawkmoon stepped out into the sunlight to greet his old acquaintance. The warrior rode up to a few feet below him and stopped, dismounting from his heavy black horse. His arms were scabbarded. His attitude, as always, was casual.

"Good morning, Duke Dorian." There was a hint of concern in his deep voice. "I am glad to see you survived the destruction of Castle Brass."

"Aye, barely. I might have survived it better, Sir Knight, had I accepted your help."

"Well, Duke Dorian, fate is fate. A moment's thought here, a quick decision there, and we might find ourselves in a dozen different situations. I am a simple Knight of the Balance. Who's to say which actions we take are ultimately for the best or not?"

"I hear there's an uprising down in old Mirenburg."

"I've heard the same, sir."

"Is that why you are here?"

The Warrior in Jet and Gold lowered his helmeted head as if in thought. "It might be one reason. Yes, perhaps you guess correctly. I am, as you must know by now, a mere messenger. I obey the Balance and, in doing so, serve the Runestaff."

"The Runestaff, eh? That mythic artefact. And what is this balance? Another mythical device?"

"Perhaps, sir. A symbol, at any rate, of the whole quasi-infinite multiverse."

"So it is Good against Evil? Pure and simple?"

"That struggle is neither pure nor simple, I think. I suppose I am here to help you make a connection in the cosmic equilibrium."

"Tell me—have you served Granbretan?"

"In my time, sir."

Hawkmoon began to move back into the cave. "A turncoat. As I suspected."

"If you like. But I said things were not simple. Besides, you have trusted other turncoats. D'Averc, for instance . . ."

Hawkmoon knew the truth of this. Even he was considered a turncoat by some.

"Do you serve what you believe in, Sir Warrior?" he asked.

"Do you, my lord duke? Or do you fight against what you do *not* believe in?"

"They are the same."

"Not always, Duke Dorian. The multiverse is a complex thing. There are many shades of meaning within it. Many complexities. We find ourselves in a million different contexts, and in each situation there are subtleties. In some we are great heroes, in others, great villains. In some we're hailed as visionaries, in others as fools. Were you a man of strong resolve when you refused my help at Castle Brass and allowed Meliadus to defeat you, destroying almost everything you loved?"

Hawkmoon felt something like a knife thrust to his belly. He sighed. "You betrayed us. You stole the crystal when we had defeated the Mad God. What else could I think?"

"I do not propose to tell you what you should think. But I assure you, I am here to help you."

"Why should you help me?"

"I do not help you for any sentimental reason, but because you serve the interests of the Balance."

"And that purpose?"

A pause. Then the Warrior in Jet and Gold said slowly, "To maintain itself. To sustain the equilibrium of the world. Of every world."

"Every world? There are others?"

"An almost infinite number. It was into one of these I offered you the chance to escape."

Hawkmoon dropped his head in thought. "Worlds where our history has taken a different turn. Where the empire never rose to power?"

"Aye—and where that power has been divided or successfully resisted."

"Where I accepted your help in defence of Castle Brass?"

"Indeed."

"What happened there?"

"Many things. From each event sprang many others."

"But I won?"

"Sometimes at great cost."

"Yisselda?"

"Sometimes. I told you. I do not serve individuals. I could not. I serve only the Runestaff and, through that, the Balance. Which determines only equilibrium. The Balance is destroyed and restored as it is needed. In one world you are its saviour, in another its destroyer. Now it is needed again and must be remade. But there are those who would remake it and use it not in the interests of humanity but in their own evil interest."

"The Balance is not a force for good?"

"What is 'good'? The Runestaff serves the Balance. Some believe they are one and the same. Equilibrium. The form of justice on which all other justice is based."

"I was once told that justice had to be created by mankind's efforts."

"That is another form of justice. That is within your control. But only fools seek to control the Balance or any of its components. It is no more possible to do that than for an individual to control a whirlwind or the tides. Or the direction in which Earth goes round the sun."

Hawkmoon was confused. He was not an intellectual. He was a soldier, a strategist. For most of his life he had been a man of action. Yet he knew in his bones that he had not best served his cause by refusing the help of the Warrior in Jet and Gold.

"And you have brought me the crystal?"

"A crystal breaks and becomes many crystals. I have brought you a piece of that crystal."

Oladahn, hearing the conversation, crept out of the cave and greeted the Warrior in Jet and Gold with a friendly hand. His red fur still bore some of the signs of the fire which had almost consumed him as he and the others fled Castle Brass through the old underground tunnels. But now he moved with all the energy he had feared gone for ever.

"What's that crystal do, Warrior?" Oladahn asked.

"It enables its holders to step in and out of this world and into many others. It enables you to move a whole army from one continent to another in an instant. It enables its possessor to challenge fate."

"Much as the amulet I lost summoned help from other worlds?" said Hawkmoon, accepting the pyramid-shaped fragment. "I'll need such help if I'm to fight the empire again."

The warrior seemed satisfied. "You'll go to Mirenburg, then? With you to lead them, there is a good chance of the uprising succeeding. Mirenburg now produces the most advanced ornithopters and weapons."

"I shall have to seek the opinions of my companions," Hawkmoon told him. "I have responsibilities. We suffered much in the fall of Kamarg."

"You have my sympathy," said the warrior, remounting his horse. "I will return tomorrow for your decision."

Hawkmoon was frowning when he went back into the caves, the fragment of crystal clenched in his fist.

II

Elric was now convinced that the child he sought was not in that Mirenburg where he had helped create a rebellion. He had returned to the Mirenburg he had first visited, which existed contemporaneously with the house in Ingleton where Oonagh's parents waited anxiously for his news. Here he was able to telephone Mr and Mrs Beck. He learned from them that his daughter, Oona, had also disappeared into the Mittelmarch, looking for Oonagh.

Mirenburg's beauty had faded under communism, but she was fortunate in that she had suffered little during the Second World War, having been swallowed by the Nazis with no more fighting than it took to gobble up Czechoslovakia. Her great twin-steepled cathedral of St-Maria-and-St-Maria continued to dominate the centre of the city, which was built on two hills divided by a river. The old city was chiefly on the east bank, and the new one on the west. Its great, brutal monuments to communist civic planning, tall, near-featureless apartment buildings and factory chimneys, rose above the primarily eighteenth- and nineteenth-century building with its astonishing mixture of architectural styles, including many from Mirenburg's last great shining period. Around the turn of the twentieth century her prince had commissioned some of the great modern architects such as Charles Rennie Mackintosh, Shaw, Wright, Voysey and Gaudí to design new municipal buildings.

Elric sensed an atmosphere of depression everywhere. Civil war had touched Wäldenstein. Rivalries between families of Slavic and German origin flared up as soon as the communist heel had been lifted. Throughout the Soviet empire and its satellites time had frozen in the 1930s. Civil rights and a radical change in public consciousness had marginalised race and culture as a means of distinguishing peoples. Only in the backward regions of the world did these things continue to inform the views of the majority.

The war had been short; the UN had interceded with help from the von Beks as mediators. The von Beks had good will in Mirenburg, though their family had not lived there for many years. Mirenburg had suffered many attacks by would-be conquerors, from the Huns to the Austrians and the Germans and, the last time, from her own people.

It became characteristic of the post-Soviet wars that ancient rivalries, encouraged by those who wished to divide and rule, culminated in the grudges only now being settled. Industrialised, turned into one of the most productive cities in the Soviet empire, exporting the Popp, the only car to rival the VW, Mirenburg had been a showcase. Vehicles, plane parts, light weapons, poured from her factories. Today she produced Fords for the local market. Wäldenstein's labour was cheaper and her pollution laws were not yet as rigorous as Germany's, so the cars were produced at a more competitive price. Thus her great chimneys belched black smoke and glowing cinders into the sky night and day, and her ancient houses grew dark with the soot of over fifty years. Elric had known the city since the fourteenth century, but he had not known it to stink so much since 1640, when the river had run dry and sewage had filled the bed.

Elric employed what skills of divination remained to him in this world, and became convinced that Oonagh had returned to this, her own sphere, assuming she had not been killed in the catastrophe whose realities he had originally witnessed under ground.

He had not been pleased to abandon his horse or his clothes en route to this sphere. Samson would be well cared for, however, in Mu-Ooria. Elric never felt entirely comfortable in the dress of our own period, which was why he affected evening clothes so often, but he had no need for secrecy, at least. Here he was recognised as a member of Mirenburg's old ruling class, and it suited most citizens to address him as "Count." Not that they were entirely unsuspicious of him. The local legend of Karmesinaugen was still remembered as involving the most sensational crimes reported in Wäldenstein in the nineteenth century, and the role was always attributed to him by the tabloid newspapers, who believed he might share his ancestor's tastes. He remembered how in earlier centuries they had pursued him through the narrow streets, brands flaring in their fists, baying for his blood. In those days he had still possessed his sword, and on occasions it had suited him to release the power and feed off their uncouth souls. But of late he found commonly available medicines to sustain him. His taste for raw lifestuff was only a memory. He remained amused, however, by the evident fear of him some superstitious souls betrayed.

Yet for all his familiarity with the citizens, not one could tell him where the little girl might be. "We would have heard, Count Zcabernac," they insisted, "if an unaccompanied English girl were living here."

"But what if she appeared to have her father with her, say, or a couple of uncles?"

"I'd know. So would many others." This from the overweight landlady of his pension. She had suggested he return to England, perhaps leaving an email address or telephone number where he could be contacted.

Then, just as he had begun to enquire about the availability of flights from Munich, something happened which made him determined to stay. He was sitting reading the *Mirenburg Zeitung* in a café not far from his pension when he looked up and saw a tall man making his way hastily across the busy Ferngasse, barely missed by a clanking Number 11 tram. He recognised the man at once as Klosterheim, whom he had last caused to be imprisoned in that other Mirenburg. Full of alarm, Elric immediately set off in pursuit, through the streets and alleys and into the old thieves' quarter, now the home of bohemians and students. Klosterheim disappeared into a traditional hostelry, Raspazian's, and was ordering a drink at the bar when Elric walked in and seated himself in the shadows near the door.

If Klosterheim was in this world, decided Elric, then there was every chance he had come here to look for Oonagh. It was very likely that Klosterheim had escaped from the St-Maria-and-St-Maria and come directly here. It suggested the girl was not yet in his power. At last Elric might discover why Klosterheim and von Minct pursued the child and why all the omens had been so terrifying.

Elric decided to confront Klosterheim before there was any chance of losing him again. He rose slowly and walked to where the gaunt man stood, paying for a Rottbier.

"Good morning, Herr Klosterheim."

Klosterheim turned but did not seem surprised. "Good morning, count. I had heard that you were here again. Have you retired from—um—'showbiz'?"

"My family has some old associations with this city. Being a sentimentalist,

I visit whenever I can. And you, Herr Klosterheim? Are you here on some sort of evangelical business?"

Klosterheim seemed to enjoy this. "Of sorts, yes."

"I believe I just missed you in Ingleton." Elric said nothing of their mutual deceptions in that other Mirenburg.

"An unusual coincidence. As is this one."

"You were looking for my daughter's granddaughter, I understand."

"We had some idea she could help us find an easy way into the Mittelmarch."

"You have always succeeded before, Herr Klosterheim."

"My capabilities are limited of late." The gaunt man offered him a sour yet oddly humorous look.

"I hope you'll let her parents know when you find her," Elric said. "I spoke to them yesterday. They are naturally anxious."

"Naturally." The grey lips touched the ruby sheen of the Rottbier.

Elric could tell that Klosterheim, his gaunt features tensing, his dark eyes hard and bright in the depths of his skull, would have been quite happy to kill him if there had been some means or excuse. But here the long-undead ex-priest was forced to remain civil. He looked up in some anticipation, however, as a huge man entered the bar and greeted him. It was Gaynor von Minct, of course.

This unregenerate Nazi had pursued Elric through his thousand-year dream since the eleventh century and was now grinning down on him ferociously like a wild beast about to kill its prey. He scowled when Elric offered to buy him a drink. The tension between the three men was so considerable that the barman went over and murmured significantly to the manager, who was serving a customer at the far end of the bar. Elric saw the manager pick up his mobile phone and put it in his hip pocket, as if ready to call the police.

Gaynor von Minct also noted this. "Perhaps we should talk elsewhere," he said. "Would you care to meet later, Prince Elric?"

"Where would you suggest?" The albino was amused. He often felt this amusement when his sixth sense warned him of danger.

"How about the Mechanical Gardens? Do you know them? They are fascinating. There's a little coffee place there, by the Steel Fountain."

"Would four o'clock suit you?" Elric hoped he could get some further clue from Gaynor. The man was arrogant enough to reveal himself by accident.

"Four would be perfect." Gaynor did not wish to be humiliated in public, so did not offer his hand, but he smiled that thin, unpleasant smile of his as he turned back to speak to the glowering Klosterheim.

Mirenburg's famous Mechanical Gardens were public enough to be safe. Making sure he was not followed, Elric returned to his pension. Here he armed himself with an old black, battered Walther PPK 9mm automatic. The two men would gladly kill him if the opportunity arose. He took his lunch at the Wienegatten and wrote the notes he would send to Mrs Persson at her poste restante in Stockholm. He had developed this habit since they had first met in the early part of the twentieth century, when they had become good friends, possibly lovers, though Mrs Persson was, as always, discreet about her liaisons.

The Mechanical Gardens had first begun operating in the 1920s, the creation of the Italian Futurist Fiorello De Bazzanno. During the communist period they continued to function, even if a little run-down. The futurist-deco style of the gardens was reminiscent of a period when the machine inspired a distinctive aesthetic. The large park, on the far bank of the river, covered a number of acres and was filled with mechanical men, trees, flowers and animals, some of them, like the gleaming *Tyrannosaurus rex*, truly monstrous. The park was dominated by an enormous, jovial grinning head made entirely of machine parts, with rolling eyes nodding back and forth as if in approval. Everything moved by systems of cogs, levers, belts and wheels. Most used electricity, though a few were still steam powered. There was an elaborate funfair, with Ferris wheel, merry-go-round, "whip," helter-skelter and a number of roller coasters, though these were not the chief attraction. Everything was mechanical, including the old-fashioned automat, the coffee shop and even the souvenir shop, where big robot "assistants" talked to customers by means of pre-recorded tapes and gave change after notes were inserted into their mouths.

With the old spires, domes, roofs and turrets of Mirenburg in the background, the art deco world of cogs, levers and engines presented by the Mechanical Gardens had a quaintness of its own. Great cogs resembling faces flashed and grinned. Massive hands constructed of rods and pistons waved overhead. The watery sunlight reflected off steel, brass and tin, and a mechanical organ played Strauss waltzes and polkas.

Most of the people in the park at that hour were couples who looked as if they had been coming there for years. At the Steel Fountain, Elric got himself a cup of café au lait and a rum pastry, which he took to one of the green tables overlooking the lawn which ran down to the river. Soon Klosterheim arrived. He wore a black trench coat and a wide black hat. His hands were shoved deep in his pockets. Gaynor was next, his big body swathed in a herringbone raglan coat, a feathered Tyrolean hat on his head. Underneath his coat was a suit of dark green tweed. The two men went to the automat and returned with coffee. Klosterheim's long, bony hand reached out for the bowl and began to place lumps of sugar in his cup. Von Minct sipped his unsweetened. "This place seems changeless. I remember when I first came. It had just opened. Mussolini had completed the March on Rome, and the king had asked him to become prime minister. Splendid days, full of optimism. How quickly the golden years go by! Are you enjoying your pastry, Prince Elric?"

Elric placed his fine, long-fingered white hand on the lattice metal of the table. "You seemed to suggest you wanted to talk about the missing girl," he said.

"My dear Prince, you certainly like to get straight to the heart of the matter. I like that, sir."

"I would guess you have not found her." The crimson eyes narrowed beneath half-shut lids. "You think she's somewhere here, perhaps?"

"You are presuming a great deal, my lord prince," said Klosterheim. "What if we, too, have only the young lady's safety at heart? Given that she no doubt trusts you, we thought she might reveal herself to you, whereas . . ."

"Indeed?" Elric sat back in his chair. He fingered his chin. He still seemed amused. "So you hounded her through the Mittelmarch in order to ensure her safety? And now you think I'll be bait for your trap?"

"Hounded?" said Klosterheim. "That's a strong word, sir!"

"I am here to warn you to give up your pursuit."

Von Minct became suddenly alert. "You're not exactly fair to us, Prince Elric."

"Perhaps." Elric saw no reason to give them any information. "So you expected to find her here? And planned to use me as a lure to bring her out of hiding!"

"We were informed we might find her at Raspazian's; that is all. But it was clear she had never been near the place. He said the fox had her."

"He? Who informed you?"

"A fellow wearing black-and-yellow armour. He did not leave us his name."

"Where did you meet him?"

"We were lost on the moonbeam roads. We are not entirely skilled in negotiating those roads in this universe, and he helped us."

Elric knew of the Warrior in Jet and Gold. Their paths had crossed once or twice, to their mutual benefit. Why would the warrior confide in Elric's enemies?

"Did he propose exactly where she could be found?"

"He said to seek her on the wheel." Klosterheim indicated the Ferris wheel. "Can you think what she might be doing there? One or the other of us has watched the wheel most of the time."

Elric was disbelieving. Von Minct and Klosterheim must be lying to him. He said nothing. He had hoped to learn something from them. Doubtless they had hoped even more of him. Leaving his cake uneaten, he finished his coffee and rose. "I'll bid you good afternoon, gentlemen."

They were nonplussed. They had expected to benefit from the meeting.

Elric left them talking to each other in low voices. As he walked out of the Mechanical Gardens he felt disappointed. Had he failed to note an important clue to the child's whereabouts? He glanced back and was surprised to see Klosterheim and von Minct paying their money and pushing through the Ferris wheel turnstile. Did they expect to find Oonagh in one of the compartments, after having waited fruitlessly for so long? Should he follow?

No. They were as thoroughly desperate as he. Yet he waited and watched them. Eventually they came out through the exit. They had no-one with them.

Elric, summoning some of his old witch-sight, did his best to read the air around the giant wheel. It was agitated, possibly populated. He thought he saw other shapes, perhaps even outlines of other cities. Looking around, he could tell that only the great wheel had an unusual quality. He knew it must have some function in this puzzle. But was he going to become as obsessed as his enemies and spend weeks watching the thing?

The park closed at five, and uniformed men on bicycles blew whistles to herd customers out. It would open again in the evening, with the added attraction of a cinema show in what had been the park's original kine-theatre.

Elric returned to his pension. He had an unconscious sense of what was happening to Oonagh and why Klosterheim and von Minct were here. Nothing was clear, but his instincts told him that there was something wrong. Something that wouldn't save Oonagh, however, because that pair would act on whatever erroneous idea they had. She was still in mortal danger. The problem remained how to find her and get her to safety. That was going to be a difficult task, he admitted, smiling to himself as he changed for dinner. He tied his bow tie, adjusted it at his throat, straightened his sleeves a little and was again the dandy who had once graced the boulevards of Mirenburg and Paris in the Belle Époque. He had been acquainted with half the great poets and painters of the day. All the artists wanted to paint his portrait, but he had allowed only Sargent the privilege. The painting now hung in a certain apartment in London's Sporting Club Square and had never been exhibited. It had been reproduced once in the *Tatler* for 18 July, 1902, in a general photograph of the artist's studio. It showed a man no older than Elric seemed now, adorned almost exactly as he was, in superbly cut evening dress.

In this costume he had once gone upon the town. But he had not always been found at the parties of the rich and powerful nor in the boulevard cafés for which Mirenburg was famous in that era before war had disrupted her pursuit of pleasure. Sometimes he might have been glimpsed in the cobbled alleys of the Deep City, or even climbing up the narrow gap between buildings to make his way easily and with great familiarity across the rooftops.

But those days were over, Elric reflected with a little self-mockery. Tonight he would dine conventionally enough, at Lessor's in the Heironymousgasse.

And then, he thought, he might make a visit after hours to the Mechanical Gardens.

He dreamed. This time he led an army against a powerful enemy. All the beasts of Granbretan were massed against him, but in his mirrored helm he rallied his troops to attack. And he was Corum—alien Corum of the Vadhagh—riding against the foul Fhoi Myore, the Cold Folk from limbo . . . And he was Erekosë— poor Erekosë—leading the Eldren to victory over his own human people . . . and he was Urlik Skarsol, Prince of the Southern Ice, crying out in despair at his fate, which was to bear the Black Sword, to defend or to destroy the Cosmic Balance. Oh, where was Tanelorn, sweet Tanelorn? Had he not been there at least once?

Did he not recall a sense of absolute peace of mind, of wholeness of spirit, of the happiness which only those who have suffered profoundly may feel?

"Too long have I borne my burden—too long have I paid the price of Erekosë's great crime . . ." It was his voice which spoke, but it was not his lips which formed the words—they were other lips, unhuman lips . . . "I must have rest; I must have rest . . ."

And now there came a face, a face of ineffable evil, but it was not a confident face—a dark face. Was it desperate? Was it his face? Was this his face, too?

Ah, I suffer!

This way and that, the familiar armies marched. Familiar swords rose and fell. Familiar faces screamed and perished, and blood flowed from body after body—a familiar flowing . . .

Tanelorn? Have I not earned the peace of Tanelorn?

Not yet, Champion. Not yet . . .

It is unjust that I alone should suffer so!

You do not suffer alone. Mankind suffers with you.

It is unjust!

Then make justice!

I cannot. I am only a man.

You are the Champion. You are the Eternal Champion.

I am only a human being. A man. A woman . . .

You are only the Champion.

I am Elric! I am Urlik! I am Erekosë! I am Corum! I am Hawkmoon! I am too many. I am too many!

You are one.

And now, in his dreams (if dreams they were), he felt for a brief instant a sense of peace, an understanding too profound for words. He was one.

And then it was gone, and he was many again. And he yelled in his bed, and he begged for peace.

And it seemed his voice echoed through the entire city, and all Mirenburg heard his sadness and mourned with him.

12

I wasn't sure exactly what happened after the Sebastocrater was shot and it started raining, except that Lord Renyard, Lieutenant Fromental and Prince Lobkowitz all left the summer house and ran after me at the same time with Lady Oona. As I laboured for the high ground, Oona's Kakatanawa (suddenly awake) began yelling what I guessed were their war-cries just as a ball of bright silver light appeared over the ornamental lake, where von Minct and Klosterheim fell back, blinded.

There was a horrible roaring noise in the distance, and it began to rain more heavily. Oona picked me up and set me squarely on her shoulders. Everyone was shouting. Then suddenly there was silence, stillness. I looked back. The whole scene—summer house, Kakatanawa, Sebastocrater, guards—had frozen, as if something had stopped time again. But Oona was in a hurry, and she and I were unaffected by whatever spell had been cast. I saw the panther trotting ahead of the others, leading the way through the narrow streets of Mirenburg. The whole city was frozen. We sped on through the gates, racing in moonlight towards the heights above the city. Only when we were looking down on the towers of Mirenburg did Oona pause and lift me from her back.

Any barmy notion I might have had that Oona and the panther were the same had gone, of course. Yet I still had a sneaking suspicion in the back of my mind that they were more closely related than most would think credible.

Below us I saw a ball of golden fire approach the still-hovering ball of silver fire through slicing bursts of rain. They quivered together in the air, as if sizing each other up. They expanded, growing brighter and apparently denser at the same time, and did not touch until, in the blink of an eye, they had merged, become the same thing, a single iris the colour of polluted copper.

"Stay there!" cried Oona above the noise of the rain, and ran back down towards the city.

"Don't leave me!" My shout was impulsive. With a wave she was gone, racing back towards that baleful eye which began to grow larger as she got closer. She disappeared through the gates as I waited anxiously, watching little stars and sparks descending on the roofs, chimneys and steeples of the City in the Autumn Stars. Then the globe became a red, glowing coal and dropped earthward again.

Was Herr Clement Schnooke working the magic he had promised? Or was something else going on, maybe started by von Minct and Klosterheim? I waited nervously. Suddenly I heard the rush of water from somewhere. I looked down through the starlight and saw the glint of the river, which was rising with terrible speed. I was so fascinated that I couldn't move. Then the panther was there, pushing at me with her nose. It was wet and warm, just like an ordinary pet cat's. She seemed to want me to follow her. Reluctantly I turned and climbed to higher ground. The water had already risen above its banks and spread out through the city streets. I began to hear distant shouts when the remains of the fiery ball fell back towards the Deep City and plunged down to where I guessed Raspazian's to be. Now I was certain this was Herr Schnooke's magic at work. I had a sinking feeling that the spell had gone seriously wrong, that Schnooke had been destroyed by his own magic. How many of my friends had he taken with him? I guessed that the spell had clashed with all the other magic at work that night. I know I witnessed a genuine disaster. All the inhabitants of Mirenburg were in serious danger.

At last Oona stood beside me again as her Indians crept out of the darkness with Lord Renyard, Prince Lobkowitz and Lieutenant Fromental.

"I have to go back there," I said. "I made a promise."

"You can hope the majority survive," said Oona very wearily. "We are only minutes away from being swallowed by the thing . . . Damned amateur magicians!"

Which suggested it was definitely Schnooke.

But I had to get back to help Onric. I babbled. I insisted. I struggled to make them let me go.

Oona continued to speak softly and kindly to me, but her attention was elsewhere. In the end I had to hope the boy had saved himself from the flood. His co-workers, after all, had seemed to value and respect him.

"We must stick together," Oona insisted. The others agreed. She turned to her Kakatanawa to speak to them in their own language.

I gave it one last try: "But there's a boy back there. He's like you, Lady Oona. Like Monsieur Zodiac!"

She didn't really hear me. "We can do little here. We must assume our friends are still in pursuit. This has much to do with them, I suppose."

I felt sick as I watched the city fill with water. I now clearly heard shouts, screams and the noises of panicking animals. Oona said something again to the Kakatanawa.

I found it hard to turn my back on the flooding city. I still had friends down there. When I mentioned this to Prince Lobkowitz he put his hand on my shoulder and squeezed it. I looked up into his kindly, miserable eyes. "What we have to do is more important than the fate of those poor souls, my dear. We must get away from here as soon as possible. We have to consider the wider good."

"I would have thought Onric could have been included in the wider good," I said.

"What name?" Oona frowned at me through the rain. "What name?"

"Onric. An albino. Looked a lot like you. He had a job in a factory down there. Well, he'll probably be out of work now." I was a bit fed up that nobody had listened to me.

"A factory?"

"A steel-making place. Where everything's white-hot, you know, unless it's red-hot."

She turned to look back at drowning Mirenburg. Some factory chimneys still smoked, but it was easy to see that their fires had been dampened, flooded and were choking. "Was he my age?" she asked in a strange voice.

Lord Renyard came over to us before I could reply to her weird question. "The moon," he murmured, and looked up.

My heart began to beat all the harder, for through the rain a full moon glowed, bright, clear and blue. The rocky landscape ahead of us was bathed in a faint blue light.

Behind us on the road below we saw people and animals plunging in panic out of the city gates nearest us, heading towards higher ground. We continued on the rocky paths well above them as my friends clearly tried to gain as much height as possible above the still-rising waters.

Oona cursed the incompetent magician Clement Schnooke from time to time. I felt that more than one kind of magic had met here tonight, without actually managing to do anyone any good.

"We can't be certain how far the river will rise," said Oona. "For all we know, it won't be much. But we have to get up into the mountains if we can. They are using quicksilver against us."

I had no idea what she was talking about, and I was almost in tears again, imagining my new albino friend drowned in his factory after I had promised to help him.

"Are we going back home?" I asked.

"As soon as we can, dear," murmured my grandmother.

"You might say we have lost the path through." Lord Renyard was looking longingly back at the flooded city. I felt so sorry for him. All his people had been left behind, everything he loved, including his prized library. At least my own home was still in one piece. Or so I supposed.

The Autumn Stars were appearing over the city, forming almost a pattern around the still-glowing blue moon. I tried to look up in the sky and see where they began and ended, but I couldn't tell. I focused on a big rent in the black clouds, almost as if the light itself had created it.

Wet, miserable and tired, we kept walking all that night and by dawn were well into the mountains. Only then did Oona sign that we could stop and shelter in the pine forest while she and the Kakatanawa went off to find food for us. Prince Lobkowitz and Lieutenant Fromental built a fire. Lord Renyard, having spent much of the night in low conversation with Oona, was definitely depressed. He went over to some mossy rocks and sat down. I joined him. He seemed pleased.

"What's going on, Lord Renyard?" I asked. "I'm sure your people must have been able to save themselves. They're very resourceful. Not too many will have been hurt."

"Some, at least, are safe. Perhaps all of them. The worst flooding appears to have been in reverse. In the mirror city. In the world below. Our path was between the worlds."

He didn't seem to have seen what I had seen, yet I believed him.

"What happened?"

"A clash of magics, almost certainly. Those men who seek you are ruthless. They'll risk anyone's life to capture you. But nobody expected them to try to flush you and Oona out with a water spell. That went wrong for them when their spell clashed with Clement Schnooke's. You saw the result."

"What was Schnooke's spell?"

"His was a time spell, with elements of fire and water spells, intended to release us and divert our captors. But two kinds of magic being wrought at the same time—well, people will always suffer." He sighed. "And it is always the innocent who suffer most. Had I been free, I might have prevented this."

"Isn't there somewhere else—some other . . . you know . . . world—where you can go, where things are more or less the same?"

"I am something of a monster, my dear. Few places on the surface find me acceptable. I must eventually seek either fabled Tanelorn or return to Mu-Ooria and the Off-Moo, who seem to appreciate my company."

"Where are we going now?"

"To find a new gateway to the moonbeam roads, the old one being blocked for us by von Minct's cruel and bloody sorcery."

"What do all these people want from me, Lord Renyard?"

"They think you can lead them to what they seek."

"Which is?"

"Well, ultimately it amounts to what someone from a pre-Enlightenment culture might describe as power over God and Satan. Whatever you call it, that's what von Minct and Klosterheim want. Power. Immense power. Power over all the worlds of the universe. What Prince Lobkowitz calls the multiverse, that is, all the versions of all the worlds."

"I know what it means," I said. "I read a lot of comics, and my dad gets *Scientific American*. What, billions of them?"

"Oh, billions of billions—we call this quasi-infinity because while it is not an infinite number, we cannot know a finite number."

"Why would they want so much power?"

"To rival God and Satan, as I said."

All my family and most of their friends were of a secular disposition, so I was inclined to be amused by the ideas of God and Satan as such. "Isn't that Satan's job?" I asked.

"It was," said Lord Renyard seriously. "But Satan no longer wished to be God's rival. He sought and found reconciliation with God. This reconciliation was not in our enemies' interest. They want, if you like, to take the job Satan renounced. To return to a state of cosmic war."

"So if they got what they wanted, they'd rule an infinite number of worlds of evil?"

"They would not call it evil. They believe that an ideal universe is one in which their priorities are uppermost. It is almost impossible for us to understand. Perhaps someone else can understand them better. They are not like us. They have no self-doubt. They believe that what is best for them is best for everyone. For everything. At least, they think that every 'normal' person wants to do what is best for von Minct and Klosterheim. Anyone who disagrees with them or resists them is abnormal and must be re-educated or eliminated. If they have God's power, they can set the cosmos to rights."

"Even though God created it?"

"Even so."

"They're mad," I said.

Lord Renyard laughed at this. "Ah, the directness of children. How I envy you!"

I found this condescending. "So how are you planning to get them sorted?"

"We can only oppose them. As effectively as possible. And protect those they would harm."

"How on earth could I give them that kind of power?" I was even more baffled. "I'm a little girl."

"A rather brave and clever one," he said gallantly. I wanted to hug him.

"But still—"

"We need to discover what it is you have," he said quietly. "We do know that the Sword, the Stone and two cups are involved. All the things called 'objects of power.'"

Oona and her men were returning through the woods. They carried several gamebirds. Lord Renyard began to salivate. "Here's our breakfast," he said. "I wonder if mine might be a little more underdone . . ."

I realised that I was very hungry, too.

After we'd eaten we packed up and moved on across the hills. It felt like Yorkshire again. I was enjoying the smell of the heather, the glint of the sunlight on limestone, the cool shade of the woods. Hunting hawks sailed high above us. Every so often we passed streams and groves of wild flowers. I began to hope we might already be on our way home.

I had to give up that idea when we reached a well-trodden road and saw an old-fashioned coach drawn by six black horses, pounding along at a dangerous speed, with its driver cracking a whip and yelling at the top of his lungs. I recognised the crest on the coach's door. It belonged to the Sebastocrater and must have come from Mirenburg. It went past too fast for us to catch up or see who was in it. If it was Klosterheim and von Minct, they might have seen us. Prince Lobkowitz frowned. "That's the Munchein road," he said.

"How long will it take them to reach the city?" asked Lieutenant Fromental.

"Another three days if they can get changes of horses."

"Must we follow them?"

"Of course not," said Oona. "Our first duty is to protect the child. In doing that we shall also thwart their plans."

"So which way should we go?"

She hesitated. "I don't know, but we should try to get home before this gets any worse."

"That would be my preference," I said.

One of the Kakatanawa who had been scouting ahead of us on the other side of the hill came running back. He spoke rapidly to Oona, who shook her head in disbelief. Then she and the others followed the Indian. I ran after them.

We stood looking down on a pleasant valley with a stream running through it and a few cows grazing. Nestled between a small copse of elder trees and may bushes was a house.

The others did not know what it was, but I did. So did Lord Renyard. He put his large, warm paw on my shoulder. He could probably tell how frightened I was.

The house was the twin of the one I had first "met" in Mirenburg. With blinds down and shutters closed, it had the appearance of being asleep.

"This could be good news, you know," murmured the fox. "Mrs House is not your enemy." His tone was reassuring, but I could sense he was as mystified as I was.

"How could it—she—get here from there?" I asked.

"Well, first you should consider that the same builder put up more than one house of the same type, mademoiselle," he suggested gently, as if preparing me for disappointment.

"No, it's the same," I said. "Same windows, doors, blinds, slates, chimneys. Same patches on the walls. It's her face, all right."

"Her?" Prince Lobkowitz came to look down at the house with us. "Face?"

Lieutenant Fromental fingered his prominent chin. "I've always thought of houses as having faces, too." He chuckled at his own whimsical imagination. "What children we are, eh?"

"I *am* one," I said. "And that house does have a face. That's Mrs House, I'm certain."

"Mrs House?" Oona drew her brows together as if summoning an old memory. She brought her Kakatanawa to a halt. The tall, bronze-coloured men murmured among themselves, occasionally laughing. They were as surprised as the rest of us at finding such an old, seemingly well-established house in this countryside.

"Mrs House—should it indeed be her—is an old friend of mine," explained Lord Renyard. "The little mademoiselle also met her before."

"She's the one who mentioned the Staff and the Stone," I said. "And talked about the blind boy. It was all a bit vague, but I'm pretty sure that's what she was saying. That's why I was asking you those questions."

"Someone you met inside the house?" asked the burly legionnaire. His big face frowned, as if he did not quite understand what was being said.

"No," said Prince Lobkowitz patiently. "You mean the *house herself*, do you not, Miss Oonagh?"

"That's what I mean," I said. "That's what I remember."

As we continued to approach her, Mrs House opened her eyes.

The effect on my friends, apart from Lord Renyard, was almost comical. They came to a stumbling stop. The door, which was Mrs House's mouth, moved. Her rich, slightly echoing voice sounded through the valley.

"Ah, it's good to see you're still safe, dear girl. You escaped the floods, as did I. I knew in my bones I would soon be on the move again, but I did not think the journey would occur so soon—and what's more, under threat of flooding. It's folk with basements I feel sorry for. I know Lord Renyard, of course, but I haven't had the pleasure of being introduced to these others."

Stammering, as I had done originally, I introduced my friends. All, including the Kakatanawa, returned respectful greetings.

"Hmm," declared Mrs House, turning her smoky eyes towards Oona, "the famous dreamthief's daughter. I heard you were retired."

"So I thought, my lady," said Oona. "But circumstances dictate—"

"Explain no more. Circumstances dictate most of our recent actions. I understand. And you, little girl?" she returned her attention to me. "Did you come by the Staff or the Sword yet?"

"Not yet, madam."

"No blind boy?"

"Almost, but . . ." I shook my head. "I found him, then lost him again."

She sighed. "Time falls away. Falls away. You must try harder."

I found myself smiling. I liked Mrs House better since she had left Mirenburg. I wasn't sure why. "I'm not sure how."

"My girl, sometimes we must give Fate a nudge in the right direction."

"Do you know the right direction, ma'am?"

"Well, I suppose I do. I have some experience in these matters. I'm not sure I'd say it was *exactly* the right direction. Where are you off to now?"

Most of my party were pretty stunned by this dialogue. I tried to explain a bit more, admitting I didn't have the faintest idea where we were going. After I'd done my best, I added, "So you see, we're escaping from Mirenburg, like you, and have no clear idea where we're going. I'd like to get home, of course, as soon as possible . . ."

"Our gateway was blocked by the flood," Oona told her. "But you think we should have found the Staff there, do you?"

"The Staff preserves itself. That is its essence. If it was in Mirenburg when the flood came, it would not be there now."

The Kakatanawa had seated themselves in a row and were regarding Mrs House with some respect while Prince Lobkowitz puzzled and Lieutenant Fromental scowled thoughtfully, as if they might, by concentration, come up with a logical explanation for the phenomenon.

From the heights above came the sound of a familiar voice. Turning, we saw the outlines of Herr Klosterheim and Gaynor von Minct, and they had a small army of cut-throats with them. Men with dark olive skins, wide-brimmed hats, bandoliers of cartridges and big boots, so evidently mountain brigands that we did not need to see their brandished pistols and muskets to know who they were. They lined both sides of the valley and had crept closer to us while we talked to Mrs House.

"You'll note that we have you covered," called Gaynor von Minct in a mocking voice. "It would be unfortunate should you resist us and harm come to the young lady."

"I'm a fool," said Oona through her teeth. She looked from one end of the valley to the other, unable to find decent cover. "I should have guessed they'd find help and return after they saw us on the road."

At a word from her, the Kakatanawa rose and surrounded me. Prince Lobkowitz, Lord Renyard and Lieutenant Fromental laid their hands on their weapons.

"Any bloodshed will be unnecessary." Von Minct and Klosterheim were now astride large horses. They came cantering down the slope towards us.

Oona whispered to me: "You might have a chance if you could get into that—house—somehow. Is that possible?"

Mrs House's voice spoke softly from behind us. "You might *all* have a chance if you came inside. The door is open. All you have to do is step into me, you know."

For a moment I wondered what the consequences might be. Then I had backed towards her mouth, her door, and skipped inside. It was cool in her dark hall, but the vivid floral wallpaper was comforting and it was only a little damp, rather as if I stood in someone's throat. Quickly the others all tumbled in after me. I looked to one side and saw another door. A few more steps, and I was in a pleasantly furnished front parlour. There was richly coloured William Morris paper on the walls, big easy chairs with Victorian floral prints, a lovely old horsehair sofa matching the chairs, even a potted aspidistra. Carpets were also floral, including that which covered the stairs, disappearing up into comfortable darkness. I was soon joined by Oona, some rather baffled Indians and my other three friends.

"This is most unusual," said Prince Lobkowitz, walking over the soft, yielding carpet to part the dark velvet curtains and look out at our pursuers. They were still standing there. They had clearly not decided what action, if any, to take. They looked, every one of them, dumbfounded.

"I rarely have guests these days," said Mrs House from somewhere. "People have poor manners and can be so destructive. But I suppose I have little choice in the circumstances. You had best leave by the back door, as soon as you get the opportunity."

Outside, the brigands were approaching cautiously. Klosterheim and von Minct stood with pistols in their hands, looking up at the windows.

Quite suddenly the scene changed subtly. The landscape was almost identical, but our enemies were no longer there, and the trees in the copse looked slightly different.

"It has been quite a while since I have done something like this," said Mrs House. "I'm afraid you will have to forgive me for any mistakes." I almost thought I heard her giggle to herself.

The landscape changed again. And again. Trees and shrubs appeared. Rocks were differently placed. "I have no very clear idea where I'm going, my dear," came Mrs House's rather exhilarated voice from the roof. "But it seemed wiser not to wait until those violent men tried to come in as well. I have always disliked violence, haven't you? And I never look forward to repainting afterwards."

Once again the scene outside changed.

"She's moving through the multiverse," whispered Prince Lobkowitz. "She's taking us to safety."

"Are we going home, Mrs House?" I asked.

"We are escaping from danger, my dear," she replied. "I can promise you nothing else for the moment."

"We're grateful," said Oona. "But do you know where we are?"

"I do not move with any direction in mind, I must admit," said Mrs House. "Just through time and space. As I always do when threatened. But I believe I will bring you a little closer to the blind boy. Or so my seventh sense suggests."

My friends were obviously disappointed, even though they were relieved for the moment to be out of harm's way. "By the back door," Mrs House reminded us as we prepared to leave. "To be on the safe side. You never know who's watching."

"Is it the back door to the past and by the front to the future?" asked Lieutenant Fromental, with some curiosity.

"Quite often," replied Mrs House. "Goodbye, all of you. I hope you stay safe and well. Keep looking for the blind boy. He will be expecting you now, dear."

Some of the others were already through the door. "Where shall I look?" I asked.

"Where you've looked before," she said. "Where blind boys work."

At these references to the blind boy, my friends grew alert. Significant looks passed between them. They were at once puzzled and suddenly keyed up.

"I've been trying to tell you," I said.

Prince Lobkowitz made as if to speak to me, then changed his mind. Instead, he uttered a long, deep sigh. He laid a hand on my shoulder.

The sun was setting behind the hills. Large-winged birds as big as cranes sailed against the crimson light. It was getting colder.

There was now a deep, green wood at the back of Mrs House. Reluctantly I left her strange embrace and stepped out of the door. It creaked as I left, almost a human voice. Cautiously we entered the peaceful gloom of the trees, walking slowly in single file. When I next looked back, Mrs House was out of sight. She had saved us from our worst enemies, but I felt in my bones she would not be able to help us again.

13

Darkness came before Oona decided it was safe to stop and make camp. Her Kakatanawa still had plenty of game in their bags, so we ate well before we were ready to sleep. I curled up with Lord Renyard, who removed his elaborate jacket, waistcoat and shirt and allowed me to cuddle against his ample red fur. I don't think I've ever known anything as soft! I slept better than I had since I had first found myself under ground.

We woke in the morning to the smell of a fresh fire and roasting meat. I felt far more relaxed and certain of seeing my mum and dad again. Lord Renyard's protective paws had kept me safe and warm, and the soft sound of his breathing had made me feel almost like a baby. I smiled at everyone and even got responses from the normally laconic and stern Kakatanawa.

We were camped on a hillside near a freshwater spring bubbling out of the ground to form a stream and run over rocks to join a river in the valley below. The trees were in their first full leaf of summer, and the whole of the hillside bloomed with blue, yellow, red and purple wild flowers like a brightly coloured map. I don't think I've ever seen so many flowers together in one place. In the valley were copses of dark green oaks and cedars casting dawn shadows. The pale blue sky flushed with gold as the sun rose, and a single large hawk hovered overhead, to the consternation of thrushes, blackbirds and finches. The place was idyllic, a fairyland. The sense of security was all-prevailing.

Prince Lobkowitz whistled as he dressed himself. Lieutenant Fromental buttoned up his rather battered uniform jacket and glowed with the pleasure of his cold dip in the river.

"All we need to do now," Oona said, "is to find out where we are and then see if we can discover a town where we can make a fresh orientation."

"We could be anywhere in the multiverse," said Lieutenant Fromental.

"Even in a world where humans do not exist at all. We might have to begin our species all over again . . ."

Lord Renyard remarked that this would be rather difficult for him. As it was, he had abandoned one of the best libraries in Europe, with many first editions of the finest Encyclopaedists, some personally signed to himself. He was not sure that he could remember every single word they had written, though he had memorised Corneille and several of Voltaire's shorter works. Lieutenant Fromental admitted that Lord Renyard was indeed the best-read gentleman he had ever met. "You would have to tell everything you know to our children!"

"My point . . ." began Lord Renyard.

Oona interrupted this fantasy, arguing that she would remain faithful to her husband and I was far too young to get married; and in the circumstances we had better not spend the day talking but push on in the hope of finding a human settlement!

So we were soon on our way. I had the privilege, with my short legs, of being carried on the backs of every one of the Kakatanawa as well as the other men, while Oona, with an arrow nocked to her bow, trotted ahead looking for a trail.

She soon picked up a good, metalled road, which suggested we were in the twenty-first century or at least the late twentieth. I began to look forward to civilisation again. We rested for lunch not far from the road we hoped would take us to a main thoroughfare.

Then, just as we were preparing to move on, we heard a roaring, clanking and hissing noise so loud it threatened to burst my eardrums. We ran rapidly for the relative safety of the rocks. Over the horizon flew the strangest plane I had ever seen in my life. As it sailed above us, with great wings beating steadily, it threw out a trail of ash and cinders stinking of sulphur, like the old-fashioned steam train my family had taken from Settle to Carlisle on my last birthday. Shaped like an enormous bird with a beak of brass and steel, clashing metallic feathers, enamelled green, red and yellow and seemingly about the size of a jumbo jet, its vast wings lifted and fell, creating a downdraft nearly flattening the lot of us!

I caught a glimpse of what might have been the crew. Goggles and masks gave them an equally birdlike appearance. The plane flew low and was lost from sight over the nearby north-eastern hills.

"An ornithopter!" declared Lieutenant Fromental in some delight. "Can their power source actually be steam? Such a vessel's never been made to work before. The power-weight ratio problem is thought to be insurmountable. You know Leonardo's designs?"

"It appears to be steam," agreed Prince Lobkowitz. "Eh?" He looked at Oona. "There's only one culture I know of in the multiverse which successfully used steam and ancient science in combination to produce a working ornithopter . . ."

"The Dark Empire," murmured Oona with some concern. "The Empire of Granbretan." She sighed. "We appear to have escaped the frying pan and landed in the fire."

"The Dark Empire?" Lieutenant Fromental was curious; his big, dark eyes looked from face to face. "Grand Bretagne? Britain?"

"In this world," said Prince Lobkowitz, "London—or Londra—is the hub of one of the most evil empires history has ever known."

Lieutenant Fromental said nothing, but a look of peculiar satisfaction crossed his face for a moment.

"So how did they get here?" I asked.

"I think the question is, how did *we* get here?" answered Oona.

"I've never accidentally stepped into this world." Prince Lobkowitz seemed concerned. "Still, there have been more histories of its particular culture than any others I've come across. Perhaps in this one they have learned the error of their ways."

"We must hope so and make the most of things. That ornithopter does not necessarily mean they actually rule this part of the world. At least we can be fairly certain we're in Europe!" Oona was anxious, I could tell, and trying not to alarm me.

"We have more chances of finding someone who can help us. Remember, the Dark Empire arose after the Tragic Millennium. Before the Tragic Millennium, people had more knowledge than almost any other culture."

"A wisdom King Huon and his sorcerer-scientists perverted," murmured Prince Lobkowitz. "They are a mad, cruel, stupid, unpleasant people. Their sadism is infamous. They have tortured the populations of whole provinces to death. And with refinement, too."

He looked at me and seemed to regret what he had just said.

"Prince!" Lord Renyard glared at him, indicating me. I was worried and fascinated at the same time. I must admit, my stomach had turned over a bit. On the other hand, I don't think I was as scared as they expected me to be. Now I've been through that whole thing, I know what's involved. Then I couldn't imagine what really, really evil people could be like.

That night we kept a low fire and put it out as soon as our food was cooked. We would eat the rest of it cold in the morning, when the Kakatanawa went hunting and scouting.

At dawn the massive clanking, booming, smoke-spewing ornithopter flew over low and took a look at us. We were in open country, with no chance to hide before the flying machine saw us. This time it swooped down and circled before disappearing over the ridge ahead.

We had no choice but to move on. The Kakatanawa were alert, with arrows on their bowstrings. Oona explained that if this was only a scouting craft it would probably not offer any special danger. However, if we had wandered into one of Granbretan's conquered nations, they might see us as a threat to be eliminated.

A little later our questions were answered. We saw two more aircraft soaring into the sky overhead and attacking the first ship we'd seen. Their guns gushed and smeared fire over one another's fuselages. The pilots, protected by transparent canopies, were apparently unhurt and continued to manoeuvre. The two new planes, with their clanking wings and clattering rotors, were much less manoeuvrable than the first one, which outflew them, sending shot after shot into their armoured hulls until at last one suddenly lurched sideways and descended rapidly towards the ground. Seeing this, the second ship turned and limped away through the sky. The first screamed down to land, with a massive bellow of steam, on the rocky side of the hill and turned over slowly, rolling sideways. Its rotors and wings flopped crazily, finally buckling and coming loose as it fell, metal screeching and groaning, until the whole contraption burst into flame.

The wreck was unapproachable, and Lobkowitz shouted at all of us to get back and get down. We barely made it into a shallow dip in the ground as the thing blew up and fragments of red-hot metal showered around us. Lieutenant

Fromental's jacket caught fire but was swiftly put out. There was a faint smell of singed hair. Lord Renyard flicked something away from his foreleg.

Nearby, the victorious machine descended to land. We wondered what the fight had been about. Rather than run, we thought it best to wait and see what would happen. The plane extended hydraulic legs and sank down onto them, for all the world like a settling bird. She stopped her engines and emitted a massive hiss of steam. The canopy slid back, and the crew of heavily suited and masked pilots and gunners climbed out. Once on the ground, they took off their masks and, shading their eyes against the noon sun, stood waiting for us as we approached.

"It's all right, I think," said Prince Lobkowitz. "No Granbretanner would ever take off his mask in public. They seem to be the Dark Empire's enemies."

After a quick discussion, we decided to send Prince Lobkowitz forward. The rest of us watched as the men talked. I breathed a sigh of relief when Prince Lobkowitz and one of the pilots shook hands.

The prince came back smiling. "They are insurgents," he said, "based in Mirenburg. They've driven the Granbretanian armies back beyond Munchein, and hundreds of thousands of mercenaries have come over to them, along with large numbers of recruits from all the conquered territories. Well-trained soldiers." The rebels, he said, had taken control of the factories and were turning out their own improved war machines and weapons in large numbers. Granbretan, fundamentally decadent, was being forced back to her heartlands. The empire was too used to relying on its superior weapons. When they were met with weapons of equal or better power, they were confounded. They were, however, by no means defeated; they might never be defeated, but at last their conquests had been successfully resisted.

In a German I didn't really understand very well, Prince Lobkowitz and the pilots talked at length. Eventually he said in English, "They want us to come back to Nürnberg and then go on to Mirenburg with them. I think it's our last chance to resume our journey and try to get"—he indicated me—"this young lady reunited with her parents."

So that's why we turned around and began our journey back. It was, as it turned out, a pretty iffy decision.

We were rather knackered by the time we arrived in their version of

Mirenburg. This city was totally different from the one we'd left. It was half-surrounded by huge chimneys belching out smoke, just like the first one, but there were so many more of them! Each chimney was carved in some grotesque representation of humans or beasts or both. The buildings were like something out of a Gothic movie, all weird shapes and sizes, and the streets were full of people in the most bizarre costumes and armour! I had never seen anything like it in a book, game or movie. The colours were mostly dark and rich. Many people rode horses, while others were carried aboard big rail-travelling trams driven by steam and also shaped like various animals. It seemed that no human artefact should be allowed to resemble itself! It was the coolest place I'd ever visited. Better than the best theme park, a mixture of London during the Notting Hill carnival, a big funfair and a fancy-dress party. I had the feeling I was enjoying it more than my friends, apart from Lord Renyard, whose long mouth grinned and whose eyes glistened. I held his big paw while he loped along, using his tall dandy cane for support. Some of the people seemed a bit surprised by him, but most gave him no more attention than the rest of our party. Maybe they were used to seeing six-foot-tall foxes in eighteenth-century finery eyeing them through an ornamental quizzing glass.

"I was only aware, mademoiselle, of the *theory* of parallel or 'alternate' worlds," he said as he strolled along. "But this demonstration is incontrovertible, is it not? I must admit that while I miss my home and my library, our expedition is providing me with a considerable amount of intellectual stimulus. I continue, naturally, to be sympathetic to your terrible situation, but find myself fascinated, especially when it occurs to me that this could be a world where the superior species resembled myself, and your own—forgive me—might be considered monstrous, eh?"

I told him that he had been such a kind friend to me that any pleasure he got cheered me up. If I knew that my mum and dad weren't worrying, I'd be enjoying the adventure a lot more myself.

His large, warm pad closed gratefully on my fingers. I realised at that point that we'd become real friends, and I felt rather proud of it. I wished everyone at school could see us together. There wasn't anything much cooler than having a talking animal as your best mate, especially when he was probably the most intelligent person you'd ever known—and a king of thieves to top it all off!

Later we found an inn for the night. I asked if I could share a room with him. No-one objected. Oona seemed almost relieved at my choice.

We were greeted as friends by the people of Mirenburg. Their morale was high. They had driven back a force said to be unbeatable. They had word that Dorian Hawkmoon, a local legendary champion against the Dark Empire, was heading their way with an army. They had never before believed they could defeat their conquerors, but now it seemed highly likely they were going to drive them back to the sea and beyond. They had by no means destroyed the threat—they might never entirely destroy it—but they now knew it was possible. They were determined to do their best.

Tomorrow, we were told, we would be granted an audience with Prince Yaroslaf Stredic, who had recently become protector of this city and the province it commanded. He was also chief of their armies. His destiny was to save the whole of Europe from Granbretan and confine the perverted, sorcerous evil empire to her own shores. She would be contained thereafter by the superior arms Mirenburg now possessed.

Meanwhile there was a feast to attend, an affair hastily thrown together by the mayor. I apparently fell asleep halfway through and was carried back to the hotel by Lord Renyard, because I woke up next morning in a beautiful little hand-carved bed with roses painted all over it, and found that the fox was already dressed.

"An important day for us, mademoiselle," he said, handing me a cup of tea. "I have ordered your breakfast. This morning we meet the saviour of Mirenburg."

And that was how I found out how this revolution had effectively been started by a red-eyed albino who bore a strong resemblance to the man I knew best as Monsieur Zodiac.

Soon we were back at the palace, seated at a big formal table. There was a bit of a preliminary ceremony while we were greeted officially as friends of the revolt, and then we started this lovely lunch. Most of the ingredients were unfamiliar to me, and some I really didn't like much, but I did my best with it, sticking mostly to salad and hot veggies. I noticed also that most of the Kakatanawa didn't look too happy with the food, which seemed unfair since they had supplied us with so many delicious meals on the trail.

Prince Yaroslaf Stredic, according to tradition, was at the head of the table, and we all sat clustered around him while various other officials and notables spread out along both sides. At the far end of the table, clearly taking an interest in us but refusing to join in any discussion, was a monk. He wore a cassock with a deep hood, and his face was impossible to make out. His broad shoulders could not be disguised by his habit, however. Prince Lobkowitz wondered if he was a renegade from Granbretan, whose people couldn't bear to have their faces exposed.

The prince was a pink, round-headed, good-natured young man with an air of confident power and was full of "Lord Elric's" praises. We learned how they had met, the trick played to get them here, Elric's cleverness, his support for the revolution, the flight of Klosterheim and von Minct, and Elric's following them in the belief that they meant me harm and might lead him to me.

I felt incredibly important when Prince Yaroslaf told me of Elric's concern, of his having the city turned upside down in search of me. We asked if Elric had left a message for us, but of course our coming hadn't been anticipated.

"Clearly," said the prince, "your friend didn't expect you to follow him. He'll regret not having stayed longer, but he has been gone for a year now, at least." He concentrated as he calculated the length of time Elric had been gone. "He is a brave, noble man, if an unusual one. Sorcery has always made me uneasy, I suppose because I associate it with Granbretan."

I wondered what spell the albino had cast that disturbed Prince Yaroslaf, but clearly the Protector of Mirenburg didn't want to discuss it any more.

Elric had told them nothing of where he was going, Prince Yaroslaf said, but moments before he said farewell, he had mentioned the "moonbeam roads." Everyone in our party knew what this meant. "He has crossed between the worlds, still searching the multiverse for this young lady," murmured Oona a bit doubtfully. "I hope he is careful. He lacks much experience of the roads themselves . . ."

Great! The one man who seemed to have some chance of getting me home had not only disappeared but had put himself in extraordinary danger as well. I did my best to remain positive when I heard this news. I was flattered that so many important people cared about me, but all I really wanted in my heart was to see my mum and dad again and then mooch off down to the stream and mess about looking for crayfish. On my own. With them to go home to. Would I ever see them again? *Don't think about it!* warned my inner voice. I knew it was pointless, but that was the level of depression I got flashes of from time to time.

"Tomorrow," promised the Prince of Wäldenstein, "we will be able to talk more casually." He apologised for the formality and the brevity of our time together. He was delighted that we were comrades of the albino, he said. "That man will go into our history as the hero who began the revolution against the Dark Empire. Without him, none of this could have happened, and we should never have sounded the trumpet call which brought us our other great hero—"

I followed his eyes, and I saw the hooded man shake his head very slightly as Prince Yaroslaf changed the subject. The mysterious lunch guest didn't want to be known to us. I tried to work out why he was so familiar to me. Surely this wasn't another trick of Klosterheim's. But Klosterheim's shoulders were narrow.

I had another thought: Gaynor the Damned?

Once again I was suddenly alert. If there was something going on here, I wanted to know about it. I kept my own counsel, though. I trusted my friends, but I didn't know these new people. I decided to bring the subject up later and see if anyone else had ideas.

"How I long to hear your stories," said the Protector of Mirenburg. "I look forward to learning how you became friends with the albino. He remains a mystery to me. Yet without him—" Again he stopped, as if he felt he was saying too much.

Meanwhile, he added regretfully, they were coping with a fresh counter-attack from Granbretan in the region of Lyon, and he had to oversee the battle plans. "The momentum of this war has been unbelievable. So ill-prepared was Granbretan, so careless in not creating defences against their own latest war ma-chines, that a revolt in one key city set off a chain reaction. Those who had once compromised with the Dark Empire, as Count Brass began by doing, learned to trust nothing they were promised. Almost everyone had lost a loved family member to the savage cruelty of those neurotic masked warriors. They wanted revenge."

After a bit more ceremony at the end of the lunch, I looked down the table and saw that the cowled man had already left.

We returned to our inn, and Oona disappeared into the city. She came back a while later with a little more news of Elric. She had talked with other citizens. "My father was certainly here," she said. "And he seems to have instigated the revolution almost by accident. His chief motive was to find you, Oonagh. They all mention how he constantly asked after you."

"Your father?"

"Didn't I tell you?" she asked.

I hadn't quite put it all together. Of course, there was every chance she and Monsieur Zodiac were related, but I hadn't realised how closely. I was starting to get a dim idea why some people didn't seem as old (or as young) as they ought to be. We were all in danger of meeting grandchildren who looked older than we did! Not that it made complete sense. For instance, if there were millions of possible versions of my world, there were millions of possible versions of myself—or Oona, or Prince Lobkowitz, Klosterheim and, indeed, Elric! Or was that what set us apart from most other people? The fact that we were *not* reproduced on every "plane." Was that why we could move so readily between the worlds, while others couldn't?

I would like to have explored this very different Mirenburg, but everyone else felt it was too dangerous for me to go out on my own. Our inn was called the Nun and Turtle. A very well-known place, I was told. I was sure that if we had enemies hiding in the city, they would be bound to know that we had arrived. There was even a chance they were staying at the same inn!

Even when they explained the old folktale behind the Nun and Turtle's name I didn't understand it any better. But the inn was clean and comfortable, a bit like an English B&B. Eating at communal tables seemed the rule here. We all sat down to supper together in the dining room, and it was then I put my theory about time and the multiverse to Prince Lobkowitz.

"Is that it, prince?" I asked.

He nodded seriously.

"It's something I've considered myself, Miss Oonagh. It could be that we are somehow separated in time as well as space. The Dark Empire of Granbretan, for instance, probably exists in our distant future. Lord Renyard's Mirenburg seemed to be about two hundred years in your past. We might accidentally be meddling with, or even changing, history, or perhaps we are being changed by it. We know that time is by no means as simple as we were taught it was—neither linear nor cyclic. Some even argue that time is a field, acted on to produce a whole sequence of events occurring coincidentally and thus producing divisions, changing directions, new dimensions. Why does the multiverse have to be in a permanent sense of flux, for instance? What would be gained from a perfect and constant balance between Law and Chaos?" He went on a bit longer and rather lost me, but I understood the general drift.

I was very sleepy, but when, before bedtime, Lord Renyard asked if I wanted to go for a walk, I agreed. He was fascinated by how like his own city the older buildings, the layout of streets and so on, were. However, the differences were what commanded his attention. He found most of it, especially the fashion for creating buildings which looked like grotesque creatures, absolutely vulgar and was relieved that next to a more modern building called The Oranesians, the old cathedral of St-Maria-and-St-Maria was still standing. We climbed twisting cobbled stairway streets to reach it. Once at the doors of the ancient Gothic church, Lord Renyard took off his hat and bowed his head as if in prayer while I looked around, seeing the whole city spread out below, its huge factory chimneys, with their glaring or tormented faces, like besieging giants.

Mirenburg was clearly on a war footing. The city walls were lined with guns and ornithopters. They squatted on every available flat space, on roofs and in squares. People told us that Wäldenstein had successfully driven back the Dark Empire and that its armies were now in Frankonia and Iberia, trying to drive the Granbretanners back into the sea. Already—to serve a strategy, most suspected—the empire troops had retreated back across the Silver Bridge that spanned thirty miles of sea, and were now massed in their land stronghold. But the enemy would not give up its empire easily. So far they had not begun to take stock of their old knowledge or set their sorcerer-scientists to work.

Two names, Bous-Junge and Taragorm, were whispered. These were apparently the empire's greatest sorcerer-scientists, who both studied the old lore and added new.

"This is a dark world, mademoiselle," said Lord Renyard. "Darker, I think, than my own."

"You believe some worlds are darker than others?" I asked. "I mean naturally darker and more evil?"

"I suspect it. Where evil has had longer to take root, in soil more conducive to its growth. Surely only the first universe, the first world, where all the avatars of all our heroes dwell, was innocent. No new worlds begin afresh. They are developments of earlier worlds. So therefore it could be possible that some universes develop a kind of *habit* of evil . . ."

14

The interior of the church was disappointing. Clearly it had been a thousand years or more since Christians had worshipped there. Now it was full of strange pictures and even stranger idols. I began to understand a little of what Lord Renyard said. Neither of us wanted to stay there. We both preferred the building's familiar exterior. As we came back out into the fading sunlight I asked him if he thought this world had developed that habit of evil. It was possible, he said, but he hoped not. The forms people worshipped or used as channels to their own souls were not always what we would regard as beautiful or artistic. "Taste," he said. "I had considered a scholarly discourse on the subject. *Sartor Resartus?*"

"Law and Chaos?" I said. "They're not the same as good and evil, I'm told."

"Merciful heavens, no! Not at all. Not at all. Evil is a cruel and selfish thing. Chaos can be wild and generous, and just as some Lords of Law are self-sacrificing and concerned for others, so are some Lords of Chaos. Did you never hear of Lady Miggea of Law or Lord Arioch of Chaos? Both are selfish and calculating. Both would sacrifice anyone else to their ambition. Yet Armein of Chaos is jolly and open-handed by all accounts, as is Lord Arkyn of Law. They would be friends in other circumstances, I'm sure, those Lords of the Higher Worlds."

"Then why on earth are they at odds?" I asked.

"Their duty demands it. We all serve Fate in some way. We all have loyalties and predispositions. We all have different remedies for the world's pain."

"Do these lords and ladies fight all the time?"

"Some do. Some do not. They do their duty. They are loyal to their cause. Only rarely do you hear of a renegade like Gaynor."

"And does anyone serve these lords and ladies from choice?"

"Certainly. The Knights of the Balance. Born to struggle in perpetual battle."

"Have you met any of these knights?" I was beginning to wonder if Lord

Renyard's faith in the so-called Balance, which my mother had talked to me about as well, was as needy as that of the people who had filled St-Maria-and-St-Maria with such hideous idols.

"I believe I have met some. I believe you have, also."

"My grandmother? Can women . . .?"

"Absolutely. There are many great champions, I hear, who are women. There are some who are androgynous. All colours and tastes." He uttered that strange, barking laugh. "Your grandmother, Oona, is a quasi-immortal. Her blood, of course, is that of champions."

"But she isn't a champion herself?"

"I do not know, and it is not my place, dear mademoiselle, to speculate. Her father, who is sometimes called Count Zodiac—"

"Which would make him my great-grandfather. He seems immortal."

"By no means. Only in his dreams, from what my friend Lobkowitz tells me!"

"Is Prince Lobkowitz a champion? Lieutenant Fromental?"

"They carry the wisdom which sometimes helps a champion. Or so I'm told. Companions of the Order, perhaps? Like their friend and, I hope, mine, the Chevalier St Odhran. But Colonel Bastable is almost certainly a knight, as well as a member of the Guild of Temporal Adventurers."

"And what's Gaynor, then?"

"Like Klosterheim, Gaynor allowed his selfish greed and egomania to possess his whole being. Both once served nobler causes. Both renounced those causes. You know, my dear, that I am a rationalist. I am of the Enlightenment. It is my whole being. Much of what you are asking should best be asked of Lobkowitz himself. Or your grandmother!"

I knew I was pestering him as we walked back down the steps. It was dusk and he wanted to get back to the inn. He had my hand in his paw as we hurried along. But I had a lot of questions. "Herr Klosterheim was once a Companion of that Order?"

"Yes, but not loyal to Chaos or Law. Now he embraces Evil, which is a much lesser thing. A petty thing, though dangerous and often powerful. Yet I suspect that he, if not Gaynor, serves the purposes of Law while not necessarily sharing its ideals."

"I heard someone mention the Lords of Hell, the Lords of Entropy. Who are they?"

"Names, nothing else. Lords, like Arioch, who are greedy and cruel, are sometimes called the Dukes of Hell by humans, but they are a miscellaneous crew. Lady Miggea, though she be a corrupted servant of Law, is called by many who have confronted her a Duchess of Hell. And some of the great elementals are also mistakenly identified with Lucifer."

"So does Lucifer exist?" I asked.

Lord Renyard looked troubled at this. "We no longer know," he said.

The shadows were gathering. We had walked further than we realised, and it was a long way back.

"So who's the most powerful?" I wanted to know. "Law or Chaos?"

"Neither," he said after a little thought.

"Okay. Then what single quality do you associate with them?"

Perhaps to keep his mind off the potential dangers of the city at night, Lord Renyard gave my question some thought. At last he answered, "Love is one."

"And the other?"

"Greed."

We had taken a wrong turn. Lord Renyard paused as we came out of an alley. Across from us was an old bridge. We were down where the river made a radical curve. Lord Renyard set out for the bridge.

"But the inn's on this side," I said.

"It will be quicker if we take this bridge, cross through the old factory quarter, and then cross again. A short cut."

"How could you get lost in your own city, Lord Renyard?" We were both becoming nervous.

"I thought I recognised landmarks, streets. I was wrong. I do apologise, dear mademoiselle. Sometimes I wish I were a mere fox and used my nose a little better."

"Why don't you?"

"Snobbery. I used to think such means uncivilised. I think I'm a little wiser now. Too late, you might say."

He was right about the short cut. We were hardly in the industrial part of the city for a few minutes before he spotted another bridge. Below it and to the left and right along the embankment, presumably for the factory workers, was some sort of recreation park, with a menagerie and sideshows. I love fairs and carnivals, though I find it hard to enjoy old-fashioned circuses. There were even a few mechanical rides. A big Ferris wheel but no roller coasters, and some really funky steam-operated bumper cars made in the form of wild animals. A sinister-looking helter-skelter stood beside an oddly fashioned merry-go-round, whose riding beasts were totally fantastic and like nothing I'd ever seen. We had to traverse the park to reach the bridge. I didn't complain. I knew I couldn't ask to take some rides, but it was hard to pass them *all* by. The Ferris wheel overlooked the river and turned slowly to the music of a distant steam organ. It reminded me of the London Wheel, which I'd already ridden several times. If we were here for a while, I'd definitely ask someone to take me. But it wasn't fair to ask Lord Renyard, who clearly found it very distasteful.

More and more people came into the park, cackling and grinning and laughing themselves silly. Evidently they came to enjoy themselves after work. Dressed in their best finery, they looked as strange to me in those odd clothes as I did to them. The park's lights had come on. The gas jets spread a warm, yellow aura.

Suddenly I thought I saw Monsieur Zodiac disappearing into one of the sideshows. I remembered he had worked in the theatre in England. Maybe he hadn't left Mirenburg, after all. Maybe he had been waiting for me.

With a quick word to a startled Lord Renyard, I broke free of his protective paw and ran into the booth. Pushing past the grubby white flap, I found myself in the gloom of the tent's interior.

I saw someone ahead of me. Someone with long white hair who could be Monsieur Zodiac, though he seemed too short as I got closer.

I called out, "Monsieur Zodiac, is that you?"

The figure looked up, as if he heard me. Then he was gone again. But there was a strangeness about his stance which alarmed me. Was it the blind boy? I became suddenly frightened, and when I heard Lord Renyard calling my name I went outside again and found him. The last thing in the world I wanted to do was worry that kindly beast. He was greatly relieved to see me and begged me not to do that again, especially in the dark park. I told him what I'd seen.

"Could Monsieur Zodiac only have pretended to have left, to confuse Klosterheim and Gaynor, maybe?"

Lord Renyard fingered his long muzzle. "I did not think he was in this realm. He travelled on, across the moonbeam roads. I thought his business was . . . elsewhere. Yet fate could have sent him here as readily as we were sent. But would he not have sought us out by now?"

"Only if he knew we were here. Maybe he didn't want to be spotted."

"We are not close acquaintances, my dear girl. I know of him, of course. But our meeting was only brief and under ground."

"He would have known me if he'd seen me. He's looking for me."

"But you are rather small, mademoiselle, if I may say so."

"Well, you're not likely to blend in with the crowd," I pointed out. "He'd surely have remembered you."

It was now completely dark. Flares and lamps were burning orange-yellow against the night. Lord Renyard grew agitated, his long whiskers quivering.

"We must hurry," he said. It was hard for him to tug me. "We must rejoin the others." He led me back through the thick press of the evening. There was a peculiar vibrancy to the busy crowd as we made our way to the Nun and Turtle. Lord Renyard sensed it, too. He had noted how, in wartime, people were inclined to make the most of their leisure. He might even call it a kind of madness, a lust for life and its pleasures because they could be taken away for ever at any moment. The atmosphere actually made me slightly uncomfortable. I was glad to get into the warmth and relative peace of The Nun, where old Herr Morhaim busily took orders for supper, apologising in his thick Turkish accent that his menu was limited somewhat by the exigencies of war.

For all that, we ate very well. We had another audience scheduled with Prince Yaroslaf the next day. We hoped he would allow us to remain in the city and pursue our own quest. We were a little afraid he might decide to enlist us for the war effort.

I had a lot on my mind and was surprised I slept soundly and peacefully. Once again my friends had thrown a great invisible shield around me. Lord Renyard came to his bed at some point. He didn't wake me in the process. Then, in the early part of the morning, I had some alarming dreams which did wake me. I'd seen the white-haired man again, only this time he wasn't a man but the youth who looked so much like my great-grandfather, and he smiled, beckoning me towards him. I wasn't frightened by the boy, but I was suddenly filled with a sense of dread—a sense that he was in great danger and that only I could save him. Then I felt both Lord Renyard and Oona standing nearby.

The dream faded. It was dawn. I could see Lord Renyard fast asleep, his long legs sticking off his bed at an angle. Observing him more closely, I realised he was sleeping perfectly comfortably, like a large dog. He had drawn the quilt over him for the sake of propriety. His clothes were all neatly folded or hung on hangers near him, and his dandy pole lay alongside the bed. Very occasionally he snored and his whiskers twitched. Affection for him welled up in me to see him there, so vulnerable and peaceful.

Though the fox's presence was reassuring, I could not go back to sleep.

I saw that someone had left a set of clean clothes for me. This was luxury. I got out of bed and went along the passage to the bathroom to use it first. I pulled the cord which would bring up a maid with some hot water, and though the water was cool by the time it arrived, I had a delicious and uninterrupted bath. I got into my fresh clothes and went down to breakfast on my own. I knew we had to be ready to meet the protector at his palace, and I felt an obscure pride in not having to be hassled along, as usually happened at home when we were going out early for some reason.

I had the satisfaction of seeing the look of surprise on Oona's face when she came down. She laughed. "I was giving you a few more minutes. I thought you were still in bed. Did you sleep well?"

"Mostly," I said.

Our carriages arrived while we were still eating. We tried to hurry, straightened ourselves as best we could and got into the waiting four-wheelers, which set off at a clip over the cobbled streets, threatening to bounce the life out of us.

It was the kind of grey, drizzling morning for which I'd always had a perverse taste. I enjoyed the ride through streets now packed with vendors and soldiers. The soldiers had the grim, staring look you saw on the news where they showed people who had been fighting too long in places like the Middle East. Quite a lot wore the masks and goggles of airmen, while others carried huge, thick-hafted, platinum-tipped flame lances on their armoured shoulders. A few wore the baroque animal armour identified with the clans and societies of Granbretan. It felt very odd for your own country to be the enemy; it was hard to get my head around the idea. I'm not saying Britain always behaved herself properly, and I knew a fair bit about Empire, but these people seemed to have come up with the ideas and methods of Adolf Hitler combined with the imperial instincts of Cecil Rhodes.

I shared a carriage with Lord Renyard, Prince Lobkowitz and Lieutenant Fromental. Oona followed with some of her Kakatanawa, who, of course, hadn't been able to fit into one carriage. My companions weren't very talkative this morning. They explained the normal protocol for visiting Mirenburg's royal leader at an audience rather than at a meal. It was quite different, they said, to how one would behave, for instance, in the presence of the perhaps now drowned Sebastocrater.

"Possibly more formal," said Prince Lobkowitz. "New states set high store by such things, as do new statesmen." He had already approved of my dress, which was very nice, given that I hadn't even shopped for it. In the carriage I worked on the hairdo Oona had tried to give me on the run. I thought I looked pretty good, all in all. Not that I usually cared.

The carriages moved up a wide avenue to what Oona called the Krasnya Palace, although the drivers called it something else. It was much fancier than the Mirenburg I'd left. The palace had a French rather than a classical style and reminded me of Versailles.

We left the carriages and ascended the wide steps up to the front doors, which were guarded on both sides by women in very bulky armour, with flame lances held at the slant. Next we were greeted by an elaborately dressed major-domo with a magnificent black beard shot with grey, who asked us to follow him through the marble corridors, past freshly painted walls. The entire place had been elaborately redecorated from top to bottom. It smelled of paint through-out. The predominant colour was now vivid green. Most vivid of all were the curtains, drawn back from the long windows, but the trim on the wood was a pretty violent green, too.

Door after door opened, was entered, then closed behind us until we stood in a small throne room filled with people. Sitting on the white alabaster throne itself was the nice-looking gentleman who had entertained us to lunch the day before. He had the same straightforward, almost naïve manner, and we got the impression again of an honest man of action. He had been elected to his position of protector, but apparently the right was his by blood. He rose from his throne and came down the steps to greet us, standing on the lowest step while the major-domo introduced us one by one. He had the most trouble with getting his tongue around the Kakatanawa names and in the end resorted to letting them introduce themselves, which they did with all the grace and style of born diplomats.

"Good morning to you, honoured visitors," he said. "We are especially glad to greet gentlemen from far Amarehk, who do not disappoint us, for our legends say the Amarehki were great warriors and handsome people." He spoke in a low, respectful tone.

It was an odd understanding of America, but I rather liked it. I realised there had been a time, and possibly was still a time somewhere in the multiverse, when Native Americans governed their own country. He seemed to have the idea that we were all from America, and nobody told him otherwise. He might as well think we were from there as from anywhere. In this "brane" or "realm" of the multiverse America had not been colonised by Europeans except in certain iso-lated places.

"Any friends of the great Lord Elric, of course, are friends of ours. You already know this, and I am again glad to welcome you here." He had climbed a few stairs and now sat down again. "He alone is responsible for what was begun here."

"It is a shame he left no forwarding address," said Lieutenant Fromental rather sardonically, without insulting the young protector.

"I agree," said Prince Yaroslaf. "But he had already done so much for us, I could ask him no more. It seemed clear to me that he did not wish to tell us where he went, save to find the 'moonbeam roads' he spoke about."

The conversation lost me after that, but the others seemed to be getting something out of it. In the end I gave up listening and decided to enjoy myself as best I could. About the only interesting bit was when we were shown a dis-play of captured armour and weapons from Granbretan. It really was weird stuff, especially the mantis armour of King Huon's guard, which looked as if a whole lot of giant insects had been wiped out. At some point refreshments were brought in, and I had the best glass of lemonade I'd ever tasted. Yet I still couldn't help thinking of the white-skinned boy I'd seen. I really wanted to get back to the fairgrounds and find him. I wondered if, later on, I could persuade Lord Renyard to help me.

Meanwhile I continued to find Prince Yaroslaf's formal court rather funny. In their padded clothes they were like a hall full of Renaissance Michelin Men. I knew it was wrong to laugh, but it was hard to keep from giggling sometimes. These people were fighting for life and freedom against a terrible evil, and all I could do was laugh! I decided I must be shallow. And this made me even more amused. The guiltier I felt, the more I wanted to giggle. In the end I asked a footman where to find the bathroom. This turned out to be a sort of inverted pyramid in the floor. At least I didn't really need it. Once inside, I almost exploded with laughter, giggling myself silly.

The door had a kind of grille in it so that people inside could see if someone was waiting outside, without anyone being able to see in. After about ten minutes I was all right. I put my eye to the grille and watched the people coming and going along the passage. No-one needed the toilet, so I relaxed and collected myself. The next time I looked through the grille, however, I got a shock.

Passing the door, as bold as brass, was Herr Klosterheim! So the man in the cowl *had* been Gaynor! I was totally astonished and almost fell backwards. When I peered out through the grille again he had, of course, gone.

For a while I was too terrified to leave. Yet I knew I had to warn my friends. Was Klosterheim in league with Prince Yaroslaf? I had no way of knowing. And now I felt sick with anxiety.

Eventually I pulled myself together, left the bathroom, and hurried to look for one of my companions.

Fortunately Oona found me before I found her. She, too, seemed scared, and I had another reason to feel guilty.

"I'm really sorry," I said. "But I've got something important to tell you. If I hadn't gone to the bathroom, I'd never have found it out." I was panting. "I saw Herr Klosterheim and had to wait until he was gone. Then—"

"We thought you'd been kidnapped," she said. Then she paused. "What? You've seen Klosterheim? Where?"

"In the hall. Passing the bathroom," I told her. "In that corridor. Back there. He didn't know I saw him. Did you know he had followed us?"

"The prince thinks they left with Elric following *them*. What can this mean? My guess is that they're working for the empire and don't even know we're here. Yet Prince Yaroslaf knows them both. He knows they are probably his enemies. Why hasn't he had them arrested?"

"Perhaps he's playing a more complex game than we think," I said, feeling a total idiot.

She nodded absently. "The sooner we get out of here, the better."

Since the reception was in our honour, it was some time before we were able to leave. Our carriages hurried through the late-morning streets of Mirenburg. I was hungry, as I hadn't even had much chance to look at the buffet. That lemonade had improved my expectations of Wäldensteiner food.

Back at the inn my friends conferred. One of us must find out if von Minct was here and if he and Klosterheim had the confidence of the protector, who had declared that Elric was his friend. We feared, of course, a repetition of the events in that other Mirenburg.

"And repetition," said Prince Lobkowitz, "is very much a norm in the multiverse. It's a sign of order, as in music. Our lives, personalities and stories all tend to repeat themselves, as do the composition and arrangements of the stars and planets."

"Surely such repetition is the natural state of Law," suggested Lord Renyard.

"And the antithesis of Chaos?" said Lieutenant Fromental.

"So does Klosterheim serve Law or Chaos now?" I asked.

"In truth, he makes the alliances which suit him, but he and von Minct tend towards a corrupted form of Law," answered Oona.

I still couldn't see why those two would have anything to do with me. As far as I knew, I had no understanding, affiliation or interest in Law, Chaos or anything else supernatural. All I wanted was to get home and be able to tell my mum and dad about my adventures. I was pretty sure that was all Oona wanted for me, too.

"We need to get in touch with the man who essentially got this whole war going," said Prince Lobkowitz. "Hawkmoon and his people recently retook Kamarg, as you have heard. We should contact him. He is a manifestation of the Champion Eternal, a Knight of the Balance who is beginning to understand the nature of the multiverse as well as any of us. Hawkmoon is bound to know a scientist who can help us."

"Are they still in Kamarg?"

"I assume so. But his army moves with supernatural speed."

"How far is it?" asked Oona.

"We should have to cross a fair bit of Europe," said Prince Lobkowitz. "Parts of which are still at war, as we have seen. Our journey would take us across the Switzer mountains, which are full of bandits, or via Italia and Frankonia. A dangerous path, for which we should need a guide, I think." Prince Lobkowitz was shaking his head. "Even if we were loaned enough ornithopters to fly us there—and we know they have none to spare—it would be a long journey."

"Is there no other alternative?" asked Lord Renyard. I had the feeling he didn't want to leave Mirenburg, however different it was from his own city.

"There is only one solution which makes sense," said Lieutenant Fromental after a while. "Some of us must go to Kamarg by land, and the rest must take the young lady there by air."

I didn't want us to separate, but I *did* fancy the idea of having a ride in one of those weird planes, so before anyone else could say anything I cried: "I like the idea!"

"I'm not sure . . ." began Oona.

"It would get me to safety quicker, wouldn't it?" I said. "And Mr Klosterheim and Mr von Minct would be less able to follow."

"You speak sense, I think, little mademoiselle." Lord Renyard put his two red-furred paws on the table to emphasise his assent.

"But what if you did not see Klosterheim?" said Oona. "What if you only saw someone who resembled him?"

"Then who was that monk at lunch yesterday? I'm pretty sure it was Gaynor."

"I saw him, too," she admitted. "But I didn't assume it was Gaynor. Hmmm . . ." She sighed. "We must wait," she said, almost to herself. "We must wait."

"Oh, please!" I lost my cool altogether. "*Why?*"

"No spare flying machines, for a start," she said. "Our best hope would be to get you and someone else onto an ornithopter already bound for Kamarg."

"We haven't time to see how the war goes," said Prince Lobkowitz. "I've talked to people here. They say there are still battlecraft in the area. The Dark

Empire makes raids. They've been driven out, but they're not defeated. There's every possibility of a flying machine being attacked. It would be too risky."

"But my mum and dad will be worrying," I said. "I don't want to miss a chance of getting home."

"I understand." Oona looked so worried, I felt sorry for her. "Travelling to Kamarg, however, won't necessarily get you all reunited sooner. It would just be a chance that Duke Dorian or one of his people could help. If, for instance, they have the crystal which gives them access to other dimensions, they could offer us real protection. While I can travel the moonbeam roads, I need to find a route through before I can try to find Elric or a way to your home that's reasonably safe. If Mirenburg hadn't been flooded by that fool's spell . . ."

"I know you will do whatever you can," I told her. "But if there's *any* way of getting home . . ." I was repeating myself and stopped.

"Hawkmoon has his own concerns," she said. "He won't sacrifice them for our interests. Only if those interests coincide with his duty. Like us, he has enemies all around him. We have to stick together. Watch one another's backs. That's how we'll survive until we get that chance you want." Suddenly, affectionately, she had reached out to me. I realised how carefully she was guarding her emotions. I knew then how much she loved me. I knew she had to be my mother's mother, no matter how impossible it seemed. I so badly wanted to ask her how she had kept so young, but I knew it wasn't the time.

My emotions began to roller-coaster again. I forced myself to calm down. I felt suddenly better. Now all I could do was enter the safety of my grandmother's embrace.

15

Next day I sat in my room trying to make conversation with Lieutenant Fromental, who had obviously been left on guard in case Klosterheim came looking for me. By now none of us was completely sure I had actually seen him.

Fromental was a kind, gentle giant who took his job seriously, but he wasn't very good company. He knew a lot about French comics and American thrillers, especially the Jack Hammer mysteries, but we had almost nothing in common. We didn't even like the same movies. He had been in the French Foreign Legion and had wandered into Mu-Ooria years ago while exploring in Morocco. There he'd met Prince Lobkowitz, but he didn't like to talk of their adventures fighting what they called "the Lost Nazis." I needed something to take my mind off everything, like a trip to the pictures. How *did* these people relax? I wasn't as much worried about Klosterheim as they were. I was thinking of those pleasure gardens, wishing they had TV in this weird world and consoling myself that it would probably be totally weird TV anyway. There wasn't even a book I could read. Some of them seemed to be written in English, but the spelling was all different, and I didn't understand a lot of the words. I tried translating, with Lieutenant Fromental's help, but he was puzzled, too. He thought some of the language was more like French than English. Even the books with pictures didn't make much sense, so I asked Lieutenant Fromental if he felt like going to the fair. He was very serious when he apologised, spreading his huge hands.

"Little mademoiselle, we have to be sure no harm befalls you. If Klosterheim is in the city, you are in considerable danger. Considerable danger. I cannot impress on you enough how much danger . . ."

"I understand," I said. "It's dangerous. I know." The problem was that the dreams were beginning to fade again. I knew I couldn't put myself in peril and frighten my friends, and I wasn't about to let boredom get to me, but I was also thinking of the person I'd seen in the tent who so resembled both the missing Monsieur Zodiac and the blind boy, Onric.

Another day dragged slowly by. And another. I waited eagerly for news of the war, hoping someone would tell us it was over. Everyone else went out whenever they wished. Once a week the whole Kakatanawa troop stayed with me. They had a game with beads and a large hollowed-out piece of wood which one of them told me was called the "canoe," and I became obsessed with playing it for a while.

My friends had begun to think I had made a mistake about seeing Klosterheim in the palace. Prince Yaroslaf had clearly not invited him to Court. The prince remained adamant that he considered Klosterheim and von Minct enemies, who would serve themselves at every turn and serve the Dark Empire if it suited them. They had been seen elsewhere, however. One report placed them in Kamarg itself, fleeing shortly before Hawkmoon's army retook the province. Another put them on the northern coast.

I think I eventually wore Oona down. She finally came to the conclusion that Klosterheim and von Minct had moved on, if indeed they had been here at all. I didn't get my ornithopter ride, but she did allow me to go to the fairgrounds as long as all the Kakatanawa and Lord Renyard went with me. It was better than sitting inside.

Thus, in the company of twelve Americans and a gigantic fox, I found the tent where I had seen the boy, only this time I went in the front entrance. Bright yellow and black displays announced something translated into English, I assumed, as a "Cornucopia of Thespian Skills." Lord Renyard paid for all our entrance tickets. None of us could read the rest of the sign, which was in a language about as far removed from the English I understood as Chaucer's, but we were all pretty sure it *was* English. It reminded me that I was still puzzled about how people, admittedly with some very strange accents, seemed to know a more or less common language. Lord Renyard said it was the lingua franca of the multiverse, which, through a series of very peculiar circumstances, was spoken by people who could walk between the worlds.

Under the canvas, a medium-size pit had been dug into the ground. It was surrounded by long benches, and an old man was standing in the pit, telling a story whose point I missed entirely.

I waited patiently, hoping that the albino boy would be next to perform, but the old man was replaced by actors wearing animal masks and doing something called *Adalf and Eeva*, which made no sense at all. Lord Renyard, who seemed pretty bored, said they reminded him of Greek players. The scene went on for hours, it seemed to me, and in the end we had to leave. I didn't see the boy anywhere. By the time Oona turned up to take us home I was actually looking forward to getting back to the Nun and Turtle.

Oona laughed at my expression and comforted me by saying how she and Prince Lobkowitz had been trying all day to find a way under ground. She was now pretty certain this version of the city didn't have a mirror image, and she had decided that it was time for us to move on. In Munchein, Barkelon or Parye, she said, we might have better luck. But not here.

Everyone seemed a bit down. All of us there preferred action of almost any kind to no action at all. As we left the tent we found ourselves surrounded again by revellers in fanciful costumes dancing in a long line, their hands on the waist of the person ahead of them. People were laughing and singing, and some staggered a bit. We stuck together but couldn't avoid getting caught up in the cheerful crowd enjoying the ritual dance.

And then, as we danced by a gap in the tents, I at last spotted the albino boy again: a young man with glittering red eyes staring straight out of hell and straight into mine. I tried to wrench myself free of the crowd and wave to him. I had a clear view of his face this time, and though they were clearly related, it was not Monsieur Zodiac. It was Onric!

I wriggled out of the mob and ran back to the tent to find him. All of my friends were shouting and following, but the youth had disappeared. I stopped running to let everyone catch up with me. But before they could do so, a figure wearing a papier mâché Red Riding Hood wolf mask darted from the crowd and grabbed me. I don't think the black-clad man had any idea how strong I was as I kicked and bit him, clawing for his eyes and dislodging the mask to reveal the cadaverous face of Herr Klosterheim.

I had been right! I felt triumphant even as he tried to drag me away and Oona, Lord Renyard and the Kakatanawa converged on him. Uingasta, one of the Americans, got hold of Klosterheim, who had dropped me, but the man, abandoning his mask, slipped free and ran off into the crowd, pursued by everyone but Lord Renyard and me.

The dancing people seemed entranced as they re-formed their ranks and danced on, as the Kakatanawa and Oona straggled back, disappointed.

"So I wasn't barmy, see?" I declared.

"You weren't barmy, dear, that's true." Oona was out of breath. She kept her bow strung and an arrow nocked on it. "We've got to get you out of the city. He knows you're here. He's been waiting his chance. I'm sure he's told von Minct, and one of them is sure to try this again. We can guard against *him*, of course. But what about those others? Klosterheim is bound to resort to supernatural aid at any moment, as soon as he can, and that will endanger the city and all of us—including what the city represents to those who oppose Granbretan." She spoke in low, urgent tones. "We'll leave as soon as we can. Come on. Let's get back to the inn."

I couldn't work out why she was reacting like this. Had she never believed Klosterheim was here? Had she been humouring me? Perhaps she thought Klosterheim had lost the power to travel through the realms. Perhaps his desperate attempt to kidnap me indicated that something else was going on, that our enemies were becoming more desperate and therefore more dangerous.

Next morning we put our affairs in order and, with help from the palace, slipped out of the Nun and Turtle, through a private gate in the city, taking the Munchein road. Oona and Prince Lobkowitz had tried to get the use of some ornithopters, but none was available. Though they were producing new machines all the time, those factories were having to be moved and, wherever possible, hidden. They were the main target for any squadron the Dark Empire sent over. There was some chance Granbretan would be trying again to destroy the factories, perhaps in the next night or two, so we accepted his need and made other arrangements. Prince Yaroslaf, respecting our danger, sent some of his best guards with us. He did everything he could to accommodate us.

Oona and the Indians rode in carriages, because the Indians didn't know much about horses. I sat inside with her part of the time, and the rest I had a pony I could ride, so long as I remained close to Prince Lobkowitz or Lieutenant Fromental. Lord Renyard, of course, also rode in the coaches.

While seated in the carriage with Oona I told her what I'd been thinking about the desperation of our enemies. She leaned over from the seat across from me and rumpled my hair. "You're a smart young lady. Our enemies grow increasingly less subtle. That means there's a clock ticking somewhere for them. You're right; they're losing time and patience and becoming more dangerous."

"And yet you still have no idea what they want me for?"

"I'm getting a bit of an idea, but nothing too clear yet." My granny's ivory beauty continued to amaze me. She was like one of those stunning 1920s figurines fashioned in ivory and bronze. At night her skin had a faint, pale glow, and her red eyes carried an expression not entirely different from her father's when he seemed troubled. In the light of early morning she was like a Greek statue come to life.

"I wonder where he is." I spoke without thinking. "Your father—Monsieur Zodiac?"

"Elric? I fear he might be lost, or that people might even be deliberately misdirecting him. Somewhere in his own world where he was born, he's suffering horribly. He's the prisoner of a cruel enemy who would bring the unchecked reign of Chaos down upon them all. He has seen Chaos in all its aggressive variety, and he fights it, though he is also dependent upon it for his very life. Should he be killed in this, his dream, then he dies in his own world, too. Every action he or his enemies take in one realm, he takes in a million others, save that these selves, as substantial as you or me, are the creation of a particularly powerful form of dreaming. Every other world but his own is a dream to him. He hangs, dreaming even now, on the yardarm of a ship, desperate for that one thing which sustains him, which will free him."

"Which is?"

"A sword," said my grandmother with weary bitterness. "It has taken him a thousand years to earn that blade. And now, to save us, he risks everything, when salvation for him could be hours or days away." And she fell into such a silence that I couldn't bring myself to ask her another question.

Later she began talking again. Elric, she said, was clearly her father, as I'd guessed, and not just an average multiversal adventurer! His destiny was some-how linked to the destiny of every world he had touched in his thousand-year search for his sword. There was some trouble with the carriage, and we had to get out while someone saw to it. We were still less than half a mile from the city, and the walls remained in sight. Prince Lobkowitz brought up a pony for me to ride.

"What's so special about my great-granddad's sword?" I asked him.

He looked at me in complete bafflement. "Elric's sword? Aha! The Black Sword. There is an aspect of it in every world I know, yet the sword itself, capable of generating hundreds of versions of itself, is elusive. Without it, our work can never be completed. Elric's destiny in this complex equation is to use the sword to bring a halt to a multiversal phenomenon which has grown out of control."

"Which is . . .?" My persistence made him smile. He guessed that this was all Oona would tell me.

"She knows how important it is for Elric to reach the end of his thousand-year dream with that sword in his hand. That has been the whole point of his dream. Yet so strong are his feelings for those he regards as his descendants that he is risking his own chance of salvation. A noble thing to do, but in the scheme of things, it is a very dangerous thing to do, putting many at risk. He does not, of course, know what he risks, save his own life and soul. Yet you are also important to him because you are his great-granddaughter, and Klosterheim and von Minct and those they represent would gain a great deal from diverting Elric and capturing you. I am beginning to guess that they deliberately led the albino on a wild-goose chase while going back to Mirenburg, perhaps knowing you would return. Yet," he mused, "you also have something they desire. As has that boy."

"So von Minct was the cowled man at the table?"

"We could presume so. But remember, there are many players in this game, and not all of them are fulfilling the roles they seem to have been assigned . . ." He laughed rather bitterly.

The carriage fixed, we were off again. My pony was used to a different kind of handling, I think. Every country has slightly modified habits of riding, so the pony and I took a while to adapt to each other. Still it was a pleasure to be riding again, even if there was no chance of a gallop or even a canter. We had to stick close together, said Prince Lobkowitz, especially at the moment. If we needed to scatter, then we could enjoy a gallop!

I think von Minct realised too late that we were leaving. Behind us I saw a single cowled figure which ran frantically in our wake before abandoning the chase. We had escaped the city just in time.

For the first fifty miles or so Prince Yaroslaf's guards accompanied us until we were well into the mountains and on our way to Munchein. This whole country, they said, had been taken from the Granbretanners, who were still making attacks on Mirenburg's factories from bases on Jarsee and elsewhere. Sometimes non-military parties would be attacked or bombed just because the enemy ornithopters failed to reach their targets and preferred to lighten their machines before returning home. Also some defeated groups of Dark Empire soldiers and their supporters lived now as bandits, preying on anyone who looked weak enough to attack safely.

I had asked Oona why we were taking these risks, but she had been too busy to answer. Now I had no opportunity. She assured me that we should be safe enough when we arrived in Munchein in two or three days' time. The ancient city had sustained some damage in the fierce fight to free her, but her old spirit of defiance lived on.

During one of the spells I spent in the carriage we rode by towns which were in ruins, some from the recent battles and some from earlier conquests of the Dark Empire, whose policy was to attack from the air, killing anything that moved before landing its troops. I had only ever looked at scenes like these on the TV. And then it had always been our side making most of the ruins, and I'd felt differently about it—often angry, sometimes guilty, but not like this. This was a feeling of furious frustration and a deep hatred of the cowardly people who did this, flying out of the clouds to bring destruction to whole families. You could still smell the smoke and ash. There was something stale and disgusting about the way it clogged up your nostrils and lay on your skin. Oona put a scarf up to her mouth as we passed through a valley where the country people were doing their best to rebuild their villages, putting up frames and walls, re-slating their roofs. They waved to us as we went by, and appeared cheerful under the circumstances. They obviously assumed we were a war party, and cheered us on, urging us to give back to the Dark Empire the hell they had experienced themselves.

Once or twice an ornithopter bearing the black-and-red roundels of those opposing the Dark Empire flew low to take a look at us, but we flew the same banner on a long spear carried by Shatadaka, another of the American warriors. The ornithopters would rise, their pilots waving to us, and go on about their business. We were careful, however, not to wave our flag until we saw the aircraft's markings first.

When a machine bearing no markings passed overhead, we felt sure it was an empire ship. It flapped down to identify us, then soared up again, rotors roaring, and disappeared, heading for Mirenburg. I could tell Oona was alarmed by the way she tensed in the carriage and called for one of the spare horses. I think she felt more in control when mounted.

We made camp that night in a wood near the road. Oona posted extra guards and would not let me move a foot from her. To be honest, I didn't much feel like moving. I slept, as before, curled up beside Lord Renyard's soft red chest.

In the morning we hurriedly saddled our horses, hardly stopping for breakfast. The Kakatanawa had become better at handling the carriages and harnessed them in no time. Oona was suddenly in a great hurry to get to our destination. We ate lunch on the move in the carriage: bread and sausage with some water from a nearby stream. Emerging from a sweet-smelling pine forest, we rode beside a small lake rimmed by hills and distant mountains. Again there were flowers everywhere, though not the same as I'd seen earlier. I tried again to ask Oona about the albino boy. Did she know who he was?

"I'd like to talk to him as much as you would," she said rather noncommittally.

"Do you think you might be related?"

"It's entirely possible." She grinned. "Since you say we're so alike. And it's obvious I'm my father's daughter. I do, after all, have a long-lost twin." Then her mood changed rapidly, and she fell into that frowning silence again, staring out of the window at the faraway peaks. At the next break, I switched again from the carriage to the pony.

The country, though bearing terrible scars, was absolutely beautiful. Occasionally I spotted a tower, and sometimes an entire castle, among the trees and rocks. One stood on the very edge of the lake, completely desolate. Like so much of the ruin Granbretan left behind her, it was a monument to the evil which had destroyed it.

I wondered if there were people in Granbretan who hated what their own country was doing. You heard a lot about the evil ones but not much about the good ones.

"That's because there are so few good ones left," Prince Lobkowitz told me. "That culture has bred to particular traits, and they don't allow much sentiment about 'Do unto others as you would have them do unto you'! Naturally there are those over there who hate what Granbretan is doing, who hate wearing masks and all the other aberrations they encourage. Would they dare as much as breathe criticism of the empire and King Huon? I very much doubt it. Would they nurture a revolutionary movement? With spies to betray them at every turn?" He looked thoughtfully at the surrounding landscape. "It would require many brave and intelligent people to overturn the empire from within. No, the best we can hope for is that it will collapse as quickly as it arose. The nature of empires, whether they be Roman, British, Russian or American, is that they are expensive and uneconomical to maintain, requiring a vast standing army and its equipment. It only makes sense if you are fond of lists, codes and filing cards. There are so many better ways of investing your time and money, most of which do not involve so much noise, violence, bombast and cruelty."

"And Elric—Monsieur Zodiac—does he come from that empire or another one?"

Prince Lobkowitz smiled and stood up in his stirrups to stretch his legs and give his bottom a rest.

"Your great-grandfather is from a very different kind of place, an ancient civilisation which gradually compromised with Chaos to give it power over the whole world. But it had not always compromised, as Elric learned. Once it had been an enemy of Chaos, a respected trading nation, famous for its probity. But as trade spread elsewhere, Melniboné became increasingly inclined to maintain her relationships with sword and fire rather than honest coin. So she kept her empire, at the cost of many of the softer mortal qualities. For Melnibonéans, though mortal, were not human. They belonged to a race which had come to our world many thousands of years earlier and made compacts with the great elemental kings of fire, water, earth and air, compacts with supernatural entities we have no means of describing. And they were supported by their dragons, the Phoorn, who spoke the same language as they did—flying monsters impossible to defeat, with venom that became fiery poison when exposed to the air. Dragon venom alone sank many a Young Kingdoms ship."

"Wow! Dragons? Really?"

"All this sounds very exciting to you, young lady," said Prince Lobkowitz, "but believe me, it's no fun to be terrorised by a living creature the size of a sperm whale, which can fly and spit venom on you. It's like being attacked by a really big, heavily armed military helicopter, only the thing has a vast tail, which can knock the mast off a good-sized ship and destroy a house in a single flick. How does it fly? How do those ornithopters fly? They fly, I think, by different logic to a jumbo jet, but we know they fly."

"I'd still like to see one of those dragons," I said.

"Pray you never get the chance!" Smiling, he reached over to clap my shoulder. He was smiling. But like most of the smiles I saw these days, there was something else under it. I guessed they had enough pieces of the jigsaw puzzle now to realise the kind of game being played by our enemies, and how much danger we were in.

Again I'd been politely cut off before I could ask all my questions. I wanted to know what the Black Sword was, if it was something more than just a sword. A kind of magic blade, was it? Like Excalibur?

Our road now wound along the shores of yet another lake. In the far distance at the very end of the flat stretch of water, surrounded by hills steep and high enough to be small mountains, was what looked like a good-size town.

"Oona told me he was looking for some sort of sword . . ."

"He already had the Black Sword. I imagine he left it behind in Ingleton for a reason. Perhaps its magic is so powerful it can be detected anywhere, or perhaps he doesn't trust it . . ."

"Trust it?"

"I'll not add that to your burden," he said firmly. Then to me: "That's right."

"So why do Klosterheim and von Minct want me? Oona doesn't really know. Have *you* worked that out yet?"

"I can't be sure. I think they believe you to be some sort of key, perhaps to the Sword itself, possibly to the Grail, given your name and background. The best thing is not to get caught by them and never find out. The less you know about any of that, the better off you'll be."

"Now you've made me even more curious," I said.

"Well, you'll have to live with that for a while. We tell you what we think you need to know in order to survive. These are secrets usually much better kept to a few of us."

"All right. Then what about my mum and dad?" I asked. "That's mostly what's on my mind. How are they mixed up in this? And Gertie and Alfy? And my granny and granddad?"

"You know your grandmother is Oona, the dreamthief's daughter. She's the only one actually mixed up in anything with us, and she's trying to make sure all of us are kept safe. But since the enemy has focused on *you*, you are her chief concern. You should never have been involved, and honestly I have yet to work out why you are."

"Have they mistaken me for someone else?"

"That's my guess. Not, of course, that I'm in any position to tell them so or be believed by them. I don't know how the misunderstanding began . . ."

"You mean everything's been an accident—wandering into the caves and everything?"

"I don't mean that. Not at all. There's the boy, after all . . ." Again a sense of something shutting down.

"So who are they really after? You sound like it's someone in a witness protection programme!"

He laughed heartily at this. A moment later Ujamaka, who was driving the first carriage, lifted his lance and pointed with it. There in the distance, from the far shore of the glassy lake, a shape could be seen descending between twin peaks. A big ornithopter.

My saddle became suddenly uncomfortable. The flying machines scared and fascinated me at the same time. I wanted to get down and walk but decided to ride back to Lord Renyard's carriage and travel with him rather than go with a silent Oona. The Kakatanawa made room for me as we watched the big flying machine descend. I was terrified and hugely curious. All kinds of conflicting emotions roiled inside me. The thing was *huge* and very noisy!

The sun was getting low in the sky, its light diffused by thin, white cloud, as the powerful machine turned against its disc and skimmed the water, steam shooting from its curving exhausts. The prow was in the glaring shape of a hawk; its rotors turned slowly as the jointed wings beat with relentless rhythm. It had no roundels and was by all appearances an empire ship. We did not raise our own flag but came to a halt as we watched the thing circling us. There was no way we could find cover against its guns now. We hoped they wouldn't waste fuel or ammunition on people they couldn't identify.

"Damn!" I heard Oona curse as she looked out and up. "And Munchein not fifty miles from here!" She looked back at the woods. She knew we couldn't make it. Even if we got there, the ornithopter could burn us out of the forest.

"We'd better keep going," she ordered. "The town's our best cover. But don't go too fast or they'll *know* we're enemies." At that, the dark bulk of the clanking flying machine flew over again, steam and cinders spewing from those exhausts. Oona smiled and waved at it as it passed so low we could see the mask and goggles of its pilot glaring down at us, the heavy heart of its engine pumping. The ground vibrated as it went over. I held my ears.

Then it was gone, back the way we had come. We picked up speed and entered into the relative safety of a ruined house. That terrible stink of ash and death was everywhere. Nothing was alive. No paper or cloth had survived, so there was no record of what had happened. Just another passing victim of Granbretan's efforts to bring order to a world it found disorderly and therefore threatening.

"They know we're here," said Oona. "So there's no point in trying to hide at this stage. Lord Renyard, get out of sight as soon as you can. The rest of you look as if you're setting up camp. If they see we think they're no threat, they might assume we're at least neutral!"

The massive, clattering, hissing thing was overhead again, blotting out the sky. Oona waved a second time. This time she was answered by a burst of flame from a turret. The flame splashed against a nearby wall. The air was filled with the smell of burning kerosene.

"Flame cannon," said Lord Renyard, who automatically lifted me behind him with his powerful paws.

"We're sitting ducks," said Lieutenant Fromental. From the depths of a voluminous overcoat he produced a pistol. We had no long-range weapons with which to retaliate.

"It's almost as if they were tracking us and picked the best place to ambush us," said Prince Lobkowitz, checking a revolver of his own. "Klosterheim was in Mirenburg! He was able to get word to this aviator!"

"But he won't want to risk killing me, will he?" I pointed out. "Not if they want me alive."

It was a good argument, they all agreed. The Kakatanawa prepared their spears and bows. Their expressions told me that if there was any way of destroying a steel ornithopter with those weapons, they would find it!

At Oona's instructions the Kakatanawa formed a tight circle around me, their war-boards used like a Greek shield-wall. Then we watched as the ship took another turn about and again came in low—even lower this time than the last—its huge clawed feet dragging the water and setting up a wake which lapped at the town's remaining pier. I felt horribly sick. The craft made a third turn and seemed to be preparing to land on the water. I thought it was bound to sink, but maybe it was wide enough and boat-shaped enough to float. Water hissed all around it, and steam shrieked as it spewed from the vents. Then, almost on cue, two more Dark Empire ships came thundering over the horizon, and Oona gave the order to seek any cover we could!

We darted desperately through the ruins. From ahead came a sudden blinding flash. The two aircraft were dropping bombs on us!

Some of the horses were better trained than others and held steady, but most of them bolted, threatening to drag the carriages to destruction. Oona yelled for her men to cut the traces, letting the horses run from the explosions. It probably saved their lives.

More bombs. All around us blazed the same white, blinding light. None of us could see any more. There was an acrid stink, and my throat began to burn and my eyes water. I blundered on through the confusion. There was shouting and clanking of arms and armour, jingling horse-gear, the guttural voices of the Kakatanawa and the Dark Empire pilots yelling through the flares.

In the confusion I lost contact with the others. Now I was really scared and started calling for Oona. I could hear her somewhere nearby. I knew that if I stayed where I was, I might be better off, but it was very hard to do in all that chaos. When I grew dizzy and found it hard to keep my balance I began to realise that they weren't just using flares. There was something else in those bombs: poison gas.

I tripped. I fell. I tried to get up. I became dizzier. I lost all sense of whether I was rising or falling. From my knees I looked up. Was the brilliant mist clearing? I heard sounds, saw shadows moving. I tried to rise, but I was even weaker. I saw huge, black eyes, a snarling muzzle.

And then I passed out.

PART THREE

THE WHITE WOLF'S SON

Near six foot tall was Lord Rennard,
All dressèd in silk and lace,
Walk'd he prowde into the farmer's yarde
Fillèd with cunning courtesy and grace.

> —*The Ballad of Lord Foxxe*
> Coll. Henty,
> *Ballads of Love and War*, 1892

From corners four rode our bold heroes
No self or selfish meaning to their muse
To meet again in Mirrensburg
Strong justice there to choose.

> —Henshe,
> *The Great Battle of*
> *Mirrensburg, 1605*
> Wheldrake's tr., 1900

16

Across the Silver Bridge that spanned thirty miles of sea came the hordes of the Dark Empire, pigs and wolves, vultures and dogs, mantises and frogs, with armour of strange design and weapons of obscene purpose. And imprisoned in his Globe of Thorns, curled like a foetus in the fluid that preserved his immortality, drifted the great King Huon, all his present helplessness symbolised by his situation. Hatred alone sustained him as he schemed the punishment he would bring upon those who refused the gift of his logic, of his sublime justice. But why could he not contrive to manipulate them as he manipulated the rest of the world? Did some counterforce aid them, perhaps control them in ways he could not? This latter thought the mighty King Emperor refused to tolerate.

—The High History of
the Runestaff
(Tr. Glogauer)

I felt terrible when I woke up and realised that I was aboard one of the Dark Empire aircraft. The whole thing shuddered and shouted as the metal wings beat at the air and the rotors laboured to help keep us aloft. Inside, the ship was much noisier than outside, and the stink of whatever chemicals fired the boilers was very powerful. I found I was not tied up but just very stiff from lying in the cramped space behind one of the pilots' seats. Two pilots and, I supposed, a gunner and a navigator shared the cockpit. When the unmasked "navigator" turned to look at me, I wasn't surprised to see Klosterheim.

He sported the air of a man who had seen all his schemes and plans reach fruition. How much had our recent actions actually been manipulated by him and Gaynor? And not only *our* actions, of course, for there were many players in this game. More, probably, than we knew. Klosterheim and Gaynor had tricked Monsieur Zodiac into pursuing them. Rid of him, at least for the moment, they let us escape from the safety of Mirenburg, then pounced. Surely Prince Yaroslaf hadn't been in league with them! Yet at that moment everything stank of treachery to me.

Where were my friends? Had they been killed? There wasn't room for anyone else in the plane's cabin. Lieutenant Fromental wouldn't have been able to get in at all.

I felt sick.

I felt awful. Not just physically, from the fumes and cramp, but mentally as well. I wanted to vomit, but if I was going to throw up, it would be, if I could manage it, all over one of my captors. I didn't say anything, in case I sounded too feeble, but I glared into Klosterheim's eyes and was rewarded with a sense of endless vacuum, as if the entire multiversal void were encompassed within that gaunt, unhappy creature. Strangely, I felt a kind of sympathy for him. What must it be like to live with that emptiness?

By now I'd picked up a bit of his history from my friends. If he wasn't immortal, he had lived for a very long time and survived more than one experience of death, unless, as Prince Lobkowitz had told me, he had an avatar in a number of multiversal realms, who knowingly carried on the agenda of his dead selves. Was *that* what immortality might be? Not one body living for ever, but one personality living through hundreds or millions of versions of the same body? Herr Klosterheim had seen scheme after scheme fail. He had been defeated more than once by those who Prince Lobkowitz had referred to as being on "our side." Indeed, defeat of one sort or another was almost all he had experienced. Why didn't he give up?

I think he read something of this in my eyes, for he turned away, muttering and snarling to himself. The ornithopter banked sharply, and for a moment I thought I wasn't going to be able to keep from throwing up. Then I sank into unconsciousness again.

When I next woke we were on the ground. I was alone. The engines had stopped. I heard distant voices and looked up to see a crow mask peering down at me. I stared back. I tried to hear what was going on outside the cockpit. Klosterheim was talking to someone in the guttural tones of Granbretan, a strange mixture of French and English. I wondered if, at some point, the French had conquered England again and left this language as their heritage. Or was I hearing Norman English from a world where William the Conqueror's speech had come to dominate Anglo-Saxon rather than compromise with it?

Then Klosterheim and the others came clambering back in. I think we had stopped to refuel.

"What did you do with my friends?" I asked him. I was hoarse. My eyes still burned. I don't think he even understood my words. He settled himself in his seat as the canopy closed and the pilot began to get the machine's steam up. The rotors whirred, and the wings began beating as we lumbered up into the air.

After a few minutes in flight the ornithopter banked suddenly, its wings labouring, and I caught the flash of something that could only be the sea, and a wide silver arc which might have been a bridge. I think it was dawn. As the light increased, my eyes hurt even more. Whatever they had gassed us with was powerful stuff.

I think the altitude had something to do with my dizziness, because I soon passed out again, still feeling sick and still determined to vomit, if I could, on Herr Klosterheim.

If this was his last chance to gain whatever it was he wanted, he deserved it, given the cleverness of his deceptions. But needless to say, his success didn't bode at all well for me.

The journey had already taken more than a day, I guessed. I woke and passed out again intermittently. I did have the momentary satisfaction finally of throwing up over someone's boots, and by their dull, cracked blackness I have a fairly good idea they belonged to Herr Klosterheim. Of course, given his history, it couldn't be the worst thing that had ever happened to him.

The last time I woke up, someone or something was lifting me out of the narrow space behind the pilots' seats. I felt fresh air slap me in the face. I opened my eyes, shaking my head as if I'd surfaced in water. It was dark again but a substantially different kind of darkness. I felt it all around me, populated, unquiet and encroaching. I glimpsed slimy greens and browns, ochre and murky blue, shadows which revealed cruel, mad eyes full of suppressed glee. I had a strong impression of flames billowing black-grey smoke. Suddenly there was a gushing roar, and I was blinded by a light again, though this was a vivid red and yellow flame, almost healthy in comparison to the other.

I heard more oddly accented voices. Klosterheim replied in the same dialect. Grunts, snuffles, barks and growls sounded as if we were in some sort of menagerie. I realised the animal noises came from various masked people who surrounded me, looking down at me. A hand stroked my body, and I shuddered.

A brazen-headed wolf spoke. A familiar voice. "She must not be harmed."

That, at least, was reassuring.

"Until the time is ready," the same wolf added. "She must stay a virgin or she's no use to us at all. The Stone is ours. Our friend has brought us the cups as a sign of his good faith. She'll bring us the Sword, and the boy will bring us the Staff. But only if we are careful to follow every aspect of the ritual. Blood for blood, cup for cup. The law of like to like . . ."

"Bah! That's mere superstition. Her only use is as bait for the albino and his pack." A high-pitched, unfamiliar yap. They spoke a form of English which was becoming easier to understand.

"They won't take the bait." That was Gaynor von Minct. I knew his voice well. "They'll have guessed what we're up to." Cynical, brutal, bleak, its tone mocked his companions. "No, there has to be more to the child's power."

"Let us first discover if the worm attracts the fish." Another voice I didn't recognise at all, like the sharp hiss of dry leaves. "If it does not, we shall investigate the nature of the worm."

"Do as you will."

The voice came closer. I opened my eyes and looked into the face of a huge cobra, its stylised mouth open as if to strike, its fangs at least a foot long, its crystalline eyes winking and sparking in the darkness, its metallic scales flashing bright green and red. "Awake, is it, little worm?" This last to me.

"Bugger off," I shouted. It was the strongest swear word I knew at the time. "You can't hurt me—"

"Oh, but we can, little worm." The cobra drew back, threatening to strike me. "We can. It is only our restraint that saves you sweet, exquisite pain. For you have come to the capital of the world's pain, the land of perpetual torment, where your kind is privileged to know the very rarest of agonies. We possess a special vocation for turning pain into pleasure and pleasure into pain. And we shall turn your courage into the most abject cowardice, believe me."

He was trying to frighten me, I think, but there wasn't any real need. I was already so terrified, a false calm had settled over me. It made me appear braver than I was, because I laughed, and the cobra reared back again, raising a green-gauntleted hand, then letting it drop to his side.

"We must not hurt her," Klosterheim said urgently, "not yet. Not yet."

"There's no entertainment in frightening children." A woman's voice. I looked for the speaker. A bird in steel, gold and rare gems; a stylised heron. "Your triumph is unseemly, gentlemen."

"My lady," returned the cobra, "we are, of course, your servants in this matter. She shall be placed in your charge, as Baron Meliadus has ordered. However, if she fails to bring us our prey, you understand that she will become our property . . ."

"Naturally. I assure you I have more slaves of her age and sex than I can afford. The war effort has forced us all to make sacrifices."

"Sacrifices," repeated the cobra. I expected to see a forked tongue come flicking out of that gaping mouth. He savoured the word.

"These days, dear Baron Bous-Junge, it is our duty to make as many as possible," said the woman. She sounded quite young. Her voice had a cool, mocking edge to it. I think I was more afraid of her than of the others.

They were all wary of her, I could tell. I guessed she was more powerful than the rest of them. I was probably in Granbretan, but of course in those days I knew nothing of their social structure. I had heard that King Huon was hideous and that Baron Meliadus, his chancellor, was ambitiously cruel. Baron Bous-Junge was some sort of court alchemist. Details of their lives were sparse on the Continent. Few of our kind who crossed the Silver Bridge from Calais to the city they called Deau-Vere ever came back to speak of what they had seen.

Intellectually I knew all this, of course, and I seemed to have reached a point where I couldn't feel any more fear, although there was plenty to be afraid of.

I began to see more details in the gloom. The room had a low, domed roof and smelled of something rotten around its edges. In a brazier suspended from the ceiling by brass chains, incense burned with a faint glow. Judging by the waft of musky air, it had only recently been lit. Outlines of armoured, beast-masked figures moved around the walls and congregated near the door. The swirl of colours came from the walls, which were made of glass. As I got more used to them I realised we were inside an aquarium. What I was seeing through the glass was liquid and the shadows of water creatures. I thought I glimpsed a mermaid, or something that might have been a shark with arms. I guessed they were genetic experiments or maybe clones gone wrong. What I hadn't realised was that this was also to be my prison cell!

Von Minct and the others began to talk among themselves. They dropped their voices so I couldn't hear. I felt they were talking in code. But why would they be doing that here, in their own capital city?

How many elaborate plots, I wondered, were being hatched in Londra? I had the sense that they relished scheming, in spite of the risks! Some people are like that. I was pretty much the exact opposite. I liked everything straightforward and above board, but I suspected that I was going to have to learn a bit of cunning quickly if I had even the slightest chance of surviving. I was probably on my own now, since I couldn't see that Klosterheim and company would have left Oona, Lobkowitz, Lord Renyard and the rest alive. Monsieur Zodiac had gone off on a wild-goose chase, and everyone else was simply too busy fighting their own particular battles to have much time for me.

I was puzzled why I wasn't grieving the loss of my friends. In the past I had been upset by a lot less. I suspect when your own life is at stake, you're inclined to defer emotional outbursts until you can afford them.

I didn't want to look too closely into the aquarium. I slept again, and when I woke up my eyes had adjusted so that I could simply sit in the middle of that strange, domed room and look at the water swirling and churning with what appeared to be a merman, with a great fishy tail where his feet should be. He put his odd, grey-green face to the glass and peered at me blankly without attempting any kind of communication. When I rose and walked towards him, he darted off. Something with huge teeth and brilliant eyes replaced him in a flash, and I recoiled. I decided to stay in the centre of the room and watch. I sat on the floor, although there were plenty of chairs. The chairs were carved with even more grotesque creatures than I saw in the aquarium. I actually felt slightly more secure on the floor. I also had a feeling that it wasn't only the merman watching me, though what those people thought they could learn from me I wasn't altogether sure!

Hungry, I wondered if they planned to starve me until I was too weak to run. That way they wouldn't have to worry about me escaping. Not that I knew where to go if I *did* escape!

Almost as soon as I'd thought of food something moved, and a young woman in a red woollen one-piece suit, a blank mask hiding her face, her head closely shaved and embedded with what looked like precious jewels, appeared behind me with a tray in her hands. She had passed straight through the aquarium walls to reach me. There must be a door there, but I couldn't see one.

"This is certainly the best prison I've ever been in," I told her as she set the tray down on a small table beside one of the chairs. Of course, I'd never been in any prison before that. "What's your name? I'd like to be able to thank everyone personally when I write my memoirs."

That sounds ridiculous to me now, but I distinctly remember saying it. Bravado? Sheer terror, probably. "Why don't you take off your mask and have supper with me? Or maybe it's breakfast . . ."

I made myself stop talking. I was on the verge of hysteria. The girl bowed. The wall began to move; one section of the aquarium slid past another. She bowed again as she stepped through. Another shimmy of watery light, and she was gone.

The food was delicious, and I don't think it was just because I was hungry. But I probably would have eaten it no matter what it was. Only afterwards did it occur to me that it might be poisoned. Sure enough, as soon as I put down my spoon, having cleaned a plate of what I assumed was a sweet dessert, I felt sleepy again.

The next time I woke up I was no longer in the aquarium room. A white light, bright enough to blind me, hit me full in the eyes. I couldn't easily see outside the circle of light as my eyes tried to adjust, but it was clear I was being observed again. I had the impression of more shadowy beast masks and a murmur of conversation. I got to my feet and found I was dressed in a filmy silk frock. I had on fresh underwear and was wearing thick tights. Everything was a shade of soft green. Someone had obviously cleaned me up while I was knocked out, because even my hair had been washed. Then a big man walked into the circle of light and hauled me up bodily before I could object.

The substance in the food also served to calm me. Either that, or I was in total denial about the fate of my friends and the fact that I was unlikely ever to see my mum and dad again.

The man carrying me was dressed in armour. It was like being lifted by one of the robots out of *Star Wars*. My clothes weren't heavy enough to give me much warmth, and I shivered against his metal-covered body. I was carried down a short corridor and then out into a street, where a tall wheeled machine, hissing and puffing out steam, waited for us. Shaped like an animal and about the size of a double-decker bus, it had a single huge wheel in the front and several small ones at sides and back. In what I assumed was a driving seat, on the top and at the rear of the thing, sat a figure whose armour and livery were identical in design and materials to the carriage. His head was enclosed in a snarling horse's head with sharp-filed teeth like a dinosaur's. He could just see over a tower in the roof made of copper and brass and glass. It looked like a mobile observatory with a telescope to me!

The driver signed to the man who held me. A door opened in the windowless side of the vehicle, and I was put in rather gently before the door was closed and locked.

A dim light was produced by gas jets. I could hear it hissing faintly. I was in a compartment with seats arranged around the sides. In the centre of the floor was a circle of light in which I could see a busy street, people riding horses, and even what looked like a kind of huge motorbike. These were dwarfed, however, by buildings erected in the shape of ugly, squatting humanoid figures with beast heads. They reminded me of something I'd seen in the Egyptian Book of the Dead.

Watching the scene immediately outside, I found that by moving a wheel near the big circle of light, I could see everything around me for some distance. It was a mobile camera obscura. I had come across something like it in Oxford, when I visited my uncle Dave, also in Bath, where one of my mum's sisters lived. But they had been fixed versions. Like many of the Dark Empire's inventions, it was a very awkward way of achieving the privacy they seemed to crave, but science had obviously developed very differently since that period they called "the Tragic Millennium." Their economics had to be radically different, for a start; but I suppose when you are bent on looting everyone else's goods and land, you don't have to worry too much about efficient costings.

As we moved, I turned the wheel, trying to get as good a picture of the city as I could. I was sure it was London—what they called Londra—though there wasn't a single familiar building or street. A busy, baroque city, with everything anthropomorphised. Slaves, naked but for masks, hurried on errands. Shops displayed their wares, most of them pretty ornate and many of them impossible to identify. Groups of warriors marched together along narrow thoroughfares over which those same grotesque buildings loomed. The bus was soundproofed, so I could hear the street noises only faintly.

We were soon joined by a guard of mounted soldiers in the livery and masks of what I guessed to be the Order of the Dog. They were heavily armed, though I wasn't likely to escape, since the door I had come in by seemed to be the only way out, unless you were the size of a mouse.

Ahead of me was a riot of statuary the size of the Empire State Building, all of it populated, judging by the windows and doors and the tiny figures I could see leaning over balconies or crossing walkways. It was very impressive because it dwarfed the tallest of the other buildings and dominated the city with its various towers, ziggurats and domes in a crazy profusion of quartz, obsidian, marble and ebony. This could only be King Huon's palace. When the carriage drew up inside a covered courtyard lit by naked flambeaux I saw mantis masks of rank upon rank of warriors, carrying the banners and insignia of the "King-Emperor." I recognised them from trophies which Prince Yaroslaf displayed in his own palace. But on living men, the armour and masks truly resembled the carapaces of insects.

Huge as the courtyard was, I still had a strong sense of claustrophobia. One of the leaders stepped forward. I watched the door open from where I sat inside, and there he was, just as he had been in the camera obscura, only, if anything, a bit larger. He reached in and signalled me to come to him. As soon as I stood beside him, he picked me up and took me out to a four-wheeled sedan chair, pushed and pulled by slaves. He put me into this, then joined the entire legion, who surrounded me to march us through King Huon's palace. We finally came to a set of doors, very tall and studded with jewels, bas-relief, painted panels, all depicting what seemed to be the mythical history of Granbretan and stories of her more recent conquests. The guards divided, each section pushing on one of the doors, which moved gradually open, revealing an even more fantastic scene inside.

It was a hall you could have placed a small city in, with room to spare. From the distant heights of the vaulted ceilings hung great woven sheets embroidered with all kinds of brilliant and grotesque devices. Judging by the proliferation of animals on many of them, I guessed they were the banners of Granbretan's leading clans, interspersed with the insignia of the conquered lands.

Their backs against the richly decorated walls, hissing, murmuring soldiers and courtiers intermingled, showing a strong interest in me. I pretended I couldn't see them. I wasn't there to entertain them but to offer my defiance.

It must have taken half an hour to move all the way to the end of the hall. There in mid-air hung a large globe, rather like a Christmas tree decoration, its insides swirling with murky colours shot through with sparks of gold, silver and emerald. I saw the faintest suggestion of eyes staring out at me. The coldest, hardest, nastiest pair of eyes I had ever seen, they contained the malice and greed of ten thousand years.

We reached the steps below the globe. As one, the mantis guards flung themselves face down with a deafening crash. I looked around and saw that everyone was in the same prone position. I sat there, refusing to join in, watching as the contents of the globe gradually eddied and swirled, became agitated, began to form a shape. At first I thought these people were more insectlike even than the guards, because what I saw was a sort of egg, and within the egg was an incredibly wizened and wrinkled homunculus, the owner of those terrible eyes, who curled a long, prehensile tongue from its disgusting, toothless mouth and touched something within the globe.

A voice, startlingly beautiful and sweet, came from the floating creature within the globe.

"Good morning, child. Few of your kind are as honoured as you. Are you aware who I am?"

"You're King Huon," I said. I had nothing to gain by being polite to this disgusting thing. "And you used to think you could conquer the world."

A vast susurration and clucking arose behind me. The sound was immediately silenced, presumably by a gesture from Huon's captain. Almost in amusement he said, "You seem aware of your importance to us, little creature. Or are you mad, like so many of those we make captive?"

"It could be both," I said. "I know I'm some sort of bait for a trap you're setting, and I know you're going to try to win back the power you've lost."

Now there was nothing but silence in that incredible throne room.

Courtiers waited to see how the king would react.

An unpleasant, beautiful chuckle came from the Throne Globe. "You are our route to the Runestaff. You understand, at least, that you have no more personal worth than a grub on a fisherman's hook. Or do you hope to deceive Huon, who sees and knows everything?"

The tongue flicked again, and the curtain to the right opened to reveal the shape of a man pinned against a board. His skin hung in strips from his body, which resembled the pictures you see in an anatomy book. Only his face, still masked, was not a bloody map. From within the wolverine helm came a whimpering groan.

Gloating, greedy, full of a glee I found more horrible than anything else, King Huon whispered, "Here is one of our favourite subjects, who came to warn us of your revolt. His name is Lord Olin Desleur. This is his reward."

The curtain closed. "We are less kind to our enemies," he said.

My stomach turned over. I couldn't erase that image from my mind. I tried to control my breathing and contain the sense of horror I felt, the pity I had for the crucified man.

King Huon remained amused. "I gather you have met your brother, young Jack D'Acre, only recently. We await his arrival with interest. Yes, yes, our servants have found him. Do not fear, my dear. You will be reunited with him soon. And when that event takes place, we shall be conquering far more than a single continent or even a single world. When that happens, my dear, sweet child, the entire multiverse will be ours."

I was completely baffled. This was the last thing I'd expected.

"Who on earth is Jack D'Acre?" I asked.

17

King Huon did not reply. His insect tongue flicked out to touch what I supposed was a control panel. The globe grew murky, as if it filled with dirty blood, and then he was gone. They wheeled me out of the throne hall again. This time, when we reached the first anteroom, we turned in a different direction, into unfamiliar passages and halls.

Could I really have a brother I didn't know about? A dark secret of my mum's? Impossible. Mum just wasn't that mysterious. She and Dad had met at university and become sweethearts; then they'd separated for a bit because my dad got a Mellon Fellowship to study at Yale, and she'd had a few boyfriends, as he'd had girlfriends, but they always said they were made for each other, they got on so well. And who was Mr D'Acre, anyway? Not my brother! Jack had to have another dad.

Needless to say, the masked guards wouldn't respond to any of my questions. Though I put a brave face on it, I was beginning to have a distinct sense of dread. Something especially nasty was being planned. Luckily, my imagination couldn't summon up the dimmest picture of what was in store. Even the sight of that poor, dying Lord Olin Desleur aroused pity and horror in me, rather than fear.

Did I secretly hope that somehow the armies of Europe would come pouring over the Silver Bridge to rescue me? Even though they were winning, it was unlikely their famous hero Hawkmoon would arrive in time to save me, and it would be a very long while before Granbretan itself fell. They would fight to the death to defend their capital. There was every chance, in fact, that Granbretan was already planning a counter-attack. I suspected I might be involved in that plan. Was I a hostage, maybe?

The odd little four-wheeled carriage rolled and bumped its way through a series of tunnels. They were low, dank and smelling very strongly of perfume, which didn't cover the stink of mould. It reminded me of those really strongly scented candles you could buy in tourist places. In fact, the flambeaux and other sources of light had largely been replaced by big, fat scarlet candles, guttering in their holders as a hot breeze blew through the tunnels. The walls here were painted with faded hieroglyphics rather than being carved or moulded, and I was again reminded of Egypt, the only other culture I knew which had so many beast-headed men and immortals in its mythology. Yet how could a mythology like that ever have come to Britain? In a way, the masks and obsession with personal privacy made some sort of ghastly sense, but nothing else did. Dark, internalised, repressed and aggressive, these people reminded me more of twentieth-century Nazis than twenty-first-century Brits. For a moment I thought of football rowdies, wearing team colours, decorating their faces, supporting teams with names like Wolves or Lions. But I still found it difficult to believe I was in London. Maybe England had been conquered by aliens, and my own people killed!

At last my transport stopped, and I lurched forward in my seat. Through the window I saw we were outside a door made of lumps of sparkling granite and slate. It creaked and whistled as it opened very slowly to admit the carriage. The mantis guards stood to attention while guards in other masks, resembling the hoods and heads of rearing cobras, took over. The naked slaves strained to drag the chair through the door as it thumped shut behind us.

Even murkier passages, lit by dim red globes of some kind. I couldn't work out what powered them. They displayed that bizarre mixture of advanced science and backward medievalism which characterised Granbretan.

We were now in another hangarlike building. This one was crammed with a profusion of very odd-looking machines. Many of them were monstrous, with snouts, dials, levers, wheels, cogs and engines whose purpose was totally unfamiliar to me. Some of the machines glowed faintly; others pulsed with colour through layers of thick dust. The place resembled a museum more than a working factory. Perhaps these were some of the machines found since the end of the Tragic Millennium, and no-one had discovered how they were used. It wasn't hard to arrive at that conclusion. My logic was that if they could use them, they would have used them. I would have seen them on the streets. The ones which looked like weapons would have been used against Hawkmoon's Continental army.

I took a long look at the things as we rolled by. The metal was all in weird colours: electric blues, glowing reds, vibrant greens. There was that smell you sometimes get from old wiring when it overheats. It was so strong, it stung my throat and eyes. I started to cough. The sound echoed through the vaulted ceilings high above and bounced off the metallic monsters on both sides of me.

The little vehicle stopped again. I peered out. A group of men stood in the shadows at the end of the hall. They wore cloaks made of snakeskin, mottled, dry, stretching from head to foot. Deep cowls hid their heads, but I caught a glimpse of eyes and the faint outline of the masks they wore, a dull sheen of dark metal.

A brusque command sent the slaves running from the place, and I was left, still sitting in the sedan chair, wondering what was going to happen next.

The door opened. One of the cowled men reached out an old, skinny hand, covered in papery yellow skin, and signalled for me to get out. I did. My knees were trembling. The cowled men then surrounded me, and I was led through several more doors until we entered a laboratory of some kind, with benches, retorts, smoking test tubes, all of very unusual shapes. Miles of twisting glass pipes ran with evil-coloured liquid and issued thick, smelly steam.

Now we were in a much smaller room, and the door closed behind us again. One of the figures sat on the far side of a desk and signed for me to sit down on a three-legged stool with thick padded arms.

"Good afternoon, my dear," said the cowled one who had been taking the greatest interest in me. "I hope you are enjoying your time as our guest."

I made some sarcastic remark. He chuckled at this. "I am Baron Bous-Junge of Osfoud. No doubt you have heard of me. I am the chief of Granbretan's scientists."

The first thought that came into my head was *Vivisection!* They were going to cut me up!

He came closer, dry cloak rustling, snake head peering, snake eyes glittering. "We shall have to make some tests, but you seem very healthy. Are you a strong little girl?"

"Stronger than you think," I told him. "And I've never had a day's illness in my life." Which wasn't remotely true. I'd had dozens of the usual complaints, from chicken pox to flu.

Again I heard a certain sort of amusement. "We were told you were a child with a mind of its own. Do you understand why our great King-Emperor was so tolerant of your rudeness, little girl?"

"Because you need me," I said bluntly.

"Has anyone told you what you are needed for?"

"By the look of things here, I'd say you want some fresh ingredients for a stew. I haven't seen past those masks you wear, like cowards, to hide your faces, but I'm beginning to suspect you file your teeth."

There was a moment's silence. Maybe Baron Bous-Junge was collecting himself. Had what I said struck a chord with him?

"Do you know where you are?" he asked, and then answered his own question. "You are in my quarters. This is where we perform some of our most useful experiments. Many are on living captives, from the youngest baby to the oldest man, and very, very few survive, sadly. It is all in the name of science. They gladly contribute to the great sum of human knowledge, without which we should never have risen above the animals."

I almost laughed at that. "You seem bent on getting lower than the average animal," I told him. "I mean, you're dressing up like them and behaving worse than them. Hasn't anyone ever told you what idiots you look in all that gear?" I sniffed. "I'm not surprised how bad you smell, either."

Now his hand spasmed, as if he controlled himself from striking me. All this was proving that for the moment, at least, I was safe. Either they needed to keep me in one piece for use in a planned ritual, or something else was stopping them from doing what I guessed they would normally do to someone who gave them that amount of cheek. A reedy, nasty chuckle came out of the mask. "I doubt if we have made a mistake. I have heard of your family's arrogance. You Germanians have given us a great deal of trouble, one way and another, what with Duke Dorian and the rest. It will be a relief to me to bring this matter to an end at last, though I must say I have not been bored by your escapades. I gather your grandmother and her father have already been neutralised. Just as well. Just as well. They had become impure, what with one thing and another. Now only you and your brother remain. The Blood is strong and clean and will be best suited for our purposes."

"So you really are a bunch of blood-sucking vampires, are you?" Why on earth did he think I was German? They seemed to have a lot of confused information! Their confusion could get me killed.

"I don't recognise the word. But the expression is crude. Have you eaten?"

"As much of your rotten food as I can stomach!"

"Go through that door." He lifted an arm. The ranks of cowled figures parted. I knew they had the power to carry me through if they wanted to, even though I felt that for every door which shut behind me, my chances of escaping became less and less, so I walked through with as much dignity as I could.

The room on the other side was rather surprising, reminding me of some old professor's study. Pictures of sorts on the walls, a fireplace, a mantelpiece, a big, high wooden desk, wooden bookshelves, all carved with those same grotesque faces and creatures. Every surface was covered in books, notes, scraps of paper, scrolls. There were even some clay tablets covered in hieroglyphics not dissimilar to those on the walls. There were two big, comfortable armchairs and signs of other creature comforts, like a pot of what looked like tobacco, a long-stemmed pipe (presumably for smoking while wearing a mask), several more or less identical cloaks on hooks, what were probably spare masks, a conical hat with a wide brim, which reminded me inevitably of an old-fashioned wizard, and what appeared to be a string of desiccated rats hanging from a central hook in the ceiling and rotating slowly above the flames from the fire, which smoked in the grate and heated the room to an almost intolerable temperature. He indicated that I should sit down and then, to my great surprise, reached up with both hands and removed his mask.

The face I saw was pale, of course, and not very wholesome. He was younger than I might have believed from his hands alone, but still getting on. There were little branches of veins under his eyes, and his lips were an odd blue colour, as if he had been chewing blackberries or something. He had a white beard almost to his chest, which appeared to have unrolled from under the mask, and white hair falling almost to his shoulders. Yet the face actually had quite a kind look to it, and his eyes had wrinkles I'd have sworn were laughter lines. When he did smile, his eyes twinkling, I responded almost with a jolt. I was getting used to sinister threats in ordinary gestures.

"Do you have children of your own?" The words came without my really thinking about them.

"Ah," he said, settling back into his own chair. "Children. Now, there's a thing. It is a century or two since my last child died, young lady."

"So you're older than you look!"

"If you wish. How old do I look?"

"About sixty," I said.

He huffed at this, the way a cat does. "Sixty? That must seem very old to you."

It didn't, particularly given my granny's age, but I wasn't going to tell him. "What did your children die of?" I asked him.

"Oh," he said vaguely, "old age, mostly. They lacked the genes, you see."

"Why was that?"

"Because I needed them. We maintain ourselves as best we can. That is why so many of us have children. They keep you young. They have kept me young for several hundred years. But sadly, the time is coming when not even the genes of my own progeny will help. I suppose I must reconcile myself to death."

"That would probably be a good idea," I said, "since my friends aren't likely to want you alive for any reason."

He chuckled. "Oh, I doubt that. I doubt that. I have so much wisdom they could use. Not, of course, that I am offering it. My loyalties are to my king and country."

I wasn't sure if I believed him, but I let it go. Baron Bous-Junge picked up a hand-bell from the table beside him and rang it twice. Immediately one of those poor, naked slaves stepped smoothly in. She was a pretty woman, but she wouldn't look at either of our faces, as if she had been trained to avoid direct eye contact. He murmured something to her, and soon two more slaves, who might have been related to the first one, brought in trays. They placed them on a table erected for the purpose and began pouring something into two beakers, while placing what looked like cakes and big, fat crumpets on irregular-shaped plates. Everything smelled good, just as if we were having tea at home. My mouth watered, and then, to my own astonishment, my eyes began to water, too. I wasn't going to let him see, but I think I was crying. Again I was suddenly missing my mum and dad, and I wished I weren't, because it made me too vulnerable. I did what I could to stop the tears.

Almost sympathetically he handed me a plate with some pastries on it and a beaker full of what I'd swear was ordinary tea. But I found it hard to eat or drink at that moment.

"They are not poisoned," he said.

"I can't see why they would be," I replied. "You or one of your soldiers could kill me easily."

He seemed to like this answer. "You have all the spirit I expected. You are your mother's daughter. And you're intelligent, too. Your people must be proud of you."

Alfy was the smartest in our family. "You should meet my brother," I said. I began to eat, partly to disguise how I was feeling.

"I hope to, quite soon. Our allies have gone to seek him now. We're sure he's in the building." This really did startle me. Then I remembered enough to keep my own counsel. Was this the "brother" Huon had already mentioned? Jack D'Acre. A funny name. I hadn't seen it spelled out then. Huon might have been saying "Jacques Dacra" as far as I knew. It sounded vaguely French. But then, everything they said sounded vaguely French. I really wanted to find out what they thought they knew. I had already given away too much in the throne hall. I couldn't resist one chance to misdirect them.

"So they haven't found my brother yet?"

"Perhaps you know where he is hiding. He would need someone like you to help him. Those barefaced incompetents tracked him down in Mirenburg, I hear. More than once. Now he's gone again. He can't be far. We need to move more swiftly, given the state of affairs elsewhere in the multiverse."

Alfy had never been to Mirenburg and wasn't likely to be going in the near future. Bous-Junge had to be talking about the mysterious Jack D'Acre. But how could all of them have got that so thoroughly wrong? Was this whole thing a horrendous mistake on everyone's part? Were they hoping to find this Jack in Ingleton? Did they plan to trade him for me?

"He won't co-operate with you any more than I will," I said.

Baron Bous-Junge chuckled. "Oh, that's not the problem at all. Everyone co-operates with us when we persuade them. The problem is that he is elusive. Given what a peculiar little chap he is, I suspect your twin has help from more than just you."

It was beginning to dawn on me that they really did think this Jack fellow was my twin brother. Realising how far off the mark they were and that this perhaps gave me a certain power, I started to smile, then checked myself. "Who, for instance?" I asked.

"Oh, I think you know, my dear. Your grandmother, your great-grandfather, no doubt your father. There's a whole clan of your kind here, who never ventured to Granbretan before. The Austerite, the Frankonian . . . We have trapped prisoners. They have eagerly told what they know. Baron Meliadus took charge of them and used his special skills to extract that information. No doubt King Huon will persuade him, in turn, to share with us."

This alerted me, too. So there were rivalries here. Factions. I could tell by his tone.

"Baron Meliadus is still in Europe, eh?"

"Leading our soon-to-be-victorious forces. Hawkmoon took us by surprise. We did not know he had learned the secret of multi-dimensional travel."

Was that it? Were they trying to find out how we moved from one "realm" of the multiverse to another? Of course! If they had that power, they could contemplate conquering endlessly, combining forces with their alter egos on all the other worlds, threatening the structure of existence itself. They knew some of us had the ability to call upon the powers of Law and Chaos. Presumably they thought my brother could do it. They didn't seem to know I had absolutely no means of doing it myself, that I needed help from someone else.

"And then there is the other albino, Zodiac. Evidently a relative, also? He could help us. There is some indication, from my own readings of the multi-dimensional skrying globes, that he might be induced to join forces with us. That would be ideal. And might save your brother's life, as well as yours."

"You'll never get him to help you," I said.

"I think that's a little optimistic of you. His interests lie just as much with us as they do with you. We understand how to unite the swords. We have discovered the emerald stone. We know how to divide the cups. Our science has achieved this. All we require now is the agent which will bind them and make them re-form. Then we control everything."

"I thought only God could do that."

Again he chuckled, his round, rather jolly face lighting up. "Oh, dear! What makes you think God has any power? Or Lucifer, for that matter? It has been a very long time since those two forces had any means of exerting their will upon the Dark Empire. They died, you see, when so many died, during the Tragic Millennium. Some believe that the Millennium would never have occurred had it not been for those deaths. I think you must accept, young lady, that King Huon is the greatest power in the universe!"

I didn't understand exactly why this depressed me. I'd never known any sort of formal religion. I thought of God and Lucifer as ideas, representing certain human and spiritual qualities, not real entities. If I'd given them any consideration at all, it had been in response to the self-involved, anxious, miserable evangelicals who turned up from time to time at airports and railway stations to ask if I "knew Jesus." Those poor, desperate individuals caused so much harm in my world. Those fundamentalists, with their suspicion, their sentimentality, their anxious superstition. They constantly thank God for helping them win gold discs or gold medals (apparently accepting that God favoured them over any other contestants). This was the antithesis of the kind of rigorous selflessness I associated with my family. Their motto in Germany had always been "Do you the Devil's work," which had something to do with protecting family relics, lost, as I understood it, during the Second World War, recovered and sent to America for safe-keeping. Granddad kept something at his London flat, but I'd never seen it. Certainly for several generations we hadn't taken any of that stuff very seriously, except as rather funky stories with a vaguely Wagnerian ring. Yet I had the sudden feeling that I was actually sensing some great revelation, something important about the human condition, about mankind's relationship with the supernatural, and it seemed to involve not only my family's honour and survival, but everyone's—and many of the things I most cared about. If it wasn't a religious feeling, it was definitely profoundly mystical. Maybe that was what real religious experience felt like.

I was in no doubt, however, that the Dark Empire represented something close to pure evil. I just wasn't so sure that our side represented anything like pure good! And surely one was needed to combat the other.

"I wouldn't reckon any of your chances once my family find out where I am," I said defiantly.

This amused him even more. "My dear child! My dear child! Do you really expect Monsieur Zodiac to come whirling to your rescue with his mighty black blade?"

"It's a possibility," I said.

"I scarcely think so!" He chuckled again. "I understand Monsieur Zodiac finds it rather difficult to walk across the room without that sword's support."

"Which is hardly the point." I put down my beaker and finished my cake. I thought I had a sense now of what they feared. "Since he possesses the sword."

"Ah!" His eyes twinkled. "You have not heard?"

"What?"

"The albino no longer owns the sword. He left it behind when he went looking for you."

"It won't be much for him to go back for it!"

"I'm sure he's a very skilled traveller between the worlds, my dear, but you see, Messrs Klosterheim and von Minct already have it. That was why they were able to come here and negotiate with us. The sword was their payment for the aid and special skills we gave to them."

"Klosterheim's got it?"

"Not at all. The Black Sword is now in our safe-keeping. I think it highly unlikely your great-grandfather will want to risk very much."

Emotion suddenly flared in me. "He'll get it back. He'll show you he's not so easily tricked! He'll be here!"

"Oh, my poor child. Of course he'll be here. He's bound to try to help you. That is why we have let slip where you are. But without his sustaining hellblade, I fear he will not be of any great advantage to you."

And suddenly I knew that white-bearded wizard for what he really was: a conniving, cruel, disgusting man.

Our eyes met. He saw what I thought of him. He threw back his head and began to chuckle heartily.

"He'll be here, my dear. He'll be here. But whether he arrives in time to find you fully alive, I very much doubt. You see, the sword needs special food if it is to be useful to us. Special food . . ." He looked up at me, and now there was an indefinable lust in his eyes. "Young and fresh."

And as his cackle rose and his shoulders shook, I understood how thoroughly my friends and family had been defeated by his and Klosterheim's cunning.

I flung my plate and cup at him. Again I was close to tears, but I turned my fear into anger. "You nasty, dirty old man!"

The liquid from the beaker stained his beard, so that it looked as if blood ran down his chin and chest. His eyes hardened for a second, and then he burst into laughter again.

"I must admit," he said, as he dabbed at himself with a napkin, "that this is certainly one of the most complex and successful traps I have laid in all my many, satisfying centuries. We have you. We have the sword. Now all we need is young Jack. And I am certain he will join us again soon."

He cast a calculating eye over me and once more was all avuncular twinkles and chuckles. "You're a spirited child, my dear, and will take some keeping, I can see. We have allowed for that. You will be put in the custody of Flana Mikosevaar, Countess of Kanberry. She is of the blood royal, a possible heir to the throne, and the widow of Asrovak Mikosevaar, the hero who died by Dorian Hawkmoon's hand at the first Battle of Kamarg. She has had twelve husbands, several of whom met bloody ends, not always in war, and one of whom was Baron Meliadus, the King's Chancellor. She has no love for mainlanders, though she keeps the name of that infamous Muskovian renegade, her most recent spouse. Best you curb that tongue with her, since she has been given permission to begin punishing you in certain ways not permitted to the rest of us. Do not expect her to be lenient because you are of the same gender. Countess Flana is famous for the pleasure she takes in inflicting pain on others."

Baron Bous-Junge's features now beamed in a fat smirk as he replaced his mask and summoned the slaves. A sigh like escaping steam came out of his mask, as if he was already tasting the revenge he would have on me.

The old-fashioned hand-bell summoned his slaves as he turned his back and pored over some old books. He had forgotten me entirely. That might have been my chance to try to get away, but I left it till too late. The slaves surrounded me. They escorted me back to the same carriage, and I had no choice but to climb in again.

After another incredibly long journey through passageways, halls and tunnels, arcades and covered streets, we finally arrived at the Heron Palace, home of Flana Mikosevaar, Countess of Kanberry, who was to become my jailer. The Heron Palace was built around a beautiful courtyard. Unusually for the Dark Empire's taste, it was open to the roiling sky. Its water garden fed green lawns and richly scented flower beds full of blossoms I had never seen before, as well as roses, hydrangeas and lupines, familiar from home. The garden was comforting in spite of the bizarre blooms. I had the impression that given the complete absence of insects and birds, the plants were flesh-eaters.

I was left alone in the small antechamber looking out over the garden and, since I had no other way of calming myself, took an intense interest in the flowers. Although the windows were wide open, they were covered by screens so that it was impossible to go out.

After what seemed hours, Countess Flana and her entourage entered the room. She was tall and slender. She covered her head with a magnificently wrought heron mask, with a long, sharp beak and a half-raised crest, all in silver and ebony. From it two large golden, cool and unreadable eyes regarded me.

"I hear you have strong opinions of your own, Mademoiselle von Bek." The voice was humorous, vibrant. If I hadn't been warned by Baron Bous-Junge what she was really like, I might have thought I would find sympathy there. I kept my own counsel. I was still planning to escape. I felt it was almost my duty to try, since I seemed so crucial to whatever Dark Empire plan was in place to conquer the multiverse.

Of course, I hadn't taken them and their plans seriously, but even their reconquering of the Continent would be bad enough. I might manage to stop something if I escaped.

I decided to pretend to be deceived by Countess Flana, who sent her slaves from the room and came to stand over me where I sat on an uncomfortable, asymmetrical couch facing the garden.

"You like my little private garden, child?"

"I love it," I said as innocently as I could. "Do you work in it yourself?"

This brought a soft laugh. "As it happens, I do, when I am alone. Which is all too rare."

Slender-fingered hands reached to remove the elegant mask, revealing one of the most beautiful women I had ever seen, on or off the screen. She had a fair, glowing skin, platinum hair and dark red lips. There was a kind of wondering, dreaming quality to her as she turned those eyes, the shade of sunflowers, upon me. Her colour was higher than I would have expected, and the flush took time to leave her cheeks. It was very hard not to trust and like someone who looked so beautiful, even vulnerable. I wondered how she had handled twelve husbands. Twelve. She seemed to belong to the wrong Order. Was there an Order of the Spider? She contradicted everything I knew about her. I wondered about her kind's potential longevity. She looked twenty-five, but she must be more than one hundred.

For all her reputation, I found myself warming to her as she drew back the screens from the French doors and led me into the tranquillity of the water garden. The sky above was awash with speeding dark clouds, which flung their shadows over black towers, domes and turrets. Once a big, black ornithopter flew over the city, its engine pounding, throwing out the usual trail of smoke and sparks.

"So you are Jack D'Acre's sister?" We walked among the flower beds and the streams of water. "There is little family resemblance."

"I agree," I said. "You'd never know we were related."

She frowned at this. "Oh, no, I think the prophecy was accurate. I miss little Jack. He lived with me, you know. An odd experience, no doubt, for us both." She stared into the fountain. A tribe of stylised bronze merpeople rose onto rocks, water spewing from their metallic mouths. They rode dolphins and carried tridents and nets, yet, for all their classical origins, they were distinctly Granbretanian: faintly grotesque, faintly aggressive and possibly alive. Her voice became distant as she remembered something. She raised her head and watched the disappearing ornithopter as it flew between the towers. "Then he ran away."

If I hadn't known better, I would have thought she recollected a lover who had left her.

"But now I have you," she said. She reached to stroke my hair. "Poor Jack. Poor blind Jack."

"Were you the one who blinded him?"

"He sang so beautifully. And he knew the future. He was a seer, as you know, my dear. And you are aware, I'm sure, of the fate of such folk."

I couldn't stop myself from repeating, "How was he blinded?"

"By the light. They needed him to listen for the demons in the steel, you see." Her voice faded and became almost inaudible. "They didn't know his true value. They took him off to Mirenburg. My informants tell me they were trying to make a particular kind of sword." Perhaps she was thinking back to when it had happened. I couldn't be sure. I had never been with anyone as mysterious, as impossible to read. "Taragorm, you see, had these machines . . . But originally I bought him for his voice."

"*Bought* him?"

She frowned, puzzled. "Taragorm had other purposes for him, and no sense of his talents. He cost me the fortune of one of my husbands." She laughed softly. "But he was worth it. Until he went away." She sighed. "The king's orders, of course. Now this . . . I'm sure he'll be discovered eventually. But this time they will tear out his tongue. If he is lucky. They'll ruin him."

I knew a second or two of hope. "I didn't think anyone could escape from Londra."

"Oh, he hasn't escaped the city," she said. "He is still here, somewhere. He must be. I can almost smell him. After all, he can't go back to Mirenburg now, can he? I'm told your presence will make him reveal himself, once he knows his sister is in our power. What do you think?"

"I think he'd be an idiot to risk it," I said.

She found this amusing. She smiled and reached for me again. I let her stroke my neck and shoulder, but she could tell I was tense. She withdrew her hand. "I miss him. I suppose you do, too."

"Not as much as you, I think."

Her expression became strangely grateful. I found it very difficult to believe her a husband-killer, but I could have been seeing only one side of her. Or maybe all these Granbretanner aristocrats were like that. I had the impression that half these people only barely repressed hysteria. Something about their taste for masks and enclosed spaces was associated in my mind with that kind of madness. I had read the expression "my blood ran cold" and had never really thought what it meant. Now I knew. In spite of the warmth, I found myself shivering in her water garden as she led me down crazy-paving paths, staring thoughtfully into vivid, fleshy blooms and pretending, I supposed, to frame her thoughts.

"You didn't know him as I knew him," she said. And she sighed deeply, then laughed. "Who could?"

"You really think he'll come back to you just because I'm here?"

"Oh, no, my dear, he won't come back to me because of you. In fact, because of you he is even more likely to stay away."

She looked at me blankly for a moment, then turned away. "That's absurd. Jack is my adopted son. I intend to make him King-Emperor someday."

"But King Huon's immortal, isn't he?"

She looked at me in surprise, as if I had overheard her speaking to herself. "Of course he is." She smiled as she stopped to point out an especially magnificent variety of lily: purple caps, not dissimilar to deadly nightshade.

We wandered back to the French doors, and she again surprised me when she asked, "Have you any preferences for food this evening? There are certain shortages, because of the war, but I can have almost anything prepared for you."

I shook my head.

Her voice softened. "You're not enjoying your stay in Londra. Why is that?"

"I miss my mother and father."

"They turned you out?"

"No. That Klosterheim and his friend chased me all over the place. Under ground. All through the dimensions. Across half of Europe. And as a result I lost touch with them."

"Where are they? Still alive?"

"In England," I said. "In Yorkshire."

"Oh!" she exclaimed, brightening. "What a coincidence. We have provinces here in Granbretan which bear very similar names."

"I shouldn't be surprised." I yawned. It had been a long, long day. The sun was in its final quarter, spreading red, agitated light across the rooftops and domes. Maybe I liked this woman because she *was* unstable. It suggested a kind of vulnerability. "How long are they going to keep me here?"

"Not long, as I understand it. They have the Sword; they have the Cup; they have the Stone. Now they need the Blood and the Staff to perform the ritual. And you and Jack, of course, will provide those."

"Why is that?" I hardly wanted to hear her reply.

"Male and female fluids are needed, and of course, they must come from your veins. For you traditionally guard the Grail. Keepers of the Stone, as they say. The Blood must come from twins of that old von Bek strain. Taragorm, who is still a good friend of mine though we were married once, told me all about it. To gain control over the Balance, virgin blood of the twin Grail children must spill and mingle, while the essence of what is male and female must combine in ritual bloodletting . . ."

"Ritual bloodletting?" I was beginning to get a clearer picture. Not a very pleasant one. I shivered.

"Yes, of *both*. That is very important. I'm sure you understand, being of that blood. But much of this is new to me. I have never studied magic, you see, and know few who do. Taragorm has machines which speak to him. They are perfectly clear about what has to be done. Like to like. Same to same. Shape to shape. Blood to blood. It is the absolute fundamental of their science as well as their magic and medicine. We follow the principles of similarity. The principle of the Balance itself. Opposites in balance. The principles upon which all life is based. But Taragorm explained this to me and will no doubt do the same for you."

"Taragorm?" I wanted to know more about him.

"He is the Master of the Palace of Time. He can travel in time, they say. At least he can see into the past and future. The world's greatest scholar in the Doctrine of Signatures. What our ancestors called *Signatura Rarum*. Like affects like. The fundamentals of science. He searches the dimensions, back and forth through history, seeking to restore all the wisdom we lost when the Tragic Millennium descended upon us."

"And what brought that disaster?"

"Who knows, child? Perhaps a similar sequence of events. What is done in one time and place repeats and repeats, yet with each repetition comes a subtle change. There is a legend of a sword, a stone, a cup, I understand, which no doubt dates from the same period. It would be ironic, would it not, if we repeated the same mistakes which brought that long, dark age from which we so recently emerged." Her laughter was sweet and light but with an edge of weariness to it. "How boring if that turned out to be the truth."

I must admit, a lot of this magic stuff went over my head. Countess Flana didn't seem to notice.

"When does this ritual take place?" It seemed reasonable for me to ask a question about their plans for my death.

"When all the worlds are in conjunction," she said. "Smaller conjunctions appear fairly regularly. A hundred spheres. A million spheres. Over the past two or three centuries there have been a series of such conjunctions. Repeating and repeating. And at every repetition, Taragorm tells me, an opportunity has been lost. On this occasion they intend to be certain. They will preserve the Balance, and they will control it." She smiled almost tenderly at me and reached out her hand to me again. This time I avoided it. "They intend to gain control over both Law and Chaos."

"Isn't that a bit over-ambitious?"

"It seems so, doesn't it, my dear? What is in such men that they must control so much?" She smoothed her dress over her legs. "They say Hawkmoon or some avatar of his is destined to destroy the Balance. But if they control it, they will take control of the Grey Fees . . ."

"The DNA of the multiverse?" Wasn't that what someone had called it? I hardly knew what they were talking about.

"You are a well-educated child. They believe they can re-create the multiverse in their preferred image. When the mainlanders Klosterheim and von Minct came to them with the plan, they were sceptical. However, they were at last convinced, partly by the ease with which those two moved between the various realms of the multiverse. Our people only had the vaguest of notions of such worlds, though they have been working on a means of travelling to them for some time. In the *Signatura Rarum* there's evidence our ancestors had this power and lost it. If Granbretan is able to pass between one world and another easily, we will find and kill those who conspire against us. Until now, the ability to travel at will between the dimensions has belonged only to others. That is why you and your brother are so valued, of course, as are your great-grandfather and your grandmother. Not only does your blood possess the magical properties required to perform the ritual, but your physical capture will bring the others to us at the right time. And they'll reveal their secrets because we'll be able to experiment on them in the optimum conditions."

Something nagged at the back of my mind. There was a flaw somewhere in her logic.

"So you want half my family in on this. Are we all going to die?"

"Your bleeding," she said, "would not mean your dying in the conventional sense. But, of course, it will not be pleasant. I almost feel sorry for you."

I suddenly had an image of Mrs Ackroyd, the farmer's wife up at Chapel-le-Dale, hanging the pig and slitting its throat in order to make black pudding. The poor thing squealed horribly while its blood poured into a big bucket. I remember her pushing her hands down into the bucket, stirring the blood and pulling out strings of some impurity. Even my friends the Ackroyd girls thought it was gross. I ran away. I didn't wait for a lift. I ran almost three miles non-stop and was in a bit of a state when I got to Tower House. My mum and dad were furious when they heard I'd seen this. They very nearly refused to let me go and play with the Ackroyds after that.

I had this image of myself hung like Mrs Ackroyd's pig, and I suddenly felt sick. I asked where the toilet was. One of the slaves took me to a similar cubicle to the one in Mirenburg, and I threw up some bile, but I wasn't really that ill. I stayed there for a bit, just trying to collect my thoughts and wondering how on earth I was going to escape. It might have seemed hopeless, but it never occurred to me that I really was in extreme danger. The image of that pig prepared me for it, though.

I opened the cubicle grille to look out. The young slaves were waiting for me. I couldn't see a way of escape at that stage, but I was beginning to get an idea, based on these people's psychology. The mysterious Jack had got away. He must be very clever to have done it, considering they'd blinded him. Or did he have friends among the King-Emperor's lackeys?

For the time being, until I got a better idea of my surroundings and my chances of escape, I decided I'd better just go back. When I returned to the court-yard, Countess Flana was wearing her silver, gold and platinum heron mask again. She had a visitor. The man had his back to me but wore no mask. I recognised him at once.

She was saying, "The boy is lost again. Would the girl know where he is? If so . . ."

I heard him reply, "That's what I came to warn you about. Don't even break her skin, if you can avoid it. She must stay a virgin or the blood's no use to you. With luck, the albino and his bitch-whelp will lead us to the boy. The boy will bring you the Staff. Without it, the other objects are useless." He turned as I came in. His eyes narrowed and hardened.

I looked into the handsome face of a man I had thought our friend, who had been so charming and delightful when we first met, who had brought Elric to Ingleton and enjoyed our hospitality. A man I had liked and trusted. The balloonist bowed in that exaggerated way of his, and his smile was hypocrisy itself.

"Good afternoon, young mademoiselle. So pleasant to see you again." The Chevalier St Odhran doffed his elaborate bonnet.

18

Now Hawkmoon, Count Brass and his daughter Yisselda, Oladahn of the Bulgar Mountains, all dressed in mirrored, flashing armour, again led their forces against the armies of Meliadus and his barons. Meliadus fumed. What power did these rebels have that they could appear and disappear at will, forever choosing the place and time of the most crucial battles . . .?

Meanwhile, as Lord Taragorm and Baron Bous-Junge contemplated the ritual which was to end in Oonagh's terrible death, Elric, searching the worlds of the moonbeam roads, determined for himself that Klosterheim and von Minct had tricked him. He returned to the world in which the Dark Empire forces were at bay, and learned from Yaroslaf Stredic that his daughter and the others had arrived and headed for Munchein. He arrived at the lakeside ruins and found his friends only a few hours after the Granbretanian ships had left.

The stink of the ornithopters was still in the air. The party had been raided with poison-gas bombs; Elric recognised the kind. The bolting horses had escaped the worst of the gas. They now stood some distance away from the ruins, cropping the grass, carriages abandoned. Two of the party were gone: Oona and Oonagh. The rest had been left to die. Using his own considerable skills in sorcerous alchemy, Elric quickly revived his friends, learning from them the possible fate of the others.

Lord Renyard was the most agitated. He blamed himself for what had happened. Elric was able to reassure him. "Plots and counterplots, Lord Renyard, are in the nature of this particular game, where even the loyalties of one's closest friends are tested. We have all been deceived by that pair and their allies. I understood Bastable tried to reach you and failed. This complicates our game. Given the way in which all the realms of the multiverse now arrange themselves in conjunction, I would guess Granbretan plans to begin their blood ritual very shortly."

The great fox scratched himself behind his left ear. "Why is that so important to them? Do they serve Chaos or Law? What do they want?"

"Oh, they're playing for pretty high stakes, I think. They play for more than either Chaos *or* Law."

"There's something more than that?"

Elric turned for help to his friend, Prince Lobkowitz, who walked slapping at his clothing and wrinkling his nose against the smell. "Something more indeed. They seek the 'consanguine conduit,' bringing together all the scattered manifestations of the Balance itself."

"The Cosmic Balance? It's broken?" The fox found his hat and licked at the dusty felt until he was satisfied it was clean enough to readjust on his head.

"The Cosmic Balance can't be broken, though perhaps it can be destroyed. It is an idea. But those elements which represent it only rarely come together. Frequently they take unfamiliar forms." Prince Lobkowitz watched as the Kakatanawa rather inexpertly rounded up the horses and, helped by Lieutenant Fromental, harnessed them to their carriages. "Of course, the Balance itself is merely the symbol of the forces which work to control the multiverse, but it is a useful and powerful symbol. Control the symbol, many believe, and you control both Law and Chaos. Since rational people have never wanted such control, and irrational people were incapable of achieving it, the theory still to be tested."

"It has never been tested? Never? What is this balance, then? How is it comprised?" Lord Renyard looked on intently as Elric began to pick through the ruins where the ornithopter had landed, perhaps hoping to find concrete clues to where his daughter and great-granddaughter had been taken. It seemed obvious that they had been carried off to Granbretan. Probably to Londra. Few escaped that island, he guessed. He cocked his gloomy head to hear Prince Lobkowitz's reply.

"Traditionally the Balance comprises a stem, a crosspiece and two bowls suspended on golden chains from the crosspiece. It combines the essence of both Order and Entropy. The stem is rooted in a great rock sometimes popularly called the Rock of Ages. Others merely call it 'the Stone.' In some parts of the multiverse these elements are themselves individually venerated, even worshipped. One found its way into legend as Excalibur, Arthur's sword, which was embedded in a rock before he pulled it free. Other tales speak of the Stone as the

Grail, a giant emerald—not always a magnificent cup—which has the power to cure the world's pain. Some believe it is the same thing as the Runestaff, which appears to have the Grail's properties and can reveal itself in many forms."

The fox opened his mouth in a puzzled grin. "I fear, sir, that as a rational creature, 'tis hard for me to understand such strange logic . . ."

Prince Lobkowitz nodded slowly, watching the others and mopping at his neck. Like them he was sweating, probably as a result of Elric's potions. "Throughout the multiverse, intelligent, imaginative beings ascribe differing powers and forms to these symbols," he said. "The cups, the swords, the rocks, are merely the more familiar forms we choose. Manipulation through representation is the quest of every alchemist, for instance. That's the peculiar logic by which we control the elements, which some condemn as sorcery. Represented by elementals—sentient beings with the power of the tornado or the forest fire, the earthquake or the storming heavens—these forces are far stronger than anything we can invent or hope to control. Even those above the elementals, the Lords of the Higher Worlds, who represent our vices and virtues as well as our ambitions and temperaments, our intellect, our courage, even our morality, would not challenge the power of the Balance. They, too, understand how they must perpetually struggle, Law against Chaos, in order to maintain the life of the multiverse, to ensure that it grows neither moribund nor too fecund. Either state is antipathetic to our existence. What's more, we are ourselves manifestations of those conditions. That's perhaps why we exist at all. Through our stories, which are formed from our desires and fears, we create order and ensure our own existence. The multiverse protects her own security and her own continuing growth by creating those forces which will, in balance, sustain her. We represent such forces in symbols which we use to interpret and organise that small part of the multiverse we inhabit and understand."

Elric came back, having found nothing. "And then," he said, by way of augmenting Prince Lobkowitz's explanation, "there are the Grey Fees." He allowed himself a thin smile, to which, by way of acknowledgement, Lobkowitz responded.

"The Grey Fees, it's believed, is the primordial matter which can be given shape entirely by thought and desire," he said. "Some who have studied the magical arts are convinced that control of all other elements is as nothing if you control the Grey Fees. The Balance is the regulator. Destroy that regulator and you personally become regulator, with control of all creation."

"Aha!" The fox was at last enlightened. "You become God!"

"And that, we are convinced, is the obscenity which the Dark Empire and their allies, von Minct and Klosterheim among them, wish to manifest, believing that both God and Satan, in their reconciliation, no longer have interest nor the power to manipulate and control."

Lord Renyard found this easy to understand. He murmured something about epicureanism and stoicism. "And there will always be those, too, who by creating conflict manage to take advantage of all sides."

"This began some centuries ago," Prince Lobkowitz concluded, "when Prince Elric's distant relative, Ulric von Bek, was commissioned by Satan to seek the Holy Grail and thus cure the world's pain. Your friend, Manfred von Bek, got himself involved in a plot by the Duchess of Crete and her associates, who wished to find the ultimate alchemical power over nature, which involves, of course, the ability to control the elements, thus turning lead into gold and so forth. Still later, the present old Count Ulric forestalled a Nazi plot to gain that power. But Klosterheim and Gaynor, who cannot easily die, because of their own experiments and skills, continued to seek control of the Grail. That is what they believe they are doing now, but I suspect Bous-Junge, Taragorm and all those other brilliant, poisoned minds of Granbretan have even more ambitious plans."

"If they gain that control—"

"Then we all cease to exist, I fear. However, they are more likely to fail and bring catastrophe down upon themselves. But even that prospect does not greatly concern our friend Klosterheim. It is *oblivion* he desires, I suspect, and this is his means of finding it. *Annihilation*. Even Gaynor has decided that he would rather die than lose his chance at controlling the very lifestuff of existence. Not that he fully comprehends what that death will mean for him: an agony of 'now' in which he relives the moment before his death for eternity. For if you would abolish time, you abolish all that makes you a living creature, as opposed to an atomic particle, which has no history but is re-created over and over again." Prince Lobkowitz let out a melancholy sigh. He could tell that not all the assembled party followed his reference to physics. But the expedition was reassembled at last. He looked to Elric. "What now, old friend?"

Elric was troubled. "Apparently, we've been outmanoeuvred by our enemies. Granbretan and her allies now possess at least two of the elements they seek, and will do everything they can to gather the rest. Even the Black Sword isn't safe from them. We gamble everything on this game—as, I suspect, do they."

"And our time grows short," said Prince Lobkowitz. "Now every Knight of the Balance, in every manifestation of our world, comes together to defeat those greedy forces, the combined power of the Dark Empire, Klosterheim, Gaynor and the rest. We must outwit them, as they have just outwitted us. They have a habit of cunning, which most of us lack. And that little girl's well-being, her very life, depends upon what we do next."

"I would give my life for the child," said Lord Renyard simply.

"As we all would," agreed Prince Lobkowitz. "But we do not wish Prince Elric, for instance, to give his life, for that would mean that he could not fulfil his destiny elsewhere. So you see, dear Lord Renyard, we act out of necessity, not sentiment, nor always decently, nor always courageously, in a highly complex conflict, full of subtle attack and counter-attack. Imagine a large orchestra, in which every instrument must be in perfect tune if a particular piece of music is to be played, also perfectly and at a specific moment. Yet each member of that orchestra can be separated by thousands of miles or even thousands of years, scattered across the multiverse, which, if not infinite, appears to be infinite. If only one of our heroes does not act as he is supposed to act, if events do not happen exactly when they are due to happen, if Elric and his avatars do not do what they must all do precisely at the right moment, then there is no hope for any of us. Life will be extinguished. The multiverse will collapse into inchoate primal matter, *and there will be no intelligence, this time, to give it form.*"

"You refer to the death of God. The death of an idea. Even so, it takes a certain courage to continue to live in such circumstances," said Lieutenant Fromental, his open, friendly face graver than usual. "Any fool can throw up his arm with his fist around a sword and cry 'Liberty or Death!' but it takes a special kind of hero to know that it is not for him to choose the time of his death, or even choose his own weapons. You know that, I think, old friend." He came up to the others, dusting his hands and smiling sympathetically at Elric. "But what I am seriously curious about is who betrayed us? Too often, it seems to me, our enemies have anticipated our moves, known where we were going and what we planned."

Elric ran his pale hand through his milk-white hair. "Aye. As if we had a spy in our midst. Yet the idea is anathema. Everything we do and say is based on mutual trust and mutual hatred of a common enemy. Who would have either the motive or the means of betraying us?"

The albino paused and shrugged. He rubbed his chin. "I have come from a world where betrayal and lies are commonplace, where anything is said and done in order to win at all costs, where people have grown used to hypocrisy and deceit and regard them as natural, legitimate instruments of trade, politics and daily intercourse, unable to distinguish truth from falsehood. They embrace the sentimental lie with the enthusiasm others bring to religion. Indeed that habit of mind has *become* their religion. Yet those of us who came together so recently to avert this plot are all habitual enemies of Gaynor, Klosterheim and their kind. We must reject the Prince of Lies. It is in our self-interest to remain loyal to one another." He sighed. "Well, there is nothing to do now but go to Granbretan and see if we can find the children before those creatures begin mingling their blood with those sacred objects."

"Children's blood!" The fox was shocked. "They are sacrificing children? How disgustingly barbaric! But why?"

"The corrupted practices of sorcery," said Prince Lobkowitz. "You begin by believing that like affects like. Like then *becomes* like. Therefore, like *controls* like. Pure blood of near-immortals is the material they hope to use to produce their new reality. When the multiverse melts and collapses into its unformed and uncontrolled fundamentals, they will absorb the blood, making it their own, and ensure that they survive to re-create the multiverse to their own design. Even if they fail, as I suspect they must, it will destroy all that regulates the multiverse. Meanwhile many heroes will die for nothing, believing themselves to be dying for a cause, dying to rebalance the elements, dying in defence of God himself. Every avatar of the one we call the Champion Eternal will perish."

"The destruction of the Knights of the Balance," murmured Lieutenant Fromental. "Even Satan did not seek that." He spoke with strong feeling, as if from experience. "We must go there. We must save our little mademoiselle."

Prince Lobkowitz drew his greying brows together. "But how on earth can we reach Granbretan undetected?"

"That is not our chief problem," Elric told him. "We can scavenge masks from the many corpses Duke Dorian has left us. I'm told the Dark Empire forces have retreated back to their Silver Bridge which spans the sea between Karlye and Deau-Vere. Even if Colonel Bastable cannot help us, as I believe he intends to, it would be easy for most of us to join groups of refugees. It will be considerably more difficult to find and rescue young Oonagh and my daughter."

Lord Renyard was a little perplexed. "I must go with you, gentlemen. How do you propose to disguise me?"

A new voice chimed in from behind them. "At last! Thank the Lord we are still to some degree synchronised. I would have been here sooner, but I had some minor problems with a timing device. I am sorry I was unable to keep our appointment in Mirenburg, Monsieur Zodiac. I simply couldn't leave the job at that point. The machine shops and factories are the only ones in this extraordinary world where I could find the engineers and craftsmen I needed. And as usual, they were behind schedule. Anyway, she's ready now. I gather you got my message."

Elric turned, recognising the voice, but it was Prince Lobkowitz and Lieutenant Fromental who spoke first, together. "Good afternoon, colonel."

The strong, open features of the newcomer brightened in a grin. "Good afternoon to you, too, gentlemen!" He stepped forward to embrace Prince Lobkowitz and shake the hands of his fellow Knights of the Balance. With heavy goggles pushed back over a military cap, he wore something very close to a uniform, in light blue and scarlet. In certain worlds he would have been recognised immediately as a member of His Majesty's Imperial Merchant Air Service.

Colonel Oswald Bastable was glad to see his old friends. He told them quickly of his time in Mirenburg, how he had thought it unwise to reveal himself to the party there, because he, too, had seen Klosterheim and Gaynor in the palace. "I decided to let them focus on you, gentlemen, whom they had already detected. This allowed me the time I needed to complete my 'infernal machine.' Of course, without Prince Yaroslaf's help, nothing would have been possible. Your word, Monsieur Zodiac, went a long way with him.

"I tried to tell Countess von Bek to wait, that I was preparing a better means of travel, but she left precipitously while I was at the factory clearing up some details of my ship. Young Oonagh almost recognised me when I joined you briefly for that first meal at Prince Yaroslaf's reception. The prince was sworn to secrecy, but I couldn't resist making brief contact with you. It was a bit of a toss-up, you see. I could have told her who I was and risked old Klosterheim and company guessing what I was up to, or I could keep my identity secret and risk your party, Prince Lobkowitz, leaving before I could contact you. That, of course, is exactly what happened. When I heard you had gone, I ran after you, but you were already some distance from Mirenburg. I was a little too late, it seems. I guessed they were waiting for you to leave the safety of the city, where they'd be able to take a crack at you. I tried to warn you, but unfortunately you misinterpreted me. Anyway, she's completed now and at your disposal. Training the crew was the hardest part. They have a very different theory of aeronautics. They're not British, you see. However . . ."

With a modest gesture of his gauntleted hand, Colonel Bastable pushed back his cap, turned and indicated low hills behind them.

Flying low, casting a long shadow on the ground, her engine droning softly, hull glittering with newly doped canvas, bright metal and fresh paint, flying a Union Jack from her aft-lines, came a slender airship, the glass portholes of her armoured gondola winking like round, innocent eyes.

"Gentlemen, may I present HMAS *Victoria*. She's our prototype. A nifty little bus, though I do say so myself. Carrying some pretty powerful ordnance. And I think we can slip across the channel in her tonight, what, and do what we need to do."

Prince Lobkowitz nodded gravely, staring hard into Colonel Bastable's face. "I suspect, sir, that you have a personal agenda in this matter."

Wide-eyed, Bastable returned his stare. "To protect the well-being of this world, sir? How does that sound?"

Elric, unable to determine the nature of their exchange, turned away in some impatience, leading the party towards the airship as she began to settle in the air a few feet above the ground.

19

The sight of the Scots balloonist made me feel suddenly sick and helpless. St Odhran's crooked smile told me all I needed to know. He had betrayed us. We were as good as finished. I remembered how Monsieur Zodiac had trusted him, even leaving his sword in the traitor's hands!

"You rotten . . ." I couldn't come up with a word bad enough. I was close to tears.

Countess Flana had better things to do. She had grown bored with me. Asking the chevalier to sit down, she summoned slaves and ordered them to wheel me out of her little sanctuary. Before I had the chance to recover my composure, I found myself in a set of apartments which, the slaves told me, had been prepared for me.

Certainly it looked as if my capture had been anticipated for quite a while. There were changes of clothes in my size, a neat little bed with a fluffy down comforter, and everything was made for a person of my height. Everything but the doors and windows, that is. They were, if anything, oversize, and all discreetly locked, barred or both. The windows were so high, I couldn't see out of them. Only when I managed to clamber on top of a piece of asymmetrical furniture (which vaguely resembled a hippopotamus) could I see a few roofs, the odd chimney against a black and scarlet sky full of perpetual, restless movement, clouds of smoke creating sinister half-familiar shapes. The glass was thick and blemished. It helped produce the effect of warped menace. I was glad to get down and have a look around my cell.

As prisons went, it was luxurious. There was a little sitting room with funny-looking chairs and another of those weird toilets. The cupboards revealed more clothes, many of them really beautiful, a couple of plain masks, which fitted me, some books made of light, silvery stuff which was neither paper nor plastic. Pictures in the books gave the impression of movement. The script was in a language I could scarcely understand. I tried to do a bit of reading, but the strain was too much.

At some point a slave brought me my supper, which consisted of a cup of salty soup, several different kinds of fish in thin strips laid on the plate in rows, some fruit and a very sweet drink which reminded me of that apricot nectar which Mum would never let us have because she said the sugar in it would rot through bone, let alone our teeth. I felt quite a lot better after I'd eaten, though. I was ready to face, if not the worst Granbretan could throw at me, then something close. They had shown me that poor, ragged creature, his skin hanging in ribbons from his body, so that I could sit and think of the similar fate in store for me, but in spite of the evidence, I refused to believe they were going to do anything so cruel.

I think I was in shock or denial, because I had become pretty unemotional, in spite of all I knew of their intentions. I shed no more tears. I had a cold hatred for St Odhran. My duty was to get away from him, to spoil his plans as much as possible. I exercised by running around the room shouting pop songs to myself, then jumping up and down on the bed, then trying some of my mum's T'ai Chi and yoga positions. By the time I stopped I had worn myself out and lay on the comfortable feather bed, panting and staring up at the heavily decorated ceiling, which had masked, naked people doing things which were not so much obscene or sexual as impossible to interpret, which was probably just as well. The walls, too, were decorated. They showed a painted forest through which a procession of people and monsters marched. All the colours were the usual dark greens, browns, reds and purples. Pretty oppressive.

As I looked around my room, I found myself nodding off in spite of my determination to try to stay awake and think through my situation. I was soon fast asleep, dreaming of cows with animal heads, of Lord Renyard dressed like an old-fashioned Victorian nanny, of Elric/Monsieur Zodiac carrying a huge black sword, which I thought at first streamed with blood until I saw that there were glowing letters engraved in the metal, red as the albino's eyes. Then came my grandmother, Oona, with her bow and arrows, loosing one shaft after another into the carcass of a monstrous wolf which pranced and snarled at the edges of my bed, gathering courage to pounce.

It was very dark in my room when I heard a scratching at the door, which swung open at my mumbled greeting. I didn't see anyone come in until a large face with green-yellow eyes was close to mine. A rumbling purr broke from the throat of the beast I recognised as our black panther. Then the door opened again. A female slave stood there, holding a tray on which was a steaming beaker of liquid like tomato juice. This slave was masked and naked, like all slaves of the upper orders. She had a really lovely body, all rounded muscular curves, and her soft, glowing skin seemed unnaturally pink in the faint light coming through the high windows. I realised I didn't know how to turn a light on in the room, and was surprised by the soft radiance which slowly filled it.

The slave made no attempt to offer me the tray but put it on the nearest surface and crossed back to the door. Was she checking to see if she'd been followed? Meanwhile the panther sat down between us. I felt sudden relief, a sense of gratitude. I wasn't really surprised when the panther's companion stripped off her mask and revealed herself as Oona, wearing what I now saw was a flesh-coloured body stocking. She had obviously worn it to hide her albino skin, which would have been easily detected even in the murk of corridors lit primarily by flaming torches.

"I thought you were dead," I whispered, "or at least that they'd left you behind. How did you get here?"

My grandmother smiled. "By ornithopter, the same as you. I didn't inhale much of the poison gas which knocked you all out. I was able to hold my breath and pretend to be overcome. Both empire ships took off at the same time. One carried von Minct, and the other left with you. But they had forgotten our ship, which returned and found us. I flagged it down and persuaded the pilot to fly me to Karlye, where a major battle was taking place. In the confusion I disguised myself and joined troops retreating over the Silver Bridge. Things were so confused on the other side, with soldiers and fighting machines everywhere, that I easily made it to Londra." She grinned. "So unused have the Granbretanners become to attack by those they conquer that they have few defences in the city. With a little help, I slipped through the gates and reached the palace."

"But you didn't have any keys . . ." I looked at the door she had entered by.

"I am not above using the odd manipulation." She reached down to pat the panther. Another vast purr rumbled in the cat's throat as she looked up at my grandmother, who answered her with a kind of *huff* which the panther responded to by half closing her eyes in a friendly way.

"Where did she come from?" I asked. The panther hadn't been with us when we fled Mirenburg.

"Oh, she always knows where to find me." My beautiful grandmother smiled. "We have a rapport. Sometimes we might almost be the same creature. Come, get dressed quickly. I'm taking you away from here."

"Escaping!" I was excited. Maybe this was why I had not felt total terror at the Dark Empire's plans for me. Maybe I had always known she would come for me. "Do you know about that traitor, St Odhran?"

"Oh, yes," she said, "I know all about St Odhran." She seemed too disgusted to say more.

The Heron Palace was alive with sound. Were we under attack? The building itself was moaning and whining, and the fluttering flames of the overhead flambeaux made the corridors seem alive, organic. Oona and the panther trotted swiftly over the uneven flagstones, keeping me between them. We went past doors from which came all kinds of animal noises, suggesting this was some sort of private zoo. It smelled like the zoo, too. In reply to my whispered question, my grandmother put her thumb up, indicating I had hit it in one.

When she got the chance, she murmured into my ear, "This is the menagerie of Asrovak Mikosevaar. He was a keen collector. Many powerful people here keep menageries."

"I'm used to barred cages and all that sort of thing. Or at least big ditches and glass!"

"These are not for public view," she whispered, "but for private pleasure."

Before she could tell me more I felt the warm night air on my face and smelled that mixture of soot, scorched metal and burning coke which was the predominant smell of the city. "This brings us out near the river, which is exactly where we need to be."

"Won't they be looking for me? I mean, you might be able to disguise yourself as a soldier, but nobody would believe I was one. Not even a little Gurkha."

She smiled. "We're not going back the way we came. I'm hoping to follow the trail of Klosterheim and von Minct. I found their prisoner."

"The boy? Jack?"

"Yes."

"How did they get Jack here? He wasn't with them in Mirenburg."

"They know a way of travelling between Mirenburg and Londra," she said. "But I can't use it. The wheel. Anyway, Jack's out of harm's way for the moment."

While we held that whispered conversation we hurried along the galleries. Only once was our way blocked, by a couple of masked male slaves who weren't really suspicious of us but were curious. Oona's response was to reach out and bang their heads together so that they slipped gently to the floor. I was very impressed.

"You'll have to show me how you do that, Granny," I said. I was taking a perverse pleasure in using the term to this attractive young woman, who really was my grandmother!

"Later," she said. "When we are all safely back in Ingleton, there's a lot I do want to show you. Wisdom that has to be passed on."

I was no longer certain we'd ever make it back to West Yorkshire, but I was heartened by her promise even though I suspected she made it to reassure me. The galleries were getting more populated, busier, with slaves bustling back and forth, carrying everything from trays of food to furniture. I was surprised they didn't notice the panther, but when I looked for her she had disappeared.

"Where are we?" I asked the first time we paused.

"We have left Mikosevaar's and are now approaching the apartments of Taragorm, Master of the Palace of Time."

"Isn't he one of our worst enemies?"

"Which is why we went this way rather than another," she said. "I'm guessing they'll first try searching the streets surrounding Flana's when they find you gone in the morning."

"What happened to your panther?"

"Oh, she's become absorbed in someone else, don't worry." It was the only answer she gave me. I wondered just how much magic was around. I caught a distinctive odour I associated with both electricity and the sulphur stink that matches make when you strike them. For some reason, I thought of it as the smell of magic.

We descended, by steps and slopes, lower and lower into the palace depths. This part was deserted. Then Oona opened a small door in the side of a very narrow passage, and even I had to duck to enter. She closed the door carefully behind us. She felt around in the dark. I heard something rustling, and it scared me. I stuck close to my grandmother. "What's that . . .?"

A Bic sparked. A conical yellow candle burned with a smell like fried fish.

Gradually I made out a small room. It seemed to have been used as a sort of store cupboard. In the far corner, a figure stirred.

He yawned as he turned over on a dark grey mattress, blinking awake.

It was the young man I had seen before, whom I'd tried to track down without success in Mirenburg's Mechanical Gardens. I saw his face clearly now. He had the same high cheekbones, almond eyes, strong mouth and chin, the gently tapered ears, that I had seen on Oona and my great-grandfather. The young albino turned his head towards us.

"Jack," murmured Oona. "I've found her. You must lie low here for a day or so. Then we'll try to get away."

He nodded. He hardly seemed interested in what she said. "My father . . ." he began, then stopped. He frowned. "Who are you, girl?"

"My name's Oonagh," I told him. "Are you Jack D'Acre?"

"That's close," he said. "It's what they call me at home. I know your voice. The girl in the factory . . ."

"That's right." I wondered where his home was, and was about to ask him when Oona said, "Jack's from London. Not Londra. He lived in Clapham before Klosterheim and von Minct got news of him." She moved back towards the door. "I must find some clothes and a better mask or I'll be of no use to anyone. I'll return as soon as I can. Should something happen and I don't get back, let me show you this." She went to the far wall of the little room and pulled away some boxes and sacking. She pointed to a short door down in the wall. "You'll have to lead Jack to safety, Oonagh. If you are in danger, go through there. It will take you to the river, where I think you'll be able to find a boat. The panther will help. It's the only way to escape the city now."

Then she was gone. When I next looked, I saw that the panther was sitting guarding the door, her eyes closed, her head hanging slightly as if she slept on her feet.

"Are you the female principle they keep talking about?" The boy stood up, came towards me. He stumbled, almost fell, his hands grabbing at air.

His red eyes stared at me without seeing. I remembered Mrs House's oracular remarks: "*You have been in danger since the day you were born!*" He was the same boy from Mirenburg. I racked my brains to try to think of what else Mrs House had told me. "*The Blood,*" she had said. "*You have the Blood.*" Well, I knew that from the Countess Flana, too—whatever it *meant*!

I didn't know what a female principle was exactly. "I spoke to you in the factory. Then I saw you later in a sideshow. Aren't they still looking for you? What happened?" I went up to him and reached out my hand and took his. His soft, gentle fingers followed the contours of my face.

"You're young," he said. "Younger than me. The one who helped me. I heard Klosterheim talking about 'the female principle.' They seem almost scared of us."

"I kept my mouth shut. Did you say anything?"

"No," he said, "but then, I have no secrets. Klosterheim and Gaynor have been holding me prisoner off and on for quite a while. They found me in London and then brought me here. That was ages ago. Then they took me to Mirenburg, where the wheel is, so they could move through various different versions of our world. That's how we managed to escape the big flood. Did they take you to Mirenburg?"

"No," I replied. "I think they were using you to try to trap me, as well as Monsieur Zodiac. After I talked to you in the factory, I saw you a couple of times, in different places. They almost captured me once, but Oona saved me."

"She's a saint, that woman," he said. "Were you part of McTalbayne's gang?"

"I don't know the name."

"Worst bastard that ever was on the street," he said. "Charged you rent for the cardboard box you lived in."

"You were homeless?"

"I told you. I had a home. A decent-sized box." He grinned to himself as he felt his way over to a small chest which had been placed against the wall. "Want something to eat?"

"No, thanks," I said, watching him open the chest and take out what looked like a pie made of green pastry and bite into it.

"These are good," he said. "Meat. Sure you won't have one?"

"Maybe later. I'm not that hungry. So when did they first capture you?"

"First? A while ago. I don't know exactly. McTalbayne had us up west on a run. I was always used as the diversion, see, because I'm blind and look sort of funny. So that was my job. I was in Marks and Spencer's, having a bit of a fit, while the rest of them stripped the racks near the door. We'd done it a hundred times before. Then, suddenly, I felt myself grabbed. I thought it was the Old Bill, the cops, but it turns out to be Klosterheim and that filthy wanker von Minct. They pretended they were police. Only when I was in the car I realised they were bullshitting me. They got me down to the river and over the bridge, and before I knew it, it was 'Three, please' for the London Wheel."

"You've been on it?"

"Well, only that time. A waste of money in my case. Next thing I knew, I was in Mirenburg. Weird place, isn't it? Are you a Londoner, too?"

I was fascinated. "Yes," I said hurriedly. "What? You mean the London Wheel took you to Mirenburg?"

"That's how they travel," he said. "What part of London?"

"Well, I was born in Notting Dale, but we moved to Tufnell Hill. Near the old windmill."

"Oh, I know it," he said. "McTalbayne used to take us up there on the way to Hampstead. We did the fair and that. Apparently it's the last working mill in London. Owned by a recluse of some sort. I know McTalbayne had his eye on the place but got put off when he went to see if he could break in . . ."

I had the strangest sensation, talking to that blind albino boy who looked so much like my grandparents and Monsieur Zodiac. The panther was still sleeping by the door.

"Do you know who your mum and dad are?" I asked him.

"I'm told my father was Elric and my mum was a dreamthief. Then there's my sister."

"They think I'm her."

His hand came out again to explore my face. "Oh, no," he said. "There's no resemblance at all."

"So it's mistaken identity, is it? Because we've got the same relatives?"

He shook his head. "Don't ask me. That pair didn't tell me much. I found out from Oona almost everything I *do* know. Which isn't much! How are you related?"

"Oona," I said, "is really my grandmother."

"Oona?" He burst into laughter. "Oona? You mean the woman who brought you here, right?"

"Right." I was a bit upset by his response.

"Well, I don't know what she's been saying or what anyone else is telling you," he said, "but we can't be *that* many years apart." He spoke in a coarse, rather aggressive tone. Maybe, I thought, he is just defensive. He must have had a terrible time since he was a baby.

"Eh?"

"Oona just can't be your granny," said Jack D'Acre. "She's far too young."

"Well, that's what you'd think—"

"I know it. Far too young. You've got it *completely* wrong. Oona's my *sister*." He put his hand to his mouth. "Oops. I wasn't supposed to tell anyone that. Keep it dark, okay, or we could be in trouble."

20

I decided Jack's ordeal had addled his mind, so I didn't press the subject. A bit later my grandmother returned briefly with a further warning to lie low. "Hawkmoon's made impressive advances. They say he has supernatural help. A crystal whose facets resemble the multiverse itself, the light representing the moonbeam roads. He is capable of moving whole armies across space and time. His army vanishes for a while and then reappears hundreds of miles deeper into enemy territory. Meanwhile the empire makes finding you two its priority. Huon has offered rewards and punishments. Some of the punishments have already started. Flana herself, I understand, is suspected."

King Huon had ordered an intensive search for me and the blind boy. The biggest operation Oona had ever seen. We were more important to the Dark Empire than the defence of its city. I tried to ask how Jack D'Acre could be her twin brother, but she had no time to explain, she said. "It's to do with the relationship of one world of the multiverse with another. The closer they are in conjunction, the closer their timelines. We grow used to these discrepancies when we travel the moonbeam roads. I suspect that is the secret Hawkmoon has. Klosterheim seems to know something about the duke's source of power. The empire wants to find anyone who has the ability to travel in that manner—you and Jack in particular."

At least I now understood how she looked roughly the same age as her father. So it really was possible, for a special few at least, to go back into history and meet their own parents before they were born! Did it mean you could manipulate events? Change the course of history? From what she said, this power was granted to you only if you were one of a kind, or at least a manifestation, like Elric, of a recurring hero called the Champion Eternal.

When Oona left to scout out our escape route, she took the panther with her. She had given me plenty to think about.

Those resonances began to make sense of so much that had been a mystery to me. If I ever got back to school and passed my A-levels, I decided to specialise in mythology and anthropology at university. Then came a fresh anxiety: Had the school holidays ended? Was I being missed at Godolphin & Latymer? It's stupid the kind of things you think of when someone is threatening to hang you upside down and bleed you to death like a pig!

Jack D'Acre wasn't Oona's brother's real name. He had been homeless, hanging out in Covent Garden and Long Acre, when his mates called him that as a joke because they thought he had a French accent. He didn't know where he was from, though he vaguely remembered a time before he was blind. He might have dreamed that he'd lived in a cottage in the country, he thought, with woods all around. He remembered "a kind of brilliant darkness," he said. He had lived there with Oona, his sister, and in those days they had been exactly the same age.

It was odd talking to my great-uncle who was probably no more than five years older than I. He still seemed more like a brother. He had a restless, boyish manner. His white hair was cropped short, and he wore a pair of sunglasses to hide his eyes, but his resemblance to Elric and Oona was uncanny.

"They also called me Onric," he told me, "in Mirenburg. A weird name. I prefer Jack, don't you?"

"Well, it's easier to remember. I'm a bit inexperienced at all this between-the-worlds travelling. I'm not sure I'd be able to do any of it without help. How did you go blind? Were you always on your own?"

"Oona says it was during the empire's first experiments. I was only little when I was blinded. Some agent of Taragorm's found me out on the moon-beams apparently. I must have been abandoned there. After that I was never on my own for long. I don't know how I got away from Bous-Junge before. There was always someone offering to help me who I could be useful to. One bloke in Oxford used to take me out with him as a leprosy victim."

He laughed. "We got a lot of money thrown at us—from a distance. Mc-Talbayne wasn't the first by a long shot. I've done worse than he wanted me to do. At least I got regular food and my own box." He chuckled again, his whole face opening up into an honest and at the same time very sad expression. Then he withdrew again. "All I had to do was be myself and create a diversion, wher-ever we were. Sometimes it was shops, sometimes streets. Mostly it was stealing from institutions, big stores, those who could afford it, though I didn't really like doing *any* of it. After that bastard Klosterheim found me again he took me to Bous-Junge, as I said. Then to Mirenburg, where they were trying to forge that sword. Then back here. They know how to get onto the moonbeam roads, though they find it hard to use them. Klosterheim knew who my mum and dad were, he said. He claimed he would make it his business to get us together again. I think they might even have bought me from McTalbayne. I suspect money changed hands because I heard them talking later. I've got this very sensitive hearing. Five hundred quid, maybe? Only a couple of hours after we got off the Ferris wheel we weren't in London any more, as I said. That bloke Gaynor met us in Mirenburg. For a while they had me in the local fairground. I guess it was a way of hiding me from anyone else who might be looking for me. It wasn't a bad scam, all in all. But things got more and more restrictive. They wouldn't let me go anywhere without at least two minders, and not very far, at that. I heard them talking. The Dark Empire wanted to find out how to use the moonbeam roads. Klosterheim and Gaynor let them use me to listen to the sword blades. They wanted some other bloke to see me. They called him 'our mutual friend.' Never said his name. They made me work, testing those swords by their resonances. They were trying to make this one special blade, see. For a special customer they hoped to trick. At least that's what I guessed. Anyway, we spent some time in that weird-smelling city, and then they brought me back here and locked me up in a filthy storage room of some sort. I think it had been a warehouse. I couldn't get out. Mainly wanted me as bait for their trap . . . I didn't know what had happened to my sister then, and I didn't, of course, know about you or my father. Then I met you and guessed it was you they were after next."

"Do you know why?"

"Some big war or science project they've got on? What would your guess be? Human bombs? I've heard lately that the empire's losing ground every day. They were so confident of their own superiority, they never expected their slaves to rise up. They certainly didn't realise the momentum that revolt would give Hawkmoon and the others. I heard Klosterheim talking about it just before Oona found me. Hawkmoon's got a secret weapon, I think. That crystal my sister mentioned. The armies were actually fighting on the sea bridge, last I heard. Whatever it is they want from us, they want it *bad*."

"They want to kill us for our blood," I said. "At least they want to kill *me*. Maybe they'll let you live; I'm not sure. They're falling back on witchcraft as they lose battles. Not human bombs but human sacrifice. Which, I suppose, is much the same thing in the end. And they don't have any game plan for failure!"

Jack nodded. "That makes a lot of sense. It's all the new weapons they're producing in Eastern Europe that's nobbled 'em. Weapons they designed themselves but were too busy and conservative to build in their home factories, where they're still turning out the old models. It's all they're tooled up for. When that chap Hawkmoon turned up he was still alive, he gave heart to millions. He must be a pretty amazing person. Everyone but the empire thinks he's the cat's meow. Even Meliadus is scared of him."

Jack's features were expressive. He had learned to hate and to control his hatred in a way I'd never had to. "From what I heard before my sister got me away, he's got them off balance. They're still trying to get their breath back. A year ago they wouldn't have believed they would have to worry about all these guys banding together against them. Up to then they'd had a lot of success with their divide-and-rule policies."

"How do you know all this? Just from listening?"

"Sharp ears, I told you. I've been luckier than you. Because I'm blind, even Klosterheim, von Minct and Taragorm talk in front of me. They think I'm deaf, too." He grinned. "But they keep quiet about meaning to sacrifice us to one of their gods, if that's what they're up to. Funny. I thought they were atheists."

There wasn't any point in telling him more of what I knew. At least, not yet. Why scare him? But it was on the tip of my tongue more than once to reveal the grimmer truth. Of course, I was also a bit mixed up about their motives. "Anyway," I said, "we're valuable to them. They could have killed us at any time. How did *you* get away?"

"Oona found me eventually and brought me here. The London Eye's the secret, all right. I don't think I ever want to ride another Ferris wheel again. You wait for hours to get on, and then there's just a mild sensation of going up and down. Then you get off and you're in Mirenburg or here or somewhere. I suppose it's cheaper than running a plane of your own. I'd love to find out what that was all about."

"Well," I said a bit harshly, "we might soon. I know they are ruthless and cruel. They'd kill us at the drop of a hat if they felt like it, but right now they need us a lot more than we need them."

"I wonder why," he mused. "I mean, apart from throwing fits in the middle of Oxford Street shops and hearing voices in swords, I'm not exactly much good for anything." He grinned into the middle distance. "They don't think I've got royal blood, do they? Why sacrifice *us*? We're not especially important. Apart from Oona, I haven't got any family. All my friends have been killed. My sister's the only one looking out for me." He laughed again. "Klosterheim really didn't expect her to turn up. He thought she was dead. She must have followed him here. Now we'll wait and do what she tells us. If anyone can beat 'em, she can. She's playing a tricky game, I reckon."

"So are they," I said. "She's a brave woman, isn't she?"

"A bloody diamond," he agreed.

After that, neither of us had any clear idea how much time passed. When we got hungry, we ate from the small store of food and water Oona left us. We slept on piles of old fabric and talked about our lives. Jack said that Oona had called him Onric when she first recognised him. Their mother had gone off, he said, though he was unclear why and where. He repeated how he thought Oona and he had lived together in a country cottage for a while, when they were little, in the days before he was blinded. It had been some sort of explosion, he thought. For a while he remembered only darkness and confusion. "It was like I was blown out of one world into another. One time into another." Maybe his father had rescued him . . . He next wound up in Bristol, adopted by a junkie named Rachel Acker, who kept him as a sort of talisman. She claimed he was her son. They both knew she was lying, but he got his food and keep, and she got her heroin. He said she was sweet to him when she wasn't totally out of it. Then Social Services discovered them and wanted to take him in, so she took him and ran off to Oxford first and then London. He and Rachel worked out a reasonably unambitious little shoplifting scheme, which kept them going for some time, but eventually Rachel disappeared, probably overdosing somewhere. And that's when McTalbayne had recruited him.

I asked him what he thought of being part of a gang run by a modern Fagin, and he laughed. "It beats being banged up in some orphanage. I've heard about those places, and I know what they do to you. At least I was my own boss. Well, partly. It's important to be your own boss. McTalbayne says it's the secret of the British Empire's success, our will to entrepreneurism." He shook his head. "What do you reckon? Is this lot here"—sightlessly he lifted his head and waved his arms to indicate, I supposed, the whole of Granbretan—"I mean, are they the best the British can be?"

I think this was an argument he had been having with himself. He didn't seem to mind that I couldn't think of an answer.

"Don't worry, kid," he said, lowering his arms. "I'm not barmy. I'm just getting bored and sick of this smelly hole. Do you think she's been caught and isn't coming back?"

I had to admit I feared the worst. We were running out of candles. What food there was didn't taste very good any more, and by the next meal we would have no water. "It's got to have been a couple of days, at least," I told him. "Maybe we should do what she told us to do and head for the river. She seemed to think we'd know what to do. But there's no Ferris wheel any more, is there?"

"I'm not sure. Maybe she has friends who'll know us." He felt his way to the far wall and cocked his head, listening as I dragged stuff away from the little secret door. "Where does that lead to?"

"Somewhere better than this," I said. "It couldn't be worse, could it? I don't want to starve to death in here, do you?"

He agreed enthusiastically. Since we didn't know where our next meal was coming from, we decided to wait until there was nothing left to eat or drink. "I think our best bet is down there, from what I've heard," he said. "It's supposed to be full of escaped slaves, crooks and old con men, but I bet it's not a patch on what I was used to . . ."

"No cardboard boxes?" I asked a bit nastily. And he laughed.

I took his hand.

I became increasingly convinced that my grandmother had been captured or dangerously delayed. Soon after I made up my mind that she probably wasn't coming back for us, there was a thump on the outside door. Nobody came in, but I heard guttural voices, the clank of armoured men. A search party! The snuffling of large dogs. Another thump. Guards in conference. They were going to find a key and come back. We now had no choice.

I took the two remaining candles from the shelf. Jack held them while I wound as much spare fabric as I could around both of us, in case we needed to keep warm. Then I opened the tiny back door, pushed Jack through and clambered in myself, pulling it and other stuff behind me. I hoped the searchers wouldn't necessarily guess we had been there.

The passage fell away steeply. It was dank, smelling strongly of foul water. From the fresh scrapes on the walls and floor, probably my grandmother had been there at some earlier point. The path was so slippery that we found ourselves sliding quite rapidly downwards, almost like a helter-skelter, as the corridor curved and twisted radically. It must have been some kind of old garbage chute, as it still smelled of what had been poured through it.

We were a long way down before I heard a hint of voices above. They came closer. Men were shouting over the menacing noise of growling dogs. At last we hit fresh air, so cold it made us gasp and shiver. We stood on cobblestones. High overhead were the restless clouds which sat forever above the towers of Londra. Before us was a maze of little alleys, some of them blocked with rusted, rotting bars which were easily pushed down.

Jack stood there shivering, wrapped in rags, listening and staring around with his unseeing eyes while I kicked in several different grates, on the basis that if we were followed we didn't want to give them an easy clue to the way we had gone. Those dogs sounded businesslike.

I grabbed Jack by the hand again and pulled him through the nearest alley, imagining I could already smell the river. But the maze was endless, twisting back and forth on itself, even though the river, surely the Thames, was only a few yards away some of the time! Every so often I heard distant explosions and saw whole squadrons of big, old-fashioned ornithopters lumbering through the air.

Dimly I realised that a battle was taking place somewhere, though not directly over us. Jack's ears were superb. He heard the different notes of engines and described air fights he thought must be happening over on what he called "the Surrey side" of the river, the South Bank. Were the Dark Empire clans breaking up under threat? Fighting among themselves? Were we witnessing the opening engagements in a civil war?

The empire must have been rotten through and through to have collapsed so thoroughly. Or had it always been stretched too thin, its power maintained by illusion, its victims too used to its dominance to realise their own numerical strength?

We finally reached a small cut in the river, where a couple of old, filthy rowboats were tethered. Everything looked as if it hadn't been used in years, and the Thames was dirtier than I had ever known it, with bits of nasty-looking débris floating in it. The water, reflecting lights and far-off explosions, was a murky crimson.

As I pulled Jack onto a slippery little jetty a shadow rose from one of the skiffs. Our black panther! Now I knew which boat to use. "Good girl," I whispered, rubbing her broad head as we climbed in with her. She looked expectantly towards the far bank. Maybe from there we could make our way to the coast, in the hope that Dorian Hawkmoon's army had already invaded.

It was not something I knew much about, but Jack couldn't believe it, either. "What did my sister say about a crystal helping them?"

"That's all she *did* say. What is the crystal, anyway?"

"I only know what I overheard Klosterheim and Gaynor saying. There's some sort of crystal shard which allows you to move yourself and sometimes whole chunks of real estate through the dimensions. What purpose that has, I don't know. Most of these people don't seem to need a crystal to get from one world to another. Maybe it's what allows you to bring something enormous through with you. Like an army. You know, not just yourself but tanks and planes or houses or something."

I could see how it would help Hawkmoon's cause, at least in minor ways, to own such a device. With my grandmother almost certainly killed or captured, I should be grateful for any advantage. If we could keep out of their hands for a while, maybe Hawkmoon would save us. Gingerly I tested the rowboat, bouncing the end of an oar in the bottom to see if it was still river-worthy. The panther moved to the prow.

The boat was sounder than I had any right to expect. All those years rowing on Grasmere were at last proving useful. I helped Jack sit down, put the oars into the rowlocks and manoeuvred slowly down the cut, which was thick with filthy, smelly flotsam and jetsam, steering us in the shadow of a long wooden jetty. The stink of the river made me feel sick.

Jack sat holding the tiller ropes, tugging them left or right at my command, so we got out fairly easily. I rowed under a series of jetties, making as little noise as possible. It grew pitch-black quite quickly, except for the sky, illuminated by the flickering red glow from the Surrey bank, the occasional spurt of flame or a gouting explosion. The sky was thick with flocks of flying machines, their metal wings clashing, their clawed landing gear stretched out as if they stooped on their prey, but we saw no direct fighting. I had the impression the battle order had changed. Perhaps Hawkmoon's people were being forced back as the empire rallied its strength.

Eventually I judged it safe to push out into mid-water and attempt a crossing. A horrible fog was rising, but I had spotted a potential landing place under cover of the jetties on the other side. As I crossed, the river would carry me down, and with luck I would wind up where I wanted to be. We were nearing the opposite bank when suddenly a white, brilliant light illuminated the whole scene. I thought we would be spotted for certain, but nobody shot at us.

We landed and went ashore, scrambling to a low, narrow landing platform, up some steps to the main jetty, the panther leading and me pushing Jack as he groped for handholds. A narrow lane ran between two sets of tall warehouses, which looked as if they had fallen against one another and were now offering mutual support, like old drunks.

And then the panther vanished again! All around us were chimneys and factories, just like in Mirenburg, and if anything, the stench was worse. We moved between rotting tenements, where not one person gave us a second glance. We were still bundled in our rags and looked just like everyone else on this side. This must be where they kept the drones of the Dark Empire anthill, without masks and, by the look of them, without hope.

I led Jack deeper and deeper into the mass of wretched apartment buildings and thundering factories. His bone-white face was turned to the sky, which still raced red, and his skin reflected the flames. His hair was the colour of cream, and his eyes were the colour of blood. In the weird, sluggish, wavering light, he looked as if he were on fire. He sniffed his way through the swaying buildings, his head cocked for any threatening sound, but he missed the danger when it eventually came.

Suddenly Jack stopped.

"Soldiers!" he hissed.

Too late. "Oh, bugger!" We turned instinctively. Behind us crept half a dozen warriors in the snarling war helms of the Order of the Vulture, Asrovak Mikosevaar's own legion.

I heard a stomping sound in front of me. Rounding a corner came a score of hounds bearing flame lances. They were led by the Chevalier St Odhran, in all his bizarre Scottish finery. I dashed into another alley, dragging Jack, but there was no way of escape.

They seemed to have known where to capture us. St Odhran recognised us both. We couldn't hope to fool them. We were trapped. At any moment we'd be back in the hands of enemies who planned to kill us in the most disgusting and painful way imaginable.

Oona *had* to be dead or captured! I had led her brother into a trap! All our efforts had brought us no advantage. I felt that I deserved what they were going to do to me, that I had betrayed my friends in a profound way.

Jack yelled a warning.

St Odhran put his hand out towards me.

But instead of grabbing me—he pushed!

Suddenly Jack and I were falling.

21

We fell slowly for what seemed a mile or more. I could see Jack's white hair standing straight up from his head, just below me as he sank in slow motion. Once he turned, staring upwards. His blind eyes had an expression of pure pleasure.

In other circumstances I might have enjoyed the sensation, which was like riding in a hot-air balloon—a cushioned weightlessness.

It was impossible to judge the time. We could have fallen for hours. My mouth was very dry. My heart stopped pounding from the terror of the encounter with St Odhran. I was determined to get my nerve back.

Someone *had* to have known where we were. Had the traitor deliberately set things up so that he could push us into the pit? But who had warned them? The panther?

I heard Jack land first. I drew a deep breath. He grunted with surprise, sprawled flat on his back. "Bugger! I was enjoying that. What's happening?"

I came down with a thump beside him. The ground yielded slightly, like a sponge. But it wasn't grass. Deep moss? I got up and helped Jack to his feet. All the stench of the city had disappeared. The air was clean, sharp, even a little bitter. I took big gulps of it, the way a near-drowning person might. I tasted it on my tongue. After all the horrible, suggestive smells of the city above us, this air was a welcome relief.

I still had a candle in my pocket. I decided to risk lighting it.

"That was awesome!" Jack said enthusiastically from nearby. I saw his pale skin in the fluttering yellow light. "A lot better than the London Wheel! I wouldn't mind doing that again." He treated the experience as he had treated a ride in a theme park. He hadn't seen St Odhran. He didn't even know how profoundly we'd been betrayed. Again, it seemed churlish to spoil his moment. He wouldn't benefit from any outburst of mine.

I was thirsty. I thought I heard water running somewhere nearby. The candle illuminated what appeared to be a ventilation shaft or maybe, in an earlier epoch, a goods chute for whoever lived down here. Hadn't there been something like it in *The Time Machine*? A sort of gravity regulator. Of course, I half-hoped we had accidentally returned to the land of the kindly, courteous Off-Moo, who would surely know how to help us. But St Odhran wouldn't have sent us into the arms of our allies.

I held the candle up as high as I could. There was glittering dust in the shaft. Magic? Vestiges of an older science, as Flana and most of her kind believed? Another invention from before the Tragic Millennium? The surrounding walls were the same spongey, pink-red rock as the floor: tough, elastic and made of no material I had ever experienced. It felt faintly damp. Its smell was almost familiar. Fishy yet pleasant. I put my palm on the wall and brought it to my nose. What *was* that smell? Skin? Hair after you've washed it? Definitely something organic.

"Over there," said Jack. "The air's different."

Ahead of us I saw an even smaller passage leading off to one side and poked my candle in so that I could see where it led. It gleamed back at me, reflecting the light, but I couldn't easily tell if it went anywhere or had been blocked off.

"I'm not sure. If we got stuck . . ." I began nervously.

"We won't." He was totally confident. Now Jack took the lead. Anything was better than just sitting around, so I followed him. I told him to let me know if he needed my eyes, and blew out the candle, squeezing after him through the slightly yielding rock, along a short passage until I breathed a sigh of relief as we emerged into a much larger cavern, full of thin, spikey stalactites and stalagmites, with a rather beautiful, pastel-coloured luminous fungus growing over everything, enabling me to see quite a long way in all directions. Strangely familiar territory. Could this really be the way to Mu-Ooria? Or, in this world, had Granbretan conquered so thoroughly that all the Middle March was theirs, too? No. The Middle March, by its definition, was common territory to all. Once there, we'd be free.

I described it to Jack, and he nodded. "I've been somewhere like it, I think. God, doesn't it smell clean after that horrible crap?"

I felt we needed something more than "clean" to reassure us, since St Odhran had deliberately pushed us down here and I couldn't see a friendly, elongated Off-Moo face anywhere. We appeared to be on our own.

"Have we lost 'em?" asked Jack.

"I doubt it," I told him. St Odhran had surely known what he was pushing us into. Where exactly were we?

I took Jack's hand. The floor of the cavern was unusually smooth. An underground river had once run this course. As my eyes became used to the soft glow I saw the walls of the cavern rising in a sequence of terraces and ledges. The cavern was a natural amphitheatre, with the terraces forming seats and walkways. The perfect place for a bit of human sacrifice. The Dark Empire had certainly been here. Many of the outcrops of limestone were carved in their typical designs, of animal faces and grotesque, bestial figures, only partially human. I was surrounded by an audience of gargoyles, their stone eyes glaring, their stone lips curled in cruel, triumphant sneers. I could hardly believe we hadn't been deliberately lured into a trap.

My hand tightening on Jack's must have alerted him. He turned his sightless eyes on me. "What's up? I can't hear anyone."

"We're still in empire territory," I told him. "And I have a horrible feeling this is where they've wanted us all along. It's some sort of theatre or ceremonial temple." I didn't speculate further for him.

"Are we the first act on?" He was trying to make light of the situation, with the dawning understanding that we might not get clear. "Or are we the grand finale?"

"They want our blood, remember? Mumbo-jumbo, but that doesn't make it any better for us!"

"Well, if it's only a pint or two, they're welcome to mine. Let's get the transfusion over and go home. I fancy a nice big plate of Dover sole and chips. How about you?" Jack had become unnaturally amiable.

It wasn't really in my nature to make jolly quips as the great big saw drew nearer and nearer, but I could not be irritated with him. I knew why he was doing it. I was pretty nervous, too. I thought that our only hope of getting out of this cavern alive was to leave at once, before the people chasing us realised we were down here. Again, as we made our way along that ancient riverbed, I was impressed. These images, corrupted and warped as they were, reminded me of what I had seen when we had gone with my parents and grandparents on our trip to Egypt. Strangely, I wondered if we were on the inside of a pyramid. The walls did slope slightly inward as they disappeared out of sight into the gloom above. Heads of birds and fish, reptiles and mammals, stared down. But they lacked that peculiar integrity which you found in Egypt. Perhaps they had derived their ideas from a more barbaric source. History and the human imagination being what they were, maybe they'd come up with it all themselves, developing it out of the football tribes, as I mentioned before, who had once ranged urban England and the Continent, looking for trouble.

I had another thought. Was this, in fact, an old sports arena? Were we going to be pitted against real lions or gladiators or something? Was this reserved just for football—only with our heads as the balls?

"Should we be keeping quiet?" Jack's voice was just audible in my ear.

Whispering back, I told him what I thought. "I can't see how they would have made a mistake, given what's happened. St Odhran pushed us down here deliberately."

"Who's St Odhran?" he asked.

"He used to be a friend of mine," I said. "Turns out he's the worst villain of all."

"Scottish bloke, is he?"

"Why, yes!"

"He's been around for a while. He's the one got me the original job in the forge testing those swords, I think. 'Our mutual friend'? I heard him talking to Klosterheim before Oona got me out of there. Something about a sword, now I come to think of it! They seemed to be bargaining. I was part of the bargain, though I wasn't always sure it was actually *me* he was talking about. What's the Stone?"

"I've heard them mention that, too. A religious object of some kind. With a lot of jewels in it, which is why it's so valuable. The Runestaff?"

"That's the word. Only I thought they said 'Moonstaff.' I guessed they'd lost it and thought I could find it for them."

I explained what little I knew. The whole time I talked I scanned our surroundings, trying to see if anyone else was here. In this part of the amphitheatre, the rock had a more volcanic appearance, as if lava had poured over the terraces and hardened. They gleamed, reflecting all the grotesque heads, reminding me of my first impressions of the World Below. Maybe we weren't just under ground, but in a bizarre mirror image of the World Above. We were definitely in a river-bed. Or maybe even a lake bed. Were our pursuers going to flood the place, as Mirenburg had been flooded? It seemed an unnecessarily elaborate plan, even for the baroque tastes of Granbretan.

I was desperately looking for another tunnel like the one which had brought us in here, but the closer to the ground things were, the harder they were to see. Eventually I gave up and began looking for a way down into those terraces. It didn't look as if anyone on our level was meant to climb up into the seating areas. We were definitely the performers, rather than the audience.

There didn't seem much point in trying to retrace our steps. I decided to move us closer to the smooth side, so that we'd be harder to see in the shadows. I honestly felt sorrier for Jack D'Acre at that moment than I did for myself. At least I hadn't been blind most of my life.

"Aaahhhh!" It was a hiss of pleasure from above. I looked up. I couldn't see anyone.

I stopped. Although I found it hard to tell, we seemed to have reached roughly the middle of the amphitheatre. Out there, at the centre, was an enormous square block of green stone, taller than me. It might have been a monstrous emerald. Slightly opaque, it reflected the light from the pastel mould growing in patches along the rising tiers of that inverted cone. And now at last I saw eyes glittering, too. Not many. A pair here. A pair there.

A wet snuffling, a grunting, a whine or two. It was truly horrible, as if we two were about to become entertainment for a bunch of salivating beasts. Wet, slobbering noises. Little cackles and croaks. None were sounds I'd ever heard in the throats of real animals, for they still had a trace of human origin.

Was the theatre filling up with the nobles of the Dark Empire? I still couldn't actually see any people. I drew Jack with me to the side, into the deepest shadows. I surveyed the frozen lava of the tiers for signs of those beast-headed Granbretanners, but only saw the odd shadow which, blending with the carved figures, might have been a household god, might or might not have been human.

An echoing voice confirmed the worst.

"No need to be shy, my dears. All that we have sought is at last in place, save for the Runestaff. But that will manifest itself soon. Like answers to like. Child answers to child. Blood answers to blood. You will bring it to us. The Staff cannot remain hidden, just as you are now unable to remain hidden. That much we know. We have waited what seems centuries for this moment. Now the Consanguinity is assured. See!"

A yellow light played over the great block of emerald stone. On it, laid out like an altar with its vestments, sat two shallow golden bowls. And what I had not immediately seen was the huge black broadsword piercing the glowing green stone from left to right. Scarlet symbols twisted and turned in the blade near the hilt, like sombre neon. Like smoke trapped inside a jar. The colours were incredibly vibrant, as if the objects had not just a life of their own but a soul as well.

Around me, overhead, I heard a creak, a jingle, a suppressed cough. There was no doubt we had a small audience.

I heard Jack sniff. "Ugh. Bous-Junge's here."

"We can smell you, Mr Bous-Junge," I said. A cheap shot, but I had a feeling I wasn't going to be up for anything much better.

"And that other one. I can smell him, too. What's his name? I bet they're thick, those two." Jack had some difficulty speaking. His mouth was dry. "Just as bad as each other."

But no King Huon? I thought. No Baron Meliadus? Was the Countess Flana still a prisoner? And what about St Odhran? Shouldn't he be here to relish his triumph?

I heard a sort of *phut*, a swish. I looked down at a dart sticking out of my arm. Another sound, and Jack was similarly shot. Quickly I pulled the thing free of my arm, then yanked the other dart from Jack's. But I was already feeling woozy. I leaned against the wall, trying to hold steady. Those cowards! We might as well be feral cats!

"Bloody hell," I heard Jack say. "The animals are shooting us." And then he crumpled to the hard, smooth, glassy surface of the amphitheatre.

A moment or two later I went down, too.

Was I dreaming it, or did Bous-Junge's unpleasant, tittering laugh fill the auditorium until the sound drowned out everything else, including my consciousness?

When I came to, I thought I heard the last vibrations of that voice, fading away. But I guessed more time had passed than that, because I was tied up, spreadeagled on one side of the stone itself. I guessed Jack must be on the other side. My arm was very sore but not in the place where the dart had gone in.

Baron Bous-Junge wasn't wearing his mask. His round, sly face smiled at me as he held up two glass vials with something red in them.

It was blood. And I had a fair idea whom it belonged to.

"We are in time. We are in time!" This was an unfamiliar voice. Beyond Bous-Junge I saw a really peculiar, globular mask, with four different styles of clock face, one like Big Ben, the famous London landmark. Hanging from it, extended over the wearer's body, was a wide pendulum, moving backwards and forwards so steadily that I thought they might be trying to hypnotise us. The legs and arms extending beyond it were skinny and mottled with brown spots, like those of a very old person.

Baron Bous-Junge giggled. "What? I can see it in your eyes, child. Did you think we'd be wasteful with your blood? That which flows in your veins makes you what we wish to be. When your blood flows in *our* veins, we become something of what you are. We take on your inherited power. We become guardians of the Grail. First we try its potency *without* killing you. We'll bring the Staff to us. We have read all the appropriate books. The Staff heals all wounds and resurrects the recently dead. We have to keep you fresh. You're good for another few pints yet."

"That's the smelly bastard talking." Jack's voice came from the other side of the stone. "But who's the ticking bastard with him?"

"He means me." The voice was curiously bleak, without nuance. "I'm Taragorm. We saved you from the moonbeam roads, didn't we? Onric, isn't it? Or do you prefer Jack?"

"I don't remember you!"

"Oh, you saw me once, Jack. Just the once."

"You're the bastard who blinded me!"

Taragorm's silence didn't deny the accusation.

"What did you do that for?" Jack wanted to know. He sounded calm.

"We needed to be able to find you," said Taragorm. "If you escaped, you'd hardly get far blind. Our mistake. We had no notion how many clever friends you have! Ah, here are our *own* clever colleagues at last." There came a faint boom as if he struck the hour.

A little behind him I saw Klosterheim. His frame was dramatically thin compared to that of his bulky companion, Gaynor von Minct.

"You are late, Prince Gaynor." Bous-Junge sounded disapproving. "The time is near. There's not a moment to be lost. We must test the Stone and the Sword. Then we must fill the bowls. One with the male blood, one with the female. All countertypes are prepared for the Balance. The intellectual"—he bowed to Klosterheim—"and the practical brute." He bowed. "Greetings, Prince Gaynor the Damned."

"I wasn't always this brute," muttered Gaynor dully. I thought he mourned some other state, some time in his life when he had fought nobly with us, rather than against us. This rogue Knight of the Balance glared over at me. Something unreadable shone in his eyes. He sighed. "I have just come from the surface. It was difficult. I think we shall be safe for long enough. And then it will be easy for us to reverse our losses."

"Losses?" Bous-Junge raised an eyebrow. "They had crossed the sea bridge. Are they now in the capital? There can be no doubt the crystal aids them. Yet I thought it smashed . . ."

"They have a fragment. They only need a fragment. The fraction is as great as the whole, remember? Hawkmoon's killed or badly wounded. He's disappeared, but Count Brass has taken Londra," Klosterheim told him. "They summon armies from nowhere. And so many of your own have gone over to his cause! King Huon is destroyed. Meliadus pronounced himself king for about half an hour. The little red-haired brute, Oladahn, killed him. The last I heard, they were trying to find where you'd imprisoned Flana. They wanted to make her queen."

"She'll not be queen, that traitress. Her mask sits on a spike at the river gate, and her head's food for her dead husband's pet beasts."

"Then who—?" began Taragorm.

"We'll form a republic," said Bous-Junge. "And rule without responsibility . . ."

Prince Gaynor the Damned gave out a great snort of laughter. "Aye. Kings and queens have a habit of carrying the blame for whole catalogues of injustices."

"Count Brass will not have long to relish his victories," sniggered Bous-Junge. "Within the hour we'll be masters of the multiverse. Merely with a thought, any one of us will be able to destroy entire worlds and create fresh ones. We shall each of us take the four quarters of our stations and rule those quarters by agreement. And by agreement, none shall enter nor seek to influence the quarter of the others. So we maintain our own balances, without need of that thing . . ."

He pointed towards me. Obviously he meant the rock Jack and I were slung over like two parts of a saddlebag.

The square emerald rock grew noticeably warmer, and I could have sworn I heard it give a faint moan. It felt like flesh against my own skin. It quivered in time to the sword vibrating within its green depths.

Klosterheim came to stand, regarding me, his cold eyes full of unreadable despair. He uttered a deep sigh. "Now do you still think my colleague was wrong in refusing to accept the reconciliation of Heaven and Hell? Look what has become of it all. Hysteria of self-knowledge, monotony of self-analysis, introspection spreading like a disease. What is all that but the infection communicated over the unpurified borders of death? The spirits of the mortal world were never meant to be so neighbourly with the spirits of the other. I have done all I can for you now. You have used my knowledge to ensure not only the death of God but the death of Lucifer, too. So be it."

With a grunt of impatience, Prince Gaynor reached towards the hilt of the black sword, which I could just see from the corner of my eye. Even as he began, Baron Bous-Junge's hand moved out and laid itself on Gaynor's wrist. "You know that only one of their blood can handle the damned blades. First you must *become* of their blood. That's why drinking their blood is so important for other reasons. Bide your time."

St Odhran stepped jauntily into the arena. He was, for all his treachery, very attractive.

"All you wanted was to trick the albino. Bring him under ground." St Odhran was smiling that mocking, crooked smile. "You have almost all you seek."

"We're grateful to you, sir," Klosterheim said.

"You'll be well rewarded, Scotchman," said Prince Gaynor, his big face full of other thoughts. "But you'll not get a fifth of the power we share. That's divided between us. We concocted this scheme together from the beginning, Klosterheim, Bous-Junge, Taragorm and I. Years it took. We knew the Conjunction of Conjunctions would come. We knew we could gather together all the elements of the Balance. We found the Stone, which some have called the Grail, and brought it from von Bek's in London. Down here. Waiting. You, St Odhran, supplied the Sword. You, gentlemen, brought the two golden bowls. The children will give us the blood of twin immortals to represent all the opposites and complementary elements of the world, Law and Chaos, which must be taken from twins who share shamanistic ancestry. All we lack is the Staff. I know in my bones that the Staff will be inexorably drawn to the other elements, for it cannot exist without them. It will manifest itself as a result of our ritual. Yet what form it takes, we do not know."

"It will come. When we bleed the twins, it will come. It will be drawn to heal its defenders."

"Twins?" I said. "What on earth makes you think we're twins?"

And this *did* stop them in their tracks! I think they realised for the first time how unlike each other Jack and I were. Not twins. Not even the same age. How had they rationalised that? Then I remembered my grandmother. Could she actually be Jack's twin, and could he actually be Zodiac's son? In all the convolutions of the multiverse, I suppose it was possible . . .

Shaking his head, as if to say it was too late to consider this now, Bous-Junge drew his long knife and advanced towards me. I had made a serious mistake in speaking out. I had caused him to change his mind. I knew he was going to slit my throat, let my blood pump all over that rock and then test its properties.

I closed my eyes, trying to be brave.

"You have made such wonderful mistakes, gentlemen." I heard a new voice, edged with irony. I recognised it. I strained to see where it was coming from. "I was almost inclined to let you play the farce through, but sadly your threat to the child's life means there's too much at stake to let you run unchecked any further. First, Baron Bous-Junge, perhaps you would oblige me by releasing the girl and my son. You'll find I'll be a little more lenient with you if you obey quickly."

I peered into the shadows of the lower tiers of the amphitheatre. There, looking relaxed and almost cheerful, with a peculiar light in his eye which said that he was enjoying himself, was my mother's grandfather, Monsieur Zodiac, otherwise known as Elric the albino.

"Damn you, Silverskin!" Disdaining ritual, Gaynor tossed back the vial of my blood into his throat, swallowed it and ran for the black sword, which vibrated steadily in the stone. He emitted a shriek of triumph that echoed throughout the cavern. It pierced my head. I wanted nothing more in all the world than to see what happened next, but as hard as I tried, I could not remain conscious.

Gaynor's hand closed around the hilt of the sword. The scream intensified. And I fainted.

22

I was not unconscious for very long, because when I woke, Gaynor was still screaming. The sound of the sword had somehow combined with his voice. He was glaring down at his right palm. Across it was a raw red welt, as if he had gripped a bar of white-hot metal.

He looked utterly baffled. "But, the Blood . . ." he said.

Elric drew an identical black sword from his scabbard. He held it aloft in both hands. The thing moaned and muttered; scarlet writing blazed out of the black steel and reflected on his ivory skin, in his own crazed, laughing eyes. His long, fine white hair rose and floated in a misty halo around his head, and I understood at last why he was feared. I feared him. And I was on his side.

Gaynor grabbed the other vial of blood from Bous-Junge. The baron made a half-hearted effort to hold on to it. The dirk forgotten in his hand, he looked up at Elric and the Black Sword. He was fascinated by something he had probably only ever heard about in legend. The two Granbretanners, as well as Klosterheim, shared the same attitude of astonishment. They had never encountered Elric or anything like him before, and they no doubt saw their defeat in that laughing apparition with his shrieking weapon, threatening everything they thought already theirs. They had been so triumphant, so certain that their great game had been played and won. And now it became apparent that Elric and his friends had anticipated them. I saw St Odhran step back to join the albino. I still didn't trust him. Was he going to try to wriggle out of his involvement in our capture?

Gaynor narrowed his eyes, steeled himself and drew his own sword, a long, silvery blade with a plain hilt. He forced his wounded fingers around it. "You know this blade, too, do you, Lord Elric? It is Mireen, Lord Arkyn's Sword of Law. I paid that Scottish traitor a high price to possess her. With Taragorm's help I turned back time. All this I did to defeat you and take possession of the Balance. I shall own both, once I have dealt with you. One of those blades is counterfeit, forged in Mirenburg. I suspect it is the one you hold, since the other pierced the Stone when St Odhran brought it here." And he put both hands around his hilt and moved forward as my kinsman vaulted down into the arena to confront him.

"The Sword of Law against the Sword of Chaos!" chittered Baron Bous-Junge, almost with relish. "I have yearned to witness this for so long. It is perfection. The Balance is doubly personified. Thus we shall make it our servant!" He moved closer to me, the long poniard drooping in his hand. He had not forgotten me. He meant to draw more of my blood, even if it killed me this time. That blood had to be absorbed by the stone if his sorcery was going to work. Even I knew that. Taragorm was out of my line of vision. I guessed he was preparing to spill Jack's blood.

Gaynor gulped down the second vial of blood, seeming to relish it. He wiped his lips on the back of his hand and examined his palm with evident satisfaction. The wound had healed. "Ah," he said. "It tastes so pure." And he cast a crafty eye towards Jack.

Then Elric was on him, the Black Sword howling and screeching with a voice all its own, like a live thing. His thrust was parried by Gaynor. Another thrust. Another parry. A counterblow from Gaynor, which sent the physically weaker Elric stumbling backwards. The white sword had no voice but possessed a blue radiance. Blue letters in the same foreign alphabet flickered along its length. Then, as Gaynor aimed another massive swing at him, Elric flung up the black blade to block it.

"Ach!" swore the big man as the white steel shattered and bouncing shards clattered to the floor of the arena.

"The forgery! It could not even hold its colour, eh?" Elric grinned into Prince Gaynor's twisted face as Gaynor flung the remains of the sword behind him.

"One of 'em must have the right blood. What's simpler than that consanguinate sorcery . . .?" The brute stamped back to the emerald stone, reaching for the black sword still embedded in it. He put his hand back on the hilt, and this time, although there was pain, as I could tell from his face, he had the strength to pull the thing free. "Ha! Now we are evenly matched, Lord Elric. I know this sword. She is called Ravenblade, the Black Sword's sister!"

Gaynor had charge of the sword in the stone. He wrapped his two hands around it, gritting his teeth as he did so.

"Mournblade I call her." A terrible half-smile was still on Elric's lips. His eyes flickered like furnaces. "Well, not for the first time have the sisters fought, though you master your blade with borrowed blood. We must hurry, Prince Gaynor, for I have another appointment with these swords I would not wish to miss."

My ancestor's lunatic laughter was something I hope never to hear again. It was the humour of a man who relished the taking of life and staking his own in the process. As if risking death and dealing it had become his sole pleasures.

Gaynor grunted, and he hefted the sword, watching the scarlet letters squirreling up and down the black iron.

Then this sword, too, was moaning and yelling like a living creature. Two black swords! One pitched against the other. What did it mean?

Gaynor renewed the attack. From where I hung, helpless against the stone, I watched the two men make flying leaps over the barriers, fighting back and forth, up and down the tiers of the amphitheatre, sometimes in the light, sometimes in shadow. Often it seemed to me that the swords themselves fought and the men were merely adjuncts to their battle. I knew I watched four sentient entities up there.

I was not the only one fascinated by the fight. All other eyes were on it. Beast-masked warriors had entered the upper tiers and were poised above the combatants, watching them intently.

Elric went down, and Gaynor pressed his advantage. Stormbringer flew free of Elric's hand.

Gaynor stood over his opponent. "Here's blood for the block!" he snarled. "Enough for a dozen rituals!" And he lifted the yelling sword to bring it down on the albino. "Miggea!"

He would have cut Elric in two if the blow had landed, but Elric rolled clear, regained Stormbringer and staggered to his feet as Gaynor recovered himself.

Elric began shouting weirdly accented words into the air, in a language that sounded a bit like Hindi. I guessed the words were represented in the letters on the blades.

Gaynor glared around him, suspecting some other kind of attack. He lumbered down on the albino, swinging Mournblade in an arc which left an aura of black and crimson light streaming behind it. The two were shouting almost in unison.

I heard Gaynor say, "Would you rather have the Balance destroyed, Elric? Would you rather there were no control at all? Merely the Grey Fees, the abolition of time, the destruction of space?"

Elric was still smiling. "The Balance is not for us to use, but for us to serve, Prince Gaynor the Damned, as well you know. It is an idea and can never truly be destroyed. Anyone who has ever attempted to enforce his power over its constituent elements has only failed. They have gone to the ultimate hell, never free of themselves or their own frustrations. Put down that other sword, Gaynor. I demand you obey me. Mournblade has no loyalty to your own blood, only to that you have stolen. You temporarily deceive her. Do you think she is not aware of that? She will soon lead you further towards your own just fate."

Gaynor was jeering. "Weakling! You betray everything. You betray that which makes you strong! You are *all* Betrayal, Elric of Melniboné."

Elric's expression changed, and he took up the attack, just as Gaynor had hoped he would.

But Elric was tired. It had cost him dearly to get here in time, to confront them and hope to rescue us. Still, he *was* here to save me; I knew that. If he lost this fight, whatever happened to him in that other world, I was almost certainly finished. As was this world. Maybe all the worlds.

Then I saw another, much older man standing above Elric. Another albino. Who . . . ? A strong family resemblance. He could have been my granddad. Elric in a different time? Impossible.

Then I realised it actually *was* my grandfather. Ulric von Bek reached out and touched Elric as he backed away from the relentless Gaynor. Then Granddad had vanished. Briefly I thought I saw still another white face staring out of the shadows. Then it, too, had gone.

Elric had more vitality now. I knew the older man had given it to him. Elric used it to advantage. Back Gaynor went against a blinding flurry of sword strokes. I couldn't believe the speed. All I know about is fencing, which we do at school. This was like fencing with claymores, those massive broadswords the Scots liked to slaughter one another with. How did they achieve that speed of reflexes, let alone the strength needed to swing so many pounds of steel with such ease? My respect for both antagonists increased. This was no ordinary medieval bludgeoning match.

And there was no clash of metal in the air, just that sickening vibration, the moaning and shouting of sentient, living steel.

Again the opponents drew apart, panting, eyeing each other, the blades resting on the glassy surface of the seats. They spoke to each other, but their voices were too low for me to hear. I strained forward.

Suddenly Bous-Junge of Osfoud fell to his knees, squirming onto the floor of the amphitheatre, clutching at his back. He dropped the long, greenish knife he had planned to use on me. Sticking out between his shoulder blades was the feathered shaft of an arrow. I looked to one side. Oona, my grandmother, stood in the shadows on another tier of the amphitheatre, her own skin grey rather than white, her eyes held steady by sheer effort of will. She smiled at me, dropped her bow, and fell sideways onto the slippery rock. She had anticipated Bous-Junge's intention to throw the knife into Elric's back and had killed him first. But the action had obviously cost her dearly.

I wanted to run to her. I struggled to get free. "Oona!" I shouted, but of course I was still tied up and could do nothing.

Then I saw the Chevalier St Odhran coming straight for me, his own dirk in his hand, a weird smile on his face.

In panic I looked around for help. I screamed. I've never screamed like that before or since. St Odhran reached me, raised the knife and cut my bonds. As I sank, sighing, to the ground, he took my weight. I was numb and weak, but I knew that sensation would come back soon, since I was uninjured. Leaving me to recover, St Odhran moved around the other side to free Jack.

At this point Klosterheim hissed his hatred and frustration and, seeing that I was helpless and unprotected, drew his sabre to take advantage of my situation. "Your blood *must* feed the rock, child. There is still time for us to succeed. See how they weaken by the second."

He was two steps away from me before St Odhran came back. Klosterheim glared at the Scotsman, muttered an insult, and then began to run, hauling himself up over the barrier and beating an erratic path up into the darkness of the heights. St Odhran made no attempt to follow him. Was he giving the German a chance to escape?

Klosterheim had been wrong. The fighters didn't look particularly weak!

Elric and Gaynor clashed again. Muscle against muscle, flesh against flesh. I smelled the particular stink of predatory animals, mingled with something altogether less familiar.

Down went Gaynor, spinning wildly to avoid the weaving runesword, blocking Elric's long, slashing blow to his torso. Up he came again, his own runesword gibbering and squalling down at Elric's unhelmeted head. He caught the albino a glancing blow as he slipped to one side. Unwounded, Elric drove back his attacker. Gaynor grunted and cursed yet grinned at Elric's skill, just as Elric smiled respect for his opponent's proficiency. So familiar were they with the nearness of death, or worse than death, that they actually took pleasure in it. Their only alternative, after all, was to fear it. And fear wasn't there in either of them.

This was a horrible game and one I would have stopped if I could have, but the glee of the fighters, the noise of the swords and some understanding of the stakes which they were duelling for overrode my repugnance. I was fascinated.

Thump! Thump! Their bodies were like battering rams in ordinary travelling clothes. Neither man was armoured.

Grunting, breathing in high, painful gasps, the two separated again, rested again, clashed again.

Gaynor lifted his head and took several steps backward.

Elric frowned, staggering.

Taragorm had intervened! I saw it happen. Chimes boomed from his body, from somewhere within his architectural mask, and they were totally out of sync. It was like watching a beautifully choreographed ballet whose music was a cacophony, one element absolutely at odds with another. Elric and Gaynor were each thrown by the sounds, just enough to increase the risk of being cut by the other. Gaynor was ready. Stuffing something into his ears with his left hand, he backed away. He had anticipated this.

The sounds from the clock mask grew more jangled and out of tune. Taragorm was using a pre-arranged strategy, formulated no doubt long ago to help Gaynor in some other battle. The air around him spangled and faded, and I recognised magic at work.

Elric's movements became increasingly disorganised, yet he kept his grip on the sword. His glance towards Taragorm told me he knew what was happening to him. I struggled to get up, yelling that I was coming to help. The circulation had not yet returned to my arms and legs. At the same time I feared I might still be in danger from St Odhran. I watched, probably a bit like a hypnotised rat, as Taragorm disappeared around the rock, presumably to dispatch Jack.

Elric stumbled.

St Odhran reached me, lifting me up to put me on my feet, caught me as I fell, and then pushed me down onto the ground so hard that I was winded. "Stay there," he said urgently. "For your life, stay there!"

Big Ben's hammers bounced against her bells. Boom! Boom! Boom! Boom! The familiar sounds of the Westminster chimes hideously off-key. It was madness. Elric wobbled and fell as the still-grinning Gaynor moved in swiftly beside him, with Mournblade raised again to strike. This time Gaynor would not be distracted, and I still could scarcely move.

All at once Elric rolled, sprawling spreadeagled on his back. Stormbringer was still in his left hand while his right tried to find purchase on the glassy rock as he willed himself to stand. Gaynor took his time as he stalked forward, his huge mouth open in a roar of pleasure.

Then Elric pointed upwards with his right hand, and lights streamed out of it. Green, red, violet, indigo, the colours poured from his mouth and fingertips. His lips writhed and snarled, uttering incomprehensible words. Morbid shadows formed around him.

Gaynor was openly contemptuous. "Conjuror's pranks, Lord Elric. Nothing more. You'll not deflect my attention as you have that of previous enemies, who lacked defences against you. I can match you spell for spell, Sir Sorcerer-King!"

The tentative smile on Elric's face broadened. He raised his head and called out in his own language. He called on the ancient gods of his people to help him save his soul.

With a noise like bursting rockets, Elric was suddenly plucking at the air, as another might pluck at the strings of an instrument. A red glare surrounded him. Blue fire continued to pour from his mouth. In response to his spell-making, sword after sword began to appear before him. And every one of the swords was black, pulsing with runes, identical to those grasped in the fists of the two fighters. Yet even now, with so many identical sentient swords, Stormbringer and Mournblade were subtly different, subtly more powerful. Stormbringer had an extra quality to it, impossible to identify. It was clear that there was only one true Stealer of Souls.

A forest of swords surrounded Gaynor now. Hundreds of them, all rustling and clashing together in their eagerness to engage the former Knight of the Balance.

Gaynor had no doubts about what was happening. His eyes held a bleak understanding as he spat on the floor, glaring at Elric, who stood with folded arms on the other side of that mass of swords. "Well, I reckoned without your particular powers, I suppose, Elric." He sneered at his own folly. "You didn't spend all those thousands of years on your dream couches in order to learn a few entertaining magic tricks for the provincial stage. I should have considered better what I was facing. Still, one symbol is destroyed and another takes its place. You'll perish yet, Lord Elric, if it's not at my hand. You have death all over you."

"I welcome it," said Elric, still gasping for air, "but I'd prefer to *choose* where death comes to me and what price I pay."

The black swords hovered over and surrounded Gaynor. At first the blades took tiny nicks out of him as he attempted to fend them off, like a man swatting at insects. Then the nicks became deeper wounds, and blood began to pour from him. His clothes fell away in tiny shreds of rag. Even his boots were cut from him like that until he stood there, blood coursing down every part of his head and naked body, his mad eyes still glaring defiance. The blades then carefully removed his skin and filleted his flesh, leaving his head until last. As he watched himself being cut into tiny fragments, piece by piece, his screams became no longer defiant but terrible in their desperate pleading for Elric's pity.

Elric had no pity.

Perhaps he alone knew it wasn't over. For each piece of flesh the black swords cut off Gaynor, a new Gaynor grew before our eyes. Gaynor after Gaynor, every one of them wielding a black sword and attacking Elric. An army of shadow Gaynors, each becoming gradually harder to see, fought against the albino and his army of supernatural swords.

With the same little smile playing around his handsome mouth, Elric fought on steadily. Like someone who has found the comfortable rhythm of a walk, though I'm sure he knew he could not yet anticipate Gaynor's defeat.

I watched in relief as one by one, Elric began to defeat his shadow enemies, who drew on the decreasing resources of the multiverse. With each sword cut, an aspect of his enemy, a fragment of Gaynor's soul, was taken into Elric's blade. The original Gaynor grew rapidly older and feebler even as his many avatars continued to fight on around him. Elric drove slowly forward until he stood before that proud revolutionary, that renegade Knight of the Balance, his lips working as if he found no suitable words, until, by its own volition, Storm-bringer lunged forward and pierced Gaynor in his ambitious heart, making him drop his own sword and grasp at the black steel which entered his body. He cast one final horrified look at Elric and whimpered one last time. His huge body then dissipated to nothing. All the other Gaynors raced inward to rejoin him, to give him substance, even as that substance was drawn luxuriously into Elric's greedy Stormbringer.

I was horrified. Elric visibly bloomed and grew stronger before our eyes.

At last Gaynor was gone, in all his aspects, and Mournblade had blended with Elric's own sword. All those other swords, with their stolen souls, had blended with their great original, and Stormbringer howled out her wild song of triumph as Elric's crimson eyes blazed and he opened his mouth wide in a bloody victory grin.

"*Stormbringer!*" he cried.

And then it was very quiet.

I saw a shadow slip away through the upper tiers. Klosterheim! I opened my mouth to warn them of his escape, but then I closed it. The beast-masked warriors were throwing off their helmets, revealing themselves to be the Ka-katanawa who had travelled here with Elric. Silently the warriors surrounded Klosterheim. He died without noise.

Those of us left standing didn't move. A moment later, tiny animals started to scuttle out onto the cavern floor, pouring from unseen holes in the rock. A kind of rodent smaller than voles, they chittered around our feet, utterly oblivious of us, their tiny twitching noses leading them to the blood. I wondered what else had gone on down here, and for how long, if a breed of vermin had developed dependent on the blood and flesh of tortured human beings. Snuffling and squeaking, they found those little morsels of Gaynor which now could never be reunited, at least until the whole multiverse turned upon its axis, mirror into mirror, blending and becoming one for that brief moment of complete coupling. The animals scuttled and peeped and squabbled over the tiny bits of flesh and bone that were their anticipated feast. An hour or two earlier and it might have been Jack and me whose scattered morsels fed the scavengers.

Taragorm, Master of the Palace of Time, lay crumpled over the body of his colleague, with whom he had schemed to take the power of God. The vermin found him next. His mask had fallen forward, revealing his wizened features. The tower of Big Ben hung broken on the floor of the amphitheatre. Perhaps St Odhran thought he'd redeemed himself by killing Taragorm.

Like a character out of *Macbeth*, the Scotsman leaned, panting, his bloody knife dropped to the ground, his back resting against the emerald stone, which continued to agitate internally. Jack D'Acre stood beside him. St Odhran had his arm around the boy.

"The Stone could have brought them back to life had it not been for the schichis," he said. "Now we'll never see that miracle. That's why they chose this place, I suppose."

Having betrayed and killed his companions, was the aeronaut trying to pretend that he had been on our side all along? I wasn't about to forget what I'd seen and heard him do at the Countess Flana's or what he'd done later in that alley. He had shoved us down the chute to be sacrificed. Only after Elric arrived did St Odhran see the tide turn and change his mind.

I glared at him to show I knew what he was up to.

He looked back at me, grinned and bowed, absolutely unrepentant. I refused to look at him or Jack but went over to where my grandmother had fallen, on the other side of Elric, to try to help her.

She wasn't injured but rather weak from hunger. They had been starving her to death after catching her on her way back to us. They had planned to torture her, but Elric, dropped from Bastable's airship with the Kakatanawa, had found and released her while trying to find us. She had led him to the amphitheatre. In turn she had done whatever she could in her weakened state to help Elric.

Elric barely glanced at either of us. He was making his way back down to the floor of the amphitheatre, to the great block of emerald stone. The sword was still held purposefully in his hand, and I could tell that what he was about to do was unpleasant to him. St Odhran continued to lean back and watch Elric dully, his arm still about Jack's skinny frame.

With a shout and a grunt, Elric leaped into the air and plunged the sword into the top of the rock, where it then rested with a foot or so of its blade buried in the stone. Stormbringer vibrated gracefully now and sang to itself an utterly different song from the one it had sung while in Elric's hands. The albino released the hilt and, overcome at last with weakness, staggered down to the floor of the cavern.

Oona got up, suddenly invigorated, and moved towards him.

"The rest of you must finish this," Elric panted. "I've done what I must, and the Sword will serve me again, never fear. This is my bargain with it. But I will try to destroy the Balance. Erekosë—Hawkmoon—all that I am, was or will be . . ."

Those were the last words I would hear him say.

Oona had reached the great emerald stone. She took first one bowl and then the other and hung them by their chains from Stormbringer's guard. They were in perfect balance. She smiled, her skin bathed in the light from each of the components. She looked towards her father.

Before our eyes, Elric fell stiffly backward through a circle of crystal pillars, whose tops formed into elongated icicles racing ahead of him as he fell up an infinitely growing circle, whose slopes became increasingly angular, turning from white to dark blue to deep, pulsing green. I myself desperately wanted to follow him, to go with him into his own vanishing dream. But he faded and disappeared, as if he had never existed.

I stumbled. A hand was on my shoulder. Refusing my wish to follow him, Oona held me back. "Let them go," she said.

"Them?"

I looked up into her face. It was a mask of grief. Then I saw her grief change to alarm. To determination. I followed her gaze.

Two more men had appeared from nowhere. They were standing on either side of the Balance. One was black, handsome, massive. The other was white, wiry, grim. Yet both looked like brothers—twins, even! Were these the real siblings von Minct and Klosterheim had discovered in all their magical scrying? Both bore huge black broadswords like Elric's. The white man had a black, pulsing jewel embedded in his forehead. Slowly they turned to regard the Balance. Then, as if for the first time, they saw each other!

With a terrible cry the black man lifted his sword. Not against the white man—but against the Balance itself!

"No!" cried Oona. "Erekosë! Now is not the time!" Staggering towards the ghostly pair, she lifted her hands. "No. The Balance is needed. Without it, Elric dies for nothing!"

For a second the black man turned, frowning.

This gave the white man his moment. He drove his own sword deep into the black man's heart. Erekosë gasped. He struggled, trying to tug the sword from his body. The jewel in the white man's skull blazed with dark fire as the black man died. But there was no joy or triumph in the victor's face. Instead, he wept. And Oona wept with him.

Oona leaned back heavily against the sides of the amphitheatre, clearly relieved. I watched in astonishment as slowly the black man seemed to be drawn up the length of his enemy's blade, drawn into the metal and then into his body until there was nothing of him left. Then the white man collapsed to the ground, the Black Jewel growing dull, as if it died with him.

St Odhran walked slowly and stiffly to look down on the corpse. Then he knelt, reaching for the white man's clenched left hand. St Odhran prised the fingers open and took something from them. Whatever it was, he put it in his own pocket. Robbing the dead, I thought. But this was all over my head.

"It's done," said St Odhran. "For now, it's done."

"Who is he?" I whispered. "What is he?"

"Merely another fragment of the whole." St Odhran sighed heavily, cradling the dead man in his arms. "He's served his turn. As most of us have." He looked down at the dead man. "Eh, Hawkmoon, old comrade?" And then, to my further amazement, the white man began to fade until St Odhran's arms were empty. I felt I would never understand fully what had gone on here. The Balance pulsed, alive, it seemed to me, with the souls of those who had died in its restoration.

St Odhran stood up and went over to Jack. The look in his eyes seemed to be one of pity.

Turning her eyes from the Balance, Oona led me over to Jack and St Odhran. We were all exhausted, and I was aching horribly. She took St Odhran's hand.

He bowed and kissed her fingers. "Madame." They seemed to share a secret moment.

"What's this about?" I said. I suppose I was showing my "usual impatience," as Mum and Dad call it, with other people's intimate moments.

"I'm sorry, little mademoiselle, if I appeared to disappoint you." St Odhran drew a deep breath and smiled with all his old, sunny charm. "We told you, I think, that each and every one of us had a specific part to play if we were to succeed in restoring the Balance and defeat those who'd use it for evil.

"I elected to deceive our opponents by pretending to make a forgery of Elric's sword, because a sword had to be introduced into their equation. But the black sword I brought here was Mournblade, the twin of Stormbringer. The other, the white blade, was the forgery. We had to make them think they were winning, or those four would never have gathered in this place for their ceremony. We might never have been able to forestall 'em as we did. It was a dangerous chance, of course, but we had to take it. Everything was done according to careful calculations, considering all the risks. I couldn't let *you* know the risk, or you would not have responded in the genuine way needed. There's been nothing that's happened, nothing that's been avoided, that wasn't planned either by their side or ours. Our only grief was that while we tried to protect you at all times, we gambled with the lives of our children. A very hard decision.

"We are engaged in a momentous war, and this has been the subtlest part of our strategy. We needed to make them become self-assured and unguarded, to believe the real power was all theirs, before we could strike in unison. Hawkmoon's advance, Colonel Bastable's aerial voyage, your capture, our arriving in time—everything was planned. Everything but that final scene. Those men—"

But I didn't want him to tell me any more. I just couldn't take it.

"I told them I wasn't Jack's twin," I said lamely. I wasn't entirely happy to hear I'd been used as a cat's-paw.

"That's right, you're not," said my grandmother. "I am. But those fools never did discover the true nature of time. They would have done irreparable damage.

Of course, I am not your father's mother, as you doubtless know. Your father is one of our *adopted* children. Your grandfather and I wanted to lead normal lives as ordinary people. But I'm almost immortal, and your grandfather was not. He was, however, the most courageous man I ever knew, and the sanest. And I'm proud of your mother. We never planned to have our own children, because we hoped to lift the family curse."

"And did you?"

"Not really," she said. With the same grieving air, she reached towards Jack and embraced him. "You're my brother, Jack, as you know. A near-immortal like our own mother and father. In time it will be impossible to tell us apart by our ages. Whatever curves we followed in the moonbeam roads brought us out at a time a shade different from our original birthplace at the edge of the Grey Fees."

I saw then that Jack's blind eyes were full of tears. I was so touched for him that I didn't realise myself that I was beginning to fall in love.

"Now Gaynor's soul is trapped in the Black Sword," said St Odhran, "and the sword is more powerful, ready for the task it is to perform in Elric's world. The rest of Gaynor's physical substance is scattered and transformed. Yet it must be recognised that another Gaynor will come eventually, and another, to be first an idealist, a champion fighting for our great cause, and then a renegade, prepared to commit any savagery, any cruelty, any treachery to win power over that which he once served. But for the moment our business is done. Now only Elric lives on in his own world, to call upon his sword for that one final time, when he will bear it against the overwhelming forces of Chaos and seek, with the Horn of Fate, to herald in the dawn of another age."

I was still wary of St Odhran. I'm not one to bear a grudge, but I do have a strong sense of justice when someone's done me a wrong. "You pushed me," I said. "Twice."

He shook his head and straightened himself. "God love us, mademoiselle, but I'd relied upon you staying put. So then I had to come searching for you in the hope I'd find you before someone else did. Then, when I did discover you near one of the old elevator shafts which acts these days to ventilate this place, I had all those troops around me and was watched from afar by Taragorm as well. All I could do was push you into that shaft, knowing that at least I'd know where to find you. I was trying to buy time. I had not thought you'd escape the city, certainly not that you'd get across the river which runs overhead now. You showed more resilience and courage, the pair o' you, than anything I credited you with. And that was a fair bit."

"It's true," said Oona. She smiled, but she was still sad. Perhaps she missed her father. "We were in league. That, of course, was how I was able to rescue Jack and come and go from Countess Flana's apartments."

"Why was Flana involved with Klosterheim and the others?"

"In her case, a certain ambition to be queen, but mainly nothing more than boredom. She found solace in intrigue, since she never found it in human company. She paid a high price for her distractions. Don't grieve for her, young lady. She'd never known love and had seen twelve husbands come and go. Some of them went painfully and reluctantly. She would never have known what love was, I'm sure." Oona looked up, shrugging. "She might well have welcomed her death as another adventure."

It sounded a bit morbid to me. I had liked poor Countess Flana in spite of her part in my imprisonment.

From out of the shadows came a familiar and welcome figure. Lord Renyard looked flustered but highly delighted. His dandy pole clutched under one arm, he put his paws around me in an awkward, strong, and entirely affectionate embrace. His expression changed, however, as he addressed the others. His tone became urgent.

"We must leave here," he said. "We have only a few hours at best."

"But Londra's defeated," I said. "Isn't it?"

Lord Renyard shook his shaggy head. "Far from defeated. The diversion we created here allowed Londra's troops to re-marshal against their enemy. Seeking you proved a useful distraction, which is another reason I didn't want you to be found. The death of this lot and of King Huon allowed the soldiers to rally under fresh leadership. Lobkowitz and Fromental are gone, vanished from a world they helped create. We can only hope they're safe. Hawkmoon's dead, and his dimension-shifting crystal lost. A badly wounded Count Brass has fallen back across the Silver Bridge.

"The Dark Empire controls the city again and will defeat us if we cannot give the Balance time to restore itself. Huon may be dead, but Meliadus, it now seems, has merely disappeared. Some believe he'll return and try to make himself king again. Count Brass is content to leave the empire confined within her island home and reach an armistice. Like most old soldiers, he wants as little bloodshed as possible. He was always given to seeing the empire as a bringer of order and justice to disparate nations."

"But that's a mistake," I said.

"That's what Colonel Bastable thinks," declared Lord Renyard with a frown.

"He still means to bomb the city?" St Odhran demanded urgently.

"I believe so, sir. That's why he let me and the Kakatanawa off the ship. So we could tell you and help you get away if necessary. A mighty infernal machine, I gather."

"Oh, mighty indeed," said Oona, suddenly alert again. "He's going to drop an atom bomb on Londra."

"There has to be a way of stopping him," I said reasonably as my mind reeled. Sorcery and atom bombs? How were they able to accept all this at the same time? "Can't you get an ornithopter up there to signal to Colonel Bastable?"

"It would take too long," said Oona. "Besides, they'll be at a far greater altitude than any ornithopter could reach." She frowned. "That's what he was building in Mirenburg. In case our other plans failed. As Count Brass retreats, he believes we face defeat. We can't contact that airship . . ."

"The HMAS *Victoria*," said St Odhran softly to himself, and shook his head.

"A nuclear blast will stop them for ever," I murmured, overawed.

"I doubt it," said St Odhran, "but by Bastable's logic it will give Europe time to recover thoroughly and ensure the Dark Empire does not threaten others for many centuries to come. You'll recall what brought about the Tragic Millennium? And it was after that the empire emerged . . ."

"Come, my dear friends. Colonel Bastable was adamant. We have to leave at once." Lord Renyard's yap was shrill with anxiety. "He insists we couldn't possibly survive such a blast. If nothing else happened to us, the river would flood in and drown us. Hurry, my friends. Hurry!"

"What about the Balance?" I asked. "Who's going to look after it?"

"The Balance has gathered all its elements together," said Oona. "And they are, anyway, primarily symbolic. The blast will only facilitate its restorative powers. He's right, young lady; we'd better get moving."

"But it *hasn't* got all its elements," I pointed out. "They never had the right twins, and there's still the Runestaff! Am I the only one to see that? What about our blood? Taragorm and Bous-Junge would have won if they'd had everything properly sorted."

"I doubt that, dear." Oona sighed and reached out her hand to me. "The Runestaff doesn't exist, you see. It's a myth, that's all. A myth common to many of the worlds where the Dark Empire has had an influence. Just another image and a word to describe the Grail, which takes many forms. We were hoping to delay them a little further by letting them think they needed it, but my guess is they knew instinctively they could go ahead without it." She smiled at me. "You were in even greater danger than you ever knew! Most of us were."

"Look," murmured St Odhran. "Will you look?"

There, growing before our eyes, hung the Cosmic Balance, the sword embedded in the great emerald, the cups suspended from the sword's wide crosspieces, an aura of pale blue-green fire flickering around it. A sight so profound, so awesome, I almost felt I should kneel in front of it, the way you do in a church.

Oona interrupted this reverie. "Quickly," she said, "I promise you the Balance is now beyond harm. We have done our work. Come."

Then, with Jack's help, Oona led us back the way she and Elric had come: a series of winding tunnels, below Londra. But we didn't go back into Londra. Eventually we entered another system of caverns, untouched by the artistry of the Dark Empire, where the walls were entirely illuminated by moss and slender streams of phosphorescent water running between high banks. Jack had an instinct for the best places to ford, listening carefully and then leading us forward. Patches of pastel moss glowed here and there in the distant roof, giving the impression of ancient stars.

Soon we had left that awful amphitheatre far, far behind. I, for one, was relieved it was going to be destroyed.

"This is beginning to look familiar," I said as we stopped to rest and eat.

Oona nodded. "You *have* been in Mu-Ooria before, haven't you? We've reached the borders of their land. They are not the only folk who live under ground, but for the most part they exist in peace with the other inhabitants.

Peace, they find, ensures their longevity. Generally speaking, it seems fair to argue that those who live by the sword generally do die by it as well." And she sighed. She seemed to be recollecting her earlier sorrow.

Lord Renyard hadn't noticed any change in her expression. He came and stood beside us, looking out over the eery planes of that extraordinarily beautiful nightscape. "I will lead you from here," he said. He pointed with his pole. "That way lies Mirenburg, drowned beneath a lake of mercury, where once I studied the French." He pointed in another direction. "There lies the road I took when I was a cub, seeking a route to Paris, where I might discourse with my heroes. And this way"—again he pointed in a new direction—"lies Ingleton."

So I *was* going home. At last! I could hardly believe it. In fact I would not *completely* believe it for a while!

As I babbled my thanks to Lord Renyard and to Jack, Anayanka, one of the Kakatanawa, stepped forward and spoke to Oona. It was clear they had decided to leave us. "They know the way home from here," she told us. After a dignified and affectionate leave-taking, they made their way across a glowing field of moss and disappeared into darkness.

A little later we saw a herd of white buffalo being stalked by a pack of equally white panthers. I thought I caught Oona casting a wistful glance towards the panthers. What had happened to her own companion? Had she been left behind? I asked.

"No." Oona smiled. "She's perfectly safe."

Led by Lord Renyard and Jack, who was well adapted for the World Below, we travelled on foot for at least a couple of days, when suddenly the big cavern we were in shook with a long tremor which I feared must be another earthquake. Was I really never going to reach Ingleton?

A spear of rock detached itself from overhead and, whistling like a shell, landed ahead of us. More rock crashed from the impact. We dived for any cover we could find. Another huge fragment fell, and another, but none too close to us. I was relieved when at long last the shaking stopped.

"Bloody hell," said Jack. "What was that?"

"Bastable's bomb." Oona paused. "So he's done it at last! Targeted the seat of Empire and blown it to bits. Whether he survived or not, I guess we'll find out later."

"How do you mean? Wouldn't a blast like that just wipe an airship out?" said Jack.

"Not if it's Bastable's," she replied mysteriously. "He has a habit of being blown sideways, away from the result of his actions."

This made St Odhran smile, but it only baffled me and Jack. "This isn't the first time he's done something like this," said the Scottish aeronaut.

Lord Renyard still wanted us to hurry. We stopped and rested several more times, and although I tried to count the number of days likely to be passing in my own world, I lost track somewhere.

Eventually Jack lifted his head, hearing something the rest of us did not, and pointed. Shortly afterwards we came again in sight of that gloriously ethereal city of the Mu-Oorians, its pale, spiked towers rising into the cavernous gloom. Here we were greeted as long-lost friends and treated to the best which that strange people could offer us, including their scholarly conversation. We described our adventures, much to their awed approval. And then Lord Renyard announced his intention to spend the rest of his days among this gentle people. "I pray you will not think me ungrateful for all the offers you have made. But it would be best, I feel, if I remained with folk who see me not as an exotic sport of nature, but rather merely the last of his race."

The Off-Moo became agitated by the tale of the airship bombardment of Londra but accepted that an unspeakable evil had been forestalled. How strange, they said, that so much energy was wasted on negotiating war, when peace could be negotiated with exactly the same amount of effort and to far more profitable ends. They mourned all Londra's innocents.

Invigorated by their integrity, we took our leave of the Off-Moo. We all found their world attractive. It offered a kind of tranquillity without loss of intellectual stimuli, a tranquillity which could not be reproduced elsewhere. Lord Renyard was happy to be with these old friends, he assured us. He promised to lead us to the surface and then would return to their city after he had delivered us safely above ground.

In our final journey we crossed underground hills and valleys washed by that peculiar silvery light. Sometimes, in the distance, we saw herds of animals, pale descendants of creatures which had once roamed the surface of the world.

Less than a day later Jack lifted his head and pointed, sniffing the air, and we began the steep upward trudge to the surface. I had hoped we might emerge just above Tower House on Ingleton Common, where I had first fallen into the World Below, but that route was closed to us. Any caves which had temporarily opened up were filled in again. We finally squeezed into one of the old mine shafts and crawled out through abandoned workings that the quarry blasting had closed off as dangerous. We eventually got to the surface, emerging into one of Mr Capstick's fields, to the irritated surprise of his sheep. I forgot my own happiness when I looked at Jack's face. I never knew anyone who showed his joy so obviously. He took a deep breath of that good dales air. "Are we home?" he asked.

I was blinking back my own tears. "It certainly looks like it," I said.

Then Lord Renyard and I parted. I didn't want him to go. He was just as upset. He gave me a lot of advice, most of it to do with reading Rousseau and the Encyclopaedists, and then he was gone, loping back into the darkness of the Middle March to continue his lonely life among a people even stranger than himself. I was never to see him again.

We walked into a perfect dales morning, bright, crisp and clear. It was good to get some healthy northern air into my lungs.

"Come along," said my grandmother briskly, stripping off her weapons and bits of her costume so she looked as if she were wearing a fancy tracksuit, "let's get down there, then. Your parents will be wanting to see you."

A mile or so down the hill we soon spotted the grey granite tower of our house, where Mum and Dad were waiting for us with some very bad news.

23

My grandfather had died the night before. He had waited in London to see if there was anything he could do to help, my parents said, but they thought the anxiety had been just too much for his heart. Strangely, when they found him, he had seemed very much at peace and had written, perhaps to cheer himself up, a note on his scratch pad. "She's safe." Nobody was entirely sure who "she" was. He'd lived a fine life to a good age.

My grandmother, of course, took the train to town at once. She was very sad but soldiered on and made all the funeral arrangements herself. It was amazing how many people came to old Count Ulric's memorial service. The funeral picture appeared in most of the papers, and they had it on TV. Granny didn't come back to Yorkshire. She had some family business to sort out in Mirenburg. She said we weren't to worry if we didn't hear from her for a while.

Jack D'Acre was living with us. Oona had asked my mum and dad to make him part of our family. She left it to me to offer them what details seemed relevant, but they were happy to have him. They assumed he was homeless, an orphan, the natural son of some distant relative. He certainly had the family looks, they said. Alfy and Gertie came back with us from London. They got on well with Jack.

Colonel Bastable had missed the funeral. He phoned from London later, then caught the train the following day. Dad picked him up at the station. Bastable's big Bentley tourer was still parked under canvas on the common. Red-eyed and laconic, he asked if it would be all right if he stayed overnight and then drove out early the next morning, after he'd helped St Odhran inflate his balloon and get airborne. He needed a break, he said. Mum and Dad fussed over both men while they were at our house. As they understood it, Bastable and St Odhran had contributed enormously to my rescue when I was lost under ground.

My parents were sorry they had missed Monsieur Zodiac, who had an engagement, St Odhran told them, and sent his apologies. They were glad to hear we wouldn't be bothered by Klosterheim and Gaynor again. Those two had clearly been dynamiting new routes down below.

Privately, I still missed Lord Renyard, but he had probably been right. My parents, though broad-minded and sophisticated, weren't ready for a man-size, talking, eighteenth-century-educated fox.

Colonel Bastable had apologised on behalf of Messrs Lobkowitz and Fromental. He said some important national business had taken them away.

I had one last conversation with St Odhran. We went for a walk together over the tranquil hills above the house. I wanted to know a bit about the Balance.

"The Balance was destroyed. Both sides wished to restore it for their own reasons," he told me. He looked down at me. Those eyes, which had managed to deceive me, were now frank, serious.

"Who destroyed it?"

He smiled sardonically and looked away up the fell. "The Champion," he said.

"And the Champion restored it?"

"It looked that way, didn't it?"

"Is nothing permanent? Even the Cosmic Balance? I thought it was the ordering mechanism for the multiverse!"

"It's a symbol," he said. "A useful one, but a symbol. Sometimes we fight to restore the Balance, sometimes to maintain it, and very occasionally, to destroy it."

"What point is there in all that? What logic?"

"The logic of context," he said simply. "Context is all-important. One set of views, one faith, one idea, can be useful and good for us at a certain time. At another, they threaten our destruction. The Eternal Champion fights to maintain equilibrium between Chaos and Order. But his fight is not always a clear one. Not always sympathetic to most of us."

St Odhran was graceful as always in his leave-taking. A small crowd of locals and tourists gathered around the balloon. He left as the sun got high, scattering what looked like golden confetti down on the cheering crowd. It turned out to be handfuls of the little fake gold coins they throw over the bride and groom at Egyptian weddings. A few hours later, Colonel Bastable made his excuses. He had another appointment he was bound to keep, he said. He roared off in his Bentley. And then it was just us, the family. I think we were all a little glad to be together again with no-one else around.

That next night was Midsummer's Eve, and St Odhran had told us to expect a great battle as Law and Chaos fought for the Balance across all the realms of the multiverse.

From our Ingleton tower we watched the War amongst the Angels, as it was described in our part of the world. All of us were crammed into those few square feet with windows all around, so that we could see inland up Ingleborough and across the rolling hills out to sea at Morecambe Bay. The glaring silver-and-black sea was lit by the most intense sheet lightning I had ever witnessed in Texas or the tropics. And silhouetted against the lightning (some would later describe them as intense black clouds of unusual shape) were the forms of angels.

These weren't the conventional Christian variety of angels, but the Lords and Ladies of the Higher Worlds, closing in pitched battle, Law against Chaos, while elsewhere Elric's struggle echoed theirs as he fought to herald in the Dawn. Lord Arioch, Duke of Chaos, and Lady Inald, haughty Countess of Law, leading their troops, faced each other across the boundary of the Middle March, fighting once again for control of the Balance.

I witnessed the chivalry of Law opposed, as ever, to the chivalry of Chaos, when they met on that Midsummer's Night in the worst summer storm England had ever known and which equalled, in the course of twenty-four hours, other huge storms across the world.

A rather florid anonymous account appeared in the *Craven Herald* and was quoted extensively in later literature. It described an assembly of winged horsemen, wielding fiery swords, who clashed in the heavens: one side representing howling Chaos and one side for stern, relentless Law.

As angels fought and fell, I tried to make out their true shapes: Lord Arkyn pointed his white sword Mireen. Lady Xiombarg, spitting black blood and blue fire, challenged him with her massive twin-bladed axe.

Jack's strongest memory, he says, is hearing the terrible smack of a winged body, the weight of an elephant, striking the limestone pavement above Chapel-le-Dale.

It was Lady s'Rashdee falling down when half her left wing was severed. You can still see cracks in the rock. Large trees grow up through them now. Locals call it the Devil's Pavement.

In America, two doctor friends of my parents, living in Inverness, California, reported the extraordinary view over the moody marshland shallows of Tomales Bay. They were sitting on their deck that night, enjoying the clarity of the weather, when they heard distant thunder and then watched a slowly darkening sky until, against it, a series of grey clouds formed the shapes of twelve Amerindian warriors in great detail. These were without doubt tribesmen not of the west but of the north-east, every one of them slightly different in costume and features as they ran out of the sunset sky and headed inland.

I also heard how the folk of Marazion, the little port across from Saint Michael's Mount, observed a gigantic figure in gold-and-ebony armour ride his warhorse over to the castle, a blazing brand in his right hand and a shard of flashing crystal in his left, make his horse rear, then bow in triumph and gratitude before galloping off across the water towards France.

I know most of it's true, because I heard the parts I didn't experience myself from Una Persson, as she calls herself now, that mysterious adventuress who spends so much of her time in Eastern Europe and never seems to age.

Sometimes I think of putting a book together of all the accounts, but this is probably all I'll write. To be honest, I've had enough of supernatural adventures in other worlds, and so has my husband. We have two young children now. We've resolved to live ordinary lives and let the fantastic past fade into an incredible dream, as we become plain old Mr and Mrs John Daker.

Mum and Dad live full-time in Ingleton, where they work at their computer business. Jack and I are thinking of moving up there to get the kids a decent education and some fresh air. London changes faster than I can take sometimes, and the price of houses is ridiculous.

When I get crabby and think the world is becoming too heavily populated, though, I let myself remember the vast population of the entire multiverse, in which nothing really ever dies, or can ever die, while the original universe still lives, where there is always some other version of you and me. Then everything falls into perspective, and I cheer up again.

I prefer not to consider that too much, though. I'd rather think of myself and all those living souls within my extended family who know that they can be pretty much whatever they want to be but who also know, better than anyone, that there really are no free lunches, that wherever you are in the multiverse, everything must be paid for, usually with hard work.

Lately, Jack's been having some bad nights. I think it's stress. I'm beginning to wonder if the stock market is represented by too few principled warriors like him. He gets sick of the lies and deceptions in the modern business world. We could do with a bit more courage and determination in public life, not all this Hollywood-style brand-name politics too many people fall for. People don't take enough responsibility for themselves or their actions.

We, too, have our ups and downs, of course. Jack says he remembers his life on the bum rather than our interventions or adventures in the multiverse. He think it's for the best. Some of us can absorb that amount of information. Some can't. Personally, I understand his denial. I don't bring the past up very often.

I'm looking forward to moving. The first morning we get back to Tower House, we'll go for a walk in grass which the fresh summer rain has sweetened, and I'll show Jack Daker the real world his eye surgery has let him see again. It will be sparkling and beautiful in the golden sun, the evergreens dark against the pale blue sky. I'll pretend it's all as it was on that first day of my adventures, before I went looking for crayfish in the brook and met the most evil man in the multiverse. It now seems such a dream. As I often say to Jack, it takes a lot of courage and nerve just to face the terrors and anxieties of bringing up a couple of children in our modern world. Today's realities are violent and fantastic enough for us! He heartily agrees.

EPILOGUE

As he fell he knew that Law and Chaos both still pursued him and that somehow he was becoming an important piece in their perpetual battle. Struggle as he might to move against the Higher Worlds' plans for him, he was never entirely free of their influence. His enemies wanted lives which were absolutely free to expand and express themselves without any form of hindrance. He could not share that lust. He valued the power and compassion of the many over the individual power and greed of the few. This set him apart from his father and family but reconnected him with his forebears who had practised his virtues and vices with more questioning of the moral uses of power.

He could not believe that it was enough to preserve Melniboné, and so he had come to think that only death could save his people. Every advance in his journey to this moment had been earned and had brought him some unwanted burden of knowledge, some dreadful doom. His fate had been to destroy an ancient nation and take on an ancient curse in the form of a blade which served itself by appearing to serve certain masters. Yet his very struggle contained both the elements which warred in the Higher Worlds, making him an unlikely Knight of the Balance, one of those few representative champions chosen to fight the fight of the many.

And still he fell until he felt a sharp salt wind in his face and warm iron in his fist, and knew he breathed with a new vitality. A vitality he had earned as he and his kind had earned it over and over again down the centuries, across all the worlds of the moonbeam roads. This understanding faded as he woke, screaming:

"*Stormbringer!*"

Hearing a curse from beneath him, Elric saw Jagreen Lern pointing up at him. "Gag the white-faced sorcerer, and if that doesn't put an end to his babbling, slay him!"

"*Stormbringer!*" called Elric again into that void, that terrible moment between life and death. "Stormbringer! Your master perishes!"

One of his guards reached up to tug at his bound foot. "Silence! You heard my master!"

But Elric had to take his remaining chance, his last knowing breath, to cry: "*Stormbringer!*"

The guard put the sharp edge of his sword to Elric's naked feet. He made to slice off his toes. But Elric paid him no heed. There was still breath enough.

"*Stormbringer!*"

The guard had climbed the rigging and was almost face-to-face with Elric. His coarse features grinned in stupid triumph as he drew back his arm to stab at the albino's throat.

"*Stormbringer!*"

With an appalled gasp the warrior fell, his cutlass dropping from his fingers as he raised his hands to grapple with something invisible, which had him by the throat. Suddenly his fingers parted from his hands in little fountains of blood.

Flinging the lifeless corpse to the deck, the sword stood before its master for a moment. Then, in a series of rapid movements, it slashed at the bonds holding him to the mast, leaped into his hand and fed him the lifestuff they, in their dreadful union, sucked from their victims, making man and sword symbiotic predators.

Elric's story was moving towards its ultimate tragedy. Those who had fought to deny him his destiny were defeated. He could fight his way to the ruins of his own past, betraying all who sought to help him, to find at least a kind of tranquillity, one Champion among many in whom morality and bleak necessity continually made war.

And now the objects of power are in fresh configuration upon an Earth where Tanelorn may sometimes be found. Old friends go there to meet and rejoice, and enemies go to be reconciled. Another name for that city is the Old and the New Jerusalem. And it is all your soul desires.

I hope I will see you there.

An End and a Beginning

THE ELRIC SAGA: A READER'S GUIDE

BY JOHN DAVEY

Elric of Melniboné—proud prince of ruins, kinslayer—call him what you will. He remains, together with maybe Jerry Cornelius, Michael Moorcock's most enduring, if not always most endearing, character.

This guide attempts to provide a title-by-title breakdown of the novels together with omnibuses in which each appeared, all in a chronological format, listing omnibuses as individual titles rather than including them within the main books' descriptions.

Elric began life sixty years ago, in response to a request from John Carnell, editor of SCIENCE FANTASY magazine, for a series akin to Robert E. Howard's Conan the Barbarian stories. What Carnell received, while steeped in sword-and-sorcery images, was something quite different. All in all, nine Elric novellas appeared in SCIENCE FANTASY between June 1961 and April 1964, the last four "serialising" (in effect) the novel *Stormbringer*, while the first five were collected as *The Stealer of Souls* (1963). These five were later split up and re-collected in, or absorbed into, *The Weird of the White Wolf* and *The Bane of the Black Sword* (*q.v.*, both 1977) and were also, as a result of this assimilation, slightly revised. Collectors should note that the true first edition of *The Stealer of Souls* (subtitled by its publishers as "*. . . and Other Stories,*" against Moorcock's wishes) was bound in orange boards; an otherwise identical but less collectable second printing had green boards.

Stormbringer (1965), conceived as a novel, was first published as such when abridged and revised from the four remaining SCIENCE FANTASY novellas. It was later restored to its original length and further revised, in 1977. The original abridgements basically condensed the first two novellas (plus part of the third) into one long section, "The Coming of Chaos."

The Singing Citadel (1970) was a collection of four other novellas originally published in various anthologies and periodicals between 1962 and 1967. They were later split up and all but one were re-collected in, or absorbed into, *The Weird of the White Wolf* and *The Bane of the Black Sword* as their events interconnect with those of *The Stealer of Souls*. They were also, as a result of this assimilation, slightly revised. The unused novella, "The Greater Conqueror" (sometimes erroneously listed as "The Great Conqueror"), was subsequently collected in *Moorcock's Book of Martyrs* (1976, a.k.a. *Dying for Tomorrow*, 1978), *Earl Aubec and Other Stories* (1993), *Elric: To Rescue Tanelorn* (2008) and *Elric: The Sleeping Sorceress* (2013).

The Sleeping Sorceress (1971) was expanded from a novella of the same name, although it was originally commissioned as a serial for Kenneth Bulmer's magazine, SWORD AND SORCERY, which never appeared. One of its sections retells, from Elric's viewpoint, a part of the Corum novel, *The King of the Swords*. In 1977, *The Sleeping Sorceress* was retitled, with minor textual amendments, as *The Vanishing Tower* (q.v.).

Elric of Melniboné (1972) is a prequel to all other Elric novels. *The Dreaming City* (1972) was a version of *Elric of Melniboné*, published with unauthorised changes. Collectors should note that, in 1977, *Elric of Melniboné* was one of three Elric books sold as illustrated editions in slip-cases. This first (in a red case) also had a smaller, limited edition (in a brown case) signed by the author, artist (Robert Gould) and publisher. In 2003, *Elric of Melniboné* was the first novel of Moorcock's to become an unabridged audiobook.

Elric: The Return to Melnibone (sic, 1973) remains, despite its comparative irrelevance to the overall series, one of the scarcest and most sought-after of

Elric books. This is the result of its somewhat chequered history, a saga complex enough to rival Elric's own. It is actually little more than a showcase for the exquisite artwork of Philippe Druillet, beginning life in 1966 as double-spread colour illustrations for the only issue of a French magazine, MOI AUSSI, with text by Maxim Jakubowski. In 1969, Druillet illustrated an omnibus called *Elric le Necromancien*, and in 1972 some of this (and new) artwork was put into a twenty-one piece portfolio as *La Saga d'Elric le Necromancien*, this time with text by Michel Demuth. All of this work up until then was unauthorised, but when the portfolio was reprinted and bound (less one piece) in the U.K. as *Elric: The Return to Melnibone* (text by Moorcock), Druillet threatened to sue. Moorcock was forced to step in on behalf of the British publishers, pointing out that permission had never been granted for Druillet to draw Elric in the first place. In order to avoid messy litigation, it was decided to allow the small print run to expire, never to be reprinted. However, a republication was finally agreed, the book made available again in 1997 as *Elric: The Return to Melniboné*, and it was later collected (alongside James Cawthorn's 1976 graphic adaptation of *Stormbringer*) in 2021's *Elric: The Eternal Champion Collection*.

The Jade Man's Eyes (1973) was a separate novella which, in order to bring it in line with the developing series, was revised and absorbed into *The Sailor on the Seas of Fate* as "Sailing to the Past."

The Sailor on the Seas of Fate (1976) originally slotted, chronologically, between events in *Elric of Melniboné* and *The Weird of the White Wolf*. One of its sections retells, from Elric's viewpoint, a part of the Hawkmoon/Count Brass novel, *The Quest for Tanelorn*. In 2006, *The Sailor on the Seas of Fate* also became an unabridged audiobook.

The Weird of the White Wolf (1977) is a chronological arrangement of selected contents from *The Stealer of Souls* and *The Singing Citadel*, compiled in order to bring them in line with the developing series.

The Vanishing Tower (1977) is a retitling, with minor textual amendments, of *The Sleeping Sorceress*. Collectors should note that, in 1981, *The Vanishing*

Tower was the second of three Elric books sold as illustrated editions in slip-cases. This edition (in a pictorial red case) also had a smaller, limited edition (in a brown case) signed by the author, artist (Michael Whelan) and publisher.

The Bane of the Black Sword (1977) is a chronological arrangement of selected contents from *The Stealer of Souls* and *The Singing Citadel*, compiled in order to bring them in line with the developing series.

The somewhat misleadingly titled **Six Science Fiction Classics from the Master of Heroic Fantasy** (1979) was a boxed set of six American paperbacks: *Elric of Melniboné, The Sailor on the Seas of Fate, The Weird of the White Wolf, The Vanishing Tower, The Bane of the Black Sword* and *Stormbringer*.

Elric at the End of Time (1984) was a collection of short fiction and non-fiction which actually contained only three Elric-related items among its contents of seven (excluding the introduction). The title story was also published separately in 1987 as a large-format novella (*q.v.*) illustrated by Rodney Matthews.

The Elric Saga Part One (1984) was the first Elric omnibus, and contained *Elric of Melniboné, The Sailor on the Seas of Fate* and *The Weird of the White Wolf*. *The Elric Saga Part Two* (1984) was the second omnibus, and contained *The Vanishing Tower, The Bane of the Black Sword* and *Stormbringer*.

Elric at the End of Time (1987) was a separate, large-format novella illustrated by Rodney Matthews for whom it was originally written some years earlier. Collectors should note that it was published simultaneously in both hardcover and paperback formats.

The Fortress of the Pearl (1989), the first Elric novel for thirteen years, expanded the saga and slots, chronologically, between events in *Elric of Melniboné* and *The Sailor on the Seas of Fate*.

The Revenge of the Rose (1991) slots between events in *The Sleeping Sorceress/ The Vanishing Tower* and the stories from *The Bane of the Black Sword*.

In 1992, Moorcock began an ambitious project of re-ordering, revising and re-publishing much of his back-catalogue in a large set of omnibuses in the U.K. under the collective title of "The Tale of the Eternal Champion." The first of these to feature the albino prince was *Elric of Melniboné* (1993), containing *Elric of Melniboné, The Fortress of the Pearl, The Sailor on the Seas of Fate* and selected contents from *The Weird of the White Wolf*. The omnibus was retitled in the U.S.A., when the "Eternal Champion" series began to appear there, as *Elric: Song of the Black Sword* (1995).

The second British omnibus to feature Elric was *Stormbringer* (1993), containing *The Sleeping Sorceress, The Revenge of the Rose*, selected contents from *The Bane of the Black Sword*, and *Stormbringer*. This omnibus was retitled in the U.S.A. as *Elric: The Stealer of Souls* (1998), not to be confused with a later volume of the same name (*q.v.*).

Collectors should note that, in the U.K., "The Tale of the Eternal Champion" omnibuses were published simultaneously in both hardcover and matching paperback formats. In the U.S.A., hardcover editions appeared ahead of their paperback versions.

Elric: Tales of the White Wolf (1994) was an original anthology of Elric stories by Moorcock and others, edited by Edward E. Kramer & Richard Gilliam.

Michael Moorcock's Multiverse (1999) was a graphic novel illustrated by Walter Simonson, Mark Reeve & John Ridgway, originally serialised in twelve parts (1997/'98). It contained three interconnecting tales (each illustrated by a different artist), one of which—Ridgway's—is "Duke Elric."

The Dreamthief's Daughter (2001) was the first volume of a new Elric trilogy—in fact the only preconceived Elric trilogy—linking the albino with some of the many and various members of the Family von Bek. (When revising his books for the "Eternal Champion" omnibuses, Moorcock had the opportunity to change several character names in order to bring them in line with the developing "Von Bek" series, which had begun in 1981 with *The War Hound and the World's Pain* although the name's derivation goes back as far as Katinka van Bak in 1973's *The Champion of Garathorm*.) Collectors should note that, also in 2001 (after the true first edition), *The Dreamthief's Daughter* became the last of three Elric books sold as illustrated editions in slip-cases. This limited edition, signed by the author and artists (Randy Broecker, Donato Giancola, Gary Gianni, Robert Gould, Michael Kaluta, Todd Lockwood, Don Maitz & Michael Whelan), was followed two years later— still dated "2001"—by a smaller limited edition which was leather-bound and tray-cased. In 2013, *The Dreamthief's Daughter* was retitled and revised (in the U.K.) as *Daughter of Dreams* (*q.v.*).

Elric (2001) was another omnibus, containing *The Stealer of Souls* (or rather its five component novellas) and *Stormbringer*, as part of a "Fantasy Masterworks" series. In 2008, it was repackaged as part of the same publisher's more exclusive "Ultimate Fantasies" sequence.

The Elric Saga Part Three (2002), another omnibus, contained *The Fortress of the Pearl* and *The Revenge of the Rose*.

The Skrayling Tree: The Albino in America (2003) is the second part of the trilogy beginning with *The Dreamthief's Daughter*. In 2013, *The Skrayling Tree* was retitled and revised (in the U.K.) as *Destiny's Brother*.

The White Wolf's Son: The Albino Underground (2005) is the third and last part of the trilogy. Although this Elric sub-series can be read as a standalone adventure (as, indeed, can each volume), brief mention is made of events slotting, chronologically, into those described within *Stormbringer*. In 2013, *The White Wolf's Son* was retitled and revised (in the U.K.) as *Son of the Wolf*.

The Elric Saga Part IV (2005), another omnibus, contained *The Dreamthief's Daughter*, *The Skrayling Tree* and *The White Wolf's Son*.

Elric: The Making of a Sorcerer (2007) was a graphic novel illustrated by Walter Simonson, originally serialised in four parts (2004–'06), and is a prequel to the novel *Elric of Melniboné*.

Elric: The Stealer of Souls (2008) was the first volume in a series of six Elric omnibuses published (in the order the main novels were written) under the collective title of "Chronicles of the Last Emperor of Melniboné," each containing fiction and non-fiction. The first volume's fiction includes *The Stealer of Souls* and *Stormbringer*. *Elric: To Rescue Tanelorn* (2008) was the second volume, a collection of Elric (or Elric-related) short fiction. *Elric: The Sleeping Sorceress* (2008) was the third volume, including the novels *The Sleeping Sorceress* and *Elric of Melniboné*. *Duke Elric* (2009) was the fourth volume, including *The Sailor on the Seas of Fate*, the *Duke Elric* graphic-novel script and a novella, "The Flaneur des Arcades de l'Opera." *Elric in the Dream Realms* (2009) was the fifth volume, including *The Fortress of the Pearl*, the *Elric: The Making of a Sorcerer* graphic-novel script and a short story, "A Portrait in Ivory." *Elric: Swords and Roses* (2010), the sixth and final volume, included *The Revenge of the Rose*, a *Stormbringer* (unmade) movie screenplay, and the first of two new novellas, "Black Petals" (2008), the second being "Red Pearls" (2011). At the time of writing, these novellas are being revised and incorporated, with much new material, into a brand-new Elric novel (due 2022).

Elric: Les Buveurs d'Âmes (2011) was an original, collaborative novel (in French) by Moorcock and Fabrice Colin, for which there seems no imminent sign of an English-language edition.

Daughter of Dreams (2013) was a revised retitling of *The Dreamthief's Daughter*; *Destiny's Brother* (2013) was a revised retitling of *The Skrayling Tree*; *Son of the Wolf* (2013) was a revised retitling of *The White Wolf's Son*.

Elric of Melniboné and Other Stories (2013) was the first volume in a set of seven Elric omnibuses published (in narrative-chronology order) as part of a larger series, "The Michael Moorcock Collection," each containing similar long & short fiction and non-fiction to the "Chronicles of the Last Emperor of Melniboné." It was followed by *Elric: The Fortress of the Pearl* (2013), *Elric: The Sailor on the Seas of Fate* (2013), *Elric: The Sleeping Sorceress and Other Stories* (2013), *Elric: The Revenge of the Rose* (2014), *Elric: Stormbringer!* (2014), and *Elric: The Moonbeam Roads* (2014) containing *Daughter of Dreams, Destiny's Brother* and *Son of the Wolf*.

In 2019, Centipede Press began publishing limited editions of nine Elric novels—which have all (to date) sold out prior to publication—each accompanied by the relevant shorter fiction required to create an overall narrative chronology. At the time of writing, these volumes have been *Elric of Melniboné, The Fortress of the Pearl* and *The Sailor on the Seas of Fate (*all 2019), *The Sleeping Sorceress* (2020) and *The Revenge of the Rose* (2021), with *Stormbringer, The Dreamthief's Daughter, The Skrayling Tree* and *The White Wolf's Son* to follow. The first three volumes have also been produced as outsized, slip-cased hardcovers offered to subscribers only.

Which brings us at long last to Saga's Elric saga volumes. Unlimited and therefore available to all, Saga Press's three uniform omnibus editions—published from 2022 to commemorate sixty glorious years since the character's very first appearance in print—contain eleven novels in order of narrative chronology: *Elric of Melniboné, The Fortress of the Pearl, The Sailor on the Seas of Fate* and *The Weird of the White Wolf* in **The Elric Saga Volume One: Elric of Melniboné**, *The Vanishing Tower, The Revenge of the Rose, The Bane of the Black Sword* and *Stormbringer* in **The Elric Saga Volume Two: Stormbringer**, and *The Dreamthief's Daughter, The Skrayling Tree* and *The White Wolf's Son* in **The Elric Saga Volume Three: The White Wolf**.

FIRST EDITIONS AND
FIRST APPEARANCES

The Stealer of Souls:

"The Dreaming City," originally in SCIENCE FANTASY No. 47 (edited by
John Carnell), U.K., June 1961

"While the Gods Laugh," in SCIENCE FANTASY No. 49, Oct. 1961

"The Stealer of Souls," in SCIENCE FANTASY No. 51, Feb. 1962

"Kings in Darkness," in SCIENCE FANTASY No. 54, Aug. 1962

"The Flame Bringers," in SCIENCE FANTASY No. 55, Oct. 1962

Neville Spearman hardcover, U.K., 1963

Lancer paperback, U.S.A., 1967

Stormbringer:

"Dead God's Homecoming," orig. in SCIENCE FANTASY No. 59, June
1963

"Black Sword's Brothers," in SCIENCE FANTASY No. 61, Oct. 1963

"Sad Giant's Shield," in SCIENCE FANTASY No. 63, Feb. 1964

"Doomed Lord's Passing," in SCIENCE FANTASY No. 64, Apr. 1964

Herbert Jenkins h/c (abridged & revised from the "serialised" novellas),
U.K., 1965

Lancer p/b (ditto), U.S.A., 1967

DAW p/b (full length & revised), U.S.A., 1977

Granada p/b (ditto), U.K., 1985

The Singing Citadel:

"The Singing Citadel" (novella), orig. in *The Fantastic Swordsmen*
(anthology edited by L. Sprague de Camp), U.S.A., 1967
"Master of Chaos," in FANTASTIC Vol. 13 No. 5 (ed. Cele Goldsmith),
U.S.A., May 1964
"The Greater Conqueror" (non-Elric), in SCIENCE FANTASY No. 58, Apr.
1963
"To Rescue Tanelorn . . .," in SCIENCE FANTASY No. 56, Dec. 1962
Mayflower p/b, U.K., 1970
Berkley p/b, U.S.A., 1970

The Sleeping Sorceress:

"The Sleeping Sorceress" (novella), orig. in *Warlocks and Warriors*
(anthol., ed. Douglas Hill), U.K., 1971
New English Library h/c (expanded from the novella), U.K., 1971
Lancer p/b (ditto), U.S.A., 1972
DAW p/b (as *The Vanishing Tower*), U.S.A., 1977
Archival Press h/c (as *The Vanishing Tower*, no dust-wrapper, in pictorial
red slip-case [also limited in brown slip-case]), U.S.A., 1981
Granada p/b (as *The Vanishing Tower*), U.K., 1983

Elric of Melniboné:

Hutchinson h/c, U.K., 1972
Lancer p/b (unauthorised changes, as *The Dreaming City*), U.S.A., 1972
DAW p/b (unchanged, as *Elric of Melniboné*), U.S.A., 1976
Blue Star h/c (ditto, no dust-wrapper, in red slip-case [also limited in
brown slip-case]), U.S.A., 1977

Elric: The Return to Melnibone (illustrated by Philippe Druillet):

Unicorn outsize p/b, U.K., 1973
Jayde Design outsize p/b (as *Elric: The Return to Melniboné*), U.K., 1997

The Jade Man's Eyes:
Unicorn p/b, U.K., 1973

The Sailor on the Seas of Fate:
Quartet h/c, U.K., 1976
DAW p/b, U.S.A., 1976

The Weird of the White Wolf:
DAW p/b, U.S.A., 1977, comprising:
    "The Dream of Earl Aubec" (a.k.a. "Master of Chaos")
    "The Dreaming City"
    "While the Gods Laugh"
    "The Singing Citadel"
Granada p/b, U.K., 1984

The Bane of the Black Sword:
DAW p/b, U.S.A., 1977, comprising:
    "The Stealer of Souls"
    "Kings in Darkness"
    "The Flamebringers" (a.k.a. "The Flame Bringers")
    "To Rescue Tanelorn . . ."
Granada p/b, U.K., 1984

Six Science Fiction Classics from the Master of Heroic Fantasy:
Six DAW p/bs, boxed, U.S.A., 1979, comprising:
    Elric of Melniboné
    The Sailor on the Seas of Fate
    The Weird of the White Wolf
    The Vanishing Tower
    The Bane of the Black Sword
    Stormbringer

Elric at the End of Time (collection):

NEL h/c, U.K., 1984, comprising the following Elric-related items:

"Elric at the End of Time," orig. in *Elsewhere* (anthol., ed. Terri
Windling & Mark Alan Arnold), U.S.A., 1981

"The Last Enchantment," in ARIEL No. 3 (ed. Thomas Durwood),
U.S.A., Apr. 1978

"The Secret Life of Elric of Melniboné" (non-fiction), in CAMBER No.
14 (fanzine, ed. Alan Dodd), U.K., June 1964

DAW p/b, U.S.A., 1985

The Elric Saga Part One:

Doubleday (Science Fiction Book Club) h/c, U.S.A., 1984, comprising:

Elric of Melniboné
The Sailor on the Seas of Fate
The Weird of the White Wolf

The Elric Saga Part Two:

Doubleday (SFBC) h/c, U.S.A., 1984, comprising:

The Vanishing Tower
The Bane of the Black Sword
Stormbringer

Elric at the End of Time (novella, illustrated by Rodney Matthews):

Paper Tiger large-format h/c & p/b, U.K., 1987

The Fortress of the Pearl:

Gollancz h/c, U.K., 1989
Ace h/c, U.S.A., 1989

The Revenge of the Rose:

Grafton h/c, U.K., 1991
Ace h/c, U.S.A., 1991

Elric of Melniboné (omnibus):

Orion/Millennium h/c & p/b, U.K., 1993, comprising:

Elric of Melniboné
The Fortress of the Pearl
The Sailor on the Seas of Fate
"The Dreaming City"
"While the Gods Laugh"
"The Singing Citadel"

White Wolf h/c (as *Elric: Song of the Black Sword*), U.S.A., 1995

Stormbringer (omnibus):

Orion/Millennium h/c & p/b, U.K., 1993, comprising:

The Sleeping Sorceress
The Revenge of the Rose
"The Stealer of Souls"
"Kings in Darkness"
"The Caravan of Forgotten Dreams" (a.k.a. "The Flame Bringers")
Stormbringer
"Elric: A Reader's Guide" (non-fiction by John Davey)

White Wolf h/c (as *Elric: The Stealer of Souls*), U.S.A., 1998

Elric: Tales of the White Wolf:

White Wolf h/c, U.S.A., 1994, comprising the following Moorcock items:

"Introduction to *Tales of the White Wolf*" (non-fiction)
"The White Wolf's Song"
plus Elric stories by Tad Williams, David M. Honigsberg, Roland J.
Green & Frieda A. Murray, Richard Lee Byers, Brad Strickland,
Brad Linaweaver & William Alan Ritch, Kevin T. Stein, Scott
Ciencin, Gary Gygax, James S. Dorr, Stewart von Allmen, Paul W.
Cashman, Nancy A. Collins, Doug Murray, Karl Edward Wagner,
Thomas E. Fuller, Jody Lynn Nye, Colin Greenland, Robert
Weinberg, Charles Partington, Peter Crowther & James Lovegrove,
Nancy Holder, Neil Gaiman.

Michael Moorcock's Multiverse:

DC Comics large-format p/b, U.S.A., 1999

"Moonbeams and Roses" (non-Elric), illustrated by Walter Simonson

"The Metatemporal Detective" (non-Elric), illustrated by Mark Reeve

"Duke Elric," illustrated by John Ridgway

The Dreamthief's Daughter:

Earthlight h/c, U.K., 2001

American Fantasy h/c (in slip-case [also limited in tray-case]), U.S.A., 2001

Gollancz p/b (as *Daughter of Dreams*), U.K., 2013

Elric:

Gollancz p/b, U.K., 2001, comprising:

"The Dreaming City"

"While the Gods Laugh"

"The Stealer of Souls"

"Kings in Darkness"

"The Caravan of Forgotten Dreams"

Stormbringer

The Elric Saga Part Three:

SFBC h/c, U.S.A., 2002, comprising:

The Fortress of the Pearl

The Revenge of the Rose

The Skrayling Tree: The Albino in America:

Warner h/c, U.S.A., 2003

Gollancz p/b (as *Destiny's Brother*), U.K., 2013

The White Wolf's Son: The Albino Underground:

Warner h/c, U.S.A., 2005

Gollancz p/b (as *Son of the Wolf*), U.K., 2013

The Elric Saga Part IV:

SFBC h/c, U.S.A., 2005, comprising:
The Dreamthief's Daughter
The Skrayling Tree
The White Wolf's Son

Elric: The Making of a Sorcerer (illustrated by Walter Simonson):

DC Comics large-format p/b, U.S.A., 2007

Elric: The Stealer of Souls: Chronicles of the Last Emperor of Melniboné: Volume 1:

Del Rey p/b, U.S.A., 2008, comprising:
"Putting a Tag on It" (non-fiction), orig. in AMRA Vol. 2 No. 15
(fanzine, ed. George Scithers), U.S.A., May 1961
The Stealer of Souls
"Mission to Asno!" (non-Elric), in TARZAN ADVENTURES Vol. 7 No. 25
(ed. Moorcock), U.K., Sep. 1957
Stormbringer
"Elric" (non-fiction), in NIEKAS No. 8 (fanzine, ed. Ed Meskys), U.S.A.,
1964
"The Secret Life of Elric of Melniboné" (non-fiction)
"Final Judgement" (non-fiction by Alan Forrest), in NEW WORLDS No.
147 (ed. Moorcock, as "Did Elric Die in Vain?"), U.K., Feb. 1965
"The Zenith Letter" (non-fiction by Anthony Skene), in *Monsieur
Zenith the Albino*, U.K., 2001

Elric: To Rescue Tanelorn:

Del Rey p/b, U.S.A., 2008, comprising:
"The Eternal Champion," orig. in SCIENCE FANTASY No. 53, June 1962
"To Rescue Tanelorn . . ."
"The Last Enchantment" (a.k.a. "Jesting with Chaos")
"The Greater Conqueror"
"Master of Chaos" (a.k.a. "Earl Aubec")

"Phase 1: A Jerry Cornelius Story," in *The Final Programme*, U.S.A.,
    1968 (U.K., 1969)
"The Singing Citadel"
"The Jade Man's Eyes"
"The Stone Thing," in TRIODE No. 20 (fanzine, ed. Eric Bentcliffe),
    U.K., Oct. 1974
"Elric at the End of Time"
"The Black Blade's Song" (a.k.a. "The White Wolf's Song")
"Crimson Eyes," in NEW STATESMAN & SOCIETY No. 333, U.K., 1994
"Sir Milk-and-Blood," in *Pawn of Chaos: Tales of the Eternal
    Champion* (anthol., ed. Edward E. Kramer), U.S.A., 1996
"The Roaming Forest," in *Cross Plains Universe: Texans Celebrate
    Robert E. Howard* (anthol., ed. Scott A. Cupp & Joe R. Lansdale),
    U.S.A., 2006

Elric: *The Sleeping Sorceress*:

Del Rey p/b, U.S.A., 2008, comprising:
The Sleeping Sorceress
"And So the Great Emperor Received His Education . . .," orig. spoken-
    word introduction to *Elric of Melniboné* (audiobook), U.S.A., 2003
Elric of Melniboné
"Aspects of Fantasy (1): Introduction" (non-fiction), orig. in SCIENCE
    FANTASY No. 61, Oct. 1963
"Introduction to *Elric of Melniboné*, Graphic Adaptation" (non-fiction),
    in *Elric of Melniboné* (by Roy Thomas, P. Craig Russell & Michael
    T. Gilbert), U.S.A., 1986
"El Cid and Elric: Under the Influence!" (non-fiction), in
    COMIQUEANDO No. 100, Argentina, Aug./Sep. 2007

Duke Elric:

Del Rey p/b, U.S.A., 2009, comprising:
"Introduction to the AudioRealms version of *The Sailor on the Seas of
    Fate* (audiobook), U.S.A., 2006
The Sailor on the Seas of Fate

Duke Elric (script)

"Aspects of Fantasy (2): The Floodgates of the Unconscious" (non-
fiction), orig. in SCIENCE FANTASY No. 62, Dec. 1963

"The Flaneur des Arcades de l'Opera," in *The Metatemporal Detective*,
U.S.A., 2008

"Elric: A Personality at War" (non-fiction by Adrian Snook)

Elric in the Dream Realms:

Del Rey p/b, U.S.A., 2009, comprising:

The Fortress of the Pearl

Elric: The Making of a Sorcerer (script)

"A Portrait in Ivory," orig. in *Logorrhea: Good Words Make Good
Stories* (anthol., ed. John Klima), U.S.A., 2007

"Aspects of Fantasy (3): Figures of Faust" (non-fiction), in SCIENCE
FANTASY No. 63, Feb. 1964

"Earl Aubec of Malador: Outline for a Series of Four Fantasy Novels"

"Introduction to the Taiwanese Edition of Elric" (non-fiction), in *Elric
of Melniboné*, Taiwan, 2007

"One Life, Furnished in Early Moorcock" (by Neil Gaiman), in *Elric:
Tales of the White Wolf*, U.S.A., 1994

Elric: Swords and Roses:

Del Rey p/b, U.S.A., 2010, comprising:

The Revenge of the Rose

Stormbringer: First Draft Screenplay

"Black Petals," orig. in WEIRD TALES No. 349 (edited by Stephen H.
Segal & Ann VanderMeer), U.S.A., Mar./Apr. 2008

"Aspects of Fantasy (4): Conclusion" (non-fiction), in SCIENCE FANTASY
No. 64, Apr. 1964

"Introduction to *The Skrayling Tree*" (non-fiction), written for Borders,
Inc., 2003

"Introduction to the French Edition of Elric" (non-fiction), in *Le Cycle
d'Elric*, France, 2006

"Elric: A New Reader's Guide" (non-fiction by John Davey)

Elric: Les Buveurs d'Âmes (with Fabrice Colin):
Fleuve Noir p/b, France, 2011

Elric of Melniboné and Other Stories:
Gollancz p/b, U.K., 2013, comprising:
"Putting a Tag on It" (non-fiction)
"Master of Chaos"
Elric: The Making of a Sorcerer (script)
"And So the Great Emperor Received His Education . . ."
Elric of Melniboné
"Aspects of Fantasy (1)" (non-fiction)
"Introduction to *Elric of Melniboné*, Graphic Adaptation" (non-fiction)
"El Cid and Elric: Under the Influence!" (non-fiction)

Elric: The Fortress of the Pearl:
Gollancz p/b, U.K., 2013, comprising:
The Fortress of the Pearl
"Aspects of Fantasy (2)" (non-fiction)
"Introduction to the Taiwanese Edition of Elric" (non-fiction)
"One Life, Furnished in Early Moorcock" (by Neil Gaiman)

Elric: The Sailor on the Seas of Fate:
Gollancz p/b, U.K., 2013, comprising:
"Introduction to the AudioRealms version of *The Sailor on the Seas of Fate* (audiobook)
The Sailor on the Seas of Fate
"The Dreaming City"
"A Portrait In Ivory"
"While the Gods Laugh"
"The Singing Citadel"
"Aspects of Fantasy (3)" (non-fiction)
"Elric: A Personality at War" (non-fiction by Adrian Snook)

Elric: The Sleeping Sorceress and Other Stories:

Gollancz p/b, U.K., 2013, comprising:

"The Eternal Champion"

"The Greater Conqueror"

"Earl Aubec of Malador: Outline for a Series of Four Fantasy Novels"

The Sleeping Sorceress

"The Stone Thing"

"Sir Milk-and-Blood"

"The Roaming Forest"

"The Flaneur des Arcades de l'Opera"

"Aspects of Fantasy (4)" (non-fiction)

Elric: The Revenge of the Rose:

Gollancz p/b, U.K., 2014, comprising:

The Revenge of the Rose

"The Stealer of Souls"

"Kings in Darkness"

"The Caravan of Forgotten Dreams"

"The Last Enchantment"

"To Rescue Tanelorn . . ."

"Introduction to the French Edition of Elric" (non-fiction)

Elric: Stormbringer!:

Gollancz p/b, U.K., 2014, comprising:

Stormbringer

"Elric" (non-fiction)

"The Secret Life of Elric of Melniboné" (non-fiction)

"Final Judgement" (non-fiction by Alan Forrest)

"The Zenith Letter" (non-fiction by Anthony Skene)

"Elric: A New Reader's Guide" (non-fiction by John Davey)

Elric: The Moonbeam Roads:

Gollancz p/b, U.K., 2014, comprising:

Daughter of Dreams

Destiny's Brother
Son of the Wolf

Centipede Press (limited edition h/cs, U.S.A.):

Elric of Melniboné, 2019, comprising:
　"Master of Chaos"
　"And So the Great Emperor Received His Education . . ."
　Elric of Melniboné

The Fortress of the Pearl, 2019, comprising:
　The Fortress of the Pearl
　"The Black Blade's Song"

The Sailor on the Seas of Fate, 2019, comprising:
　"Introduction to the AudioRealms version of *The Sailor on the Seas of
　　Fate* (audiobook)
　The Sailor on the Seas of Fate
　"The Dreaming City"
　"A Portrait In Ivory"

The Sleeping Sorceress, 2020, comprising:
　"While the Gods Laugh"
　"The Singing Citadel"
　The Sleeping Sorceress

The Revenge of the Rose, 2021, comprising:
　The Revenge of the Rose
　"The Stealer of Souls"

Stormbringer, 2022, comprising:
　"Kings in Darkness"
　"The Caravan of Forgotten Dreams"
　"The Last Enchantment"
　"To Rescue Tanelorn . . ."
　Stormbringer

The Dreamthief's Daughter, The Skrayling Tree, The White Wolf's Son (all
　forthcoming)

The Elric Saga Volume One: Elric of Melniboné:

Saga Press h/c, U.S.A., 2022, comprising:

"One Life, Furnished in Early Moorcock" (by Neil Gaiman)

Elric of Melniboné

The Fortress of the Pearl

The Sailor on the Seas of Fate

The Weird of the White Wolf

"The Elric Saga: A Reader's Guide" (non-fiction by John Davey)

The Elric Saga Volume Two: Stormbringer:

Saga Press h/c, U.S.A., 2022, comprising:

The Vanishing Tower

The Revenge of the Rose

The Bane of the Black Sword

Stormbringer

"The Elric Saga: A Reader's Guide" (non-fiction by John Davey)

The Elric Saga Volume Three: The White Wolf:

Saga Press h/c, U.S.A., 2022, comprising:

The Dreamthief's Daughter

The Skrayling Tree

The White Wolf's Son

"The Elric Saga: A Reader's Guide" (non-fiction by John Davey)

MINUTIAE

In both of the variant omnibus editions called *Elric: The Stealer of Souls*, as well as all subsequent appearances, the version of *Stormbringer* is presented in a definitive, re-revised form, retaining its full, four-novella length but also incorporating some of the pertinent changes from its 1965 abridgement which were lost during its 1977 restoration to full length.

Non-Elric items contained within the *Elric at the End of Time* collection include "Sojan the Swordsman" (a composite of short tales featuring Moorcock's first ever fantasy hero), "Jerry Cornelius & Co." (two essays on that character) and the short story "The Stone Thing."

The essay "The Secret Life of Elric of Melniboné"—between its first fanzine appearance (1964) and its collection in *Elric at the End of Time*—was also in *Sojan* (Savoy Books p/b, U.K., 1977). That collection additionally contained another piece of non-fiction, "Elric," which originally appeared in the fanzines NIEKAS No. 8 (ed. Ed Meskys, 1963, as a letter) and CRUCIFIED TOAD No. 4 (ed. David Britton, 1974).

The French omnibus, *Elric le Necromancien* (Éditions Opta h/c, 1969), collected *The Stealer of Souls* and the full version of *Stormbringer*—plus the novellas "The Singing Citadel" and "To Rescue Tanelorn . . ."—all arranged in correct chronological order some eight years before any English-language equivalents. More recently, in France, the mammoth omnibus, *Le Cycle d'Elric*, collected in a single volume *Elric of Melniboné*, *The Fortress of the Pearl*, *The Sailor on the Seas of Fate*, *The Weird of the White Wolf*, *The Sleeping Sorceress*, *The Revenge of the Rose*, *The Bane of the Black Sword*, "The Last Enchantment," *Stormbringer* and "Elric at the End of Time."

Moorcock and Elric are particularly well served in France, where individual and omnibus volumes remain permanently in print, and a two-volume edition of *Elric: Tales of the White Wolf* appeared as well as another anthology of original stories by hands other than Moorcock's (although he introduces it), *Elric et la Porte des Mondes* (2006),which seems unlikely ever to receive an English-language edition (although some stories were translated for the 2017 anthology, *Michael Moorcock's Legends of the Multiverse*).

Many graphic adaptations of the Elric saga have appeared over the years, mostly starting as comics. Moorcock himself, together with James Cawthorn, plotted a two-part strip in 1972, in which Elric and Conan the Barbarian join forces ("A Sword Called Stormbringer!" & "The Green Empress of Melniboné" in CONAN THE BARBARIAN Nos 14 & 15). Cawthorn also produced a one-off graphic adaptation of *Stormbringer* for Savoy Books (1976). Several other Elric one-offs have appeared over the years, drawn by various hands, but the most widely available series for some time were Pacific/First Comics' *Elric of Melniboné* (6 parts), *Elric: Sailor on the Seas of Fate* (7 parts), *Elric: Weird of the White Wolf* (5 parts), *Elric: The Vanishing Tower* (6 parts) and *Elric: The Bane of the Black Sword* (6 parts), all serialised throughout the 1980s. The first three sets were also compiled as bound graphic novels. The sequence was stopped by Moorcock before *Stormbringer*, due to deterioration in the quality of the art-work, although a new graphic version of that novel, adapted by P. Craig Russell, was finally serialised in the U.S.A. for Topps/Dark Horse Comics in 1997 (compiled as a bound graphic novel a year later). All of these and other adaptations have more recently been bound and published by Titan Comics.

The two Moorcock-scripted tales, *Duke Elric* and *Elric: The Making of a Sorcerer*, have of course developed the saga further still, and also more recently there have been both *Elric: The Balance Lost* (2011/'12, an original 12-part graphic series by Chris Roberson & Francesco Biagini) and a French sequence of loose adaptations comprising (to date) *Le Trône de Rubis*, *Stormbringer*, *Le Loup Blanc* and *La Cité Qui Rêve* (2013–'21) by Julien Blondel, with Didier Poli, Robin Recht, Jean-Luc Cano, Julien Telo, and others.

Also heavily and ornately illustrated are the various rule books and supplements for Elric-related role-playing games from the American companies Chaosium (whose best-known *Stormbringer* has itself been revised and massively expanded several times) and more recently Mongoose Publishing with their *Elric of Melniboné*. There are also French RPGs in existence, and a Swedish video game in development.

Elric ephemera has become quite a major industry and, if a long-awaited Elric movie ever comes to fruition, such things can only be expected to blossom further still. There have already been collectable cards, die-cast miniatures, dolls, jigsaw puzzles, model-kits, posters, T-shirts, "replica" swords and, of course, records.

Moorcock's musical involvement with several rock bands, including his own, is well known. He wrote an Elric-related song, "Black Blade," for Blue Öyster Cult, but it is Hawkwind who have used the albino prince to the best effect. In 1985, they released the album *The Chronicle of the Black Sword*, and went on an accompanying theatrical concert tour—sometimes featuring Moorcock on stage with the band—which also gave rise to a live album, *Live Chronicles*, and video/DVD, some versions of which include Moorcock performances.

Quite what the ever-taciturn Elric would make of all this attention, I am not sure. Sixty years on, he has already endured far more than those first nine SCIENCE FANTASY novellas would have had us believe possible. Only time will tell us where else he goes from here . . .

ELRIC

MYYRRHN

TARKESH
the Plains of Toraunz

Banarya   Nio

Vale of
Xanyaw

Sequaloris   DHARIJOR
Gromoorva
The Hewn City
of Nihrain   Nargesser
JHARKOR

Cadsandria   Dhakos
Thokora·

SHAZAAR

Marshes of the
Mist

THE
SILENT LAND   'Aflitain

△△△ The Serpent's Teeth

THE
PALE
SEA

STRAITS OF CHAOS

Nwamgaart·   PAN
The City of the   TANG
Screaming Statues

THE DRAGON SEA

Vilr

SORCERER'S ISLE

MELNIBONÉ
Isle of the Dr—
Imrryr,
The Dreaming City

Hiding Place
of the
Sealord's Fleet

Rlin K'ren Aa   Ramasaz

THE BOILING SEA

L'ashma

Dhoz-Kam

ASHANELOON   Al-River OIN
YU LORN

N

W   E

S

to KANELOON
and
WORLD'S EDG